Praise for

DEVIL'S BROOD

"For those who like their historical fiction as complex and tightly woven as a medieval tapestry, this book cannot fail to please. Highly recommended." —*Library Journal*

"Teeming with characters and authentic period detail, the novel is part splendid pageant and part history lecture." —*Booklist*

Praise for

WHEN CHRIST AND HIS SAINTS SLEPT

"The magnificent combination of history and humanity that Penman's readers have come to expect. . . . Perhaps the most impressive feature of the narrative is Penman's skill in showing how essentially good people can end up doing great evil." —*Publishers Weekly*

"[A] marvelous medieval pageant of a novel . . . Another jewel in [Penman's] already glittering crown." —*Orlando Sentinel*

"Penman once again tells a tale of kings and queens, singular destinies, and double-crosses. . . . [She] inventively animates a large cast [and] continues to base her narrative on the firm ground of fact."
—*Kirkus Reviews*

"[Penman] brings to life a vast array of unforgettable characters, both historical and invented, all of whose loyalties are being constantly tested by the chaos of the times. [This novel] should win new readers for Penman and delight her longtime fans. It belongs in all public libraries, large and small." —*Library Journal*

DEVIL'S
BROOD

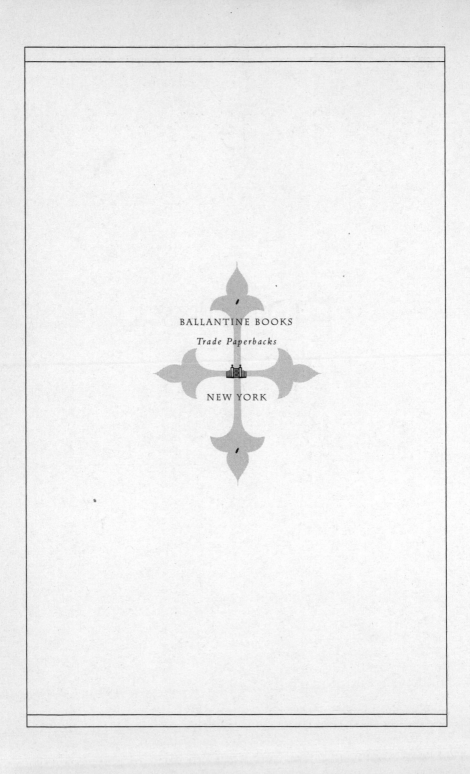

BALLANTINE BOOKS

Trade Paperbacks

NEW YORK

Sharon Kay Penman

DEVIL'S
BROOD

2009 Ballantine Books Trade Paperback Edition

Published in the United States by Ballantine Books, an imprint of
The Random House Publishing Group, a division of Random House, Inc., New York.

BALLANTINE and colophon are registered trademarks of Random House, Inc.
RANDOM HOUSE READER'S CIRCLE & Design is a registered
trademark of Random House, Inc.

Originally published in hardcover in the United States by G.P. Putnam's Sons,
a member of the Penguin Group, in 2008.

LIBRARY OF CONGRESS CATALOGING-IN-PUBLICATION DATA
Penman, Sharon Kay.
Devil's brood / Sharon Kay Penman.
p.   cm.
ISBN 978-0-345-39673-0
1. Henry II, King of England, 1133–1189—Fiction.
2. Eleanor, of Aquitaine, Queen, consort of Henry II, King of England, 1122?–1204—Fiction.
3. Great Britain—History—Henry II, 1154–1189—Fiction.
4. Marriages of royalty and nobility—Fiction.
5. Great Britain—Kings and rulers—Family relationships—Fiction.   I. Title.
PS3566.E474D48   2008   2008029451
813'.54—dc22

Printed in the United States of America

www.randomhousereaderscircle.com

2   4   6   8   9   7   5   3   1

Book design by Judith Stagnitto Abbate/Abbate Design
Map by Jackie Aher

TO VALERIE PTAK LAMONT

AND LOWELL E. LAMONT

CAST *of* CHARACTERS

✦

ROYAL HOUSE OF ENGLAND

Henry Fitz Empress (b. 1133), second of the name to rule England since the Conquest; also Duke of Normandy, Count of Anjou, Maine, and Touraine

Eleanor (b. 1124), Duchess of Aquitaine in her own right; Henry's queen; former consort of Louis VII, King of France

Their children

William (1153–1156)

Hal (Henry, b. February 1155), their eldest surviving son, crowned King of England in 1170

Richard (b. September 1157), Duke of Aquitaine and Count of Poitou

Geoffrey (b. September 1158), Duke of Brittany upon his marriage to Constance

John (b. December 1166), youngest son, known as John Lackland

Tilda (Matilda, b. June 1156), Duchess of Saxony and Bavaria

Leonora (Eleanor, b. September 1161), Queen of Castile

Joanna (b. October 1165), later Queen of Sicily

Geoff, Henry's illegitimate son (b. c. 1151)

Hamelin de Warenne, Earl of Surrey, Henry's illegitimate half brother

Emma, later Princess of Gwynedd, Henry's illegitimate half sister

Rainald, Earl of Cornwall, illegitimate son of Henry I, Henry's uncle

Rico, Rainald's illegitimate son

Ranulf, illegitimate son of Henry I, Henry's uncle

Rhiannon, Ranulf's Welsh cousin and wife

Morgan and Bleddyn, Rhiannon and Ranulf's sons

Roger, Bishop of Worcester, Henry's first cousin

Maud, widowed Countess of Chester, Henry's cousin and Roger's sister

Hugh, Earl of Chester, Maud's son

Rosamund Clifford, Henry's concubine

William Marshal, Hal's household knight

ROYAL HOUSE OF FRANCE

Louis Capet, King of France

His wives

Eleanor, marriage annulled in 1152

Constance of Castile, died in childbirth

Adèle of Blois, sister to Thibault, Count of Blois, and

Henri, Count of Champagne

Philippe, Louis and Adèle's son and heir

Louis's daughters

Marie, Eleanor's daughter, wed to Count of Champagne

Alix, Eleanor's daughter, wed to Count of Blois

Marguerite, Constance's daughter, wed as a child to Hal

Alys, Constance's daughter, betrothed to Richard

Agnes, Adèle's daughter, later Empress of Byzantium

Robert, Count of Dreux, Louis's brother

BRITTANY

Constance, Duchess of Brittany, Geoffrey's betrothed

Conan, late Duke of Brittany, her father

Margaret, sister of Scots king, her mother, wed to English baron, Humphrey
    de Bohun
Raoul de Fougères, André de Vitré, and Roland de Dinan, Breton barons

ENGLISH AND FRENCH BARONS

William de Mandeville, Earl of Essex, Henry's close friend
Robert Beaumont, Earl of Leicester
Peronelle, Countess of Leicester, his wife
Maurice de Craon, Angevin baron
Simon de Montfort, Count of Evreux
Henri, Count of Champagne, and Thibault, Count of Blois,
    Louis's sons-in-law and brothers-in-law

AQUITAINE

Petronilla, Eleanor's sister, deceased
Isabelle and Alienor, her daughters, wed to Counts of Flanders and
    Boulogne
Raoul de Faye, Eleanor's uncle
Hugh, Viscount of Châtellerault, Eleanor's uncle
Aimar, Viscount of Limoges, wed to Sarah, Rainald's daughter
André de Chauvigny, Richard's cousin and household knight
Raimon St Gilles, Count of Toulouse, enemy of Dukes of Aquitaine

FLANDERS

Philip, Count of Flanders, wed to Eleanor's niece Isabelle
Matthew, Count of Boulogne, Philip's brother, wed to Eleanor's niece
    Alienor

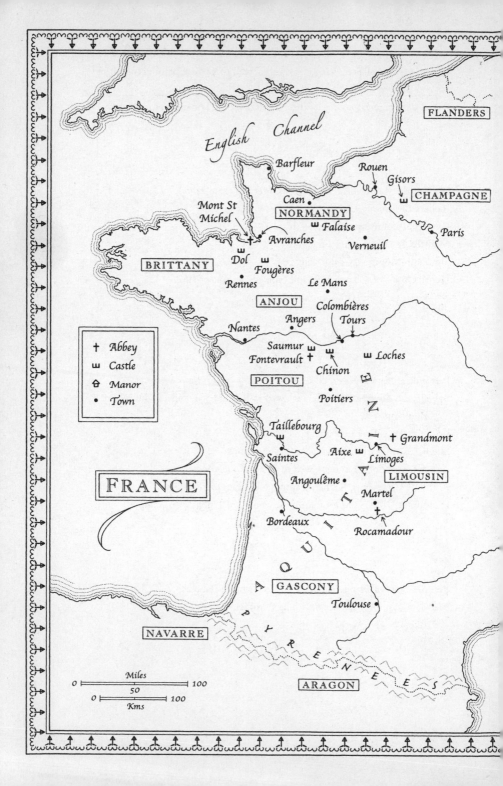

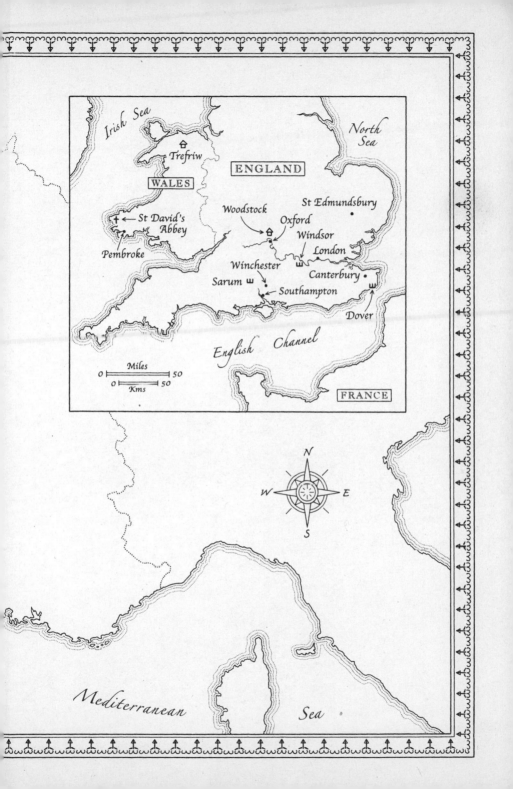

Devil's Brood

PROLOGUE

⚜

*H*E WOULD BE REMEMBERED long after his death, one of those rare men recognized as great even by those who hated him. He was a king at twenty-one, wed to a woman as legendary as Helen of Troy, ruler of an empire that stretched from the Scots border to the Mediterranean Sea, King of England, Lord of Ireland and Wales, Duke of Normandy and Aquitaine, Count of Anjou, Touraine, and Maine, liege lord of Brittany. But in God's Year 1171, Henry Fitz Empress, second of that name to rule England since the Conquest, was more concerned with the judgment of the Church than History's verdict.

When the Archbishop of Canterbury was slain in his own cathedral by men who believed they were acting on the king's behalf, their bloodied swords might well have dealt Henry a mortal blow, too. All of Christendom was enraged by Thomas Becket's murder and few were willing to heed Henry's impassioned denials of blame. His continental lands were laid under Interdict and his multitude of enemies were emboldened, like wolves on the trail of wounded prey. The beleaguered king chose to make a strategic retreat, and in October, he sailed for Ireland. There he soon established his lordship over the feuding Irish kings and secured oaths of fealty from the Irish bishops. The winter was so stormy that Ireland truly seemed to be at the western edge of the world, the turbulent Irish Sea insulating Henry from the continuing outcry over the archbishop's death.

But in the spring, the winds abated and contact was established once more with the outside world. Henry learned that papal legates had arrived in Normandy. And he was warned that his restless eldest son was once more chafing at the bit. In accordance with continental custom, he had been crowned in his father's lifetime. But the young king was dissatisfied with his lot in life, having the trappings of shared kingship but none of the power, and Henry's agents were reporting that Hal was brooding about his plight, listening to the wrong men. Henry Fitz Empress decided it was time to go home.

CHAPTER ONE

April 1172
Dyved, South Wales

SOON AFTER LEAVING HAVERFORD, they were ambushed by the fog. Ranulf had long ago learned that Welsh weather gave no fair warning, honored no flags of truce, and scorned all rules of warfare. But even he was taken aback by the suddenness of the assault. Rounding a bend in the road, they found themselves riding into oblivion. The sky was blotted out, the earth disappearing under their horses' hooves, all sound muffled in this opaque, smothering mist, as blinding as wood-smoke and pungent with the raw, salt-tang of the sea.

Drawing rein, Ranulf's brother Rainald hastily called for a halt. "Mother of God, it is the Devil's doing!"

Ranulf had a healthy respect for Lucifer's malevolence, but he was far more familiar than Rainald with the vagaries of the Welsh climate. "It is just an early-morning fog, Rainald," he said soothingly.

"I can smell the brimstone on his breath," Rainald insisted, "can hear his cackling on the wind. Listen and you'll hear it, too."

Ranulf cocked his head, hearing only the slapping of waves against the rocks below them. Rainald was already shifting in the saddle, telling their men that they were turning back. Before Ranulf could protest, he discovered he had an ally in Gerald de Barri, the young clerk and scholar who'd joined their party after a stopover at Llawhaden Castle. Kicking his mule forward, Gerald assured Rainald that such sudden patches of fog were quite common along the coast. They'd soon be out of it, he promised, and offered to lead them, for this was a road he well knew.

Pressed, too, by Ranulf, Rainald reluctantly agreed and they ventured on, slowly and very warily. "Now I know what it's like for your wife," Rainald grumbled, glancing over his shoulder at his brother. "Poor lass, cursed to live all her days bat-blind and helpless as a newborn babe."

Ranulf's wife, Rhiannon, was indeed blind, but far from helpless. Ranulf took no offense, though; Rainald's tactlessness was legendary in their family. Slowing his mount, he dropped back to ride beside Rainald's young son. The boy's dark coloring had earned him his nickname, Rico, for upon viewing him for the first time, Rainald had joked that he was more an Enrico than a Henry, swarthy as a Sicilian. Rico's olive skin was now a ghostly shade of grey, and Ranulf reached over to pat him reassuringly upon the arm. "Horses do not fancy going over cliffs any more than men do, and Welsh ponies are as sure-footed as mountain goats."

Rico did not seem comforted. "Yes, but Whirlwind is Cornish, not Welsh!"

Ranulf camouflaged a smile, for the placid hackney hardly merited such a spirited name. "They breed sure-footed horses in Cornwall, too, lad." To take his nephew's mind off their precarious path, he began to tell Rico of some mischief-making by his youngest son, Morgan, and soon had Rico laughing.

He missed Morgan, missed his elder son, Bleddyn, and daughter, Mallt, above all missed Rhiannon. But he'd agreed to accompany Rainald to the holy well of St Non, even knowing that he'd be away for weeks, for he knew the real reason for Rainald's pilgrimage. Rainald had claimed he wanted to pray for his wife's soul. But Beatrice had been ailing for many years, hers a malady of the mind that only death had healed. Rainald's true concern was for his other son, Nicholas, who had not been blessed with Rico's robust good health. Frail and sickly, Nicholas was not likely to live long enough to succeed to his father's earldom, as evidenced by Rainald's desperate decision to seek aid from saints, not doctors.

Rainald's pain was all the greater because Nicholas was his only male heir. Rico was born out of wedlock, and thus barred by Church law from inheriting any of his father's estates—even though Rainald himself was bastard-born. The irony of that was lost upon Rainald, who was the least introspective of men. It was not lost upon Ranulf, who shared Rainald's tainted birth, both of them natural sons of the old King Henry. Neither of them had suffered from the stigma of illegitimacy, though. As a king's son, Rainald had been judged worthy to wed the heiress of the earldom of Cornwall, and Ranulf had long been the favorite uncle of the current king, Henry Fitz Empress. Henry would gladly have bestowed an earldom upon him, too, but Ranulf, who was half-Welsh, had chosen to settle in Wales where he'd wed his Welsh cousin and raised his family—until forced into English exile by a Welsh prince's enmity.

His Welsh lands were forfeit and his English manors were meager in comparison to Rainald's vast holdings in Cornwell, but Ranulf had no regrets about turning down a title. He was at peace with his yesterdays, and he'd lived long enough to understand how few men could say that. For certes, Rainald could not. Nor could the king, his nephew, absent these many months in Ireland, where he'd gone to evade Holy Church's fury over the slaying of Thomas Becket.

Gerald de Barri's voice floated back upon the damp morning air. A natural-born talker, he was not going to let a bit of fog muzzle him, and he continued to engage Rainald in conversation, not at all discouraged by the earl's taciturn, distracted responses. Ranulf listened, amused, for Gerald was an entertaining traveling companion, if somewhat self-serving. The nephew of the Bishop of St David's, he was returning to England after years of study in Paris, and he reminded Ranulf of Thomas Becket, another worldly clerk blessed with great talents and even greater ambitions.

Becket had been a superb chancellor, wielding enormous influence because of his close friendship with the king. What a pity it was, Ranulf thought, that Harry had taken it into his head to elevate Becket to the archbishopric. But who could ever have expected the man to undergo such a dramatic transformation? He wasn't even a priest, had hastily to take holy vows just days before his investiture. But once he was Canterbury's archbishop, he'd devoted himself to God with all of the zeal he'd once shown on behalf of England's king. Henry hadn't been the only one discomfited by Becket's newfound fervor. His fellow bishops had often been exasperated by his provocations, his refusal to compromise, his self-righteous piety. Even His Holiness the Pope had been confounded at times by Becket's intransigence.

All that had changed, of course, as he bled to death on the floor of his own cathedral, and when the monks had discovered their slain archbishop's vermin-infested hair-shirt under his blood-soaked garments, none had doubted they were in the presence of sainthood. Acclaimed as a holy martyr in death, even by those who'd considered him to be a vexation and an enigma in life, Thomas Becket was sure to be anointed as the Church's next saint. Already people flocked to his tomb at Canterbury, seeking healing cures and buying little vials of his blood as precious relics. More than fifteen months after Becket's death, Ranulf still marveled at it all. Was Becket truly a saint?

He smiled wryly, then, remembering his last meeting with his nephew the king, just before Henry's departure for Ireland. Over a late-night flagon of wine, Henry had challenged him, wanting to know if he believed Becket was a saint. He still recalled his reply. "I cannot answer your question, Harry, doubt that anyone can. I do know, though, that saints are not judged like ordinary men. That is, after all, what makes them saints." Henry had reflected upon that in silence, then said, sounding both skeptical and regretful, "Saint or not, Thomas got the last word for certes."

Menevia was the name given to the small settlement that had sprung up around the cathedral of St David. Its houses were outnumbered by shabby inns, stables, taverns, and a few cook-shops, for the shrine of the Welsh saint was a popular choice for pilgrimages. Because of its remoteness and the difficulty of travel in Wales, the Holy See had decreed that two pilgrimages to St David's were the equivalent of one to St Peter's in Rome. The cathedral itself was situated just west of the village in a secluded hollow, out of sight of the sea raiders and Norsemen who had pillaged the coast in bygone times.

The men expected to be accosted by villagers proclaiming the comforts of their inns, the superiority of their wines and mead, the bargain prices of their pilgrim badges. To their surprise, the streets appeared deserted. Advancing uneasily, they finally encountered an elderly man in a doorway, leaning heavily upon a wooden crutch.

"Where have all the folk gone?" Rainald called out, and when he got only a blank stare in response, Ranulf repeated the question in Welsh, to better effect.

"To the harbor," the ancient replied, hobbling forward a few steps. "Sails were spied and when word spread, people went to see. Most pilgrims come on foot, but we do get some who sail from Normandy and Flanders, even a few Frenchmen who lack the ballocks to brave Welsh roads." He grinned, showing a surprising mouthful of teeth for one so old, but Ranulf knew the Welsh were particular about tooth care, cleaning them with green hazel shoots and polishing them with woolen cloth.

Flipping him a coin for his trouble, Ranulf interpreted for the others, translating the old man's "Frenchmen" into "English" to avoid confusion. It was not always easy to live in lands with so many spoken tongues. To many of the Welsh, the invaders from England were French, for that was the language they spoke. To the French, those who dwelled on the rain-swept island were English. But those descendants of the men who'd followed William the Bastard to victory in God's Year 1066 thought of themselves as Norman, and his nephew Henry was Angevin to the core.

Having no interest in incoming ships, they continued on toward the cathedral, where they received the welcome worthy of an earl, although Gerald de Barri was disappointed to learn that the bishop, his uncle, was away. They were escorted to the guest hall and were washing off the grime of the road when they heard shouting out in the close. Ranulf and Rainald hastened to the window, looking down at a man sprinting toward the bishop's palace. As several canons hurried to meet him, he sank to his knees, chest heaving.

"The king . . ." He gasped, struggling for breath. "The king is coming! His ships have dropped anchor in the harbor!"

BY THE TIME their party reached the beach, Henry and his companions had come ashore and were surrounded by a large crowd: villagers, pilgrims, and the local Welsh. It always amazed Ranulf to watch his nephew with his subjects, for he had not enough patience to fill a thimble and yet he showed remarkable forbearance when mobbed by supplicants, even those of low-birth. Ranulf had seen many people undone by the lure of power, so many that he'd long ago concluded it was a sickness in and of itself, one as dangerous in its way as the spotted pox or consumption. Harry, he thought, had come the closest to the mastery of it . . . so far.

"Your Grace!" Rainald bellowed, loudly enough to hurt nearby eardrums. Henry turned toward the sound, for at thirty-nine, he still had the keen hearing of a fox. He beckoned them forward and they made the public obeisance due his rank and then were enfolded into welcoming embraces, for Henry had never been one for ceremony.

Henry showed no surprise at their appearance upon this remote, rocky shore. "My fleet anchored safely at Pembroke," he said with satisfaction. "But how did you guess that I'd be landing at St David's?"

Rainald looked puzzled, but Ranulf joked, "All know I have second sight," before admitting that they'd not passed through Pembroke, knew nothing of the landing of the king's fleet, and their meeting upon this westernmost tip of Wales was pure happenchance.

"Well, it is an auspicious omen, nonetheless," Henry declared, "getting my homecoming off to a good start." Several canons from the cathedral had arrived by now and Henry allowed them to lead the way from the beach, explaining piously that he'd sent his fleet on ahead yesterday, but had refrained from traveling himself on the holy day of the Lord Christ's Resurrection. The canons murmured approvingly at such proof of their sovereign's reverence. Ranulf and Rainald, who knew their nephew far better than these credulous clerics, exchanged amused grins. Henry's campaign to placate the Church had already begun.

St David's was only a mile distant, but their progress was slow because of the crowds pressing in upon them. Henry did not seem to mind; leaning upon a pilgrim's staff, he turned their trek into a procession, good-naturedly acknowledging the greetings of the villagers, even bantering with a few of the bolder ones. But the friendly, relaxed atmosphere changed abruptly when they reached the cathedral close.

More of the canons were clustered at the gate, making ready to welcome the king. A muddy stream grandiosely known as the River Alun bordered the northern side of the churchyard, bridged by a large marble stone, its surface polished and worn by the tread of countless pilgrim feet. As Henry approached, an elderly woman stepped forward and cried out in a hoarse, strident voice.

Henry had a good ear for languages, but Welsh had always eluded him, and he turned to the canons for enlightenment. Obviously flustered, they sought to ignore the woman's ranting, insisting she was babbling nonsense and not to be heeded. Henry knew better; one glance at the spectators told him that. Some looked horrified, others embarrassed, and a few—those with the dark coloring of the Welsh—eagerly expectant.

"What did she say, Ranulf?" he demanded of the one man he could trust to give him an honest answer.

Ranulf answered reluctantly, yet truthfully. "She called upon Lechlaver to revenge the Welsh upon you."

Henry scowled. "Who the Devil is Lechlaver? Some heathen Welsh god?"

"No . . . it is the name of yonder rock." Realizing how bizarre that sounded, Ranulf had no choice but to tell Henry the rest. "Local legend has it that Merlin made a prophecy about Lechlaver. He foretold that a ruddy-faced English king, the conqueror of Ireland, would die upon that rock."

It was suddenly very still. The crowd scarcely seemed to be breathing, and more than a few surreptitiously made the sign of the cross. Some of Henry's own companions cautiously edged away, in case Merlin's prophecy involved a celestial thunderbolt. Rainald reached out as if to keep Henry from advancing any farther. Ranulf did not consider himself to be particularly superstitious, but even he did not want his nephew to set foot on that slick marble stone.

Henry looked from one tense face to another and then, slowly and very deliberately, strode forward. Leaping nimbly onto the rock, he crossed without a misstep. Turning back to face the spectators, he said in a voice pitched loudly for all to hear, "Who will believe that liar Merlin now?"

There was a collective sigh as breathing resumed and the world of shadows receded before Henry's scorn and certainty. Beaming, Rainald made haste to follow, as did the others. People trooped over Lechlaver, the depths of their unease revealed now by the intensity of their relief. Only the Welsh bystanders stayed on the other side of the shallow river, their disappointment etched in the down-turned mouths, the averted eyes. One youth could not endure to see Merlin shamed before these arrogant foreigners and called out in heavily accented French:

"You are not the king in Merlin's prophecy, for you are not the conqueror of Ireland!"

Henry swung around to confront the young Welshman, and for a suspenseful moment, his audience wondered if they were to see his notorious Angevin temper take fire. But then Henry laughed. "If your Merlin thought anyone could truly conquer Ireland, lad, he was a poor prophet, indeed!" Adding under his breath to Ranulf as they resumed their progress toward the cathedral, "How do you defeat a people who lack the common sense to know when they're beaten?"

Ranulf smiled, knowing that Henry was speaking, too, of the Welsh and his disastrous campaign of six years past. His ambitious plans to bring the rebellious Welsh lords to heel had come to naught, thwarted by the erratic weather, the rugged mountainous terrain, and phantom foes who refused to take the field, preferring hit-and-run raids, evasive maneuvers, and nightfall forays that recognized their weaknesses and played to their strengths. Faced with a rare military defeat, Henry had withdrawn his army back across the border and changed his tactics, forging an alliance with Rhys ap Gruffydd, the most powerful of the Welsh princes. So far this stratagem had proven successful; Wales was more peaceful than it had been in years.

Glancing over at Henry, Ranulf hoped that his nephew would apply the lessons he'd learned from the Welsh in his current battle with His Holiness the Pope and the mighty Roman Church. But it was just that—a hope—for he of all men knew how dangerously stubborn Henry Fitz Empress could be. There were faint bloodstains upon the tiles in Canterbury Cathedral testifying to that.

CHAPTER TWO

✦

May 1172
Savigny Abbey, Normandy

*J*T WAS DUSK WHEN the Bishop of Worcester rode through the gatehouse of the Cistercian abbey of Our Lady. Although a prince of the
Church, Roger traveled without an entourage—only a servant, his clerk, and
four men-at-arms, their presence required on the outlaw-infested roads. He did not
think an ostentatious display was appropriate, for he was living in exile, having left England in protest over the English king's contest of wills with Thomas Becket. Few had
emerged unscathed from that cataclysmic conflict between Church and Crown, but
Roger's loyalties had been shredded to the bone. Becket was more than a fellow prelate
and the head of the English Church; he was also a close friend. And Henry Fitz Empress was more than Roger's sovereign; the two men were first cousins and companions since childhood.

Roger had been one of the few men who'd dared to tell the king the truth in the
turbulent aftermath of Becket's murder: that Henry might not be guilty of the actual
deed, but neither was he innocent. But he had also been one of the bishops sent to
Rome to plead Henry's case before the Pope, denying that the archbishop had died at
his order. Now he was once more thrust into the role of peacemaker, riding to Savi-

gny's great abbey to bear witness to this meeting between two papal legates and his cousin the king, knowing full well how high the stakes were for all concerned.

In addition to the two cardinals, a number of Norman and Breton bishops would also be present. By Roger's reckoning, at least eight were men who could be expected to support the king. In truth, many of Becket's fellow bishops had been less than enthusiastic soldiers in the Archbishop of Canterbury's crusade to vanquish the English king, feeling that he'd been needlessly provocative and acrimonious, always scorning compromise in favor of confrontation. Until his ungodly murder had transformed him from often-irksome zealot to blessed holy martyr, Becket had found his strongest advocates among the bishops of France, his warmest welcome at the court of Louis Capet, the French king. Two of his most steadfast allies had been the Bishop of Rheims, Louis's brother, and the Archbishop of Sens, who'd laid Henry's continental lands under Interdict, and whose sister was Louis's queen.

It did not surprise Roger that neither of these prelates would be present at the Savigny council, for he knew Pope Alexander wanted—nay, needed—to mend this dangerous rift with the most powerful monarch in Christendom, just as Henry needed to make peace with the Holy See. It would be a great pity, he thought, if Harry's foolhardy pride thwarted that rapprochement.

Roger *was* surprised, though, by the absence of John des Bellesmains, the Bishop of Poitiers. He would have expected John to be there, come what may, for his friendship with Thomas Becket had gone back many years, begun in their youth as clerks in the household of the Archbishop Theobald. But Poitiers was the capital of Poitou, the domains of the Lady Eleanor, Henry's controversial queen and Duchess of Aquitaine in her own right. Roger wondered now if Eleanor had deliberately kept Bishop John away from Savigny, knowing his sympathies lay firmly with the slain archbishop. If she had, then mayhap the rumors of her estrangement from Harry were not true.

But with Eleanor, there could be other reasons, other motives as yet undiscovered. Even though his sister Maud, the Countess of Chester, was one of Eleanor's intimates, Roger had always been rather wary of his cousin's queen, a woman who dared to meddle in those matters of state best left to men. And if Harry spun webs to make a spider proud, Eleanor could entangle archangels in her snares. Roger suspected that she intrigued even in her sleep.

The hosteller was waiting to welcome Roger, and grooms had materialized to lead their horses to the stables. After an exchange of courtesies, Roger was turning to follow the monk toward the abbey guest hall when his attention was drawn by a flash of color. Unlike the unbleached white habits worn by the Cistercian monks moving about the abbey garth, this man was garbed in a cope of bright blue silk, decorated with wide embroidered borders, and a matching blue mitre, the points ornamented with scarlet thread. The processional cope and mitre proclaimed him to be a prelate of Holy Church, and the fleshy, ruddy face was vaguely familiar to Roger, but to his embarrassment, the name eluded him.

Fortunately, his gaze then fell upon the bishop's companion, a slightly built man, no longer young, starkly clad in the black cowl and habit of the Benedictines, abbot of one of Christendom's great jewels, the island monastery of Mont St Michel, and a friend of long standing, both to Roger and his cousin the king. And as he warmly returned Abbot Robert de Torigny's greeting, Roger recalled the identity of the mystery bishop: the abbot's neighbor, prelate of the city across the bay, Richard of Avranches.

Bishop Richard wasted no time in breaking the bad news. "I fear your journey has been for naught, my lord bishop," he declared dolefully, his sorrowful visage almost but not quite disguising the relish that people invariably take in being the bearer of evil tidings. "The king met this afternoon with the Holy Father's legates, but it did not go well. King Henry balked at renouncing his Constitutions of Clarendon, and when no progress could be made on this contentious issue, he stalked out in a rage, saying he had matters to tend to back in Ireland."

By now others had gathered around them. Roger recognized the abbot of Savigny, utterly dismayed that this disaster should occur on his watch. He was flanked by the equally flustered Bishops of Bayeux, Sées, and Le Mans, theirs the doomed expressions of men trapped between Scylla and Charybdis, owing their allegiance to Henry, and their obedience to Pope Alexander. Bishop William of Le Mans felt a flicker of hope, though, with Roger's arrival, and at once entreated him to seek out his cousin the king.

"His Grace will heed you, my lord, for he has great respect for your good judgment. Surely you can convince him of the folly of abandoning the talks with the Holy Father's legates?"

Roger was past the first flush of youth, and a day in the saddle had taken its toll; his back ached and his muscles were sore and cramped. He'd been looking forward to a bath and a nap before he changed his travel-stained clothing and presented himself to the cardinals and the king. Suppressing a sigh, he looked at the circle of expectant faces and agreed to do all in his power to keep his cousin from returning to Ireland.

Savigny's abbot had turned his own quarters over to his royal guest, and Abbot Robert offered to show Roger the way. Observing the older man's sedate pace and calm demeanor, Roger realized that he did not seem nearly as disquieted as the bishops. "I'd almost forgotten," he said, "how well you know the king," and Abbot Robert's mouth hinted at a smile.

"I know this much," he said amiably. "The king does not like to make war. But when he does, he does it very well, and sometimes the wisest tactic is a strategic withdrawal."

"Indeed," Roger agreed, and they entered the abbot's great hall, overflowing with the king's servants, household knights, barons, and clerics. Roger was running the gauntlet of greetings, had just reached the Bishop of Evreux, when the bedchamber door opened and Henry strode into the hall.

As usual, he did nothing to call attention to himself and his clothing would have been remarkably plain and unadorned for a minor border lord, much less the man who ruled the greatest empire since Charlemagne. But Henry had no interest in the trappings of power, only in the exercise of it. Nor did he need to strut and preen as Roger had seen other men of rank do, as Thomas Becket had done during his years as the king's elegant, worldly chancellor. Yet Henry was always the focus of all eyes, even upon those rare occasions when his identity was not known. Even as a youth, he'd had it, the force that gave him the mastery of other men. It was as if he were a lodestone, a magnet that attracted light and luck, not metal.

That was so fanciful a thought that Roger laughed softly to himself as he moved toward his cousin the king. Henry was delighted to see him, reaching out to clasp Roger's hand in both of his, forestalling a formal obeisance. "At last! I'd begun to fear you'd been waylaid by bandits or Breton demons!" Adding with a gleam of mischief, "Not that one so virtuous and worthy would have anything to fear from the forces of darkness. What evil spirit would dare to defy a bishop?"

"Your Grace's faith in my sanctity is most heartening," Roger said dryly, "given that some claim your lineage can be traced to the Devil."

Henry's grey eyes flashed, but with amusement, not anger. "Ah, yes, the righteous Abbot Bernard once declared that my lord father was the Devil's spawn, or words to that effect. As I recall, my father laughed at him, much to the sainted Bernard's indignation."

Roger knew that story well; it was legendary in their family. The man Henry sardonically called "the sainted Bernard" was likely to become a genuine saint, as the Holy See had begun the canonization process. But impending sainthood had not tempered Henry's disdain, for Abbot Bernard had been a bitter enemy of the counts of Anjou, claiming that the Angevins sprang from a depraved stock, doomed and damned. Roger did not doubt that Abbot Bernard was a holy man, blessed by the Hand of the Almighty, but neither did he deny that Bernard's earthly behavior had not always been saintly. God's Lambs were not always meek, mild, and forgiving, and for a moment, he thought sadly of his friend and martyr, Thomas Becket.

Shaking off the memory, he reminded himself that today's needs must take precedence over yesterday's regrets. Meeting Henry's gaze evenly, he said, "I hear, my lord king, that you've a sudden yearning to see the Irish isle again."

Henry's expression was not easy to read, for he had the irritating ability to appear utterly inscrutable when it served his purposes. "Yes," he said, "you've heard right. Come on in," jerking his head toward the open bedchamber door, "and I'll tell you of my travel plans."

SEVERAL MEN WERE GATHERED in the bedchamber, only one of whom Roger was pleased to see, his uncle Rainald, Earl of Cornwell. The others—Arnulf, Bishop of Lieieux, Geoffrey Ridel, Henry's acting chancellor, and Richard of Ilchester, Archdeacon of Poitiers—were trusted royal councilors, but they had also been avowed enemies of Thomas Becket. Fending off his uncle's bear hug of a greeting, Roger acknowledged the bishop and archdeacons with cool civility, and then turned to face Henry.

"You are not truly ending the talks ere they begin, Harry?"

"Of course not." Henry accepted a wine cup from Rainald, gesturing for Roger to help himself. "On the morrow, Arnulf will seek out the legates and offer to mediate our differences."

"And what are those differences?"

"They demanded that I repudiate the Constitutions of Clarendon." Henry's smile was without humor. "And you know how likely I am to agree to that, Cousin."

Roger did. Henry had attempted to define and clarify the ancient customs of the realm by putting them down in writing, a radical proposal to his conservative bishops, who had been accustomed to vague, ambiguous terms that could be accepted or repudiated as circumstances warranted. But they were practical men for the most part, well aware that there must be accommodation between Church and Crown; if the king refused to unsheathe his secular sword to enforce spiritual penalties, how effective would those penalties be?

Compromise was anathema, though, to the Archbishop of Canterbury. Thomas Becket had refused to accept the Constitutions in any form whatsoever, arguing that the Church, not the king, was the giver of laws. But Henry had forced the issue, for accommodation was possible only if there was trust on both sides, and Henry no longer believed he could trust his former friend and chancellor. Becket had eventually given in and ordered the bishops to accept the Constitutions, only then to repent and recant his sworn oath. Within less than a year, Becket had fled into French exile, and the Pope, reluctantly dragged into this dangerous dispute, had backed Becket's position and came out in opposition to the Constitutions of Clarendon. The stalemate had endured for the remainder of Becket's life, looming ahead of them now like an uncharted rock, threatening to sink all hopes of a peaceful settlement.

That would not happen, though, as long as Roger drew breath. He was going to steer this ship into a safe harbor if it was the last thing he ever did. "When I was in Rome last year to plead your case at the Holy See, I spoke at some length with several of the cardinals. I gathered that the Church's objections to the Constitutions were not so much based upon the contents; they accepted your argument that the customs set down were indeed the traditional practices of the realm, more or less. Their concerns were with the oaths that you demanded of all the bishops. Never had such oaths been required by any of your predecessors. We balked at taking vows that might conflict with canon law, as you well remember, Harry. It was only when Thomas's resolve briefly weakened, that we had to agree—"

"His resolve 'briefly weakened,' did it?" Henry echoed sarcastically. "That is a very kind way to phrase it, Cousin. I believe his exact words to you and the other bishops were, 'If the king would have me perjure myself, so be it. I will take the oath he demands and hope to purge the sin by future penance.'"

Roger winced, sorry but not surprised that someone had broken the confidentiality of the bishops' conclave; informants clustered around kings like bees at a hive. "I admit that was not Thomas's finest hour and his behavior at Clarendon is not easily defended. But I need not remind you, Cousin, that your behavior has not always been defensible either. What matters is how we settle this issue now. Would you be willing to agree not to demand such an oath of your prelates in the future?"

When Henry nodded, Roger glanced toward the Bishop of Lisieux. He had no liking for the other man, but he did not deny that Arnulf was highly intelligent, well educated, and an accomplished diplomat. "That would be a beginning, my lord bishop."

Arnulf's smile was both confident and complacent. "Indeed, it would," he said and gestured toward a parchment sheet filled with scribbles, scratched out words, and ink splatters. "My lord king and I were discussing this very matter ere you arrived. There must be a way to satisfy the cardinals without making an explicit renunciation of the Constitutions. How does this sound? 'The King of the English vows to abolish any new customs which have been introduced into his realm to the prejudice of the Church.'"

Roger considered the wording. "Yes, that might do it." Shooting his cousin a sharp look, he said, "This vow is acceptable to you, Harry?"

"Of course. I do not see this as a controversial issue, for I am confident I have not introduced customs detrimental to the Church, for certes not knowingly," Henry said blandly, and Roger sighed, for he'd expected as much. Fortunately, the papal legates would expect as much, too. They'd not be going into this blind. Remembering that he held a cup of claret, he took a swallow, warmed as much by a surge of optimism as by the wine. It was beginning to look as if both sides might win this war.

Setting his cup down on the table next to Arnulf's draft, he asked to be excused so that he could wash away the dust of the road. Henry let him reach the door before he asked the question Roger had hoped to avoid.

"Do you not want to know what the cardinals told me about Becket's killers?"

Roger already knew the answer to that deceptively innocuous query. "It is my understanding that the killers are on their way to Rome to do penance for Thomas's murder."

"Yes," Henry said, "and what penance do you expect the Pope to impose?"

"I would not know," Roger said untruthfully, a lie that Henry pounced upon with zest.

"What penance *can* he impose, Roger? To take the cross and journey to the Holy Land. Does that seem sufficient punishment to you for the murder of an archbishop?"

Roger frowned, for Henry had just demonstrated the logical absurdity of the Church's insistence upon disciplining their own. The Constitutions of Clarendon had been the result, not the cause, of the conflict between Henry and Becket. It had begun with Henry's desire to make clerics subject to secular law. The Church had long claimed sole authority to judge the offenses of men in holy orders or the crimes committed against them. Even men who'd merely taken religious vows must be tried in ecclesiastical court, not the king's court. No matter how heinous his transgression, a clerk was beyond the reach of royal justice, and the harshest penalty the Church could impose was degrading, depriving him of his orders.

Henry had been outraged by these mild punishments, and he demanded that clerks convicted of serious crimes in an ecclesiastical court should then be stripped of the Church's protection and handed over to his courts for sentencing. Roger still remembered the litany of horrific crimes Henry had assembled to bolster his argument: more than one hundred murders committed by clerics in the eight years since he'd become king, including the scandalous case in which an archdeacon poisoned the Archbishop of York and, as punishment, was deprived of his archdeaconry.

Roger remembered, too, the case that sometimes troubled his dreams even now. A clerk in Worcestershire had raped a young girl and slain her father. When Henry insisted that the man be turned over to a royal court, Becket had ordered Roger, as Bishop-elect of Worcester, to imprison the man so he could not be seized by the king's justices. Roger believed in the principle defended so passionately by Thomas Becket, that the clergy had Christ alone as their king and were not subject to royal jurisdiction. It was easier to argue, though, when the consequences of that principle—the abused daughter and widow of the murder victim—were not kneeling at his feet pleading for justice.

"A pity," Henry said coolly, "that Thomas was so adamant, so scornful of compromise on the issue of jurisdiction. Had he been more reasonable, his murderers would not have gone free. Ironic, is it not, Cousin?"

Roger could have pointed out that Becket would not have been murdered if Henry had not lost his temper and spoke those fatal words that sent four men to Canterbury Cathedral, thinking they were fulfilling the king's wishes: *What miserable drones and traitors I have nourished and promoted in my household, who let their lord be mocked so shamefully by a lowborn clerk!* But he did not, for what purpose would it serve? It would change nothing. He looked at Henry, hearing an echo of his cousin's hoarse, desperate denial. *As God is my witness, those men did not murder him at my bidding.* The real pity, he thought, was that Harry's remorse had faded so fast.

WITH THE MEDIATION of Archbishop Rotrou of Rouen, Bishop Arnulf of Lisieux, and the Archdeacon of Poitiers, peace was made between the English king and the Roman Church. It was agreed that Henry and the papal legates and bishops would ride south to Avranches and Henry would there do public penance for his part in the murder of the Archbishop of Canterbury and receive absolution of his sins.

FROM THE CASTLE BATTLEMENTS, Henry had a superb view of the bay and, in the distance, the celebrated abbey of Mont St Michel. It was one of the marvels of Christendom, built upon a small, rocky island that was entirely cut off from the mainland at high tide. It had a dreamlike appearance, seeming to rise out of the sand and sea foam like a lost vision of God's Kingdom, its high, precarious perch above the waves so spectacular and dramatic that at first glimpse, pilgrims did not see how it could have been the work of mortal men.

It was low tide now and the dangerous, shifting sands had been laid bare. Henry could see a few tiny figures trudging across those sands toward the abbey, but not as many as would be expected. He knew why, of course. Many of the pilgrims had delayed their crossing upon hearing that the King of England would be doing penance upon the morrow at Avranches's cathedral of St Andrew the Apostle. That would be a sight to behold, a rare tale to bring back to their towns and villages upon completion of their pilgrimages.

Henry narrowed his eyes, as much at that unwelcome thought as at the unrelenting gusts of sea-borne wind, belying spring's calendar with its chill. Glancing at his closest companion, he said, "It has been far too long since I visited your abbey. Mayhap we can make time ere I must depart for Caen. When was I there last—when I came with Louis?"

Abbot Robert pretended to ponder the question; as if he did not have every one of the king's stays seared into his memory like a brand! A royal visit was the greatest honor imaginable, but it was also a great expense and a great strain, for the striving after perfection on such an occasion was both exhausting and utterly elusive. Thinking of Henry's sojourn with the French king, he smiled at the memory, for it had always amazed him that Henry should have been able to win over the man who'd been Eleanor's first husband. Of course that unlikely peace had not lasted, but it had endured long enough for Henry to arrange an even more unlikely marriage between his eldest son, Hal, and Louis's daughter, Marguerite, child of the woman he'd wed after divorcing Eleanor.

"I believe that was indeed your last visit, my liege," he confirmed, all the while marveling at the vagaries of fate. He had devoted much of his life to a history of his abbey and his times, and he wondered what future historians would make of the improbable story of Henry Fitz Empress and Eleanor of Aquitaine.

A great heiress and a great beauty, she'd wed the young French king at thirteen, easily winning his heart, for he'd been pledged to the Church at an early age, would have happily served the Almighty if his elder brother had not died in a fall from his horse, and he retained a guileless innocence, a monkish simplicity that was ill suited to the worldly sophistry of the royal court. Their marriage had been neither happy nor fruitful, for they were as unlike as fire and milk. In fourteen years of wedlock, Eleanor had given birth to only two children, both daughters, and when their union was finally dissolved on the grounds of consanguinity, the true reason was her inability to give him a male heir.

Barely three months later, she had shocked their world by wedding Henry, then Duke of Normandy, who was nine years her junior. Louis the king was horrified that so dangerous an adversary as Henry should have access to the riches of Eleanor's Aquitaine, and Louis the man was mortified and hurt that Eleanor should have defied him by choosing such an unsuitable husband, one ambitious, bold, clever, and lusty. Their swift, secret marriage had led to war with France, and Louis's humiliation was complete when Henry needed but six short weeks to send his army reeling back across the border, and but two years to claim the English crown. Eleanor then proceeded to salt Louis's wounds by giving Henry five sons and three daughters, losing only William to the deadly perils of childhood.

At least Louis had the consolation of envisioning his daughter as Queen of England. But even that had not gone as planned. Two years ago, Henry had mortally insulted Thomas Becket by allowing the Archbishop of York to crown his fifteen-year-old son, a coronation that Becket had futilely forbidden. But in the chaos and confusion, Marguerite had not been crowned with her young husband, giving Louis yet another grievance against his Angevin rival.

A sudden clamor turned Henry's attention from the abbey to the town below them. The streets were winding and narrow, accommodating the hilly terrain, and he could only catch glimpses of riders and horses. But then the wind found a fluttering banner of red and gold and he smiled. "My son is riding into Avranches," he announced. "I should have known from the cheers." He glanced toward the abbot, wanting to share his pride and pleasure with his friend. "You've not seen the lad for years, have you, Rob? Wait till you see how he's grown—already taller than me and he's just three months past his seventeenth birthday!"

Others had followed Henry onto the battlements: his uncle Rainald, his cousin Roger, his justiciar, Richard de Lucy, and Hamelin de Warenne, his half brother. Hamelin was the illegitimate son of Henry's father, Geoffrey, Count of Anjou, taken under Henry's wing after Geoffrey's untimely death. Hamelin had flaming red hair, an open, freckled face that made him seem much younger than his thirty years, an impulsive nature and, thanks to Henry, a very wealthy wife who'd brought him the earldom of Surrey. His affection for Henry was equaled only by his awe, and he beamed now to see his elder brother in such good spirits.

"Does Hal know why you summoned him to Avranches?"

Henry shook his head. "He thinks he is here just to swear to those agreements I am making with the Church." Seeing Abbot Robert's puzzled look, he explained, "I have a surprise in store for the lad."

Below them, men were riding into the castle's inner bailey. There was no need to point out the young king. Everything about him— the spirited grey stallion and ornamented saddle, the costly mantle of fine scarlet wool, the white calfskin gloves studded with pearls, the stylish pointed cap with a turned-up brim embroidered in gold thread, the gilded spurs attached to his boots with red leather straps—proclaimed him to be of high birth and one of God's favorites. He'd been blessed, too, with uncommonly good looks, tall and well formed, with vivid blue eyes and gleaming golden hair, cut short around his ears, one lock allowed to curl fashionably onto his forehead. Catching sight of his father up on the battlements, he doffed his cap in a gesture both graceful and dramatic, and Henry grinned.

Staring down at this handsome youth, Abbot Robert blurted out, "If he is not the very image of Count Geoffrey!"

"He has my father's coloring for certes," Henry agreed, "and his sense of style. He has my father's ready wit, too. Did you hear, Rob, what he said at his coronation feast? To honor him, I myself carried the great boar's head dish to his table. The Archbishop of York commented that it was not every prince who was served by a king. And Hal said, quick as a flash, 'Yes, but it can be no condescension for the son of a count to serve the son of a king.'"

Abbot Robert did not see the humor in that flippant remark, but he laughed dutifully because Henry was laughing. As he had been no admirer of Count Geoffrey of Anjou, though, he hoped that Hal had inherited nothing from his grandsire but his striking good looks.

SWINGING EASILY FROM THE SADDLE, Hal soon joined his father up on the battlements, choosing to climb a wooden ladder rather than gaining access to the ramparts by entering the keep. Spotting William Marshal, the head of Hal's household knights, Henry beckoned for him to come up, too, and then gathered his son into a welcoming embrace. After exchanging hugs with his kinsmen, Hal courteously greeted the justiciar and Abbot Robert, who gave him credit for having much better manners than Count Geoffrey.

"Tell him, Brother," Hamelin prompted, nudging Henry in the ribs, and Hal was instantly alert.

"Tell me what?"

Henry feigned a scowl at Hamelin's impatience, but he was not one for waiting, either. "I have a surprise for you, lad."

Hal had retained a child's love of surprises, but some of his father's surprises had seemed more like ambushes. Moreover, he did not like to be called "lad" now that he was a man grown and an anointed king. "What?" he asked, with more wariness than anticipation.

"Marguerite is here."

Hal blinked in disappointment. He'd known Marguerite for most of his life; they'd been wed when he was five and she was two and a half. He tended to think of her as a little sister, when he thought of her at all. "Oh?" he said politely, wondering what he was supposed to say.

"Well, her presence is but half of the surprise. It is my intention to have her crowned this summer at Winchester. Archbishop Rotrou will preside and your cousin Roger has agreed to take part, too," Henry said, with a playful smile at Roger. "And because of the furor that Becket caused about your coronation, I have decided that you will be crowned again—a gesture of good will toward the Church."

Hal's interest was now fully engaged; he loved pageantry and rituals and revelries. His first thought was that they could hold a tournament afterward, but he decided not to share that idea with his father, knowing that Henry disapproved of tourneys as frivolous, wasteful, and a threat to the public order. His next thought was even better: the realisation that his coronation would be the ideal opportunity to achieve a long-delayed desire.

"And I could be knighted, too!"

Henry was already shaking his head. "No, lad, not yet. You know I think Louis ought to be the one to knight you. That would mean a great deal to him and go far toward mending the breach between us."

"But I do not care who knights me! All that truly matters is that it is done. I am already seventeen; how much longer must I wait?"

"Some events are worth waiting for," Henry said, giving his son a reassuring pat on the arm. "You are still young for such an accolade. How old were you, Will, when you were knighted?"

Caught off balance, William Marshal stiffened; the last thing he wanted was to be pulled into this ongoing squabble between father and son. "Twenty and one," he said reluctantly, feeling that he'd somehow let Hal down by speaking the truth.

Hal was not easily discouraged, though. "And how old were you?' he demanded of Henry, providing the answer himself, a triumphant "Sixteen!"

Not for the first time, Henry wondered how he could have sired such obstinate offspring, for Hal's brother Richard was even more headstrong and mulish, and thirteen-year-old Geoffrey was already showing signs of the same willfulness. Only little John and his Joanna were biddable and easily pleased. But a man wanted his sons to show pluck and spirit, and so he did not deny Hal outright, promising vaguely to give his request serious consideration.

Hal had heard this before, for they'd been having this same argument since Henry's return from Ireland last month. He was coming to the conclusion that his father's promises were counterfeit coin; they looked genuine, but they could not be spent. He was opening his mouth to protest further when Roger intervened.

"Hal," he said quietly, "I believe that is Marguerite coming out of the hall. You'd best go down and greet her, lad, ere she feels slighted. You know how sensitive lasses can be."

Hal almost asked Roger how he knew that, what with him becoming a priest at such a young age. But he was angry with his father, not his cousin, and his sense of fairness stifled the gibe. Nor did he want to hurt Marguerite, and he nodded grudgingly. Turning toward the ladder, his gaze came to rest upon the girl below in the bailey and he came to an abrupt halt.

"That cannot be Marguerite!"

At the sound of her name, she glanced upward. Hal had not seen her in more than a year; she'd left England in April of 1171 and had spent most of her time since then at her father's court. He'd remembered to send her gifts for New Year's and her saint's day, but she'd always been on the periphery of his life, the child-wife who'd eventually share his throne and bear his children—one day far in the future. Until then, he would not lack for female company; girls had been chasing after him since he was thirteen and he usually let them catch him. Now he gazed down at the heart-shaped face framed in a linen barbette, the chin-strap made newly fashionable by his mother, her fair hair covered by a gauzy veil of saffron silk, and he was stunned by the changes in her. She was so stylish of a sudden, slim and curvy where she'd been skinny and flat, so . . . so womanly.

He sketched a bow, she responded with a graceful curtsy, and he pantomimed that he'd be down straightaway. When he looked back at the men, they were all grinning. He was too amazed to take offense. "She is lovely," he marveled, counting surreptitiously on his fingers.

Henry spared him the trouble. "She is fourteen now, lad, and as you say, very lovely, indeed."

Hal hesitated. "Um . . . is she old enough to—?" He flushed slightly, but grinned, too, and his father laughed.

"Um . . . I would say so. But if you have doubts, you can always ask her."

Hal usually did not mind being teased, could give as good as he got. "I will," he said, winked, and headed for the ladder, descending to the bailey so rapidly that they half-expected him to land in a heap at Marguerite's feet. Instead, he sprang lightly to the ground and was soon gallantly kissing his wife's hand as she blushed prettily and cast him adoring looks through fluttering lashes.

"Well," Henry said, "I do believe the lass is answering him without even being asked," and they shared smiles, remembering what it was like to be young and bedazzled by a come-hither look, a neatly turned ankle. For Henry, memory took him back to a rain-spangled garden in Paris, an afternoon encounter with Louis's queen that would change lives and history. He could still remember how breathtakingly beautiful Eleanor was that day. He'd have been content to gaze into her eyes for hours, trying to decide if they were green with gold flecks or gold with green flecks. She had high, finely sculpted cheekbones, soft, flawless skin he'd burned to touch, and lustrous dark braids entwined with gold-thread ribbons he yearned to unfasten; he'd have bartered his chances of salvation to bury his face in that glossy, perfumed hair, to wind it around his throat and see it spread out on his pillow. He'd watched, mesmerized, as a crystal raindrop trickled toward the sultry curve of her mouth and wanted nothing in his life so much, before or since, as he wanted her.

She'd known that Louis was heeding his council's advice, planning to divorce her, and then compel her to wed a man of their choosing, a pliable puppet who'd keep her domains under the control of the French Crown. In that soaked summer garden she'd taken her destiny into her own hands, offering him Aquitaine and herself, and he was so besotted that he could not say which mattered more to him, the richest duchy in Europe or the woman in his arms.

They'd agreed to wait, though, for she shared his pragmatism as well as his passion, and they both knew even a glimmer of suspicion and Louis would never set her free. Nine months later, they were wed in her capital city of Poitiers. Never had he been happier, not even on the day he became England's king. Lying entangled in the sheets on their wedding night, she'd confided that their lovemaking had been like falling into a fire and somehow emerging unscathed, laughing huskily when he showed he was not yet sated and murmuring, "My lord duke, tonight all of Aquitaine is yours for the taking."

Henry returned to reality with a start, staring blankly at Roger as he realized he'd not heard a word of his cousin's question. Eleanor's alluring ghost receded into the past, leaving him with a sense of wonder that twenty years could have passed since that torrid May night. He also felt an odd sense of loss, although he wasn't sure why.

"I want to talk with you, Will," he said abruptly, and the young knight, who'd been sidling toward the ladder, straightened his shoulders and braced himself for what he knew was coming. "I've been warned," Henry continued, "that my son has been consorting with the wrong company. I cannot do much about his association with Raoul de Faye as he is the queen's uncle. But Hal has gathered around him a band of youths who are rakehells and idlers, light-minded, callow malcontents. Several of them accompanied him to Avranches: Juhel de Mayenne, Simon de Marisco, Adam d'Yquebeuf, and Hasculf de St Hilaire. You know them for what they are, Will, know that barnacles clinging to a ship's hull can slow it down, even render it unseaworthy. Why did you not alert me that he was being led astray?"

"My lord king . . ." Will was miserable, knowing that whatever he said, he was sure to be in the wrong, either with his young lord or his sovereign.

"Why do you think I chose you to tutor my son in the arts of war and chivalry? Because you sit a horse well and can wield a sword? There is no shortage of knights with those skills. I chose you because you are steadfast and honest, because you have more mother-wit than most men, because I thought I could rely upon you to watch over my son, to keep him safe."

"I would give my life for the young king," Will said simply, with such sincerity that none of those listening could doubt him. "I do watch over him, my liege. I've done my best to teach him what he must know, and I am proud of his prowess, for he is an expert rider and has mastered both sword and lance with admirable ease. But I cannot spy on him, not even for you, my lord king. I am his sworn man, and my first loyalty

must be to him. To do less would be a betrayal he would not forgive. Nor could I forgive myself."

The silence that followed was stifling. Girding himself to bear the king's wrath,
Will raised his head and met Henry's gaze. The king's eyes were the color of smoke, his
mouth tightly drawn, as if to stop angry words from escaping. "Keep him from harm,
Will," he said at last. "Do not let me down."

Will swallowed, knelt hastily, and then retreated just as hastily, vastly relieved by
his reprieve but not fully understanding it. Rainald did not understand, either. "The
impudence of the man! Why were you so forbearing with him? Had he dared talk to
me like that, I'd have dismissed him straightaway."

"If I did that," Henry said, "Hal would lose the one trustworthy and honorable
man in his service, the one man who'd be loyal to his last breath. How would that benefit my son, Rainald? Do you not know how rare such men are? Men who put loyalty
above ambition and greed and royal favor?" And even Rainald realized that Henry was
speaking not only of William Marshal, but of Thomas Becket, the false friend who'd
betrayed him for reasons he could never comprehend.

PEOPLE HAD BEGUN TO GATHER at dawn before the Cathedral church
of St Andrew the Apostle, not wanting to miss the spectacle of a king brought low,
forced to do penance like all mortal men. They were to be disappointed. Henry arrived
with the papal legates and barons and bishops beyond counting. They'd all gone into
the cathedral, where Henry swore upon the Holy Gospels that he'd neither commanded nor desired that the Archbishop of Canterbury be slain, and that when he was
told of the crime, he was horrified and truly grieved for the death of Thomas of
blessed memory. He admitted, though, that the killing was the result of his heedless,
angry words, and he pledged to honor the commitments made to Holy Church on
this, the last Sunday before Ascension in God's Year 1172, the eighteenth year of his
reign. His son the young king then took an oath to honor all those commitments that
did not relate only to Henry. But all of this was done out of sight and sound of the
waiting crowds.

When Henry finally emerged from the church, the spectators were disappointed
anew, for he was not bareheaded and barefoot and clad only in his shirt. A few men explained knowingly that he was spared the usual mortification because he'd not been
excommunicated, but most of the bystanders took a more cynical view, that kings
were always accorded special treatment, even by the Almighty. Henry knelt upon the
paving stones, only then removing his cap, and received public absolution by the Cardinals Albert and Theodwin. When he rose, the cardinals and the Bishop of Avranches

led him back into the cathedral, a symbolic act of reconciliation with the Church and the Almighty.

The dissatisfied onlookers dispersed when they realized the show was over. Roger, Bishop of Worcester, stood alone for a moment before slowly reentering the church, for he had been close enough to Henry to hear him say softly after the absolution: "Check, Thomas, and mate."

CHAPTER THREE

✦

June 1172
Poitiers, Poitou

*F*ROM AN OPEN WINDOW of the queen's solar in the Mauber-
geonne Tower, Maud, Countess of Chester, looked down upon a garden
vibrant with summer flowers and echoing with youthful high spirits.
Eleanor's son Geoffrey was playing quoits with two friends, a game that was by its very
nature boisterous and somewhat hazardous. When the players were youngsters of
thirteen and fourteen, it was guaranteed that the horseshoes would be flung about
with abandon, missing the targeted hob more often than not, scarring the grassy mead
and scaring songbirds from budding fruit trees and overhanging willows. The shouts
of the boys and the barking of their dogs had drawn an audience of giggling girls, all
of them highborn and destined for the marriage beds of princes.

The oldest of the girls was Maud's daughter-in-law, Bertrada, who'd wed her son
Hugh three years ago, becoming at thirteen countess of one of England's richest earldoms, the Honour of Chester. The prettiest was Geoffrey's sister Joanna, only in her
seventh year but already showing signs that she'd inherited her mother's fabled beauty.
Eleven-year-old Constance, dark-haired and whip-thin, was a great heiress in her own

right; betrothed to Geoffrey in early childhood, she would bring to him the Duchy of Brittany. And Alys, also eleven, was a daughter of the French king, plight-trothed to Geoffrey's older brother Richard, one day to rule with him over the vast, lush domains of Eleanor's Aquitaine.

Eleanor and Aquitaine. Maud always thought of her friend in those terms, for it was Aquitaine that had defined Eleanor, that had conferred upon her the queenships of France and then England. Few brides had ever brought such a dowry as Aquitaine to their husbands. Eleanor's duchy comprised the counties of Poitou, Berry, Saintonge, Angoulême, Périgord, the Limousin, La Marche, the Auvergne, the Agenais, and Gascony. Stretching from the Atlantic Ocean to the Massif Central and the Rhone Valley, from the Pyrenees to the River Loire, it encompassed much of southwestern France, dwarfing the lands controlled by the French king, and it had been blessed by nature and God with a mild climate, fertile soil, deep river valleys, ancient oak forests, and some of the best vineyards in Christendom. By taking Eleanor as his queen, Louis had gained greatly in stature and the French coffers had overflowed with the riches of Aquitaine. Maud thought that her cousin Harry might not even have won his crown had he not wed Eleanor as soon as she was free. Aquitaine had been his stepping-stone to the English throne.

Maud's friendship with Eleanor had endured for almost twenty years, but she'd never spent that much time in the other woman's domains, for neither had Eleanor. For much of her married life, she'd been traveling with Henry or acting on his behalf in Normandy and England or occupied with her many pregnancies. It was only four years ago that she'd taken up residence again in Aquitaine, holding her own court at Poitiers and gathering the reins of government into her own hands.

Turning away from the window, Maud wandered restlessly about the chamber. Eleanor had excused herself to confer with Saldebreuil de Sanzay, her constable in Poitou, and Maud was growing bored with her own company. Several charters were spread across a trestle table and she scanned the top one briefly. It was a routine act of patronage, remitting taxes for a citizen of La Rochelle in exchange for his agreement to pay rent to the abbey of Fontevrault. What caught Maud's attention was the change in the form of address. Instead of the usual *Fidelibus Regis et suis*, it read: *Fidelibus suis*.

Maud gazed down thoughtfully at the parchment. Eleanor's charters had always begun "To the king's faithful followers and hers." This one was addressed simply to "her faithful followers." Did it matter? A careless mistake by her scribe? Or another feather in the wind, a subtle but significant indication that Eleanor was asserting her independence and her authority? Her right to govern in her own name?

A sudden spate of cursing drew her back to the window. Geoffrey's friends had begun to quarrel over a throw and before long, they were rolling around in the grass as Geoffrey and the girls cheered them on. Maud watched serenely; with two sons of her own, she knew how little such youthful squabbles meant.

She didn't hear the opening door, did not realize she was no longer alone until Eleanor joined her at the window. Eleanor, the mother of four sons, paid even less heed than Maud to the garden brawl. "Petronilla's daughter has just ridden in," she said, hazel eyes luminous with pleasure. "I was hoping she'd arrive in time to witness Richard's investiture."

Maud jogged her memory. Isabelle was the elder of Petronilla's two daughters, wed as a child to the Count of Flanders; Alienor, who'd wed Isabelle's brother-in-law, the Count of Boulogne, a few years ago, was already here. As far as Maud knew, Eleanor had not spent much time with her sister's children. That she had taken the trouble to make sure both girls were present in Poitiers showed Maud how much her friend missed Petronilla, whose death that past year had robbed Eleanor of her last living link to a sun-drenched, blissful childhood, to a time when she'd been indulged and pampered and cherished as her father's favorite in this exotic land she so loved.

Below in the garden, Joanna had decided the tussling had gone on long enough and, with an authority that would have done credit to a girl twice her age, she demanded that the boys stop fighting. They did, probably glad of an excuse to end their pummeling, but Maud was amused by the little girl's aplomb, thinking that the young Eleanor must have been just as self-assured and poised. Smiling at Joanna's mother, she said, "Are the rumors true about Joanna? That she may soon be plight-trothed to the King of Sicily?"

"There have been talks," Eleanor confirmed. "But we're still in the preliminary stages of negotiation, so it is too soon to tell how it will go. There is no hurry, after all, for Joanna will only be seven in October. I see no reason for her to grow up in a foreign court," she said, so emphatically that Maud thought of Joanna's older sisters. Tilda had been the first to go, wed two years ago in far-off Saxony at the age of twelve. Then it was the turn of Eleanor's namesake, known as Leonora, wed to the young King of Castile at the age of nine.

The two women looked at each other, the same thought in both their minds. In their world, princesses were born to be bartered for foreign alliances, and although the Church officially disapproved of child marriages, it was a common occurrence. Henry's mother had been sent to Germany at the age of eight. Marguerite had been wed to Hal before she was three. Eleanor had been thirteen when her father's unexpected death set in motion the events that would give her the crown of France and a life in exile. Maud had been older than Eleanor, but not by much, when she'd been married to the Earl of Chester, a man utterly lacking in either honor or mercy, but one of the great lords of the realm. Because she was quick-witted and resilient and pragmatic, Maud had learned to live in relative peace with her savage, unstable husband, to take solace and joy in her children, and, eventually, to revel in the freedom of widowhood. But she had made sure that her daughter would be no child bride; Beatrix had not wed Ralph de Malpas until after she'd celebrated her nineteenth birthday.

As the only daughter in a family of sons, Maud had often longed for a sister, and as she gazed at Eleanor now, it occurred to her that this woman was as close as any blood-sister could be. They had much in common, both beautiful in their youth, both strong-willed, proud, and confident in their powers to charm, both now within hailing distance of their fifth decade, for they would celebrate their forty-eighth birthdays that summer.

"I had an interesting conversation this morn with your niece Alienor," Maud commented, with a wry smile. "She wanted to know why I had never remarried after Randolph's death."

"I hope you did not shatter all her illusions about marriage," Eleanor said, no less wryly. "You must remember that her parents were that rarity, a couple who'd wed for love . . . or lust. And Alienor seems content enough with her own husband . . . so far."

"No, I was circumspect . . . for me. I said merely that my memories of Randolph were too vivid for me to contemplate taking another husband."

Eleanor laughed approvingly. "It is no easy feat for a wealthy widow to escape her legion of suitors. You must have been very fleet of foot, indeed, dearest."

"I made sure," Maud acknowledged, "never to leave my lands without a sizable escort, one large enough to discourage any ambitious young lordlings with ambush and marriage on their minds." Knowing that Eleanor had fended off two such attempts to force her into matrimony as she'd journeyed back to Aquitaine after her marriage to the French king had been annulled, she indulged her curiosity to ask: "If you could have been certain, Eleanor, that you need not fear being remarried against your will, would you have remained unwed?"

Eleanor's mouth tightened, almost imperceptibly. "You do not truly think that the French court would have permitted that? No sooner was the ink dry upon the annulment decree than Louis's advisors were arguing amongst themselves, deciding which French puppet to place in my bed. Had they even suspected I'd so hastily wed a man of my own choosing, they'd never have allowed me to return to my own domains. But yours was a conjectural question, was it not? So in that spirit: 'Be not entangled again in the yoke of bondage.'"

Maud blinked, for Eleanor rarely let her bitterness show so nakedly. "Your interpretation of Scriptures is somewhat uncanonical," she said dryly. "That is from St Paul, is it not? If my memory serves, he also said it was better to marry than to burn, hardly a rousing endorsement of wedlock."

"I have never understood," Eleanor confessed, "why the Church sees lust as so great a sin. Why would the Almighty have made coupling so pleasurable if it were so wrong? But when I tried to argue that point with Louis, he was horrified that I dared to question the teachings of the Holy Fathers, and it convinced him that we were a depraved and wanton lot, we southerners. He could never forgive himself for the carnal pleasures he found in my bed. He was not much of a husband, or a king, either, for that matter, but by God, he'd have made a superb monk."

Eleanor's face shadowed, for even now, memories of her marriage to the French king were not welcome ones. "He may well have been right, though, about the people of the south. We view lust as we do wine and food and laughter, as essential ingredients for a joyful life. My grandfather . . . ah, how he loved to vex his priests and distress his confessor! He wrote troubadour poetry, you know, and some of it would have made a harlot blush. He liked to joke that one day he'd establish his own nunnery and fill it with ladies of easy virtue. On our wedding night, I told Harry some of the more scandalous stories about my grandfather, and he laughed until he nearly choked, gasping that between us, we had a family tree rooted in Hell."

This last memory was both more pleasant and more painful than those from her marriage to Louis, and Eleanor fell silent for several moments. "I think," she said at last, "that I would have wed Harry even if I were not threatened with a husband of the French court's choosing. I wanted children, for I knew Louis would never let me see our two daughters, and indeed, he did not. I needed an heir for Aquitaine and I wanted to give Harry sons, to prove wrong those who'd dared to call me a barren queen. I always knew it was Louis's failing, not mine. How could I conceive if I so often slept alone?"

"And I am assuming that you had no trouble getting Harry into your bed?" Maud queried, so blandly that Eleanor could not help smiling.

"You could safely say that," she conceded, and Maud felt a surge of sadness that things had gone so wrong between her cousin and his queen. She remembered how it had once been, remembered the early years of their marriage, when they'd been so sure that the world, like the English crown, was theirs for the taking, lusting after empires and each other, striking such sparks with their quarreling and their lovemaking that the air around them always seemed charged, as if a storm were about to break.

Eleanor's attention was focused again upon the gardens. She was still a very handsome woman, but even queens were vulnerable to the passage of time. Now, though, her smile was dazzling, chasing away the years, cares, even regrets. Maud glanced over to see what she found so interesting.

Another youth had sauntered into the garden, accompanied by a huge wolfhound. Maud guessed him to be about sixteen, for he was already taller than many grown men, and he moved with the athletic grace of one utterly comfortable in his own body. Maud knew how unusual it was for one so young to have such physical presence; both of her sons had been as clumsy and gangling as colts when they were this boy's age. He had curly red-gold hair and a scattering of freckles, and she would later marvel that she had not known his identity at once, but it was not until Joanna gave a delighted squeal and flung herself into his arms that she realized she was looking at Eleanor's second son, Richard, who would on the morrow be invested as Duke of Aquitaine.

"Jesu, that is Richard!"

"Indeed it is." Eleanor glanced curiously at her friend. "Why do you sound so surprised?"

"Because the last time I saw him, he was a boy, not a man. He looks older than his years, for he will not be fifteen until the autumn, no?"

"September. He was born on the Nativity of Our Lady. The first and only time that Harry was present for one of my confinements."

Maud grinned at the memory, for she'd been present, too, at Richard's birth. "I remember now. Harry's brother Will later told me that they'd been hard put to keep him from bursting into the birthing chamber. Harry was never one for waiting."

Below in the garden, Richard was swinging Joanna in circles, making her shriek with laughter. The other girls had clustered around him, but Geoffrey and his friends did not seem as pleased by his arrival in their midst. Maud could not blame Geoffrey for his discomfort. Although only a twelvemonth separated the birthdays of the two boys, Geoffrey looked like a child next to his brother, his slightness of build and his lack of height cruelly accentuated by Richard's adult appearance. Maud's two sons had been allies from earliest childhood. She suspected that was not the case with Richard and Geoffrey.

The sight of Eleanor's sons reminded her that all of the royal brood was not accounted for. Hal and Marguerite were in Normandy with her brother Roger, making plans for their coronation at Winchester. But no mention had been made of Eleanor's youngest nestling, John. The lastborn, the afterthought, the child jokingly dubbed John Lackland by his father.

"Is John here, too?" she asked, and Eleanor shook her head.

"He is with the nuns at Fontevrault," she said, and while her words were matter-of-fact, her tone was dismissive.

Maud was saddened but not surprised by the other woman's indifference, for she had been there for John's birth. She'd been summoned in haste by Eleanor's sister;

Petronilla had been panicked, fearing that Eleanor might die in childbirth. Her fears were understandable, for Eleanor was forty-two and the older a woman was, the greater the risks she faced in the birthing chamber. But the real reason for Petronilla's alarm was guilt. She had made a grievous mistake. She had told Eleanor about Henry and Rosamund Clifford.

Maud turned her head aside, not wanting Eleanor to read her thoughts. It was more than five years since Eleanor had suffered so to give John life, but to Maud, those grim memories would never fade. She knew Eleanor had not expected her husband to be faithful. She was worldly enough to know that a man with an itch would scratch it. But Rosamund Clifford had not been a passing fancy, a bedmate whose name he'd not remember come morning. The daughter of a Welsh Marcher lord, Rosamund had been favored with a pretty face, golden hair, and a gentle, docile nature. And to the surprise of all but her ambitious, conniving father, she had stirred in Henry more than lust.

Maud supposed she should not have been so surprised by his liaison with this biddable girl-woman. But she'd expected better of her cousin. A man worthy of Eleanor of Aquitaine ought not to be susceptible to fluttering lashes, flattery, and bedazzled adoration.

Be that as it may, he had taken Rosamund to his bed, a pardonable sin. But he'd then grown careless and indiscreet, so much so that their trysts were soon an open secret. Heedless of Eleanor's pride, he had installed Rosamund at Woodstock, a favorite royal manor. And soon afterward, Petronilla had decided—for reasons known only to her and the Devil—to tell Eleanor, then in the seventh month of a difficult pregnancy, of her husband's public infidelity. Eleanor had reacted as anyone but Petronilla could have predicted. Although it was the dead of winter, she took ship for England and headed straight to Woodstock.

Maud had not been witness to the meeting between her cousin's queen and his concubine. All she knew of it came from Petronilla, who had confided in baffled frustration that nothing had happened. Encountering the girl on the snow-covered path to the spring, Eleanor had spoken only four words. *How old are you?* And when Rosamund, as yet unaware of her identity, had said she was nineteen, Eleanor had said nothing else. She had, Petronilla reported indignantly, just turned and walked away!

Maud had understood Eleanor's response even if Petronilla had not. A woman heavy with child was at her most vulnerable, clumsy, and awkward in a stranger's body. It would be adding insult to injury for an aggrieved wife to discover that her husband was smitten with a girl young enough to be her own daughter. Eleanor had refused to remain at Woodstock, retreating to her palace at Oxford, and it was there that she'd gone into labor weeks before the baby was due. The birth had been a hard one, and they had not been sure either mother or child would survive it. But eventually Eleanor's last son was born, a small, dark creature who could not have been more unlike her other infants, so sun-kissed and robust and golden. John had been fretful from the first, almost as if he sensed his entry into the world had been unwelcome, and when the exhausted Eleanor had shown no interest, Maud had been the one to instruct the chaplain to baptize him for the saint whose day it was, St John the Evangelist. Maud had understood that John was a living reminder to Eleanor of pain and humiliation and betrayal. She had hoped that in time a mother's instincts would prevail over a wronged wife's resentment. She was no longer sure that would ever happen.

In the years since John's birth, Eleanor and Henry's marriage had suffered. On the surface, all seemed well. But the telltale signs were there for those in the know. Eleanor had begun to pass most of her time in Aquitaine, ostensibly to soothe the rebellious inclinations of her restive, recalcitrant barons. Henry's liaison with Rosamund Clifford continued, although he'd taken care to be much more discreet after his Woodstock blunder. Their separations stretched out for months at a time; it was no longer a certainty that they'd hold their Christmas and Easter Courts together. Most troubling for Maud, Eleanor had kept her distance in the aftermath of Thomas Becket's murder, offering no comfort to Henry at a time when he desperately needed it. It was no surprise, therefore, that there was much gossip and speculation about their possible estrangement.

When she'd learned from Eleanor that they had never discussed Rosamund or Woodstock, Maud feared that they had crossed their Rubicon. From what little Eleanor had confided and from all she'd left unsaid, Maud had concluded that there had been a communication breakdown of monumental proportions. Eleanor, proudest of the proud, had waited for her husband to broach the subject of Rosamund, to offer her an apology for flaunting his mistress so openly. But Henry had utterly misread her silence, vastly relieved that she had not given him an ultimatum, had not demanded that he banish Rosamund from his bed and life. Not understanding that she was unwilling to risk the humiliation of a refusal, he'd assumed that his worldly, pragmatic wife did not see his infidelity as so great a sin. Grateful that she'd chosen to deal with the problem of Rosamund Clifford by not even acknowledging there was a problem, he'd eagerly entered into their conspiracy of silence, never once detecting the scent of burning bridges in the air.

If her cousin Henry had allotted Rosamund Clifford too little significance, Maud's other male kin had given her too much. Her uncles Rainald and Ranulf and her brother Roger were well aware that Henry's relationship with his queen had taken a turn for the worse, but they blamed Rosamund for every fissure, every crack in the foundation of the royal marriage. Maud knew better, for she understood that it was far more complicated than a king's careless adultery. Eleanor's greatest grievance was not a simpering lass with flaxen hair and smooth skin. It was Aquitaine, always Aquitaine.

It puzzled Maud that her male relatives could not see this. Was it that men could not believe a woman might share their ambitions, their need for power? Eleanor saw herself as more than Henry's queen, mother of his children. First and foremost, she was Duchess of Aquitaine, never doubting that she could have ruled as well as any man and better than most. She knew the importance of the dowry she'd brought to each of her marriages. But the expectations she'd brought to those marriages were very different. She'd been given no say in her marriage to Louis, but in daring to wed Henry, she'd taken her destiny into her own hands. She had no intention to be subservient to her new husband. What she'd had in mind was a partnership.

It had not come to pass, of course. She'd underestimated Henry's strong will and overestimated the influence she could wield over him. It was not that he believed, as most men did, that women were, by their very natures, incapable of exercising power or acting without male guidance. No son of the Empress Maude could ever look upon women as mere broodmares, and Eleanor had counted upon that. She had not realized, though, that Henry was, by *his* very nature, unable to share power. He had occasionally allowed her to act as regent in his absence, but he always kept a firm hand on the reins. Nor did he accord her opinions the respect she felt they deserved, utterly ignoring her warnings against elevating Thomas Becket to the archbishopric of Canterbury. Too often, she'd found herself relegated to the sidelines or the birthing chamber, more and more aware of the ultimate irony—that the husband she'd discarded had paid her more heed than the one she'd chosen for herself.

But Henry had done more than circumscribe Eleanor's role as his queen. He'd usurped her role as ruler of Aquitaine. Within two years of his coronation as England's king, he'd demanded that her barons do homage to him, homage previously reserved for her alone. The riches of Aquitaine had gone into his coffers. The coins issued in her domains bore his name, not hers. When their daughter had wed the King of Castile two years ago, he had given the province of Gascony as her marriage portion, not consulting Eleanor as he disposed of lands she'd expected to go to her heir, to Richard. Even after he'd permitted her to return to Poitiers, he continued to control her financial and military resources, keeping the real power in his own hands.

No, Rosamund Clifford was only one of Eleanor's grudges. The girl may have ignited the fire, but the fuel was already stacked up, awaiting such a spark. The saddest aspect of it all to Maud was that she was sure her cousin was utterly unaware of the depths of his wife's resentment. She thought that he was undoubtedly the most brilliant man she'd ever known, with one great failing. He seemed unable to view their world from any perspective but his own. Just as he'd been oblivious to Eleanor's discontent, he could not comprehend why his eldest son was so unhappy to be a king in name only. Maud had seen the damage his blindness had done to his marriage. She could only hope that it would not prove as harmful with his sons.

Another quarrel had broken out in the gardens below them, this one between Richard and Geoffrey. Richard had demanded a turn in their game of quoits, Geoffrey had refused, and now they were debating the issue in loud, belligerent voices. Glancing at Eleanor, Maud said diplomatically, "I imagine the lads are too near in years to get along with each other. I'd wager they both are closer to Hal."

"Not really," Eleanor admitted. "Hal and Geoffrey have their differences, though they usually patch them up. But Richard and Hal are like chalk and cheese, squabbling over the most minor matters. I keep hoping they'll outgrow it," she added, not very convincingly.

Maud was surprised, for Hal was very easygoing, with a flair for friendship. "It is only natural," she ventured, "that Richard would be jealous of Hal. It must be difficult for a youngster to understand why his older brother inherits the crown and the—" She got no further, for Eleanor had begun to laugh.

"Jealous? Richard? Good Lord, no! Richard cares not a fig for England." Gazing down at her second son, she said, with absolute certainty and great satisfaction, "Richard does not begrudge Hal his crown or kingdom, not as long as he gets Aquitaine."

On the following day, the Sunday after Pentecost, as church bells pealed and the citizens thronged to watch, Richard was escorted through the city streets to the abbey of St Hilaire. There Archbishop Bertram of Bordeaux and Bishop John of Poitiers offered him the lance and banner that were the insignia of the duchy, and he was officially recognized as Count of Poitou and Duke of Aquitaine.

Maud had attended many opulent feasts in her life: Christmas fetes, weddings, a coronation. She soon decided that Eleanor's revelries in her son's honor would rank among the most memorable. The great hall was shimmering in light, sun streaming from the open windows, and ablaze with color, the walls decorated with embroidered hangings in rich shades of gold and crimson. New rushes had been strewn about, fragrant with lavender, sweet woodruff, and balm. Because the hearth had not been lit, the guests were spared the aggravation of smoke spiraling up toward the rafters, and the air was sweet to breathe, perfumed with honeysuckle and violet, their seductive scents luring in from the gardens butterflies as blue as the summer sky.

The tables were as splendid as their surroundings, draped in snowy white linen cloths, set with silver wine cups and salt nefs and delicate finger bowls. Maud, her son Hugh, and daughter-in-law Bertrada were among the honored guests seated at the high table, giving her an ideal vantage point to observe her fellow diners and the happenings in the hall. Clearly Eleanor had spared no expense to make Richard's day as perfect as possible. A small fountain bubbled with wine, candelabras flared with candles of wax, not tallow, and Maud was impressed to see that every guest had been provided with a knife, for it was normally expected that people would bring their own utensils.

The food and drink were equally praiseworthy. Eleanor had ordered rich red wines from Cahors and Gascony, costly sweet wine from Cyprus, and for the fortunate guests at the high table, the celebrated Saint Pourçain from her Auvergne, a wine so outrageously expensive that even Maud had rarely tasted it.

A trumpet fanfare announced the arrival of each course, followed by ewers bearing lavers of warm, perfumed water so guests could wash their hands. The dishes were carried in on large platters and then ladled onto smaller plates called tailloirs at each table so that the diners could help themselves. It was common practice for three people to share a tailloir, but here, too, Eleanor had been lavish and each dish was meant for two guests, with those at the high table accorded an unheard-of honor, individual dishes for each one. Maud could not recall such a luxury at her cousin's coronation, not even at the famously extravagant fetes hosted by Thomas Becket in his days as Henry's chancellor.

She was so delighted by the quality of the food that she contemplated, half-seriously, bribing Eleanor's cooks to join her household. The guests were offered goose stuffed with herbs, garlic, grapes, and sage. There were grilled oysters and a lamprey torte with walnuts, mint, cloves, and saffron. A delicate soup of almond milk and onions, with sops of bread. Pike in a white wine galentyne sauce. A blancmange of venison meat, blanched almonds, rice, and sugar. The cooks had done themselves proud with the lighter dishes, too, providing an almond tart doucette and another of cream custard, and the sweet wafers known as angel's bread. Eleanor had even imported oranges from Spain so that her cooks could prepare a comfit with the candied rind, honey, and ginger.

When the meal was finally done, Eleanor's almoner collected the trenchers—stale bread used as plates—to be distributed to the poor, and the trestle tables were dismantled so there would be room for entertainment. Harpists and flutists had played while the guests were eating, but now livelier diversion was provided: tumblers and daredevils juggling torches and swords. Maud had been invited to join Eleanor and Richard upon the dais, so she had one of the best seats in the hall, but she found her fellow guests more interesting than the performers.

Virtually all of the highborn of Aquitaine and the lands farther south were present. Eleanor's own family was there, of course, to share Richard's triumph. Raoul de Faye, her maternal uncle and seneschal. Her other uncle, Hugh, Viscount of Chatellerault, his new wife, Ella, and his son, William. Her two nieces, Petronilla's daughters, Isabelle and Alienor. Her sister by marriage, the Lady Emma of Laval, Henry's half sister, recently widowed, but so beautiful that it was unlikely she'd remain unmarried for long. If anyone but Maud thought it odd that Henry was absent, that opinion was not voiced. According to Eleanor, Henry had gone into Brittany to deal with yet another rebellion, but it was obvious to Maud that he was not missed.

The lords of Poitou were well represented. Saldebreuil de Sanzay, constable of Poitou. The Count of La Marche. Count William of Angoulême and his son, Vulgrin. Geoffrey de Rançon, Lord of Taillebourg. Porteclie de Mauzé, a distant cousin of Eleanor's, and Sir Hervé le Panetier, her steward. Aimar, Viscount of Limoges, and his wife, Sarah, a daughter of Maud's uncle Rainald. Maud was particularly interested in the presence of the Counts of La Marche and Angoulême and the Viscount of Limoges, for they'd been the ringleaders in a rebellion against Henry just four years ago. She wondered if they were signaling by their attendance that they were hostile to Henry, not Eleanor and Richard. Or had they simply not wanted to miss such a celebrated fete? The Archbishop of Bordeaux and Bishop of Poitiers were present, as was the abbot of Tournay. And there was a large contingent from the lands to the south of Aquitaine.

Just as Henry cast a long shadow, so, too, did the other conspicuous absentee: Raimon St Gilles, Count of Toulouse, the most powerful lord of the south and the most hated. Like his father before him, Raimon was ambitious, ruthless, and always dangerous. Count Raimon had long been a sworn enemy of the Dukes of Aquitaine, for Eleanor's father had a claim to Toulouse. Maud thought the claim to be rather tenuous, arising out of a disputed inheritance involving Eleanor's grandmother. Eleanor took it very seriously, though, enough to have convinced both of her husbands to assert her claim by force. Neither Louis nor Henry had succeeded in prying Toulouse from Count Raimon's grip, but their failures had not discouraged Eleanor and she continued to consider Toulouse as rightfully part of her domains, part of Richard's inheritance.

The jugglers had completed their performance, and a troubadour had taken center stage. The audience quieted, and he began to sing a lover's plaint, imploring his lady that she could make of him a begger or richer than any king, so great was her power over him.

Maud joined the other guests in applauding enthusiastically. "That was wonderful," she exclaimed. "Who is he?"

"That is Levet, Raimbaut d'Aurenga's joglar." Seeing Maud's blank look, Eleanor leaned over to explain further. "A joglar is similar to a jongleur, a court performer. Most troubadours do not sing their own compositions, not those of high birth like Raimbaut or Countess Biatriz."

Maud had glanced curiously toward Raimbaut d'Aurenga, regretting that she was no longer young, for this southern lord was as handsome as he was talented. But her head swiveled back toward Eleanor at the mention of Countess Biatriz. "The Countess of Valentinois? She is a troubadour, too?"

"She calls herself a trobairitz, but yes. She is very gifted and I hope that we'll hear some of her songs tonight. Raimbaut's sister the Lady Tibors, is a trobairitz, too, I believe."

Maud was fascinated, for it was very unusual in their world for women to compose poetry. The only female writer she knew was Henry's half sister, the Abbess of Shaftsbury, who wrote skillful lais and fables under the name Marie de France. And here were two women poets as guests at Eleanor's table. Why did women troubadours flourish here and not elsewhere?

A slender, dark-eyed woman followed the joglar, and Maud's interest sharpened, for surely she must be going to perform one of the compositions of the Countess Biatriz. Much to her disappointment, the song was in the *lengua romana,* the language of the south. "Is she not going to sing in French?"

Eleanor shook her head. "I forgot that you do not know the *lengua romana.* In my grandfather's youth, the dialect of Poitou was very similar to the *lengua romana* or *lemozi,* as they call it, but nowadays Poitevin is more like the French of the north. Most of those in my lands speak both tongues, and I made certain that Richard was tutored in the *lengua romana.* Slide your chair closer and I will translate for you."

"I've lately been in great distress over a knight who once was mine," she quoted. "She says she loved him to excess, but he betrayed her because she could not sleep with him. Night and day she suffers, lamenting her mistake."

Maud's eyes widened. "Is it common for women of the south to be so bluntspoken?"

Eleanor grinned. "In one of the other verses of that song, she declares that she'd give almost anything to have her handsome knight in her husband's place!"

Maud shook her head in bemusement. "Life is truly different in these southern regions, especially for women!"

"Women are more free to speak their minds," Eleanor agreed. "And men even listen to us at times, for power is not solely a male preserve. Here we do not follow the practice of primogeniture. The eldest son does not inherit his father's estate; it is divided up amongst all the sons. And often it is bequeathed to a daughter. Take the Countess of Mauguio over there. She inherited Mauguio upon her father's death and held it in her own right through two marriages. Last year her son dared to call himself Count of Mauguio and began to intrigue with the House of Montpellier, long an adversary of her family. She was outraged by what she saw as his betrayal."

"I do not blame her," Maud exclaimed. "I have so often heard sad stories like this, women swept aside like so much chaff by male kin unwilling to wait for their inheritance."

"Ah, but this is not France or England. The Countess of Mauguio struck back swiftly, disinheriting her impatient son in favor of her granddaughter."

Maud was amazed. "She could do that?"

Eleanor's eyes reflected the closest candle flame, taking on greenish glints in its flickering light. "This is not England or France," she repeated proudly, and Maud could only nod, thinking, Indeed not!

Raimbaut d'Aurenga's joglar had taken up a gittern again, making ready to sing another of his lord's compositions. His earlier French rendition had been a courtesy for the Poitevin guests, but now he chose his own language, the lyrical *lengua romana* of the troubadour.

"*Cars, douz e fenhz del bederesc*
M'es sos bas chanz, per cui m'aerc;
C'ab joi s'espan viu e noire."

Without Eleanor to translate for her, the words held no meaning for Maud. She discovered it was easy to be caught up in the flow of the language, though, for it held a melodic harmony that French or English lacked, putting her in mind of the softer sounds of Spanish or Italian. It was a beautiful tongue, this *lengua romana*, but an alien one. And as she listened, she fully comprehended for the first time that this was an alien world, too, Eleanor's Aquitaine.

CHAPTER FOUR

✦

November 1172
Gisors Castle, Norman Vexin

*M*ARGUERITE WISHED that she did not feel so shy with this stranger who was her father. She did not doubt that the French king was a kindly man, a good man, quick to smile, slow to find fault. The vices of his youth—his temper, his stubbornness—had been mitigated by the passage of time and his piety was acclaimed by all. She knew he was in his fifty-third year, an age that seemed ancient to a girl not yet fifteen. His flaxen hair was sparse around his crown, like a monk's tonsure, and his eyes were heavy-lidded, but still as brightly blue as a summer sky; she'd always been thankful that she'd inherited his fairness and not the unfashionable dark coloring of her dead mother, a Spanish princess she could not remember. She'd heard it said that he'd been comely in his youth, and she supposed it might well be true. But if she could visualize Louis in his prime, she could not see him wed to her husband's mother. Each time she'd tried to envision Louis and Eleanor together, her imagination failed her.

It occurred to her that she could count on the fingers of one hand the times she'd been alone with Louis, for she'd been sent to King Henry's court before she'd celebrated her first birthday. But she'd grown up knowing that she was the daughter of the

King of France, knowing what a proud heritage that was, and never doubting that this father she'd so rarely seen had not forgotten her. Now, though, she was discovering that they had little to say to each other and when Louis suggested that they seek out her husband, she felt a surge of relief, for Hal was never at a loss for words.

A TILTYARD HAD BEEN set up in the northern end of the upper bailey, and the young King of England had drawn an admiring audience. A skilled rider, Hal had made several successful runs at the quintain, hitting the target dead-on each time, whereas his competitors were not so fortunate. As Louis and Marguerite approached, a knight struck the shield a glancing blow and was unhorsed when he was smacked by the sandbag attached to a wooden pivot. When it was Hal's turn again, he drove his ten-foot lance into the shield with enough force to set the quintain post vibrating.

"Well done!" Louis called out, loudly enough for Hal to hear, and then, in a lower tone, to Marguerite, "The lad could not look more like a king with the blessed crown of Jerusalem upon his head."

"I think so, too," she agreed, so ardently that Louis smiled, pleased that she seemed to have found such happiness in her marriage. At that moment Marguerite happened to notice the boy watching from the sidelines, a pale, solemn child with an untidy shock of brown hair, her half brother, Philippe. So jubilant had Louis been upon Philippe's birth on an August evening seven years ago that he became known as Philippe Dieu-Donné, the God-given. Louis had already sired four daughters, but Philippe was his heart's joy, an only son born late in life to a man who'd long despaired of begetting a male heir. Never had Marguerite seen such a doting father and, as she glanced over at her little brother, she found herself thinking unkindly that no one would ever say of Philippe what Louis had just said of Hal.

Once Hal caught sight of them, he tossed his lance to a squire and swung from the saddle. He greeted Louis with a flourish, acknowledging their kinship both by marriage and vassalage, for he'd done homage to the French king for the duchy of Normandy. Slipping his hand into Marguerite's, he entwined their fingers together, a silent but subtle declaration of unity that Louis noted approvingly. He was very pleased with this young son-in-law of his, for Hal was good-natured and gallant, but also malleable and overly eager to claim his kingship, chaffing at the bit like a finely bred stallion ready to run.

"Come, walk with me," Louis said, shepherding them in the direction of the gardens, bare and fallow under a pallid November sun. Passing through the wicker gate, he seated himself upon a wooden bench, gesturing for them to join him. "Your invitation to meet me at Gisors gladdened my heart," he murmured, "and was a most welcome surprise, for I'd heard that you planned to remain in England into the new year, holding your Christmas Court at Winchester."

"That was our intent," Hal admitted, hesitating before confirming what Louis already knew. "But my lord father summoned me to return to Normandy." Adding, after another, longer pause, "And of course I obeyed."

But not willingly, Louis thought, not willingly at all. "Marguerite told me that you came to Gisors straightaway from the harbor at Barfleur. How long shall I have the pleasure of your company ere you must seek out your lord father?"

Hal's shoulders twitched in a half shrug. "In truth," he said, "I am in no hurry to see my father." Finding a smile, he said wryly, "The Church holds that fighting during Christmastide is a sin, a violation of the Truce of God."

"Are you so sure that you and your father will quarrel once you are together?" Louis asked, and Hal raised his head, his eyes searching his father-in-law's face. He seemed to be making up his mind how much to confide, and Marguerite leaned over, whispered something in his ear too softly for Louis to hear.

"Am I sure that we will quarrel?" Hal said at last. "No . . . it need not be. I have only to defer to my father in all matters, stifle my complaints, accept his judgment without question or qualm, and we will be in perfect accord."

Louis was faintly surprised that the wound had already begun to fester. The lad was like his father in one way if no other—their mutual lack of patience. "If you were to defer to Henry in all matters," he said mildly, "you would be a puppet prince, not an anointed king."

Hal stood up suddenly, began to pace. "If you see that so clearly, why cannot my father?"

"Well, we shall have to make him see." Turning then to his daughter, Louis suggested that she make sure that her little brother Philippe did not get into any mischief whilst he and her husband continued their discussion.

Marguerite had been taught that obedience was a woman's duty, and she did not object to being dismissed so summarily. As she exited the garden, she glanced back and smiled at the sight meeting her eyes—Hal and her father talking quietly together, their heads almost touching, their faces intent. He has found an ally in Papa, she thought, and with a light step, she went to find Philippe.

NORMANDY WAS A LAND honeycombed with castles, but none were as formidable as the cliff-top stronghold overlooking the River Ante. Beneath the walls of Falaise, the village straggled down the steep slope, its narrow street deserted in the chill November twilight. From a window in the upper chamber of the castle's great keep, Meliora looked in vain for signs of life. The villagers were huddled by their hearths, secure in the shadow of the royal fortress as night descended over the Norman countryside.

Meliora pulled the shutters into place with a shiver, went to stand by the chamber's sole source of heat, a brazier heaped with charcoal. She knew her mistress did not like Falaise and she understood why. The castle had dominated the valley for one hundred years, and had been designed for defense. The towering rectangular keep was impregnable, but not particularly comfortable. Rosamund Clifford's chamber was neither spacious nor well lighted, although the wall hangings were made of costly Lincoln wool and the canopied bed was piled high with plush coverlets. Since Henry was so rarely there to keep her warm at night, he at least saw to it that she did not lack for fur-lined blankets.

Rosamund was seated before a wooden frame, working upon an altar cloth of finely woven Spanish linen. She was an accomplished needlewoman and passed much of her free time embroidering church vestments. She had recently finished a beautiful cross-stitched chasuble for the priest at Godstow priory, and Meliora supposed that the altar cloth was meant for Godstow, too, as Rosamund was very generous to the nunnery where she'd been educated. She looked up with a quick smile as Meliora drew near and the older woman smiled back, wishing that Rosamund did not look so pale, so fragile.

When the king had engaged her for Rosamund, she had accepted eagerly, for she was a widow twice over with grown children and she preferred life on a larger stage than her home village back in Cornwall. She'd assumed that the king wanted her to act as a shepherd, keeping his little lamb safe from wolves. She'd not expected, though, that his lamb would become so dear to her.

Nor had she expected that her employment would last so long. Far more pragmatic than the convent-reared Rosamund, she'd assumed that the king's passion for the girl would soon flame out. But seven years later the fire still burned, although she wondered cynically if their frequent separations played a role in that. She often thought Rosamund must be the most neglected concubine of all time, for her royal lover practically lived in the saddle, patrolling the length and breadth of his empire with a speed that seemed to defy the laws of nature. When the French king had remarked sourly that he could almost believe Henry had learned how to fly, he was speaking for legions of frustrated adversaries and thwarted rebels. But to Meliora, Henry's remarkable mobility meant only that most of Rosamund's nights were lonely ones.

"I do not suppose," she said, "that the king told you how long our stay at Falaise will last?"

Rosamund shook her head. "I doubt that he knows himself. He expects to be in Normandy for the rest of the year, and so it makes sense for me to be here. Falaise is conveniently located, accessible from most areas of the duchy."

Meliora agreed that Falaise was well situated, but she suspected that Henry's choice had also been influenced by the fact that it was not a castle favored by his queen; he would not want to risk another awkward Woodstock encounter. Given Falaise's history, Meliora found it rather ironic that he should have tucked his mistress away here of all places, where one of Christendom's most notorious liaisons had begun. From these castle battlements, a Duke of Normandy had noticed a young girl washing laundry in the village stream below. Bedazzled by her beauty, he took her as his bedmate, and the following year she gave birth to a son. Marriage was out of the question for Arlette was only a tanner's daughter, but the duke recognized their son as his, and when he later took the cross, he named William as his heir. Against all odds, the boy known as William the Bastard would lay claim to the duchy and end his days as King of England. As for Arlette, she'd married well after her lover's death, and this tanner's daughter would be remembered as the mother of a king, a bishop, and a count.

During these past weeks at Falaise, Meliora found herself thinking often of Arlette, her duke, and their bastard-born son who would become the great-grandfather of England's current king. She wanted to believe that Rosamund would be as lucky as Arlette, but she did not think it likely. Arlette had been strong enough to defy the world, prideful enough to ride through the main gate of the castle when the duke summoned her; no back alleys for her. Whereas Rosamund reminded Meliora of a flower set down in alien soil; she was too tender, too delicate to thrive at the royal court. The two women were unlike in another way, too; Arlette had been fertile, while Rosamund was barren.

Meliora supposed that it was not entirely accurate to apply that cruel term to Rosamund, for twice she'd gotten with child, only to miscarry in the early weeks of the pregnancy. What saddened Meliora the most was Rosamund's lack of hope. As much as she yearned for children, even children born out of wedlock, she had no expectations of motherhood. She loved Henry enough to live in sin with him, but she never forgot that they were sinning, and she saw her failure to conceive as God's punishment for those sins.

Rosamund's head was bent over the altar cloth, and Meliora reached out, brushed aside the long, blond braid dangling across the embroidery frame. She was not usually given to whimsical notions, but it seemed to her that she could sense Arlette's bold spirit in the chamber with them, a ghostly presence watching over Rosamund with that most condescending of emotions—pity.

Rosamund's breathing had quickened, coming in audible gasps, and she was clutching at the sheets like one grasping for a lifeline. When Henry gently shook her shoulder, she jerked upright, eyes wide and unfocused, and he said soothingly, "It was but a bad dream, love, no more than that."

She rolled over into his arms, clinging with such urgency that he gazed down at her in surprise. "You truly are disquieted. What did you dream to give you such a fright?"

"I do not remember," she lied. In truth, she remembered all too well, for this was a recurrent nightmare, one that troubled her sleep several times a year. It was always the same: she was lost in the woods, alone and afraid as darkness came on. "It matters for naught," she assured him, "just a silly dream. I am so sorry, beloved, for awakening you!"

"I was not asleep," he admitted, and she strained to make out his features in the shadows. A faint glimmer of lamplight filtered through the slit in the bed hangings, not enough to illuminate his face. He'd arrived long after nightfall, as usual without warning, and wasted no time in carrying her off to bed, so the only conversation they'd had so far was carnal in nature.

"What chases away your sleep?" she asked, so solicitously that he brushed her mouth with a quick kiss.

"My eldest son." Sitting up, he shoved a pillow behind his shoulders. "Hal came back from the French court with a head full of foolish notions and saddle bags stuffed with laments. The lad has begun to collect grievances like a miser hoarding coins."

"I cannot imagine what grievances he might have with you. You made him a king!"

"Well, he now sees that as an empty honor. He complains that I have not provided him with income adequate to his rank, that I have given him naught but promises, that I continue to delay his knighthood and to refuse to allow tournaments in my domains, and above all, that I treat him like a raw stripling instead of a man grown."

Rosamund was not deceived by his matter-of-fact recital of Hal's complaints. "I think," she said indignantly, "that he owes you more gratitude than this."

Henry's mouth tightened. "Hal insists that he be given the governance of either England or Normandy, and I know full well who planted that baneful seed. The lad has always paid heed to the wrong people, and when he opens his mouth these days, the French king's words come tumbling out."

"You refused him, of course."

"Of course. He is far too young to govern on his own. Nor can his judgment yet be trusted. His susceptibility to Louis's blandishments proves that all too well."

"What happened when you denied his demand?"

"He went off in a rage, is sulking with the little Marguerite at Bonneville." Henry was both angered and hurt by Hal's willfulness, and with Rosamund, he had the luxury of candor. "I had no choice but to refuse him, Rosamund. He is not ready for such responsibilities. After his coronation, I'd instructed him to meet with the Canterbury monks. It is past time for the archbishopric to be filled again. But the monks have balked at accepting my nominee, the Bishop of Bayeux, and I'd hoped that Hal might make them see reason. He met with them only briefly at Windsor, showed little interest in resolving the dispute. It grieves me to say it, but he seems more intent upon the pursuit of pleasure than in learning the duties of kingship."

She did not need to see his face now. She could hear the unhappiness in his voice, and she wanted desperately to offer comfort. It was her private opinion that Hal was flighty, spoiled, and immature, but she saw no reason to share it with Henry. "He is very young," she ventured, and as she'd hoped, Henry seized upon that.

"Aye, that he is. He kept reminding me that I was just seventeen when my father turned Normandy over to me. But I doubt that I was ever as young as Hal." He sounded more bemused now than irate. "It is not his fault. Life has been so much easier for him. I had to fight for my kingship, and Hal . . . well, Hal has always known he would be king after me. Mayhap it is not so surprising that he'd take longer to reach manhood."

"Not surprising at all," she said, knowing that was what he needed to hear, and when he slid an arm around her shoulders, she could feel that some of the tension had ebbed; his muscles were no longer so tightly corded.

"He's a good lad, you know, a son to be proud of. He is too easily influenced, but that is a fault of youth and inexperience. He'll learn better. He has the makings of a fine king, Rosamund. He does not lack for courage or wit, and he is amiable, spirited, and very generous . . . too much so."

Although she could not see his face, it sounded as if he was smiling. "It is expected that a lord be open-handed and bountiful. Next to valor, that is the most admired of virtues. But Hal's generosity is rapidly becoming the stuff of legend. He bestows his largesse upon his followers as if he were Midas, one reason why he has attracted so many drones, idlers, and parasites. But he ought not to be blamed for the greed of others. It is commendable that he wants to take care of his household knights. I only wish he were not quite so lavish, since the money he's spending is mine!"

He laughed softly. "But it is his nature to share, and I doubt that will ever change. Last year he was out hunting with some friends and they stopped at a pond to water their horses and eat a meal. When Hal discovered that he did not have enough wine for them all, he emptied it into the pond so they all could have a taste!"

Laughing again, he gave Rosamund an affectionate hug. "Say what you will, the lad has a knack for the grand gesture! As king, that will stand him in good stead. He just needs seasoning, needs time."

She murmured agreement, grateful that she'd been able to ease his mind. What harm did it do if he made allowances for his son's bad behavior? If he was right and Hal's shortcomings were those of youth, time would remedy them. And tonight at least, his sleep would be untroubled.

THE WELSH LOVE of their homeland ran deep and they often sickened when uprooted from Welsh soil. They had a word for this heartfelt longing—*hiraeth*—which expressed the sorrow of exile, the sadness for what had been lost, a yearning for what could have been. Two years after their banishment from Gwynedd by a vengeful Welsh prince, Rhiannon and Ranulf had found little contentment in England.

Rhiannon's pain was keener, for her husband was only half-Welsh, and he'd not adopted her country as his own until he was grown. Rhiannon had never known another world. Trefriw called to her in her nighttime dreams and in her daylight reveries. Her aged father was there, as was her younger sister and her newly married daughter. Her mother was buried in the tiny graveyard at Llanrhychwyn, the chapel in the hills above Trefriw where she and Ranulf had been wed. She'd gone blind in childhood, and the few memories she had of sight were visions of Gwynedd. England was an alien land, would never be hers.

But her love for her husband was greater than her love for Wales. When he'd told her that he was loath to tear her away from the only life she'd known, she had quoted Scriptures to him: *Entreat me not to leave thee, for whither thou goest, I will go, and where thou lodgest, I will lodge. Thy people will be my people and thy God my God.* If she had not been able to make his people hers, as she had pledged, she never regretted her decision to follow him into English exile. And because she knew how restless he was, how dispirited, she had not objected when he wanted to answer the English king's summons. Even though it meant venturing into a world more foreign to her than England, she agreed to accompany him to his nephew's Christmas Court at Chinon Castle in Touraine.

HENRY HAD FALLEN IN LOVE with Chinon as a young boy, and his affection for the castle had only deepened over the years. He liked its location—rising up against the sky on a high hill overlooking the River Vienne. He appreciated its ancient history, for the site had once been occupied by a Roman fort. He valued its formidable defenses, protected on three sides by steep cliffs and blocked on the fourth side by a chasm of his making. He'd spent considerable sums on Chinon; the round Tour du Moulin was his work, as was the square Tour du Tresor, where Crown revenues were stored, and he'd renovated the royal residence and great hall along the south side of the castle bailey. When it had come time to choose where to hold his Christmas Court, his decision had been an easy one.

On the day before Christmas, the great hall echoed with the clamor of laughter and music. After a lavish midday meal, guests were dancing that popular favorite, the carol, while others preferred a less energetic activity, engaging in conversation enlivened by the region's excellent wines. From his seat upon the dais, Henry watched the pageantry, a vibrant panorama of color and sound and motion. He was playing a rare role for him, that of a bystander, for he'd twisted his ankle spearing the wild boar that would grace his Christmas table, and he'd propped his injured leg upon a footstool, reluctantly acquiescing with his doctor's orders, at least for a day or two. He did not mind missing the carol, for dancing was not one of his passions. But he did mind the enforced idleness; even during Mass, he was restless, impatient, known to pick his priests for the brevity of their sermons.

Hobbled now by a strained ankle, he could only occupy himself with mental musings. It puzzled him that he'd not found more pleasure at Chinon. It had been several years since he'd had so many of his family under one roof: his queen, his sons Richard, Geoffrey, and John; his daughter, Joanna; his uncles Rainald and Ranulf, his half brother and half sister, Hamlin and Emma; his cousins Roger and Maud. Only his eldest son was absent, expected daily to arrive from Normandy. Virtually all of his English and Norman and Angevin barons were there, most of his bishops, even many of Eleanor's lawless Poitevin lords. His Christmas Court was a resplendent success, a dazzling reflection of his power and prestige, tangible proof of his status as the greatest king in Christendom. So why was he not better pleased by it?

His gaze swept the hall, coming to rest upon the regal, elegant figure of his wife. They'd often been apart during their two decades of marriage, but never so long as this last separation, nigh on two years. He hadn't been sure what to expect, but so far their reunion had gone well enough. No woman could act the queen more impressively than Eleanor; even after all these years, he was still proud to enter a hall with her on his arm.

As he watched his wife, the corner of his mouth curved and pleasurable warmth began to spread throughout his body, centering in his groin. Their night's lovemaking had left him sated, scratched, and wondering how he could have stayed away from her bed for so long. In his thirty-nine years, he'd had women beyond counting or remembering, but none had ever stirred his lust so easily as the one he'd wed. He'd often joked that she could kindle a flame quicker than summer lightning and last night she'd done just that, radiating so much heat that he'd half-expected to find scorch marks on the sheets.

In some ways, she was still an enigma to him: strong-willed, passionate, stubborn, worldly, too clever by half, infuriating, seductive, prideful, daring, even reckless. Tallying up her vices and virtues, he was amused to realize he could not be sure which were which. But on this Christmas Eve at Chinon Castle, he was more than willing to give her the benefit of every doubt, for he missed their easy intimacy, the mutual, instinctive understanding that had been theirs since that rainy afternoon in a Paris garden. It had been a long time since he'd felt that they were in such natural harmony.

Beckoning to a servant, he instructed the man to fetch his queen and then, on impulse, his uncle. He'd planned to give Ranulf his surprise on Christmas morn, but he saw no reason to wait. Ranulf hastened over, shepherding his wife and young son Morgan up onto the dais. Henry ordered chairs to be brought out for them, watching from the corner of his eye as his servant caught Eleanor's attention. She would not come at once, for she was not a woman to be summoned; she would wait just long enough to make it seem as if she were obeying a whim of her own. Stifling a smile, for he was pleased that he could still read her so well, he began to exchange the usual courtesies with Ranulf and Rhiannon.

As always, Henry was intrigued by Rhiannon's ability to follow the sound of his voice; her head tilted, she turned her brown eyes toward him so unerringly that few would have suspected her blindness. After he'd inquired after their other children, a recently wed daughter and a grown son, he directed his attention to Morgan, asking his age and grinning at the boy's answer, "Eight years, ten months," for he could remember when he, too, had marked birthdays as milestones.

In accordance with custom, boys of good birth were sent to live in a lord's household to receive their education, and Henry was surprised that no such provisions had been made for Morgan. When Ranulf admitted that they had not yet chosen a lord to supervise his son's instruction, Henry suggested that Morgan join the royal household. Ranulf was momentarily at a loss, both honored and conflicted by the offer. He was well aware what a great opportunity this would be for the boy. But it was complicated by Morgan's Welsh-Norman blood. His elder son had chosen Rhiannon's world over Ranulf's, even changing his baptismal name of Gilbert to the Welsh Bleddyn, and he'd chosen, too, to remain in Wales. With Gilbert's example in mind, Ranulf was not sure what was best for Morgan.

For Rhiannon, it was much simpler. She did not want to be separated from her son, yet she knew it was inevitable. Sons were sent away at an early age; in Wales, too, that was the practice. Because she'd steeled herself for just such a moment, she kept silent, waiting with outward composure for Ranulf to decide their son's future; only the tightening of her hand on Morgan's shoulder revealed her inner turmoil.

Ranulf opened his mouth, still not sure what he would say. But Morgan was quicker. He'd overheard his parents discussing his education on several occasions, knew that they were deciding between the households of the Earl of Cornwall, the Earl of Chester, and a Welsh lord named Cynan ab Owain. Glancing from his father to his cousin the king, he made his own choice. "Say yes, Papa," he entreated, "say yes."

Ranulf knelt so they were at eye level, his eyes searching the boy's face. "Are you sure?" And when Morgan nodded, he said, "Well, Harry, it seems to be settled."

"Good. I'll keep an eye on the lad, never fear. Now we have another matter to discuss. I've had an interesting offer recently from a Welsh prince you love not—Davydd ab Owain." Henry broke off then as Eleanor drifted over to the dais, and invited her to join them. Once she was seated beside him, he said, "You are just in time, love. We were talking about a prince of North Wales, Davydd ab Owain."

"The one who banished Ranulf?"

"The very one. I never understood, Uncle, just why he was so out of sorts with you. What did you do to earn his disfavor?"

"I was a friend of the man he killed, the man who ought to have been ruling Gwynedd in his stead."

"Ah, yes, Hywel . . . the poet prince. A good man, a far better one than Davydd." Henry shifted in his seat, turning toward Eleanor. "I am not sure if you remember, love, but Hywel and Davydd were both sons of Owain Gwynedd, Hywel being the eldest, the most capable, and the best-loved. But Davydd and another brother Rhodri lay in wait for Hywel after Owain's death, and he was slain in their ambush. Owain's surviving sons then divided up his lands. Davydd is no longer content with his share of the pie, though, is casting a covetous eye upon his brother Maelgwn's portion, the isle of Anglesey. So in order to war upon Maelgwn, he wants to make peace with England, having figured out that only a fool would fight battles on two fronts."

"That sounds like Davydd." Ranulf shook his head in disgust. "Make him pay dear for his peace, Harry."

"I did," Henry assured him. "He must truly be hungry for Maelgwn's lands, as he agreed to all my terms without argument. I think you'll be particularly interested in one of his concessions, Uncle. You are welcome to reside again in his domains, welcome to return to your manor at . . . Trefriw, was it?"

"Truly?" Ranulf stared at Henry incredulously. "He agreed to this?"

Rhiannon's French was quite serviceable by now, for she'd been wed to Ranulf for more than twenty years. But she was suddenly unsure of her mastery of his language, afraid to believe what she thought she'd heard. "We can go home?" she asked doubtfully, and when Henry confirmed it, she buried her face in Ranulf's shoulder and wept for joy. Ranulf was blinking back tears himself, holding her in an embrace that was oddly private in such a public setting; for that moment they were oblivious to the crowded hall, the curious stares, even their wide-eyed young son.

Watching with a smile, Henry brushed aside their euphoric expressions of gratitude, joking that he feared they'd misunderstood him. It was Wales they'd be going back to, not Eden. Eleanor, who was fond of both Ranulf and Rhiannon, leaned over and murmured an approving "Well done." But then she said, "Harry," in a very different tone.

Glancing toward her, he saw that she was looking across the hall at a new arrival, a tall figure still clad in traveling clothes, a mud-splattered hooded mantle. Even at a distance, Henry recognized him at once—William Marshal, his son Hal's sworn man—and fear caught at his heart. His injured ankle forgotten, he was on his feet by the time William Marshal reached the dais. He knelt, saying "My liege, my lady" in a low voice.

"My son . . ." Henry swallowed, for his mouth was suddenly dry. "What have you come to tell us, Will?"

The younger man's head came up sharply. "Ah, no, my liege! Your son is well, I swear it!"

Relief rendered Henry speechless for a moment. "What did you expect me to think?" he said angrily, for anger was an emotion he could acknowledge. "You arrive in our midst like the Grim Reaper's henchman, looking as if you bear the weight of the world on your shoulders. Christ Jesus, Will, I've seen happier men about to be hanged!"

"I am indeed sorry, my lord king, to have alarmed you for naught." Although Henry gestured impatiently for him to rise, Will stayed on his knees. "If I seem troubled, it is because I am loath to deliver this message. Your son . . . he bade me inform you that he will not be attending your Christmas Court at Chinon. He is holding his own court at Bonneville."

"I FEAR," HENRY SAID, "that I could not get out of this bed if the castle caught fire. Jesu, woman, are you seeking to kill me? My very bones feel like melted wax."

Eleanor cocked a skeptical brow. "If lust could kill, Harry, you'd have been dead years ago."

"I never claimed to be a monk, love. That was your first husband, as I recall."

Amused in spite of herself, she hid her smile in the crook of his arm. "Mock him if you will, but poor Louis has you beaten in one race at least—his sprint toward sainthood."

"I grant you that," he conceded. "But unlike Louis, I never wanted a halo, only a crown." Propping himself up on an elbow, he entwined his fingers in the dark river of her hair. He loved it flowing loose like this, his mind still filled with erotic images from their lovemaking: her long tresses tickling his chest, a silken rope looped around his throat, whipping wildly about her face when she tossed her head from side to side. "You realize," he said, "that we've likely scandalized the court, disappearing in the middle of the afternoon for a daylight tryst."

"What truly scandalized the court is that you were off bedding your wife and not your concubine. What sort of example is that to set for your barons?"

Henry was instantly alert, not sure if she was being sarcastic or playful or finally throwing down the gauntlet about Rosamund. He felt a prickle of resentment, for it was very unsporting to ambush a man in the aftermath of sex. "What concubine?" he asked warily, trying not to sound defensive.

"'What concubine?'" she echoed mockingly. "Come now, Harry, you do not expect me to believe that you've been sleeping alone these two years past. I think it is safe to assume that you found a bedmate or two or three in the course of your travels."

His first reaction was relief that this was not about Rosamund, after all. She was gazing up at him serenely, with just the suggestion of a smile. But those greenish-gold eyes had never looked more catlike, utterly inscrutable, and he found himself thinking of the way cats played with their prey before moving in for the kill. "I plead guilty," he said. "I did occasionally take a woman to warm my bed. But surely you would not fault me for that, Eleanor? You might as well blame a man for eating when he's hungry."

"I could not agree more. You need not fret, Harry. I know full well what matters and what does not." It was interesting to see that she could so easily make him squirm over his little trifle, but she had no intention of pursuing it further. That ship had sailed.

Henry chose to take her words at face value, for that allowed him to preserve their marital peace without paying too high a price for it. "I do not say it as often as I ought, but you hold my heart," he said and then grinned. "And any other body parts you care to claim . . . as long as you give me a chance to get my strength back first."

"A most tempting offer, my lord husband, but one best deferred till tonight." Sitting up, she shook her hair back, and then, because she'd always faced her fears head-on, she added, with studied nonchalance, "In truth, Harry, you've worn me out. I am not as young as I once was, after all."

Henry yawned, his gaze lazily tracking the curves of her body, so familiar and still so pleasing to the eye. "Surely you know, love, that fruit is sweeter once it has ripened," he said, thinking that the female body must surely be one of God's greatest works, a treasure trove that never lost its allure, no matter how often he explored its riches.

Eleanor studied his face. It was true he could play fast and loose with the truth when it served his purposes, but he'd never been gallant, never been one for courtship compliments. He'd once admitted that he could see no reason for lavish flattery, for if a woman was beautiful, she already knew it, and if she were not, she'd know he lied. So when he said he still found her desirable, she did not doubt him. Of course he had no notion of the effort it took to keep the years at bay, or that she'd come to see time as the enemy.

Yawning again, Henry swung his legs over the side of the bed. His mellow mood notwithstanding, Eleanor had not expected him to remain abed with her, not with so many daylight hours remaining; to keep him idle, he'd need to be shackled to the bedpost. Not bothering to summon a servant, he'd begun to collect the clothing they'd discarded in such haste. Wrapping her arms around her knees, she remembered how much she'd liked to watch him naked, for unlike her first husband, he'd always been quite comfortable in his own skin. She still enjoyed the sight of his nudity, for his constant activity had kept him fit. Deep chested, with well-muscled arms and the bowed legs of one who'd spent much of his life on horseback, he was, she thought, a fine figure of a man. She'd missed having him in her bed.

Of the secrets she kept from him, none of them involved their lovemaking. She'd never had to feign pleasure with him. If her satisfaction was bittersweet, it was because she'd felt the need to compete with his little sugar-sop, to prove she knew his body and his wants far better than Rosamund Clifford ever could. It shamed her that she could not dismiss the Clifford chit as easily as she had the other sluts he'd bedded. But as well as she lied to others, she could not lie to herself, and she'd become acutely aware of their age difference. In the beginning, it had not troubled her at all that she was nine years older. That was no longer true, not since he'd taken up with a girl young enough to be her daughter. Watching as he shrugged into his shirt and pulled his braies up over his hips, she was angry with herself for her lack of pride and angry with him for his lack of loyalty. She could forgive his physical infidelity. His emotional infidelity, she could not.

Gathering up her gown, chemise, and silken hose, he deposited them within reach, at the foot of the bed. "Shall I call for one of your ladies, love?"

She'd need help taming her tousled, tangled hair, but she was not ready to rejoin the world waiting beyond that bedchamber door; there were matters still to discuss, matters more important than desires of the flesh. "What mean you to do about Hal's latest defiance?"

Henry was pulling his tunic over his head and his voice was muffled in its folds.

Once he was free, he said ruefully, "I was hoping you'd have some suggestions, Eleanor. What ails the boy? He is a king, for the love of Christ! Why is that not enough for him?"

"He wants more than privileges and prestige, Harry. He wants to exercise power. Can you truly blame him? At his age, you'd have demanded no less."

"At his age, I'd been fighting for two years to claim the crown stolen from my mother. He keeps throwing that at me—the fact that I was younger than he is now when I took command of Normandy. But we both know that is a false comparison. For all the love I bear him, Hal is not ready to rule on his own. When left to his own devices, he passes his time playing those damnable tourney games, carousing with dubious companions, and spending money like a drunken sailor. If one of those coxcombs who cluster around him like bees to honey expresses admiration for his new mantle, like as not, he'll strip it off and hand it over. Whilst he was in England, the Exchequer could not keep track of all the bills submitted by merchants for his rash expenditures. Look at that foolishness at Bonneville last month. He threw a feast restricted to knights named William, for the love of God! They came out in droves, too, more than a hundred of them eager to wallow at the trough, eating and drinking enough to feed an entire town for a week."

Eleanor could not keep from smiling. "And you see no humor at all in that?"

"No, I do not," he insisted, but the corner of his mouth was twitching, and after a moment, he conceded, "Well, some . . . but I'd find it much more amusing if I were not paying the bills!" He was scanning the floor rushes for his leather belt and dagger sheath. "After Christmas, I go to Auvergne to meet with the Count of Maurienne."

"I know," she responded, irked by his sudden change of subject. She was familiar with his newest scheme—to secure a future for their youngest nestling by marriage to the count's daughter and heiress. The arrangements had been made months ago. He would journey to Auvergne, meet the count while mediating a dispute between the King of Aragon and her personal bête noire, Count Raimon of Toulouse, and then he'd escort the count and his young daughter to Limoges where the marriage contract would be sealed. But it was Hal she wanted to discuss, not John, and she was about to steer the conversation back to their eldest son when Henry's next words showed his mention of Auvergne was not a digression, after all.

"We'd agreed that you'd continue on to Limoges with our sons and await my arrival. But there has been a change of plans. Hal comes with me to Auvergne, like it or not. I sent word to him this morn, a command, not an invitation. I mean to keep him on a short leash until he proves he can be trusted off-lead."

Eleanor exhaled a soft breath, almost a sigh. He still did not understand what a sharp sword he'd given his enemies by crowning Hal. He'd claimed he was merely following the custom of his continental domains, and it was indeed traditionally done in

France; she did not doubt Louis would crown his son Philippe in due time. But she knew that there was more to Henry's controversial decision to crown Hal, never before done by an English king. He'd seen his mother cheated of her queenship by her cousin Stephen, had seen the suffering that resulted from Stephen's usurpation and the resulting horrors of civil war, a time so wretched that the people had whispered that Christ and his saints must surely be asleep. He'd had to fight fiercely for his own inheritance, both in Normandy and England, and such a turbulent childhood had left scars. He was bound and determined to spare his sons what he'd endured, and that was his true reason for insisting upon crowning Hal in his own lifetime—to make sure that there'd be no doubts about the legitimacy of his heir's claim to the English crown.

But in acting to protect Hal, he'd made himself dangerously vulnerable. The future would always exert a more potent pull than the past, and Hal now represented the glowing promise of tomorrow, while Henry was reduced in the eyes of many to the status of a caretaker king. The risk he'd taken would not have been so great had he not such a multitude of enemies, men eager to use the weapon he'd unknowingly given them. As she watched him moving about their bedchamber, Eleanor felt an unwanted surge of sadness at the terrible irony of it all. Before she could think better of it, she resolved to make one final attempt to reach him, to make him understand that if he did not learn the art of compromise and conciliation, he was courting his own ruin.

"Hal is not entirely in the wrong, you know," she said quietly. "You do not give him sufficient income to maintain a royal household, which makes it inevitable that he should go so deeply into debt. And there is something to be said, too, for his other grievances."

He turned toward her, his surprise evident upon his face. "And what would that be, pray tell?"

She ignored his sarcasm, choosing her words with care. "You keep saying Hal is too young, too callow to rule in his own right. I do not deny that he may well make mistakes. But how else will he learn, Harry?"

"Do not make it sound as if I am fretting over the usual mishaps of youth— tavern brawls, getting a village girl with child, playing the fool with his friends. The stakes are far higher for Hal, and you well know it."

"It is rather late to complain about that, is it not? The truth is that this is a coil of your own making. Hal is a king because you would have it so. You cannot change what is done, can only learn to live with it."

"I could do that . . . if he were not taking his lessons at the French king's knee!"

"You've forfeited the right to bemoan that, too. If you did not want Louis to have a say in Hal's life, you ought not to have married him off to Louis's daughter. Instead of deploring Louis's malign influence, you need to do what he does—listen to the lad."

"I do listen to him, Eleanor. The trouble is that I like not what I hear. I love him as my life, but I cannot trust him to rule on his own—not yet."

"And when will that day come? When he reaches twenty and one? Thirty? Every apprenticeship has a set term. How many years do you mean to keep him a king in training?"

"I cannot answer that," he said, so abruptly that she saw his temper was catching fire. "How can I? I know not what the morrow holds."

I do, she thought, no less angry now than he was. If he were blessed to reach Scripture's three score years and ten, Hal would still be on that "short leash." Even on Harry's deathbed, he'd be figuring out a way to rule from the grave. He had ever to keep his hand on the reins, which meant that Hal would be doomed to ride pillion behind him. And how much freedom would he permit Richard? She knew well the answer to that, too. She had never been allowed to be more than his surrogate in her own domains. It would be no different for Richard. Just as Hal was a shadow king, Richard would be a shadow duke, answerable to Harry, always to Harry.

Henry's anger was cooling as fast as it had sparked. He supposed it was only natural that she'd come to Hal's defense; all knew how protective a lioness was of her cubs. He did wish she could be more understanding of his plight, more like . . . well, like Rosamund. But if a man wanted comforting or cosseting, he'd need to look elsewhere. Those soft curves of hers hid some very sharp edges. He did not want to tarnish the afterglow of their lovemaking, though; this had been one of the best afternoons they'd had in a long while.

"Let's not quarrel, love. We both want the same for Hal, differ only in how to achieve it. I daresay the lad and I will be working well in tandem long ere Louis goes to God."

He'd touched unwittingly upon Eleanor's greatest fear—that her sons would not be well settled in their own lands by the time they would face a more formidable foe than Louis. By all accounts, his Philippe was a sickly little lad and might not reach manhood. The boy's death would pass the French crown to one of his sisters, the main reason that Henry had angled to wed Hal to Marguerite. But Marguerite had two older sisters, Eleanor's daughters by her marriage to Louis, and they were both wed to highly competent, ambitious men, the Counts of Champagne and Blois. Eleanor had discussed this with Henry on several occasions, but there'd been no meeting of their minds. Henry thought the best way to counter the French threat was to keep power consolidated in his hands, a strategy that would work, she thought tartly, only if he did not intend ever to die. She said nothing, though, for why waste her breath?

Fully dressed now, he crossed the chamber and gave her a lingering kiss. "I shall see you, love, at supper, I trust?" He'd taken a few steps before turning back toward the bed. "I almost forgot to tell you. I've settled upon a successor for the Archbishop of Bordeaux: William, the abbot of Reading. I thought we could have him consecrated during our stay at Limoges."

She drew a sharp breath. "I thought I told you," she said, "that I favored the abbot of Tournay for that position."

"Did you? It must have slipped my mind. But I daresay you'll be well pleased with William, for he is a good man, pious and well educated."

And English. She almost spat the words out, somehow held them back. This was not the first time he'd preempted her choice of prelates; the recently deceased Archbishop of Bordeaux and the Bishop of Poitiers were both his men. But her tolerance was no longer what it once had been, and slights like this stung more than they had in the past. Seething in silence, she was even more affronted that he seemed unaware of her outrage. Grasping for any weapon at hand, she asked him with poisoned politeness if he'd made any plans for the morrow.

Henry paused at the door, glancing over his shoulder. "No . . . why?"

"I thought you'd want to have a Requiem Mass said for his soul. Surely you have not forgotten, Harry? Tomorrow will be the second anniversary of Thomas Becket's murder."

He was very still for a moment, staring at her as if she were a stranger. "No," he said tersely, "I have not forgotten."

She knew she'd wounded him when he'd least expected it, and her satisfaction lasted until the door had closed behind him. Once he was gone, it ebbed away along with her anger, leaving her with naught but the ashes and embers of a dying hearth fire.

CHAPTER FIVE

✦

February 1173
Near Limoges, Aquitaine

*E*LEANOR'S EYES INTENTLY SEARCHED the sky. It was the blanched, faded blue of midwinter, leached of color and utterly empty barren of clouds and her missing peregrine. Her vexation was all the sharperbecause the hunt had begun with such promise. When a heron had been flushed from the rushes along the river, she'd detached the leash and the falcon launched itself from its perch on her leather glove, soaring up into the sun as it sought to gain height over its prey. And then it was diving down upon the heron, faster than any arrow, a dark angel bearing death in its talons. But the heron veered abruptly and the falcon missed. As it hurtled past, the heron turned upon its attacker, and suddenly the falcon was the one in flight, fleeing before the larger bird's thrusting beak. The triumphant heron checked its pursuit and flew toward the safety of its river refuge, while Eleanor's thwarted peregrine disappeared over the horizon.

Her falconer had repeatedly issued the recall and swung the lure up into the air, to no avail. A quarter hour had passed by now, with no sign of the errant falcon, but Eleanor continued to probe the sky, as if she could compel its return by sheer force of will, all the while muttering some of the most colorful, creative obscenities that the Countess of Chester had ever heard.

Moving her mare in closer, Maud looked at the queen with mock horror. "What language, my lady! Luckily my brother the bishop is not within earshot. Does your lord husband know you have such a command of curses?" she teased, and Eleanor tore her gaze away from the sky long enough to give Maud a look that was more impatient than amused.

"Who do you think I learned them from?" Her falconer had come back into view, shaking his head in defeat, and she swore again, as angry with herself as with the lost bird. "She was not ready," she admitted, "needed more training. But I only brought two from Chinon and the other falcon is ailing with a catarrh."

"Then you had no choice," Maud pointed out, "for your royal guest was keen to go hawking. And he seems well pleased, so the day has not been a total loss."

Following Maud's gaze, Eleanor saw that the King of Navarre was indeed in a jovial mood, bantering with their host, the Viscount of Limoges, and Maud's brother. Roger had taken no active part in the hunt, one of the few bishops who obeyed the Church's ban on hawking for those in holy orders, and Sancho was joking about his abstention with the heavy-handed humor permitted to kings. Feeling the women's eyes upon him, Roger sent a smile winging their way, and then turned back to deflecting the royal gibes.

"He does look content," Eleanor conceded, and that was no small achievement, for the Navarrese king had been growing restless and irritable as the days passed and Henry did not arrive.

"Madame!" Aimar, the Viscount of Limoges, was guiding his stallion in her direction. "I am so sorry about the loss of your falcon," he said, unhappy that the day's success would be marred by this setback. "I took pains that all would go well, had my chaplain begin the hunt with a prayer that the birds would not stray. But I can assure you that she will be found. Each time I've been unlucky enough to lose one of my falcons, it has always been retrieved by the local villagers."

Eleanor knew he was probably right. Any peasant spotting a belled hawk with leather jesses would know at once that it was a lord's bird and worth a goodly reward. But she could not shake off her chagrin, for she never willingly relinquished something that was hers.

With an effort, she brought her attention back to the conversation. Viscount Aimar was telling them what he'd just learned from King Sancho: that the Saracens were as avid hunters as Christians, and even though they were infidels, they'd come up with a most intriguing means of controlling their hawks—by covering their heads with leather hoods until they were ready to be set upon their prey. Eleanor was no less interested in this new method than Aimar, and made a mental note to mention it to Henry, whose passion for hawking bordered on obsession. Aimar's servants had begun to unload the wagons, setting up trestle tables and unpacking stools so the hunting party could take refreshments in comfort, and Eleanor did her best to dismiss her wayward falcon, holding out her hand so the viscount could help her dismount.

Rainald assisted his daughter from her mare, and then hastened over to do the same for his niece, wanting to know if Maud would be journeying with him, Ranulf, and Rhiannon when they returned to England. To his surprise, she refused, and with his usual tactlessness, he blurted out, "Why? You've been here for months. Are you not ready to go home yet?"

"The queen has kindly extended an invitation to remain at her court, Uncle, and I was glad to accept. Why not? I am a widow with grown children, and Bertrada is old enough now to act as Hugh's lady, does not need a mother-in-law to dog her steps. Besides," Maud added, with a grin that belied her years and any claims to matronly dignity, "what fool would prefer Chester to Poitiers?"

Rainald still looked baffled, but Maud and Eleanor traded smiles, both well content with the role that the Countess of Chester had chosen to play: a surrogate sister for the queen who still grieved for her blood sister. Viscount Aimar was hovering close by, waiting to escort her to the table, and Eleanor was turning toward him when her uncle stepped between them, murmuring a deferential "A moment, if I may, my lady."

Eleanor allowed Raoul to draw her aside, and as soon as they were out of the viscount's hearing, he said, "Harry and Hal are likely to be arriving any day now, and we may not have many opportunities for private conversation. Do you think this time together has served to mend the rift between them?"

"No, I do not."

"A pity," Raoul said, because convention seemed to demand it; a father's estrangement from his son would be considered tragic by most people. For him, it would be a blessing, a God-given chance that might never come again. His loathing for his niece's Angevin husband was not personal. He'd not liked her French husband either. He wanted Aquitaine to be ruled by their own, wanted no more foreigners over them.

Eleanor was regarding him with a sardonic half smile. "You really ought to get Harry to teach you how to mask your thoughts, Uncle. If you were any more eager to see the breach widen between them, you'd be panting like yonder greyhounds."

He shrugged. "I've never lied to you, lass. You know what I want and why I want it."

She was the first to look away. "I just wish," she said, so softly he barely heard her, "that you were not quite so happy watching the death throes of my marriage."

It was then that the bearers shouted and a grey heron broke cover near the river, powerful wings taking it up into the sky over their heads. Most of the hunting party had already relinquished their falcons and were moving toward the tables. But Richard's bird of prey still perched upon his leather glove. His reaction was instantaneous and his gyrfalcon exploded into the air with breathtaking speed. Like the peregrine, it rose rapidly, and then it was plunging earthward, its sleek white body blurring into a streak of light as it caught up with its quarry. They collided in midair and then plummeted to the ground, out of sight in the marsh grass.

"Release the dogs!" Richard yelled, but the greyhounds were already in motion, racing to subdue the heron before it could escape from the much smaller gyrfalcon. Richard had slid from his saddle and was running toward the death-struggle. When he and the bearers finally emerged from the reeds, he had the bloody heart of the heron in one hand and his beautiful, lethal hawk in the other. Eleanor had never seen him so excited, and she felt a surge of fierce pride as he headed straight for her, eager to share his triumph.

"Did you see her stoop, Maman? That was so fine a kill, well-nigh perfect!"

"Indeed it was, dearest," she agreed, her own disappointment dispelled by Richard's jubilation. Others were gathering around them, and Richard basked in the attention, feeding the heart to the gyrfalcon as he accepted their plaudits, whistling for the greyhounds so they could get their well-earned praise, too. Only Geoffrey stood apart, watching with an expression surprisingly jaundiced for a youngster of fourteen.

The men were as willing as Eleanor to prolong the moment, remembering the pride of their first kills. It was only with the arrival of a messenger for the Viscount of Limoges that they began to disperse, turning toward the tables now laid out with wine and food. Eleanor stayed where she was, though, flanked by her uncle and her son, for the expression on Aimar's face was not that of a man who'd just received welcome news. After conferring briefly with the messenger, he moved hastily in her direction.

"Madame, I've just gotten word that King Henry has ridden into Limoges."

That was no surprise, for Henry had sent word that he would reach Aimar's city within a day or two of the start of Lent and this was Shrove Tuesday. Eleanor inclined her head, waiting for him to reveal what had disquieted him about her husband's arrival.

"Your son the young king is with him, of course, as are the King of Aragon, the Count of Maurienne, and his daughter." Aimar paused, obviously unhappy with what he would say next. "He is accompanied, as well, by the Count of Toulouse."

No one spoke. Eleanor could see her suspicions mirrored on the faces of Richard and Raoul. She would sooner have broken bread with Lucifer than with Raimon St Gilles, and her husband well knew it. So why had he brought the count to Limoges?

HENRY, COUNT RAIMON, and the young King of Aragon had been ushered to the castle chambers set aside for them and were washing away the grime of the road. But Hal had remained in the great hall. His hair was tousled, there was a smear of dirt on his cheek, and his clothes and boots were mud-splattered, yet he still looked like one of the heroes in a troubadour's song or geste, the handsome, dashing young knight who was without peer and existed only in a storyteller's imagination. He was surrounded by those guests who'd not gone hawking, commanding their attention so completely that few at first noticed the hunting party had returned.

Following in Eleanor's footsteps, Marguerite forgot etiquette and brushed past the queen in her haste to welcome her husband. At the sound of her voice, Hal sprang to his feet and swept her into a close embrace, a display of public affection that would have been considered unseemly in others but earned Hal indulgent smiles from even the most judgmental.

Hal showed more decorum in greeting his mother, his host, and their companions, but wasted no time in drawing Eleanor aside for a more private conversation. "I had an inspired idea," he confided, "but I will need your help to bring it about, Maman. How often do so many of high birth gather together like this? We have no less than four kings, two queens, and a multitude of counts, earls, barons, and their ladies. What better setting could we have for a knighting ceremony? And what better time? We could do it next Wednesday . . . my eighteenth birthday," he explained, as if Eleanor had been elsewhere on that auspicious occasion and needed reminding. "Will you talk to him, Maman? Will you make him see how perfect it would be to do it here, to do it now?"

As usual, Hal's enthusiasm was contagious, and Eleanor found herself agreeing even though she did not think Henry would heed her. She knew she should remind Hal of his father's stubborn insistence upon having him knighted by the French king, but she hadn't the heart to interject reality into his dream. It was her son's strength and his weakness that he could not conceive of defeat.

Having gotten what he wanted—his mother's backing in this coming clash of wills with his father—Hal announced that he was greatly in need of a bath, and he and Marguerite exited the hall with an eagerness rarely shown for bathing. Eleanor turned to find her constable, Saldebreuil de Sanzay, at her side.

"You ought to have heard the lad, Madame," he said, with the fond familiarity of one who'd known Hal all his life. "He was telling us some highly entertaining, if rather improbable, tales about past hunts. He claimed that one time he'd set a young gyrfalcon upon a crane, but the bird had a large fish in its beak and dropped it as the gyrfalcon began its stoop. His hawk shot right by the crane and went after the fish!"

The constable laughed so heartily that he began to wheeze, and Eleanor felt a pang, for this man had been her rock, her mainstay since her days as Queen of France. He'd always refused to reveal his exact age, and he'd gone to war against time with the same valor and fortitude he'd mustered against other foes, but it was a battle he was doomed to lose, and she was coming to understand that it would be sooner than either of them had anticipated. As their eyes met, his smile faded away.

"Have you heard, my lady? The Count of Toulouse rode in with your lord husband, the king. Do you know why he would bring the count here?"

"No," she said grimly. "But I intend to find out."

H ENRY HAD ALREADY BATHED and changed his clothes and was getting his hair and beard trimmed when Eleanor entered his bedchamber. "Ah, there you are, love," he said cheerfully. "How was the hawking? I'd wager your hunting was nowhere near as successful as mine."

Eleanor felt a prickle of foreboding, for he sounded much too smug for her liking. She gestured in dismissal and the servants emptying the bathing tub abandoned their buckets and withdrew. The barber hesitated, scissors poised in midair. When Henry nodded, he quickly retreated, flustered by his queen's icy demeanor. Henry showed no such misgivings, though, holding the scissors out to Eleanor with a grin.

"If you are chasing my barber away, you'll need to finish the task he began. I assume you want a private conversation, although I'd not be adverse if you intend to jump my bones." When she reached for the scissors, he surprised her by catching her hand and pressing his mouth to her palm. Past experience had taught her to suspect such high spirits, a reliable indication that he was up to something, and as she began to clip the curly bright hair at the base of his neck, she stared at the back of his head, wishing she had the power to see into his skull, into the serpentine, convoluted byways of his brain. It was surely one of God's inexplicable jests that she'd taken both a lamb and a fox to her marriage bed.

"Did you meet the Count of Maurienne yet? He's a likable man, amiable and quite reasonable. We struck a very advantageous deal for Johnny. If Count Humbert dies without a male heir, Johnny and his daughter . . . Adela, I think, no, Alice . . . will inherit Maurienne and Savoy. If the count does manage to sire a son, then he'll settle the principality of Rousillon upon our lad. So whatever the outcome, there'll be no more talk of John Lackland." Henry swung around in the chair, so abruptly that

Eleanor nearly sliced his ear. "Maurienne controls the Alpine passes, the trade routes into Italy. We're gaining so much for so little, Eleanor . . . just four thousand silver marks and the pledge of alliance."

"I am familiar with the marriage terms, Harry, and with your ambitions in Italy. The count is not the guest I've come to discuss, and you well know it."

Henry's mouth twitched as he suppressed a smile. "Ah, you mean the King of Aragon. A fine lad, although I do wish he were not so young. Once Hal discovered that Alfonso will be able to rule on his own when he turns sixteen next month, he pounced upon that like a starving hound upon a bone, and gave me no peace. I will say this of our son, he does not lack for perseverance!"

"I do not give a besan for the King of Aragon! Why did you not warn me that you'd be bringing that weasel St Gilles back with you?"

Not at all put out by her flare of temper, Henry turned in his seat so they were face-to-face. "If it is any consolation, Count Raimon is no happier to be here than you are to have him."

"Need I remind you, Harry, that I have a weapon in my hand? If you do not speak soon, I will not be responsible for what I do."

Laughing openly now, he claimed the scissors, tossing them into the floor rushes. "I'd not want to lead you into temptation." Without warning, he snaked an arm around her waist and pulled her down onto his lap. "Thirteen years ago, I made you a promise that I was not able to keep. Now I grant you that I rarely lose sleep over broken promises, but this is one wrong I am delighted to right."

"Just what are you saying?"

"What happened thirteen years ago, love?"

"You went to war against Raimon St Gilles, asserting my claim to Toulouse. And you failed . . ." Her voice trailed off, her eyes widening. "You cannot mean that he has agreed to do homage for Toulouse?"

She was staring at him incredulously, and it occurred to Henry that he'd never before seen her at such a loss for words. "That is exactly what I mean, Eleanor. Now you understand why I said Count Raimon is not overjoyed to be here."

"What I do not understand, Harry, is how you did it. I'd not have thought even Merlin could have wrought such a miracle!"

"Actually, love, it was not so difficult. For all his vices, Raimon is no fool and is quite capable of reading a map. On one side lie the lands of King Alfonso, my young ally who loves Raimon not, and with good cause. On his other, lie the lands of Count Humbert, soon to be my kin by marriage. These alliances had begun to pinch Raimon in his most vulnerable male parts, for he was becoming convinced that I was aiming to encircle and isolate him, with God knows what mischief in mind."

Henry laughed again. "I had no intention of waging war, but Raimon expects others to be as false and treacherous as he is. And he could not rely upon the French king to pull his chestnuts from the fire this time, since he is no longer wed to Louis's sister. So he decided that homage was a cheaper price to pay than blood, and he—"

He got no further, for Eleanor stopped his words with a passionate kiss. "You ought to have told me," she chided, "but I forgive you." She could forgive a lot for Toulouse. It had long been the litany of her House that the St Gilles family had stolen Toulouse, disregarding her grandmother's rightful claim, and she'd persuaded both husbands to assert her title to the county. Neither had succeeded and Maud had given her some mordant, incisive advice: resign herself to its loss unless she meant to try again with a third husband. But Toulouse was not just her inheritance, it was Richard's.

She kissed Henry again and then slid off his lap. "You may just have made amends for giving Gascony away."

"Gascony?" Henry was genuinely puzzled. "I did not give Gascony away. It was our daughter's marriage portion, and I specified that it would not happen whilst you still lived."

"I know." He had taken care to preserve her rights, but what of Richard's? Passing strange, but he'd never understood that the succession to Aquitaine mattered no less to her than the succession to the English Crown did to him. She'd wanted a generous dowry for her daughter in far-off Castile, just not at Richard's expense. But Gascony was yesterday, Toulouse was today.

"I'd best find Richard and let him know." At the door she paused to favor him with the sort of smile he'd not gotten from her in several years—utterly spontaneous, admiring, and affectionate. "I'd given up hope that the day would ever come when I'd see Raimon kneel to do homage to me," she admitted. "I only wish my father were alive to witness it, for he died thinking that Toulouse was lost to us."

Henry started to say something, then stopped. But his expression was suddenly so guarded that Eleanor froze, her hand on the door latch. "Harry?"

It was not so much a question as a demand, and he acknowledged it by exhaling a pent-up breath. "Well . . . the truth is that he has not agreed to do homage to you, Eleanor."

"I see." She leaned back against the door, regarding him in silence that threatened to stretch into infinity. "He does homage to you, but not to me. What about Richard?"

Henry was thankful that he could reassure her on that point, hoping it would allay her disappointment. "Of course he'll do homage to Richard."

After another uncomfortable silence, she said, "It gladdens me to hear it." But once she was out in the stairwell, she sank down on the stone steps, not wanting to face others until she was sure her rage was under control. It did not surprise her that Raimon St Gilles would dare to insult her like this. He was not a man to humble his pride before a woman, not unless forced to it. But Harry had not done that. He'd chosen to accommodate the Count of Toulouse because it was easier that way, easier for him.

Standing up, she brushed the dust from her skirts. When Maud had urged her to relinquish her hopes of claiming Toulouse, she'd offered other advice as well, no less pragmatic and unsentimental. *You cannot change a man, Harry least of all. You will always come second with him, for his kingship will come first.* And there in the stairwell of the Viscount of Limoges's castle, Eleanor could hear her own response echoing down through the years, and Maud's uncompromising reply: *So you are saying, then, that I must accept Harry as he is. But what if I cannot? Then learn to love him less.*

THE VISCOUNT OF LIMOGES had given Maud a tour of his kennels, where his favorite greyhound bitch had recently whelped. As he escorted her across the bailey afterward, he offered her the pick of the litter once the puppies were old enough to be weaned. When Maud demurred, he insisted, saying with a smile, "You have been a Godsend to my wife. Sarah's nerves were on the raw at the prospect of entertaining so many highborn guests, and you and our duchess have gone out of your way to put her at ease, doing what you could to make sure that nothing went amiss."

Maud thanked him, thinking that only in Aquitaine would a duchess outrank a queen. They were passing the open doors of the stables, and she came to a sudden halt, having caught sight of a familiar figure standing by one of the stalls. Excusing herself, she stepped into the shadows of the barn.

Hal was currying a beautiful white stallion, so occupied in his task that he did not hear Maud's approach. He swung around in surprise when she spoke his name, and then smiled in recognition. "Cousin Maud! Come take a look at my new palfrey. Shield your eyes, though," he added with a grin, "lest you be dazzled by his radiance."

His jest was not far off the mark; the horse was as perfect a specimen as Maud had ever seen. Hal had begun to comb out its silky mane, saying that it was as soft as his wife's hair, playfully begging her not to repeat that to Marguerite, and then declaring that he'd settled upon a name: Morel.

Maud was not surprised by his choice; that was a popular name for knightly steeds in chansons de geste. "Dare I ask how you could afford such a magnificent beast? Have you taken to banditry in your spare time?"

Hal laughed. "Do not think I have not been tempted, Cousin. But Morel did not cost me even a denier. He is the product of a benign conspiracy between my mother

and King Alfonso. He'd visited her at Poitiers last summer to discuss their mutual enemy, Count Raimon, and she arranged for him to bring Morel to Limoges. Spanish
horses are the best in Christendom," he said happily, "so she could not have given me
a finer birthday present!"

"Indeed," Maud agreed, reaching out to pat the palfrey's muzzle. "You made mention only of your mother. Was Morel not a gift from both your parents?" She hoped
that was so, for separate gift-giving was not an augury of a healthy marriage, but he
was already shaking his head.

"No, Morel was my mother's present. My father promised me four Iceland gyrfalcons when one of his agents next goes to Norway."

Iceland gyrfalcons were quite literally worth a king's ransom, so that was a very
lavish expenditure from a man not noted for extravagant spending. "That was a most
generous gift," Maud said, feeling suddenly sad although she wasn't quite sure why.

"Yes." The terseness of his response made it seem incomplete, and Hal appeared
to sense that. Raising his head, he met Maud's eyes over the stallion's back. "Assuming
that he remembers," he said, but without malice; she thought he sounded sad, too.

"Hal . . ." Maud was not sure if she should venture onto such unstable ground,
but she'd begun to realize that there was no one to speak on her cousin Harry's behalf;
the only voices Hal heard these days were those hostile to his father. "I know you are
disappointed that Harry refused to knight you."

"I am disappointed that the weather did not allow us to go hawking today. I am
disappointed that I lost three straight games of hazard to Hasculf de St Hilaire yesterday. But when my father denies me the rite of passage to manhood, I think a stronger
term is needed than 'disappointment,' Cousin Maud."

"He does not mean it that way, Hal, truly he does not. His intent is not to slight or
demean you, nor to cause you pain. He has it in his mind that you need to be knighted
by the French king, for that would do honor to you both. Limoges cannot hold a candle to Paris, lad. Surely it is worth waiting for a splendid ceremony at the French
court?"

"No," he said, "it is not worth the wait, not to me." He'd not raised his voice, not
showed any anger, but there was a finality in his words that discouraged Maud from
persisting. Father and son were more alike than they knew, and that was not a thought
to give her any comfort.

THE COUNT OF TOULOUSE made such an exaggerated obeisance before
Eleanor that it bordered upon mockery. "My deepest sympathies, Madame," he said
blandly. "I can only imagine how disappointed you must be."

Eleanor's son was standing so close that their shoulders were touching, and she could feel the jolt of tension that shot through Richard's body. Putting her hand casually on his arm, she gazed coolly at her adversary. "And why would I be disappointed, my lord count?"

Count Raimon's eyebrows rose in feigned surprise. "Why because of the loss of your falcon, of course. I heard about your ill-fated hunt. Very bad luck, indeed."

"Not at all. My falcon was found two days ago, none the worse for her mishap. You are not as well informed as you think, my lord count."

Bending over her hand again, he said, "I rejoice in your good fortune, my lady." He had oddly colored eyes, a pale golden-brown with yellowish glints. Wolf eyes, Eleanor thought, and as the count sauntered away, she said as much aloud.

Richard looked startled, and then laughed. "Great minds think alike, Maman. Alfonso calls him *el lobo loco*. The crazed wolf."

Eleanor smiled. "*El lobo loco* . . . I like that." It was no surprise that Richard and King Alfonso had struck up an easy friendship, for they were of an age—fifteen— with many interests in common—a shared love of hunting and horses, a mutual loathing for Raimon St Gilles. Their rapport pleased Eleanor, for friendships of youth often forged the alliances of manhood.

"Alfonso has been teaching me how to swear in his language," Richard confided. "Spanish curses are very satisfying, for they roll right off the tongue. Alfonso has a number of colorful names for *el lobo loco*: *cabrón*, *huevón*, and my own favorite, *hijo de mil putas.*"

Eleanor had an inkling of its meaning, but she did not want to deny Richard the pleasure of instructing her. "Dare I ask you to translate or is it too crude for my maidenly ears to hear?"

That amused Richard greatly. "You could teach a soldier to swear, Maman! It means 'son of a thousand whores.'"

"Amen," she said, and Richard grinned, making the sign of the cross. It was then that her uncles, Raoul and Hugh, reached them, with Saldebreuil de Sanzay a few steps behind. She was touched by their loyalty; they'd seen her talking with Raimon St Gilles and hastened over to offer their support. Viscount Aimar was also making his way toward her. She'd decided not to join Henry upon the dais while Raimon swore homage, not wanting to see his smirk, his silent gloating. But she was warmed now by the hatred filling the hall, all of it aimed at Raimon's arrogant, dark head. And at least she would get to watch *el lobo loco* humble himself before her son; at least she would have that satisfaction.

A sudden stir indicated Henry's entrance. Wasting no time with preliminaries, he took his seat upon the dais. Hal followed, looking very regal and very unhappy. Richard gave his tunic a quick tug, and hastened to join them. A silence settled over the crowded hall as the Count of Toulouse began his walk toward the dais.

Eleanor knew he must be dreading the ceremony to come, but no emotion showed in his face. Mounting the steps of the dais, he removed his sword, knelt before Henry, and placed his hands together, palm to palm in the universal gesture of submission. "My lord king and liege lord, I, Raimon St Gilles, Count of Toulouse, do willingly enter into your homage and faith and become your sworn man, and to you faithfully will I bear body, chattels, and earthly worship, and I will keep faith and loyalty to you against all others."

Henry was as impassive as Raimon. "We do promise to you, as my vassal and liegeman, that we and our heirs will guarantee to you and your heirs the lands you hold of us, against all others, that you may hold said lands in peace."

Rising then, he raised Raimon to his feet and gave him the ritual kiss of peace. Richard's gaze briefly caught his mother's, and he made a comic grimace, for he'd been complaining, only half in jest, that he'd sooner kiss a badger than his new vassal. But when Raimon glanced his way, he was appropriately solemn, showing the gravity that the occasion required.

What happened next, however, took him utterly by surprise. Instead of kneeling to him, Raimon moved toward his brother, knelt, and swore homage to Hal. Richard's mouth dropped open; he looked bewildered and, then, enraged. When Raimon finally did homage to him, he made no effort to hide his fury, slurring his words in his haste to get his oath said, giving his kiss of peace with the distaste of one embracing a leper.

Eleanor was utterly still, heedless of the turmoil swirling around her. Her kinsmen and her vassals had watched in disbelief, and now they were turning to her, dismayed and angry.

"Eleanor!" Raoul was so close she could feel his breath on her cheek. "What in hellfire just happened?" He'd been outraged that St Gilles would be swearing homage to a man who was Duke of Aquitaine only by marriage, while ignoring the woman who was Duchess of Aquitaine by blood right and the anointing of the Almighty. He'd consoled himself that St Gilles would be accepting Richard as his liege lord, but he'd never expected that homage would be done to Hal, too. There was no legal basis for it: Hal had been crowned as King of England, Duke of Normandy, and Count of Anjou. He had no claim to Aquitaine, no claim to Toulouse—until now.

"Christ on the Cross," he sputtered. "What sort of double-dealing was that?" He already had his answer, though, sure that Eleanor's hellspawn husband was seeking to add Toulouse to his own domains, to make it part of his Angevin empire. Glaring at his niece, he found himself wondering how much she'd known. But he dismissed that suspicion as soon as it surfaced, for all the color had drained from her face; even her lips were white.

"Eleanor?" he said again, alarmed by her pallor and her continuing silence. Eleanor ignored him, ignored them all, never taking her eyes from the dais, from the husband who had betrayed her yet again.

HENRY STARED AT HIS WIFE in exasperation. "It never occurred to me that you would object. It is but a formality, after all, and I thought it would please Hal."

"And did you spare even a thought as to how Richard would react?"

"For the love of Christ, woman, sometimes you act as if Richard is the only child of your womb and the rest are foundlings!"

"I am not speaking as Richard's mother, but as Duchess of Aquitaine. Did you not see the reaction of my barons in the hall? You rekindled all of their suspicions, all of their mistrust in one grand gesture, Harry, and for what? If it is indeed an empty honor, as you allege, then why should Hal be pleased by it? And if it is not, better you tell me now if you have designs upon Toulouse. I have a right to know!"

Henry shook his head in disgust. "I am beginning to wish I'd never heard of Toulouse! No, I do not harbor any great scheme to annex it. Not that I expect your ranting, rebel lords to believe me. Aquitaine is one large lunatic asylum, and you clearly have been spending too much time there, Eleanor, or you would not have needed to ask me such an insulting question."

"I would not have needed to ask you any questions at all if only you'd told me what you had in mind."

"More fool I, but I thought you'd want St Gilles to do homage to Hal as well as Richard—to honor both your sons."

More fool you. But the words never left her lips, for she knew now that the time for talking was done.

LENT WAS ALWAYS the season of dread for cooks; not only was meat banned from every table, but so were eggs, milk, butter, and cheese. The cooks of the Viscount of Limoges had shown considerable ingenuity, though, offering up a seafood feast that pleased even the demanding palates of his royal and highborn guests. Only Henry took no enjoyment from the meal meant to celebrate the betrothal of his youngest son and the Count of Maurienne's daughter.

In truth, Henry had never displayed much interest in food, eating and drinking sparingly even in those months when the menu was not so restricted. But on this last Sunday in February, it was Henry's sour mood that was spoiling the revelries for him. His eyes swept the high table, coming to rest morosely upon the Count of Toulouse. He was beginning to think the man was accursed. For certes, he'd brought naught but trouble to Limoges.

Taking a swallow of wine without really tasting it, Henry tallied up the grievances he could lay at the count's door. Richard had provoked a public quarrel with Hal over that ill-fated act of homage, and so now Hal was out of sorts, too. But instead of finding fault with Richard, Hal had concluded that his father was to blame for the botched affair. Henry was beginning to think that his eldest also held him accountable for the Great Flood and the Expulsion from Eden. In this at least, Hal and Richard were united, for Henry hadn't gotten a civil word from his second son since the ceremony. It would seem, Henry thought, that Richard had inherited his share of the Angevin temper. The sad truth was that he did not know Richard well at all. He was Eleanor's, had always been Eleanor's.

As for his queen, he had no illusions that they'd made peace. They were operating under a truce at present, no more than that. Her public pose notwithstanding, he knew she was still aggrieved, for reasons that made no sense whatsoever. He could almost believe there was something in the water or air of Aquitaine that caused people to act so moon-mad. It was just as well that he'd be going into Brittany in a few days whilst she returned to Poitiers. Some time apart would give both their tempers time to cool.

The thought of Brittany diverted his attention to his third son. Mayhap he ought to take Geoffrey with him. It might be good to pass some time with the lad in the lands he'd one day rule. He did not know Geoffrey all that well, either, and he'd never meant it to be that way. He had wanted the same easy rapport with his sons that he'd enjoyed with his own father. Despite his best intentions, though, his children had been relegated to the outer edges of his life, unable to compete with the myriad duties and demands of kingship. But he'd remained confident that there would be time to make amends for those lost, early years, to forge a bond with his sons that could never be broken. He did not understand why it was now proving so difficult.

Fidgeting restlessly in his seat, he shifted so he could see his youngest son. John had been permitted to sit at the high table next to his future father-in-law. He was a solemn child, the only one of their brood with Eleanor's coloring, a stranger not only to Henry but to his family, for John had passed the first years of his life with the nuns at Fontevrault Abbey. Henry thought he looked ill at ease, doubtless overwhelmed by all the unaccustomed attention. There was something about this forlorn little boy that touched Henry's heart, and he was glad he'd been able to arrange such a promising future for the lad. Too often a younger son was shunted aside, valued more cheaply than his older brothers.

Henry's gaze flicked from John, roaming the hall until he located William Marshal at one of the lower tables. The young knight was surely the ultimate example of the sorry fate that could befall a spare son. Will had been offered up by his father as a hostage, a pledge of John Marshal's good faith. Marshal, a man of no scruples whatsoever, had promptly broken his oath, and when warned by King Stephen that his small son would pay the price for his treachery, his response had been so cold-blooded, so pitiless that it had soon passed into legend. Go ahead and hang Will, he'd told Stephen. He had the hammer and anvil with which to make other and better sons. Will's life had been spared only because Stephen could not bring himself to hang a five-year-old child.

It was a story Henry had never forgotten; he was not easily shocked, but that had shocked him profoundly. Once he'd chosen Will as one of Hal's household knights, he'd wondered occasionally how Will had dealt with a memory like that, wondered if his ambition and steely sense of purpose could be rooted in that sad history. Turning his gaze back to John, he watched the child play with the food on his trencher and felt a surge of pride that he could provide so well for all his sons, thankful that Johnny would prosper in a world so often cruel to unwanted children.

Once the meal was finished, servants began to clear away the trestle tables so there would be room for the entertainment Viscount Aimar had arranged: performances by troubadours, tumblers, and, he promised, an amazing act involving a dancing bear. Seats were positioned on the dais for all the royal guests, Count Humbert, and the Count of Toulouse. Henry stopped a nurse from ushering John off to bed, swooping the boy up onto his lap. "There you go, lad, the best seat in the hall," he said fondly, and John, regarding him gravely with Eleanor's enigmatic eyes, perched on the arm of his chair like a bird about to take flight. The little boy seemed more comfortable once Joanna joined them, for she'd often been with him at Fontevrault, and she was so outgoing and confident that Henry thought she could coax a turtle from its shell. Smiling into her upturned, laughing face, he wondered why sons could not be as easy to please as daughters.

"My lord king?" Count Humbert had risen from his chair. Seeing that he wanted to talk, Henry rose, too, allowing Joanna and John to share his seat. The count made amiable, polite conversation for several moments before raising the one issue still to be settled between them. "We have agreed that your son and my daughter will inherit Maurienne and Savoy when I die. But we have not yet discussed what young John will bring to the marriage. What lands do you mean to confer upon him prior to the wedding?"

Henry had anticipated this demand, knowing that he'd have to offer something of value since the marriage contract was weighted so heavily in his favor. "Of course," he said affably. "It is my intention to endow John with three castles: Chinon, Loudun, and Mirebeau."

The count had spent time poring over maps of Henry's domains, so he was familiar both with the castles and their strategic location, forming a triangle between Normandy and Aquitaine. "That is satisfactory," he said, smiling.

Henry had no time to savor the moment, though. Hal was on his feet, staring at them accusingly. "You cannot give those castles to John. They are mine!"

Henry swore under his breath. "We shall discuss this later," he said hastily, intent upon reining Hal in before the other guests took notice of their dispute. "It is true these castles are in Anjou, but you will not be the loser for it," he assured his son. "I will make other provisions for you."

"Promises can be broken." Hal glared at his father, fists clenched at his sides. "I was invested with Anjou and it cannot be partitioned without my consent—which I will never give!"

Henry's face flamed. "I told you this is neither the time nor the place. We will discuss this later!"

"There is nothing to discuss." And to Henry's fury and frustration, his eldest son turned away, stalking down the steps of the dais and shoving his way through the suddenly silent crowd. Flushed with embarrassment, Henry could only watch. But Hal never looked back.

HENRY PACED THE SOLAR as if it were a cage, his fury rising with each step. Eleanor had made herself comfortable in the window-seat, sipping from a wine cup as she watched her husband's fuming. When Hal finally entered, Henry crossed the solar in three strides, slamming the door shut with enough violence to reverberate out into the stairwell.

"How dare you shame me like that before the court!"

Few men could stand up to Henry in one of his Angevin furies. Even kinsmen like Ranulf and Rainald feared getting scorched by those flames. Only his cousin Roger was not daunted by the royal rage; during their clashes over Thomas Becket, they'd once had a public shouting match that earned Roger a reputation as a man who was utterly fearless and utterly foolhardy. But Eleanor saw now that Roger had a rival in recklessness, for Hal did not flinch.

"How dare you give away my castles!" he shot back. "And without even a word to me beforehand!"

"I told you," Henry snapped, "that I'd make sure you were compensated for their loss!"

"I do not believe you," Hal said flatly. "Why should I? You handle the truth carelessly, and your promises ebb and flow like the tides. I reach for one, and all I grasp is a handful of foam and sand."

Henry could not remember the last time anyone had dared to defy him like this . . . not since Thomas Becket. "I am done with making excuses for your rash, heedless behavior. For too long, you have been playing the fool instead of learning the duties of kingship. You have done nothing to earn my trust . . . or my respect. Until you do, you'll be kept on a short leash, and that is a promise you *can* rely upon."

Hal flushed, hot color surging into his face and throat. "Say what you will. Your threats and insults and mockery will change nothing. I will never agree to relinquish those castles—never!" Blinking back tears of rage, he whirled then, fled the chamber before his emotion could overcome him, before Henry could stop him.

With a powerful thrust of his arm, Henry cleared the table, sending wine cups, flagon, and candles flying. Eleanor rose without haste, tilted her cup and poured wine onto the smoldering floor rushes. "I think the viscount would rather we did not burn his castle down," she said, and Henry gave her a look that all but ignited the air between them.

"I suppose it was too much to hope that you'd be helpful," he said scathingly.

She did not respond at once, regarding him pensively. Hal had nothing of his own, neither castle nor crofter's hut. Yet now he planned to give three valuable Angevin castles to six-year-old John and he did not think Hal would be resentful? How could he be so blind?

"I could not take your side, Harry," she said, "for I believe Hal is in the right. I would do all I could to mend this breach between you, I swear I would, if only you could see that . . ."

" 'Hal is in the right'?" he echoed. But because there had been no anger in her voice, his own anger began to ebb away. "He is a credulous, idle spendthrift, and, God pity him, a lamb amongst wolves. How can *you* not see that, Eleanor? I will not let my son become a puppet for the French king, and if he blames me now, so be it. In time he will understand that I was acting in his best interests."

She was taken aback by the sadness that swept over her. It was both unexpected and unwelcome. She looked at him, this man who'd been husband, lover, partner for more than twenty years, and she felt such a confusing welter of emotions—regret, resentment, a painful sense of loss—that her words caught in her throat.

"I am sorry, Harry," she said, and there was such sincerity in her voice that he forgave her with a fleeting, mirthless smile.

"So am I, love. Life would be far more peaceful if you'd given me only daughters as you did for Louis. Mayhap we could make a trade—Hal for Louis's little Philippe. He seems like a docile, biddable lad."

Even now he could still make her smile. "'A docile, biddable lad' would drive you to drink, Harry. It would be like riding a timid, meek gelding who shied at every shadow."

"You're right," he admitted, wryly amused by how well she knew him. He did indeed prefer a mettlesome stallion, but he also wanted one that was broken to the saddle. Fortunately even the most spirited horse could be tamed with enough patience.

A GALE WAS BREWING, and by dark, the winds had picked up, rattling shutters, tearing off shingles, and testing the castle walls for points of entry. A fire roared in the hearth of Henry's bedchamber, but he could still hear the muted sounds of the storm, wailing into the night like the cries of the damned. That was an unusually morbid thought for him, but his confrontation with Hal had inflicted some deep wounds and he was still brooding about it hours later.

"Your move, Harry," his cousin prompted, and with an effort, he forced his attention back to the chessboard. His distraction had cost him; Roger, a skilled player, had maneuvered him into an untenable position. To gain time, he signaled for wine, and one of his squires hastened over with a flagon.

Ranulf stood and stretched. He'd smothered several yawns and had begun to drop hints about the lateness of the hour. But Henry did not want him to leave, not yet. These two kinsmen of his could be relied upon to give sound advice, for Roger had a good head and Ranulf a good heart. Once he'd summoned them, though, he'd found himself reluctant to unburden himself, not wanting to start the bleeding again. His son's defiance hurt more than he was willing to admit, and talking about it would change nothing.

But if he did not want to confide in them, he still wanted them to stay, trusting them to keep his ghosts at bay. Pushing away abruptly from the table, he said, "I cannot keep my mind on this game tonight. Sit in for me, Uncle."

Taking the seat Henry had vacated, Ranulf studied the chessboard and whistled softly as he saw his predicament. "You are too kind," he said dryly. "You could at least provide me with a flag of surrender."

"When did a Welshman ever roll over and play dead?" Henry perched on a corner of the table, but he was too restless to sit for long and soon was wandering aimlessly about the chamber, picking up and discarding items at random. This was going to be a long night. He briefly considered going to Eleanor's bedchamber, but if he was no longer wroth with her, he was still disappointed by her stubborn defense of the indefensible. A pity Rosamund was so far away. Tumbling a wench might make it easier to sleep. But he could not very well ask Aimar to find him a bedmate, not with his queen under the same roof. Jesu, she'd stab him with his own dagger, like as not!

A soft knock at the door drew all their attention, given the hour, and they watched as one of the squires hurried over to open it. After a brief exchange with someone out in the stairwell, he turned back toward Henry, frowning in perplexity.

"The Count of Toulouse is without, Your Grace, seeking a few words with you. Shall I admit him?"

Raimon St Gilles was the last man Henry had expected to see, the last one he wanted to see. His curiosity got the better of him, however, and he nodded. Entering the chamber with his usual swagger, the count made a perfunctory obeisance, then said brusquely, "I have urgent information for you, my lord king. But it is not meant for other ears, must be given in private."

Henry hesitated, but boredom won out. "Go down to the hall," he told his squires, "and see if you can find some mischief to get into." He stopped his kinsmen, though, as they started to rise. "The Bishop of Worcester and Lord Ranulf are staying. I would trust them with the surety of my soul."

"With all due deference, my liege, I do not," Raimon objected.

"With all due deference, my lord count, it is not open for debate."

Raimon scowled at Roger and Ranulf, who looked back at him coolly. "Very well. I shall rely upon your discretion and honor, my lord bishop, Lord Ranulf, for I am putting my life at risk by coming to the king."

As he'd expected, that riveted their attention upon him. "When I swore homage to you, my liege," he said, "I vowed to keep faith with you until my last breath, and I am here to prove my sincerity."

His words and his delivery were too theatrical for Henry's taste. "What have you come to tell me?"

"You are in peril, my lord. A conspiracy is forming against you, and the conspirators are very highborn and very dangerous. It is a plot that crosses borders, involving the King of France, the Counts of Flanders, Boulogne, Champagne, and Blois. They are casting a wide net, my liege, are seeking to draw in the King of Scotland, too."

"What you call a 'conspiracy,' my lord count, they most likely would call 'statecraft.' So they are forging another alliance, hoping to protect their interests. How is this any different than what they've done in the past?"

"Because in the past, they did not have a rival claimant for the English crown."

Henry's eyes narrowed. "Go on," he said coldly.

"I am sorry, my lord, but your son, the young king, is an eager participant in the plot against you. The French king and the Count of Flanders have played skillfully upon his lack of experience and his poor judgment, convincing him that he can gain power only by rebellion. He has been persuaded that there is no other way to claim his just due."

Henry opened his mouth to deny St Gilles's accusation, to insist that his son would never betray him like that. But he could not, for there was a chilling plausibility about the count's revelation. "How do you know all this?"

"I have many enemies, my liege, so I try to make sure that I am rarely surprised. I am sure you have spies at the French court, just as Louis has spies at yours. Mine are better informed, for they are better paid."

Until now, Roger and Ranulf had kept silent. But Ranulf could no longer restrain himself, his suspicions feeding upon his inherent dislike of Raimon St Gilles. "You have made a most serious accusation, my lord count. I do not doubt that the French king is scheming with others to thwart the king at every turn. But I do not believe that Hal would ever connive to harm his father, and if that is what you are alleging, you will need more convincing proof than the whispers and conjectures of paid spies and informers."

Raimon would have ignored Ranulf's challenge had Roger not chimed in, too, saying skeptically, "I agree with Lord Ranulf. What proof can you offer?"

"To you, my lord bishop—nothing. I care not if you doubt what I say. My concern is for you, my lord king," he said, swinging back to Henry. "I do not know the ultimate aim of their conspiracy. It may well be that the young king intends only to compel you to give him a share of your domains. Rumor has it that he has demanded you turn over England or Normandy to him. And I doubt that the French king wants to see you dethroned. That would set a fearful precedent, after all. As for the others, I daresay they have less interest in preserving the sacred inviolability of kingship."

He paused then, for dramatic effect, well aware of the impact that his next words would have. "Alas, my liege, I have not told you all of it. You are nurturing vipers in your own nest. The young king is not the only one to heed the blandishments of your enemies. Your sons Richard and Geoffrey are implicated as well, doubtless swayed by their mother. For as much as it pains me to say it, your queen is involved in the conspiracy, too, doing all she can to turn your sons against you and stir up rebellion in her lands."

Ranulf choked on his wine, began to cough so violently that he sounded as if he were strangling. Roger had long cultivated the polished persona of a prince of the Church, rarely giving others a glimpse of his inner self. Now he gaped at Raimon, too stunned to hide his dismay. Gratified by their reactions, the count glanced toward Henry, but here he met with disappointment, for the king's face was utterly impassive, an inscrutable mask that revealed nothing of his thoughts.

"Is there more?" Henry asked, and his voice, too, was dispassionate. When Raimon shook his head, he said, "I will remember what you have done, my lord. Never doubt that."

This was not the response the count had been expecting, but he'd obviously been dismissed and he withdrew reluctantly, disquieted and dissatisfied. Henry strode toward the door, slid the bolt into place with a loud thud. Only then did he turn back toward the other men, who were watching him mutely, no more able to read his expression than the Count of Toulouse.

"Well," he said, "now we know where the snake went after it was thrust out of Eden."

"Never have I heard such poison spewed from a man's mouth," Ranulf said indignantly. "Thank God you were not taken in by his malice, Harry!"

"I daresay there is some truth in what he said," Roger cautioned, anxious lest his cousin dismiss the count's warning out of hand because he'd gilded it with lies. "I do not doubt his claim that a conspiracy exists. Nor do I doubt that St Gilles has seized upon it to settle a few grudges of his own."

"Eleanor warned me that he had an evil heart and a corrupt soul. I ought to have paid her more heed." Henry had begun to pace, too angry and agitated to keep still. "I knew he hated her, of course, but it never occurred to me that he would dare to strike out at a queen, my queen. And he was not content with that, he must malign my sons, lads of fourteen and fifteen. A wonder he did not think to throw Johnny into the fire, too!"

Ranulf and Roger traded glances, for they both caught the omission—no mention of Hal.

Henry's shock was giving way to rage. "I swear by the Rood that St Gilles will rue this day. I can only deal with one enemy at a time, but his reprieve will not be for long. That, too, I swear upon the Holy Cross."

"What will you do, Harry?"

Henry had stopped before the hearth, standing so close he was in danger of being singed by the leaping flames. "On the morrow, Uncle, I shall go hunting," he said, and at another time, he would have been amused by their bewilderment. "All know how I love the chase, so that will arouse no suspicions. Whilst I am off 'hunting,' I will send word to the castellans of my border castles, instructing them to lay in supplies, enough to withstand a siege, and to strengthen their garrisons. When Louis moves against me, he will find that we are expecting him."

As Roger's eyes met Ranulf's again, he saw that they shared the same concern. And because he knew his uncle was too kindhearted for utter candor, Roger realized that it would be up to him, "Only a madman would credit St Gilles's venomous accusations against your queen and younger sons. But I very much fear that there is some truth in his charges against Hal."

Henry was silent for so long that they thought he was not going to answer. When he finally turned away from the fire, they saw there was no need for words; his answer was plainly writ in the anguished slash of his mouth, the glimmering grey eyes, the first time that either man had seen him on the verge of tears.

"I know," he said huskily. "God help us both, I know."

E LEANOR'S DREAM WAS UNRAVELING, besieged by an undercurrent of noise and flashes of light. She came back to reality with reluctance, instinctively aware that these were still the hours of night, the hours of sleep. As soon as she moved, she winced, for her thigh muscles were sore. Memory came flooding back—her husband's return from his hunting trip, long after dark, after she'd gone to bed. She'd awakened to his embrace, his mouth hot upon hers, his beard scratching her throat. His lovemaking had been impassioned, intense, and yet oddly impersonal, for she suspected that any soft female body would have satisfied his need. His side of the bed was empty, but still warm, and she jerked the bed hangings aside, blinking in the glare of torchlight.

A quick glance at a notched wax candle confirmed her suspicion that it was much too early to be awake. Henry was already dressed, though. Sitting on a coffer, he was pulling his boots on, and she wondered if he meant another day's hunting. "Why are you up at such a God-forsaken hour?" He glanced over his shoulder at the sound of her voice, but offered no explanation, and she sat up with a sigh, knowing sleep was lost to her now, too.

A servant had fetched wine and bread to break their fast, and Henry poured a cup, carried it across the room, and handed it to Eleanor. "I want you to take Geoffrey with you when you go back to Poitiers," he said, and she looked up at him in surprise.

"I thought he was accompanying you into Brittany. Has there been a change of plans?"

"Yes." But he did not elaborate, instead began to buckle his scabbard belt, further proof that he had a journey in mind. Eleanor tugged at her hair, finding it caught under her hip; she'd braided it before going to bed, but Henry had unfastened it during the night. Drinking her wine, she wondered where he meant to go if not into Brittany. The festivities at Limoges were over. The Kings of Aragon and Navarre had departed for their own lands, as had many of the attending barons and their ladies. John had been sent back to Fontevrault Abbey to resume his studies; his little bride-to-be would accompany Eleanor to Poitiers, there to be raised with Constance and Alys and Joanna. Only the Count of Toulouse still lingered, uncaring that none wanted him there, putting Eleanor in mind of a vulture hovering over carrion, awaiting his chance to swoop down to feed. She was sure he was up to no good, and she was glad she would soon be seeing the last of Limoges, glad she would be going home to Poitiers, favored of all her cities. Watching Henry as he moved around the chamber, she was jolted to realize that this might well have been the last time she'd share his bed.

"Where do you go from here, Harry?"

Before he could respond, the door swung open and Hal entered. "Why did you summon me so early, Maman?" he complained, yawning. "I'd hoped to remain abed for—" He stopped abruptly as Henry moved into his line of vision. His eyes cut from his father to his mother in the rumpled bed, and to Eleanor's surprise, he flushed deeply. She was astonished; surely he could not be embarrassed by this proof that she'd spent the night with Harry? And then, as he gave her a look of silent reproach, she understood. To Hal, she'd been sleeping with the enemy.

"The summons was mine," Henry said, regarding his son with a lack of emotion that Eleanor found troubling. "I am returning to Normandy this morn, and you are coming with me."

Hal was still off balance, but he tried now to regain his footing by saying emphatically, "I think not."

"You are not being given a choice." Henry's voice was toneless, and to Hal, his gaze was as piercing and predatory as those Iceland gyrfalcons he'd promised but would never deliver. Hal glanced back at Eleanor, seeking guidance. But this woman seemed like a stranger to him, clutching blankets to cover her nudity, her hair tumbling about her shoulders in wanton disarray, utterly unlike the coolly poised, elegant mother who was his lodestar and mentor. As their gazes crossed, she shook her head, almost imperceptibly, signaling that she did not know what his father intended.

"You need not look to your mother for assistance," Henry said, still in that matter-of-fact manner that Hal found more disturbing than outright anger would have been. "It is only natural that a mother bird should protect her chicks, but when it is time for a fledgling to leave the nest, he is on his own."

Hal was quick to seize his father's metaphor and turn it back against him. "But that fledgling cannot learn to fly if his wings are clipped."

"Clever lad," Henry said softly, and it was not a compliment. "Lest you've forgotten, I warned you that you'd be on a short leash until you prove it is no longer needed. So for the foreseeable future, you'll be closer than my own shadow. And since you've been keeping dubious company of late, I am dismissing those self-seekers and syco-phants who are leading you astray, men such as Hasculf de St Hilaire, Adam d'Yque-beuf, and Juhel de Mayenne."

Hal's outraged gasp was audible to both his parents. "You cannot do that!"

"It is done," Henry said tersely, and his son whirled to face his mother, an involun-tary, stunned cry of "Maman!" escaping his lips.

Eleanor's eyes locked with his, sending a message that was both reassurance and warning. "I understand your reluctance, Hal," she said, "but you are not in a position to resist. You must do as your father commands."

NORMALLY A KING'S LEAVE-TAKING was a chaotic, noisy event, but those who'd gathered in the inner castle bailey to watch Henry's departure were sub-dued and somber. Some of Hal's knights lurked in the shadows, unwilling to call the king's attention to themselves, but William Marshal strode out into the chilly March sunlight, a silent affirmation of loyalty to his unhappy young lord. Eleanor noted the gesture and approved. Marguerite and Hal were embracing; he brushed tears from her cheeks with his fingers before taking his stallion's reins. His defiant gaze raked the bai-ley, finding sympathy from most of the onlookers, for this was Aquitaine; these were his mother's vassals. Only the Count of Toulouse looked satisfied with his disgrace. As their eyes met, Hal leaned from the saddle and spat.

Seeing that they were about to depart, Eleanor moved forward, trailed by her un-cle, constable, and Viscount Aimar. "My lord husband," she said, "go with God," and Henry acknowledged her farewell with a formal "Madame," brushing his lips to her outstretched hand. Searching for his other sons, he found them standing on the steps of the great hall, and gave them a grave salute, then signaled his men to move out.

Hal had recovered his aplomb by now and he blew kisses to his wife, winked at his cousin Maud, and smiled at his mother before putting the spurs to his stallion. The last glance he cast over his shoulder, though, was a long, meaningful look aimed at William Marshal.

Marguerite had begun to sob in earnest, and Maud put a supportive arm around the girl's shaking shoulders. But it was then that her eyes came to rest upon Henry's queen. Eleanor was standing with her uncle Raoul and her son Richard, and as Maud looked at them, it seemed to her as if their faces were carved from stone. She instinc-tively made the sign of the cross to ward off a superstitious sense of foreboding, and then turned back to console Hal's weeping young wife.

CHAPTER SIX

⚜

March 1173
Chinon Castle, Touraine

*T*HE DAY WAS OVERCAST and, at first sight, Chinon Castle seemed under siege by encroaching clouds. Gazing up at its mist-shrouded towers, Henry felt a weary sense of relief. He was back in his own domains now, back in the land of his birth and, as always, returning to Chinon was a homecoming.

As they approached the village, people crowded into the streets to watch, although theirs was a meager royal procession, disappointing for those yearning for spectacle or pageantry: travel-begrimed household knights, three solemn earls, and two troubled kings who'd barely spoken a word since leaving Limoges. Reining in before the stone bridge that spanned the River Vienne, Henry glanced at his son's averted face. Hal had withdrawn into a cocoon of sullen silence. When compelled to acknowledge Henry's existence, he did so with exaggerated deference, addressing his father as "my liege" in a voice dripping with sarcasm. Henry's half brother Hamelin had done his best to restore family harmony, but his lectures on filial duty had fallen on deaf ears and Hal was soon treating his uncle with the same mocking courtesy he offered his father.

Henry was fond of Hamelin, but he'd never valued his brother's advice, and so it was no surprise when Hal did not, either. He had more respect for the Earl of Essex's judgment, and as they crossed the bridge, he debated asking the other man to try his hand at peacemaking. Essex was a renowned knight and Hal might pay more heed to his counsel. As difficult as it was for Henry to ask for help, he was realizing that with Hal, he needed all the help he could get.

Once they'd ridden up the limestone cliff to the castle, Henry hastened to his bed-chamber. He'd gotten wet while fording a stream earlier in the day and his chausses were clinging clammily to his skin. Stripping them off, he rubbed his legs briskly with a towel while Fulke, one of his squires, rooted around in a coffer for dry clothing. His other squire, Warin, was supervising servants as they lugged a second bed up the stairs, for Henry trusted his son so little now that he insisted they sleep in the same chamber, thus guaranteeing that their nights would be as disquieting as their days.

An older man had just entered, bearing Henry's favorite falcon on his out-stretched arm, and Henry smiled, his mood momentarily lightening. "See that a chicken is fresh-killed for her meal," he instructed the falconer, making up his mind to fly her on the morrow. The season was ending, but he'd still have a few more after-noons to rejoice in the pure joy of the open air, the boundless sky, and poetry on the wing. He was tempted to ask Hal to join him, but that was a fool's fantasy. It would take more than a shared love of hawking to bridge the chasm yawning between them.

He was pulling on a dry tunic when the Earl of Essex sought entry. Henry waved him in without ceremony, for Essex was more than a loyal vassal. Eleanor had once compared Henry to a well-defended castle, claiming that he let some people into his outer bailey, very few into the inner bailey, and none at all into the keep. For whatever reason, he remembered that now, and acknowledged that Essex had earned access to the inner bailey. Somehow managing to circumvent those barriers set up after Thomas Becket's betrayal, Essex had become a friend.

There was comfort in that realization, and surprise, too, for Essex was surely an unlikely candidate to become a king's confidant. In so many ways, he was an anomaly. Tall and slender and fair-haired, he looked more like a court fop than a warrior, but his languorous manner could not be more deceiving; he wielded a sword with lethal skill, and was one of Henry's most capable battle commanders. He held an English earl-dom, but he'd been raised in Flanders, growing to manhood at the court of the Flem-ish count, Philip. In the six years since he'd inherited his brother's title and returned to England, he'd been besieged by ambitious mothers hoping to snare him for their mar-riageable daughters, but he'd shown no interest in taking a highborn bride. Only Henry knew that he'd given his heart to a Flemish mistress he could never wed, and doted upon an illegitimate daughter who could not inherit his lands. And he'd gained a well-deserved reputation for loyalty, despite being the son of one of the most treacherous, disloyal barons ever to draw breath, the worst of the lawless lords who'd ravaged England during those wretched years when King Stephen had fought with Henry's mother, the Empress Maude, for the English crown.

Geoffrey de Mandeville could have taught Judas about betrayal and Herod about cruelty. He had abandoned King Stephen for the Empress Maude, deserted Maude to pledge his allegiance again to Stephen, and was contemplating yet another breach of faith when Stephen struck first, stripping him of his base of power, the Tower of London. As always, though, Stephen's punishment was halfhearted and he'd allowed the earl to remain at liberty. He'd promptly rebelled and unleashed hell upon the innocent and the defenseless. Burning, pillaging, raping, his men devastated towns and churches alike, inspiring such fear that it was said the grass withered where he walked. He'd died assaulting one of Stephen's castles, not long after he'd been excommunicated for seizing Ramsey Abbey. Since he could not be buried in hallowed ground, the Knights Templar had hung his coffin in a tree so as not to pollute the earth.

His son and namesake was allowed to inherit the earldom once Henry ascended the English throne, serving Henry faithfully till his death, when his title and lands passed to his younger brother, William. Geoffrey de Mandeville rested today in consecrated ground, the Pope having granted a posthumous absolution at his family's behest, but his reputation could never be restored, and his name was still a byword for treachery and betrayal. Yet this same man had sired two sons of honor and integrity. Henry did not understand it, any more than he'd understood how John Marshal could have begotten a worthy son like Will. He could only be thankful for it.

"If you'd hoped for an idle afternoon, my liege, those hopes are about to be dashed." Essex's smile was wryly sympathetic. "Word of the king's arrival invariably spreads faster than a summer brushfire, and the great hall is already filling with petitioners, claimants, plaintiffs, supplicants, and self-seekers of every stripe. Some have cases pending before your Curia Regis, others want you to resolve local disputes, and all of them are entreating that they be heard."

Henry sighed, but he was accustomed to this, for a king's time was almost as valued as his favor. "I'll grant audiences this afternoon and hold court on the morrow," he said, casting a regretful look in his falcon's direction.

"The priest of St Maurice's has asked to see you, too." Knowing that Henry had paid for the construction of the church, Essex guessed that he'd take a personal interest in its progress. "Do you want to see him first?" When Henry nodded, the earl started for the door, then paused. "Shall I ask your son to join you in the hall?"

Henry hesitated. He knew that the earl was trying, in a more subtle fashion than Hamelin, to reconcile father and son. Would Hal be pleased by the invitation? But when had he ever shown interest in the more mundane duties of kingship?

"No, Willem," he said, using the playful nickname he'd bestowed upon the earl in affectionate acknowledgment of the other man's boyhood in Flanders—"Willem" being Flemish for "William." "More likely than not, I'd have to command his presence, and that would defeat the purpose, would it not?"

Willem took his candor for what it was—a declaration of trust—and made a discreet departure, for he was wiser than Hamelin, knew better than to push. When the king was ready to talk about his son's wayward behavior, he would pick the time and place.

Henry's squires had been quietly conferring, for they were constantly engaged in a losing battle to make their lord look more regal, and they offered him now a choice of two short cloaks called rhenos, one lined with sable, the other with miniver. Henry cared only for staying warm in the great hall, and selected at random, then fended off their efforts to get him to change his plain green tunic for a more fashionable one with a diagonal neckline. When a knock sounded on the door, he seized the opportunity to escape their ministrations and strode over to answer it himself. He was expecting Willem and the priest of St Maurice's. He was not expecting to see his son.

"May I come in?"

Henry stepped aside to let Hal enter, and his squires at once dived for the door, murmuring vague excuses as they fled. "Passing strange—people usually enjoy watching bloodshed." Hal's joke was a lame one, but it was a joke, nonetheless, and Henry's initial surprise gave way to astonishment. They'd not been on speaking terms for days, and suddenly the lad was making jests? After considering his possible responses, he chose silence, waiting warily for Hal to reveal his intent.

Hal seemed ill at ease. Wandering about the chamber, he lavished attention upon Henry's falcon before picking up one of the discarded cloaks. "May I borrow this sometime?"

"I thought you were aiming higher than a cloak," Henry said coolly, and Hal let the garment slip through his fingers onto the floor.

"I hate this," he blurted out, for the first time meeting Henry's eyes.

"What do you hate, Hal? That we are estranged? Or that you were dragged away from Limoges against your will?"

"Both," Hal admitted, with a flickering smile. "I have the right of it in our quarrel, Papa. But it serves for naught to fight like this. Even if we cannot agree, we need not turn words into weapons. I have said things in anger that I now regret, and I hope that is true for you, too."

"This is a remarkable change of mood. Just a few hours ago, you were acting as if I were the Antichrist. If you have experienced a divine revelation, like St Paul on the road to Damascus, I will be most interested to hear about it." Henry's sarcasm was so sharp because he'd been affected in spite of himself by his son's use of "Papa," an echo of simpler, happier times.

Color rose in Hal's face, but he did not look away. "I suppose I deserve that," he conceded. "I ought to have found a better way to express my objections to the marriage contract. For that, I am indeed sorry." Continuing quickly, "I do not want you to misunderstand what I am saying, though. I am apologizing for my bad manners, not for my protest. As for what caused my 'remarkable change of mood,' the credit—or blame—for that must go to Uncle Hamelin."

At Henry's obvious surprise, Hal could not help grinning. "I know how unlikely that sounds. But even a blind pig finds an acorn occasionally."

"And what acorn did Hamelin dig up?"

"He reminded me of the date. Today is the fifth of March . . . your birthday."

Henry was taken aback. "So it is," he said, for he'd indeed been born on this day forty years ago at Le Mans. "It had entirely slipped my mind . . ."

"Mine, too . . . until Uncle Hamelin spoke up." Hal was looking discomfited again. "He made me see that I owe you better than this," he said in a low voice. "I hope that you can forgive my public rudeness. I promise you that it will not happen again."

Henry wanted very much to believe him. "Yes, I can forgive you," he said cautiously. "But you must understand, Hal, that nothing has changed and nothing will change until you prove to me that you can be trusted."

"I know that. And I'll not mislead you, Papa. Nothing has changed for me, either. I am never going to agree to the loss of Chinon and the other two castles. Nor am I going to stop demanding my just due as an anointed king. But in the future I will try to keep our quarrels private and I will accord you the respect you deserve as my father and my king." Hal paused before saying hopefully, "Fair enough?"

Henry nodded slowly. "Fair enough."

Hal's relief was palpable. "I was afraid," he said, "that you'd not believe me." They regarded each other in silence for a few moments, neither knowing what to say next, fearful of taking a misstep onto such very thin ice. Reaching down, Hal retrieved the cloak from the floor rushes and fastened it around his shoulders. "Since we just agreed to a truce," he said cheerfully, "that must mean that I can borrow your clothes, no? Now I'd best get down to the hall and find Uncle Hamelin. I am going to make him very happy by telling him that he single-handedly brought about our reconciliation!"

At the door, he halted. "There is one more thing, Papa. I need to request a favor."

Henry said nothing, all his suspicions flaring up again. Hal did not seem to read anything ominous in his silence, though, for his smile did not waver. "It was not just my anger that has kept me so quiet since we left Limoges. I've been coping with a wretched toothache. It comes and goes, but is worse when I eat or drink."

Henry's response was skeptical, not sympathetic. "And I suppose you want to go into the village in search of a barber who'll pull it."

Again, Hal surprised him. "Good God, no! I'd not let a barber get within a mile of me with a pair of pincers." He gave a shudder of mock horror. "I would like you to send for an apothecary. Surely there must be herbs that I can take to ease the pain?"

So Hal had not been conniving to leave the castle. Henry had rarely been so happy to be proven wrong. "Yes . . . cloves might help. I will tell the steward to fetch the village apothecary straightaway."

Hal looked pleased. "Thank you. For this fine cloak, too." He ran his fingers admiringly over the softly woven material. "I suppose you'll want it back . . . eventually." This time his smile was full of mischief, and it called up memories Henry had been seeking to suppress, memories of the boy who'd been so quick to laugh, to tease, so proud to be a crowned king, not yet corrupted by the siren songs of the French court.

Henry stood motionless for a time after Hal's departure, deliberately calling up echoes of the Count of Toulouse's warning. *They have played skillfully upon his lack of experience and his poor judgment.* He'd spoken a harsh truth when he'd told Hal that nothing had changed. But he could not deny that the faintest of sparks had been kindled, a feeble glimmer of hope in the dark that had descended upon his world at Limoges.

D INNER, normally scheduled at noon, had been shifted to a later hour as part of the Lenten abstinence and was not served until after Vespers had rung. It turned out to be a pleasant surprise for Henry's household knights and the castle garrison, who'd been anticipating gloom and bleak silence. Instead, the meal that evening was informal, enjoyable, and raucous in the absence of women. Hal was in high spirits, and had the men laughing uproariously over his extravagant account of what he called the Saga of the Royal Tooth. He claimed that Chinon's barber, hearing of his malady, had stalked him relentlessly all afternoon, urging him to have the tooth extracted.

"He vowed that he need not use the pincers if I was skittish about them, that there were other ways. Only these 'other ways' made the pincers sound better and better. One method was to coat the ailing tooth with the ashes of earthworms. Another was to mix up a powder of ants and their eggs and blow it through a quill onto the tooth. Or smear on a concoction of newts and fen beetles. When I questioned where he'd find newts or ant eggs, he assured me that all the necessary ingredients were at hand. By then I realized that he and Master Gervase, the apothecary, were partners in crime, and I began to fear the worst!"

Chinon's castellan, blinking back tears of mirth, offered to send to the nearest city, Tours or Angers, to find a surgeon who made his living by pulling teeth. Hal hastily made the sign of the cross, as if to ward off evil. "Jesu forfend, Sir Robert! My new friend, the barber, told me more than any man would want to know about their methods. He described a 'popular procedure' in which they cauterize the skin behind the victim's ear, then heat henbane and leek seeds over hot coals and have him inhale the smoke through a funnel. Since I know henbane is a poison, I assume the next step in the process would be to hide my body afterward!"

Several knights chimed in with horror stories of their own, but Hal was not ready to yield center stage, and it occurred to his amused father that he'd have made a fine minstrel or player. Adroitly recapturing control of the conversation, Hal launched into the next chapter of his narrative: his meeting with Master Gervase, the apothecary.

"He said they think pain is caused by worms breeding in the tooth. That reassured me greatly, of course. He explained that the worms could be driven out by lighting a candle made of mutton fat and burning it as close to the ailing tooth as I could endure. Meanwhile, he'd hold a basin of cold water under my jaw and the worms would seek to escape the heat and fall into the water. I considered it, but then I started to wonder how we could be sure that the worms could not swim," Hal said, with such tongue-in-cheek seriousness that the hall erupted into hilarity again.

When the laughter subsided, Hamelin provided more fuel for the fire by asking Hal what treatment he'd finally settled upon. Hal grimaced and shook his head ruefully. "By that point, Uncle, I'd begun to fear that the only choice open to me was to drown the worms—and my sorrows—in drink. But when he saw that his sale was in danger, Master Gervase offered a few recommendations more tolerable than ant eggs or powdered newts. At first he suggested that I rub the oil of the box tree on the afflicted tooth, and I was tempted. But then he let slip that this remedy also cured piles, which I found right curious. Did I really want to put a potion meant for the arse into my mouth?"

With an actor's innate sense of timing, Hal paused for the audience to react and was not disappointed. "Seeing that I was not keen on the box tree oil, Master Gervase advised me to rub the tooth and gum with betony or cloves—which was what my lord father had suggested hours ago!" Slanting a facetious glance toward Henry, he said, "So if you ever tire of governing, my liege, you can always earn a living as an apothecary."

This time his sally was met with cautious silence, his audience waiting to see how Henry would react, for under the circumstances, that could have been a harmless jest or a barbed gibe. It was only after Henry smiled that the other men felt free to laugh, and he realized that some of their merriment was due to sheer relief that father and son seemed to have made peace.

Hal continued to amuse with his comic commentary, expressing his doubts about the draught that the apothecary had eventually prescribed to ease his pain and help him sleep, a blend of henbane, black poppy, and bryony root, for they were all poisons. He wondered, too, why the martyred maiden Apollonia was the patron saint for toothaches when she'd had all of her own teeth cruelly extracted by her pagan tormentors. Wasn't that, he mused, rather like picking a virgin as the patron saint for whores or a miser as the patron saint for spendthrifts?

Henry enjoyed watching Hal's performance; it had been a long time since he'd seen his son so lighthearted, so carefree. This meal was in such stark contrast to the tense, unpalatable dinners they'd endured since leaving Limoges that he found himself savoring the bland Lenten fare, even eating a few mouthfuls of salted herring, a despised dish that rarely appeared on a royal table. Chinon's cooks had offered up a particularly mediocre menu, confident that Henry was not likely to notice. The final course was a soupy pudding made with almond milk and dried figs. But before the men could push away from the tables, Hal rose and banged on his wine cup with a knife to attract attention.

"I want to end dinner with a salute to my lord father," he announced, and on cue, a servant entered with a flagon and two silver wine cups. Reaching for one, Hal handed the other to Henry. Puzzled, he followed his son's lead and leaned over so Hal could ceremoniously clink their cups together. Taking a swallow, he looked at Hal in surprise, for the vessels were filled with hippocras, a costly spiced wine that was served only upon special occasions even by the wealthy and highborn.

Looking pleased with himself, Hal lifted his cup high. "You may not all know that this is a special day . . . my lord father the king's birthday. I would have you drink to his health and good fortune!"

The men raised their own cups and the hall resounded with cries of "To the king!" Glancing back at Henry with a sly grin, Hal signaled for silence. "I am grateful to my uncle, the Earl of Surrey, for reminding me, as this is not a birthday to go unmarked. It is not every day, after all, that a man reaches the venerable age of fifty."

Henry inhaled the wine he'd been about to swallow and began to cough. Again the audience quieted, watching Henry to see if he was amused or annoyed by his son's jape. Getting his breath back, he laughed, and the men burst into applause and cheers, so grateful were they that the rift between their lord and his son was on the mend. None wanted to be forced to choose between them, for how could a man weigh the present against the future?

Rising, Henry lifted his cup as Hal had done. "Let's drink now to my son, who has every attribute of kingship except the ability to count." Midst the laughter, his gaze came to rest affectionately upon his beaming brother. Hamelin had given him a birthday gift more valuable than gold, silver, or myrrh: a new beginning.

HENRY DID NOT LINGER long in the great hall, for his hours in the saddle had caught up with him, and he felt unusually tired. After joking with Willem that his son's jest had been on target, for tonight he felt far closer to fifty than forty, he withdrew to his bedchamber in the keep. Hal had already retired, losing much of his earlier animation once his tooth began to pain him again, and when Henry entered the chamber, his son was sound asleep, an empty vial of the apothecary's draught in the floor rushes by his bed. Henry's squires were awaiting him, yawning behind their hands as they drowsily assisted him to undress. Glancing from their drooping eyelids to the flagon of night wine on a nearby table, Henry smiled, guessing that Hal had shared it liberally with them. None had ever faulted his son's generosity. It was his good heart that had gotten him into trouble; he was too trusting, a troubling flaw in a king. He would have to be taught the lessons Henry had learned at an early age.

THE BEDCHAMBER WAS LIT only by the flickering flames of the dying hearth and there was no sound but the even breathing of Hal's father and his squires. It was difficult to lie still, to wait. Too much was at stake, though, for impatience, and Hal did not fling back the bedcovers until he was sure that the other occupants of the chamber were asleep. He was fully dressed, save for his boots, and he hastily pulled them on, fastened his belt, and slid his sword into its leather scabbard, as silently as a ghost. He held his breath as he raised the door latch, stifling a triumphant laugh when none of them stirred as he slipped out into the stairwell.

His father preferred to sleep in the keep rather than in the royal apartments he'd built along the south wall. Emerging into the bailey, Hal stood motionless for a moment, his eyes searching the darkness, but he could detect no lights, no signs of life. A few men might still be awake in the great hall, though, and he quickened his pace until he'd gotten past it. Ahead of him lay the gatehouse, flanked on each side by stone towers. There he found the guards, sharing a flask and throwing dice.

They sprang to their feet in alarm as he entered, for gambling during sentry duty could bring the wrath of the castellan down upon them. But their dismay lessened once they recognized Hal, as he was not known to be a disciplinarian.

"How may we serve you, my lord?"

Hal had a good memory for faces, and he'd been at Chinon often enough in the past to become acquainted with the garrison. He called them by their given names now, a familiarity that he knew they'd find flattering. "Giles, Daniel, and Mauger, is it not? I could not sleep." He pointed at his jaw, knowing that even if they'd not been in the great hall during dinner, they'd have heard by now of his afternoon encounter with the barber and apothecary. "It seems that not even poppy and bryony root are strong enough to vanquish a toothache. I was wandering about the bailey like a lost soul, and then I saw the light from the gatehouse window."

Giles was their spokesman and he said expansively, "We would be honored to keep you company, my liege. Alas, we lack those comforts that a king has every right to expect." With a wave of his hand, he took in the barren, dimly lit guard chamber. "We've not even a stool to offer you, and the only wine we have tastes like verjuice."

"If you can take my mind off this wretched toothache, Giles, that will matter more to me than all the luxuries of Constantinople. As for the wine . . ." With a grin, Hal reached under his mantle and produced a wineskin. "Now," he said, glancing down at the dice, "what game are we playing? Hazard or raffle?"

The hour that followed was one the guards would never forget. They could scarcely believe that they were gambling with the young king, sharing his wineskin and bantering with him as if he were one of their own. Hal lost more than he won and joked that he had worse luck than a cuckolded husband. He asked them about their families and their bedmates, for they were too young to afford wives, and told them stories of hunts and tournaments, giving them glimpses of a world that was as fascinating to them as it was foreign. And when Mauger complained of his father's strict ways and heavy-handed discipline, Hal offered him sympathy and the knowing smile of one who'd walked in Mauger's shoes. They were sorry, therefore, when he stretched and got to his feet, for they were not yet ready to return to reality.

"I've kept you from your duties long enough," he said, wincing as he gingerly touched his sore jaw. "You are good lads, the lot of you. Seek me out on the morrow and I'll find a way to show my appreciation."

They thanked him profusely, dazzled by visions of silver coin and fine wine and a king's favor, and assured him that it had been their pleasure to be of service. Hal smiled, tossed his wineskin to Mauger, and took a step toward the door before pausing. "There is something else you could do for me," he said, and they vowed that he need only name it.

"I'll not be able to sleep tonight. It is not just this accursed tooth. In truth, I've an itch that only a woman can scratch."

They grinned, for that was an itch they well knew, and suggested that any maid servant in the castle would be honored to swive him. "I suppose so," he said, with becoming modesty. "But I have a particular lass in mind, one who lives down in the village, the young widow of the blacksmith." Lowering his voice, he winked. "I am depending upon your discretion, for she'd not like to have her name bandied about the garrison. But I can assure you that no man sharing her bed will have any thoughts to spare for teeth!"

They were quiet, looking at him in consternation, and Hal hid a smile, for he read their faces and their minds as easily as a monk could read his Psalter. They wanted to please him, were eager to be part of this benign conspiracy, knowing they could dine out on this story for the rest of their lives. They'd heard the whispers of his disgrace, the rumors that he and his father were feuding. But he'd certainly seemed to be on good terms with the king during dinner. And he was famed for his generosity, not one to forget a favor.

It was Giles who found the solution. "We can lower the drawbridge for you, my lord. But you'll have to go on foot." Hoping he'd come up with a compromise that accommodated the young king whilst protecting themselves, he waited anxiously to see if it was acceptable to Hal.

To his great relief, Hal laughed and clapped him on the shoulder. "Why would I need a horse? Her house is but a stone's throw from the bottom of the hill." And it was as easy as that to escape from his father's formidable castle at Chinon.

THE NIGHT WAS COLD, but the day's clouds had been swept from the sky by a brisk west wind and the darkness was lit by stars beyond counting. Hal supposed he should be nervous, yet all he felt was excitement. It had been hard to wait calmly as the guards manned the chains and winches, first raising the iron portcullis and then lowering the drawbridge, for the noise seemed loud enough to awaken the dead. But no one came out to investigate, and Hal was soon standing on the causeway, waving jauntily at his unwitting accomplices. He hoped they'd not pay too high a price for their misplaced trust. But to his father's credit, he did not make scapegoats of those who could not defend themselves. No, his anger would not be turned upon the hapless guards. There would be one person he'd blame, and only one.

At the bottom of the hill, he hesitated, then decided to head for the Grand-Carroi, the village crossroads. He could only hope he had not long to wait. What he would do if his wait were in vain, he refused to contemplate. The village street was deserted; even the dogs were asleep. Hal had just passed the silhouette of St Maurice's church when figures stepped from the shadows into his path.

Hal felt no surprise as the moonlight revealed their identities: Peter Fitz Guy, Simon de Marisco, and, of course, William Marshal. These men were far more than members of his retinue; they were good friends, and he embraced them like brothers.

Peter and Simon shared his jubilation, but Will was somber, his expression showing both resolve and recognition of the great risk they were taking. Hal knew the older man was conflicted, for unlike the others, he still saw Henry as his king, not his enemy. But his loyalty to his liege lord had proved stronger than his misgivings, and Hal was deeply touched by his steadfast devotion. Flinging his arm around Will's shoulders, he hugged the knight again, and privately vowed that Will would be well rewarded for his staunch, unwavering allegiance.

"I knew you'd be here," he exulted, "I knew it!"

Simon and Peter grinned and began to tell him of the troubles they'd had in their race to reach Chinon before the king, interrupting each other freely as they complained happily about taking lesser-known roads and getting little sleep and having to hide in the nearby woods as they kept the castle under surveillance. It was Will who cut their premature celebrating short, reminding them tersely that time was of the essence.

They knew he was right and followed him hastily back into the safety of the shadows, explaining to Hal that the others were waiting in a copse of trees on the edge of the village. "What about fresh mounts?" Hal wanted to know. "We're going to need them, for we'll not be able to spare our horses."

"I sent a man ahead to Alençon," Will said, "so they'll be ready for us when we get there."

That had been Hal's main concern, for he knew how fast his father traveled under ordinary circumstances; in times of need, he'd shown an uncanny ability to put wings to his horse's hooves. "Bless you, Will," he exclaimed, rejoicing that a few whispered words to Marguerite could have set in motion such a perfect plan. He'd not doubted, though, that Will would understand the cryptic message she'd borne—one simple word, "Chinon." How could he fail when he had right and God and such valiant knights on his side?

When they wanted to know how he'd gotten out of the castle, he grinned and promised to tell them all about his ruse as soon as they were safely away. He was eager to share, for not many men could claim to have outwitted his father with such ease. Will's concern about delay was justified, though, and it would have to wait.

He liked the looks of the stallion they'd chosen for him; it was pawing the grass, eager to run. So was Hal and he swung up into the saddle with a laugh of pure pleasure. His eyes moving from face to face, he felt such a surge of affection for these men that his throat tightened and his eyes misted. "Songs will be sung and tales told of the events of this night. We'll soon have my father's hounds on our trail. But this is one fox that will not be caught!" He put spurs to his horse, then, the wind carrying echoes of his laughter back through the silent streets of the sleeping village.

"My lord! wake up, my lord!"

Henry opened his eyes, quickly closed them to shut out the glare of torchlight. His head was throbbing and he wanted only to spiral down into sleep again. But the voices were insistent. Filtering the light through his lashes, he saw tense faces floating above him.

"Harry!" This was his brother's voice, and he guessed that it was Hamelin's hand clamped upon his shoulder. Opening his eyes again, he gazed blearily at the men hovering around the bed. What was the matter with him? His head felt as if it were stuffed with cobwebs.

"My lord king, you must get up." Willem was standing beside Hamelin. "Your son is gone. He has fled the castle."

Henry blinked, his gaze sweeping the chamber. Nearby, his squires lay on their pallets, snoring peacefully. But Hal's bed was empty. "What do you mean he is gone? What time is it?"

"Nigh on dawn, my liege."

Sitting up with an effort, Henry saw that his castellan was in the chamber, too. Why was he having so much trouble making sense of this? He'd always awakened like a cat, instantly on the alert. "Fetch that basin," he ordered and when Hamelin brought it to the bed, he splashed water onto his face. It was frigid, a thin sheen of ice coating the surface, and the shock chased away the last of his grogginess.

"What are you saying? How could Hal have gotten out of the castle?"

"These dolts lowered the drawbridge for him." Glaring over his shoulder, the castellan gestured and three terrified young men were shoved forward. Shrinking back, they stared mutely at the king as the castellan gave Henry an angry summary of the night's events. "So they stood there, grinning like jackanapes, and waved him on his way," he concluded caustically. "And it took half the night ere they realized that he was not coming back, and then another hour or so until they mustered the courage to summon me."

One of the youths stumbled forward and fell to his knees by the bed. "Forgive us, my liege," he pleaded. "He wanted to tumble a wench, and we could see no harm in it. We did not let him take a horse." He swallowed, looking up at Henry with silent tears streaking his face. "He played us for fools, sire . . . I am so sorry!"

"He played us all for fools," Henry said, but he was still struggling with disbelief. Could Hal have truly done this? Could he have been so cunning, so false? So heartless? "I am a light sleeper," he said. "How could he have been sure that I'd not awaken . . ." And then he caught his breath, comprehension coming like a blow. His eyes moved from the flagon of night wine on the table to his squires, still sleeping in the midst of turmoil, and for a fleeting moment, he saw, too, a silver wine cup filled with hippocras.

"He put it in the wine," he whispered. They looked at him blankly, and he said it again, needing to hear the words spoken aloud, for only then could he believe them. "The sleeping draught." Sweet Mary, Mother of God. "The sleeping draught for that convenient toothache of his."

"My lord king . . ." Willem reached out, clasped his hand in a warm, firm grip. "What would you have us do?"

Henry's head came up. "Saddle the horses."

The castellan at once headed for the door. Hamelin was trying to awaken the squires, without any luck. Willem, glancing toward the forgotten guards, dismissed them with an abrupt gesture. They fled the chamber, not daring to look back, and Willem began to gather up clothing for the king. Henry was already on his feet. Grabbing garments from the earl, he dressed quickly and silently. Willem waited, wisely saying nothing, but Hamelin could not hold his tongue.

"How could he do this? I would never have thought him capable of such treachery." Moving toward his brother, he came to a hesitant halt, not sure what to do next. "Harry . . . Harry, I am so sorry!"

Henry looked at him. "So am I," he said at last, and then added in a voice that sent chills along Hamelin's spine, "but not as sorry as that traitorous whelp will be."

CHAPTER SEVEN

✦

March 1173
Poitiers, Poitou

*T*HE WINDOW-SEAT WAS CUSHIONED, and sunlight was filtering into the solar over Maud's shoulder, for they were double windows and covered with thin sheets of horn, which admitted more light than the usual linen screens. A blazing hearth and woolen wall hangings shut out the chill, and the fireplace had a feature that Maud had not seen before: a stone hood that kept the smoke from escaping into the chamber by funneling it up the chimney. The floor rushes were fresh and fragrant; Maud had been impressed to learn that they were changed weekly, for she knew some English barons who'd consider it extravagant to replace them more than once a year. One of Eleanor's musicians was strumming a plaintive melody on his gittern, two of her ladies were embroidering pillow covers, and her favorite greyhound was sprawled, belly-up, before the fire. A third attendant was reading aloud for their entertainment the sorrowful tale of star-crossed lovers Tristan and Iseult. It was a pleasant, peaceful scene, and Maud thought again that they knew how to live well in Aquitaine. Little wonder Eleanor had yearned for her homeland during her years of marital exile, for neither Paris nor London could match the splendors—or the comforts—of Poitiers.

Eleanor was not stitching as her ladies were, and Maud realized that she'd never seen her friend with a needle in her hand. Her aunt, the Empress Maude, had not been one for embroidery either. Maud supposed it was a small but subtle form of rebellion, for even queens were expected to do needlework, to occupy themselves with womanly tasks.

As for herself, Maud did not object to this particular domestic duty. She was a skilled seamstress and enjoyed exercising her imagination with needle and thread. Her current project was an elegant chrysom cloth of fine linen. In four years of marriage, her daughter-in-law Bertrada had already given birth to three children, and so Maud thought it only logical that there'd be a need again for christening attire in the coming twelvemonth. She was sorry Bertrada was not with her at Poitiers, for she'd become quite fond of the girl, but her daughter-by-marriage had insisted upon returning to England with Ranulf, Rhiannon, and Rainald.

She'd been surprised that Hugh had not taken Bertrada when he'd departed on pilgrimage after Christmas to the holy Spanish shrine of Santiago de Compostela. Their separation might be for the best, though, giving Bertrada time to recover from her last confinement. She knew of no woman who'd want to face the birthing chamber every year, much less a lass who was barely seventeen.

Thinking of difficult deliveries called John's birth to mind, and she glanced toward the queen. Eleanor was seated at a table, occupied with pen and parchment, which aroused Maud's always-lively curiosity; a letter must be very private indeed if it could not be entrusted to a scribe. She was amusing herself by speculating about the nature of her friend's confidential message when the door suddenly banged open, with enough force to startle them all.

Richard swept into the chamber like a whirlwind; that was the only way Maud could describe his dramatic entrance. He was so flushed that he seemed to be feverish, and he looked eerily like his father in his rage. He was followed by Raoul de Faye and a third man who was a stranger to Maud. Slamming the door behind him, Richard strode toward his mother, paying no heed to the others in the solar.

"You'll not believe what that damned fool has done, Maman! He fled from Chinon Castle and has taken refuge at the French court!"

Eleanor rose so swiftly that her chair toppled over into the floor rushes. One glance toward her attendants was all it took; rising, they quickly departed the chamber. So did the musician. It never occurred to Maud that the queen's dismissal applied to her, too, and even if it had, she'd not have stirred from the window-seat. Nothing short of a direct command would have sufficed, given Richard's remarkable revelation about Hal. God help him, what had that reckless lad done now? And why was Richard so distraught over his brother's disgrace? From what she'd observed, there was little love lost between them.

"How do you know this, Richard?"

"He was with me when the message came from . . . Well, better we mention no names." Raoul gazed coolly in Maud's direction, seeing her not as his niece's friend but as the king's cousin. "It is true. Hal has bolted and the cat is amongst the pigeons for certes." Spotting a flagon and cups, he moved to the table and began to pour for them, saying, "Wine will not make the news go down any easier, but it cannot hurt." Glancing over his shoulder, he beckoned his messenger to come forward. "Tell the queen what you told us."

The man removed his hat with a flourish, then knelt before Eleanor. "My lord dared not commit words to parchment, Madame, lest it fall into the wrong hands. But Lord Raoul knows his identity, as do you, my lady. He bade me come straightaway with the news of the events at Chinon. Your son, the young king, did indeed take flight. When King Henry learned of it, he rode after him in all haste. But the young king made great speed, covered more than a hundred miles in less than a day and night. And he had planned ahead, for fresh horses were awaiting him at Alençon. King Henry continued on, though, as far as Argentan. But he'd gained no ground, and at Argentan, he was told that Lord Hal had suddenly veered east. He gave up the chase, then, knowing further pursuit was futile, and the young king soon reached safety in the lands of the French king's brother, the Count of Dreux."

"Hell and Furies!" Eleanor had begun to pace, her skirts swirling about her ankles. "What was he thinking?"

"When does he ever think?" Richard straddled a chair and accepted a wine cup from Raoul. "If he were to sell his brain, he could claim it had never been used."

Eleanor did not seem to be listening. Reaching the hearth, she stopped suddenly. "Morel! Jesu, I ought to have seen this coming." Seeing that they did not understand, she said, "He did not take his new stallion, left him behind with me at Limoges. He did not want to risk losing him, for he was planning his escape as early as that."

The messenger still knelt and Raoul reached out, helped the man to his feet. "You've done well, will be rewarded for your service. Go down to the great hall and get a meal, then tell the steward to find you a bed." As the man withdrew, moving with the stiffness of one who'd spent many hours in the saddle, Raoul brought a wine cup over to Eleanor. Rather pointedly, he did not offer any to Maud, but she did not notice the snub. She was dismayed by Hal's folly, but troubled, too, by the implications of this mystery messenger. Raoul de Faye had paid one of Henry's lords or knights to spy upon him, and Eleanor had known about it—and approved.

Eleanor looked at her wine cup, seemed about to drink, then set it down. "How did Hal manage to get away? It could not have been easy, not with Harry watching him like a hungry hawk."

"To give the lad credit where due, he was right clever about it. He got Harry to drop his guard by seeking his forgiveness, then feigned a toothache to be able to see an apothecary, and once he'd been given a sleeping draught, he put it in his father's wine." Raoul laughed, but Eleanor did not.

"Does it matter how he did it?" Richard sounded impatient. "What matters is that he has put us *entre la espada y la pared.*" This was another Spanish expression he'd picked up from the young King of Aragon, one he obligingly translated for them now, saying it meant "between the sword and the wall."

Eleanor seemed lost in her own thoughts and did not respond. Stepping forward, Raoul put his hand on her arm. "The lad is right. Hal's flight was a signed confession of his guilt and confirmed all of Harry's suspicions of a conspiracy with the French. This means we no longer have time as our ally, Eleanor. Hal has flushed our quarry and whether we are ready or not, the hunt is on."

Eleanor frowned. "I am well aware of that, Uncle!"

"My God . . ." Maud's whispered words seemed to echo in the sudden silence. She was staring at Eleanor in disbelief. "You are conspiring against Harry?"

Eleanor stiffened, for she'd not expected Maud to sound so horrified. "Leave us, Uncle," she said, adding, "You, too, Richard," when her son did not move. He did not look happy about it, but he followed Raoul from the solar.

As soon as the door closed behind them, Maud rose and crossed the chamber, not stopping until she was close enough to look into Eleanor's eyes. "Is it really true, then? You are part of this plot?"

Eleanor could have said that she had not fully committed herself, for it was technically true, but that was a sophistry. The conspiracy might still be in its initial stages, but she'd known since Limoges that there'd be no turning back. "Yes," she said, resisting the impulse to say more. She'd not have thought that she'd need to explain herself, not to Maud, but the other woman was regarding her now as if they were strangers.

"Whatever grievances you have against Harry, I cannot believe you want him dead!"

"Of course I do not," Eleanor snapped. "Neither do my sons, nor Louis, either, for that matter. Can you imagine Louis, of all men, plotting regicide? I daresay he hopes to bleed away some of Harry's strength, to keep him from expanding his empire at Louis's expense. He hopes, too, that my sons will be easier to deal with than Harry. That may well be true for Hal, but not for Richard, as he'll learn to his cost."

"You keep saying 'my sons.' But they are Harry's sons, too. And however you think he has wronged you, Eleanor, nothing could justify turning a man's children against him."

Eleanor was taken aback by the hostility in that accusation. "You think I did that? No, Harry handled that quite well all by himself. *My* sons love him not, and why should they? They barely know him. Richard and Geoffrey call him the Aquilon, a Norman name for the north wind. He sweeps into their lives, wreaking havoc, and then moves on, with nary a backward glance. And when he does pay them heed, it is only to make use of them in his various schemes and stratagems."

"That is what kings do. And can you truly say that you have not done it, too? That you are not using Richard to protect Aquitaine?"

"Richard's interests and Aquitaine's interests are one and the same. There is no conflict there."

"And what of Hal? It seems to me that you are seizing upon his discontent to right your wrongs. How fair is that?"

"You could not be more mistaken," Eleanor said coldly. "Hal did not need me to prod him into rebellion. That was Harry's doing, not mine. Hal is a crowned king, yet he has nothing to call his own. Harry denies him even the semblance of independence, much less any real authority. And when Hal has protested, Harry seeks to content him with empty promises. Let me tell you what Hal says of those promises—that they are counterfeit coin. And he is right."

"Harry may not be a perfect father. But he does love them, Eleanor. You know he does!"

"Yes, I'll grant you that. But he sees them as pawns on his imperial chessboard. He'll never treat them as men grown, for in his eyes, they'll always be children, children in need of his guidance and superior wisdom. He is convinced he is in the right and is utterly unwilling to compromise. Why should he? He is the puppeteer, after all, the one pulling the strings. But neither Hal nor Richard are puppets, as he is about to discover."

"I do not deny that Harry is stubborn or that he makes mistakes, some of them grievous. Certainly he has erred with Hal. But there had to be another way than this, Eleanor!"

"I thought so, too—once. I talked myself hoarse trying to reach him, Maud, trying to make him see that he is the one sowing seeds of rebellion. But he'd not listen, not if it meant sharing power. I've told him that he governs as if he never intends to die, and it is no jest. You know what happens to saplings trapped in the shadow of a massive oak; their growth is stunted. Well, I am not going to let that happen, not to my sons. Harry made Hal a king and it is time he acknowledges him as one. As for

Richard, he will rule Aquitaine with me until he grows to manhood, and then he will be accountable to the Almighty, not the King of England. And once Geoffrey weds Constance, he will—"

"Geoffrey, too? But he is just fourteen!"

"Need I remind you that when Harry was fourteen, he hired routiers and went off on his own to England, intending to help his mother fight Stephen."

"Yes, and when the routiers balked at his promises of payment and threatened to desert, leaving him stranded, he asked Stephen to lend him money to return to Normandy. Stephen was so amused by his sheer bravado that he did! Does that sound like your ordinary fourteen-year-old, Eleanor? For this is what it comes down to, does it not? How could you have forgotten the mettle of the man?"

"I do not need you to lecture me about Harry's capabilities. After twenty years of marriage, I'd say I know him far better than you do."

Maud shook her head slowly. "I am beginning to think that Harry is not the only blind one in your family. You once described Louis as 'dithering at every royal crossroads.' He is not going to defeat Henry Fitz Empress, not in this life or the next. Neither are striplings like Hal or Richard. Nor are you. Oh, I know you can match Harry in shrewdness and daring and ice-blooded resolve. But you cannot take the field against him, can you? Why do you think I am so distraught over this madness? Because this is a war you cannot hope to win!"

Henry was facing a far more formidable coalition than just Louis and her sons, but Eleanor was not about to reveal that to Maud, for it was painfully apparent that she'd greatly misjudged the other woman. She said nothing, and after a moment, Maud moved, shivering, to the hearth, feeling cold to the very marrow of her bones. "Why did you let me stay in the solar? I would to God I'd never heard a word of all this, for what am I to do now with what I know?"

Eleanor did not doubt the sincerity of her distress, but she had no sympathy to spare for Maud's misery. "There is nothing you can do."

Maud's nerves were so raw that it took very little to inflame her temper. "How can you be so sure of that?" she challenged. "How do you know that I'll not tell Harry what I've learned?"

"Because," Eleanor said, "you love your son as much as I love mine."

To Maud, there was something ominous in that matter-of-fact statement. "What are you saying, Eleanor? That my son is to be held hostage for my good behavior?"

Eleanor's eyes narrowed, the only sign that she was now as angry as Maud. "No, I am saying that your son Hugh is one of Hal's most enthusiastic allies. He has pledged his honor and the vast resources of Chester's earldom to this rebellion. So you'd best hope that you are wrong about this being a war we cannot win."

Maud gasped, losing color so rapidly that she looked ill. "I . . . I do not believe you. Hugh is in Spain! Would he have gone on pilgrimage if he were conspiring against the Crown?"

It was a feeble hope, though, and Eleanor was quick to snatch it away. "The rebellion was not to begin so soon. That is why Raoul and Richard were so vexed with Hal. Hugh expected to have plenty of time to make his pilgrimage, and I'd wager that he planned to pray at Santiago's holy shrine for victory. Not that he shares your doubts about the outcome. He sees Hal as an anointed king, one he wants to serve, and there are many young lords who share his convictions."

Maud reached out, grasped the back of the closest chair for support. She had never been so frightened as she was at this moment. If Hugh was in rebellion, her daughter Beatrix's husband might well be implicated, too, for he'd been bedazzled to be the brother-in-law of the Earl of Chester. "It is not enough that you've poisoned your own well," she said bitterly. "No, you must poison mine, too!"

"Jesus God, you sound just like Harry! He cannot admit that our sons have minds of their own, and it seems that neither can you. I did not subvert Hugh's loyalty, did not lead him astray. I never even discussed Hal's grievances with him. The choice was his."

"I love my son dearly, but I am not blind to his failings. He lacks the attributes of leadership, has always been easily influenced. It would not take much to convince him that he'd be embarking upon a great adventure. Hal would have been just as easily persuaded, and there'd be many at the French court eager to do the persuading. But you could have put a halt to it, Eleanor. If you'd warned Hal that this rash intrigue could be his ruination, he'd have listened to you. But you did not, and I'll never forgive you for that."

She was turning toward the door when Eleanor spat, "You have not been dismissed yet, my lady countess."

Maud paused, then dropped a deep, mocking curtsy. At that moment, she wanted only to strike out, to make Eleanor hurt as much as she was hurting, and she had the weapon at hand. "What is there left to say, Madame? Unless you wish to discuss those rumors of your involvement in the conspiracy?"

"What are you talking about?"

Maud feigned surprise. "Harry did not tell you, then? The Count of Toulouse sought him out at Limoges and warned him that you were plotting with the French king against him."

Eleanor stared at her. "What sort of game are you playing, Maud? Why should I believe you? Even if that swine St Gilles did come to Harry with his suspicions, how would you have known about it?"

"I know because my brother and my uncle were in Harry's bedchamber when St Gilles brought his baneful offering. Roger held his tongue, of course, having had practice in keeping the confidences of the confessional. But Ranulf knew that I could be trusted with secrets, mayhap because I'd kept so many of his, and he told me what happened. Should you like to know Harry's response? He was outraged that St Gilles should dare to malign you like that. Not for a heartbeat did he wonder if it could be true, as he proved by sending Richard and Geoffrey back with you to Poitiers."

Eleanor's throat had tightened, but she was not about to let Maud see that her words had wounded. "That does not surprise me. His pride would keep him from believing it."

"Not pride," Maud said, "trust." And confident that she'd gotten the last word, she made her departure.

Eleanor exhaled a ragged breath and sat down abruptly on the settle. She'd been shocked by Maud's judgmental response, and she felt betrayed by a woman she'd long trusted. She was hurt and disappointed, but above all, she was angry, and there was no dearth of targets for her fury—Maud for her disloyalty, Hal for his foolhardy flight from Chinon, Raoul for taking pleasure in the wreckage of her family, Louis for simply being Louis, Raimon St Gilles for being even more treacherous than she'd realized, Harry for his obstinacy, his arrogance, and his faith in her. The remainder of her rage she spilled over onto herself—for caring about his pain, pain he'd brought upon himself. She swore aloud, using all of Henry's favorite oaths, but it did not help, and when she was nudged by her greyhound, she gratefully accepted the dog's silent sympathy. She invited the animal up onto the settle beside her, and was taking what comfort she could from the abiding, absolute loyalty shining from those slanted dark eyes when the door opened and Raoul entered the chamber.

"I am guessing that you did not patch up the rift with our troublesome countess," he said, "for when I passed her in the stairwell, she drew her skirts about her as if I were infected with the pox."

Eleanor hastily blinked back the tears that had begun to trickle from the corners of her eyes, knowing her uncle would see them as womanly weakness, for he constantly feared that her regrets might give way to remorse and, then, repudiation of their plans. "No, we did not 'patch up the rift.' She greatly disapproves of our intentions and was not shy about expressing that disapproval."

"Why in Our Lady's Name did you allow her to remain in the solar, Eleanor?"

"She asked me the same question," Eleanor said, with a mirthless smile. "Because Maud is not a woman to be dismissed as if she were a maid servant." She conveniently ignored the fact that she'd tried to do just that moments ago. "Because she would have to be told sooner or later, especially now that Hal has forced our hand. And because I thought she would understand . . ."

"You ought to have known better. It was only to be expected that her kinship to the king would count for more than her friendship with you. Blood always wins out. What happens now? Will she try to warn Harry?"

"No, she will not," Eleanor said, with enough certainty to ease his qualms. "As you say, Uncle, blood will out. Her love for her son is greater than her loyalty to Harry."

D INNER WAS AN ELABORATE AFFAIR as Eleanor was entertaining William le Templier, the new Archbishop of Bordeaux, and John aux Bellesmains, the Bishop of Poitiers. The first course was being served when her steward was called aside, listened intently to the message being murmured in his ear, and, with apologies, hurried from the hall. He soon returned and hastened toward the high table. "Madame, the king is here! He has just ridden into the bailey."

Eleanor set her wine cup down with a thud. All along the length of the table, she saw her guests reacting to this startling news, none of them with pleasure. Raoul paled and Saldebreuil de Sanzay frowned and, for a brief moment, an expression of unease shadowed Richard's face. Geoffrey, less practiced in concealing his emotions, looked downright alarmed. Although she maintained her public poise, Eleanor was shaken, too, for she was not ready to face her husband. What if she'd been wrong about Maud's keeping quiet? She'd departed the morrow after their confrontation; could she have gone to Harry, after all?

The steward glanced around the table, saw the tension, and began to laugh. "Ah, no, Madame, 'tis the young king, your son!"

H AL'S UNEXPECTED ARRIVAL loosed chaos in the hall, for he had to be welcomed by the clerics and the other guests and apologies had to be made for inter-rupting the dinner. But at last they were gathered in the privacy of Eleanor's solar, all family except for her venerable constable, Saldebreuil. Hal was lounging on the settle, with Marguerite sitting so close that she was practically in his lap. Geoffrey was hov-ering nearby, eager to begin bombarding his elder brother with questions. Raoul and Eleanor's other uncle, Hugh, were also in high spirits, treating Hal as if he were re-turning from a battlefield triumph. Only Richard stood apart, and when their eyes met, Eleanor shot him a silent warning to mind his manners. She'd long been troubled by the strain between her two oldest sons, and she did not want Richard to spoil Hal's homecoming by starting a quarrel; as young as he was, his sarcasm could be lethal, and she did not want him exercising it at Hal's expense.

Hal was relating the story of his escape from Chinon, with a flair for the dramatic that would have done justice to the *Song of Roland*. He was extravagantly complimented for his cleverness, and only his mother spared a thought, however reluctant, for the injury he'd inflicted upon his father. "I never doubted," he concluded, "that I would get away, not for a moment. Just as I knew my knights would be there for me. I am indeed blessed to have such loyal men. And such a fair wife," he added, laughing and dropping a kiss upon the tip of Marguerite's nose.

She laughed, too, blushing very becomingly. "What happened once you reached my father's court?"

"I was welcomed as a king ought to be. Louis made me a new great seal and I was given lavish quarters in his Paris palace, and as soon as word spread of my arrival, the Counts of Flanders and Boulogne traveled to the French court to meet with me, as did the Count of Blois and—" Hal broke off, sat upright on the settle, and glanced over at Eleanor, blue eyes bright with excitement. "But first I must tell you, Maman. I was knighted in Paris!"

It was impossible not to share in his joy, and he was immediately inundated with praise; even Richard bestirred himself to offer a laconic congratulations. After a moment to reflect, Raoul began to laugh. "Well, it was not the way he'd expected it, but Harry got his wish. Hal was knighted by the French king!"

Hal looked over at Raoul and shook his head. "I was not knighted by the French king." That drew all their attention, as he'd hoped, and he paused to heighten the suspense. "I asked the most worthy, honorable man I know to confer knighthood upon me. I asked Will Marshal."

There were exclamations of surprise and astonishment, for they did not see why Hal would have chosen a mere knight to perform such a significant ceremony when he could have had it done by a king. Only Eleanor understood and, crossing the solar, she leaned over and kissed her eldest son on the cheek. "That was a very generous gesture, Hal. I am sure Will was greatly honored by it."

Hal separated from his wife long enough to rise to his feet and give his mother an exuberant hug. "I had trouble convincing him that I was serious, but once I had, he was overwhelmed."

"Loyalty like his should be rewarded," she said approvingly. "It does not hurt to let the world know, too, that you value fidelity. A great lord is expected to show great generosity to his vassals and knights. It makes others all the more eager to serve you."

"I suppose," he said vaguely, for the truth was that he'd not considered the political ramifications of his choice. It had been an impulsive act, a way to honor a man he greatly respected, the embodiment of knightly chivalry. Sitting down again beside Marguerite, he smiled up at his mother. "I know it was not easy for Will to defy my father. I am sure he had misgivings, and I think he overcame those misgivings because of you, Maman."

"Me? What do you mean, Hal?"

"Once we were safely in French territory, naturally we wanted to celebrate. We celebrated so much, in fact, that the next morn I felt as if the bells of Notre Dame were going off inside my head. Even Will drank enough to loosen his tongue. He started to talk about you, Maman, about how he owed you his very life, about what a great queen you were and what an honor it had been to serve you whilst he was one of your household knights." He grinned. "He sounded smitten, if truth be told!"

Eleanor was pleased, but Marguerite looked puzzled. "What did he mean about owing her his life?"

Hal slid his arm around her waist, quite happy to enlighten her. "It happened five years ago in Poitou, darling. My mother was ambushed by the de Lusignans. To save her from capture, Will and his uncle, the Earl of Salisbury, fought like demons. She got away safely, thank God, but the earl was slain and Will was wounded and taken prisoner. Will had no money for the ransom, although he lied and pretended that he had kin willing to pay it. He knew sooner or later they'd find out the truth, but he was desperate to buy as much time as he could. Then—as he described it—the miracle happened. His captors announced that his ransom had been paid by the queen and set him free. When he returned to Poitiers, grateful beyond words, my mother not only gave him a position in her household, but she provided him with a destrier and chain mail, thus winning his heart for all eternity!"

Marguerite was regarding Eleanor with wide, admiring eyes. She'd been astonished by some of Hal's stories about his mother—that she'd gone on crusade with Louis and their caravan had been attacked by Saracens, that her ship had been captured by pirates in the pay of the Byzantine Emperor, only to be rescued in the nick of time by the King of Sicily's fleet—but this one sounded as if it came straight from a minstrel's tale. "You have led the most remarkable life," she blurted out, "like Iseult or Guinevere!"

Both of those legendary queens had also been faithless wives, but Eleanor knew that her daughter-in-law's insult was an innocent one, and she smiled at the girl before turning back to Hal. "You mentioned a number of highborn lords. Have they fully committed themselves to our rebellion?"

"Indeed they have, all of them! It was very easy to come to terms with them, Maman. I promised the Count of Blois two hundred pounds a year and the castle of Amboise. The Count of Flanders shall have the county of Kent, a thousand pounds a year, and the castles at Dover and Rochester, and his brother, the Count of Boulogne, shall have the county of Mortain in Normandy and the Honour of Hay in Wales. Best of all, Louis thinks that the King of Scotland will also commit to our cause in return for Northumbria and the earldoms of Huntingdon and Cambridge for his brother. We can count, too, upon Raoul de Fougères and most of the Breton barons, and in England, the Earls of Chester, Leicester, Norfolk, and Derby. Not to forget your lords in Poitou, Maman. Has there ever been such a redoubtable alliance? Not since all those Greek kings sailed for Troy!"

At least he'd retained some of his tutor's lessons, Eleanor thought, but she was appalled by his blithe admission that he'd given away so much of his inheritance. The others were staring at him with the same amazement; only Marguerite seemed untroubled by Hal's shortsighted, misguided mistake. From the corner of her eye, Eleanor caught a glimpse of her second son. Richard's lip had curled, his disdain so obvious that she knew he was about to pounce, and that would only make matters worse. Moving quickly to forestall him, she said, "Hal, as gladdened as I am by your visit, I am somewhat surprised by it, too. I know you avoided your father's domains, but even so, the danger was great. He'd pay handsomely to get you back in his control, and our world is full of men who'd betray their own mothers for a handful of deniers. Why did you take such a risk?"

The risk had been part of the appeal, but Hal knew better than to confess to that to his mother. "I came," he said, "to bring my brothers back with me to Paris."

HAL AND MARGUERITE had been the first to withdraw; after yawning and complaining, very unconvincingly, that he was exhausted from his journey, he'd gone off to Marguerite's bedchamber, their laughter giving the lie to his professed intent to sleep. Richard and Geoffrey were the next to go, eager to start packing. Alone in the solar with her uncles and her constable, Eleanor sat down wearily on the nearest seat, an uncomfortable coffer chest. "You need not say it, Raoul," she warned. "Hal has made a grievous mistake. I know that all too well."

"A pity Hal does not," Raoul observed, but without heat. He was not heartbroken that his grandnephew should be disposing of his lands with such careless abandon, and as his eyes met his brother's, he saw that Hugh agreed with him. Aquitaine could only benefit by it. Richard had been quick to see that, too, saying scornfully before he departed that Hal could slice England up six different ways from Sunday as long as Aquitaine remained intact. "We have to look upon the bright side," Raoul continued.

"Yes, Hal is pledging to give away most of his inheritance ere he even comes into it. But when Harry hears of this, he is like to have an apoplectic fit and that would solve our troubles rather neatly."

Eleanor raised her head, and there was nothing of the niece in the look she gave him. "You have said enough," she said, and Raoul knew better than to argue, not when she sounded like that. He excused himself, and Hugh soon followed.

"Madame." When Eleanor turned toward him, Saldebreuil rose and limped over to her. "This does not bode well for a quick resolution of the rebellion. Your lord husband will never agree to honor your son's promises, and Hal's new allies will not be willing to make peace unless he does. Do you think you can talk sense into the lad, make him see that he's blundered into a den of thieves?"

Eleanor appreciated his candor, the bluntness of an old soldier who knew his days were dwindling, freeing him to speak his mind. "It is too late for that. He has already struck these Devil's deals and cannot repudiate them . . . at least not until he wins," she added, with a queen's cynical understanding of statecraft. "Damn Louis for this! The rest of them are no better than wolves on the prowl. But Hal is wed to Louis's daughter, and he owed him better than this."

Saldebreuil thought that Eleanor's analogy was an apt one, for Hal was indeed a lamb let loose amongst wolves. Thankful that their young duke was not as trusting as his elder brother, he sat down again, for his bones were beginning to ache. "What will you do, my lady? If you send Richard and Geoffrey to Paris, there will be no turning back."

"I know," she said. "But you saw the looks on their faces. They'd set out tonight if it were up to them. How could I tell them not to go? I cannot do what Harry has done, treat them like feckless, flighty children. Richard would never accept that, and Geoffrey is already very jealous. If he were not permitted to go to Paris, too, he'd never forgive Richard."

Events were taking on a momentum of their own and choices were being made for her, much to her dismay. If only she did not have to rely upon Louis. If only she could take command of this ill-assorted coalition. But men like Philip of Flanders were not likely to pay heed to a woman. And for a moment, she could hear echoes of Maud's tart-tongued reminder that she could not take the field herself.

Looking up, she saw that Saldebreuil was watching her with the protective concern allowed an old and devoted retainer, and she mustered up a smile for his benefit, before saying grimly, "Raoul was right when he said that whether we are ready or not, the hunt is on. Hal's rebellion has become a war, and it is a war we must win."

CHAPTER EIGHT

✦

April 1173
Rouen, Normandy

ENRY HELD HIS Easter Court that April at Alençon. It was one of the most miserable times of his life. His rage still smoldered, yet the object of his anger was well out of reach, being lauded at the French court. He sent Archbishop Rotrou to Paris to fetch his son, but he did not have any hopes of success. He was still waiting, too, to hear from Eleanor. He'd dispatched an urgent message, instructing her to use her influence with Hal, but he'd not yet gotten a response from her. Not that he expected she'd have any luck in bringing Hal to his senses. The youth who'd betrayed him so cruelly and then fled to his enemy's embrace was a stranger to him. It was almost enough to make him believe in changelings. And since nothing in his life seemed to be going right anymore, he was not at all surprised to get a communication from Rome informing him that on February 21 the Pope had canonized Thomas Becket as a saint.

AFTER EASTER, Henry moved on to Rouen and had Rosamund Clifford summoned from Falaise. He took little pleasure in her presence, though, for his world was out of kilter. The archbishop had not yet returned from Paris, nor had there been word from his queen. He lay awake at night, dwelling morbidly upon the events at Chinon, blaming himself for allowing Hal to delude him like that and vowing it would never happen again. Hunting offered a respite from the bleak landscape of his own thoughts, but incessant rains often robbed him of even that brief reprieve. The only happiness he had that April came with the unexpected arrival from England of his natural son, Geoff, who'd raced for Southampton and took ship for Normandy as soon as he'd gotten word of Hal's defection.

Geoff was the oldest of his children, having turned twenty that past December. He'd been raised in Henry's household, treated since infancy as the king's son, and Henry was determined that his out-of-wedlock birth would not besmirch his prospects. His grandfather had done right by his numerous illegitimate children, and Henry meant to do no less for Geoff. Intending a career in the Church for the boy, he'd put Geoff into deacon's orders at an early age and bestowed upon him the archdeaconry of Lincoln, but he had even grander plans in mind for Geoff, and was very pleased that he'd now be able to share them in person with his son.

The day after Geoff reached Rouen, the weather cleared and Henry seized the opportunity to spend the afternoon in the forest of Roumare west of the city. The season for hart would not begin until the summer, but roebucks could be hunted in the spring, and Henry was eager to try his new pack of running hounds, the best of the breed known as chien bauts. Returning at dusk with enough venison to feed a hundred of Christ's Poor, he was weary and muddied and more relaxed than he'd been in many weeks.

Geoff deserved much of the credit for his change in mood, for his son was as passionate about the hunt as he was, and just as competitive. They were still squabbling playfully about which of them had brought down the last buck as they entered the city gates and headed toward the ancient ducal castle on the south bank of the River Seine.

"I know it was my arrow," Geoff was insisting, turning in the saddle to ask the Earl of Essex for confirmation of his claim. "You saw the kill, Willem. Tell my father whose arrow brought it down!"

When Willem grinned and muddied the waters by suggesting it might well have been his, Geoff gave a hoot of derision, loud enough to startle his stallion, which shied suddenly and almost unseated its young rider, much to Henry and Willem's amusement. Geoff was a skilled horseman and soon got his mount under control. He was usually thin-skinned about being laughed at, for like many born on the wrong side of the blanket, he was very sensitive to slights. But he was so pleased to see his father laughing that this was one time when he was quite content to be the butt of their humor. If he'd thought it would cheer Henry's spirits, he'd willingly have been tossed head over heels into the Seine.

Upon their arrival at the castle, Henry ordered the deer carcasses to be turned over to his almoner, saving only a few haunches for their table that evening. He then took Geoff and Willem to the kennels to show them a litter recently whelped by Lerre, his favorite lymer bitch, and the King of England and his son were soon down on their knees, romping with Lerre's puppies.

Rising reluctantly, Henry brushed straw from his tunic and bent over to give the mother dog a fond farewell pat. He lingered, though, in the kennels, for he wanted a private moment with Geoff. "I needed a day like this, for it has been a wearisome week. The Pope has been complaining that I have left six English bishoprics vacant for far too long, and since I am now back on good terms with the Church, I felt obliged to address his concerns. So I've been mulling over candidates, hope to have the selections made by month's end."

Willem and Geoff tactfully refrained from mentioning the reason those bishoprics had been unoccupied for so long—because Henry collected six thousand pounds a year from the revenues of vacant sees. Henry went on to tell Geoff that he'd written to the Pope, assuring him that the vacancies would be filled as soon as free elections could be held. Geoff nodded politely, trying to hide his boredom. Even though he knew he was destined for a career in the Church, he had little interest in Church matters. If it had been up to him, he'd have chosen knighthood, but he'd been loath to confess this to Henry; he'd do almost anything to avoid disappointing his father.

At the mention of "free elections," Willem began to laugh. "It must be said that you have your own interpretation of what 'free election' means, my liege. May I tell Geoff about the instructions you sent yesterday to the cathedral chapter at Winchester?"

When Henry shrugged, Willem turned to Geoff. "Your lord father ordered the monks to hold a free election, and then he added, 'But I forbid you to accept anyone save my clerk, Richard de Ilchester, Archdeacon of Poitiers.'"

Geoff grinned and the corner of Henry's mouth twitched even as he protested that he was merely trying to make sure that there were no misunderstandings. "I am giving the bishopric of Ely to my chancellor, Geoffrey Ridel; he deserves it for his steadfast loyalty during the clash with Becket. I am inclining toward Robert Foliot for Hereford, as he is kin to the Bishop of London."

That was not a surprise, for the Bishop of London had also given Henry unwavering support against Becket, and Geoff nodded again. But his father's next words took his breath away. "I mean the bishopric of Lincoln to go to you, lad."

"Me? But . . . but I am not even a priest!"

"Neither was Becket until two days ere he was consecrated as Archbishop of Canterbury."

Yes, Geoff thought, and we know how well that turned out. He could not say that, though, to Henry, and he mumbled his thanks with such a lack of enthusiasm that even Henry noticed. The prospect of becoming a bishop was an alarming one to Geoff, but he was an optimist both by nature and experience, and he was soon consoling himself that his consecration could be delayed for months, even years. He could argue with perfect truth that he was too young to hold such an exalted position.

Once he was in his chamber in the keep, Henry washed and changed his hunting clothes, all the while giving some thought to Geoff's muted response. Geoff was usually so high-spirited and exuberant, grateful for the smallest favor. Mayhap he felt overwhelmed by the honor. He would have to talk to the lad, reassure him that he was worthy of it. He was bantering with his squires, who were delighted to see him so cheerful, when a knock sounded at the door.

After a whispered exchange in the stairwell, Warin glanced back at Henry. "It is the Archbishop of Rouen, my liege." Not waiting to be told, he stepped back so Rotrou could enter, for he knew how impatiently Henry had been awaiting his return from Paris.

Rotrou was not alone, accompanied by Arnulf, Bishop of Lisieux, Henry's brother Hamelin, Maurice de Craon, an Angevin baron and longtime friend, and Willem, still in his muddied hunting garb. Henry knew at once that Rotrou did not bring welcome tidings. He was an elderly man, but he seemed to have aged a decade in the fortnight since Henry had last seen him. Hamelin's face was a mirror, reflecting utter misery, and while Willem looked impassive, his very presence was ominous, for Rotrou would not have needed his support unless his news was dire indeed. But what sent a prickle of unease along Henry's spine was a memory, triggered by the sight of Rotrou and Arnulf together. They had been the ones who'd come to tell him of Becket's murder.

"Welcome back, my lord archbishop."

Henry gestured toward a chair, but Rotrou shook his head, fearing that if he sat down, he'd not be able to get up again. Never had he dreaded anything as he dreaded telling the king what he'd learned in Paris. As terrible as it had been to bring word of Becket's murder, this was worse. There was no way to soften the blow and so he did not try.

"When I met with the French king and demanded that the young king be sent back to your court so you might resolve your differences, he interrupted to ask me who sent such a message. I replied, of course, 'The King of England.' And he said that was impossible since the King of England was there with him and had no need to send ambassadors. He went on to claim that your son's coronation established him as the true king, the only king."

Henry's jaw clenched and hot color surged into his face and throat. The anger he'd felt toward Hal was submerged in the scalding rage now directed at the French king. His son was an idiot, but the true guilt was Louis Capet's. He'd taken advantage of Hal's credulous nature, poisoned his mind against his own blood, and made of him a cat's paw, a dupe of the French Crown.

With an effort, Henry found a strained smile for the aged cleric. "I ask your pardon, my lord archbishop, for sending you on a fool's errand. It was a cruel waste of your time. Little wonder you look so bone-weary."

"My lord king . . . there is more. I would give anything if I did not have to tell you this. The young king was not alone at the French court. His brothers Richard and Geoffrey are there with him."

"No, that is not possible. You must be mistaken."

"My liege, I saw them with my own eyes. I spoke to them."

Henry continued to shake his head. "That makes no sense. Even if Hal somehow bedazzled them with promises and bribes, Eleanor would not have let them join in his folly. She would never have allowed them to follow him to the French court."

The archbishop no longer met Henry's eyes. "She sent them to Paris, my lord. She has been conspiring with your enemies against you. I . . . I cannot explain how she could have so forgotten the loyalty and obedience she owes you as your wife and queen. It is almost as if the French king has cast a spell upon your entire family. But there is no doubt of her participation in this odious, unholy plot. Your sons admitted it, nay, they boasted of it."

A suffocating silence fell. When the men realized that Henry was not going to speak, they quietly withdrew, for even Hamelin understood that there was no comfort they could offer, no balm for a wound so deep.

HENRY HAD LOST TRACK of time. It could have been hours, it could have been days since the archbishop had told him that he'd lost his sons and had been betrayed by his own queen. He was not in pain, not yet. He was numb, so stunned that nothing seemed real. When he'd learned of Becket's murder, he'd been plunged into an emotional cauldron, overwhelmed with grief, anger, shock, guilt, and fear, feelings so intense that it was as if he were drowning in them. Now . . . now there was only a void, a vast emptiness filling his head and his heart.

He did not hear the knocking at first, and when he did, he could not rouse himself to respond. He did not even turn his head when the door opened, continuing to stare into the hearth's shooting flames, mesmerized by that white-gold blaze of heat and light and sheer, raw energy. Passing strange, how fire could be both a blessing and a scourge, saving life and taking it, keeping winter at bay even as it devoured the damned, the sinners condemned to the deepest pits of Hell-Everlasting.

"My liege . . . Harry."

He looked up unwillingly, saw Willem standing beside him, with Geoff hovering by the door. "We brought you some food," the earl said softly, "should you get hungry later."

A stray thought surfaced, the realization that this was the first time the other man had ever called him by his given name. He nodded in acknowledgment and waited for them to go away. But when he turned his eyes from the fire, they were still there, and after a prolonged pause, Willem began to speak.

"I was eleven when my father died. Being so far away made it harder for me, as I'd not yet come to think of Flanders as home. I'd never truly known him, not the man he really was. But I loved the man I thought he was, and I grieved for him. When I learned the truth—that he was accursed, with the Mark of Cain upon him—I fought against believing it as long as I could. As young as I was, I understood that I was losing far more than my father. I was losing my past. My memories could no longer comfort me, for they were false . . ."

Henry had never heard Willem speak of his father; he'd not so much as mentioned his name. Those echoes of that young boy's pain penetrated his haze, and he looked intently into the other man's face. "And once you did believe it, Willem . . . what then? How did you learn to live with a loss like that?"

"I tried to find answers. How could he have been so kind to my brothers and me and yet capable of such unforgivable cruelty? I well-nigh drove myself mad, looking for reasons, for justifications, for any glimmer of light."

Henry's eyes caught his and held. "And did you? Find the answers you sought?"

"No, I did not. Sometimes there are no answers to be found, Harry . . . and that was the hardest lesson of all." Willem was still holding the platter of food. Setting it down on the table, he said, "We'll leave you now. God keep you, my liege."

Henry got to his feet as he heard the door close behind Willem. The aroma of roasted venison wafted off the trencher, but he was not tempted; his gorge rose in his throat at the very sight of the sliced meat. He could not imagine ever taking pleasure in a meal again. Ever taking pleasure in anything. As he turned away, he saw that his son had not gone with Willem. Geoff still stood by the door, clutching a wine flask to his chest, looking so young and wretched that Henry's frozen heart felt the first thawing. He did not welcome it, did not want to feel again.

"You need not stay, lad."

Geoff hesitated, but he stood his ground, and then he found his tongue and his words came tumbling out in a desperate rush. "I brought you wine, Papa. I thought . . . thought it might help. Getting drunk, I mean."

Much to his surprise, a ghost of a smile flitted across Henry's lips. "Believe it or not, Geoff, I've never gotten drunk."

"I have," Geoff said earnestly, "and it does chase the hurt away." Venturing farther into the chamber, he held the wine flask out to Henry, and inhaled audibly when his father took it. Geoff was still in shock, too. He'd always liked the queen, for she'd been good to him. Her kindness had puzzled him at first, but he decided she did not mind his father's straying since it occurred whilst they'd been long apart, during those sixteen months when he'd been in England fighting to claim the crown that was rightfully his. But she was now Jezebel in his eyes, one with Delilah and Bathsheba, all the wicked women of Scriptures, and he harbored a savage hope that she, too, would end her days as Jezebel did, in ignominy and shame, carrion for hungry dogs.

"At least now you know why Hal and his brothers were so easily led astray," he said, and then tensed, afraid he'd overstepped his bounds. But his father showed no anger and he was emboldened to continue. "She turned them against you, Papa. They would never have heeded the French king's blandishments if she had not urged them on."

As unwelcome as it was, that was the first logical explanation offered for why his sons had become his enemies. Hal's defection to the French court was a festering wound, one he suspected he'd take to his grave, for it could never heal if he could not understand why it had happened. Richard and Geoffrey's treachery was even more incomprehensible to him. But if it were all Eleanor's doing, it suddenly made dreadful sense. She had stolen his sons away, turned them into weapons to use against him. And fool that he was, he'd never seen it coming, never suspected for even a moment that she was capable of such a vile, unforgivable betrayal.

"Papa . . . do you want me to go?"

Henry looked at his son and then slowly shook his head. "No, lad, I want you to stay."

THEY'D NOT TALKED, passing the wine flask back and forth as they watched the hearth log burn away into ashes and cinders and glowing embers. Eventually Geoff had fallen asleep in the floor rushes, not stirring even as Henry tucked a blanket around his shoulders. A pale grey light was trickling through the cracks in the shutters, and Henry guessed that dawn must be nigh. He'd not slept. Nor had he been able to follow Geoff's advice and drown his sorrows in spiced red wine. He'd passed the longest night of his life locked in mortal combat with his ghosts, calling up and then disavowing twenty years of memories. He would banish that bitch from his heart if it meant cutting her out with his own dagger. And when at last he allowed himself to grieve, he did so silently and unwillingly, his tears hidden by the darkness, his rage congealing into a core of ice.

Geoff was awakening, yawning and stretching, blinking in bewilderment to find himself on the floor. Remembrance soon came flooding back, and he jerked upright, his eyes frantically roaming the chamber in search of his father. "Papa? Papa . . . are you all right?" He immediately cursed his clumsy tongue. How could a man be all right with a knife thrust into his back?

But when Henry answered, his voice was level and measured, revealing nothing of the night's turmoil. "I am well enough, Geoff," he said, rising from the window-seat and moving to the hearth, where he sought in vain to revive a few sparks. "I have need of you this morning, lad."

"Anything, Papa, anything at all!"

"First, I want you to fetch my squires. Then find Willem and tell him that I shall be holding a council meeting this afternoon. Lastly, I want you to go to a house on St Catherine's Mount, close by the church of St Paul. I shall give you a letter to deliver to the lady dwelling there. Tell her to start packing her belongings, that I will be sending a cart. I want her moved into the castle by nightfall."

CHAPTER NINE

✦

July 1173
Rouen, Normandy

LETTER FROM ROTROU, Archbishop of Rouen, to Eleanor, Queen of England:

Greetings in the search for peace.

Marriage is a firm and indissoluble union. . . . Truly, whoever separates a married couple becomes a transgressor of the divine commandment. So the woman is at fault who leaves her husband and fails to keep the trust of this social bond. . . . A woman who is not under the headship of the husband violates the condition of nature, the mandate of the Apostle, and the law of Scripture: "The head of the woman is the man." She is created from him, and she is subject to his power.

We deplore publicly and regretfully that, while you are a most prudent woman, you have left your husband. . . . You have opened the way for the lord king's, and your own, children to rise up against the father.

We know that unless you return to your husband, you will be the cause of widespread disaster. While you alone are now the delinquent one, your actions

will result in ruin for everyone in the kingdom. Therefore, illustrious queen, re-
turn to your husband and our king. In your reconciliation, peace will be restored
from distress, and in your return, joy may return to all. If our pleadings do not
move you to this, at least let the affliction of the people, the imminent pressure
of the church and the desolation of the kingdom stir you. For either truth de-
ceives, or "every kingdom divided against itself will be destroyed." . . .

And so, before this matter reaches a bad end, you should return with your
sons to your husband, whom you have promised to obey and live with. Turn
back so that neither you nor your sons become suspect. We are certain that he
will show you every possible kindness and the surest guarantee of safety. . . .

Truly, you are our parishioner as much as your husband. We cannot fall
short in justice: Either you will return to your husband or we must call upon
canon law and use ecclesiastic censures against you. We say this reluctantly, but
unless you come back to your senses, with sorrow and tears, we will do so.

Eleanor did not reply.

The bishop of worcester's ship approached the Norman coast at
dusk and anchored in the Seine estuary. Two days later, Roger disembarked at the
Rouen docks, and he was admitted to the king's riverside castle as the noonday sun
reached its zenith. As usual, he traveled with only a small retinue, and they were
quickly settled in. Roger then went in search of his cousin the king.

He soon learned that Henry was absent, off hunting in the Roumare Forest. The
great hall was empty, the inner bailey all but deserted. He assumed that the barons
with Henry were part of the hunting party, and Archbishop Rotrou would be found in
his own palace close by the great cathedral. But there was something eerie about the
silence, the lack of the customary hustle and bustle and organized disorder that heralded the king's presence. Not wanting to go back to his cramped, stifling chamber, he
found himself wandering aimlessly about the castle grounds, as if movement could
keep his troubled thoughts at bay.

Had Fortune's Wheel ever spun so wildly? His cousin had begun the year as the
most powerful king in all of Christendom, only to be struck down by one calamity after another. The betrayal by his queen and sons had opened the floodgates, inundat-
ing him in wave after wave of defections and desertions. Anjou and Maine were, for
the most part, loyal, but Brittany, England, and Normandy were in peril, and Roger
could not help wondering if Henry was being punished for the death of the Church's
newest saint, Thomas of Blessed Memory.

Roger's own nephew, the Earl of Chester, had joined the Breton rebels. The Earl of Leicester, son of Henry's former justiciar, was with Hal, as was his cousin, the Count of Meulan. The Chamberlain of Normandy had treacherously gone over to the enemy, bringing with him more than one hundred armed knights. The Earls of Derby and Norfolk had thrown in their lot with the rebels, and other English lords were under suspicion, including Roger's elder brother William, Earl of Gloucester. For the most sinister aspect of rebellion was that the king's vassals need not openly declare for Hal to do Henry harm; they need only do nothing. And that was what many of them were choosing to do, waiting to see who was likely to prevail, father or son.

England was rife with rumors and speculation, fed by the news coming out of Normandy. In June a two-pronged assault had begun upon the eastern border. Philip d'Alsace, the Count of Flanders, and his brother Matthew, the Count of Boulogne, were laying siege to Driencourt while Louis led a French army against Verneuil. Should these two fortresses fall, the road to Rouen would be open to them. As alarming as that was, Henry's English supporters were alarmed, too, by his apparent inactivity. He'd been at Rouen for more than three months, the longest he'd ever been in one place during his entire reign, and by all accounts, he'd been passing most of his days hunting deer, not rebels.

Concern for Henry's mental state had been one of the reasons for Roger's trip to Rouen; the other was the cloud of suspicion hanging over his older brother. He did not want William to be tarred with Hugh's brush, nor did he want his sister, Maud, to be banished from royal favor. It was not her fault that her son had turned to treason, and he hoped to make Henry understand that.

The sun was high overhead, radiating heat rarely felt in England, and Roger was heading back to the great hall when a shout echoed from the battlements: riders coming in. He halted, hoping it might be Henry returning from the hunt. It wasn't, but the new arrival was a welcome one: William de Mandeville, the Earl of Essex.

Once they'd exchanged greetings, Willem turned his horse's reins over to his squire, smiling when Roger asked why he'd not gone hunting with the king. He'd been meeting with some of the routiers, he explained, as a new contingent had just arrived from Brabant.

Roger was not surprised to hear that, for he knew such mercenaries were the backbone of his cousin's army. Rather than relying upon the grudging military service given by his vassals, Henry preferred to hire professional soldiers, and such men were always easy to find. Despite the disapproval of the Church, routiers from Brabant and Flanders and even Wales were available for those lords with enough money to engage them. Debating that point with Roger, Henry had insisted that routiers made superior fighters because they could be mobilized at once, they would serve as long as they were paid, their desire for plunder gave them enthusiasm for their work, and their fearsome reputation often weakened enemy morale. Roger had not been convinced by his cousin's arguments, for he still thought it immoral for a man to earn his living by killing fellow Christians. But now he felt a flicker of relief, so worried was he about Henry's plight. At least he'd have routiers on hand for the defense of Rouen should it come to that.

"I hope you are bringing good news about the siege of Leicester," Willem said, and Roger was pleased to reply in the affirmative. Henry's justiciar, Richard de Lucy, and his uncles, Rainald and Ranulf, had been besieging the city and castle of the rebel Earl of Leicester since early July, and Roger was now able to tell Willem that the townspeople had surrendered. The castle still held out and a truce had been struck till Michaelmas. Roger's other news was not as encouraging, though. De Lucy had ended the siege of Leicester Castle in order to hurry north, where the Scots king had been staging bloody border raids.

"Now it is your turn, Willem. The last we heard in England, the sieges of Driencourt and Verneuil were still continuing. Tell me they have not fallen."

"I would that I could. Driencourt fell to the Counts of Flanders and Boulogne last week, and they moved on to Arques. The siege of Verneuil still goes on. The town is composed of three wards, called burghs, each with its own walls and ditch. The French have taken the first two, but the third and the castle still hold out."

Roger stared at the other man. "Jesu, how can you sound so calm? Arques is less than twenty miles from Rouen!"

"First of all, Rouen is well defended, no easy prize for the taking. Secondly, the Flemings suffered a great reversal at Arques. The Count of Boulogne took an arrow in the knee, and the wound has festered. His brother was so distraught that he halted their advance whilst Matthew's injury is treated."

Roger did not see that as such a "great reversal." He'd met the Count of Flanders, and he thought Philip was the most formidable foe that Henry was facing, far more ruthless than Louis. How long would his brotherly concern last?

"I do not understand why Harry has taken no action! Why does he linger here at Rouen, doing nothing? Why did he not try to relieve the sieges of Verneuil or Driencourt?"

Willem's smile was one of patronizing patience; he was wryly amused that people were always so quick to make uninformed judgments about military matters. As clever as Roger was, had he ever led an army, planned a campaign? "The king was wise enough to see that he had to wait for his foes to move first. Beset on so many sides, he has to fight a defensive war, and he understood from the first that Normandy must be protected at whatever cost. If he were to lose Normandy, many of his English barons with lands on this side of the Channel would join the rebellion to save those estates. Moreover, he'd be forced to choose between England and Anjou if Normandy was taken.

"Trust me, Roger, it has not been easy for him to wait like this. He is a man accustomed to seizing the initiative. Trust me, too, that he has not been 'doing nothing.' He fortified all his border castles, often using his hunting as a means of sending confidential messages or holding clandestine meetings. He has more than five thousand Brabançon routiers at his command, and he made a swift, secret trip to England this spring to bring back money from the royal treasuries at Winchester and Northampton, so he can hire more if need be. When the time is right, he'll strike back, and when he does, I have no doubt that he will prevail."

"From your lips to God's Ears," Roger said lightly, but he was greatly reassured by Willem's cool certainty, for he respected the earl's grasp of strategy and battle lore. "Tell me, Willem. How is Harry coping . . . truly?"

Willem shrugged. "It is hard to say. He has never been one for confiding, has he? I am guessing that he draws strength from his anger, at least during the daylight hours. How he fares alone at night is between him and the Almighty." The sun was hot upon his face and he touched Roger's arm, saying, "Let's find some shade in the gardens, and you can tell me about the new Archbishop of Canterbury's thwarted consecration."

Roger grimaced. "That was a disaster. All was in readiness for the ceremony and on that very day we got a letter from Hal, claiming that the archbishop's election was invalid because he'd not given his approval and warning us that he'd made an appeal to the Holy Father. So we still lack an archbishop until we hear from Rome, which is most unfortunate—although I'll admit that I thought the monks had made a poor choice in Prior Richard. Oh, the man is laudably inoffensive, with the virtue of realizing his limitations, but he is hardly a worthy successor to St Thomas."

Willem thought that Prior Richard's appeal might have been the fact that he was so very different from the volatile, intense, martyred archbishop, but he was too tactful to say so to Roger, knowing he and Becket had been friends. Opening the gate into the gardens, he asked if there was any chance that Hal's ploy could succeed and the Pope take his side.

Roger shook his head. "I see Louis's fine hand in this appeal to Rome. He was outraged that Harry was able to reconcile with the Church so easily, and he'd like nothing better than to stir up more trouble between Harry and the Holy See. But the Pope thought it was in the Church's best interests to make peace with so powerful a king and he—"

Roger stopped in mid-sentence, distracted by the sight meeting his eyes. Five boys were racing around the gardens, laughing and shrieking. The object of their amusement was a young blindfolded woman, laughing, too, as she stretched her arms out, trying to catch them as they danced around her. Both men smiled, for they'd often played Hoodman Blind themselves in their youth. Roger assumed that the children were some of the sons of the nobility being educated in the king's household, and as he drew closer, he recognized one of them from Henry's Christmas Court at Chinon: his uncle Ranulf's youngest son, Morgan.

Morgan recognized him, too, and ended the game by crying out, "Cousin Roger!" As he dashed over to embrace his kinsman, the other children began to back away, seeing that the fun was over. The woman removed her blindfold, and at once dropped down in a deep curtsy. She was very pretty, with blue eyes and fair skin, too well dressed to be a nursemaid. She was obviously known to Willem, though, for he strode forward and gallantly kissed her hand, then glanced back at Roger with a glint of mischief.

"My lord bishop, may I present the Lady Rosamund Clifford? My lady, this is the king's cousin, the Bishop of Worcester."

Rosamund flushed as she and Roger exchanged stilted greetings, and she quickly made her excuses, her withdrawal from the gardens so hasty that it was practically an escape, the boys trailing in her wake. Roger gazed after her, taken aback. So this was the infamous Rosamund Clifford.

Reading his thoughts, Willem grinned. "She is not as you expected, is she?"

"No, she is not," Roger conceded. "I thought she'd be more . . . more sultry," he said. "Eleanor was a great beauty, after all, when she was younger. I suppose I imagined Rosamund to be cast in the same mold."

"I know. The lass is comely enough, but she is no Cleopatra. She is soothing, though, and mayhap that has its own charm." Willem laughed softly. "Much has been said of the queen, but I daresay none have ever called her 'soothing,' have they?"

"Indeed not," Roger agreed. He'd heard that Henry was now openly living in sin with Rosamund, and while he deplored adultery, of course, he could understand why the king had taken such a defiant stance in light of the queen's betrayal. "Well, at least there is one who is benefiting from these tragic events."

"You mean Rosamund? I doubt it. The world is full of women eager to be the king's concubine, but Rosamund does not seem comfortable in that role."

"That is to her credit," Roger said, thinking sadly that there were no winners in this wretched family war then, only losers . . . and with the worst still to come.

R OGER WENT TO BED early that evening, and had just fallen asleep when he was awakened with a summons from Henry, who was having a late supper with the hunting party. By the time he'd dressed and gone to the great hall, the meal was done, for Henry was never one to linger at the table. He impatiently cut short Roger's formal greeting, saying, "Come with me, Cousin."

Roger did, following him out into the inner bailey. The day's heat had faded and the sky was a deep twilight turquoise, stars glimmering like scattered shards of crystal. It was a beautiful evening but Henry seemed oblivious to his surroundings. Even after they'd entered the gardens, he paid no heed to the fragrant roses, the scent of honeysuckle and thyme, or the soft bubbling of the fountain. Roger wondered if he remembered that the garden was Eleanor's creation, hoped he did not.

"So," Henry said, "have you brought me any good news from England? Or more bad tidings?"

The edge in his voice put Roger in mind of a finely honed sword blade, and he was grateful that he did have "good news" to offer. "I learned ere I sailed that the Scots king was retreating back across the border after failing to take Carlisle. The royal army was in close pursuit and burned Berwick in retaliation for the Scots ravages in Northumberland."

He could not tell if Henry had heard that already; his expression gave away nothing. "The Scots king is a two-legged viper," Henry said, after a long silence, "He offered to aid me in putting down the rebellion, providing at his own cost a thousand armed knights if I'd recognize his claim to Northumbria. I said no, but Hal was willing to promise that and more. From what I hear, he has been so open-handed with his new allies that if I died tomorrow and he had his victory, there'd be little left to govern."

"All the more reason, then," Roger said quietly, "to make sure that he does not win," and Henry gave him a sharp, searching look.

"It gladdens me to hear you say that, Cousin. I would that all of your family shared the sentiment."

Roger did not shrink from the challenge. "We are deeply shamed by my nephew Hugh's treachery. But he is an aberration, Harry, a foolish youth easily seduced to folly. The rest of us remain loyal to the true king, to you."

"I never doubted your loyalty, Roger. But what of your brother? Can you speak for him?"

"Yes, I can." Roger moved closer so that light from the rising moon fell across Henry's face. "My father was a great man, loyal to your mother and you until his last breath. It would not be too much to say that you might not have won your crown if not for his unwavering support."

"I'll grant you that," Henry said. "But we were not speaking of my uncle Robert, may God assoil him. We were speaking of your brother William."

"No one would call William a great man. If truth be told, I have always thought him to be a bit of a fool. But he is no traitor, Cousin. He is your liegeman and only yours. I bear a letter from him, assuring you of that." Reaching into his tunic, Roger held a sealed parchment out and after a barely perceptible pause, Henry took it, tucking it away in his belt. "I have a message, too, from my sister. Maud would have you know that she was deeply grieved when Hugh joined the rebellion. It broke her heart."

Henry wanted to believe Roger, for he'd always been very fond of Maud. But belief did not come easily to him these days. "I am sure you will understand if I have doubts about that, Cousin."

"Because of the friendship between Maud and your queen? That was one more casualty of this accursed rebellion." He decided not to push further. "Do you know where they are . . . your sons?"

Henry's mouth curved down. "Hal has had a busy summer with the Counts of Flanders and Boulogne at the siege at Driencourt. The last I heard, Richard and Geoffrey were still in Paris, supposedly being looked after by Raoul de Faye—hardly the ideal choice for a guardian—so God only knows how they are abusing their newfound freedom. And my devoted queen continues to spin her webs from Poitiers."

Roger sighed, having no words to assuage such bitterness. He chose, instead, to return to the conversation he'd had earlier that day with the Earl of Essex, for he needed to know that Henry shared Willem's confidence. "Willem told me that the Count of Flanders has halted his march upon Rouen whilst his brother recovers from his wound. It surprised me that Philip should show such family feeling, for I always thought the man had ice water in his veins."

"You are forgetting that Matthew is more than Philip's brother. He is his heir, too."

Roger had indeed forgotten that the Count of Flanders's marriage was childless. Passing strange, he thought, that Philip and Matthew were both wed to nieces of Eleanor, the daughters of her dead sister, Petronilla. Harry was right about the queen's webs; they covered half of Christendom. "Philip is a two-legged viper, too," he said acidly, "for all that he poses as a champion of chivalry and knightly honor."

"You do not know the half of it, Roger. Louis was stricken with his usual eleventh-hour misgivings, and when he realized that war was actually at hand, he began to waver like a reed in a high wind. My agents at the French court told me that it was Philip who bolstered Louis's quavering resolve."

"Harry . . . what happens if Verneuil falls to the French? Willem seems to think that Rouen could still hold out, but I'd rather not see England's king trapped in a town under siege."

"Neither would I," Henry said dryly, "but Verneuil is not going to be taken. I recalled Hugh de Lacy from Ireland and sent him to Verneuil ere the siege began. If need be, he'll hold the castle till Hell freezes over. But it will not come to that, not with Louis in command."

Roger sensed that Henry was talking about more than the fate of Verneuil. "You expect to win this war, then," he said, and Henry gave a short, harsh laugh.

"Should the day ever come when I cannot outwit or outfight Louis Capet, I'll willingly abdicate." Henry had begun to pace, crunching the gravel underfoot, for he still wore his hunting boots. "Archbishop Rotrou said he could almost believe Louis had cast a malevolent spell upon my family. That gives Louis too much credit. If he ever took up the Black Arts, he'd bewitch himself, as likely as not. I suppose the argument might be made that my sons are feeble-minded, and that could certainly apply to Hal, but I've seen no evidence that Richard and Geoffrey share his absurd faith in French honor."

Roger hesitated, but the answer Henry was groping for seemed so obvious to him that he could not hold his tongue. "If you are searching for the sinister force behind this rebellion, Harry, you need look no farther than Poitiers."

"My beloved wife, the Circe of Aquitaine." Henry laughed again, and to Roger, it was like the sound of shattering glass. "Instead of turning men into swine, she turns my sons into rebels. But it was so damnably easy for her, Roger. That is what I do not understand. Why were they so susceptible to her poison?"

Roger did not know, and another silence fell as he watched Henry stride back and forth on the narrow garden walkway. He was somewhat surprised that the other man was willing to discuss his family's treachery, but he was flattered, too, that Henry had chosen him as a confidant.

"Cousin . . . my confessor has another explanation for my recent trials and tribulations. He thinks that God is punishing me for Thomas Becket's death."

Roger's jaw dropped. Almost at once he dismissed the claim that this "explanation" had come from Henry's confessor, sure that he'd never have dared to suggest that to the king. He'd given up hope of ever hearing these words from his cousin's lips, but now that he had, he was quick to seize this rare, precious chance to save a soul. "That same thought has occurred to me, too, Harry."

That was not the answer Henry wanted. "Why?" he demanded. "That would make my penance at Avranches rather pointless, would it not?"

"How honest do you want me to be, Cousin?"

Henry frowned. "I asked you," he said at last, "because you are a man of God and because you were the only one with the courage to tell me that you blamed me for Becket's murder, that if I were not guilty, neither was I innocent. So, yes . . . I want you to be honest."

"Very well. I do not think you are truly contrite, Harry. Oh, you said all the right things to the bishops and papal legates. But your actions send another message. Look at the bishops you recently selected to fill those vacant sees. Four of the six were men either actively hostile to Thomas or kin to those who were."

Henry's face had hardened, but he said tersely, "Go on."

"This rebellion you are facing . . . it is inexplicable in so many ways. You yourself questioned how Eleanor could so easily have subverted your lads. And then there is her involvement. I am a student of history, Harry, and there is no shortage of tales of rebellious sons. But I know of no other queen who dared to rebel against her lord husband. So I have wondered how it came to pass, and I have wondered, too, if the Almighty has looked into your heart and saw that you have not truly atoned for your part in Thomas's death."

"Do not be shy, Roger. Hold nothing back."

Roger ignored the sarcasm. "You asked what I thought, Harry. You are the only one who knows if I am right. But I would urge you to search your conscience, and if you do indeed repent Thomas's death for all the wrong reasons, you must come to terms with that."

"Do you know what I am thinking now? That I am very glad you are not my confessor." Henry picked a rose from a nearby bush, idly tore off the petals and dropped them onto the grass at his feet. "There is one problem with your theory of divine retribution, Roger. If I accepted it, that would cast Eleanor as the instrument of the Almighty."

Roger smiled, not at all discouraged, for he was accustomed to his cousin's gallows humor. He'd planted a seed, one that might, God Willing, take root, and for now, he was content with that.

Henry had halted, head cocked to the side, and then Roger heard it, too, a familiar voice calling out, "My lord king!" They were turning toward the sound as Willem hastened into the gardens. "A messenger has just ridden in," he said breathlessly. "The Count of Boulogne is dead!"

THEY CROWDED AROUND HENRY as he read rapidly by torchlight. When he looked up, it was with a chilling smile. "Count Philip was so stricken by his brother's death that he has ended the campaign, is leading his army back into Flanders. It seems his chaplain and other churchmen told him that this was God's punishment for stirring sons to rebellion against their father."

There was a stunned silence and then the great hall erupted in cheers and laughter. Taking advantage of the turmoil, Roger slipped away. The castle chapel was empty, although candles still flickered and the scent of incense hung in the air. Approaching the altar, he knelt and prayed for the kingdom and for his cousin's troubled family.

HAL MIGHT HAVE BEEN FORGIVEN for thinking that war was good sport, as his initial foray was a highly successful one. He'd captured the castle of one of his father's vassals, Hugh de Gornai, and had taken prisoner the baron himself and eighty of his knights. This was the first time that he'd bloodied his sword and it had been an exhilarating experience. After that, he joined the army of the Counts of Flanders and Boulogne, and that, too, was exciting, for he had great respect for Count Philip, who was widely known as a preudomme, a man of prowess, the highest compliment that could be paid in their world. When Driencourt Castle surrendered after a two-week siege, it only confirmed Hal's giddy certainty that victory would soon be within their grasp.

But then Count Matthew was wounded at Arques, and within a few days, he was dead. That was a shock to Hal, for he'd genuinely liked the count, a cousin as well as an ally. Even more stunning was Count Philip's sudden decision to end the campaign and withdraw to his own lands. Shaken and bereft, Hal had ridden south to Verneuil, in need of his father-in-law's solace.

There he soon regained his emotional equilibrium. Louis had greeted him with flattering warmth, assured him that Count Philip would rejoin the campaign once he'd had time to grieve, and predicted that Verneuil was on the verge of collapse. Only the castle and one of the burghs held out and hunger was prowling the streets of the beleaguered town. It was just a matter of time, Louis said, until Verneuil was theirs.

That time seemed to have come on August 6, when a delegation of citizens ventured out under a flag of truce. Admitting that their people were woefully short of food, they asked Louis for a truce so that they could warn the English king that they must surrender if he could not raise the siege. This was normal practice, and Louis was compelled by the chivalric code to grant their request. He gave them only three days, though, an unusually brief respite. On August 9, the town must yield if Henry had not come to their rescue by then, and Louis in turn promised that their surrender would be on honorable terms, with no harm to the townspeople or their chattels or the hostages they offered up as proof of good faith.

Hal's spirits soared with yet another triumph within reach, and the next two days passed quite pleasantly, for with military operations suspended, he and his knights amused themselves with bohorts, informal tourney games. As the sky streaked with the vivid colors of sunset, Baldwin de Bethune borrowed some dice and they cleared a space so they could gamble by firelight. Hal ordered a keg of wine to be brought out, declaring that a celebration was in order, for on the morrow the town would surrender and the castle would soon be forced to seek terms, too. He did not have a chance to enjoy his impromptu festivities, though, for it was then that he was summoned to the French king's command tent.

As soon as he ducked under the canvas tent flap, Hal knew that something was wrong. The men were somber, their expressions troubled, and Louis was as white as newly skimmed milk. "He is here!" he blurted out, and Hal caught his breath.

"My father? I thought he was in Rouen!"

"He was," the king's brother Robert said testily, "but now he is at Conches with an army and he has sent us an ultimatum—that we either end the siege and withdraw or we do battle on the morrow."

Hal's stomach lurched, for he did not want to face his father on the battlefield. Louis had assured him that it would never come to that. As he looked at his father-in-law, it was obvious that Louis did not want to fight his father, either. A quick glance around the tent told him that few of the men did. Hal knew pitched battles were rare, for most lords and kings preferred skirmishing and sieges to risking all on one throw of the dice. But he sensed that there was more at work here than the usual military caution. His father cast a long shadow.

Louis was standing by an oaken trestle table. Reaching for a silver cup, he drained the wine in several deep gulps; Hal was startled to see that his hand was none too steady. "How did he get here in time?" Louis asked. "Blessed Lady, I only gave them three days!"

"How does he ever do it?" Robert snapped, for he was always ready to blame Louis when their plans went awry. "For twenty years he has been doing what mortal man cannot; you ought to be used to it by now." He could feel Verneuil slipping away even as he spoke; he doubted that his brother had the backbone for a bloody confrontation, for the war without quarter that the English king would wage on the morrow.

"Be that as it may," the Count of Blois said coolly, having little patience for Robert's rancid jealousy in the best of times, "we must decide now how we shall respond to his challenge. It is not as if we have many options. Either we retreat or we fight."

"Not necessarily." Heads turned toward the speaker as the Count of Évreux stepped from the shadows into the light of Louis's candelabra. Hal did not know Simon de Montfort all that well. A tall, balding, saturnine figure with piercing black eyes and a tongue like a whip, he was respected for his courage, but disliked for his arrogance and his slyness. Once he was sure that he had their attention, he said, "There is a third choice. Are you interested in hearing it, my liege?"

Louis did not like the count and did not trust him, either. But after a moment, he nodded. "Tell us," he said, and de Montfort did.

WHEN HAL EXITED the tent, he was surrounded by his knights, for rumors were spreading that the English king was at Conches and a battle was looming. They began to pelt him with questions, wanting to know if it was true. Hal brushed them aside. "Where is Will Marshal? Find him for me—now!"

THEY WERE ALONE in Hal's tent, for he'd barred the others from entering. "Are the rumors true, my lord? Has your father come to the defense of Verneuil?"

"Yes, he is here."

Will thought he was braced for it, but he still flinched, for this was his greatest fear. Hal was his liege lord, but so was Henry. To fight against the king's men was not the same as drawing his sword against the king himself, the *christus domini* who'd been consecrated with the sacred chrism. Scriptures spoke quite clearly on that matter. *For who can stretch forth his hand against the Lord's anointed and be guiltless?* "So we fight on the morrow," he said bleakly.

"No . . . there will be no battle."

Will blinked. "We are retreating, then?"

"No." Hal's throat was tight; he swallowed with difficulty. "The Count of Évreux reminded Louis that the townspeople do not yet know of their reprieve. He said we could take advantage of their ignorance, insist that they surrender as agreed upon."

"That makes no sense. Do they expect King Henry to watch placidly as this takes place?"

"They . . ." Hal swallowed again, aware of a sour taste in his mouth. "The Bishop of Sens and the Counts of Blois and Champagne are going to my father tonight, asking for a day's truce, and promising that Louis will meet with him on the morrow to negotiate an end to the siege. They will then summon the townsmen, tell them that their time has expired and they must surrender the town or their hostages will be hanged. My father's army is encamped at Conches, about ten miles north of here, so by the time he learns that he has been deceived, it will be too late. The town will be ours."

Will's was an easy face to read, and Hal's fair skin reddened. "Do not look at me that way. This was not my doing!"

"Did you protest?"

"Yes . . ." Hal ducked his head in embarrassment. "They laughed at me, Will.

Louis's brother and Simon de Montfort told me that I was still learning the lessons of war, that I was not seasoned enough to understand. They pointed out that guile is always an acceptable tactic, that ambushes are not dishonorable, that if the enemy can be tricked, so much the better. They reminded me that the first tenet of warfare is to lay waste the land, to burn the crops in the fields and torch the villages, to starve the enemy into submission. They said this was merely another stratagem . . ."

"And did you believe them?"

"No," Hal confessed, "I did not. What they mean to do . . . it is not honorable, is it, Will?"

He looked so unhappy and vulnerable at that moment that Will felt a protective pang. Hal was his king, his companion, his comrade in arms, but there were times when he seemed like a younger brother, too, one in need of guidance and counsel. The answer he gave Hal, though, was utterly uncompromising, brutally honest.

"It is more than dishonorable. It is despicable and cowardly, and the French king will carry the shame of it to his grave."

THE EARL OF LEICESTER had a castle at Breteuil, midway between Conches and Verneuil, but he'd fled at the approach of Henry's army and Henry ordered the castle razed to the ground. He chose Breteuil as the site for his meeting with the French king, meaning to use the smoldering rubble to convey a message in and of itself. But the morning dragged on, and Louis still had not arrived.

Henry was stalking back and forth, casting frequent glances up at the sun, almost directly overhead by now. Willem and the Earl of Pembroke had just made a wager as to how much longer Henry would be willing to wait. Sauntering over to the king, he joked, "Seems like Louis overslept. I'd be willing to fetch a mangonel from Conches if you want to give him a wakeup he'll not soon forget."

"Do not tempt me, Willem." Henry waved aside a wineskin being offered by one of his squires and shaded his eyes for another look at the sun. "Louis is prone to inconvenient attacks of conscience and remorse. Mayhap he is suffering from one this morn and is ashamed to face me after—Jesus God!"

Willem spun around, his eyes following Henry's gaze. Billowing black clouds of smoke were spiraling up into the sky, coming from the south, from Verneuil.

GEOFF HAD NEVER SEEN a sight as sorrowful as the town of Verneuil. Much of it had been destroyed in the siege, and the one surviving ward was in flames. A few men were trying to drag tables and bedding to safety, and a few others had formed a bucket brigade in a futile attempt to fight the rapidly spreading fires. But most had gathered in small groups, watching in stunned silence as their homes and shops were consumed. Geoff was close enough now to see bodies lying in the street, and nearby a woman with a torn, bloodied skirt knelt in the dirt, weeping as she clung to a small, terrified child. The stench of death overhung the town, a sickening, rank smell of blood, urine, fear, and burning flesh, and Geoff would later mark this August Thursday in God's Year 1173 as the day when he'd forever surrendered any youthful illusions about the glory and majesty of war.

The arrival of armed men in their midst panicked some of the townspeople, but others were too dazed to react, staring at Henry and his knights with hollow, empty eyes. But as the wind caught the king's red and gold banner, one man stumbled forward to clutch at Henry's stirrup. Gazing down into that upturned face, streaked with smoke and tears, Henry recognized him as the mercer who'd carried to Rouen the town's plea for rescue, and he swung from the saddle.

"I tried to stop them, my liege, from opening the gates. I kept telling them that you'd sworn you were coming to our aid. But they feared for our hostages and they thought they could save themselves by surrender." The man's mouth had begun to tremble. "We did what the French demanded, but it availed us naught. They'd promised we'd not be harmed. Then their soldiers swarmed into the town like mad dogs, stealing whatever they could carry away. We'd not hidden our women, thinking they'd be safe. The hellspawn paid no heed to the pleading of respectable wives and mothers, dragged them from their houses into the street as if they were whores, and when their men tried to protect them, they were slain. And then they set the fires, so many that there was no hope of putting them out. Why did they do that, sire? Why did the French king not keep his word?"

Henry shook his head, so angry he could not trust himself to speak.

Willem had joined them, not wanting to interrupt the mercer's anguished account of his town's betrayal, but now he touched Henry's arm, gesturing toward the castle. "The drawbridge is coming down." As they watched, the gates were swung open and men came racing out, with the castellan, Hugh de Lacy, in the lead.

"Thank God you are here, my liege!" Gasping for breath, de Lacy fell to his knees before Henry, as much an act of exhaustion as one of obeisance. "But if only you'd come a few hours sooner. We could do nothing, had to watch from the battlements as the townsmen surrendered and that treacherous French Judas turned the town over to his soldiers for their sport. But we were dumbfounded when we saw what was happening in the French camp. They were pulling out, leaving behind tents, carts, livestock, even their mangonels and other siege engines. We'd expected them to launch another attack on the castle, and instead they were retreating!"

Getting stiffly to his feet, de Lacy winced, for he'd incurred several minor wounds in the defense of the castle. "It makes sense now, though. They saw your banners, my liege, and fled like rabbits, the craven whoresons. They'll never get over the shame of this—"

De Lacy broke off, for his king had whirled and was running for his horse. The other knights were quick to follow. Watching as they galloped away from the burning ruins of Verneuil, the castellan shouted after them, "Catch the bastards! Make them pay!"

THEY DID NOT RETURN to Verneuil until nightfall. The castle garrison came out to greet them, but asked no questions. The torch-fire playing upon the weary, grim faces told them all they needed to know. "We've run out of most of our provisions," de Lacy said to Henry, "but what we have is yours, my liege. We would be honored to give you shelter tonight."

"That is kind of you, Sir Hugh," Willem interjected, "but we will continue on to Conches where we left our supply wagons." He wanted to get Henry away from Verneuil, knowing the sight of the town's charred remains would only salt his wounds, but Henry gave him a quelling look and shook his head.

"No," he said curtly. "We stay here tonight."

Willem knew better than to argue. Taking de Lacy aside, he told him that they'd overtaken the French army's rearguard and killed those they'd caught. But Louis and his knights had gotten across the border to safety. "For now," Willem added coldly, and then told the castellan of the day's treachery. De Lacy was outraged. If the town had been taken by storm, the French would have been justified in pillaging, raping, even burning it to the ground. But once they'd made a truce, they were honor-bound to keep it. And the deceit they'd practiced upon Henry was such a flagrant violation of the conventions of war that it threatened the very foundations of their society. Sworn agreements of respite and truce were like the Peace of God, ways that the Church and kings sought to avoid *guerre à outrance*—war to the extreme, to the death.

When men heard of the French king's shameless duplicity, de Lacy snarled, they would not be willing to serve such a lord. Willem hoped that was so, but he had a more jaundiced view of his fellow men and their flexible concept of honor. "This," he said tiredly, "will be remembered as a day of infamy." And he went in search of Henry.

He found the king walking with Geoff through the wreckage of Verneuil, and fell in step beside them. They passed the blackened shells of houses and shops, an occasional body draped in cloth and awaiting burial. The flames had been extinguished but the wind still swept embers up into the air and they glowed in the dark like scorched fireflies. The night was hot and still. Now and then there came to them muffled wailing, muted sobs, the sounds of mourning. They walked for what seemed like hours to Willem, and in that time, Henry spoke only once, saying in a flat, tight monotone that went beyond anger, "I want this town's walls rebuilt. Find men to see to it, Willem."

"I will, my liege," Willem said, and they continued on in silence.

F ROM THE TWELFTH-CENTURY *Annals of Roger de Hoveden:*

The King of France neither restored to the burghers their hostages nor preserved the peace as he had promised, but entering the town, made the burghers prisoners, carried off their property, set fire to the burgh, and then, taking to flight, carried away with him the burghers before-mentioned into France. When word was brought of this to the King of England, he pursued them with the edge of the sword, slew many of them, and took considerable numbers. . . . But in order that these events may be kept in memory, it is as well to know that this flight of the King of France took place on the fifth day before the idos of August, being the fifth day of the week, upon the vigil of Saint Lawrence, to the praise and glory of our Lord Jesus Christ, who by punishing the crime of perfidy, so speedily avenged the indignity done to his Martyr.

CHAPTER TEN

✦

August 1173
Rouen, Normandy

GILBERT FOLIOT, Bishop of London, was pleased, but not surprised, to be given such a warm welcome by the king. Of all England's clerics, he had been the most steadfast in his support of Henry and the most critical of Thomas Becket during their acrimonious clash between Church and Crown. He'd been twice excommunicated by Becket, the second time for taking part in the coronation of Henry's son, and this ecclesiastical censure had set off Henry's fateful rage, leading to Becket's bloody murder upon the floor of his own cathedral. Gilbert had been absolved by Rome seven months after Becket's death, but had been restored to his bishopric only that past May, for his hostility to the martyred archbishop was a stain upon a previously unblemished reputation. Once widely admired for his austerity, his estimable intellect, and masterly knowledge of canon law, he would now go to his grave known as the bishop who'd defied a saint, and for a proud man like Gilbert Foliot, that was not easy to accept.

It was some consolation, though, that he stood so high in the king's favor, and he gratefully accepted a seat beside Henry upon the dais in the great hall. Sipping a cup of spiced red wine, he listened with enormous satisfaction as Henry related the flight of the French king from Verneuil. He was equally pleased to hear that Henry had sent a detachment of Norman knights and Brabançon routiers into Brittany to deal with the Breton rebels, for his desire to see the king triumph was greater than his disapproval of hired mercenaries.

Henry turned the conversation then to the bishoprics still vacant because of Hal's appeal to Rome, and Gilbert was happy to reassure him that he could rely upon the backing of the Church. He did not doubt that His Holiness the Pope would approve the elections, pointing out that the papal legates had instructed the electors to choose men who would preserve "the peace of the realm" and reminding Henry that the only prelate to cast his lot in with the rebels was that perpetual malcontent, the Bishop of Durham.

"And the Bishop of Lisieux, may God damn his treacherous soul to Hell," Henry said bitterly, for that was still a fresh wound.

Gilbert had never liked Arnulf of Lisieux, considering him to be a self-server and far too devious and cynical for his own good, but he was surprised, nevertheless, that Arnulf should have made such a major miscalculation, concluding that the bishop was most likely trying to keep a foot in both camps. He was even more surprised by what Henry said next, asking if it was true that he'd founded a hospital in honor of Thomas Becket, for the slain archbishop was usually a topic that Henry assiduously avoided.

"No, my liege. The hospital of Holy Trinity at Southwark was founded by Thomas himself. After his canonization, we changed the name to St Thomas the Martyr and I offered sinners a remittance of thirty days of penance if they contribute to the hospital." Since the king had been the one to bring the subject up, Gilbert now felt free to mention a recent action of Henry's. "I heard, my liege, that you have named Thomas's sister Mary as Abbess of Barking."

That was a signal honor, for abbesses of Barking were normally daughters of kings, but Henry shrugged it off, saying that he was merely righting a wrong. "I ought not to have sent Becket's family into exile," he admitted. "It was done in anger and was unjust to hold them to account for his transgressions."

This was the first time that the king had confessed to making mistakes of his own in his war of wills with Becket. "It is a generous gesture, nonetheless," Gilbert said.

Henry shrugged again. It had not escaped him that Gilbert no longer made use of the slain archbishop's surname. Thomas had always been thin-skinned about his family's merchant origins, preferring to call himself "Thomas of London" rather than the more pedestrian "Thomas Becket," a sensitivity his enemies had been quick to seize upon. He'd always been "Thomas" to Henry until their falling-out; after that, he'd managed to make "Becket" sound like an epithet.

"You never liked him, did you, Gilbert?"

"No, my lord king, I did not."

"In fact, when I chose him as archbishop, you said that I'd performed a veritable miracle, turning a worldly courtier and soldier into a man of God."

Gilbert blinked; he'd not known that his angry sarcasm had reached Henry's ears. "I am sorry, my lord—"

"For what? You were right." Henry's smile was rueful. "You can hardly be blamed for disliking him. He had a tongue like an adder, calling you 'a hapless Judas and a rotten limb,' calling your fellow bishops 'priests of Bael and sons of false prophets.'"

"He was never one for forgiving his enemies," Gilbert agreed, wondering where Henry was going with this.

"You of all men know how vengeful he could be, how prideful and stubborn. Most of those who are so certain of his sanctity never even laid eyes upon him. But you're in a unique position to judge, Gilbert. Can you truly accept the Church's canonization of him as a saint?"

That was a question Gilbert has often asked himself in the months after Becket's murder. "Yes, my liege," he said quietly. "I can."

"Why?" Henry asked, but he sounded more curious than skeptical.

"It is true that Thomas's life was not a holy one. But none can deny he died a martyr's death."

"And is that enough to confer sainthood upon him?"

"His martyrdom . . . and the miracles that have been reported at his tomb and elsewhere in the months since his murder."

"Miracles can be faked, as you well know, for reasons of politics and profit. How can you be sure they are genuine?"

"I daresay some of them are not. But there have been too many to discount, my liege. You may be sure I investigated these reports with great care, for if truth be told, I did not want to believe in them. Even when Thomas cured my fever, I continued to doubt."

Henry had heard of Gilbert's own miracle. Eight months after Becket's murder, he'd fallen gravely ill, lay near death until his friend and fellow bishop, Jocelin of Salisbury, prayed to Thomas for his recovery. "So what convinced you, then?"

"The manner of his death could not be dismissed out of hand. Nor could the discovery that he'd worn a hairshirt and braies under his garments, infested with vermin and lice that had burrowed into his groin, or the revelation of his confessor that he'd mortified his flesh with daily penitential whippings. I was told that his back was scarred with the marks of past scourging. Can there have been more painful proof of sanctity?"

Henry could not argue with that. "I admit I thought he was a hypocrite until I learned that he'd worn those filthy, lice-ridden braies next to his private parts. After that I did not doubt his sincerity, however misguided it was."

Gilbert nodded his agreement. "And then there are the miracles. They began almost as soon as he drew his last breath. The wife of a Sussex knight was cured of her blindness after praying to Thomas. Eight days after the martyrdom, Father William de Capella, a London priest who'd been stricken with palsy was cured after drinking water mixed with the saint's holy blood. I spoke with Father William myself, could find no other explanation for the recovery of his speech. A local woman's palsy was healed after her husband applied rags dipped in the martyr's blood to her afflicted legs. People are said to have been cured of lameness, deafness, withered limbs, and deadly fevers."

Gilbert leaned forward, so caught up in the intensity of his recital that he did not notice as wine splashed from his cup. "Even the brother of one of the men implicated in the murder was cured after drinking the 'waters of St Thomas'!"

"Water mixed with his blood? Remarkable that he bled enough to keep filling those little tin phials that the monks pass out to those who make offerings," Henry said dryly. "That is almost a miracle in itself."

"Surely you do not doubt the existence of miracles, my lord king?"

"Of course not. But it cheapens them to be accepted too readily. Is it true that Thomas punishes those who fail to keep promises they make to him?" And when Gilbert confirmed it, Henry said with a crooked smile, "Now that sounds more like the Becket I remember."

Gilbert was not deceived by the flippancy; it was obvious that Henry had been paying closer attention to the martyr's miracles than he was willing to admit. Before he could respond, though, there was a stir at the other end of the hall. Henry's steward was pushing his way toward the dais. "My liege, a messenger has just arrived from Brittany."

"Have him come forward," Henry commanded, and a disheveled youth, muddied and bedraggled, soon approached the dais. Kneeling, he looked up at Henry with a gleeful grin that conveyed his message better than any words could have done. "I bring you glad tidings, Your Grace. My lord, William du Hommet, bade me ride to Rouen as if my horse's tail were on fire, and by God, I did. We engaged the Breton rebels yesterday morn in open country near the town and castle of Dol, which they'd taken by bribery. It was a total triumph, my lord. We captured seventeen of their knights and killed most of their men-at-arms. Some got away, but Lord Raoul de Fougères and the Earl of Chester and sixty or so knights retreated back into Dol Castle. Lord du Hommet said to tell you that they are penned up like lambs for the slaughter, but he lacks the siege engines to take the castle and urges you to come straightaway."

By now the man was surrounded by Henry's lords and knights, and as soon as he was done speaking, he was barraged with congratulations and praise for his amazingly swift ride. Even allowing for Henry's posting of fresh horses at his castles and abbeys for the use of royal couriers, his was a remarkable achievement; Dol was more than one hundred fifty miles from Rouen.

Henry was delighted. Ordering wine for the messenger and promising a generous reward, he broke the seal on William du Hommet's letter and began to read rapidly. Geoff had entered the hall after the courier's arrival and he was shoving his way through the crowd, eager to learn what had happened. Catching sight of the Earl of Essex and the elderly Earl of Arundel, he veered in their direction, and when they told him that the Earl of Chester and the Breton rebels were trapped in Dol, he gave a jubilant shout that was more often heard on the hunting field.

"This accursed rebellion is in its death throes," he predicted joyfully. "First the Count of Boulogne is struck down, then the French flee from Verneuil like thieves in the night, and now Hugh of Chester is caught in a snare of his own making!"

The men smiled at the enthusiasm of youth. "Well, not yet," Willem said. "But I'd wager he'll be shut up in a royal castle by week's end."

"You mean by next week, do you not? We will not even reach Dol till then, and if the siege lasts—" Geoff paused in surprise, for the two men were laughing at him.

"Clearly you have never ridden with your lord father when he is in a hurry to get somewhere," Willem said with a grin, and when Geoff conceded he had not, they laughed again.

"Ah, you are in for a treat." Arundel was grinning, too. "Fortunately for these old bones, I'll be left behind, for the king knows that I could never keep up with him. As you'll soon see, lad, it is the closest that men can get to flying. I remember when—" He broke off then, for Henry was shouting for silence.

"Why are we wasting time?" he demanded, and Willem jabbed Geoff playfully in the ribs before asking innocently when the king wanted to depart. Henry looked at him as if he'd lost his wits. "When do you think, man? Now!"

T HE YOUNG EARL of Chester was baffled and heart-sore that his luck could have soured so fast. At first all had gone according to plan. Joining Raoul de Fougères, they'd launched a highly successful chevauchée, burning and pillaging the lands of those Bretons who'd remained loyal to Henry. Hugh had enjoyed himself enormously, finding that his first taste of war was even more fun than a tournament. But it had not lasted. Warned that the king's routiers were on the prowl, they'd decided upon a direct challenge, and both sides met on the battlefield on August 20. The experience taught Hugh why prudent commanders avoided pitched battles when at all possible, for it turned into a debacle. Their lines broke, and because men were never so vulnerable as when in flight, the slaughter that followed was terrible. Retreating in confusion, Hugh and the Breton lords found their only escape route blocked by the routiers and they had no choice but to withdraw back into Dol.

The three days that followed were utterly wretched. They'd watched helplessly from the battlements as the townsmen surrendered their city to Henry's commander, Lord du Hommet, and to add insult to injury, they then had to watch as other Bretons joined in the siege, for they'd alienated much of the countryside with their raiding and plundering. Hugh became so disheartened that Raoul de Fougères had turned upon him in anger, berating him for his lack of fortitude. The siege would soon be lifted, he'd insisted. Those lowborn routiers were little better than bandits. They knew nothing of true warfare, lacked even the most rudimentary siege engines. It would not be long until they'd lose interest and move on, seeking easier prey. Hugh very much wanted to believe him, but he was not encouraged when Raoul then put the knights and garrison on half-rations. If the siege was not going to drag on, why did they need to worry about running out of supplies? Wishing that Hal were there to bolster his sagging spirits, Hugh tried to ignore his growing chorus of regrets by getting thoroughly drunk.

He awoke the next morning feeling feverish, queasy, and utterly out of sorts. As he stirred and groaned, the bedcovers beside him rippled and a girl's head popped out. Hugh looked at her blankly, having no idea who she was. He swallowed with a grimace, becoming aware that his mouth tasted like vinegar. The girl was gazing at him curiously. "Do you want me to answer that, my lord?" she asked, and only then did he realize that the thudding noise in his head was actually a pounding on the door. When he nodded, she slid from the bed, hastily pulling a chemise over her head. He recognized her now as one of the castle kitchen maids, although he did not remember her name. Concluding that he was still half drunk, he lay back against the pillow.

"Hugh, wake up!"

Grudgingly opening his eyes to slits, he saw Raoul de Fougères's son Juhel standing by the bed. "Go away," he mumbled, and felt a dulled throb of indignation when Juhel would not. "Damn you to hell, leave me be . . ." And then he gasped and shot bolt upright in bed, for Juhel had poured a basin of washing water over his head. Sputtering and cursing, he lurched from the bed, seeking to bury his fist in Juhel's belly. He never even came close; the other man sidestepped easily.

"Stop it, you fool! Are you going to face Judgment Day as a drunken sot?"

"What are you babbling about?"

"I am trying to tell you that the English king is in the city, making ready to assault the castle!"

Hugh decided that Juhel must be mad. "I think you're the one who's drunk. We fought on Monday and this is only Thursday. There is no way in the world that he could get here that fast."

"No? Suppose you tell him that." Juhel grabbed Hugh's arm and, before he could protest, propelled him across the chamber toward the window. Fumbling with the shutters, he flung them open and pointed. "See for yourself!"

Hugh squinted against the sudden blaze of painful light, his eyes focusing blearily upon the banner flying from the enemy encampment, a gold lion emblazoned across a background of crimson. "Holy Mother of God!"

RAOUL DE FOUGÈRES awaited Hugh in the great hall. Taking in the younger man's pallor, he said coldly, "I hope you can sober up by noon. You'll make a better impression if your eyes are not so bloodshot and your hands are not shaking as if you have the ague."

Hugh was secretly intimidated by the Breton lord, who'd never shown him the deference he was accustomed to receive from his English vassals. Making an attempt at dignity, he said, "I assure you, my lord, that I am quite sober. What happens at noon?"

"We are surrendering the castle to your cousin, the king."

Hugh's mouth dropped open. "We cannot do that! If I fall into his hands, I am doomed, for he'll never forgive me!"

Oliver de Roche, Raoul's seneschal, gave a harsh laugh, and raised his cup in a mock salute; clearly Hugh was not the only one who'd been sampling the wine kegs. "If he puts rebels to death, there'd not be a lord alive in all of Brittany," he said in a slurred voice. "For us, rebellion is a sport. What man in this hall has not risen up against the English king more than once?"

Hugh glared at de Roche, who was not as formidable a figure as Lord Raoul. "It is different for me," he snapped. "He forgives vassals because he thinks it is wise to do so, keeping men from fearing they have nothing to lose and fighting to the death. But I am his cousin, his blood-kin. He'll not forgive *me*."

"He will forgive you," Raoul asserted, "as long as we surrender. But if he takes the castle by force, he can do with us as he pleases. King Stephen once hanged the entire garrison of Shrewsbury Castle."

"Harry has never done anything like that!"

"Has he ever faced a rebellion by his own sons? How do you know what he'll do if we give him the excuse to seek vengeance? You do not know, my lord earl, and that is my point. It is not a risk we are willing to take."

Hugh shook his head stubbornly, for at that moment, he feared nothing so much as the thought of facing his cousin at noon. "You talk as if the castle's fall is inevitable. I say we hold out, that we fight instead of shamefully surrendering!"

There was a low, angry murmuring, and as he looked around, Hugh saw that the others agreed with Raoul; even his own knights seemed ready to surrender. Raoul was regarding him with unfriendly eyes, and suddenly Hugh was acutely aware of the great gap between them. The Bretons were like the Welsh; they did not truly trust those not of their own blood.

Raoul was not known for his patience, but he tried now to remind himself that this English earl's rank deserved respect, even if the man did not. God save him from these callow youths who knew as much about war as a nun did about whoring. "As Oliver said, we Bretons are well seasoned in rebellion. We know when to fight and we know when to cut our losses, which is why we have survived so long. Henry Fitz Empress is the most dangerous foe I've ever faced. He never adheres to the conventions of warfare. Instead of laying waste to his enemies' lands, he strikes fast and hard at their castles.

"Need I remind you of the strongholds he's taken over the years? Chinon from his rebel brother, Chaumont-sur-Epte from the French king, and Chaumont-sur-Loire from the Count of Blois. Thourars was said to be impregnable; he took it in three days. Castillon-sur-Agen fell in less than a week. The tally is even more impressive here in Brittany. He razed my great castle at Fougères to the ground, captured Josselin and Auray from Eudo de Porhoët, seized Bécherel Castle from Roland de Dinan, and just two years ago, he descended upon the Viscount of Léon like a thunderbolt, reduced all of his castles to rubble . . . *all* of them. So when you tell me we ought to hold out at Dol, I do not find that a convincing argument."

Hugh was suddenly overcome with fatigue; feeling as if his legs would no longer support him, he sank down onto the closest bench. "There has to be another way beside surrender."

Raoul de Fougères regarded him unblinkingly. "You have until noon to think of one."

THE TOWNSPEOPLE HAD GATHERED to watch the surrender and there was almost a festive atmosphere, for they were thankful they'd been spared the horrors of a siege, thankful the war was over for Brittany. Most of them cared little for who ruled over them as long as they were left to live in peace, and they were milling about in front of the castle, laughing and gossiping, buying fruit-filled wafers from street vendors, ducking into nearby taverns to quench their thirst, and staring with un-abashed curiosity at the English king and his lords.

Henry stood with the Earls of Essex and Pembroke, Richard du Hommet, the constable of Normandy, and his cousin William, the hero of Dol. They were watching with grim satisfaction as the castle drawbridge was lowered and forlorn figures trudged out, bearing a white flag of truce. The Earl of Chester was in the lead, followed by Raoul de Fougères, his son Juhel and his brother, Guillaume. The Bretons were sto-ical, but Henry was gratified to see that his cousin was as white as a corpse candle.

Approaching Henry, Hugh sank to his knees in the dusty street, and the others did the same. "We surrender ourselves and the castle of Dol into your hands, my lord king," he said hoarsely. "We know we have grievously offended you, violated our oaths of fealty and homage, and we are truly repentant and remorseful. We humbly beg your pardon and . . . and pray that you will show mercy even if we do not deserve it."

Henry looked at them without speaking, and when Hugh could stand the sus-pense no longer, he blurted out a plaintive "Cousin" that he at once regretted, for Henry turned upon him the full force of those glittering grey eyes. "You would do bet-ter at this moment," he said, "not to remind me of our kinship." And when he added "Cousin," he invested that simple word with so much raw emotion—reproach and rage—that despite the hot August sun, Hugh began to shiver.

L EAVING THE FRENCH KING'S palace on the isle known as the Île de la Cité, Will Marshal threaded his way through the maze of crooked streets until he reached the Grand Pont. It was the finest bridge he'd ever seen, nigh on twenty feet wide, and made of stone at a time when even London's bridge was wooden. Booths and stalls lined both sides of the bridge, most of them occupied by moneychangers. Since Will's pouch was already filled with deniers parisis, he shouldered his way past the foreigners and travelers crowding around the booths to change their money, and was soon sauntering along the right bank of the Seine, heading for the Grève, site of the weekly Paris market.

There he had no trouble finding what he sought: a small glass mirror with a lead backing. It was a great improvement over the more common mirrors of metal, and he was sure Barbe would be pleased with the gift. Stopping to buy a loaf of bread and a pork pie from a vendor, he ducked into the nearest tavern to eat it, washing it down with a henap of raisin wine, for he still had the robust appetite that had earned him the nickname of Scoff-food during his days as a squire. Once his hunger was satisfied, he fed the leftover bread to a skinny stray dog and started back toward the Grand Pont, good-naturedly rejecting the overtures of several street whores, attracted by his confident demeanor, his height, and the sword on his hip, a good indication that he could afford their services.

Returning to the Île de la Cité, he did not head for the palace, instead turned onto the Rue de la Draperie, the street of the Parisian drapers. Barbe's shop was doing brisk business, with customers admiring a new shipment of silks from Sicily, but when Will entered, she turned the trade over to her assistant, and he accompanied her abovestairs to her private chamber, where she expressed delight over her new mirror and wasted no time in showing her gratitude in bed.

Will had never been keen on relieving his male needs with whores, and knew better than to seduce virgin maidens. He preferred lusty young widows like Barbe, and because he was personable, generous, and blessed with a fine physique, he'd rarely had trouble finding worldly, accommodating bedmates. Barbe was one of the best he'd had, and he knew he'd miss her once his stay in Paris was done.

Their bedsport had left them both drenched in sweat, and she soon rose, padded barefoot to the window and opened the shutters, wrinkling her nose at the rank smell of the river. Coming back to the bed, she noticed for the first time the ripe bruise spreading across his ribs, and was at once solicitous, insisting upon rummaging around in a coffer until she found a goose-grease salve. "What did you do, dearest . . . get caught up in a tavern brawl?"

Will grinned, shifting so she could better apply the salve. "Worse . . . I agreed to some sword-play with my lord's brother Richard. He wanted to practice parrying an enemy's blow, but his enthusiasm left my old bones battered and bruised."

Barbe put the salve down in the floor rushes and climbed back into bed beside him. She loved it when he talked about court life, for that was a world beyond her ken, exotic and alien. "I thought you told me that your lord's knights did not mingle with Duke Richard's men?"

"As a rule, they do not, sharing their lords' rivalry. But my position is somewhat different, for I once served in the queen's household and spent many hours teaching Richard how to wield a sword and aim a lance. We remained on friendly terms even after the old king asked me to instruct Lord Hal."

"They are both fine-looking lads," Barbe said, "but even I can see how unlike they are. Lord Hal always stops to wave and acknowledge the cheers when he rides through the streets, and Lord Richard does not even seem to hear them. I was talking with some of the neighborhood women last week and we agreed we'd rather have Lord Hal as a lover, for he never passes a beggar without flipping him a coin. A man so open-handed would likely keep his leman draped in silks and pearls! But which do you think would make the better king, Will?"

Will had indeed pondered that question. He loved Hal, respected Richard. A pity Hal did not have Richard's iron will, or Richard Hal's generosity of spirit. His stay in Paris had given him a chance to study the third brother, too, and he'd decided that Geoffrey might be the cleverest of the three. He'd always admired the old king's ability to remain dispassionate in the face of adversity. Only with St Thomas had his sangfroid failed him, with disastrous consequences. He doubted that either Hal or Richard had inherited any of their sire's uncanny self-possession; their emotions ran close to the surface, quick to spill over. If one of the king's sons had his coolly calculating brain, it was likely to be Geoffrey. Of course he was just shy of fifteen, so only time would tell.

Will knew Barbe would have been fascinated by his musings about King Henry's sons, but discretion was both a habit and a natural inclination. A man would not prosper at the royal court if he'd not learned to govern his tongue. So not even with his bedmate would he drop his guard, and he began to speak instead of a subject that he knew she'd find of interest: a recent feast given for the king by the Bishop of Paris in honor of their victory at Verneuil.

Even as he delighted Barbe by describing the rich menu and fine gowns of the French queen, Adele, and the English queen, Marguerite, Will marveled that Louis could celebrate such a shameful episode. They'd done their best to put a favorable cast upon it, bragging how they'd outwitted the English king and left Verneuil in ruins. But word had trickled out, and Will was soon hearing the rumors discussed in Paris taverns. The citizens of Paris showed a surprising sympathy for their counterparts at Verneuil, but Will realized that they were putting themselves in the places of the Norman burghers, imagining their own shops looted and their houses burned.

Will had not often considered the suffering of citizens in war, having been taught that civilian casualties were both unfortunate and unavoidable. That was the way wars were waged, with chevauchées that served a twofold purpose by devastating an enemy's countryside: denying his army much-needed provisions and demonstrating to his people that he was failing a lord's first duty, unable to protect his subjects from harm. What had appalled Will about Verneuil was the deliberate violation of Louis's sworn oath, both to Henry and the townspeople, and his refusal to honor his own truce. Will firmly believed that the world would descend into chaos and hellish turmoil if men did not obey those laws meant to govern their behavior and tame their more shameful impulses, laws set forth by the Holy Church, by the Crown, and now by the chivalric canons. Chivalry was the foundation stone of his life, offering more than a code of conduct, offering a map which would enable men of good faith to avoid those sinful temptations that might jeopardize their chances of salvation.

Will was thankful that Hal shared this conviction, for it would have been very hard to follow a lord who did not. He just wished Hal had been strong enough to defy the French king and his evil advisors, strong enough to have prevailed. But Hal was young. He had time to develop that steel in his soul, Will assured himself. So far he had resolutely refused to listen to the seditious inner voice whispering that age was no excuse, that had King Henry been faced with a Verneuil at eighteen, he would never have allowed it to happen.

With duskfall, the day's heat slowly began to ebb. They could hear the sounds downstairs as Barbe's assistant ushered out the last customers and closed up the shop. The noise from the street continued to waft through the open window, though, for people would not retire to their homes until curfew rang. Will and Barbe made love again, and then she fetched some cold chicken, cheese, and fruit for a bedside supper. They were just finishing their apples when a muffled thumping sounded below.

Will cocked his head. "Is someone knocking at the door?"

Barbe paused to listen, too. "Whoever it is will go away."

But the pounding continued. And then a voice shouted loudly, "Will Marshal! If you're up there, come to the window!"

"Ignore him," Barbe urged.

But Will recognized the voice. Swinging his legs over the bed, he crossed to the window and peered down into the street, where Simon de Morisco was standing, hands on hips, getting ready to shout again. At the sight of Will, he heaved a sigh of relief.

"Thank God! I was sent to find you straightaway and did not know where else to look. Hurry and dress, Will. You have been summoned back to the palace."

Entering the palace's great hall, Will was surprised to see Hal and Richard seated together, for they did not often seek out each other's company. Clearly the news from Brittany must be grave, indeed. All Simon could tell him was that a messenger had arrived with word of a calamity, but no more than that. Hal and Richard were sitting with Raoul de Faye, Marguerite, the Count of Leicester, Robert Beaumont, and his wife, Peronelle. As Will approached, Richard and Hal slid over on the bench to make room for him beside them. He took his seat, ignoring the disgruntled looks he was getting from several of Hal's knights; he well knew that some were jealous of his privileged status and since he could do nothing about it, he did his best not to let it bother him.

"Simon said there was a setback in Brittany?"

Hal nodded, and Richard gave a short laugh that sounded uncannily like Henry's. "To call it a 'setback' is like calling the Expulsion from Eden a minor misunderstanding. It was a disaster, Will. Last Thursday Hugh and Raoul de Fougères and all their knights surrendered Dol Castle to my father. The rebellion in Brittany is over."

"Sweet Jesu," Will breathed, for this was far worse than he'd expected. "I did not even know King Henry was in Brittany, thought he'd returned to Rouen after . . . after Verneuil."

"He did," Hal said glumly, "but as soon as he learned Hugh and the Bretons were trapped in Dol, he hastened west, and once he arrived on the scene, they panicked and ran up a white flag."

"A disgrace," the Earl of Leicester muttered, shaking his head in disgust, and Hal, Richard, and Will exchanged glances, all of them sharing the same thought: that Leicester had abandoned his castle at Breteuil and ran for his life as soon as he'd gotten word of Henry's approach. None of them voiced that thought, though. It would never occur to Will to do so, and the brothers were learning some hard lessons in diplomacy; Leicester was a valued ally, even if they both thought he was a horse's arse.

Will diplomatically ended the silence that had followed Leicester's accusation, asking, "What happened to them after they surrendered?"

It was Raoul de Faye who answered him. "Actually, they were treated rather leniently under the circumstances. Harry let most of them go once they'd sworn homage to him again and promised not to take part in further rebellions. He even freed Raoul de Fougères after he'd offered up his sons as hostages for his good behavior, and did not declare any of their estates forfeit to the Crown . . . at least not yet."

Raoul did not sound particularly happy about the Bretons' good fortune, and Will understood why. Word of Henry's forbearance would quickly spread, reassuring other rebels that they could submit to the Crown without fearing they'd lose their lands or their lives. It was a shrewd tactic for a man fighting a civil war. "What of the Earl of Chester?"

"He was not as lucky." Hal frowned, for he was fond of Hugh. "My father sent him under guard to Falaise Castle, where he'll be held prisoner . . ."

His words trailed off, but Will knew the phrase he was reluctant to say. "At the king's pleasure." Hugh of Chester could be freed if Henry won the rebellion. He could also be held for the rest of his earthly days. And for one as high-strung as Hugh, the uncertainty would gnaw at his nerves his every waking hour. Glancing at Henry's sons, Will wondered if they feared their father might treat them as harshly as he had Hugh. He certainly did, feared for Queen Eleanor, too, since Hugh's imprisonment showed that Henry could not forgive family betrayal as easily as he could the disloyalty of vassals and liegemen.

"Poor Hugh," Hal said softly, "and poor Bertrada and Cousin Maud. I cannot give them such sad news. You do it for me, Uncle Raoul. But when you write, offer them hope for his early release. Women are not meant to bear such heavy burdens."

Will did not understand how Queen Eleanor's son could make such a nonsensical statement and, judging from the expressions on the faces of Raoul de Faye and Richard, neither did they. But as Will glanced over at Marguerite, whose hand was tightly clasped in Hal's, he decided that Hal was being protective of his young wife; Marguerite was just fifteen, after all.

"Louis was badly shaken by the news," Hal said, looking somberly at Will. "And who can blame him? In just a month, our great alliance has fallen apart. The Scots king has fled back across the border. The Count of Flanders has gone home, too. Our invasion of Normandy came to naught, and now the Breton rebellion has been quelled, and so easily. Little wonder Louis told me that he has begun to fear the Almighty is no longer on our side."

That was such a tactless admission that Will winced. It was bad enough that the French king was having such dangerous doubts without Hal letting others know of his misgivings. Another strained silence fell, this one broken by Richard. "The Almighty," he said, "is usually on the side of the best battle commander." Hal scowled at his brother, for that sounded almost sacrilegious to him. But before he could respond, the Countess of Leicester spoke up. She'd been listening with obvious impatience, and now took advantage of the break in the conversation to voice her opinion.

"The French king ought not to mourn the loss of the Bretons. They always make unreliable allies, skulk back to their own lands as soon as things start to go wrong, and so do the Scots. England is the key to victory. If we'd invaded it as my husband advised, we could have taken London by now."

Will was offended by her meddling in these military matters. It was one thing for a woman to express her opinions to her husband in the privacy of their bedchamber, quite another for her to speak out so boldly in public. He had no trouble reconciling his traditional views of the female sex with his admiration for the highly untraditional Queen Eleanor, for in Will's eyes, she was unique, not to be judged by the same standards that applied to lesser women. Glancing around the table, he saw that Peronelle's views had not gone down well with the others, either. Richard, Raoul, Hal, and Marguerite were all regarding her with disapproval. Her husband was smiling at her, though, confirming Will's suspicions that Peronelle was the master in that marriage. He knew she was a great heiress, but he did not like her any the better for it; if arrogance was a male failing, it was even more unseemly and unappealing in a woman.

"We must hope that the Count of Flanders reconsiders his rash decision to abandon our alliance," Hal was saying when the door was flung open and the French king entered the hall.

They all jumped to their feet at his approach, but he waved them back into their seats. He looked surprisingly calm and peaceful for a man who'd gotten dire news such a short time ago. "I know what must be done," he told them, with a certainty he rarely showed. "I have prayed for answers, and the Almighty has shown me the way."

H ENRY HAD CALLED A COUNCIL MEETING on such short notice that he'd begun to think it would be dawn until they all straggled in. But they were finally seated around a trestle table, looking at him expectantly, some smothering yawns, for not all men kept Henry's late hours and several had been roused from their beds by his summons. Henry waited until they'd been served a good quality Gascon wine, and then broke his news.

"I have received a remarkable communication from the French king. It seems that he now sees himself as a peacemaker and has generously offered to reconcile me with my sons."

As he'd expected, their response was explosive and incredulous. He let them vent, but when Willem called Louis the greatest hypocrite in Christendom, Henry demurred. "No, I think not. Louis has a rare gift; he is able to entertain any number of contrary thoughts at one time. Moreover, he has the dubious talent of believing whatever he wants to be true at any given moment, and should I be churlish enough to remind him that he was the cause of this estrangement he is now eager to heal, he'd be deeply wounded by my ingratitude."

They did not dispute his sardonic assessment of the French king, for most of them had experiences with Louis stretching back more than two decades. "What will your answer be, my liege?" the Archbishop of Rouen asked, although he was confident he already knew what Henry would answer.

"I shall accept his invitation, agree to attend his peace conference."

Some of the men seemed surprised, but most of them weren't. Regarding the king pensively over the rim of his wine cup, Willem said, "What are your terms for peace?"

"I mean," Henry said, "to put an end to this needless war as soon as possible. I would not offer Louis so much as a stale crust of bread. But with my sons, I am prepared to be more generous."

"How generous, my liege?" the Earl of Arundel asked cautiously, and when Henry told them, they stared at him in astonishment, shocked that he could be so magnanimous after such a grievous betrayal by those of his own blood.

"Are you sure, my lord?" Willem thought he knew Henry as well as any man did, but he'd not been expecting this. "Sure that you can forgive them?"

Henry was amazed that the question could be asked. "Of course I can forgive them, Willem. They are my sons."

After that, it was quiet in the council chamber, for none doubted he'd spoken from the heart, and none dared to ask if he could also forgive his queen.

CHAPTER ELEVEN

✦

September 1173
Gisors, Normandy

ENRY AGREED TO MEET his sons and the French king on September 25 between Gisors and Trie in the Norman Vexin, at a huge, spreading elm tree that had often been the site of peace conferences. Accompanied by the Earls of Essex and Pembroke, the Constable of Normandy, the Archbishop of Rouen, his son Geoff, and his household knights, Henry arrived at noon. The French were already there. Henry reined in his stallion, but made no move to dismount.

It had been six months since he'd last seen his sons. In the past, he'd been separated from them for longer than that, most recently during his sojourn in Ireland. But he was acutely aware now of the changes that those months apart had wrought. Richard seemed to have added a year or two to his age, for his shoulders had broadened and his stubble had become a full-fledged golden beard. A shadow on Geoffrey's upper lip and peach fuzz on his cheeks had not been there at Christmas. The sight of Hal was the most painful. The sunlight gilding his curly, fair hair, he looked regal and resplendent in a scarlet mantle and matching cowhide boots with gold turned-down tops, a natural magnet for all eyes—just as on that night at Chinon when he'd saluted Henry with a dazzling smile and a silver cup of drugged wine.

Hal was standing beside the French king, with Richard and Geoffrey close by, proclaiming to the world that they were united, allies, and he—their father—was the enemy. Henry fought back a wave of baffled hurt and anger, waiting until he was sure his voice would not betray him. Ignoring Louis, he locked his eyes upon Hal.

"I am not here to negotiate with you and your brothers, Hal, nor to bargain with you. I have come to tell you what I am willing to offer to mend this rift between us and restore peace in our family. You may choose between England and Normandy. If you choose England, you will have half the crown revenues and four royal castles. If you prefer Normandy, you will be entitled to half the ducal revenues, plus all the revenues of Anjou, and three castles in Normandy, one each in Anjou, Maine, and Touraine."

Hal's mouth had dropped open; his eyes were as round as moons. Without waiting for his response, Henry shifted in the saddle so that he faced Richard. "I am offering you, Richard, half the ducal income from Aquitaine and four castles."

Richard's reaction was more guarded than Hal's, but his surprise was still evident and Henry suppressed a smile, thinking that they suddenly looked less like defiant rebels and more like lads getting an unexpected birthday treat. Turning his gaze upon his third son, he said, "For you, Geoffrey, I am willing to be no less generous. As soon as the Pope sanctions your marriage to Constance, you will come into the full inheritance of Brittany."

A stunned silence fell, broken at last by Hal. "May we have time to think it over?"

Henry was disappointed that it could not be resolved then and there; he truly did not see why they'd need to discuss his offer. But he did not want to appear to be pressuring them. "You may give me your answers on the morrow. And know this, that I am willing to put the past behind us, as if this foolhardy rebellion had never been. Whatever our differences, you are my sons, of my blood, and nothing is more important than that."

Henry signaled, then, to his men, swung his stallion in a circle, and rode away without looking back.

H ENRY WAS STAYING at Gisors Castle, and Louis had chosen to lodge at Chaumont-en-Vexin, a formidable royal fortress just six miles away. Not long after their return, Raoul de Faye was standing on the steps of the great hall, his eyes roaming the bailey. When he finally saw his brother, the Viscount of Châtellerault, emerging from the stables, he shouted "Hugh!" so urgently that the other man looked around in alarm. By then, Raoul was halfway across the bailey. He pulled Hugh aside, his fingers biting into his brother's arm, but Hugh did not protest, for he'd never seen Raoul so angry, so agitated.

"Have you spoken yet to Richard or his brothers?"

Hugh shook his head. "No . . . have you?"

"I had just a few words with Hal. I did speak with Louis, though, and that gutless weasel wants to accept Harry's peace terms and skulk back to Paris. When I reminded him that Harry had not said a word about Eleanor's fate, do you know what he told me? He said very piously that it was not for him to meddle in the sacrament of matrimony, that what happened in a marriage was between a husband and his wife and the Almighty. He has no stomach for continuing the war and is willing to let Eleanor pay the price for his blundering, God curse his craven, sanctimonious soul!"

"Lower your voice," Hugh warned. "You're attracting attention. What of Hal? What did he say?"

"Enough to make me suspect he wants to take Harry's bait. Did you see how his eyes lit up when Harry offered him half the crown revenues? I'd wager he's already planning how to spend the money. He and Louis are together in the solar now, and if he has any doubts, you may be sure Louis will argue them away."

"He does not have a brain in that handsome head of his, does he?" Hugh said bitterly. "Does he not realize that— Wait, there's Geoffrey!"

Geoffrey looked startled to see both his great-uncles bearing down upon him with such haste; he hadn't realized men their age could move so fast. When Raoul demanded to know if he was willing to accept his father's offer, he did not answer at once; he was learning to be wary even with family. He'd talked it over with Hal and he was leaning toward acceptance, for he knew that he could not hope for more than Henry had offered, not at fifteen. He also knew that these men would not be happy to hear that, and so he temporized, saying only, "I admit it is tempting, but I have not made up my mind."

His evasion did not work, though, for they began to berate him for his indecision, but then Raoul spotted Richard coming around the corner of the mews. They immediately called out his name, hurrying to intercept him. Geoffrey was forgotten, but he was accustomed to being utterly overshadowed by his elder brothers, and he chose to overlook the slight and follow them, sure that this would be a conversation he ought to hear.

Richard had halted, although he made no attempt to meet them halfway. As soon as they'd reached him, Raoul put to him the question he'd just demanded of Geoffrey. Richard answered readily. "No, I am not willing. He offered money, and much more than I expected, but only money. Nor did he make any mention of my mother and the part she played in the rebellion."

Raoul heaved a great, gusty sigh. "Thank God Jesus that someone else noticed that! His offer is a bribe, a lavish, tempting bribe, but a bribe all the same. It is a bribe, though, that your brother seems willing to take. He and Louis are meeting even as we speak, laying their plans for the morrow—"

"Where?"

When Raoul said the solar, Richard spun around and headed across the bailey, so swiftly that the others were hard pressed to keep up with him. The great hall was crowded, and several intense discussions were going on, the most heated one led by the Count of Dreux, Louis's volatile younger brother. Robert was gesturing emphatically, his face a mottled shade of red, and those gathered around him seemed to be in agreement, for they were nodding and murmuring among themselves. The Earl of Leicester was pacing back and forth by the open hearth. As soon as he saw Richard, he swerved toward him.

"Richard! We need to talk. Your father said nothing about your allies. If you make peace with him, what happens to me or Hugh of Chester?"

Richard brushed by him as if he'd not spoken, and plunged into the stairwell. Taking the stairs two at a time, he did not pause before the solar door, shoved it open, with Raoul and Hugh on his heels and Geoffrey a few steps behind. Louis and Hal were seated at a trestle table with Henri of Blois, the Count of Champagne, his brother Étienne, the Count of Sancerre, and Louis's youngest brother, the Archbishop of Rheims. There were other men there, too, but Richard did not know their names, clerks and priests who labored anonymously for the French king since his chancellor had resigned the year before. They turned startled faces toward the door as Richard burst into the chamber.

"I am sorry I am late. The messenger you sent to fetch me must have gotten waylaid or lost. Surely you *did* send someone to find me, for this is as much my decision as it is Hal's."

It did not take much effort for Louis to imagine those barbed words coming from Henry's mouth. He was genuinely fond of Hal, but he'd never warmed to Richard, and he realized now how easily that indifference could turn into active dislike. Forcing a smile, he said, "Come in, Richard. I assure you that we were not trying to keep anything from you."

Richard ignored him as completely as Henry had done just hours earlier. "Hal, is it true you mean to accept the offer?"

Hal was irked by his peremptory tone. He chose to let it go, though, for too much was at stake for their usual brotherly squabbles. "If he'd made this offer to me at Christmas, I'd never have rebelled. So, yes, I am accepting it. Why would I not?"

"I can understand that you'd not want to be burdened with any real authority.

Having to govern would interfere with your tournament time. But did you spare even a thought for our mother's safety?"

Angry color scorched Hal's skin. "Of course I did! That was the first thing my father-by-marriage and I discussed. He pointed out that she has not taken an active part in the rebellion. All that our father knows for certes is that she let you and Geoffrey go to Paris with me, and that is easily explained. If I assure him that she did not know of my plans, that none of it was her doing, I am sure—"

"Christ on the Cross! I cannot believe we came from the same womb, for you do not have the sense God gave a goat!"

Hal shoved his chair back, coming quickly to his feet. "How dare you—"

"Enough!" Raoul shouted, loudly enough to drown out Hal's outraged response. "If you do not want to hear it from Richard, hear it from me, then, Hal. You know I have a spy at your father's court. He has reported that Harry does not believe you or your brothers would have rebelled if you'd not been beguiled into it, and he has no doubt who bears the responsibility—the French king and your mother. He does not just think she aided and abetted you. He is convinced that she was the instigator, for as long as he can blame Eleanor, he need not blame himself."

"You exaggerate," Louis said sharply. "I have spies, too, at his court, Hal, and they tell me something quite different."

Hal looked from Louis to Raoul to Richard, then back to his father-in-law. "If my mother is to bear the blame for this—"

He got no further, for the door banged open again. This time the intruder was Louis's brother Robert. His suspicions flared as soon as he saw Henry's sons, and he glowered at Louis. "What is going on up here? Why are we not discussing this in council, Louis?"

Louis glared back at him. "It is not for you to question me, my lord count," he said coldly, making use of his brother's title as a pointed reminder of their respective status as sovereign and subject. "It was my intent to summon them once I'd spoken with my son-in-law."

Robert was not impressed by Louis's assumption of kingly authority. "I am gladdened to hear that," he said, and smirked. "I shall go back to the hall and tell the others that we are about to hold a council meeting." And he exited the solar before Louis could stop him. Louis was furious, but Robert had maneuvered him into a corner and he saw no other option than to hold a council. Rising, he gathered his dignity about him as if he were donning robes of state, and strode from the solar. The others were quick to follow.

Raoul lingered behind, though, and stepped in front of the Count of Champagne as he started toward the door. Henri of Blois and his brother Thibault were the most influential of Louis's lords, his sons-in-law by their marriages to his daughters by Eleanor, Marie and Alix, and brothers-in-law by his marriage to their sister, Adèle. Raoul had not often crossed paths with them until the rebellion, and he'd been surprised to find that Henri was quite likable. His beautiful, elegant countess had joined him in Paris, eager to meet her young half brothers, and they'd developed an immediate rapport. Raoul was very taken with Marie, too, for she reminded him of a youthful Eleanor, and as she was quite curious about the mother she'd not seen since she was seven, Raoul had passed some pleasant evenings in Marie and Henri's company.

It was Henri to whom he turned now, for the count knew Louis far better than he did, and he was desperate to glean insights about the French king, to learn anything that might help him to avert this impending catastrophe. "You cannot approve of this so-called peace, Henri, for what does France stand to gain by it?" He did not ask the count how he would benefit. His brother Thibault would get Amboise Castle should they win, but rather remarkably, Henri had demanded nothing of Hal in return for his support.

"Not much," Henri admitted. "If it were up to me, I'd not be so quick to agree to terms with the English king. But it is Louis who wears the crown, and as much as that galls his brother Robert, it is Louis who decides if it is to be peace or war. And as you saw, he has chosen peace."

"Why? I do not understand the workings of that man's mind. Why go to such great lengths to stir up a rebellion against Harry and then call it off as if it were a game of camp-ball halted by rain? I know he wants to see Harry humbled, weakened. So why will he not do all he can to make that happen?"

"Ah, Raoul, you do not understand Louis at all, do you? You share the English king's view of him as somewhat simple, easily swayed by others, with sand where his backbone ought to be. But he is more complicated than that. He is very devout; his great tragedy is that he was plucked out of that monastery when his elder brother died, for he'd have been far happier as the monk he was meant to be. As a good Christian, he loathes war; as a king, he is forced to wage it. But in his heart, he believes that shedding blood is a mortal sin, so when his campaigns go awry, as they usually do, he concludes that the Almighty is punishing him for violating the commandment that states, 'Thou shalt not kill.'"

"But he started this war, not Harry. Why goad Harry's sons into rebellion if he were not willing to see it through to the end?"

Henri smiled faintly. "I said he was complicated, not consistent. Louis hates the English king almost as much as he loves God. For more than twenty years, Harry has bested him at every turn. He could not keep Harry from wedding his queen, or from winning the English Crown, or from expanding his realm until it now rivals Charlemagne's. Had he not been so starved for success, he'd not have let himself be talked into that farce at Verneuil. But you may be sure that any satisfaction he gained from it was all too fleeting, a poisoned brew by morning, for even if he does not always heed it, Louis is cursed with a conscience, a most inconvenient virtue for a king."

The count paused, as if deciding how candid he ought to be. "A man so beset with self-doubts does not deceive himself about his capabilities. He may not admit it, but he knows he is an inept battle commander, Harry a brilliant one. He thought Thomas Becket had given him the weapon he needed, a way to defeat Harry beyond the battle-field, and when the archbishop was so foully murdered, midst his grief there was sat-isfaction, too, that Harry would finally reap what he had sown. You can imagine his frustration when Harry managed to avoid excommunication and then to make his peace with the Church. You have to feel some sympathy for him, Raoul. He is like that figure in Greek myth . . . what was he called? The poor king condemned forever to roll a stone uphill, only to have it roll back down again. Well, that is Louis, constantly struggling to thwart Harry at something, anything, and constantly losing."

"I might have more sympathy for the man," Raoul said tautly, "if he were not so willing to make my niece the scapegoat for his sins."

"Does that truly surprise you? He has never forgiven Eleanor for daring to wed Harry rather than waiting dutifully for him to select a husband for her. And he has never forgiven her for then giving Harry five sons when she gave him only daughters. But if you cannot muster up sympathy for Louis, neither can I find sympathy to spare for your niece. She meant to use Louis for her own ends, so she can hardly complain once she discovers that he was using her, too."

Raoul felt resentment flicker, but he did not allow it to catch fire. He'd long known that Eleanor's French allies were of two minds about her part in the rebellion. They welcomed the aid offered by the Duchess of Aquitaine, but they were not comfort-able with the rebel queen, the faithless wife. Raoul held his tongue, though, for he'd not yet gotten what he needed from Henri. "What if we could make Louis believe that this was one war he could win? That if he held firm, he could have a great victory over Harry?"

"If you can give him that certainty, the king will prevail over the monk, to borrow that memorable phrase coined by your niece. But it will be no easy task. I know that at times it seems as if he can be led by the nose like a bridled gelding. But he can also be very stubborn, his the stiff-necked obstinacy of the weak. And between them, Robert and your young Richard have him determined to make peace on the morrow, if only to punish them for their defiance. So it will not be enough to convince him that he can finally gain that victory over Harry. You will have to offer him a way to save face, too, to reverse himself without sacrificing his pride."

Henri smiled then, signaling that the lesson was over. "We'd best go down to the hall whilst there is still time to change Louis's mind. I will be interested to see if you can put my advice into action."

Upon his return to the great hall, Raoul joined his brother, who whispered that Robert had just stormed out after a particularly acrimonious exchange with Louis. The French lords were gathered around the dais, save for the Count of Évreux, who had withdrawn to a window-seat, watching the proceedings with the detached amusement of one being entertained by minstrels or jongleurs. Louis was seated upon the dais, and a chair had been provided for Hal, but he'd not remained in it for long and was fidgeting like a horse about to bolt, although he kept his gaze fastened upon the French king and his brother all the while.

Richard was standing on the dais steps, looking at Louis with a hawk's unblinking intensity. "You still have not answered me, my liege. How would my lady mother fare under this 'peace' of yours?"

Raoul silently blessed Richard for putting the question so bluntly, for going right to the heart of the matter. But as he glanced around the hall, he could find little sympathy for Eleanor's plight, and with a chill, he realized that the only one standing between Eleanor and disaster was her sixteen-year-old son.

Louis was finding it harder and harder to maintain a civil tone with this prideful young lordling, who seemed to have inherited the worst qualities of both his parents. "I understand your concern for your mother, lad, but you must trust me that—"

For Richard, the French king's patronizing smile was the spark that set his smoldering temper ablaze. "I am the Duke of Aquitaine, not your lad! And I do not give my trust freely. It must be earned."

Louis saw no further reason to humor this impudent brat. "You need to be reminded, Richard, that you came to me as a supplicant, and you and your brothers promised to be guided by my advice and that of my council."

Richard's upper lip curled. "But not all promises are kept, my liege . . . are they?"

This not-so-subtle reference to Verneuil hit its target, and Louis's face twitched as if he'd been struck. "You are a foolish boy, and you've said more than enough!"

"Not nearly enough! Hear me on this—all of you." Richard swung around, his eyes raking the hall. "I will have no part of this so-called peace."

Louis had half risen from his chair. "Then you will stand alone!"

"No," Hal said suddenly, "he will not." Coming down the steps of the dais, he stood beside Richard and looked at his father-in-law, head high. "My brother and I do not often see eye-to-eye, but he has convinced me that he is right and it would be folly to accept our father's offer."

Richard and Louis were staring at Hal, the former with gratified surprise, the latter with angry disappointment. When Hal shot a meaningful glance toward Geoffrey, he hesitated briefly and then sauntered over to join them. "I will not be accepting the offer either."

"And how do you expect to fight your father without French help?" Louis demanded scornfully. "You'll find that your words ring as hollow as your titles!"

"They'll have my help!" Heads turned toward the Count of Dreux, standing in the open doorway of the hall. Once he was sure that all eyes were upon him, Robert swaggered forward to stand beside Henry's sons. "And they ought to have yours, for they have sworn allegiance to you for Normandy and Aquitaine, so you owe them a liege-lord's protection!"

"What would you know about a king's duties and obligations? You've never worn a crown, and that is your true grievance with me, Robert—jealousy, pure and simple!"

Paying no attention to Robert's enraged reply, Raoul shoved his way over to the window-seat where Simon de Montfort was lounging. "I need your help. I know how to get Louis to change his mind, but he'll not heed Eleanor's uncle. You have to be the one to tell him."

"I'd like nothing better than to continue the war, but Louis will not heed me, either."

"He listened to you at Verneuil!"

"Yes . . . and soon regretted it. Have you not noticed how coldly he has treated me since then? It is a wonder I have not gotten frostbite by now. No, you need someone else, someone he truly trusts . . . and that has never been me."

Raoul turned away, searching the hall frantically for the right face, one whom the French king "truly trusts." For a moment, his eyes rested upon the Count of Champagne. Henri had nothing to gain, though, nor to lose, whether it be peace or war. But his brother . . . his brother had long lusted after Amboise Castle, and a premature peace would take that glittering prize from his grasp. Within moments, Raoul had drawn Thibault of Blois aside, speaking quietly and urgently in the count's ear, and then he held his breath as Thibault strode toward the dais.

"I am astonished," he declared, "that our sovereign lord should be spoken to so disrespectfully. The Duke of Aquitaine must be forgiven, for he is young and has not yet learned to govern his temper or his tongue. But you, my lord Count of Dreux, have no such excuse."

Robert was quite willing to aim his rage at a new target, but Thibault did not give him a chance to retaliate. "May I speak to the council, my liege?" Mollified by his deference, Louis graciously gave his permission, and Thibault mounted the steps of the dais.

"We can all agree that the English king's offer was surprisingly generous, and this from a man not known for spending with wild abandon." There were some chuckles at that, and even Louis smiled. "We need to consider what that means, my lords. Henry Fitz Empress proclaimed his willingness to welcome his sons back with open arms, as if their rebellion had never been, and then to reward them lavishly for that very rebellion. What does that tell us? That he is desperate to make peace with his sons. Think about that, my liege, my lords, think about the leverage that gives us. If Henry will offer so much in his opening gambit, how much more will he concede if only we hold firm!"

Thibault paused, saw with satisfaction that Louis was listening intently. "This is a rare opportunity, my lord king. We have something that the English king very badly wants. I say we take advantage of that, deny him his peace until he is willing to pay the price we set upon it. And he will pay it, for as he said himself this morn, nothing is more important than blood, than his sons."

A hushed silence greeted Thibault's words; even Robert had the sense to keep quiet. Louis leaned back in his chair, and then nodded gravely. "As always, you are the voice of reason, my lord count, the only one in the hall. We would be fools, indeed, if we let this chance go by. On the morrow, we shall tell the English king that he will have to do better, much better."

Raoul's first reaction was the exhausted relief that so often marked the end of a bloody battle. Too weary to celebrate, he found an empty window-seat and slumped down upon the cushions, closing his eyes, not looking up until his brother was standing beside him, asking if this was his doing.

"Indeed, yes," he said proudly, and began to laugh. "How I love the way Fortune's Wheel tilts when we least expect it. I daresay you remember what almost befell Eleanor when her marriage to Louis was dissolved and she was seeking to reach safety in her own lands."

"Of course I remember. Twice she was almost abducted by overly eager grooms."

"And one of them was Count Thibault, who was sorely disappointed when she was warned that he'd planned to seize her in Blois and force her to wed him. I always thought it ironic that Louis would then marry her daughter to him. But it is even more ironic," Raoul said with a grin, "that Thibault, of all men, should now be her unwitting savior!"

As they rode from Gisors to the meeting place under that venerable elm, Henry was in good spirits, listening as Willem boasted to Geoff about their capture of Louis's castle at Chaumont-en-Vexin six years ago. "It was a great triumph for your lord father, brilliantly executed."

"He says that because he was one of my commanders," Henry interjected and Willem grinned.

"Modesty has never been one of my failings. Whilst your father tempted the garrison to rush out and engage him, Geoff, his Welsh routiers swam the river and got into the town. The garrison was soon put to flight by our men and when they tried to retreat back into the town, they found it was in flames. Chaumont was where Louis was keeping his army's provisions, so he was greatly grieved by its fall."

"Staying at Chaumont last night must have given him a bad dream or two, then," Geoff said gleefully and Henry turned in the saddle to smile at him.

"I hope so, lad, I surely hope so!"

Ahead they saw the towering branches of the elm, and beneath its vast shadow, the French had gathered. Henry was amused that they'd claimed the shade, for that much he was willing to concede to them. His sons were standing together at a distance from Louis, and he took that as a good sign, although he did not feel much need to look for favorable omens, so sure was he that their answer would be the one he wanted. How could it not be? He was offering forgiveness and substantial revenues and more independence than they'd ever had before, and he was offering it despite the collapse of their rebellion. What greater proof of his sincerity could there be than that?

Upon dismounting, he gave Louis a terse greeting, for it would be years, if ever, before he'd forgive the French king for Verneuil, and then walked over to his sons. "You've had the night to think it over. What is your answer?"

Hal seemed to have been designated as their spokesman, for he was the one to step forward. "Our answer is no. We cannot accept."

This was one of the few times in Henry's life when he was caught utterly off balance, and his intake of breath was audible to Hal. He looked at this stranger who was his son and he could not understand how it had ever come to this. "Out of curiosity," he said at last, "would you mind telling me why?"

Hal was making a disquieting discovery, that it was easier to defy Henry when he was enraged and hurling threats. For just a moment he'd seen his father's vulnerability, seen his hurt, and somewhat to his surprise, he found he could take no pleasure in it. "It . . ." Clearing his throat, he said simply and with no hostility, "It is not enough."

"Not enough," Henry echoed incredulously. "Again, out of curiosity, you understand, just how much money will it take to buy back your allegiance?"

Stung, Hal cried out that was not what he meant, but it was Richard who now drew Henry's attention. "We are not talking about money."

Henry regarded his second son, looking intently into grey eyes very like his own. "What, then?"

"You gave us no assurances that Hal will have any say in the governance of England or Normandy. Nor have you said that I will be able to rule Aquitaine as is my right."

Henry's anger was diluted by a vast weariness, for he'd had this very argument so often with Hal. "As I've told your brother more times than I can begin to count, that is because of your youth and inexperience. Why do you lads find this so hard to grasp? An aspiring goldsmith does not expect to become one overnight; he knows he must first serve an apprenticeship. Why should it be any different for young princes?"

"You did not serve an apprenticeship," Richard pointed out coolly, "before your father turned Normandy over to you."

"And you were just seventeen," Hal chimed in, "fully a year younger than I am now!"

Henry wanted nothing so much at that moment than to grab them both and shake some sense into them. "That happened because I had proved myself by then, and my father knew my judgment could be trusted."

"Yes, but you will not give us the chance to prove ourselves!"

This was an old and familiar argument of Hal's, but before Henry could respond to it, Richard stepped in front of his brother. "There is more. Even if you agree to give us a share in the governing of Aquitaine and England or Normandy, there is another obstacle in our path to peace. You said you were willing to forgive us."

"I said it and I meant it." Henry glanced from one to the other; Geoffrey, as usual, was forgotten. "I will forgive you, I swear it upon all I hold sacred."

Richard raised his chin, met his father's eyes challengingly. "Can you also forgive our mother?"

Henry stiffened and, as he looked at his sons, never had the gap between them seemed so wide to him, so impossible to bridge. "So be it," he said flatly. "We are done here."

As Henry started to turn away, there were startled murmurs from the French, and he marveled wearily at their surprise, for he'd warned them from the first that he'd not come to bargain with his sons. He'd only taken a few steps toward his horse, though, before Louis hastened after him.

"You are a fool, Harry Fitz Empress!" The French king's voice shook with fury as he confronted the man he blamed for most of his life's disappointments. "Do you not see what you are throwing away? You are losing your sons! Do you truly value your pride more than you do them?"

"They were not lost," Henry snarled, more than willing to turn upon Louis the anger he'd not wanted to let loose upon his sons. "They were lured away, and if there is any justice in this world, you'll answer to the Almighty for it. You may not even have to wait till Judgment Day to atone for this particular sin. You have a son, too. Who knows—one day he might grow restless under your tutelage, look elsewhere for advice and support. If so, I will most gladly return the favor."

"You can rant and threaten all you want, blame me, your queen, blame everyone but yourself. It changes nothing. You had a chance today to win your boys back, and you trampled upon it. It is not a chance that will come again. Do you know how we celebrated your son Richard's sixteenth birthday? I knighted him, Harry. I knighted him, not you!"

Louis's taunt drew blood. Henry looked at the other man with loathing, and then turned accusing eyes upon his second son. "My congratulations, Richard," he said scathingly. "What an honor for you, to be knighted by the victor of Verneuil."

Richard's reaction was unexpected; he grinned. But then Henry realized why; Richard had not been at Verneuil, felt none of the shame. And as their eyes met, they shared a moment of odd understanding, one of mutual contempt for the French king.

It was very different, though, for Louis and Hal. Louis turned beet-red and spun on his heel. Hal flushed darkly, too, and cried out that Verneuil was not his doing.

Henry turned back toward his son. "Yes, it was your doing, Hal. All of this is your doing. Part of being a man is taking responsibility for your actions. I hope you learn that one day. But based upon what I've so far seen, I doubt that you will."

Hal went white. Humiliated, hurt, indignant, he glared at his father, sure in that moment that he hated Henry, that he would always hate him. "It will be war then," he warned, his voice hoarse and none-too-steady. "And you may be certain of this—that I will never offer you terms as generous as those you offered me! If you want peace, you will have to beg for it on your knees!"

Henry's eyes glittered. "What do you know of war, boy? It is not dressing up in scarlet boots and wearing a sword on your hip, or promising half your kingdom to the Scots and the Flemings, or swaggering about like the hero in a minstrel's chanson. You want to know about war, you ask the Count of Boulogne, the Earl of Chester, and the burghers of Verneuil. But you cannot, can you? The Count of Boulogne is rotting in his grave, the Earl of Chester is rotting in one of my prisons, and the citizens of Verneuil are too busy grieving for their dead and the French king's lost honor."

Hal started to protest again that he was not responsible for Verneuil, realized just in time that he'd only be proving Henry's point, as Henry continued remorselessly. "I suppose you could ask the allies you have left, but they are dwindling rapidly in case you've not noticed. The Count of Flanders and the Scots king have cut you loose. So have the Breton rebels, who were only too happy to surrender to me at Dol. So who does that leave? Your brothers, who've yet to bloody their swords? Your formidable father in-law? The fearsome Earl of Leicester? Indeed, Hal, I am shaking in my boots at the very thought of facing such worthy adversaries!"

That provoked a choked cry of utter outrage, but it did not come from Hal. Thrusting aside the French lords in his way, the Earl of Leicester strode over to confront Henry. "Are you calling me a coward?"

Henry found it remarkable that his late justiciar, a man of honor and integrity, could ever have spawned such a worthless whelp as this. "I'd say your conduct at Breteuil speaks for itself," he said contemptuously.

The look Leicester gave him was murderous. "I retreated in good order when I saw that I could not hold the castle!"

That was so preposterous a claim that Henry laughed in his face. "You bolted at the first sight of my banners. I daresay I could have sent our camp laundresses to take the castle and you'd still have run like a spooked sheep."

Leicester saw Henry through a red mist of rage. "I am not running now, you Angevin son of a whore!" he shouted and drew his sword.

There was instant pandemonium. Amazed, Henry dropped his hand to his own sword hilt, making ready to defend himself. But his men were already in motion. Willem's blade caught the sun as it slid from its scabbard, and Geoff, not as experienced but just as eager, unsheathed his weapon almost as swiftly. The others were no less quick to react, though. Hal and Richard were yelling at Leicester, the Count of Champagne had darted forward to get between Henry and the earl, and Will Marshal, appearing from nowhere, was there, too. But the French king was the most horrified of all.

"Have you gone mad?" He was staring incredulously at Leicester, as if the earl had suddenly sprouted horns and a tail. "How dare you draw your sword upon a king?"

"I have a right to defend my honor!" But as he glanced around, Leicester saw this was a cock that wouldn't fight. He'd managed to do the well-nigh impossible—temporarily unite them all in a common cause, for there could be no greater crime in their world than to kill a man who was the *christus domini,* the Anointed of the Lord. Jamming his sword back into its scabbard, Leicester shouted defiantly at Henry, "This is not over! When we next meet, it will be on the battlefield in England!" Whirling then, he shoved his way through the press of men, yelling for his men and horses.

The Archbishop of Rouen had taken it upon himself to lecture them all on the sin of spilling blood during God's Truce, and Louis's brother, the Archbishop of Rheims, added his moral authority to Rotrou's, both men uneasily aware of how contagious violence could be. With that same thought in mind, Henry's men had brought over his stallion. Swinging up into the saddle, he paused to stare down at his sons and the French king.

"You wanted war?" he said. "Then by God, that is what you'll get!"

THE LADY BEATRIZ, one of Eleanor's attendants, halted in surprise as she entered the queen's bedchamber, for it was dusk but the hearth had not been lit and no lamps burned on the table. Glad that she'd brought a candle, she hastened over to light the oil wicks, intending to have some harsh words with the servants for being so neglectful. As an oil lamp sputtered and ignited, she caught movement from the corner of her eye, turned, and then recoiled in surprise.

"Oh, my lady, how you startled me! I had no idea you were here." Moving toward the silent figure in the window-seat, she gasped as her candle illuminated the queen's face. "Madame, are you ailing? Shall I fetch a doctor?"

"I am well, Beatriz," Eleanor said, but the girl was not convinced, for the older woman was ashen. Her gaze darting from Eleanor's hollow eyes to the parchment crumpled in her lap, Beatriz dropped to her knees, stretching out a hand in mute entreaty. "My lady . . . forgive me if I have overstepped my bounds, but you look so troubled. Something is wrong, I can tell. Is there nothing I can do?"

Eleanor looked down at the kneeling girl. Most of her ladies-in-waiting did not serve her for long, eager to find husbands at the royal court. But Beatriz, a young widow and distant cousin on her mother's side, had been with her for more than four years. Her uncle Raoul had recommended Beatriz, and at first Eleanor had wondered if he'd put the girl in her household to spy upon her. But Beatriz had passed every test she'd set for her, and Eleanor had no doubts about her loyalty or her love. She'd only had two female confidantes in her life, though, her sister Petronilla and Maud, the Countess of Chester, and she was not about to confess her heart's pain to a sweet child young enough to be one of her daughters. Yet Beatriz was right. She was in great need of solace, in need of one she could truly trust.

"There is something you can do for me, Beatriz," she said, and managed a flickering smile. "Fetch my constable."

As HE'D AGED, Saldebreuil de Sanzay's eyes had begun to fail him, and his vision was tolerable only at a distance these days. It did not help that the letter was in Raoul de Faye's own hand, for his scrawl was not as legible as a scribe's uniform script. He was too proud to ask Eleanor to read it to him, though, and she was too distracted to notice his difficulties. He eventually solved the problem by holding the letter out at arm's length. When he looked up, there was an expression upon his face that she'd rarely seen before, one of fear—for Richard, for Aquitaine, above all, for her.

Fear. She'd not often had to deal with it, for hers had been a privileged life. She'd been insulated from fear by her high birth, her crown, and her headstrong nature. In her forty-nine years on God's Earth, she could honestly say that she'd rarely been afraid. Even during those times when she'd been placed in physical peril—the assault by the Saracens in the Holy Land, the capture of her galley by pirates in the pay of the Byzantine Emperor, the ambush by the de Lusignans—there'd been no time to dwell upon the danger until it was over, and then there was no need. Now . . . now there was nothing but time, and as she'd sat in her darkened bedchamber after reading Raoul's letter, she'd thought of the unforgiving wrath of the man she'd married and could not deny that she was afraid of what the future might hold, afraid that she may have made the greatest mistake of her life.

"You were not told of this peace conference, then?" Saldebreuil asked quietly, and she shook her head.

"I knew nothing of it until Raoul's letter arrived." She gazed down at her clasped hands, noticing the golden glimmer of her wedding ring. Why was she still wearing it? "I expected the Count of Flanders to take charge of the rebellion. Had I thought the reins would be left in Louis's hands, I'd never have risked it."

He nodded bleakly. "It has gone wrong from the first, my lady. If Hal had not fled from Chinon when he did, we'd have had the time we needed to complete our plans, to coordinate our strategy. They ought to have attacked all at once, on multiple fronts. The assault upon Normandy began promisingly enough, but it all fell apart when the Count of Boulogne was slain, and gave your husband the chance to quell the rising in Brittany. If the Scots king had only persevered, if they'd invaded England at the same time . . ." His words trailed off, for he recognized his complaint for what it was, a soldier's lament for lost opportunities and bungled choices.

"Raoul thinks I ought to have gone to Paris with him and my sons. But how could I do that? How could I leave Aquitaine? What sort of a message would that have sent to my lords and vassals if I'd run away like . . . like a flighty, fainthearted woman?"

"In all honesty, Madame, I doubt that your presence in Paris would have changed things much. You have more common sense than any man I've ever known, and more courage. But we both know they'd not have heeded you. You're crippled by your skirts, and your lads by their years. Had he only been older, Richard could have . . ."

Again, he left the thought unfinished, for he was too much of a realist to embrace those most frivolous of regrets, the ones rooted in the barren soil of What If and If Only. Instead, he said briskly, "Well, at least we've been granted a second chance. I think it likely the Count of Flanders will soon rejoin the hunt, for he is not a man to mourn for long, not when all of Kent can be his for the taking. And when he does, the French king's mishaps will not matter as much. We must remember, too, that the Scots king is still a player in this game. And whilst he may not be your husband's equal on the field, he has something the other rebels do not—the resources of a kingdom to draw upon."

"Yes," she said, "but so does Harry. Our spies tell us he has enough to hire twice as many Brabançon routiers as he has now in his pay." As she'd spoken, she was tugging at her wedding band until it slid from her finger. Clenching it tightly in her fist, she said morosely, "I wonder how long it will be ere they come calling into Aquitaine."

Saldebreuil had no answer for her, but then she'd not expected one, and after that, they sat for a time in silence as the shadows lengthened and night came on.

CHAPTER TWELVE

✦

October 1173
St Edmundsbury, England

*U*PON LEARNING THAT the Earl of Leicester had sailed from Wissant on September 29 with a large contingent of Flemish mercenaries, the Earl of Arundel set out in pursuit, landing at Walton on the coast of Suffolk. There he learned that Leicester had joined forces with the Earl of Norfolk at Framlingham, and that the king's justiciar and constable, Richard de Lucy and Humphrey de Bohun, had hastily signed a truce with the Scots king so they could return to deal with this new threat.

THE ABBEY OF ST EDMUND'S was a celebrated pilgrim shrine, for it held the holy bones of the martyred Saxon king Edmund. Geoff hoped that he'd have time to do honor to the saint, but for now he could think only of the coming bloodshed. He had persuaded Henry to allow him to accompany the Earl of Arundel, but he was uncomfortably aware of his lack of military experience and was desperately determined that he not blunder and bring shame upon his father.

They were greeted cordially by Abbot Hugh, who promised that his guest-master would somehow find lodgings for their men, no mean feat under the circumstances; the justiciar and constable had gotten support from Henry's cousin, the Earl of Gloucester, and his uncles, Rainald and Ranulf, so the abbey and town were already overflowing with knights and foot soldiers. The earl soon excused himself, candidly admitting that his "old bones" were in need of a rest; having reached his biblical three score years and ten, he no longer felt the need for bravado. Left to his own devices, Geoff gladly accepted the offer of a young novice monk to show him around.

His guide introduced himself as Jocelin of Brakelond and took Geoff into the nave of the church to see the saint's shrine located behind the High Altar. Pilgrims came from all over England, Brother Jocelin said proudly, although honesty compelled him to admit that the crowds had fallen off in the past two years as more and more people chose to make pilgrimages to St Thomas at Canterbury. In recent weeks, most of the visitors had been local townspeople, he confided, praying that their saint would save them from the Earl of Leicester's Flemings and praying, too, that the warfare would not keep them from holding their great fair in November. Geoff bit his tongue to keep himself from reminding the young monk that there was more at stake than lost fair revenues. If they did not succeed in quelling Leicester's rebellion, England itself could be lost to the rebels.

After leaving the church, Jocelin escorted Geoff through the cellarer's gate into the great courtyard and then to the abbot's hall rather than the guest hall, for he knew that his abbot was a shrewd politician as well as a churchman and he'd want to be sure that the king's son was treated as a privileged guest. Geoff hesitated in the doorway, for he was shy with strangers. To his relief, he soon spotted two familiar faces: his father's uncles, Rainald of Cornwall and Lord Ranulf of Wales. He did not know either man very well, but they shared a common bond—illegitimacy—and he headed in their direction.

To his delight, they welcomed him with genuine enthusiasm, squeezing over to make room for him at their table. They had spent the past three months fighting beside the justiciar, Richard de Lucy, first laying siege to the town and castle of Leicester and then pursuing the Scots king back across the border, and Geoff felt a surge of gratitude that these two men, so loyal to their sister the Empress Maude, were proving to be no less loyal to her son.

Rainald would happily have entertained Geoff for hours with stories of their Scots campaign, but Ranulf deftly steered the conversation toward more urgent matters— the threat posed by the Earl of Leicester and his ally, Hugh Bigod, the Earl of Norfolk. Geoff was familiar with Bigod's history, for he was notorious for his double-dealing. He'd begun his career by committing perjury on Stephen's behalf, falsely swearing that

Maude's father had repudiated her upon his deathbed; Stephen had rewarded him with the earldom of Norfolk. But he'd soon proved that Stephen could trust him no more than Maude could, and his unbridled ambition had even led him to join the infamous Geoffrey de Mandeville. De Mandeville had paid for his treachery with death, dishonor, and eternal damnation. But Bigod had somehow escaped retribution, and seemed as indifferent to the passage of time as he was to the voice of conscience. He'd rebelled against Stephen, Maude, and then Henry, had been excommunicated by Thomas Becket for usurping the lands of a Norfolk monastery, and now, at the vast age of eighty, he was still actively engaging in his favorite pursuits—insurrection, perfidy, and marauding. Geoff thought that an alliance between Bigod and the Earl of Leicester was inevitable, the damned seeking out the damned.

"After he landed at Walton, that snake Leicester slithered off to join Bigod in his burrow at Framlingham," Rainald reported, grimacing as if he'd tasted something foul. "But he soon wore out his welcome. His Flemings thought they could take anything that caught their eye—food, livestock, women. And his countess had her nose so far up in the air that she'd have drowned if it began to rain. Bigod's wife decided she'd rather entertain starving wolves as guests, and there was so much tension that Leicester and his wife—who fancies herself his chief military advisor decided that they'd march west to Leicester Castle."

"We have to stop them!" Geoff exclaimed, with such intensity that the older men smiled and Rainald could not resist teasing him a bit.

"Are you planning to ride with us, lad? I thought Harry meant to make you a prince of the Church. As a priest, your choice of weapons is somewhat limited. I guess you could always put the curse of God upon Leicester. He deserves it if any man does!"

Geoff tensed, hurt and offended. But then he caught Ranulf's wink and relaxed, reassured that Rainald's maladroit humor was not meant to wound. "I am not a priest yet," he said, adding ruefully, "and in no hurry to take holy vows. My father believes that I'd make a far better cleric than I do, but he did agree to let me receive a knight's training. I bloodied my sword when the French army fled Verneuil, so I am not such a novice as you think, Granduncle Rainald."

"Jesu, lad, do not call me that! That makes me sound downright ancient, like a holy relic or one of those churchyard yew trees. Uncle Rainald will do just fine."

"And we will stop them, Geoff," Ranulf said. "You need not fret about that. Three days ago they took Haughley Castle. They ransomed the knights, but they burned the village to the ground. Haughley is just twelve miles east of St Edmundsbury. Leicester will not dare an attack upon the town, though, and he'll try to circle around us. Once he does, we'll strike."

"And with God's Blessings," Geoff said emphatically, although his nerves throbbed with the realization that a battle could be looming within days. "I'd risk the surety of my soul to see Leicester called to account for his sins. At Gisors, he actually dared to draw his sword on my father!"

"So that really happened? We heard the story," Ranulf said, shaking his head in bemusement, "but could scarce believe it."

"And it is not as if Leicester has youth as an excuse," Rainald pointed out, "not like my niece Maud's idiot son Hugh, doing penance these days in a Falaise dungeon. Leicester was born the year after the sinking of the White Ship, which makes him more than fifty!"

"I suppose Leicester could plead madness," Geoff commented acerbically, "for nothing less than lunacy can explain his actions. But what of his wife? If Peronelle is not welcome at Framlingham, where will she go when he heads for Leicester?"

"She'll go with him," Ranulf said with absolute certainty. "On the march to Framlingham, she rode at his side, wearing chain mail and bearing a lance and shield."

Geoff was dumbstruck, but before he could respond, Rainald gave a short bark of laughter. "That must have been a sight to behold. Ranulf says there is a Greek myth about women warriors, and I suppose Peronelle thinks she is one of those . . . Amazons, was it, Ranulf? Not even Eleanor ever dared to arm herself as if she were a man!"

Eleanor's name sank like a stone in the conversational waters and an awkward silence fell, for Henry's uncles understood her conduct no more than he did. Rainald had been impressed by her beauty and her willingness to swap bawdy stories with him, and she'd won Ranulf over by befriending his wife, Rhiannon. She was now the enemy, though, for her glamour and past kindnesses counted for little against a betrayal of such magnitude. It was Ranulf who gave voice to their bitterness. "Raimon St Gilles warned Harry at Toulouse that he was 'nurturing a viper in his nest.' He did not believe it, of course. What man would believe that of his own wife?"

"No man would," Rainald concurred. "Poor Harry. That Clifford chit is said to be a pretty little thing, but was there ever so costly a piece of tail? Not Harry's fault, though. How could he have known Eleanor's jealousy would turn her into a madwoman?"

Geoff could not defend Rosamund, for in the eyes of the Church, she was a wanton. Having met her, he did not like to hear her described so crudely, though, and since he did not feel comfortable taking Rainald to task for it, he chose to change the subject. "Is it true that the Earl of Gloucester is here with you?"

Ranulf nodded and Rainald explained cheerfully that Gloucester did not seem happy about it, but he had no choice. "He knows Harry thinks he is weak-willed, and since he is wed to Leicester's sister, Harry would naturally wonder how susceptible he'd be to the earl's blandishments. So he is here to prove that he is not as daft as his nephew Hugh."

Geoff did not like the Earl of Gloucester, thought he was pompous and just as feckless as Henry suspected. But he felt an unwelcome prick of pity for the earl now; it did not seem fair that he should be tainted by his wife's Beaumont blood. He was thinking that civil wars were the cruelest of all wars when a man stopped by their table. He was of medium height with closely clipped brown hair and beard, and looked to Geoff to be in his mid-twenties. His familiarity with Rainald and Ranulf indicated to Geoff that he was someone of substance, but he was taken aback when the introductions were made, for the newcomer bore a well-known name: Sir Roger Bigod.

"Bigod? Are you kin to the Earl of Norfolk?"

His query might have been tactless, but it was not ill-intentioned. He'd never out-grown his boyhood habit of speaking his mind. But Sir Roger bristled at the question. "The earl is my father," he said defiantly. "What of it? Are you suggesting that we are trying to keep a foot in both camps and that is why I am supporting the king?"

Geoff blinked. "Good Lord, no! The thought never entered my head. I'd be the last man in Christendom to cast aspersions upon another man's family loyalties. Look at mine. My half brothers could put Judas to shame, and whilst my lord father is will-ing to forgive them, I doubt that I ever can."

Roger was disarmed by his candor and regarded Geoff with amused approval. "A few friends and I are going into town to get something to eat. You want to come along? Afterward we'll show you the sights—taverns, alehouses, and mayhap a nunnery."

Geoff grinned, for he knew "nunnery" was slang for a bawdy-house, and knew, too, that this was Roger's way of apologizing for his flare of temper. "What are we wait-ing for?" he asked, pushing away from the table.

Roger grinned, too, but then his gaze fell upon Ranulf and Rainald. "You are also welcome to come," he said, politely but not very enthusiastically.

Ranulf declined with a smile, and watched as Geoff and Roger headed for the door. Rainald watched, too, saying indignantly, "They think we are too old and de-crepit for a night of drinking and whoring!"

"Well," Ranulf said, "we are," and after a moment, Rainald sighed.

"Yes, I suppose we are," he agreed, somewhat sadly. But then he brightened. "At least we are not too old to fight!"

Ranulf thought that was debatable, for Rainald was sixty-three and he was just weeks away from his fifty-fifth birthday. He'd much rather have spent these past months back in Wales with Rhiannon, savoring their homecoming. But his nephew's need must come first. There had been a time when he'd briefly been estranged from his eldest son, and he still remembered the pain of it. How much greater must Harry's pain be, betrayed by his own blood, by those he had most reason to trust.

"We have a saying in Wales, '*Dangos y cam a'i faddau yw'r dial tostaf ar elyn.*' It translates as 'To disclose the wrong and forgive it is the severest revenge upon an enemy.' But when it comes to those involved in this rebellion, Rainald, I find myself agreeing with Geoff, that there can be no forgiveness."

Rainald signaled to a passing servant, snared two cups of ale, and passed one to his brother. "Let's drink," he said, "first to victory and then to retribution."

T HEY WERE MAKING THEIR WAY up Churchgate Street, having been warned by the Watch that curfew had rung, but in no hurry to return to the restrictive environs of the abbey. Geoff was in good spirits, for he'd enjoyed his outing with Roger Bigod and his friends. He'd had enough ale to feel mellow but not enough to suffer from it on the morrow, and he'd had a very satisfactory encounter with a young whore named Eve, was already looking forward to a return visit. When he said as much, though, Roger laughed.

"I'd not count on that, Geoff. Chances are that we'll be leaving St Edmundsbury in the dust within a day or two at most."

Geoff turned to look at the other man. "You think it will be as soon as that?"

"I do. Our scouts are keeping a sharp eye on Leicester. Once we know which road he means to take, we can move to intercept him and— What was that?"

Geoff had heard it, too, a muffled shout. Fulk de Barnham, one of Roger's household knights, pointed off to his left. "It came from that alley." Crossing the street, they peered into the alley, hands on sword hilts. Raising his lantern, Geoff saw enough to draw his weapon. He did not know the rights or wrongs of the fight, but he did not like the odds—three to one. As he moved forward, Roger and his companions followed; they might not share Geoff's strong sense of chivalry, but they were not at all averse to ending the night with a brawl.

A young man had been backed against the wall. Bleeding and bruised, he was defending himself with a wooden stick, and getting the worst of it. But his assailants broke off the attack as soon as they realized they were no longer alone. One glance at the drawn swords and they fled toward the other end of the alley, disappearing into the night. Their victim slowly sank to his knees, gasping for breath. All Geoff could see of him was a thatch of bright hair, as yellow as primroses. "Are you hurt?" he asked, leaning over to touch the other's shoulder. When he raised his head, Geoff saw that he was little more than a boy, fifteen, sixteen at most. His words came out in a rush, and

Geoff guessed they were being thanked, but he had trouble understanding all that was being said, for he had a rudimentary grasp of English, and the boy's East Anglican accent rendered his speech all but indecipherable.

Roger and his knights were far more fluent in English than Geoff, and they soon had the youth's story. "He says his name is Ailwin," Roger related, "and he was set upon by those cutthroats as he left the alehouse up the street. They saw him as easy prey, I suppose, a lad alone, fresh from the country. Look what he was using to fend them off."

Geoff shone his lantern upon a long wooden handle with a shorter, stouter stick attached at the end by a leather thong. It seemed vaguely familiar to him, and after a moment he recognized it as a flail, a farming implement used to thresh wheat. "Why would he be wandering around St Edmundsbury with a flail? The last time I looked, there were no crops to be harvested in the center of town!"

Ailwin was struggling to get to his feet and Fulk gave him a hand, while Roger put a few more questions to him. "He says he came here to fight the Flemings. The flail was the only weapon he had."

Geoff almost laughed at the notion of this green farm lad going off to war with a flail, but stifled it in time, not wanting to hurt the boy's feelings. Roger was speaking again to Ailwin and when he glanced over at Geoff, his face was bleak. "Leicester's Flemings burned his village and killed his family."

They looked at one another and then at Ailwin. "We cannot leave him bleeding here in the alley," Geoff said finally. "Tell him to come with us back to the abbey. At least he'll have a bed for the night."

"The shire is full of Ailwins," Roger said. "Leicester has much to answer for." He did not add the words "as does my father." But the unspoken thought seemed to hang in the air between them, and Geoff could only hope that the day of reckoning would soon be coming—for all their sakes.

GEOFF COULD NOT DISMISS Ailwin from his mind, though, and the next morning while breaking his fast with his granduncles and the Earl of Gloucester, he told them about the boy's rash quest. "I cannot blame him for wanting to strike back at the men who killed his family," he concluded. "But God help him if he should actually run into some of the Flemish routiers!"

Gloucester looked at Geoff blankly, unable to understand why they were wasting time discussing the fate of a runaway peasant, but Ranulf and Rainald were intrigued by the image he'd conjured up—a country ceorl wielding his flail in the interest of justice.

"There's no use trying to talk the lad out of it," Rainald asserted, spearing a large piece of sausage with his knife. "Better he tags along after the army than to go roaming off on his own. There's safety in numbers, after all."

"Rainald is right." Ranulf helped himself to a chunk of freshly baked bread. "If he is set upon vengeance, he'll not be discouraged by anything you say. He has a just grievance, after all, and—"

"'A just grievance,'" Gloucester echoed in astonishment. "You are talking about a lowborn villein, a drudge, a . . ." He paused, groping for words, and finally settled upon "nithing," an English term of contempt. "He is no more capable of understanding the concept of honor or a blood-debt than my favorite lymer hound! What you should have done, Geoff, was report him to the sheriff, for if he is bound to the land, he has no right to run off like this and ought to be punished."

Rainald and Ranulf looked at the younger man, marveling that their beloved brother Robert could have sired such a son. Geoff had neither their patience nor their long experience in dealing with Gloucester's bad manners, and he set down his ale cup so abruptly that liquid sloshed over the rim. "That makes perfect sense," he said, with enough sarcasm to have done his father proud. "We are facing a rebel army that is far larger than ours, an army made up of Flemish routiers eager to turn all of England into a charnel house. So of course our first priority ought to be tracking down and disciplining a lad who may or may not be a runaway villein."

Gloucester scowled, but when Geoff showed no signs of being intimidated by his disapproval, he decided it was not worth his while to engage in a public quarrel with this insolent stripling. Getting to his feet, he made what he hoped was a dignified departure, ruing the day that a king's sinful spawn must be treated as if he were lawfully begotten, on equal footing with those born in holy wedlock. And his contempt for Geoff was not in the least diluted by the fact that his own father had been a royal bastard, for Gloucester had never been one to let his reasoning be undermined by facts.

As he walked away, Rainald leaned over and punched Geoff playfully on the arm. "Well done, lad. Now we can enjoy our meal in peace. Our prospects are not as dire, though, as you made out. It is true Leicester has three thousand Flemings under his command, but they are more like a pack of hungry dogs than a true army."

"But routiers are feared the length and breadth of Christendom," Geoff protested. "Look how easily my father's Brabançons overcame the Breton rebels."

"Fortunately for us," Ranulf said, "Leicester's routiers are not as battle-seasoned as Harry's soldiers. He hired them on the cheap, taking any men willing to sign on, and he was in such a rush that he had no time to separate the wheat from the chaff. A goodly number of his so-called routiers were weavers, bedazzled by the prospects of rich plunder in England. They've been stealing anything that was not nailed down on their marches, singing a cheery little ditty, 'Hop, hop, Wilekin, England is mine and thine.' But they've not yet been battle-tested, and it remains to be seen how they'll respond when they are."

Although he would not have admitted it, Geoff had been troubled by the disparity in size between the two armies, and he was heartened now to think Leicester's Flemings were not as formidable as people feared. "We've been lucky, too," he commented, "in the quality of the battle commanders we've been facing. The French king and Leicester: who'd fear either of those stout-hearts on the field?"

Ranulf and Rainald were expressing their amused agreement when there was a stir across the hall. As they turned toward the sound, they saw Roger Bigod hastening in their direction. "Our scouts have just ridden in," he reported breathlessly. "Leicester is on the move. He is making ready to ford the River Lark north of the town!"

ROGER BIGOD HAD BEEN GIVEN the honor of bearing the standard of St Edmund, and as they rode out of the town's Northgate, Geoff's eyes kept returning to that sacred banner, flaring as the wind swirled it, proclaiming to all that they were marching under the saint's protection. The sky above them was a brilliant blue, a harvest sky, and the October sun spangled the countryside in dazzling golden light, burnishing the autumn foliage so that the trees seemed on fire, ablaze with leafy flames of yellow and scarlet. Geoff had never been so aware of the physical world around him, so grateful for the beauty that the Almighty had bestowed upon them. But if his senses had been honed as sharp as his sword, his emotions were soaring like St Edmund's banner. He was caught up in the surging thrill of the hunt, eager to test his prowess and his courage, to make his father proud and see the rebel earl brought low. His nerves were vibrating like Welsh harp strings, but there was no fear in him, not yet. On such a day, defeat was impossible to imagine.

The Earl of Leicester had made a fateful decision to cross the River Lark at the hamlet of Fornham St Genevieve just four miles from the royal army at St Edmundsbury. Henry's commanders could not understand why he'd chosen to take such a risk, could only be grateful for it. They'd been ready to move as soon as they received confirmation from their scouts of the earl's whereabouts, and they raced north with the stirring words of the aged Earl of Arundel ringing in their ears, "Let us strike them for the honor of God and St Edmund!"

When they were within sight of the rebel force, not a man among them doubted that the Almighty was on their side. They'd caught Leicester in the very act of fording the river, and while his knights had already reached the west bank, his Flemish foot soldiers were still massing on the east bank, his army split in two by the rushing waters of the Lark.

THE ATTACK BEGAN as a trot, with lances held upright, trumpets blaring and pennons fluttering in the breeze, and the war cry of the English royal House erupting from countless throats, *"Dex aie!"* It seemed to Geoff that his heart was pounding in rhythm with his stallion's thudding hooves. This was the way combat was meant to be, not the ugliness at Verneuil, the broken faith and slaughter of innocents. This was a fight between equals, knights trained in war, matching skills and valor. Leveling his lance, couched under his right arm so it was held steady against his chest, he urged his destrier into a gallop as the enemy knights charged to meet them.

His target was a knight on a roan stallion. As the distance narrowed between them, he braced himself for the impact, still more excited than afraid, instinctively putting into practice the lessons learned in years of tiltyard drills. His foe struck first, but his lance hit the edge of Geoff's shield, sliding off harmlessly. Geoff's aim was better. He was rocked back against his saddle cantle as his lance shattered upon his opponent's shield, and then he gave a triumphant shout, for the force of his blow had unseated the other knight.

He hesitated then, not sure what to do next. It never occurred to him to kill the man sprawled in the trampled grass; it would be dishonorable to slay a defenseless knight, and foolish, too, for he'd be forfeiting a profitable ransom. But the battle still raged around him. Shouldn't he seek out another foe? His dilemma was solved by Fulk de Barnham. As he galloped past, he yelled, "What are you waiting for? Take him prisoner or someone else will!"

The enemy knight was struggling to sit up, holding his arm at such an odd angle that Geoff guessed he'd broken a bone in his fall. Casting aside his damaged lance, Geoff unsheathed his sword. "Do you yield?"

The man's eyes locked onto that lethal, naked blade. "I do," he said hoarsely. "I am your prisoner, sir."

Geoff frowned down into that pale, tense face. He'd heard it argued that it would now be his responsibility to escort his captive to a place of safety, but clearly that was impossible under the circumstances. He had no intention of leaving the battle, and he decided he had no choice but to trust to his enemy's honor. "You have pledged yourself to Geoffrey Fitz Roy," he declared, and spurred his stallion away without waiting for a response.

He soon found another adversary, a knight on a lathered chestnut. They exchanged inconclusive blows, but when he circled back to strike again, he was shocked to see the other man had ridden on. Glancing around, he saw that this was occurring all over the field. Men were down, riderless horses milling about in confusion. Leicester's line was wavering, his knights, outnumbered and hard-pressed, giving ground before the onslaught. And then the line was breaking, and the survivors were in flight, seeking only to save themselves.

"Leicester is getting away!" A knight galloped by Geoff, gesturing and shouting. Catching a glimpse of a streaming checkered banner in the distance, he recognized it as the earl's device and joined the chase, urging his stallion to greater speed.

"Treacherous swine! Swaggering, misbegotten whoreson! We'll follow you into Hell if need be!" No one could hear him, of course, but Geoff continued to yell threats, so outraged was he that Leicester would try to save his craven skin by bolting the field, leaving his men to die.

The rebel knights were being overtaken, one by one, for they were fleeing across marshland and they were soon blundering into bogs and sloughs. A ditch loomed ahead, but Geoff's destrier did not break stride. Gathering itself, it soared up and over, and Geoff gave a shaken laugh, for there was a second horse down in the ditch, one that had not been so lucky, floundering on three legs. He drew rein to catch his breath and heap praise upon his stallion, caught movement from the corner of his eye just in time. A man darted forward, muddied and desperate, and snatched at his reins. Geoff's stallion was well trained in the maneuvers of the battlefield—Henry had seen to that—and it reared up, dragging the man off his feet. He'd come in from the left, so Geoff could not make use of his sword. Instead, he bashed the knight with his shield, and watched with satisfaction as his assailant reeled backward, plunging down into the ditch with a resounding splash.

A horseman was approaching, very fast, and he spurred his stallion forward. He was confident that this was not one of Leicester's fleeing knights, for he was going in the wrong direction, and by now the rider was close enough for him to recognize the device on his shield—the insignia of the constable, Humphrey de Bohun.

The man reined in a few feet away. He was splattered with blood, whether his own or not, Geoff could not tell, and his chest was heaving, his face streaked with sweat and dirt. "Do you have a wineskin?" he wanted to know, and when Geoff unhooked it from his pommel and tossed it over, he drank in gulps, then removed his helmet and poured the remaining liquid over his head. "God Above, it is hot!"

It was a cool autumn day, but Geoff agreed with him; between his mail and his exertions, he felt downright feverish. "What is happening?"

He'd assumed de Bohun's knight was acting as a courier and the man confirmed it now with a flash of white teeth as he replaced his helmet. "We caught Leicester, and as easy as snaring a rabbit it was, too. He did not even try to fight us off, the milk-livered, mewling pisspot! My lord sent me to get word to the Earls of Cornwall and Gloucester."

His last words floated back on the wind to Geoff, for he was already galloping off. Geoff was tempted to continue on, so greatly did he want to witness Leicester's capture and humiliation. But common sense reasserted itself, and turning his horse around, he rode after the courier. The battle was not yet won, for there were still Leicester's three thousand Flemish routiers to deal with.

He'd not gone far, though, before he saw several horsemen gathered beside a water-filled trench. What drew his attention was their laughter, not something he'd expect to hear upon a battlefield. They turned as he rode up; one of them was a knight in Roger Bigod's household, and he assured the others that Geoff was on their side. It occurred to Geoff that warfare would be easier if all the combatants wore identifying colors or devices. A baron or lord's knights would bear his insignia on their shields, but not always, and in the heat of battle, mistakes could be made, and sometimes were. That was what had most surprised Geoff about combat: the chaos and confusion.

He started to ask the knights what was going on, but by then he was close enough to see for himself. A slight figure in chain mail was struggling in the water, while on the bank one of the knights was removing his helmet and sword before sliding down into the trench. It made sense to Geoff that they'd attempt a rescue; why not get wet for the chance of a goodly ransom? He was puzzled, though, that the would-be rescuer's companions were so amused by his efforts, and even more puzzled now when the trapped knight lurched away, refusing to take his outstretched hand.

"What . . . he'd prefer drowning to capture?" he asked incredulously and, oddly, that sent the other men into further paroxysms of mirth.

"Not 'he,'" one managed to gasp. "She!"

Geoff's jaw dropped. Once he understood what they were saying, he swung from the saddle and hastened toward the ditch, eager to see the Earl of Leicester's notorious Amazon countess. The other knights were still laughing, cheering the Good Samaritan on with cries of "Go, Simon, go!"

So far, Simon was not having much luck. "Come on, my lady," he said coaxingly. "You're getting in over your head. Surely you do not want to drown in a ditch like a dog!"

"Yes," she hissed, "I would rather drown than let you put your hands on me, you lumpish, poxy lout!"

This sent Simon's comrades into hysterics; one almost unseated himself, he was laughing so hard. The countess had gone under, came up sputtering and coughing, and when she did, Simon lunged forward. But she was as slippery as an eel and slid out of his grasp. "This is crazy, my lady," he insisted, edging closer to make another grab. "So you've lost. War is always a question of losing and winning. But if you kill yourself, you'll burn in Hell for all eternity!"

For the first time, she seemed to be listening to him, to hear what he was saying. She looked from him to the watching men, and there was such despair on her face that their laughter momentarily stilled. When Simon stretched out his hand, she hesitated, then began to splash toward him, and he'd soon pulled her to safety. But when he was about to boost her up the bank, she suddenly began to resist again. Tugging frantically at the jeweled rings adorning her fingers, she slipped them off before he realized what she was doing and flung the rings out into the depths of the ditch.

"There!" she cried triumphantly. "I'd rather the fish get them!"

With that, Simon lost all patience. "Bitch!" he growled, shoving her up onto dry ground before plunging into the ditch again, where he dove repeatedly into the murky water, seeking in vain to recover the countess's rings.

Geoff understood Simon's frustration, for there'd be no ransom for the Countess of Leicester. It did not matter how much she might offer for her freedom; she would be a prisoner of the Crown, not released until and if his father willed it. Peronelle had flung back the hood of her hauberk, removing her sodden linen coif to reveal thick braids coiled neatly at the nape of her neck. She was not at all what Geoff had expected. He'd heard such stories of the influence she wielded over Leicester that he'd envisioned her as a Jezebel, thinking theirs was the classic case of an older man doting upon a young and beautiful wife. But Peronelle de Grandmesnil was not a young woman, not a new wife. Geoff guessed she might be as old as forty, which meant that she was the mother of Leicester's four children, and indeed she did look more maternal than seductive, even allowing for her present bedraggled state.

She caught him studying her, and thrust her chin out, glaring at him with a defiance that he found both admirable and exasperating. "What are you staring at, knave?" she snapped, and Geoff felt a twinge of pity for her children; with this shrew and Leicester as their parents, they were truly doomed by their own blood.

"I was wondering," he said coldly, "if you were curious about the fate of your lord husband. Mayhap not, since he apparently was more concerned with saving himself than seeing to your safety."

It was hard to tell for sure, but he thought that she blanched beneath her coating of mud. "You know what befell my husband?"

Geoff surprised himself by wishing he could tell her Leicester was dead; he hadn't known he had such a streak of malice. "He is safe enough," he said, adding ominously, "for now," even though he knew—and she surely did, too—that Leicester was too highborn to pay the ultimate price for his treason. He was coming to realize that the guiltiest ones—the French king and his half brothers—were likely to escape any real punishment, leaving their supporters to suffer for their sins. There was only one of the conspirators who might eventually be held to account—his father's queen.

GEOFF FOUND HIS GRANDUNCLES on the bank of the River Lark. He'd not needed to worry about the Flemish routiers, they assured him. Trapped on the wrong side of the river, the Flemings had watched helplessly as Leicester's knights were ridden down, and when the royal forces began to ford the river, they'd confirmed Rainald's scornful belief that they were better weavers than routiers, and panicked. They had sought to save themselves by fleeing into the marshy meadowlands beyond the tiny chapel of Fornham St Genevieve, and what followed, Rainald reported gleefully, was a slaughter.

"It was over in less than an hour," he told Geoff. "We captured virtually all of Leicester's knights, including the lordly turd himself, and his French cousin, Hugh de Chastel. As for his greedy Flemings, they'll get some English land out of this—enough to be buried in."

Geoff laughed aloud, amused by his kinsman's flair for creative cursing; from now on, he knew he'd think of Leicester as "the lordly turd." "The Flemings did not try to surrender? They died fighting?"

"No," Ranulf said, "they died running. And they were not offered a chance to surrender."

Geoff knew that the chivalric code did not apply to lowborn routiers, and he could not muster up much sympathy for the slain Flemings, not when he remembered young Ailwin, trying to avenge the slaughter of his family with a farmer's flail. "So we killed them all, then," he said, but to his surprise, Ranulf shook his head.

"No, not us, lad. The local people did it, the peasants and ceorls. They pursued the Flemings with hayforks and clubs and flails, whatever weapons they could find, and when they caught one, they wasted no time dispatching him to Hell. Many of the routiers drowned, too, either in the river or in the ditches that cross these meadowlands. We'll be digging grave pits for some time to come."

Geoff whistled silently, and then, remembering that the slain routiers were still fellow Christians, he dutifully made the sign of the cross. But Roger Bigod's words were echoing in his ears. *The shire is full of Ailwins.* The ways of the Almighty were indeed mysterious at times. Who'd have expected Him to make use of villeins and ceorls as the instruments of Divine Justice?

"The Earl of Norfolk will be quaking in his boots once he hears about Leicester's defeat," he said happily. But before he could dwell upon the earl's discomfort, men were pushing forward, pointing and shouting. Turning, he saw the cause of their excitement. The king's constable, Humphrey de Bohun, was returning to St Edmundsbury in triumph. But the bystanders had eyes only for his captives—Hugh de Chastel, who bore the lofty title Count of Châteauneuf-en-Thimerais, and his cousin, Robert Beaumont, Earl of Leicester. What struck Geoff first was that the linen surcoat Leicester wore over his mail was still clean, unstained by blood or dirt or mud. He wondered uncharitably if the earl had even bothered to draw his sword, thinking that his countess had put up more of a fight than her heroic husband. Leicester appeared oblivious to the jeers and catcalls of the spectators. He was livid, slumped in the saddle as if his spine no longer had the strength to hold him erect, his the stunned disbelief of a man who could not understand how his God and his luck could have so forsaken him.

Geoff suspected that the wily old Earl of Norfolk would have shown more spirit. But he suspected, too, that Norfolk would find a way to escape a reckoning, as he'd so often done in the past. "At least it is over," he said. "Thank God Almighty for that!"

Ranulf gave him a searching look, but refrained from commenting even though he knew better. It was not over, would not be over as long as the French king and the King of the Scots and their allies were still free to continue the war. For they would, he had no doubts of that. For now, though, he let Geoff enjoy their triumph. It was worth savoring, after all, the victory they'd won this October day at Fornham St Genevieve.

AN UNSEASONABLE THUNDERSTORM had rolled through Rouen earlier in the evening, and Rosamund still heard occasional rumblings of thunder in the distance. She'd been embroidering another altar cloth for Godstow Priory while waiting for Henry to come to bed, but she was smothering yawns and finally laid the sewing aside. She was tired all the time these days, for Henry was sleeping even less than usual. She'd always been awed by his vigor, his ability to go to bed so late and rise so early and yet seem so invigorated, so energetic. Lately, though, his sleep habits had gotten much worse, and Rosamund was often kept awake herself by his restlessness. He would not admit it, but she was sure she knew the reason for his current unease. There had been no word from England, only a foreboding silence.

Rosamund was confident that Leicester's rebellion would be quelled, for her faith in Henry was as deep as her faith in the Almighty, and if that was blasphemous, so be it. But she sensed that Henry was beset with doubts, for perhaps the first time in his life, and she did not know how to help, just as she did not know how to heal the festering wounds caused by his family's betrayal.

She curled up in the middle of the bed and was soon joined by a kitten the color of saffron. Cats were not usually kept as pets, except occasionally by nuns, but Rosamund had a fondness for them. It was only recently that she'd confided this partiality to Henry, and much to her delight, he was willing to indulge her in it, joking that he wished he'd known earlier that she could be satisfied with stable cats rather than costly jewels. Now, when the kitten settled down on the pillow beside her, she was soon lulled to sleep by its soft, melodic purring.

She was not sure how long she'd slept, jarred back to awareness by a loud thud. At first she thought it was another clap of thunder, but then she heard Henry's voice calling her name. A moment later he pulled the bed hangings aside and enfolded her in an exuberant embrace.

"Wake up, lass. This is no time to sleep, not when we have so much to celebrate!"

"You've heard from your justiciar!" she cried, and he nodded, grinning.

"The rebellion in England is over. That whoreson Leicester is now a prisoner of the Crown, his knights pleading to be ransomed, his Flemings rotting in Suffolk graves. It was a brilliant victory, love, about as good as it gets." He hugged her again, then gave her a passionate kiss that took her breath away, in part because he was holding her so tightly.

"Beloved, that is such wonderful news!"

When Henry told her that the battle had been fought near St Edmundsbury, she resolved to make sure that its abbey benefited, too, from royal largesse. Henry was not as open-handed in his giving as she or the Church would have liked, but she knew she could coax him into showing greater generosity in the wake of such a blessed victory.

Henry was pouring them wine and she sat up in the bed to watch, unable to remember the last time she'd seen him so happy. "What of the Earl of Norfolk, Harry? Did he take the field with Leicester?"

"Of course not. That sly old fox prefers to let others do his hunting for him. But he was alarmed enough by Leicester's defeat to agree to a truce and even to dismiss his own Flemish routiers. There will be no further outbreaks of violence in England, at least not this year."

Taking the cup he was offering, she gave him a radiant smile. "What will you do with the Earl of Leicester? He is a wicked, loathsome man, Harry, ought to be punished severely for his treachery."

Henry was amused and touched that the soft-hearted Rosamund was so fierce when it came to the rebel earl; she'd been utterly unforgiving from the moment she'd learned of his behavior at Gisors. "Richard de Lucy dispatched Leicester and his quarrelsome countess to Southampton, and from there they'll be sent to keep Hugh of Chester company at Falaise."

"When we return to England, it would be a godly act to make a pilgrimage to St Edmundsbury," she murmured, for she'd just remembered that the Suffolk saint was known to show favor to barren wives.

"If you like," he said absently, joining her on the bed where he set about unfastening her long blond braids. Rosamund leaned back against him with a contented sigh, thinking that this would be their first Christmas together. She'd always passed them alone, watching from afar as he celebrated his Christmas Court with his queen.

"Harry . . . St Edmundsbury is not the only pilgrimage we can make," she ventured, and he paused in the act of running his fingers through her hair to say dryly that he hoped she was not going to suggest Canterbury. "I was thinking of Mont St Michel." She looked at him hopefully, for she'd long yearned to visit the celebrated island abbey. "Now would be the perfect time for such a pilgrimage, beloved. The Breton rebels have been subdued and there'll be no fighting elsewhere until the spring . . ."

She stopped in mid-sentence, feeling the sudden tension in the arm encircling her waist. When he sat up, she searched his face intently, worrying that she'd somehow offended. "Of course by next spring, I am sure peace will be restored and your sons will have come to their senses," she said hastily. "I did not mean to imply that this wretched war will drag on into the new year."

Henry did not seem to be listening, and when he rose and began to move restlessly around the chamber, she watched him in growing dismay. She'd always found his sudden mood swings to be disconcerting, and never more so than now, for his elation over Leicester's defeat seemed to be vanishing before her very eyes.

"Harry . . . have I said something wrong?" she asked timidly. "If I did, it was not meant . . ."

He'd begun to stir the hearth logs with an iron poker. Straightening up, he was surprised to see tears welling in her eyes. "Ah, no, love, you did nothing wrong. But I cannot take you to Mont St Michel now. My war is not yet done for the year."

She was reassured by his use of an endearment, proof that he was not angry with her as she'd feared. She was baffled, though, by what he'd just said. She knew little of military matters, but even she knew that fighting ordinarily ended with the first frost, not to be resumed until the return of mild weather. "You mean to continue your campaign?"

"I was waiting till I got word from England, but I am free now to move south into Anjou. The Count of Vendôme has been overthrown by his own son, who then threw in his lot with Hal and the French king, doubtless hoping that they'd help him hold on to his ill-gotten gains. I mean to reinstate the count and bring his ungrateful whelp to heel."

Rosamund could understand why he'd feel so strongly about putting down a son's outlaw rebellion; that was so obvious that it needed no discussion. She could understand, too, his determination to restore order in Anjou, for insurrection in the land of his birth had to be particularly galling. The tone of his voice, though, alerted her that there was more at stake than the Count of Vendôme's plight, and when he glanced in her direction, she was disquieted by the expression upon his face. His eyes were the color of smoke and yet cold enough to send a chill up her spine, reminding her that ice could burn.

"And then?" She whispered, shaken, even though she knew that this smoldering, implacable anger was not meant for her.

"And then," Henry said grimly, "I think it is time I paid a visit to my loving wife."

CHAPTER THIRTEEN

✦

November 1173
Poitiers, Poitou

ADAME, you are in grave peril. The English king's army is poised like a dagger at the heart of Poitou. By week's end, he could be at the very gates of the city and we will not be able to hold out against him."

William de Maingot was Lord of Sugeres, brother by marriage of the powerful Geoffrey de Rançon, and one of Eleanor's most trusted vassals. At the moment, though, she was hard pressed to be civil to the man. She expected such dramatic posturing from traveling players, not from one of her counselors. Nor was she impressed by his overwrought, portentous warning. Did he truly think she was unaware of her danger?

They'd all had their say by now—William de Maingot, Porteclie de Mauzé, Guillaume de Parthenay, her steward, Hervé le Panetier, and Sir Nicholas de Chauvigny, the head of her household knights. Only Saldebrueil had held his peace, knowing that she would never be bullied into making a decision. They were a pitifully small group, but this war of attrition had scattered her lords to the four winds. Her uncles were in Paris with her sons. Geoffrey de Rançon and the Count of Angoulême were making ready to defend their own lands from her husband's routiers, as were the wily de Lusignan clan. Others, like the Viscount of Limoges, had deliberately stayed out of the fray, doubtless watching to see who'd prevail before committing themselves. Her inner circle was shrinking, as was her margin of safety.

"Madame, he is right," Porteclie de Mauzé exclaimed as soon as William de Maingot had stopped speaking. "Your husband has taken the castles of La Haye, Preuilly, and Champigny—"

"And your uncle's castle at Faye Le Vineuse!" De Maingot made such a sweeping, theatrical gesture that he almost overturned his wine cup in Nicholas de Chauvigny's lap; fortunately the knight had good reflexes and caught the cup just in time. Oblivious, de Maingot slammed his fist down upon the table. "He razed it to the ground, my lady, left nothing but smoldering ruins. We must be thankful that Raoul is in Paris. I would to God that you were, too, Madame! But it is not too late. There is still time to find safety at the French court."

Eleanor said nothing. Nicholas de Chauvigny glanced in her direction, then scowled at de Maingot and Porteclie de Mauzé. "I fear it *is* too late," he said. "Better our lady should seek shelter with Geoffrey de Rançon at Taillebourg. It will not fall to the English king; there is no more formidable stronghold in all of Poitou."

Both men began to argue with him, insisting Eleanor's only chance lay in flight. She appeared to be listening, but it was a pose; her thoughts had begun to wander, for she knew how meaningless their argument was. Nicholas was right; she had waited too long. But she did not think Taillebourg was the sanctuary that Nicholas did. Yes, it was said to be impregnable, but she'd lost track of the impregnable castles taken by her husband over the years. Once he learned where she was—and he would, for she did not doubt his agents had her under surveillance—he would descend upon Taillebourg like the Wrath of God Almighty. Her chances were better on the back roads of Poitou. If she could slip undetected from Poitiers, she ought to be able to reach safety in French territory. It would be a stroke of incredibly bad luck to run into Harry's men, and luck had always been on her side. But she did not want to flee. Not to the French court, never there.

"I will give you my decision on the morrow," she said, pleasing no one, indifferent to their disapproval. They withdrew with obvious reluctance; only Saldebreuil de Sanzay dared to remain—as she'd known he would.

"I understand why you are loath to leave. Poitiers is your capital city, the very heartbeat of your realm. Yours has been a life in exile, my lady. Now that you've finally come home, it is only to be expected that you do not want to turn your back upon it."

Eleanor turned, regarding him with the shadow of a smile. "You know me, Saldebreuil, mayhap too well. Scriptures say that the heart of kings should be unsearchable."

"I know, too, Madame, that more than love of your homeland holds you here. Pride binds you as tightly as any chains could."

Her eyes narrowed, taking on a warning glint of green. "Choose your words with care, my old friend. Even you can misspeak."

"By speaking the truth?" he asked gently, and she was the first to look away, unable to deny the abiding affection in that quiet query. "I understand why you do not want to seek refuge at the French king's court. Louis will make you welcome, and his smile will be so smug that you might well choke on it. It will be no easy thing to ask for his protection; I know that. But you must ask yourself what you have greater cause to fear: Louis Capet's condescension or Harry Fitz Empress's wrath."

Eleanor did not reply. He had his answer, though, in the slumping of her shoulders, in her silence. "I will make the necessary arrangements for your departure," he said, and if she could not bring herself to acquiesce, neither could she gainsay him. She did not move, listening to the familiar sound of his footsteps as he limped toward the door. Only after he'd gone did she sit down wearily upon the closest coffer.

"Damn you, Harry," she whispered, "and damn you, Louis. Damn you both to Hell Everlasting."

CONSTANCE HAD BEGUN to drum her fingers on the table, but it did nothing to stir Alys into action. She continued to stare down at the chessboard, her brow furrowing. When she finally reached out, Constance gave an exasperated sigh. "You cannot do that, Alys. A queen can only move diagonally."

Alys was unfazed by her error. "Sorry," she said, pulling her queen back. "I forgot. I'd rather play queek or tables, anyway. Chess is boring."

"Chess makes you think." Since Constance believed that Alys thought as little as possible, she was not surprised that the other girl should find the game so unappealing. She kept the sarcasm to herself, though. She was only twelve, but she'd learned at an early age that candor was an indulgence she could ill afford.

Alys resumed her interminable study of the chessboard, and Constance sighed again. But the wait proved worth it, as Alys's eventual move placed her queen in peril. Constance hid a smile, was making ready to pounce when the door opened and the flesh-and-blood queen entered.

Alys jumped up and ran to greet Eleanor. Fawning over her, Constance thought tartly, as she rose and dropped a perfunctory curtsy. Eleanor came forward into the chamber, her gaze sweeping past the girls to search the shadows. "I was hoping that Joanna would be here," she said, sounding disappointed. "No one has been able to find her all afternoon. Do either of you know where she might have gone?"

Constance shook her head, but Alys was more helpful. "Try the gardens."

"The gardens have already been searched."

Alys smiled. "Did they search the yew tree? Joanna likes to climb into it and hide from the world."

Eleanor smiled, too, for she'd climbed her share of trees in her own childhood. Constance watched in disapproval as she thanked Alys and departed. Alys reclaimed her seat at the chessboard, then glanced up and saw the other girl's face. "What? Why are you glaring at me like that?"

"Why did you give away Joanna's secret hideaway?"

Alys looked at the other girl in surprise. "Since when are you such friends with Joanna? You always say she is a pest, too young to bother with."

Constance shrugged. Adults were the enemy, and children had so little power that their secrets were to be safeguarded at all costs. But she did not expect Alys to understand that. "It is my move," she said, and captured Alys's queen.

Alys did not seem to notice. She was regarding Constance with curiosity. "You do not like the queen, do you?" she said unexpectedly. "Why not? She's always been kind to you."

Constance's temper flared and she had to bite her lip to keep the angry words from escaping. Kind? Only a fool like Alys would think she should be grateful to the people who'd stolen her birthright. Eleanor's whoreson husband had made a puppet of her father, Duke Conan, then forced Conan to abdicate in her favor so she could be betrothed to his son Geoffrey. They meant to make Brittany an Angevin fief, staking their claims in her marriage bed. There was nothing she could do about it, but by the Rood, she did not have to like it.

Alys was still staring at her. "You do not like any of them, do you?" When Constance did not reply, she smiled. "Such a pity then, that you must marry Geoffrey, is it not?"

Constance stared back, for there was unmistakable malice in the other girl's sugared sympathy, and she suddenly realized that Alys did not like her any more than she liked Alys.

A NOVEMBER GARDEN was often a bleak place, but the Poitevin winter had been mild so far and there were still splashes of color, flowers still blooming in defiance of the season. Eleanor moved quietly along the pathway, one of her greyhounds trailing at her heels. The yew tree had been young when her grandfather had ruled in Poitou, and reached proudly toward the heavens; she had to tilt her head to see its top branches. Feeling a twinge of pride that her daughter dared to scale such heights, she gazed up into the cloud of evergreen and said, "Joanna? It is your mother. Climb down so we may talk."

There was a moment of silence, and she began to doubt Alys's information. But then Joanna's head poked out, framed by lush greenery. She was twenty feet off the ground. She showed no unease, though, and nimbly scrambled down to lower branches, landing on her feet like a cat. Her coppery curls were dusted with needles and there was a dirt smear across her nose, another on her chin. Her eyes looked very green in the fading light as they searched her mother's face. "Am I in trouble, Maman?"

Eleanor supposed she should be disciplined for risking broken bones and ripping her skirt, but she hadn't the heart to scold the girl. Why should she be punished for having a boy's spirit and daring? "No, lass. You do remember, though, that yew tree seeds are poisonous?"

"I know that," Joanna said, and Eleanor stifled a smile, for that confident young voice could have been hers, forty years ago. Leading the child toward a nearby bench, she hesitated, for she'd been loath to have this conversation, had been putting it off as long as possible.

"I wanted to tell you, Joanna, that I will be going away for a while."

"Where?"

"Paris." Adding casually, "I want to see your brothers," as if this would be a pleasure trip.

Joanna was not deceived, though. Keeping those green eyes on her mother's face, she said, "You are running away from Papa."

Eleanor was momentarily at a loss. She'd tried to shield Joanna from her involvement in the plot against Henry, warning servants and attendants and even Constance and Alys to guard their conversation in the child's hearing. She'd known it was unrealistic to expect her daughter to remain in ignorance, but she'd been stung by Maud's accusations that she'd turned their sons against Henry, and was determined that no such accusation could be made about Joanna. But even before she saw the reproach in Joanna's eyes, she knew she'd made the wrong decision.

"I am sorry, Joanna, for trying to keep the truth from you. I ought to have been candid with you from the first, but you are so young—"

"I am eight now, Maman!"

"Yes, you are. But I know you love your father, and I did not want you to feel that you had to choose between us. You are very dear to us both, and nothing will change that."

"I know Hal and Richard have been unhappy with Papa for a long time. Richard says he never listens, that he is as stubborn as a balky mule." Joanna ducked her head, staring down at her lap, and Eleanor resisted the impulse to brush the yew needles from her hair. "So you . . . you took their side, Maman?"

"Yes, Joanna, I did. But your father has led an army into Poitou, and my council has advised me to leave Poitiers for now."

The girl looked up, then. "Would Papa hurt you?" She met Eleanor's eyes steadily, but there was a quaver in her voice, and Eleanor reached out, covered her daughter's hand with her own.

"No, he would not," she said, choosing her words with care. "But he is very angry with me because I supported our sons in their quarrel, and I prefer not to have a confrontation just yet. We think it is for the best that I join your brothers in Paris. But I do not expect to be gone for long. I will be back here ere you know it, lass."

Joanna had a disconcertingly direct gaze. "What will happen after that?"

"I expect that the French king and your brothers will prevail and your father will come to terms with them." Eleanor studied Joanna closely, unable to tell if she believed it. But, then, Eleanor was not sure if she believed it herself.

"WELL?" ELEANOR ASKED. "What do you think?" She turned in a circle and Saldebreuil smiled at her transformation. She was dressed as a knight, complete with sword and scabbard, her hair pinned up under a cowled hood.

"I'd not have recognized you," he assured her, thinking that she still had very shapely legs, revealed now in close-fitting bright blue hose.

Eleanor was looking admiringly at her soft leather ankle boots. "We had trouble finding a man's boots small enough to fit my feet until I tried on an old pair of Geoffrey's." She liked the freedom of her new clothes. It was much easier to move unhampered by long skirts. She would have to get used to the unaccustomed heft of the sword at her hip, but she would be spared the weight of chain mail since most knights did not wear their hauberks while on the road.

Saldebreuil's smile had faded and his dark eyes were somber. Trying to reassure him, she evoked a smile of her own, saying playfully, "I think I make a rather handsome man, do I not? And this ought to be a foolproof way to sneak out of the city undetected by Harry's spies. They'll never expect me to don male disguise, after all."

"Indeed not," he affirmed, striving to sound hearty and confident. He did think her ruse would enable her to escape her husband's agents. He wished she would have more men with her, though. They'd decided that it would be better to travel with a small escort in order to pass as ordinary travelers, and he agreed that made sense. But he would not be going with her, as his joint evil had flared up again, making riding painful, and he knew he would worry and fret until he received word of her safe arrival in Paris.

Eleanor picked up a mirror to check her camouflage one last time. Satisfied, she turned back to him with a smile, and he said softly, "Go with God, Madame."

They looked at each other and then Eleanor said, "Propriety be damned" and gave him a quick hug before heading for the door. Saldebreuil went to the window, thrusting open the shutters. The dawn sky was the shade of soft pearl, a few night stars still glimmering to the west. The air was chill but dry; it would be a good day for travel. Eleanor's escort was below in the bailey, waiting for her. She soon emerged, pausing to give her palfrey an affectionate pat on the nose before using a horse block to swing into the saddle. Glancing up toward the window, she gave Saldebreuil a jaunty wave. He waved back, but with a sense of foreboding, and he remained at his post long after she'd ridden out. His vigil had begun.

E LEANOR WAS ACCOMPANIED by Nicholas de Chauvigny and two of her household knights. The rest of her bodyguards were Porteclie de Mauzé's men, as he had claimed the honor of escorting her to Paris. Their pace was too swift for conversation, but Eleanor could see that they were nervous, casting frequent glances over their shoulders, measuring the progress of the sun on its westward arc, swiveling their heads at every rustling in the underbrush. She did not share their unease, confident that the greatest danger was already past. Once they'd evaded her husband's spies and slipped out of Poitiers, the odds were very much in her favor that she'd reach safety in French territory.

It was not the journey that troubled her; it was the destination. She loathed the very thought of being indebted to Louis, and she knew all too well how it would gratify him to give her refuge at his court. For she had no illusions about their dubious partnership. Hers were allies of expediency, and as eager as they'd been to join forces with the Duchess of Aquitaine, they were likely now to see her as a frightened woman fleeing her husband's just rage.

B Y LATE AFTERNOON, they were deep in Touraine. Eleanor's men were showing signs of increasing strain, for this was a land congested with castles, most of them under Henry's control, and these fortresses must be given a wide berth. Going downstream to avoid Bridoré Castle, they forded the River Indre in late afternoon, and were soon swallowed up by the vast forest of Loches.

They were not far now from their destination, planning to pass the night at Sainte-Trinité de Grandmont Villiers, a small priory hidden away in the midst of Loches Forest. They'd chosen it for its isolation, but Eleanor derived a secret satisfaction from that choice, for the priory had been founded by Henry. He'd always favored the austere Order of Grandmont, a partiality Eleanor did not share. The Grandmontines scorned females as sinful daughters of Eve, reluctant even to allow them to enter their churches, and Eleanor took malicious amusement in the knowledge that she would be sheltering at this male sanctuary, outwitting both her husband and his women-hating monks.

As soon as they entered the woods, they lost the light. Although many trees had been stripped bare, a heavy growth of evergreens, brush, and entwined branches formed a canopy that the wan November sun could not penetrate, and they rode into an early dusk. The path was narrow and their horses' hooves crunched upon a carpeting of brittle, brown leaves. Squirrels darted along overhanging boughs, and once they startled a fox as they rounded a bend in the road; they caught just a blur of red fur as it faded back into the shadows. Men were usually skittish about such dark forest trails, for many believed that demons, ghosts, and revenants lurked in the gloom, and all knew that outlaws did. But Eleanor's knights welcomed the camouflage, feeling more vulnerable out on the king's roads, knowing that Henry's army was on the prowl. They were less enthusiastic about their stay at the Grandmontine priory, for the order was renowned for its asceticism and self-denial, even forbidding the possession of livestock, and the men knew that meant a meager meal awaited them.

Listening to their glum speculation about that paltry supper, Eleanor had to smile. She did not begrudge them their grumbling; both men had—like Nicholas—been in her service for years and had volunteered for this high-risk mission. The monks' hospitality would likely be an even greater privation for her, accustomed as she was to the best their world had to offer, but she did not care if they were fed bread and water, wanting only to stretch out on a bed in the guest hall and ease her aching muscles. She'd ridden astride occasionally in the past, but never for such a lengthy journey, and although she would never have admitted it to Nicholas or Porteclie, she was very tired.

"God's Legs!" Riding at Eleanor's side, Porteclie de Mauzé swore suddenly and then signaled for a halt. "My horse has gone lame," he exclaimed. "What wretched luck, with us so close to the priory." Swinging from the saddle, he began to examine his stallion's right foreleg as the other men drew rein, milling about on the pathway until he told them to dismount. Suppressing a sigh, Eleanor slid from the saddle, too, not waiting for Nicholas's assistance.

They'd stopped at a crossroads, another winding trail snaking off to their left. In a nearby copse of trees was a small thatched hut. Pointing it out to Eleanor, Nicholas said that a celebrated recluse dwelled there, an ancient known as Bernard the Hermit. He'd once earned his keep by guiding travelers through the forest, although he was now too old to venture far from his hut. But he was admired for his piety and godly way of life, and local people saw to it that he didn't starve.

Eleanor glanced over at that shabby little hut, unable to comprehend why anyone of sound mind would deliberately choose to live like that, alone and impoverished. But when Nicholas started toward the cottage, she followed, welcoming a chance to walk off her stiffness. The door was ajar and after calling out politely, Nicholas pushed it open. He came back out almost at once. "There is no one inside," he reported, sounding disappointed. "I hope he has not died."

Porteclie was still examining his horse's hoof, and Eleanor moved in his direction, with Nicholas trailing behind. It was then that her palfrey lifted his head, ears pricking, and snorted. Gérard, the elder of Eleanor's knights, was listening, too, quickly giving the alert. "Riders are coming," he warned, gesturing toward the second road that angled off toward the west.

They had not encountered many travelers on the road today; prudent people tried to keep to their own hearths during times of war. Eleanor tensed instinctively before common sense reasserted itself. Annoyed that she should be susceptible to such phantom fears, she nonetheless shifted so that she was half-hidden by her horse, for she knew that her disguise would not bear close inspection. Nicholas had tensed, too, his hand dropping to the hilt of his sword. As the riders approached, he glanced toward Porteclie, waiting for the older man to take charge. When Porteclie neither moved nor spoke, Nicholas shot him an aggrieved, reproachful look, and then stepped forward to greet them.

"Good morrow." His stomach muscles tightened as he saw how badly outnumbered they were by these new arrivals, but he forced a cheerful smile, saying as blandly as he could, "A fine day for travel, no? Have you come far?"

"No, not far . . . from Loches." The speaker was a dark-haired man in his early thirties, clad in a good wool mantle, with a quick smile and a relaxed manner. He looked eminently respectable and quite reassuring, but Nicholas's queasy stomach lurched again, for Loches was one of Henry's most formidable strongholds.

"I am Sir Yves des Roches." Plucking the names out of the air, Nicholas half-turned so that he could glare at Porteclie, who should have been their spokesman. "This is my lord, Porteclie de Mauzé. We're on our way to the abbey at Cormery."

The stranger's eyes flicked toward Porteclie, but without interest. His gaze moving from face to face, he did not pause until he found Eleanor. She'd drawn her hood forward to shadow her face, careful to keep on the far side of her palfrey, but he did not hesitate. "Welcome to Touraine, Madame." He doffed his cap in a deferential gesture that somehow seemed sincere despite the incongruity of the circumstances. "I am Sir Hervé de Monbazon, the new provost of Loches. We have been awaiting your arrival since Nones rang, had begun to fear that you'd chosen another route."

Shock rendered Eleanor speechless, and then she swung around to confront Porteclie. Even as her eyes swept from the hermit's hut to his supposedly lame stallion, her heart was unwilling to accept what her head was telling her, for Porteclie de Mauzé was one of her most steadfast barons, a distant cousin on her father's side of the family. But as she looked into his face, she saw the ugly truth written in his ducked head, his averted eyes, and his silence.

"You Judas!" Nicholas had reached the same appalled conclusion and lunged for Porteclie's throat. As they crashed to the ground, Eleanor's two knights drew their swords, urging her to flee. When she'd been ambushed by the de Lusignans five years ago, William Marshal and his uncle, the Earl of Salisbury, had done the same, offering up their lives for her safety. The earl had died and Will had been wounded and captured, but their blood had bought her the time she needed to escape. Now, though, there was nowhere to run, and even as she struggled with the enormity of this betrayal, she saw the futility of resistance.

"No!" she cried sharply. "I'll have no bloodshed, will have no men dying in vain! Lower your swords—now!"

They hesitated and then slowly obeyed. Porteclie's knights stood rooted, no one moving, not even to come to their lord's aid. It was easy for Eleanor to tell which ones had been in the know and which had not, for the latter looked stunned and the former either grim or shame-faced. The provost had swiftly dismounted and ordered two of the men to separate Nicholas and Porteclie, who were rolling about in the dirt, locked in a death grip. When they were pulled apart, Porteclie stayed down, gulping for air, his throat scratched and bruised, already showing clear imprints of Nicholas's clutching fingers. Nicholas was bleeding from a deep cut to his leg, slashed by one of Porteclie's spurs. When Eleanor told him to surrender his sword, he looked at her in anguish, dark eyes glittering with blinked-back tears, but he did as she bade, offered his weapon to the provost before limping over to stand protectively at her side.

Hervé de Monbazon passed Nicholas's sword to one of his men. "If you will, Madame," he said politely. It was a moment before she realized he wanted her own sword. Unbuckling the scabbard, she handed it to him. "Thank you. Now . . . may I help you to mount?" he asked, still so politely that she wanted to slap him. Did he think that his feigned courtesy could make this anything but what it was? He might act as if she was his queen, but she was his captive and they both knew it.

But if he could pretend that this was a perfectly ordinary encounter, then by God, so could she. "Be sure to bring my sumpter horse," she said, in the brusque tones of one who never doubted her orders would be obeyed. "It carries my clothes." When he cupped his hands, she stepped into them and swung up into the saddle, inclining her head in aloof acknowledgment of his help. When he ordered her men to be bound before they mounted their horses, she voiced no protest, knowing it would be futile. When he snapped a leather lead upon her palfrey's bridle, she kept silent, staring straight ahead as if his action was of no interest to her. And when they rode off, she never looked back at Porteclie de Mauzé, standing with his men by the side of the road.

Eleanor had never liked Loches Castle. Situated upon a rocky outcrop far above the River Indre, its stark, rectangular shape was silhouetted ominously against the evening sky. Made of grey-white freestone, it reminded her of the Tower of London's great keep, and she'd never liked that stronghold either. Loches's ancient donjon—more than one hundred twenty feet high, with walls nine feet thick, its few windows not much bigger than arrow slits—proclaimed that this was a wartime fortress, not a royal residence. It had been built by one of Henry's more infamous ancestors, Fulk Nerra, in the eleventh century, and she'd found it to be utterly lacking in comfort during her infrequent visits. But if it had always seemed primitive to her, there was something almost sinister about it now, looming out of the darkness like some hulking beast of prey.

They entered the bailey through the Porte Royale gatehouse, were soon being ushered into the great hall that occupied the second story of the keep. Unlike the provost, the man standing by the smoking hearth was well known to Eleanor. Maurice de Craon was the same age as her husband. He was of average height like Henry, and like Henry, he gave the impression of being larger than he actually was, with a wrestler's well-muscled build and stocky legs. Only in coloring did he differ from his sovereign, for he was as swarthy as Henry was fair. Eleanor's heart sank at the sight of him, for Maurice de Craon was one of Henry's intimates, a powerful Angevin baron and a battle commander of some note. His presence at Loches showed how important her capture was to her wrathful husband.

Raising her chin, she moved toward him with all the hauteur at her command. "My lord de Craon."

"Madame." If Eleanor's voice had been coolly clipped, his dripped with icicles. His eyes were almost black; they took in her appearance with a disdain he did not bother to conceal. "I am surprised that Sir Hervé was able to recognize you. You could hardly look less queenly, could you?"

When Nicholas bristled, Eleanor shook her head almost imperceptibly. "But I *am* the queen," she said, "and you'd do well to remember that. One of my men has a wound in need of tending. I wish him to be seen by a doctor without delay."

"Do you, indeed? Well . . . if wishes were horses, beggars would ride." Turning, he gestured toward two of his men. "Take these prisoners down to the dungeon." Adding "without delay," with a mocking glance over his shoulder at Eleanor.

"I'd have thought you had better breeding than that, my lord. Only a churl would not know that men of Sir Nicholas's rank are to be well treated until their ransoms can be arranged."

"Ransom?" he echoed and laughed. "What a droll wit you have, Madame. But if you are so fretful about their well-being, mayhap you should join them in the dungeon so that you can look after them yourself."

Eleanor caught her breath, quickly reached out to still Nicholas's outraged protest. But it was easier to control Nicholas's anger than her own temper, for she'd had little practice in biting back intemperate words. She opened her mouth to throw down a challenge that might well have gotten her incarcerated with her men. Before she could defy Maurice de Craon, though, Sir Hervé de Monbazon stepped between them.

"May we have a few words in private, my lord?" he asked smoothly, favoring Maurice with the same disarming smile that he'd turned upon Eleanor. Maurice did not seem pleased by his intervention, but after a brief hesitation, he nodded and followed the provost toward the stairwell in the east wall.

Eleanor gave Nicholas a critical scrutiny, her eyes flicking from his pallid face to his bloodstained chausses and boot. "Come with me," she said, taking his arm and steering him toward the closest bench. "You, too," she directed her other knights, Gérard and Guyon. Once the three men were seated, she glanced around the hall, finding what she sought when she noticed a plate of bread and cheese on a nearby trestle table. Bringing it back to them, she directed Nicholas to hold out his bound wrists and cut the rope with the bread knife, then did the same for Gérard and Guyon. She was watched all the while by the other men in the hall, but while some of them murmured among themselves, none attempted to stop her, and whenever she met an individual's gaze, he quickly looked away.

When the door opened, she stiffened warily, as did her knights. But the man emerging from the stairwell was not Maurice de Craon. The new arrival was an elderly priest, who stared at Eleanor with round eyes and open mouth. Like the others in the hall, he seemed hesitant, but after an irresolute moment, he gripped his cane firmly and hobbled toward her.

"Madame, you are truly here! Do you remember me?"

Like Henry, Eleanor had been blessed with a remarkable memory, and like him, she'd taken pains to cultivate the talent; for a prince, that was a survival skill. Now, as she studied the priest, it stood her in good stead. "Father Lucas," she said and smiled. "Of course I remember you. You were very helpful when that baby was found abandoned on the Loches Road."

Pleased color rose in his cheeks. "It was my pleasure to serve you, my lady."

"I need your help again, Father Lucas. This is Sir Nicholas de Chauvigny, a knight of my household. As you can see, he has a leg injury that ought to be cleaned and treated as soon as possible. Will you take care of that for me?"

He did not answer immediately, casting a revealing glance over his shoulder toward the stairwell. But then he straightened his shoulders and nodded emphatically. "Indeed, I will, Madame."

While he'd turned away to summon a servant, Eleanor snatched up the bread and cheese and passed it to her men. "Hide this in your tunics," she said. "I rather doubt that Maurice de Craon will prove to be a generous, open-handed host."

The priest was soon back with a basin of water and a small jar of ointment. Nicholas was scandalized when Eleanor reached for the salve, and insisted that he could clean the wound by himself. Amused in spite of herself by his outraged sense of decorum, Eleanor turned the task over to Gérard. The priest's unease was becoming more and more apparent, his gaze straying often to the stairwell.

"Madame . . ." Lowering his voice until it was barely audible, he said hurriedly, "I was praying in the chapel, must have dosed off, for I was awakened of a sudden by voices. It was Lord Maurice and Sir Hervé. I suppose they'd sought out the chapel for privacy. They were arguing about you, my lady. The lord thought you ought to be treated as a rebel, but the provost insisted it was wiser to treat you as a highborn hostage. Lord Maurice said he'd been with the king at Rouen when he learned of your . . . your betrayal. His words, Madame, not mine! He said the king was grievously hurt by your actions, that he would want you punished, not coddled. Sir Hervé said that they must not forget how unpredictable the king could be, as changeable as the winds. He advised Lord Maurice to tread carefully on such unsteady ground."

His last words came in a rush, with another nervous look over his shoulder. "I do not know which of them will prevail, my lady. It will depend upon what they think the king wants done with you."

"Yes," Eleanor said softly. "That is the question, is it not?" One not even she could answer, as well as she knew her husband. Now that she was in his power, what would Harry do?

W HEN MAURICE DE CRAON led her toward the stairwell, Eleanor felt a surge of relief when they headed up, not down. So it was not to be the dungeon. For all her bravado, she did not want to be thrust into a damp, dark cell. When they reached the third floor, Maurice turned to the right, not the left, and a grim smile flickered across her lips. Maurice had deemed her unworthy of sleeping in the king's bed; instead she was to be held in the smaller, more spartan guest chamber.

They'd been preceded by servants, who made haste to light an oil lamp and pulled back the bed hangings. Sir Hervé soon followed, accompanied by another servant carrying Eleanor's coffer. The sight of it was a welcome one, for she wanted her own clothes; she'd not liked the way the men in the hall had stared at her legs and ankles. But then Maurice made a snide comment about her male garb, saying that he'd had her coffer brought up so she could change straightaway out of her unseemly attire, and she immediately considered wearing her knight's garments until they hung on her in rags.

"Does my appearance disturb you, my lord? Alas, I am desolated by your disapproval," she said, so sardonically that his mouth tightened and she could see the muscles clench along his jawline.

Striding to the door, he paused, giving her a look of appraisal that was neither friendly nor flattering. "It is true you do not have to answer to me," he said coldly. "But you are answerable to the lord king, your husband." Not waiting for her response, he closed the door with a finality that was almost as disquieting as his words had been.

A silence settled over the room. The servants quickly and self-consciously finished their tasks and fled, leaving Eleanor alone with the provost. He seemed to be debating whether to speak or not, at last said, almost apologetically, "Lord Maurice is plainspoken, but if he lacks the polished manners of a courtier, he is a good man for all that, my lady. I hope you will not hold his rudeness against him."

Eleanor was no longer so put off by his silken civility, not after exposure to the Angevin baron's overt hostility. "As it happens," she said, "I understand Maurice better than you think I do, Sir Hervé. He recently wed Isabel of Meulan, and she is a first cousin of Robert Beaumont, the rebel Earl of Leicester."

His engaging smile vanished. "You mean he feels the need to curry favor with the king now, to prove that his loyalty has not been infected by the Beaumont heresy? You are wrong, Madame. His outrage is bona fide and many share it." He hesitated, as if to say more, instead bowed and made a discreet departure.

After a few moments, Eleanor inspected the room. It lacked the fireplace and private latrine of the king's chamber, but as prisons go, it was not so bad. They'd not provided a brazier for heat, but winters in the Loire Valley were not severe and there seemed to be an adequate pile of blankets on the bed. She wandered aimlessly from the bed to the small shuttered window, back again, and then started when a soft knock sounded at the door.

"Come in," she said resolutely, determined to keep up a bold front, and a young man entered with a wooden tray. He set the tray upon the trestle table, sketched an awkward obeisance, and hastily backed toward the door. Once he was gone, Eleanor moved to the table, looking at her meal. The food was plain, nothing fancy, not the sort of dishes to grace the royal table, but it was plentiful. She'd not go hungry, and she did not know if that would be true for Nicholas and her knights. Although she'd not eaten for many hours, she could muster up no appetite. Picking up the wine cup, she took a tentative swallow, grimaced at the taste, and set it down.

She froze then, having caught the shuffle of footsteps in the stairwell, holding her breath as she waited for the door to open. It didn't. The footsteps paused, and then she heard the click of a key being turned in the lock. It was not loud, but it seemed to echo in the silence until there was no other sound in her world but that metallic clink and the thudding of her heart. It was only then that the full reality of her plight hit home. Slumping down on the bed, she buried her face in her hands and gave way to despair.

CHAPTER FOURTEEN

December 1173
Paris, France

W HEN HAL'S LASHES FLICKERED, Marguerite leaned over and kissed his cheek, brushing his skin as lightly as a butterfly's wings. Opening his eyes, he smiled drowsily. "Is it dawn yet?"

"The sun has been up for hours. You are such a sluggard," she chided fondly, "still in bed at this time of day . . . for shame."

"There are two of us in this bed," he pointed out. "So you must be a sluggard, too."

"I could not get up," she insisted. "You were sleeping on my hair!"

Propping himself up on his elbow, Hal saw that her long, blond tresses had indeed been caught under his arm. "Well . . . I can think of several good reasons to remain abed despite the hour." Sliding his hand up from her waist, he cupped her breast. "Here is one. Ah, and here is another . . ."

Marguerite sighed with pleasure, but two could play that game. "I do believe you're right," she purred, reaching out to stroke his thigh. "I think I've found another one."

Hal's eyes half closed. "By God, you have," he said and rolled over on top of her just as a loud pounding began. Swearing, he called for his squire. "Thierry, tell whoever it is to go away, tell them I'm sleeping, tell them I'm dead . . ."

Marguerite began to giggle until he stopped her laughter with his mouth. They were too absorbed in each other to pay any heed to the sounds beyond their bed: footsteps, an opening door, a murmur of voices, and then a smothered protest, "My lord, you cannot come in—" But they were rudely brought back to reality when the bed hangings were suddenly jerked open.

Marguerite gave a squeak and dived under the covers. Hal sat up, his temper flaring at the sight of his least-loved brother. "Hellfire and damnation! Get out of here, Richard!"

"He's taken her!"

Some of Hal's annoyance ebbed in the face of Richard's agitation. "Who? What are you talking about?"

"Our mother! She has fallen into his hands, is being held prisoner in one of his Angevin strongholds."

Hal blinked, staring at his brother in disbelief. That could not be true. The Lord God would never let that happen. He was suddenly sorry he'd quaffed so much wine the night before, for his thinking was muddled. "That cannot be right. You must have heard a rumor, gossip—"

"Use your head, Hal. Why else would I be in your bedchamber at such an hour? For the pleasure of your company?"

Hal found himself at a loss for words, and Marguerite re-emerged from the blankets, pulling them modestly up to her chin even as she put her arm around his shoulders. "I am so sorry, sweetheart. But you must not despair. My father will move heaven and earth to rescue her."

Richard rolled his eyes, thinking that they were a well matched pair, both as simpleminded as sheep. Hal knew that Marguerite was only trying to comfort him. He did not have as much faith in her father, though, as he'd had before Verneuil. He was still confused, for he'd been torn from his wife's arms into a waking nightmare without any warning. It was not fair. Men should have time to come to terms with such calamitous happenings.

His brother was waiting impatiently, and he threw the covers back, swinging his legs over the side of the bed. But then he paused. "Richard . . . what can we do?"

It was a moment of odd role reversal, as if he were the younger brother, not the elder. Richard usually had answers for everything. But not this time. He hesitated, and Hal felt a chill, realizing that Richard did not know what to do any more than he did.

THEY'D GATHERED IN the French king's palace, were awaiting him in a private chamber overlooking the River Seine. Raoul de Faye had wandered restlessly to a window, and when he opened the shutters, he looked out upon a scene as bleak and cheerless as his mood. The city seemed painted in shades of grey, with looming storm clouds, a sky darkening with an early dusk, the river a dull, leaden color, its choppy surface pelted with icy rain drops. He'd let a blast of cold air into the room, and when the others began to complain, he closed the shutters and returned to his seat.

He was familiar with every man in the chamber, for they were all pillars of the French king's court. Seated closest to the hearth was the elderly Maurice de Sully, Bishop of Paris. Beside him sat Louis's younger brother, the Archbishop of Rheims, while the youngest of the brothers, the perpetually discontented Robert, Count of Dreux, was sprawled on a bench by himself. The king's two sons-in-law, Henri, Count of Champagne, and Thibault, Count of Blois, were whispering together across the table, while their younger sibling, Étienne, Count of Sancerre, was slouched low in his seat, looking bored. Simon de Montfort, Count of Évreux, was amusing himself by flipping a coin in the air and trying to coax Raoul's brother Hugh into wagering upon the outcome. Since de Montfort was known for his sharp dealings, Hugh was prudently refusing his blandishments. And sitting on a cushioned settle were Raoul's three great-nephews, the ones most affected by the momentous news out of Poitou.

Raoul's gaze focused thoughtfully upon them. Geoffrey's face was unrevealing; he was strangely guarded for one so young, and Raoul realized that he never knew what Geoffrey was thinking. That was certainly not true with Hal, whose face served as a mirror to his soul. His dismay was evident to anyone with eyes to see. And Richard was smoldering, a fire that had burned down but not out. He kept casting aggrieved glances toward the door, as if willing Louis to make his appearance.

Louis finally swept into the room, flanked by his clerk and chaplain. Waving the others back to their seats as they rose, he stopped by Eleanor's sons and squeezed Hal's shoulder in an affectionate gesture of support. Taking a chair at the head of the table, he sighed audibly, like a man with too many burdens to bear, and then looked toward Raoul.

"This is indeed sorrowful tidings. What do we know for certes and what is just conjecture?"

"The queen's constable sent a courier to me late last night. On the Friday before Advent, she left Poitiers, heading for Chartres and then Paris. She was waylaid near Loches and taken into custody by the king's men. She was being escorted by one of her Poitevin barons, Porteclie de Mauzé, and what we know comes from him. He told Saldebreuil that they were ambushed in the forest, that they were taken by surprise and so greatly outnumbered that they could not resist. So he says." Raoul's mouth twitched in a mirthless smile that conveyed without words both his own skepticism and Saldebreuil's.

Richard was more forthright. "I think his story stinks like three-day-old mackerel. He told Saldebreuil that my mother must have been betrayed and even suggested a few likely suspects. But in any hunt for the Judas, we'd do well to start with him. He lets his liege lady be taken without lifting a finger to stop it, and then he and all his men are set free to continue on their way? Does he take us for utter fools?"

"A great pity," Louis said somberly. "May the Almighty keep her safe in her time of travail."

"I am sure the Almighty will look after her, my lord king." Raoul leaned forward, his eyes locking upon the French king's face. "But prayers will not set her free. We need to make plans, to decide how best to accomplish that."

Louis glanced around at his nobles, as if seeking a consensus. Finding what he sought on their faces, he looked at Raoul and slowly, sadly, shook his head. "Alas," he said, "there is nothing we can do."

Raoul felt no real surprise, just a surge of outrage. Richard and Hal shared it. The former sprang to his feet as the latter cried out incredulously, "What are you saying, that we leave her to rot in one of his dungeons?"

"I very much doubt that she is in a dungeon, lad. Your father is not a brute, is not likely to maltreat the mother of his children."

Raoul was not impressed by Louis's reassurances, saw that neither were his young kinsmen. But none of Eleanor's allies were going to rescue her. Most men, even those who'd been bedazzled by her beauty, did not approve of her. He'd long known that to be true. He suspected that Eleanor knew it, too. She'd never cared, though, what others thought. She'd never had to . . . until now.

"I know this is not what you want to hear," the Count of Champagne said quietly, and with enough sincere sympathy in his voice to still their protests. "I was sorely distressed to hear of her capture, for I know how it will grieve my wife. It is true she has not seen the queen since childhood, but she would never want to see her mother in such dire straits. Yet there truly is nothing we can do. We do not even know where she is being held. She could be at Loches, or have been moved to Chinon by now. She could even be on her way to England."

Louis did not appreciate the reminder that his daughter Marie was also Eleanor's flesh and blood, or the suggestion that she might feel some emotional attachment to her mother, for he'd done his best to obliterate Eleanor's memories from Marie and Alix's lives. He'd been willing to marry Marguerite to Eleanor's son if that would make her Queen of England one day, but that was statecraft. This was personal, and it hurt to learn that Marie was still under Eleanor's infernal spell. He welcomed Count Henri's support, though, and he said quickly: "The count speaks true. I would like nothing more than to ride to your mother's rescue, would that it were possible. It is not."

Hal looked as if he'd been slapped in the face. "I cannot accept that," he cried, "I cannot!" And then he turned, as they all did, to stare at his brother, for Richard was stalking toward the door.

He jerked it open, and then swung around when Louis called out his name sharply, demanding to know what he meant to do. "I mean," he said, "to return to Poitiers and take command of the rebellion. There may be nothing you can do, my lord king," and in his mouth, that respectful term of address sounded like the foulest of insults. "But I am going to win this war and free my mother." And without waiting for the king's response, much less his permission, he slammed out of the chamber.

Hal had started to rise, then slumped back on the settle. Geoffrey kept silent, watching them all with alert blue-grey eyes that gave away nothing. Color was staining Louis's cheeks, but he made an effort to conceal his anger. "Lord save us from the foolishness of the very young," he said, with what he hoped was a wry, indulgent smile, and the other men began to murmur their agreement. All but Raoul, who decided it was time to burn his bridges.

Getting to his feet without haste, he looked directly at the man once wed to his niece. "Manhood is not measured in years, my liege. Some reach it at an early age, whilst others . . . others never reach it at all." And he turned then on his heel, followed after Richard without looking back.

ELEANOR HAD PASSED only two days at Loches before being taken to Chinon. There she was lodged in an upper chamber of the Tour du Moulin instead of the royal apartments along the south wall. Her gaolers had apparently decided that she was to be denied luxuries but not comfort until they heard otherwise from the king. Soon after her arrival at Chinon, Maurice de Craon had ridden away, presumably to consult with Henry about her fate. She half expected her husband to return with the Angevin baron, and was relieved when he did not. But she was soon on the move again, riding northwest under heavy guard. She refused to ask Maurice any questions, just as she refused to complain about the rapid pace and long hours in the saddle. From Chinon to Angers, the next day on to Laval, then north to the great fortress of Domfront where she'd given birth to her daughter and namesake, Leonora, twelve years earlier.

They were covering more than forty miles a day, which was a considerable distance for winter travel, and she suffered from blisters and saddle sores and cramped muscles, all of which she endured in stubborn silence. By now she thought she knew where they were heading: either to Falaise or to the port of Barfleur. The latter destination would mean that she was being taken to England, and if that were so, she could only cry aloud with Job, "Where is now my hope?" Falaise was preferable to England, but not by much. Chinon had been the repository of good memories, happier times, and it was less than forty miles from Poitiers. Falaise was deep in the heart of Normandy, a royal castle but also a royal prison, a fortress of war in a windswept, inhospitable land where she'd find few friends. Falaise, too, was not a place where hope could flourish.

From Domfront they headed northeast, and by dusk, they were within sight of the towering twin keeps of the ancient stronghold of Falaise, looking as if it had been carved from the steep cliffs that overshadowed the marshes and ravines of the River Ante. As thankful as she was to have reached the end of her journey, Eleanor could not suppress a shiver as she gazed up at those grim, foreboding walls.

AT FALAISE, she was once more treated with courtesy, not deference. She was being held in a small chamber in the keep, lit only by a single shuttered window, heated by a charcoal brazier. It was not suitable accommodations for the Queen of England, but she suspected it was preferable to the lodgings of the other royal prisoner, the hapless Earl of Chester. She was neither hungry nor cold. She was isolated, though, cut off from the normal rhythms and routines of castle life, her only contacts with the servants who brought her meals and tidied up her room. Never before had she been deprived of women attendants to assist her in dressing and to keep her company. She missed her dogs, missed her books, missed the music that had echoed throughout the halls of her Poitiers palace. She was left alone with her own thoughts, and they were not pleasant ones.

At Loches and Chinon, she had retreated behind her court mask, showing her gaolers the queen, never the woman. Aloof and remote, she'd dared them to breach the invisible wall she'd erected around herself, clothed in pride as men rode off to war in chain mail. But at Falaise, she changed her tactics, for now that the shock of her seizure was wearing off, she realized that her self-imposed solitude was not serving her interests.

In her youth, she'd been an accomplished flirt. Her mirror had not yet become her enemy, but she was no longer young. After studying her guards with care, she finally selected a lanky, gangling boy not much older than her sons. It had taken little effort to gain Perrin's good will, required no more than a few smiles and the light, teasing tone that she used with Richard.

Perrin was soon her unwitting accomplice and her conduit, sharing with her his news, gossip, and rumors. From Perrin, she learned that on the day of her capture, her husband had entered the city of Vendôme in triumph, having restored the count to power and vanquished his rebellious son. She learned that the Earl of Leicester and his rebel countess had been sent from England and were now sharing her confinement at Falaise. But Perrin could tell her nothing of what was happening in her own domains. What had that whoreson Porteclie told them? Did her Poitevins know that she had been seized by Harry's men? Did they think she was dead? Or had she just vanished, her disappearance cloaked in mystery, her fate unknown?

FIVE DAYS AFTER her arrival at Falaise, Eleanor awoke to find winter had laid claim to Normandy during the night. Opening the shutters, she stood at the window, gazing down upon the snow-coated roofs and steep, icy streets of the village. The air was cold, colder than in Poitiers, and the wind carried the damp chill of the sea, for they were less than thirty miles from the coast.

She was still at the window when a deferential knock sounded and Perrin entered with a tray—bread, cheese, and wine to break her fast. She closed the shutters, smiling to see a small branch of holly beside her wine cup. The day before, the boy had brought a fragrant sprig of winter marjoram, doubtless stolen from the castle herb gardens. The holly was a dark shade of emerald, festooned with bright red berries, a vivid flash of color midst the drabness of her confinement. But her smile faded as she glanced over at Perrin, for he was visibly perturbed.

"My lady . . ." He hesitated and then blurted out, "One of the sergeants told me that the king will be holding his Christmas Court at Caen."

"I see . . ." As their eyes met, they shared the same understanding. Caen was twenty miles north of Falaise. Her day of reckoning was coming sooner than she expected.

AFTER PERRIN HAD DEPARTED, Eleanor went back to bed. Propping a pillow behind her, she shut her eyes and tried to think calmly, objectively. She truly did not know what to expect. Her husband had been remarkably lenient with rebels in the past, for he never seemed to take it personally. Because he saw their rebellions in political terms, his detachment allowed him to forgive his adversaries in the interest of the greater good, a stable, peaceful kingdom. The clemency he'd accorded the Breton lords was not unusual for him; unlike most men, he could be dispassionate about treachery. The only time he'd shown himself to be vengeful or vindictive was the one time that he'd seen the betrayal as personal—with Thomas Becket. Eleanor had rarely been so cold; she could feel goose bumps rising on her skin, even after she'd burrowed under the blankets. Few betrayals could be more personal than that of a wife and a queen.

She did not think her life was in danger. It was true that one of Henry's more notorious ancestors, the brutal Fulk Nerra, had burned his wife at the stake for the crime of adultery. That had occurred almost two hundred years ago, though, and the unfortunate woman had not been a ruler in her own right. As Henry's wife, she was at his mercy. Errant or unwanted wives could be banished to nunneries, shut up in remote castles, meet untimely, convenient deaths, and few would protest. But the Duchess of Aquitaine could not just disappear. Her vassals, her lords and barons would demand answers. So would her sons.

Logic told her that the worst she had to fear was imprisonment, and judging by the conditions at Falaise, it would not be a harsh confinement. When Maurice de Craon had returned to Chinon and escorted her to Falaise, he was obviously acting under Henry's orders. If he'd wanted her cast into a dungeon, it would have been done already.

Logic also told her that she need not fear the violence that so many women must suffer in silence. Theirs was a world in which both Church and society sanctioned a husband's right to discipline his wayward wife. *A woman who is not under the headship of the husband violates the condition of nature, the mandate of the Apostle, and the law of Scripture.* The Archbishop of Rouen's bitter rebuke had been a blunt summary of a woman's subordinate role in the eyes of the Almighty. And she was wed to a king, a man known for his fiery temper. But in more than twenty years of marriage, he had never raised his hand to her.

She'd long ago concluded that she owed Henry's forbearance to his family history. His parents' marriage had been as turbulent as it was wretched. It had been doomed from the first, for Maude was twenty-five, the beautiful and imperious widow of the Holy Roman Emperor, and Geoffrey was fifteen, a spirited, spoiled youth used to getting his own way. She had not wanted the marriage, but her father had given her no choice. After being an empress, Maude felt it was demeaning to be a mere countess, and she was outraged to find herself yoked to a headstrong boy. Geoffrey was accustomed to females who were compliant and adoring, for he was wealthy, highborn, and so handsome that he was called Geoffrey le Bel. He was not prepared for a wife who was worldly, alluring, and disdainful, and he'd soon begun lashing out with his fists. When he decided that he'd had enough and sent her home to her father, she'd found no sympathy at the English court. The old English king cared nothing for her bruises and humiliation, blamed her for her marital woes, and persuaded Geoffrey to take her back. They'd eventually reached a tenuous truce, but Henry's earliest memories were of turmoil and discord, and those memories had left their mark.

So she should feel confident about facing him. Why, then, did she feel such unease? Because this was uncharted territory. When had a king ever been defied by his own queen? Who could predict what he would do? It was possible he did not even know that himself. Eleanor nestled deeper in the bed, vowing to stop torturing herself with conjecture and supposition that served for naught. She'd know soon enough. Despite her determination, though, she could not sleep.

Two days later, Perrin alerted her that a rider had been sent ahead to prepare for the king's arrival. The next day, though, he was absent from his duties. Another man brought her meals, and served her with a swagger, a jarring familiarity she'd not encountered before. After years of dealing with prideful Poitevin barons, she had no difficulty in putting him in his place, and he gave her no further cause for complaint. But when he delivered her dinner that afternoon, he watched her from the corner of his eye with a smug smile, and she knew then that her husband was expected at any time.

For the rest of the day she did nothing but pace and keep vigil at the window. Darkness fell, but she continued to watch, and not long after the village churches rang for Compline, she saw the flare of torches in the distance. She left the shutters open just enough to give her a view of the bailey without being seen herself, and watched as the castle was caught up in the inevitable chaos and excitement that heralded the king's coming. Henry was astride one of his favorite stallions, a big-boned grey with silver mane and tail. Riding at his side were William de Mandeville and his brother Hamelin. But Eleanor's attention was riveted upon the slender figure of a woman, clad in a fur-lined mantle of fine scarlet. She'd known that Harry had been living openly with Rosamund Clifford since he'd been told of her part in the rebellion, but it had not occurred to her that he'd flaunt his concubine at his Christmas Court. Stepping away from the window, she closed the shutters upon her husband and his harlot.

Eleanor bolted upright in the bed, her breath coming in ragged gulps, her pulse racing. The dream had been terrifying. She'd heard muffled screaming, and when she opened the window, she saw flames engulfing the buildings in the bailey. She'd pounded on the door and shouted till she was hoarse, but no one came to let her out. She'd been forgotten.

The dream still seemed so vivid, so real that she shuddered. But that was all it was, a bad dream. Memory came back in a rush, the long hours waiting for her husband, waiting in vain. She'd not settled herself in bed until after midnight, and she'd stayed fully dressed, but eventually she'd fallen asleep. Throwing back the blankets, she went to the window, was startled to see that the night was gone.

A loud rapping spun her toward the door, but almost at once she realized that Henry was not likely to knock for admittance. "Enter," she said, and felt a throb of disappointment at sight of the guard, for it was the same churl from the preceding day. Where was Perrin? He kept his gaze down as he placed her tray on the table, but he smirked when he saw that last night's meal had gone virtually untouched. Eleanor ignored him, and as he picked up the second tray, she reached for the wine cup, took several deep swallows. Her back was now to the door, and so she did not see Henry come into the room as the servant departed. When she finally turned and found him standing in the doorway, she gasped and her hand jerked, wine splashing onto the sleeve of her gown.

Henry closed the door and leaned back against it. "Your nerves are on the raw this morn."

So that was how he wanted to play it. Eleanor raised the cup in a mock salute. "I'd offer you some wine but the castellan has given me only one cup. He does not seem to think I'll be doing much entertaining."

He was still leaning against the door, his pose deceptively casual, for he seemed as taut to her as a drawn bowstring. "You are looking wan and careworn these days."

"So are you," she shot back, and it was true; his eyes were hollowed and blood shot. She'd assumed that he'd delayed their meeting to torment her, but now she wondered if he could have been as loath as she to have this confrontation. Setting the cup down, she said, "I am glad you are here. We need to talk."

"I daresay we do," he said laconically. But she noticed that he was clenching and unclenching one of his fists at his side, evidence that his nerves were on the raw, too.

"Sir Nicholas de Chauvigny and two of my knights are being held at Loches by your provost. I would hope that as a matter of fairness, you will order their release. They have done nothing to deserve such harsh treatment."

"Nothing at all, aside from treason and rebellion."

"They are loyal to me, Harry. How can you blame them for that?"

"And you know so much about loyalty." And without warning, the ice cracked, giving her a disquieting glimpse of the profound rage just beneath his surface composure. When he moved, it was so fast that she took an involuntary step backward.

"I'd always heard that women could become fickle and flighty once they're too old to breed, but I never truly believed it—until now."

Although she tried to hide it, she knew he could see that his words had wounded. They were the most dangerous of adversaries, intimate enemies who knew each other's vulnerabilities, knew how to draw the most blood. She said nothing, though, watching him warily as he strode toward her.

"Did you truly hate Rosamund as much as that? Enough to tear our family apart because I strayed?"

"You think this was because of Rosamund Clifford?" She shook her head incredulously and then startled him by laughing. "You are good in bed, Harry, but not that good!"

The expression on his face was one of disbelief. "What grievance could you possibly have other than Rosamund?"

"Aquitaine! Richard and Aquitaine!"

"For the love of Christ, Eleanor! I've heard enough of that foolish babbling from our sons, do not need to hear more of it now from you!"

"You may have heard, but you did not listen. You never do. Dear God, Harry, you think you're an easy man to live with? You suck all the air out of a chamber, leave none for the rest of us to breathe!"

He'd begun to move and she moved with him, holding her ground, so that they seemed to be engaged in an odd, deadly dance. "So you rebelled because I was not a good listener?" he jeered. "My sons are too young to know better, but there is no excuse for your betrayal. You were one of the very few people on God's Earth whom I truly trusted! Raimon St Gilles came to me at Limoges, warned that you were intriguing against me, and I would not believe him. I was furious that he dared to accuse you of such base treachery—more fool I!" He drew an uneven, audible breath. "But if I was a fool, what does that make you, my lady duchess? It makes you my prisoner, for as long as I choose to hold you. And all for what?"

"Yes, I have lost," she said, raising her chin and meeting his eyes without flinching. "But so have you. You just do not know it yet."

"Indeed? And who is going to defeat me? That quivering mound of valor, Louis Capet? Our disgruntled fledglings?"

"You may prevail on the field. You probably will. But it matters for naught. You can win battles, not the war. You've already lost what you value almost as much as your kingdom. You've lost your sons."

A muscle twitched in his cheek, and his lips peeled back from his teeth in a snarl. "That may be so, but you'll not be able to enjoy it. Whatever happens with my sons, you'll get no more chances to poison their minds against me. I will never forgive you," he spat, "never. You could beg for your freedom on your knees for all the good it will do you!"

"I'd rather die!"

"That could be arranged."

"Yes, I suppose it could. You need only return to the great hall, throw one of your celebrated fits of temper, and demand to know why your lords and barons let you be mocked and defied by your troublesome wife. Ah, wait . . . you did that already with Thomas Becket. And it did not work out so well for you, did it?"

It may have been a trick of the light, or his pupils may have dilated, but suddenly his eyes looked black to her, and she feared she'd pushed him too far. He grabbed her wrist in an iron grip, and she felt a jolt of purely physical fear. She'd known that she was subject to his power, but this was different, this chilling realization that she could not hope to match his strength, that he could do whatever he wanted with her in this chamber and she'd not be able to stop him.

He was forcing her toward the window, ignoring her struggles to break free. Holding her with one hand, with the other he jerked the shutters open. Pain was shooting up her arm. Their faces were so close now that they both could feel the other's hot breath on their skin. There had been this passion between them from their very first meeting. In the past it had always ended in bed, but she wondered now if it would end in the grave. Determined not to let him see her fear, she managed a taunting smile. "What are you going to do, Harry? Push me out the window?"

"Do not tempt me," he said through gritted teeth. Pulling her even closer, he said, "Look out at the sky. Look upon the sun, for as God is my witness, you'll not be seeing it again."

She was still trying to free herself, and when he suddenly released her, she reeled backward, would have fallen if she hadn't grabbed the table for support. By the time she'd regained her balance, he'd gone. Feeling as if her knees would no longer support her, she sank down upon her coffer. Her mouth was so dry that she could not swallow, but her hands were trembling too much to pour any wine. Jesus God, how had they ever gotten to this day?

HENRY PLUNGED INTO the stairwell so rapidly that he tripped and almost tumbled down the steps headfirst. Slumping against the wall, he sought to catch his breath, his chest heaving. His fabled temper was much more calculated than most people realized, one more weapon in a king's arsenal. But what had just happened in Eleanor's chamber was different. He'd come so close to losing control that it frightened him, for he'd always prided himself on being in command, scorning those men who could not master their own passions. A king at the mercy of his emotions did not deserve to be one.

He'd not been prepared for this, neither his own blind fury nor her defiance. Just as he'd expected his sons to accept his olive branch at Gisors, he'd expected Eleanor to seek his forgiveness, for what defense could she offer? His breathing had steadied, yet his sense of unreality remained. How had his life gone so dreadfully wrong? What sins had he committed that his own family would turn upon him like this? He slammed his fist suddenly into the wall above his head, again and again, stopping only when he saw a smear of blood on the stones. He felt no pain, but he brought his injured hand to his mouth, sucked the blood from his scraped knuckles. And then he straightened his shoulders, adjusted his mantle, and, raising his head high, emerged out into the pale winter sunlight of the bailey.

CHAPTER FIFTEEN

✦

May 1174
Poitiers, Poitou

*W*ARS WERE NOT usually fought during the winter months, but on January 1, Hal and the Counts of Blois, Perche, and Alençon struck deep into Normandy, launching a surprise assault upon the town of Sées. If Sées had been captured, Falaise would have been at risk and Henry's road south into Anjou would have been blocked. But the citizens of Sées fought back fiercely and repulsed the attack. Louis then negotiated a truce with Henry to last until the end of March and a similar truce was struck in England with the Scots king. Both sides set about preparing for the resumption of hostilities in the spring.

AFTER EASTER THE SCOTS KING crossed the border and laid waste to Northumberland. The Pope sent two legates to Paris, hoping that they could persuade the French king to reconcile Henry and his sons, but they had no luck. The Count of Flanders showed interest in rejoining the rebel alliance. And on April 30, Henry left Normandy for the city of his birth, Le Mans. From there he headed into Anjou and then into the lands of his captive queen. He met little opposition and on Whitsunday Eve, he was admitted without resistance into Eleanor's capital city of Poitiers.

TORCHES FLARED in the night, casting wavering shadows as the English king and his men dismounted in the bailey. Eleanor's steward hastened down the steps of the great hall to bid them welcome. "Sir Hervé," Henry said brusquely, cutting off the man's obsequious greeting. The steward had been secretly in his pay since the previous summer, one of several Poitevin lords who'd put self-interest before fidelity to their duchess, and while he made use of them all, Henry had no respect for a man whose loyalty was for sale to the highest bidder.

Not taking the hint, the steward continued to fawn and flatter, so unctuously that Henry was hard put to maintain even a semblance of civility. Seeing the royal temper beginning to kindle, the Earl of Essex intervened, declaring that the king was eager to see his daughter, and when Sir Hervé assured them that Joanna was waiting within the great hall, Henry pushed past the man and took the steps two at a time. The steward hurried after him, saying something about "a surprise guest," but Henry was no longer listening. His half sister Emma was standing in the doorway, with a smile so like his eldest son's that he felt a pang. And then he came to a startled halt, gazing over Emma's shoulder into the hall.

"Marguerite?" As he strode forward, the girl hastily made a deep, submissive curtsy, but he quickly raised her up. "What are you doing here, lass?"

"I . . . I came to take my sister and Constance back with me to Paris," she said, almost inaudibly.

Noting her pallor and the tears brimming behind her lashes, he smiled quizzically. "You do know that I am not going to cast you into a dungeon?"

"Yes," she whispered, "I know. But I also know that you will not let me go."

"No," he admitted, "I cannot do that—not until Hal and I have made our peace." She asked when that would be, but since he had no answer for her, he preferred to pretend he hadn't heard the question. His younger sons' future wives were standing nearby and he moved to greet them. Neither Alys nor Constance shared Marguerite's misery. The former knew that she had nothing to fear from him and the latter was indifferent to this sudden change in her circumstances, for she considered herself to be a hostage whether she dwelled in Eleanor's duchy or Henry's domains.

John's plight-trothed, little Alice of Maurienne, was sitting on the steps of the dais, clutching her favorite felt puppet. As she yawned, blinking sleepily up at him, Henry instructed her nurse to put her to bed, and then glanced around the hall. "Where is Joanna?"

Emma had followed him inside. "Over there," she said, "in the window-seat."

The hall was so deep in shadows that Henry had not noticed his daughter. Smiling, he started toward her, holding out his arms. But he stopped abruptly when Joanna drew back at his approach, staring at her in disbelief. "Surely you are not afraid of me, child?"

That stung her pride. "Afraid? No! But I am not happy with you, Papa."

Henry could only marvel at the damage wrought by the snake in his Eden. "What in God's Name did your mother tell you?"

"That you are angry with her, but it has naught to do with me. That you love me as she does. That I do not have to choose between you."

The words themselves were not objectionable. They were, in fact, so fair and impartial that Henry could find no fault with them, and that vexed him all the more. Joanna had always held a special place in his heart, for he'd imagined that she was much like Eleanor had been as a child. Now, as troubled as he was by her recalcitrance, he could not help admiring her spirit. Moving forward, he sat down beside her in the window-seat.

"Why are you 'not happy' with me, Joanna?"

Joanna gave him the look that children bestow upon adults who are being deliberately obtuse, "You are holding Maman as a prisoner!"

"Yes, I am. But she gave me no choice, lass. She plotted with my enemies against me. You do know that?"

"Yesss," she said, drawing the word out reluctantly. "But I heard . . . I was told that you are not treating her kindly."

"Yes, I daresay you were," he said grimly, raking the hall with accusing eyes. None of Eleanor's retainers met that ice-grey gaze, doing their best to become invisible, or at least inconspicuous. "They were lying to you, Joanna. Your mother is being treated as a highborn hostage, not a rebel. She is being held in a comfortable bedchamber, not a dungeon. You have my sworn word on that."

She stared down into her lap, twisting her fingers together. He saw that she'd begun biting her nails again, a habit he thought she'd outgrown. "Where is Maman?" she asked at last. This was a question being asked throughout most of Christendom, and he heard the murmur that swept the hall, knew that every ear was turned their way.

"I will tell you," he said, "but only you." And leaning over, he whispered in her ear.

Joanna looked intently into his face. "Maman has never liked it there," she said, but she was honored that he should entrust her with so great a secret. "May I see her?"

Not in this lifetime or the next, Henry vowed silently. But those sea-green eyes were watching him so hopefully that he could not bring himself to hurt her with the truth. "Yes," he said, "once the war is over," and that seemed to satisfy her, for when he put his arm around her shoulders, she did not pull away.

"What now, Papa? Do you want me to stay here?"

"No, lass, I do not," he said, thinking that he'd sooner see her thrust into a snake pit. "You and the other girls will be going to live in Rouen for now. I was thinking of having Johnny leave Fontevrault and join you there. Would you like that?" Sweeping up the fragments of his broken family, he thought bitterly, but Joanna looked pleased.

"I would like that very much," she said. "I've missed Johnny." She missed her other brothers, too, though she knew better than to confide that to him. She wasn't sure if she should forgive him for imprisoning her mother, but it was comforting to have him holding her like this, comforting to remember that she was not utterly alone. "Papa . . ." She ducked her head, leaning into his embrace. "Papa . . . I do not understand why this is happening."

Henry's jaw muscles tightened. "Neither do I, lass," he said softly. "Neither do I."

RICHARD STRODE INTO the nave of St Pierre's Cathedral and beckoned to Sir Martin de Jarnac, one of his household knights. Martin hurried over, rather nervously, for he knew Richard had been meeting earlier in the day with the Bishop of Saintes and the bishop was increasingly unhappy with Richard's occupation of his city. "My lord? How did it go?"

Richard shrugged. "The bishop had more complaints than a dog has fleas. He was particularly wroth that we've appropriated the cathedral for our own purposes." Their constant carping was taking some of the bloom off his pleasure in gaining control of the town.

His first command had not begun auspiciously, for La Rochelle had closed its gates at his approach, refusing to allow him entry into the town, boldly declaring that they were loyal to the old king, not the young one. Richard had been mortified, vowing that those overweening, impudent churls would pay for that and pay dearly, but he could do nothing at the time except retreat, his ears burning with the echoes of their scornful laughter. His only consolation was that his brother Hal's assault upon Sées had failed, too.

Fortunately, a fierce rivalry existed between La Rochelle and Saintes, and if the former turned Richard away, the latter was then keen to make him welcome. But the citizens of Saintes were soon having second thoughts about their hospitality. Richard's men had lost no time in fortifying the town, throwing up a wooden castle to guard the Roman bridge and using the cathedral for their headquarters. As troubling as these developments were, even worse was to come. Word had reached Saintes that the English king was now encamped at Poitiers, only seventy miles to the north.

Richard was not as alarmed as the citizens by his father's arrival, for he had confidence in the city walls, his new fortifications, and his own military instincts. More-over, he meant to make good use of the time remaining to him. While Henry cele-brated Whitsuntide in Poitiers, he'd dispatched riders to Geoffrey de Rançon, William de Maingot, and the Count of Angoulême, urging them to join him at Saintes without delay. They had a chance to force a decisive battle, to win a victory that would end the war and free his mother, and he meant to make the most of the opportunity.

"This morning I slipped out of the town and visited the ruins of the Roman am-phitheater," he confided to Martin. "It was an amazing sight, so much of it still intact after all that time."

Martin was vaguely aware that Saintes had once been an important Roman town, for he'd seen the huge Arch of Germanicus at the bridge, supposedly built to honor a long-dead emperor. While he didn't share Richard's interest in the past, he was a firm believer in humoring the highborn, and he asked politely what this amphitheater was used for.

Richard was surprised by his ignorance. "That was where the Romans staged their games, where their gladiators fought and felons died. My lady mother would tell me the most wondrous stories about ancient Rome. When gladiators entered the arena, they faced the audience and proudly proclaimed, '*Morituri te salutamus!*'"

Martin had never learned Latin and looked so blank that Richard translated, "'We who are about to die salute you.' Did you not study history when you—" He got no further, having noticed the archdeacon hovering nearby, waiting for a word with him. Richard sighed, for he already knew what the cleric wanted to discuss. Saintes was on the route to the great Spanish shrine of Santiago de Compostela, and its citizens were worrying that pilgrims might stay away, fearing they'd be trapped in a siege. As much as he yearned to duck out a side door into the cloisters, Richard felt it was his duty to offer reassurances and, forcing a smile, he started toward the archdeacon just as all hell broke loose.

At least it seemed that way to Richard. Heads were turning toward the sudden clamor coming from outside the cathedral. Richard spun around and ran for the door, with his men at his heels. As he emerged into the dusk, he found a scene of utter chaos. People were running in different directions, cursing as they bumped into one another, putting him in mind of an overturned ant hill. He'd seen panic like this only once be-fore, when a fire broke out in Rouen, and when he saw smoke billowing from the di-rection of the river, it confirmed his worst fears.

"Stop, you fools!" he yelled. "We need to get buckets and fight the fire!" None of the frightened citizens paid him any heed. He was shouting orders at his own men, di-recting them to find buckets and ropes and hooks so they could pull down endangered buildings if need be, when he heard his own name being called, rising above the din like the solitary cry of a seagull. The sight of Raoul was a welcome one, and he hastily started toward his kinsman, roughly shouldering his way through the crowds thronging the street.

"We're under attack! We have to get out whilst we still can!"

Richard gaped at the older man. "What are you talking about? There is a fire—"

"Yes, and your father set it! He's come calling with an army, Richard, and I do not want him to find us home!"

"That is not possible! How could he get here so fast?" No sooner were the words out of his mouth than Richard regretted them. His enemies had been asking that question of his father for as long as he could remember, and in any case, it was irrelevant. "We can keep him out," he insisted, "hold on until we get men from Taillebourg and—"

"No," Raoul said sharply, "we cannot. His men have already taken the castle we put up by the bridge and are breaking down the city gates even as we speak. Our only chance is to get out now—"

"No!" Richard was indignant. "I'll not run away—never!"

"Whilst we waste time arguing, Harry's men will be swarming into the city! The whoreson caught us by surprise, Richard, and it is too late to do anything but retreat." When Richard continued to shake his head stubbornly, Raoul swore under his breath. "Do you miss your mother so much that you want to join her at Chinon or Falaise?"

That got through to Richard, that and the changing timbre of the shouting. It was louder now, more urgent, and closer, coming from the city gates. Shaking off his shock, he said, with a composure that Raoul applauded, "Where do we go?"

"We can get out through a postern gate, then head downriver to Taillebourg. Harry was concerned about speed, not a long siege, and did not bring mangonels with him. We ought to be safe enough with de Rançon—if we can reach him."

This was the first time that Richard had been personally confronted with the unpleasant realities of war—that it was not all glory and blaring trumpets and swirling banners. It was not a lesson he'd ever wanted to learn. Looking around for as many of his men as he could find, he said tersely, "Let's go."

RICHARD MANAGED TO ESCAPE from Saintes as his father was sweeping into the town. The rebels retreated into the cathedral, held out for a day, and then surrendered. Henry captured more than sixty knights and over four hundred archers, plus all their supplies, weapons, and horses. The cathedral of Saintes and many of the nearby houses were badly damaged, the acrid odor of smoke lingering over the town long after the fighting was done.

HENRY SPENT THE REMAINDER of the spring chasing rebels and fortifying his border strongholds. The news from England continued to be bad, as one after another of his castles fell to the ravaging Scots army. After taking and turning over
the castle of Ancenis to Maurice de Craon, Henry summoned his lords and bishops to
a great council in Normandy on the Nativity of St John the Baptist.

HENRY REACHED BONNEVILLE, the site of the council, on the evening
of June 23. The castle was neither comfortable nor spacious, having been constructed
in the eleventh century, and many of his barons had been compelled to seek lodgings
in the nearby port of Toques. Henry was indifferent, as usual, to his surroundings, and
was soon settled in his bedchamber. He was tired, for he'd been in the saddle since
dawn, but these days his thoughts raced and ricocheted around his brain so wildly that
sleep was becoming a luxury, one even a king could rarely afford.

"Stay for a while," he said, and Willem smiled, took a seat on a nearby coffer as
Henry dismissed his squires. The earl made easy conversation for a time, soon saw that
Henry was not really listening, and fell silent, waiting. Henry walked back and forth,
too edgy to sit still. He was already regretting asking Willem to remain, and he was
about to tell the other man that he could go off to bed when one of his squires hurried
back into the chamber.

"My liege, men have just ridden into the bailey, are seeking an audience with you
straightaway. I told the steward that they should wait till the morrow, but when he told
me who they were, I thought you'd want to see them. It is the Bishop-elect of Winchester and your uncle, the Lord Ranulf."

Henry nodded. Richard of Ilchester was one of his most trusted officials. As
Archdeacon of Poitiers, he'd supported Henry unwaveringly in the clash with Thomas
Becket, even enduring excommunication at the archbishop's hands. His reward for
such loyal service was the bishopric of Winchester. And Ranulf was known to be very
close to the king, bound as much by affection as by blood. Their presence here in Bonneville conveyed a message in and of itself, and it was not an encouraging one.

The two men were soon ushered into his chamber. They both looked exhausted,
and as soon as greetings were exchanged, Henry told them to find seats, ordering his
squire to fetch some wine. They waited until it had been served and they were alone
again with Henry and Willem before revealing the urgency of their mission.

"My liege, we have been sent to entreat you to return to England as soon as possible." The bishop sagged back in his chair, never taking his eyes from Henry's face. "If you do not, you are in danger of losing your kingdom."

Henry said nothing, his gaze flicking from the bishop to Ranulf, who took that as his cue to speak up. "My lord king, the bishop speaks true. We have not been able to keep the Scots from ravaging the border lands, and they've been raiding into England. They have taken castles at Appleby, Leddell, and Harbottle, and Robert de Vaux has been so hard pressed that he was forced to seek a truce, agreeing to surrender Carlisle if you cannot relieve him by Michaelmas. The Scots king then sacked Warkworth and slaughtered many of the townspeople."

The bishop leaned forward, his fists clenching on his knees. "We have naught but dire news, my lord. The rebellion has flared up again in the Midlands. They attacked and burned Nottingham and the garrison at Leicester is still holding out, refusing to surrender. And bandits and masterless men are taking advantage of the unrest to commit crimes of their own. The king's roads are no longer safe; it is as if we are back in the dreadful days when Stephen ruled. There was rioting in London, my liege—in London!"

Henry's continuing silence was beginning to unnerve them, for they were accustomed to his taking command of a crisis, taking decisive action. Just when the stillness in the chamber was becoming intolerable, Henry turned and looked at the bishop as if he were seeing him for the first time. "You are half dead on your feet, Richard. Go to bed. You, too, Uncle."

The bishop did, but Ranulf stayed, sensing that Henry's need for comfort was greater than his own need for sleep. When he looked over at Willem, the earl raised his shoulders in a silent shrug, for he, too, was at a loss. They watched Henry in silence, neither one knowing what to say, and both started when he suddenly spoke out.

"Ranulf? Did you know that the Count of Flanders has sworn upon a fragment of the True Cross that he will invade England within a fortnight from tomorrow?"

"Yes," Ranulf said, "I know." He knew, too, that Count Philip had already dispatched an advance guard of three hundred knights, but he could not bring himself to say anything about it, not sure if Henry had heard, and not wanting to give him any more grief.

Henry was staring down at the ashes in the cold, empty hearth. "My French spies tell me that Louis and Philip and their lackeys hope to lure me to England so they can attack Normandy once I am gone."

"That may well be true, Harry," Ranulf said carefully. "But England is already in flames. Can you stand by whilst it burns?"

"I truly thought I'd won this accursed war last year with those victories at Dol and

Fornham St Genevieve. But this rebellion is like a snake, shedding one skin only to grow another. Does it ever end?"

"You will prevail, Harry," Willem declared. "I have no doubts whatsoever. I know Philip of Flanders well, and he is no match for you on the battlefield. As for that fool on the French throne, he is no more a leader than that beggar we passed on the road this noon. Men would not follow him out of a burning building. And your sons . . ." Here he paused, his voice trailing off, and Henry gave him a ghostly grimace of a smile.

"Ah, yes," he said, "my sons, my loyal, loving sons."

Ranulf sat up straight, remembering that he did have news that might give Henry comfort. "I can think of no better words to describe Geoff. Have you heard what he did, Harry? He called out the men of Lincoln as their bishop-elect and lay siege to Roger de Mowbray's castle at Kinnardferry. He captured Roger's son and razed the castle to the ground. He then joined forces with the Archbishop of York and took de Mowbray's castle at Kirkby Malzeard."

"Did he, by God?" This time Henry's smile was more convincing. "He is a good lad, is Geoff." He'd picked up his wine cup, but now set it down, untouched. "I thought I told you to go to bed, Uncle. You, too, Willem. I need you both alert and awake for the council on the morrow."

Willem did as he was bid, but Ranulf still hesitated. "I am not tired," he lied, "if you want to talk . . ."

"No," Henry said, "I am going to bed myself."

"Shall I summon your squires?"

"No . . . not yet. I want to be alone for a while."

Ranulf looked searchingly into the younger man's face. Priests often spoke of life as a "vale of tears," warning that "all is vanity and vexation of spirit," reminding their flocks that "man that is born of woman is of few days, and full of trouble." Yet he doubted that most Christians, sinners though they be, ever reached that dark, desolate place where hope withered on the vine and the voice of the Almighty was silent. But he had—he'd lost the woman he'd loved, a friend closer than a brother, and all sense of purpose. Stricken by grief and guilt, he'd wandered alone in the wilderness, caring for naught until he rediscovered divine mercy and his faith in a Welsh mountain valley. He had never forgotten, though, the pain of feeling forsaken by God, pain he saw reflected now in his nephew's eyes.

"God's Blessings upon you," he said, but no more than that, for he knew Harry's anguish was beyond his power to heal. He could only pray that the Almighty and Jesus, the Only Begotten Son, would take pity upon Harry, show him the path to salvation in his time of greatest need.

CHAPTER SIXTEEN

July 1174
Falaise, Normandy

*E*LEANOR HAD NOT FULLY appreciated what a charmed life she led until it was taken away from her. From birth, she'd had the best that their world had to offer, never thinking to question her good fortune. She'd chaffed under the constraints imposed upon women by society and the Church, but she'd not wondered why she'd been so blessed. People were expected to accept their lot in life as God's Will, which was easy to do for a woman born beautiful and a duke's daughter.

In the months since her betrayal in Loches Forest, though, the reality she'd known had vanished, leaving her a stranger in an alien land. The most mundane tasks were now a challenge. For the first time, she faced the normal vexations and disappointments of daily life. She'd only brought a few gowns with her, and she'd lost so much weight that they no longer fit all that well; moreover, they would eventually become threadbare and worn if she could not replace them. Accustomed to having servants who heated her baths, she now had to make do with a basin and cold water. Washing her long hair was a test of endurance. In the past, she had only to express a wish for a delicacy, however exotic, and it would appear upon her table as if by magic. Now the monotony of her meals had robbed her of her appetite, and she found herself craving oranges from Spain and wine from Gascony and spices from Cyprus and Sicily.

But her physical privations were tolerable. It was her emotional hardships that were scarring her soul. Theirs was a world in which only hermits and recluses scorned the company of others; until her captivity, she'd never slept alone in a chamber before. Her concept of privacy went no further than being snugly cocooned behind bed-hangings with her husband. Now there were days when she did not hear the sound of another human voice. She was not a woman to thrive in solitude, and the loneliness of her confinement was hard to bear.

So was the boredom. When she remembered how glibly she'd complained of the tedium of her life at the French court, she winced for the young, spoiled girl she'd once been. With nothing to occupy herself but her own thoughts, she was unable to escape the misery of her plight, reliving that harrowing confrontation with Henry and seething at her abandonment by her craven allies. At least anger provided its own en-ergy. Far more frightening was what followed—the loss of hope as she reached two unwelcome milestones. June marked her sixth month as a prisoner. And in June, she'd observed her fiftieth birthday. As a child, that had seemed such a vast age to her. Now she saw it as a death sentence, for how likely was it that she'd outlive the husband who was nine years younger than she?

You'll never see the sun again, he'd warned, and she had no reason to doubt him. In her time of greatest need, her deliverance depended upon a spiteful former hus-band and her callow young sons. How had she ever let it come to this? That was a question she could not face, and to avoid it, she'd turned to the Almighty for support and solace. Her religious faith had been the conventional kind, practiced but not pon-dered. She'd dutifully attended Mass, distributed alms, made generous donations to abbeys like Fontevrault, and felt that she'd kept up her end of the bargain. She'd rarely prayed for specific boons, except during those unhappy years when she'd been unable to give Louis a son, scorned by her critics as a barren queen, and those prayers had gone unanswered.

At Falaise, she'd asked the Almighty to let her sons win this war, knowing that nothing less would gain her release. But as summer bloomed and her hopes withered, she'd begun to offer up a more desperate prayer, beseeching God to end her confinement any way He chose, for she'd also begun to fear that in such utter despair lay madness.

JULY DAWNED WITH STORMS AND HIGH WINDS. Eleanor closed the shutters against the rain and spent much of her time trying to sleep, the only means of escape available to her. And so she was in bed on a wet, dreary afternoon when she heard footsteps out in the stairwell. It was pride rather than curiosity that induced her to sit up and straighten her clothing, for she did not expect this to be a visitor she wanted to see. It had been more than a fortnight since Perrin had waited upon her. A fellow guard had complained that he was unduly friendly with the royal prisoner, and duties had been found for him elsewhere. Losing her only link to the outside world was the final straw, and soon afterward she'd spiraled down into a deep depression.

She'd gotten to her feet by the time a brusque knock sounded and the door was pushed open to admit Maurice de Craon. She greeted him coolly, hoping she'd managed to conceal her unease; she very much doubted that his arrival heralded good news.

"Madame," he said formally. "As a courtesy, I am informing you that you should make ready to depart on the morrow. We will be leaving at first light."

Eleanor abandoned her attempt at studied indifference. "Where," she said sharply, "will we be going?"

The Angevin baron regarded her in silence for a long moment, his dark eyes alight with grim satisfaction. "Barfleur," he said, "where *you* will be taking ship for England."

E LEANOR WAS SURPRISED to find that she'd have company on her journey to Barfleur: her fellow prisoners, the Earl and Countess of Leicester and Hugh of Chester. They were just as startled to see her, apparently unaware that she was sharing their confinement, and she spared a grateful thought for her chatty young source, Perrin. Of the three, imprisonment seemed to have left the lightest mark upon Peronelle, which made sense, for she'd known that as a woman, she'd have the best chance of regaining her freedom. Her husband appeared to have aged, to have lost some of his bluster. But the one most affected by captivity was the Earl of Chester. Hugh was thin and pallid. Always high-strung, he looked almost haunted now, and Eleanor glanced away, hearing Maud's accusing words echoing on the wind: *It is not enough you've poisoned your own well. No, you must poison mine, too!*

It took nearly three days to reach Barfleur, for the downpour continued and the roads were deep in mud. Barfleur was the primary port for Channel crossings and the largest town on that rock-hewn peninsula. But the royal castle was a few miles to the south, and it was there that Eleanor expected to pass her last night on French soil. She was to get a shock, though, as the castle walls came into sight, for a familiar red and gold banner flew from the keep—signaling that the King of England was in residence.

Eleanor's tired body tensed; it had never occurred to her that she'd be sailing back to England with Henry. The other prisoners had seen the royal standard, too, much to their dismay. They exchanged nervous looks as they were escorted into the bailey, for they were no more eager than Eleanor to confront the king. Despite the chill dampness of the dusk, sweat mingled with rain drops upon the Earl of Leicester's ruddy face as he remembered his last meeting with Henry, remembered with appalling clarity that he'd drawn his sword upon his sovereign. The nasty weather notwithstanding, the bailey was crowded with spectators, nudging and jostling one another as they sought to get a good look at the new arrivals.

Eleanor knew she was the true attraction. They were there to gape at the captive queen. Well, if they wanted a show, by God she'd given them one. "My lord de Craon," she said imperiously, waving aside a groom and waiting for the baron himself to assist her in dismounting. He did, with poor grace, scowling as she took time to adjust the hood of her mantle and straighten the cuffs of her gloves. He gestured toward a corner tower, but just then the door to the great hall burst open and Joanna came flying out. Heedless of the rain and mud, she splashed across the bailey to fling herself into Eleanor's arms.

Eleanor's hood fell back, and she was soon as wet as her daughter, but she did not care, and they clung together in a wordless embrace that ended only when she glanced up and saw her husband standing in the doorway of the hall. Hugh and Leicester at once dropped submissively to their knees, but Henry never took his eyes from his wife, and she shivered, for if looks were lethal, she'd have died then and there in the bailey of Barfleur Castle.

E LEANOR WAS ESCORTED to a small bedchamber on the upper story of the keep. Her reunion with Joanna had been a brief one, cut short when Henry sent someone out to retrieve the girl, using the bad weather as a pretext. Eleanor had assured her daughter that they'd meet again, although she did not know if that were true or not. It seemed the ultimate irony to her that she could lose her children twice in one lifetime, and while she damned both Louis and Henry, she cursed, too, a society in which fathers were given so much power and mothers so little.

After realizing that she'd not heard a key turning in the lock, she dared to open the door, only to discover an armed guard. He saluted her politely, as if he were posted there for her protection, and she puzzled him by laughing shrilly. She forced herself to eat some of the meal brought by a silent servant, but she kept listening for the sounds of footsteps in the stairwell. When she finally heard a murmur of voices, she watched the door open, with mingled hope and dread, not knowing if it would be her daughter or her enraged husband.

"It's me, Maman!" Joanna's pronouncement was superfluous, her smile joyful. Eleanor had just gathered the girl into her arms when she added happily, "I brought you another visitor!" And to Eleanor's amazement, her daughter-in-law stepped, smiling, into the room.

THAT WAS THE BEST evening Eleanor had known in months. The girls were as delighted to see her as she was to see them, eager to share their news, to tell her of the fall of Poitiers and Marguerite's ill-fated visit, the capture of Saintes, and the return of the Count of Flanders to the rebel coalition. They'd been living in Rouen, they explained, until they were urgently summoned to Barfleur by Henry, and they would all be going with him to England as soon as the weather cleared. And as she listened, Eleanor felt hope beginning to spark midst the ashes of a dead fire. This sudden change of plans could only mean that the war was going badly for Henry in England.

JOANNA AND MARGUERITE had kept their visit short, understanding that they'd lose the privilege if they abused it, promising to return upon the morrow. Joanna had seemed surprised when asked how they'd managed to get permission, saying airily that "I asked Papa," as if his consent had never been in doubt. Eleanor knew better, and grudgingly gave Henry credit where due; he could easily have kept Joanna away, just as Louis had done with their daughters. But once he'd agreed, it would not be that easy to change his mind, which meant that she'd be able to see Joanna and Marguerite again. There would be opportunities, for it was not uncommon to wait days, even weeks, for a favorable wind.

They'd been stranded in Barfleur for almost a month as they'd waited to cross the Channel for Henry's coronation, finally sailing in heavy seas when his patience ran out. That was not a memory to give Eleanor comfort; it was painful to remember the jubilant woman she'd been on that November eve twenty years ago, willing to depart in a gale because she was so sure that God was on their side, so confident that she and Henry were masters of their own fate, destined to rule over the greatest court in Christendom and not to drown like those poor doomed souls on the White Ship.

The next day was even more rain-sodden and windy, and Eleanor's faith was rewarded in mid-afternoon when Joanna and Marguerite were ushered into her chamber. Joanna brought wilted flowers from the castle gardens and Marguerite, with surprising practicality, had herb packets: agrimony for fever, pennyroyal for cramps, and chamomile for headaches. Adding shyly that chamomile was also said to be useful for melancholy. She had apologies to offer, too. Alys had wanted to come, she explained, but she had lost her nerve at the last moment.

"She said she did not know what to say to you. I told her that did not matter, but she still balked, saying she'd come next time."

"You cannot blame the lass," Eleanor said dryly. "Her lessons in manners never included one on captive queens." Glancing over at Joanna, she said, "What of John? Did your father forbid him to come?"

Joanna looked uncomfortable. "No . . . Johnny would not come with us. He said Papa would not be happy with him if he visited you."

Eleanor looked away, saying nothing. She had no qualms about her older sons, feeling that they'd been old enough to make up their own minds. Her conscience was not so clear when it came to her youngest two. She'd hoped that she'd be able to keep John and Joanna out of the fray, and it was only after her capture that she'd admitted what a frail reed that hope was. She was sorry that John had felt the need to choose between them, but it stung that he'd chosen his father, for Henry had spent even less time with the boy than she had.

Joanna picked up a wafer uneaten from Eleanor's dinner, and when Eleanor nodded, she crammed half of it into her mouth. "I have a surprise for you, Maman," she announced. "I am going to fetch it now, will be back soon." And before Eleanor could object, she'd darted out the door.

Past experience had taught Eleanor that Joanna's "surprises" ought to be approached with caution. But she welcomed this opportunity to speak alone with Marguerite. Neither of them felt comfortable speaking too candidly in front of Joanna, whose loyalties were already bruised and bleeding. As soon as the door closed, Eleanor leaned forward and touched her daughter-in-law's hand in a gesture of encouragement. "How did you and Joanna win Harry over? I truly would not have expected him to let Joanna see me."

"I could see that he was not happy about it," Marguerite confided. "Once he decided he must return to England, he dared not leave any of us behind. I suppose he hoped that Joanna would not find out you were sailing with us, that she'd hear no one gossiping about your presence at Barfleur. Of course someone told her," she said, sounding so slyly satisfied that Eleanor realized she'd been that "someone," and she gave her daughter-in-law a look of startled approval; until now she'd seen only the sweet side of Marguerite's nature, had not known the girl had spirit, too.

"Once she was alerted, she kept vigil for you," Marguerite continued. "And when she looked up at her father with pleading eyes and quivering lips, he could not bring himself to deny him. But . . . but he agreed only for Joanna's sake."

"And not mine," Eleanor said flatly, bitter that Henry could declare forfeit all her rights as a mother. "What of you, lass? Has Harry been kind to you?"

"Oh, yes," Marguerite said without hesitation. "He was not long in Poitiers, though, as he sent us on to Rouen whilst he chased Richard out of Saintes. We did not see him again until he summoned us to Barfleur in such haste."

"The threat to England must be dire if he thinks he needs to take command himself. I would love to know what happened to force his hand."

"I think I do know," Marguerite said surprisingly. "Hal and the Count of Flanders are at Gravelines, waiting for favorable weather so they can invade England."

Eleanor felt a surge of excitement, for she had far more confidence in Philip of Flanders's military skills than she did in Louis's. If they could gain a decisive victory, her chances of being freed would improve dramatically. She well knew Louis and Philip would not bestir themselves much on her behalf, but Richard and Hal would never abandon her, and an English triumph would give them the leverage they needed. "There is a question I would ask you ere Joanna returns. Does Rosamund Clifford sail with us?"

Marguerite was flattered that her mother-in-law would speak to her like this, woman to woman. "No," she said emphatically, "I think not. He has been very open about their liaison since last summer, so I do not think he'd have her hidden away here." Shaking her head indignantly, she said, "I think it is shameful that men cannot be faithful to their wives. But if they must sin, they ought to have the decency to do it in secret."

Eleanor was taken aback, for she'd not realized that Marguerite thought she'd rebelled because of Rosamund Clifford. She wondered suddenly if her sons were equally ill-informed. She felt confident that Richard knew better, for he understood her love for Aquitaine if anyone did. But what of Hal and Geoffrey? "Marguerite, why does Hal think I joined the rebellion?"

"He knows you did it for him, for his kingship. He has often said how lucky he is to have a mother who would sacrifice so much for his sake." Marguerite did not doubt, though, that Eleanor's jealousy of Henry's leman had played a part, too, and she searched now for words of comfort, saying haltingly, "I've spoken to people who've seen the Clifford wench, and they say she is not even that pretty. For certes, not as beautiful as you, my lady mother."

Eleanor was both touched and vexed by the girl's attempt to offer balm to a grieving wife. She opened her mouth to assure Marguerite that it was only her pride that had been wounded, not her heart. But it was then that the door opened and Joanna rushed in again.

Her cheeks were bright with wind-whipped color, her mantle splattered with mud. She was clutching a woven basket to her chest, looking so pleased with herself that Eleanor suspected she'd been up to mischief of some sort. "I have a present for you, Maman," she said, and carried the basket across the chamber to deposit it beside Eleanor on the bed. It was covered with a white cloth that looked like a napkin, and Eleanor reached out, expecting fruit or cheese. To her surprise, she found herself looking at a tiny kitten.

"One of the stable cats had a litter, but then she disappeared." Joanna leaned over, tickling the kitten under its chin. "This is the only one who survived. I heard a groom saying he was going to drown her because she was too young to fend for herself and would likely starve. So I had a wonderful idea—to give you the kitten, Maman."

Eleanor looked dubiously at the kitten, which fit easily into the palm of her hand. It was a pretty little creature, dove-grey with gold eyes, but she'd never had a cat as a pet before. "I do not know, Joanna," she said. "I doubt your father will agree."

Joanna smiled. "He will," she predicted confidently. "You'll see."

H ENRY HAD JUST RETURNED from a trip to the harbor, where he'd had another frustrating talk with the ship's captain, who dolefully concluded that the weather was still too foul to risk sailing. Henry knew the man was right, but his nerves were shredding under the strain. Common sense told him that if he could not sail, neither could Hal or Philip. But he was heeding other voices than logic these days.

A fire had been lit in the hearth, for the relentless rain was making a mockery of the summer calendar. After he'd changed into a dry tunic and chausses, Henry tried to distract himself by playing a game of chess with Willem, but he soon abandoned the effort, unable to keep his thoughts away from the darker corners of his mind. Willem and Ranulf were watching him pace back and forth in sympathetic silence when one of his squires hastened over to answer a knock on the door. He at once opened it wide, for only two people had unrestricted access to the king at Barfleur: his son and daughter.

Joanna was clad in a silk dress that seemed inappropriate for everyday use, and her hair was neatly brushed for once, hanging down her back in two reddish-blond braids. She looked very appealing, but very solemn, and after greeting the men politely, she asked Henry if she could speak with him about a "serious matter."

"Of course, lass," he said, guiding her toward the settle. "What do you want to buy now? Did you find another carved horse or spinning top in the marketplace?"

"This is more important than playthings, Papa. Did you know that Maman does not have a lady to attend to her? At first I thought she'd been left behind at Falaise. But then I learned that she'd not had a handmaiden at all!"

Sounding shocked, Joanna looked earnestly into her father's face. "We have to do something about this, Papa. Men do not understand how much a lady needs help with dressing. Long hair like Maman's is not easy to brush or wash or braid. It is hard, too, to lace up a gown in the back. I was going to ask you if I could go to stay with Maman once we get to England so I could be of help."

Henry stiffened, but Joanna did not seem to notice and continued on guilelessly. "But after I thought about it, I knew you'd not want me to do that, not whilst you and Maman are still quarreling. So we need to get Maman a handmaiden, Papa. Will you see to it? I know you are too busy now, but mayhap later, when you have more time?"

She was regarding Henry so trustingly that he felt a rush of emotion, love for this innocent child of his flesh warring with his need to punish her treacherous mother. "Yes, Joanna," he said at last. "I will see that it is done."

"Thank you, Papa, thank you!" She threw herself into his arms, hugging him gratefully. "I will not worry about Maman so much if she is not alone."

As she embraced her father, her face was not visible to him. But it was to Willem, and he caught her triumphant grin. Why, the little vixen, he thought, and when their eyes met, he gave her a mock scowl that caused her to look at him in dismay. He winked, then, and Joanna relaxed, giggled, and winked back.

"I will not keep you, Papa," she said dutifully. "I know you have much to do these days. May I tell Johnny that you will be in to bid him good night?" When he nodded, she smiled and slid off his lap, heading for the door. There she paused, as if having an afterthought. "I almost forgot to tell you about the kitten, Papa. She was going to be drowned by one of the stable grooms, but I stopped him. I know cats are not often kept as pets, but I did not want the kitten to die. So I gave her to Maman." And with a farewell wave, she slipped out the door.

Henry glanced up to find both Ranulf and Willem watching him, and raised a hand in warning. "Do not say a word, either of you. I know very well that we have just performed a puppet show, with me playing the role of puppet."

"And a fine puppet show it was, too," Ranulf said, with as much cheer as he could muster. "If the Almighty had meant us to be able to resist the coaxing of our daughters, He'd not have made them so irresistible . . . now would He?"

Willem laughed and Henry smiled. But it seemed to Ranulf that he could see a glimmer of tears behind his nephew's lashes, and he felt a sorrowful rage that Harry was being hurt so badly by his heedless, selfish sons and his false, coldhearted queen.

ELEANOR WAS HAVING the most restful nights she'd had in months, lulled to sleep by the reassuring rhythms of the storm, each blast of wind and torrent of rain giving promise of yet another day with her daughter. She was not prepared, therefore, when she was awakened at dawn on the Monday after her arrival by an apologetic guard, who told her that she must make ready to depart as the king was sailing that morn.

E LEANOR COULD SEE NOTHING but chaos. The bailey was crowded with men and horses. Servants were dragging large coffers toward the carts, routiers carrying food from the great hall to eat on the run, dogs barking madly and getting underfoot. Whips cracked the air as horses struggled to move carts mired in mud. A stallion reared suddenly, unseating his rider and nearly trampling those who tried to grab the dangling reins. Men were cursing and shoving, shouting commands that went unheeded. A priest was berating a castle page, while a woman shrieked as her mule shied away when she was being assisted into the saddle. The Earls of Leicester and Chester were being prodded toward their waiting mounts, while Peronelle lagged behind, complaining loudly to anyone within earshot. Trying to shelter herself from the rain with the hood of her mantle, Eleanor halted on the steps of the great hall, looking about frantically. But she could not find Joanna, John, or Marguerite. Nor was there any sign of Henry.

When her guard nervously urged her on, she turned on him in fury. "I told you I am not going anywhere until I speak with the king. See to it, damn you, see to it!"

"Madame, I . . . I cannot do that!" he stammered. "Our orders were to escort you to the harbor!" Much to his relief, then, he spotted Barfleur's castellan and let out a yell, pushing his way toward the man. Momentarily abandoned, Eleanor resumed her search for Henry or her children, to no avail. And when her guard returned with the castellan, that harried individual refused to listen to her protests.

"You may want to see the king, Madame," he snapped, "but I very much doubt that he wants to see you!" Ordering the guard to follow his orders, he moved on. The guard and Eleanor looked at each other in mutual frustration. Clearing his throat, he was imploring her not to get him into trouble when she finally caught sight of a familiar figure.

"Tell Lord Ranulf I want to speak with him," she directed the unhappy guard. "Now, man, now!" As she watched tensely, he did as she bade, hurrying over to intercept Ranulf. Henry's uncle had an easily read face, his dismay and reluctance all too evident. She'd expected as much; if Henry's officials found it awkward to deal with her, how much more uncomfortable it must be for his kinsmen. But she was relying upon Ranulf's innate good manners, and she was not disappointed. Holding his mantle tightly against the gusting wind, he strode toward her, the guard following closely on his heels.

"Ranulf, thank God you're here! You can get through to Harry if any man can. You must convince him that it is too dangerous to sail in this storm."

"I cannot do that."

She stared at him in disbelief. "You want to die? I cannot believe you've forgotten the fate of the White Ship!"

"Of course I have not forgotten," he said testily. "But I have already talked to Harry and I could not get him to change his mind. The winds have shifted, are coming now from the west, and he is determined to sail ere they shift again."

"This is madness," she said, "utter madness. Let Harry go to the Devil and drown for all I care! But I'll not have him risk my children's lives!"

"I doubt that you are in a position to do anything about it," he said, so coldly that she was suddenly reminded that he was a king's son, and the blood of the autocratic William the Bastard flowed in his veins as it did in Henry's.

Abruptly changing her tactics, she laid her hand on his arm and said in a calmer voice, "I know you are loyal to Harry. I know, too, that you are angry with me. But you are a fair man, Ranulf, and a sensible one. Surely you do not want to sail in such vile weather. Speak to Harry again. Not for me. Do it for Joanna and John and Rhiannon, who does not want to become a widow this day."

Ranulf looked at her for a moment, wanting to turn away but unable to do so. Whatever her other crimes, she was still a mother. Seeing him hesitate, she said, "Harry will listen to you. I know he will."

Making up his mind, then, he grasped her arm and steered her back toward the steps. They were like a small island in a sea of bodies, as people surged past them on all sides, not even glancing their way. "I have already tried to convince Harry to wait. So have Willem and the ship's master. He told us that if his safe arrival in England will bring peace to his realm, the Almighty will guide him safely into port. But if God has turned away His Face and His Favor, may he never reach the shore."

Eleanor was stunned. "I do not believe you. I do not believe Harry said that. He is reckless, yes, but not foolhardy. And he has never deferred to anyone's will but his own, not even the Almighty's. Most of the time he thinks they are one and the same."

Ranulf's mouth tightened. "If you knew Harry half as well as you think you do, you could never have betrayed him," he said, and stalked away, leaving her standing alone on the steps of the hall, with her guard hovering nearby.

E LEANOR HAD SAILED in storms before. But nothing had prepared her for what awaited them as soon as their ships rounded Barfleur Point and headed out into open water.

The rain was being blown sideways by the force of the wind, and the Channel was churned into white-water froth. Canvas tents had been set up to shelter the passengers, and the stench was soon overpowering, for even the most experienced travelers were fighting seasickness. As Eleanor's ship sank down in a trough and then battled its way up, people were flung about like children's toys, crashing into coffers and gunwale, screaming as they slid along the wet deck. All around her, she could hear men praying with the fervor of the doomed, entreating Nicholas of Bari, the patron saint of sailors, to save them from the perils of the sea. She was too angry to pray, though, and chose to spend her last hours damning her husband to Hell Everlasting.

When she could endure the stifling, stinking tent no longer, Eleanor got up and lurched toward the open flap. Two of her guards at once staggered after her, crying out in alarm. Stumbling out into the storm, she grabbed at one of the windlass posts for support. As the ship's master screamed, "Hard on the helm!" the helmsman jerked the tiller to the left, and the deck dropped under her feet. The guards were beside her now, panting and cursing, but still loath to lay hands upon the queen. "Go back inside," they implored her, petrified that she might be washed overboard, leaving them alive to face the king's wrath.

Eleanor ignored them, never even heard them. A searing bolt of lightning cast an eerie greenish light upon the slanting deck, silhouetting sailors as they fought to tighten one of the shrouds, giving her a terrifying glimpse of that heaving, black sea. The rain and clouds obscured the masthead lanterns of the other ships in their fleet. They were alone in this Devil's cauldron, the skills of these frantic seamen pitted against the savagery of the storm, and she shuddered, thinking of Joanna and John out there in the darkness, sick and wet and scared.

After a particularly rough Channel crossing with his brother Hamelin, Henry had confided to her that a king's chess games were played with the lives of other people. It was a great and fearful power, he admitted, and did not bear close inspection, for otherwise it could never be invoked. She did not know how to reconcile that man with the one who was gambling with God's Favor, if Ranulf could be believed. What madness had infected Harry, that he'd offer up their children's lives as stakes in this accursed wager with the Almighty?

THE PREVAILING WESTERLY WINDS drove Henry's battered fleet across the Channel in record time, and they anchored safely in Southampton harbor that night. The weary passengers and crewmen sought lodgings in the castle and the town, and slept like the dead. Ranulf was so tired that he could easily have stayed abed till noon. That luxury was to be denied him, though, as he was rousted out of bed at daybreak with the unwelcome word that the king would be departing Southampton within the hour.

THE RAIN HAD FINALLY stopped, but the sky was still overcast, a foreboding shade of grey. Ranulf paused long enough to search the bailey for Henry, and then hastened into the crowded great hall, where he ran into a yawning, rumpled Earl of Essex.

"What is happening?" he asked, helping himself to bread smeared with honey.

Willem broke off a chunk of goat cheese and swallowed it in two bites. "We're all on the move this morn. Leicester and Chester are being taken to Porchester, the Lady Marguerite, the Lady Joanna, John, and the other lasses are to be escorted to Devizes Castle, and the queen . . . the queen is to go to Sarum."

Ranulf conjured up a mental image of that bleak, moorland fortress. It would not be a happy homecoming for Eleanor. "What about us? Where does Harry mean to head first? I do hope he'll set a reasonable pace. The Scots border is a long, long ride from here."

"He is not going to confront the Scots king . . . at least not yet."

"Where, then?" Ranulf asked and, to his surprise, Willem shook his head.

"Better you hear it from Harry himself," he said cryptically. "I am not sure you'd believe it otherwise."

Puzzled, Ranulf pushed away from the table and went to find his nephew. Henry was giving instructions to a man clad in mail, his hard visage and guarded eyes giving testimony to years in royal service. When he made a terse query about "shackles," Henry nodded grimly, and Ranulf blinked, wondering if that order could possibly be meant for Eleanor. But then the knight mentioned "Porchester," and he realized the command was aimed at the unhappy rebel earls, Leicester and Chester. As soon as the man moved away he stepped forward to attract Henry's attention.

Even Henry's inexhaustible well of energy seemed to have run dry. His eyes were dull, and there was such a hectic color burning across his cheekbones that Ranulf suspected he was running a fever. Taking advantage of his status as one of the king's intimates, Ranulf said with troubled candor, "Jesu, you look dreadful this morn. Surely we can afford to rest a day longer in Southampton?"

Henry didn't answer, and Ranulf yielded in a battle he'd never expected to win. "And you'll not listen to me, I know. You never do. Willem would not tell me where we are going. I hope you'll be more forthcoming?"

Henry gave him an odd look, one that Ranulf could not interpret. "Canterbury," he said, and walked away without waiting for a response.

CHAPTER SEVENTEEN

✦

July 1174
Westminster Palace, England

RANULF AND WILLEM were admitted to the king's antechamber, but when they asked to see Henry, they had to wait while his chamberlain got permission for their entry. He soon emerged from the royal bedchamber, but not with the word they wanted. He was sorry, he reported, the king had retired for the night. Although they doubted that, they had no choice but to withdraw. Outside in the gardens, they paused to review their options.

"What now?" Willem sounded disheartened, and Ranulf couldn't blame him. Since leaving Southampton, they'd tried repeatedly to talk with Henry about his intent to do penance at Becket's tomb, to no avail. They'd initially been disquieted by his plan simply because it seemed so wildly out of character for him. But they'd soon had other reasons for concern. He'd been fasting on bread and water while pushing his body to the utmost, riding as if racing his troubles, and they'd begun watching him with the alarm of men trying to catch up with a runaway wagon.

"I do not know," Ranulf admitted. "There is not much we can do, is there? No man can be forced to share what is in his heart, least of all a king."

Willem acknowledged the truth of that by bidding Ranulf good night. "You'd best get some sleep," he warned, "for he will want to depart at first light."

Ranulf remained in the gardens after Willem went off to find a bed for the night. Although he was only fifteen years Henry's senior, he'd always had a fatherly, protective love for his sister's son, and he felt that he was somehow letting Henry down in his time of greatest need. The rain had stopped and the air was cool. He had just seated himself upon a wooden bench when he saw the Bishop of London and his attendants coming toward him. Rising, he greeted Gilbert Foliot courteously, but he felt obligated to advise the bishop that if he hoped to see the king that evening, he would be disappointed.

Gilbert blinked in surprise. "But the king summoned me, sending a messenger to tell me that he'd arrived at Westminster and wanted to see me straightaway."

Ranulf apologized and then, on impulse, fell in step beside the bishop. In the antechamber, the chamberlain had obviously been briefed, for he ushered the bishop into Henry's bedchamber without first announcing him. Figuring he had nothing to lose, Ranulf entered with Gilbert. Henry was still dressed, although he'd removed his boots. He gave Ranulf a sharp glance, but he did not order him from the chamber, and Ranulf took that as tacit permission to remain.

Interrupting the bishop's pleased speech of welcome, Henry said bluntly, "I have need of your aid, my lord bishop. On the morrow I am going to Canterbury to do penance for my part in the archbishop's death. I would like you to accompany me, and speak on my behalf to the monks of Christ Church priory."

"My liege, I would be honored!" Gilbert's eyes shone; he seemed about to embrace Henry before thinking better of it; the fact that Henry had called him by his title rather than the more intimate "Gilbert" indicated the king's wish to observe the formalities this night, and Gilbert was shrewd enough to catch it. "Nothing would give me greater pleasure."

"Good. We shall be departing at dawn, so it might be easier for you if you spend the night at the palace. My chamberlain will see to your needs."

Gilbert seemed reluctant to leave, obviously eager to discuss Henry's spiritual epiphany, but he'd been dismissed. Murmuring his good wishes, he withdrew, leaving Henry alone in the chamber with his uncle. Ranulf was expecting to be dismissed, too, but it did not come. "Where are your squires?" he asked, not sure how to ease into such an intrusive conversation, for what could be more meddlesome than an inquiry into the state of a man's soul?

"I sent them off to the hall to eat," Henry said, inadvertently giving Ranulf the opening he sought.

"Are you still fasting?" Getting a brief nod, he said carefully, "Would it not be better to wait until you reach Canterbury ere you fast? If you deprive yourself too severely, you risk becoming ill."

"I thought the purpose of penance was to mortify the flesh," Henry said, with a twisted smile. "Have you forgotten that Thomas not only wore a hairshirt and braies infested with vermin, but he subjected himself to a daily scourging? Do you think he'd be impressed just because I missed a few meals?"

"Is that what you want, Harry . . . to impress Thomas?"

"I want . . ." Henry began, but then he stopped, and shook his head, like a man weary of talking. After a few moments of silence, he said, "Did you notice that Gilbert asked no questions? Nor did he assure me there was no need for such a pilgrimage. It would seem that he considers my penance at Avranches as flawed as Roger does."

"Why does Roger think that?" Ranulf asked, even though he already knew the answer.

"My cousin, the esteemed Bishop of Worcester, thinks that the Almighty has looked into my heart and found that I repented of Thomas's death for all the wrong reasons."

"And what do you think?"

Henry's shoulders twitched, in what was almost a shrug. He'd dropped down into a window-seat, and Ranulf crossed the chamber, knelt in the floor rushes by his side. "Harry, are you sure you want to do this?"

Henry rubbed his fingers against his aching temples. "I suppose I could wait for more explicit signs of divine displeasure, wait until the Thames turns to blood or a plague of locusts comes up and covers the land."

"You are not Pharaoh."

Henry raised his head, looking Ranulf full in the face for the first time. "Can you honestly tell me, Uncle, that you have not wondered if this rebellion was God's punishment for Thomas Becket's murder? If not, you are most likely the only one in Christendom who has not entertained that thought."

"What I think does not matter. Nor does it matter what Roger or Gilbert Foliot think. We are not the ones who must do public penance at Canterbury Cathedral." Reaching out, Ranulf put his hand on Henry's arm. "You are a proud man. You are a king. I know that we are told there is no greater glory than to humble ourselves before the Almighty. But that is easier for some than others. If, as I suspect, you mean to abase yourself utterly in atonement, you must be sure that this is what you truly want to do. Otherwise, I fear you will not gain what you seek—peace of mind."

"'Peace of mind'?" Henry echoed and then laughed harshly. "I have a greater need than that, Uncle. I mean to ask the Almighty and the sainted Thomas to save my kingdom. Not just for my sake, for all our sakes. The vultures are already gathering, and

God help him, but Hal will not be able to fend them off. He'll be a king in name only, whilst the Count of Flanders and the French king and the Scots king carve up my domains like a Michaelmas goose. You think the people suffered under Stephen? That will look like a golden age in comparison to the misery and anarchy that would follow my defeat."

Ranulf could not argue with that bleak assessment of Hal's kingship. He knew that men made pilgrimages for a multitude of reasons, both pure and profane. Some were reluctant penitents, ordered to it by an imperious bishop, an irate priest. Some sought God's Mercy for a loved one, a frail child, an ailing wife. Some saw pilgrimage as a way to honor God. Others were driven by guilty consciences, memories of past sins. He did not doubt that those who humbled themselves of their own free will, those who asked no specific boons in return for their suffering were the ones who came away from a pilgrimage with that "peace of mind" his nephew dismissed so disdainfully. What would Harry do if he submitted to this ordeal and nothing changed? If the victory he'd prayed for was denied him? What does a man do when he acts out of desperation and despair and even that is not enough?

"I will entreat the Almighty," he said softly, "to hear your prayers." And he tried not to think of a conversation he'd once had with his other nephew. Roger had assured him that God always answered prayers. But sometimes He said no.

ON FRIDAY, JULY 12, Henry and his companions were approaching the town of Canterbury. As they neared the lazar-house of St Nicholas in Harbledown, they had their first glimpse of the cathedral in the distance. Henry dismounted, and the hospital's master came hurrying out to meet him. Several of the lepers emerged from their wattle-and-daub huts, but they kept their distance. They were clad in long russet robes and scapulars, the ravages of their disease hidden by hoods for the men and thick, double veils for the women. Henry greeted the master and then accompanied him into the chapel to pray. After some hesitation, the Bishops of London, Winchester, and Rochester dismounted and followed, too. Most of the men remained on their horses, though, for even the bravest of knights was leery of entering a lazar-house.

Henry and the bishops soon emerged, and after he told the priest that he was granting the hospital twenty silver marks a year, to be paid out of royal revenues, the master thanked him profusely, promising that the lepers would offer up daily prayers on his behalf. If anyone thought that those poor souls needed prayers more than the king did, it remained unspoken. When Henry returned to the others, he did not remount, and seeing that he meant to walk the rest of the way, his men made haste to dismount, too.

They'd covered about half a mile when they saw the Westgate looming ahead. Henry headed not for the gate, though, but for the church of St Dunstan's by the side of the road. His squires scurried after him. The other men waited, puzzled, and when the flustered parish priest arrived, none of them had any answers for him. They could see a crowd gathering just inside the Westgate, but the church bells that would normally peal out the king's arrival were silent, for Henry had sent word that he wanted no royal ceremony.

It had been raining lightly since mid-morning, but as they waited for Henry to emerge from the church, the heavens opened and Canterbury was engulfed in a summer downpour. When Henry finally appeared, they saw that he'd stripped to his shirt and chausses and removed his boots. One of his squires was holding out the green wool cape that he wore when hunting, and the boy looked dismayed as Henry waved him away.

"He's going to cut his feet to ribbons by the time he reaches the cathedral," Willem muttered to Ranulf, who was more concerned at the moment with Henry's intention to brave the rainstorm clad only in his shirt. Striding forward, he spoke briefly with his nephew, and to the relief of the spectators, Henry reluctantly agreed to don the green cape. As he set out, the bishops and knights fell in behind him, but Willem delayed long enough to ask Ranulf how he'd convinced Henry to wear the cloak.

"I told him," Ranulf said, "that if he caught a fatal chill in the rain and died at Canterbury, all of Christendom would conclude that his sins had been too great for St Thomas to forgive."

Willem looked at him, not knowing what to say. Ranulf had moved on, and he hastened to catch up, even though he was dreading what was coming as he'd never dreaded anything in his life before.

Escorted by the city reeve and aldermen, Henry passed through the Westgate and entered the town. As he walked along St Peter's Street, his feet were soon cut and bleeding, but the rain washed his bloody footprints away. People lined both sides of the street, heedless of the weather, for they knew they were witnesses to a spectacle that none would ever forget—the sight of a highborn king, God's Anointed, offering up his pride to make peace with their saint.

Thomas Becket had not been universally loved, even in his own city, but he'd always been revered by Christ's Poor, and they turned out now in large numbers. The town's merchants were quick to recognize what a blessing Henry was conferring upon them, for once word got out that the English king had prostrated himself before the

Blessed Martyr, Canterbury's shrine would become the most popular pilgrimage in all of Christendom. But their enthusiasm was tempered with uncertainty, for they did not know what was expected of them. Should they cheer the king for submitting to St Thomas? Or jeer him for his part in the Martyrdom? The result was that, for the first time within memory, a king passed by in utter silence, even the children and beggars watching in awed stillness.

If Henry's bloodied bare feet were giving him pain, he did not show it. Nor did he seem to feel the drenching rain or take notice of the crowds. Followed by the bishops and his knights, he continued on past the churches of All Saints and St Helen's, past the king's mill, the guildhall, and the pillory. St Peter's Street had become High Street when he halted momentarily, then turned into Mercery Lane, a passageway so narrow that more than two men could not walk abreast. Ahead he could see the monks waiting by the cemetery gate. The new archbishop was still absent, having gone to Rome to get papal approval of his election, but Henry recognized Odo, the prior, and Walter, the abbot of Boxley Abbey. In the past, he'd been welcomed by the chiming of the cathedral bells and the chanting of Lauds by the choir. Now there was only the same eerie quiet that had settled over the city.

They came forth to offer a solemn, subdued greeting, and quickly ushered him into the cathedral precincts, escorting him along the path through the cemetery for laypeople. The storm had turned it into a morass, and Henry's feet and legs were soon caked with mud. He could think of few sights more desolate than a graveyard in the rain. The rest of the monks were waiting in the cathedral. He could see curiosity and anxiety and excitement on their faces, but little overt hostility. Oddly enough, Thomas had not been that popular with his own monks, had been feuding with Prior Odo at the time of his murder. It was only the discovery of his hairshirt and whip-scarred back that had awakened them to the realization that they'd had a saint in their midst.

"Show me," Henry said, and they knew at once what he meant. Holding a candle aloft, Prior Odo led the way up the nave toward the northwest transept. A small altar had been set up on the spot, and candle flames glimmered on something silvery. "What is that?"

"Those are fragments of the sword of Richard le Bret," the prior said, striving to sound matter-of-fact and almost accomplishing it. Another monk behind him, an anonymous voice in the shadows, volunteered that he was the knight who delivered the deathblow, striking with such force that he split the archbishop's skull and broke his blade upon the tiles.

This unknown informant did not repeat what the knight had cried as he stood over the archbishop's body. *Take that for the love of my Lord William, the king's brother!* There was no need, for Henry and every man in the cathedral knew what had been said. Thomas had refused to grant William a dispensation to wed Isabella de Warenne, and when the twenty-seven-year-old William died suddenly soon afterward, his friends had contended that he'd died of a broken heart. Henry had blamed Becket, too, for Will's death, but as he gazed at the pieces of that broken sword, it seemed so long ago to him, part of another man's life. Kneeling, he prayed earnestly to God for forgiveness, and then leaned over and kissed the ground where Thomas died.

Rising to his feet, he looked over at the prior. "I would like to see his tomb now." "Of course, my liege. The stairway to the crypt is right behind you."

With the prior again leading the way, they all descended to the cathedral undercroft. It was deep in shadows, and Henry's eyes had to adjust before he could make out the outlines of the archbishop's tomb. A wall had been built around the sarcophagus, rising a foot above the coffin, covered by a large marble slab. In each side of the wall two windows had been cut so that pilgrims could lean inside and kiss the coffin. Henry knelt again and began to pray.

THE BISHOP OF LONDON stepped forward to join Henry beside the tomb. "It is my honor to speak on behalf of the lord king. He orders me to declare his unreserved confession on his behalf, which I and others have heard in private. He declares before God and before the martyr that he did not cause St Thomas to be slain, but freely admits that he did use such words as were the cause of his being murdered. He begs the saint to forgive his offense, and he agrees to return all her holdings to this holy church. He has already pledged to give the cathedral the sum of thirty pounds each year, and he now adds an additional ten pounds per annum, so that candles may always be kept lit at the archbishop's shrine. He asks you to pray to the true martyr lying here, beseeching him to lay aside all anger. The king has come here to make atonement."

When Gilbert was done speaking, Henry gave him an approving nod. "Thank you, my lord bishop." Turning back toward the monks, he said, "I hereby affirm all that the Bishop of London has said. I ask now for your forgiveness."

Prior Odo smiled. "Gladly, my lord king, gladly." And embracing Henry, he gave him the kiss of peace while many of the monks applauded.

There was a lessening of tension after that, as most of the men assumed the worst was over. As Henry's eyes moved from face to face, he saw that only two knew what was coming, Gilbert Foliot, who'd been forewarned, and Ranulf, who sometimes seemed gifted with second-sight. "I regret the Blessed Martyr's death more than words can ever say. But actions speak louder than words. It is for that reason that I restore to the cathedral and priory all of their rights and privileges. It is my pleasure to offer to St

Thomas four marks of pure gold, a silk pall, and forty librates of land in Kent. I have asked the prior to send for the archbishop's sister so that I may make amends to her as well, and I pledge to found an abbey in honor of the archbishop. And now . . . so that there may be no doubts as to the sincerity of my repentance, I willingly submit to the punishment I deserve for my part in this tragedy and ask that I be scourged for my sins." With that, he unfastened his cloak and removed his shirt.

As they realized what he intended to do, a loud murmur swept through the spectators, expressions of shock and distress and satisfaction all mingling as one, like a river fed by smaller streams. Ignoring these ripples, Henry glanced from the bishop to the prior. "I would have each of the bishops and Abbot Walter give five lashes and then three from each one of the Christchurch monks."

Prior Odo hastily whispered to one of the monks, who quickly fetched a penitential whip, a leather thong attached to a short handle. When he offered it to the Bishop of London, Gilbert took it as if he'd been handed a live snake. Seeing that he'd have to be the one to initiate the scourging, Henry said tersely, "Do it," and then knelt by the tomb, thrusting his head and shoulders into one of the wall openings. It was an awkward position and his back began to ache before the first touch of the whip, but it had the advantage of shielding his face from his audience, one small indulgence that he hoped the Almighty would not begrudge him.

With a murmured *"Deus vult,"* Gilbert struck his king's bared back. It was a light blow, as were those that followed, for all of the bishops seemed determined to make the scourging a symbolic one. Prior Odo was no less gentle, and the first few monks to wield the whip were either intimidated by the circumstances or were never partisans of the archbishop, for their lashes barely touched Henry's flesh. In the beginning, Henry was trying to keep count of the blows, but he'd soon given it up. There were at least seventy monks, which added up to more than two hundred strikes, and he decided that was enough to know. When the first blow sliced into his skin and drew blood, there were indignant protests from some of his men that subsided only when he demanded silence.

He discovered he could measure a monk's devotion to St Thomas by the strength of his blows. Most were cautious or prudent, but occasionally one of the monks would employ the whip with enough enthusiasm to raise welts. Despite the care that the majority were taking, his back was soon stinging from the sheer number of the strokes. But his real discomfort came from his hunched posture, and before long, he felt as if his spine were breaking in two. The trapped, musty air of the tomb was bothering him, too, bringing on several prolonged coughing fits. At the start of the scourging, he'd sought solace in prayer, but it was difficult to concentrate when his body was anticipating the feel of the lash, and eventually he stopped trying to think altogether, just focused upon enduring the ordeal. It actually came as a surprise when he heard Prior Odo declare that it was done.

It was not easy to straighten up, so stiff had his body become. For a moment, he felt light-headed and had to grip the tomb for support. Staggering over to the central pillar, he squatted down upon the floor and refused those who would have offered water or wine. "My penance is not over," he said hoarsely. "I shall stay here all night, offering up my prayers to the Almighty and St Thomas."

After they hurriedly conferred, Prior Odo announced that they would be honored by his presence and they would make sure that other pilgrims were kept away so he might pray in private. When Henry interrupted with a curt, "No, let any enter who wish," Odo looked troubled, but he assured Henry it would be done. He beckoned then to two new arrivals, and Henry watched as an elderly woman and a younger man timidly drew closer.

"My liege, this is Mistress Rohesia and her son John. You sent for them," the prior added, and only then did Henry realize they were Thomas Becket's sister and nephew. She had none of her brother's innate assurance, the poise and polish that had made it so easy for him to walk with kings and talk with princes of the Church. When Henry had reacted with fury to Becket's latest outrage and expelled all of his family and retainers from England, this stooped, shy woman was one of the chief victims of his vengefulness. He was shamed now by that memory, further disquieted by the recollection of a heated quarrel he'd had with Eleanor, who'd argued in vain against the expulsion, claiming that "This interminable feuding with Becket has well and truly addled your mind!"

"You may approach," he said, as kindly as he could, called her "gentle sister," and asked for her pardon and grace. She stammered out something unintelligible, and he realized that he was only frightening her all the more, for she did not know how to treat a king like a supplicant. "I deeply regret the wrong I've done to you and your family. I would make amends the only way I can—by granting you the king's mill that stands by the River Stour. You ought to be able to collect at least ten marks a year in rental payments. Take it with my blessings."

Rohesia looked dumbfounded, but her son's smile was bright enough to light the darkest shadows of the crypt. He began to declare their eternal gratitude, but Gilbert Foliot accurately read the exhaustion on Henry's face and tactfully steered them away.

"My lord king?" Willem was leaning over, looking so concerned that Henry somehow managed to find a smile for him. "What would you have us do now?"

"You may go, Willem. There is no need for any of you to remain."

The earl frowned. "I do not want to leave you alone, my liege."

"I will not be alone," Henry said, stifling a cough. "I will have St Thomas to keep me company." Once Willem would have been sure that was a jest; now he no longer knew.

ALL AFTERNOON and well into the evening, pilgrims were admitted to the crypt, where they made offerings to the monk keeping vigil by the shrine, prayed to St Thomas, and watched the King of England do penance. Some were surreptitious about it, others gawked openly, but Henry was always aware of their eyes upon him. Kneeling by the tomb of the man who'd once been a beloved friend, then a hated enemy, he'd silently entreated the Almighty to forgive him, interspersing these pleas with the Latin prayers he'd learned in childhood. Refusing to eat or drink or even to pass water, he lay full length upon the cold floor of the crypt as he uttered the familiar words of the Confiteor.

The other pilgrims did not share his knowledge of Latin, but they knew the responses to the Mass and so when he whispered, *"Confiteor Deo omnipotenti, beatae Mariae semper Virgini, beato Michaeli Archangelo, beato Ioanni Baptistae, sanctis Apostolis Petro et Paulo, et omnibus Sanctis, quita peccavi nimus cogitatione, verbo et opere: mea culpa, mea culpa, mea maxima culpa,"* they understood that he was confessing to God, the Blessed Mary, the archangel, the apostles, and the saints that he had "sinned exceedingly, in thought, word, and deed."

He'd begun by alternating pleas to God and St Thomas, but after a while he'd stopped praying to Thomas, for he felt as if his words were falling into a void. The archbishop did not seem to be listening. His fatigue was beginning to affect his thinking; when he recited the Litany of the Saints, he found himself unable to remember who came first, the patriarchs and prophets or the apostles.

After Vespers, the tide of pilgrims slowed to a trickle. But a new monk had taken up the vigil and he was a talker. Introducing himself as Brother Benedict, he informed Henry that he was collecting accounts of St Thomas's miracles so that they might be saved for posterity. Pointing to a pile of crutches stacked in a corner, he explained that they had been abandoned by cripples who'd been healed by the saint's mercy. With his own eyes, he'd seen people cured of leprosy, blindness, the palsy. A canon of Oseney was cured of the falling sickness, and a Templar from Chester was healed of a bowel ailment. But he only included those miracles that could be verified, he assured Henry. He did not intend to report one of his favorite stories, alas, for he could find no witnesses to confirm its accuracy. He then proceeded to tell Henry a preposterous tale of a starling that had been taught to recite a prayer to the Blessed Martyr. The bird had been attacked by a hawk—a kite, he believed it was—and invoked the prayer as it was caught in the kite's talons. The hawk was at once struck dead, he recounted breathlessly.

Henry did his best to block out that droning voice, unwilling to give way to anger during his time of penance. Brother Benedict was not making it easy, however. As the night wore on, his body ailments were becoming more and more difficult to ignore. His lacerated back was throbbing; so was his head. His gashed feet had begun to bleed again, and his bladder felt full to bursting. Although he'd eaten nothing but bread for almost a week, he was not hungry. But his thirst was well-nigh intolerable. He'd put his shirt on again; it did little to shield him, though, from the damp chill of the crypt. With a flicker of very grim humor, he recalled Ranulf's warning and entertained himself by imagining the great scandal should he be found dead on the morrow.

With an effort, he came back to the here and now, troubled that his thoughts were wandering like this. He ought to be thinking only of his sins. His muscles were cramping and stiffening, so that he had to pull himself upright by holding on to the marble top of the sarcophagus. Brother Benedict was still chattering on, describing the drowning of a little boy of Rochester; he'd fallen into the River Medway in mid-afternoon, had not been dragged out till Vespers had rung. But his mother refused to despair and measured his body with a thread and promised St Thomas a silver thread of the same length if he saved her son. And lo and behold, the child moaned and stirred and vomited up a barrel full of river water, even though they'd first hung him by his feet and not a drop did he spit out.

"Not that the Blessed Martyr is one to be trifled with. There have been sinners who sought his aid, and then did not fulfill their vows as promised, and retribution was always swift. I myself witnessed a sad case where a lame boy fell asleep with his head on the tomb. He had a vision of St Thomas, who rebuked him for his disrespect, and said, 'Go hence, I will do nothing for you.' His parents pleaded, but our saint would not relent."

Henry began to recite the Pater Noster, the first prayer to come to mind, in hope of drowning the monk out. *"Fiat voluntas tua, sicut in caelo et in terra,"* he murmured, the words coming from memory as his thoughts began to stray again. Was there a way to murder Brother Benedict and make it seem as if he'd been smitten by the wrath of the unforgiving Thomas? A vengeful saint was surely a contradiction in terms, but he alone seemed to think so. He was no longer shivering, and when he put his hand to his forehead, it felt hot. He'd been running a fever intermittently for days now, and he supposed neither the drenching nor the hours spent on his knees had done his aching body any good. Focusing again upon prayer, he began to repeat the Litany, almost at random. *"Agnus Dei, qui tollis peccata mundi, miserere nobis."*

And to his great relief, the Son of God heard his plea and showed mercy, for Brother Benedict rose from his post and excused himself, saying that there would be no more pilgrims that night and he hoped to get a few hours sleep before Matins.

Gathering up his offerings, he politely wished Henry God's Peace and shuffled off to bed, leaving Henry alone in the crypt with the dead and the ghost of the murdered archbishop.

At least, it seemed that way to Henry. He had not been able to invoke the saint's presence, but it was easier to imagine Thomas's earthly spirit lurking in the shadows, watching his abasement with sardonic amusement. For Thomas had once had a quick wit, a playful humor, a droll sense of mockery. He'd lost that humor, though, as soon as he'd put the sacred pallium about his neck, yet another mystery that Henry could not fathom. Had the man he'd known and trusted and loved ever truly existed? Or had he been a fiction from the very first, a chimera conjured up out of cobwebs and moonbeams? Henry desperately wanted to know the answer, an answer only Thomas Becket could give him.

"It is just the two of us now, Thomas. No one else can hear our secrets, so why not talk to pass the time? We have hours to go till dawn, time enough for honesty if nothing else."

Pushing himself away from the tomb, he walked toward the center of the crypt, noting with bemusement that he left a trail of blood and mud. "Ranulf said something once that I've never forgotten. He thought that his Welsh friend Hywel—you remember the poet-prince—saw you with the clearest eye, saying that you reminded him of a chameleon, changing your color to reflect your surroundings. The perfect clerk. The perfect royal chancellor. And then the perfect archbishop. Was he right, Thomas?"

He cocked his head, hearing only the silence of the grave. "I suppose you'd rather talk about the killing. Fair enough. I never wanted your death. I swear this to you upon the lives of my children. But you know that already. Why am I so sure? Because Roger showed me a letter written by your subdeacon, William Fitz Stephen. I've restored him to royal favor, by the way. In fact, he and his brother Ralph are co-sheriffs of Gloucestershire now. Life goes on.

"What was I saying? Ah, yes, the letter. Fitz Stephen wrote that you told the killers that you did not believe they came from the king, from me. So there really is no reason to swear my innocence upon holy relics, is there? You know the truth. Of course Roger knew the truth, too, and was the one man with the ballocks to say it straight out to my face. I may not be guilty, he pointed out, but neither am I innocent. I daresay you agree with him, no?"

He waited, heaving a sigh that echoed in the stillness. "Come, Thomas, hold up your part of the conversation. You need not do anything dramatic, like loosing a thunderbolt or performing one of your miracles. But at the least, you could extinguish a few candles to show me you are paying attention. Surely that is not too much to ask?"

He was feeling light-headed again, and sank down upon the floor, slumping back against one of the pillars. "I sound like a drunkard or a madman . . . mayhap both. But just between you and me, talking to a ghost makes as much sense as talking to a saint. What else do you want to know, Thomas? Did I grieve for you? No, I did not. My grief was for myself, for I knew at once that you'd trapped me well and truly. For you are not innocent either, my lord archbishop. You sought your martyrdom, you craved it, even lusted after it for all I know. You could have escaped, Thomas, had so many opportunities to evade your killers. But you did not, did you? You had to confront them, had to taunt them. Was it true that you called Fitz Urse a pimp?"

Henry laughed unsteadily, ending in a cough. "They went unpunished, you know. You insisted that only the Church could punish its own, so I could do nothing to them, and the Pope could only send them off on pilgrimage to the Holy Land with a stern warning to mend their evil ways. Christ Almighty, Thomas, surely you see the irony of that? The lunacy? For I will not lie to gain your pardon. I was right to want to try degraded priests in my courts. Your way turned justice into a farce, and I will never understand why you could not see that."

Henry leaned forward, rested his head upon his drawn-up knees. He was either burning up with fever or losing his mind. "*Sancte Thoma*," he mumbled, "*requiescat in pace*." But there was as much pain as mockery in his voice, and when he looked up, he saw the crypt through a haze of hot tears. "Do you know why I did not grieve for you when you died, Thomas? Because I'd already done my grieving. I trusted you, I had faith in you, I loved you more than my own brother. And then you turned on me. But it need not have been that way. You could have served both me and the Almighty, and what a partnership we could have forged, what we could not have done together!"

Getting to his feet with difficulty, he had to hold on to the pillar, for his head was spinning. "When I told you that I would raise you up to the archbishopric, you said you would not want to put our friendship at risk. And I assured you that it would not happen, that I was not so prideful that I saw God as a rival. Do you remember what I said? That the Almighty and I would not be in contention for your immortal soul. Why could you not believe me, Thomas?"

His tears were falling faster now, but there was no one to see them. "I am truly and grievously sorry that our path led us to this place, this night. I do mourn you, Thomas. But do I think you are a saint? God's truth, I do not know. You are the only one who can answer that question, my lord archbishop. We both know you could never resist a challenge. So take it up. Prove my doubts are unfounded. Prove me wrong."

Dropping to his knees, he winced at the pain that action caused his fevered, battered body. "St Thomas," he said in a low, husky voice, "guard my realm."

H ENRY HEARD MASS at daybreak the next morning, warned the citizens of Canterbury that there was danger of a Flemish invasion, and advised them to move their goods beyond the River Medway. He set out for London then, reaching the city the following day, where he was welcomed enthusiastically by the citizens, who escorted him through the streets to his palace at Westminster. By this time he was running a high fever, and utterly exhausted, body and soul, he took to his bed.

H ENRY HAD BEEN BLED by his physician earlier in the day and advised to rest until he regained his strength. But even when he was ill, he found it hard to stay abed, and by the afternoon, he was up and dressed, conferring with his court officials and getting reports from his scouts, who were watching for the Flemish fleet. The soles of his feet had been badly bruised and cut by the Canterbury cobblestones, and so he made one concession to his body's needs and remained on the settle in his bedchamber while he conducted affairs of state. He was still awaiting word from the North, where the Scots king was menacing the royal castle at Alnwick, but he was finding it difficult to recapture his sense of urgency. He felt numb, depleted of all his reserves, as if he'd gambled everything on one roll of the dice and lost.

Soon after Vespers, the arrival of the Bishop of Worcester was announced. Roger swept into the chamber like a summer wind, dark eyes glowing, as elated as Henry had ever seen him. Striding forward, he engulfed Henry in an exuberant embrace, behavior so unlike Roger that Henry voiced no complaints, although his cousin's hug was pressing painfully against his injured back. Releasing him at last, Roger sank to his knees and kissed Henry's hand.

"I have never been so proud of you, Cousin," he said. "I know what courage it took to humble yourself like that. Whatever else you may accomplish in this life, I truly believe Friday was your finest hour."

"So you are saying that from now on, it is all downhill?" Henry's attempt at humor could not disguise the pleasure that Roger's words had given him; his cousin had never been one for lavish, effusive, or fawning praise. Retaking his seat, he gestured for the other man to join him on the settle, and signaled for wine.

Roger had fully intended to discuss Henry's penance at length, wanting to hear all the details of this blessed reconciliation. But as he looked more closely at his cousin, he was startled into blurting out tactlessly, "Jesu, you look like you've been camping at death's door! I'd heard you were ailing, but I did not realize how ill you truly were. You have seen a doctor, I trust?"

When Henry brushed off his concern with predictable impatience, that reassured Roger somewhat. "I'll not stay long," he said, "for you ought to be in bed. Ere I go, though, what is the news from the North? Has Alnwick fallen yet?" He realized at once how pessimistic that sounded, as if he expected defeat, but it was too late to call his words back. To his surprise, though, Henry did not react, and he did not take that to be a good sign.

"The last I heard," Henry said, "William de Vesci is still holding out at Alnwick. I suppose you know that the rebels have seized Norwich, Northampton, and Nottingham. You may not know that my son and the Count of Flanders have been waiting at Gravelines, intending to launch their invasion once the weather clears. For all I know, they could be landing on English beaches even as we speak."

He delivered this alarming news with an eerie lack of emotion, almost as if he were relating another man's troubles, and Roger felt a chill that seemed oddly out of place on a summer evening. When had Harry ever sounded listless or fatalistic? "I'll go now," he said, "so you may get some rest. But I'll be back in the morning."

Henry had not meant to ask. But as Roger reached the door, he heard himself saying suddenly, "Roger . . . do you think Thomas forgave me?"

Roger turned, with a surprised smile. "I know he did," he said, and Henry, who'd never had reason to envy other men, felt a sharp pang, wishing that he shared Roger's utter certainty, his steadfast faith, and his serene acceptance of God's Will.

HENRY WAS STRETCHED OUT upon the settle, dozing. One of his squires was sitting in the floor rushes beside the settle, gently rubbing ointment into the wounds on his king's feet. Others moved quietly around the chamber, making as little noise as possible. It was still early for one who kept night-owl hours, but Henry's weary body was asserting itself after days of abuse and neglect. As he drifted down into sleep, the last sound he heard was the distant chiming of church bells.

When he awakened, he had no idea how much time had elapsed. Candles still burned, and Warin was still tending to his injured feet. He propped himself up on an elbow, and it was then that he heard the voices, the clamor that had chased away his sleep. "What is it?"

"Someone wanted to see you, my liege," Warin explained, "and when the chamberlain said you were sleeping and he must wait till the morrow, he began to argue. I am so sorry that you were disturbed."

"Who is it?" Henry called out, and the chamberlain came into his line of sight.

"It is a messenger, my lord, from the North. I told him to come back, but he is most insistent. He says you know him—Brien, one of Sir Ralf de Glanville's men."

"Let him enter," Henry commanded, his voice even more raspy than usual. Sitting up, he swung his legs over the side of the settle, but Warin was close enough to see that he'd lost color; his feverish flush fading into an ashen pallor as he watched the door.

The man ushered into the chamber was indeed known to him. He looked as haggard and gaunt as his king, and he dropped to his knees like one thankful for a moment's rest. "Forgive me, sire, but I've scarcely eaten or slept these four days gone, so urgent was my news."

Henry closed his eyes for a heartbeat. "Tell me," he said grimly. "Hold nothing back."

Brien had been given a wine cup and drained the contents in several swallows. When he lowered the cup and looked at Henry, there was such blazing joy upon his face that Henry caught his breath. "My liege, I bring you wondrous news, as good as you could wish. The Scots king has been taken captive by my lord de Glanville, and with him all his barons."

One of Henry's squires let out a jubilant shout, and the other men in the chamber began to exclaim and praise God. Henry was not yet ready to believe, though. "Is this true, Brien? Swear to me it is so!"

"Yes, sire, by my faith, it is so! Soon after dawn on Saturday, we surprised the Scots king in the meadows before the walls of Alnwick Castle. My lord de Glanville and the sheriff of Yorkshire met William de Vesci at Newcastle on Friday last, where he'd gone to seek aid for Alnwick. He told us that the Scots king had sent the bulk of his army off to ravage Northumbria, and he had remained behind with only sixty knights. We set out at once, had ridden more than twenty miles before the sun had risen. A thick fog settled in during the night, but we continued on, sure that God was with us. When we emerged from the mists, we saw the Scots king breaking his fast with his knights. At first he thought we were his own men returning, and by the time he realized the truth, it was too late."

"God's Bones," Henry breathed. "What proof have you of this?"

Brien grinned. "My lord knew that was the first question you'd ask, my liege. I bear a letter from Sir Ralf, attesting to all that I've told you. And on the morrow you ought to receive further confirmation from the Archbishop of York, for he was dispatching a messenger, too. He was not as fast a rider as me, though!"

Henry snatched up the letter Brien was holding out, but he made no attempt to read it. "Tell me the rest," he said, and Brien needed no urging.

"I have to admit, sire, that he fought valiantly, spurred his stallion into our midst once he realized he was trapped between us and the castle. But one of our men speared his fine grey destrier, and the king's legs were pinned when the beast fell. He surrendered to my lord de Glanville, and was taken under guard back to Newcastle and then, on to Richmond. That traitor Roger de Mowbray fled like a hare before hounds, but none of the Scots knights would abandon their liege lord, and surrendered when he did." Brien was not happy at having to compliment his Scots foes, but he was a fair man, and he added, "They acquitted themselves well, my liege, brave men all."

He was being offered more wine, which he accepted happily. "You are indeed favored by God, my lord king. I am honored to be the one to bring you such glad tidings."

Henry laughed. "Ah, Brien, you will want for nothing for the rest of your born days," he promised. "Land, gold, it will all be yours for the asking."

Brien laughed, too. "For now, my lord, I ask only for a bed and a meal to fill my empty belly!"

Others were crowding into the bedchamber now, drawn by the uproar, and in the ensuing pandemonium, it was left to Henry's squire Warin to realize the full significance of Brien's message. "My lord," he cried, tugging on Henry's sleeve in his urgency to be heard. "Brien said that the Scots king was captured on Saturday, around dawn. My liege, that was when you were completing your penance at St Thomas's tomb!"

There were exclamations of wonder and most of the men made the sign of the cross. Henry stared at the squire, and then sat down abruptly on the settle. "You are right, Warin," he said in awe. "This is indeed his doing."

WORD WAS SPREADING LIKE WILDFIRE throughout the palace, and Henry's bedchamber was soon thronged with celebrants, both jubilant and reverent. Willem and Ranulf had pushed their way through to Henry's side, and Gilbert Foliot had also succeeded in reaching the king. "My lord," he cried, "should we ring the bells to awaken the city?"

"No," Henry said, "let them sleep. The morning will come soon enough." Glancing around, he knew that none of these blissful, boisterous men would get a wink of sleep. Neither would he, for his exhaustion was magically vanished, his fever forgotten. "We might as well move these revelries over to the great hall," he said, grinning when his declaration was met with raucous cheers; he knew these men would have cheered if he'd announced they must all take holy vows.

"I do want to awaken my cousin, the Bishop of Worcester," he said. "Send someone to fetch him, Gilbert. And once he gets here, I want to go to the abbey church and give thanks to St Thomas for our victory, for his miracle."

FOR HIS TWO-HUNDRED-SEVENTY-MILE DASH, Brien was rewarded by Henry with "ten liveries of land" and an estate in Norfolk.

HAL AND THE COUNT OF FLANDERS had decided to send their fleet on ahead of them, and their ships had sailed into the same storm that had inundated Canterbury. During those hours that Henry did penance for his sins, their fleet was scattered by the high winds, and the threat of invasion was over. Just as people gave credit to the martyred archbishop for the capture of Henry's greatest enemy, they saw the dispersal of the Flemish fleet as yet another proof of St Thomas's favor.

CHAPTER EIGHTEEN

✦

July 1174
Northampton, England

ANULF HALTED ON THE STEPS of the great hall, watching as a large group of horsemen rode into the castle bailey. When he recognized their leader as Henry's illegitimate son, he hastened over to bid Geoff welcome and as soon as the latter dismounted, they embraced with the euphoria that all of Henry's supporters shared these days.

"I've brought seven hundred knights with me," Geoff said proudly. "Can we find beds for them all?"

"We'll manage," Ranulf assured him. "Your men are going to be disappointed, though, for the fighting is done."

Geoff blinked in surprise. "All done?" he asked, trying to conceal his own disappointment. "I heard that the garrison at Huntingdon Castle surrendered. But what about Hugh Bigod and the Earl of Derby?"

"Hugh Bigod skulked out of his lair and pleaded for the king's mercy two days ago. And on Tuesday we will be receiving the submissions of the Earl of Derby, the Earl of Leicester's constable, Roger Mowbray, and our disgruntled bishop, Hugh of Durham."

Geoff could only shake his head in amazement. "Then the rebellion in England is truly over!"

"I think that happened the moment the Scots king was taken at Alnwick. For all the talk of rats deserting a sinking ship, they have nothing on rebel lords trying to save their skins. They damned near trampled themselves in their rush to make peace with the king. Speaking of kings, you missed quite a spectacle this morn—the arrival of the Scots king."

"I would have enjoyed seeing that," Geoff said, with vengefulness that he knew did not befit a bishop-elect. But he did not care, wanting to savor every moment of their victory over Henry's enemies. "Was he taken before my lord father in shackles?"

"No, but he arrived with his feet tied under his horse, an affront not usually inflicted upon kings. For all that he calls himself William the Lion, he seemed more like a docile stable cat to me. He managed to cling to his dignity, but there was no bravado, none at all. He is going to have to pay a huge price for his freedom, and he well knows it."

Leaving the castle steward to figure out where to lodge these new arrivals, they started across the bailey. "You'll be a sight to gladden your father's eyes," Ranulf said. "He was right proud of your triumphs in the North. Who knew you had the makings of a first-rate battle commander?" he joked, amused when Geoff actually blushed. "I should warn you, though, lad, that your father is hobbling about with a crutch, and he is as bad a patient as you'd expect him to be."

"Was he wounded in the siege of Huntingdon?" Geoff asked, sounding so alarmed that Ranulf hastened to offer reassurances, explaining that Henry had been injured the day before when the Templar Tostes de St Omer's horse had lashed out suddenly, striking the king in the leg.

That allayed some but not all of Geoff's concerns, for he knew how easily wounds could become infected; he'd never forgotten the fate of a boyhood friend, who'd died in agony after stepping on a rusty nail. Once they entered the great hall, he headed for the dais, so eager to see his father that he barely heard the greetings and congratulations trailing in his wake. Henry was just as delighted to see his son, and waved Geoff up onto the dais so they could talk with a modicum of privacy. He brushed off Geoff's concerns for his injury, saying wryly, "It is downright embarrassing, getting kicked by a horse at my age. And it was not even my horse!"

Ordering chairs for Geoff and Ranulf, he did his best to get his aching leg comfortable on a cushioned footstool, and then made his son very happy by asking to hear all about Geoff's military exploits. Geoff needed no further urging and launched into a detailed account of the captures of Roger Mowbray's castles at Kinnardferry and Kirkby Malzeard and his success in penning up the rebel garrison at Thirsk. Henry listened attentively, asked all the right questions, and waited until Geoff was done before sharing his own news with his son.

"A messenger reached me this morn with unwelcome word from Normandy. After learning that I'd sailed for England, the French king recalled Hal and the Count of Flanders and they are now laying siege to Rouen."

"You'll be returning, then, to Normandy," Geoff exclaimed, his eyes alight. "May I go with you? It may be our only chance to fight side by side!"

Henry had never understood the appeal that war held for other men. Even in his youth, he'd not been bedazzled by dreams of glory, had always looked upon war as a necessary evil, a king's last resort. "You're sounding rather bloodthirsty for a bishop, lad," he teased. "Speaking of that, we will have to get the Pope's approval of your election once the rebellion is finally over. Would you fancy going to Rome yourself? Let me know if so, and I'll make the necessary arrangements."

Geoff's face shadowed, and he glanced away, saying nothing. Henry did not notice. Ranulf did, though. He knew most people would share Henry's view, that he was bestowing a great honor upon his son, especially one born out of wedlock. But Ranulf had learned a hard lesson with his own eldest—that sons did not always share their fathers' aspirations, and he understood, as few others did, that an unwanted honor could be a heavy burden. Giving the reluctant bishop a sympathetic look, he sought to change the subject before the silence could become awkward, and admitted that he hoped to go home to Wales now that the rebellion in England was won.

"I wish there were a way to lure you and Lady Rhiannon to my court and keep you here," Henry said. "But I know I cannot compete with the siren songs of Wales. Go with my blessings, Uncle. You've more than paid your dues. As have your Welsh countrymen." Turning to Geoff, he lavished praise upon his Welsh ally, Rhys ap Gruffydd.

"Not only has he kept the peace along the marches, Rhys even led a contingent of Welshmen to fight for me in England, laying siege to Derby's stronghold at Tutbury."

Geoff was impressed. "The Welsh are usually ones for taking advantage of English strife." At once regretting his candor, he glanced apologetically at Ranulf. "No offense, Uncle. How will you reward Rhys for his loyalty, Papa?"

"By giving him what he most wants—a free hand in Wales. I wish it were so easy to reward your rogue prince, Ranulf. Davydd ab Owain has been no less steadfast for me than Rhys. But now he is asking for a boon in return, one I'd rather not bestow upon him."

"What does he want?" Ranulf asked curiously. "Horses, cattle? Gold? Surely not a border castle? I doubt even Davydd would be that brazen."

"What he wants," Henry said, "is my sister. Did you notice that Benedictine monk over there, Ranulf? That is Brother Simon, sent from Basingwerk Abbey to ask for

Emma's hand in marriage. Davydd wants to be able to boast that he is the King of England's brother-in-law, I suppose. He also knows that she'd bring a few English manors as her marriage portion. I daresay he's heard that she is a beauty, too, and that never hurts. I'd as soon tell him nay. I liked Hywel, the brother he killed, and I agree with your dismal view of his character. But I will probably have to give my consent if I hope to keep the peace along the border. As thin-skinned as Davydd is, he's like to take a refusal as a mortal insult."

"Yes," Ranulf agreed reluctantly, "he would." He did not know Emma well at all, remembered her as very fair and rather prideful, but he sympathized with any woman yoked to Davydd ab Owain. "What will Emma think of this?"

Henry shrugged. "She probably will not like it much at first. My family seems cursed with strong-willed women, and Emma is definitely one of them. But it is a good match for her. Whatever his other failings, Davydd is a prince. If she bears him sons, they can expect to rule over most of Gwynedd one day."

Geoff did not know the Welsh prince at all and barely knew his aunt Emma, so he did not have any real interest in whether they wed or not. "Do you know what I find most miraculous, Papa? That the Scots king was captured at the very same hour that you were concluding your penance at Canterbury!"

Henry laughed, a laugh Geoff had not heard in quite a while. "Thomas was ever one for showing off," he said with a grin, "and he always had a flair for drama. He wanted there to be no doubts whatsoever that he and the Almighty had forgiven me. Not even Louis Capet can argue otherwise now." Glancing from his son to his uncle, he surprised them, then, by offering a rare, unguarded glimpse into the depths of his soul, saying quietly, "It is a blessing to be at peace with God again—and with Thomas."

"I shall honor St Thomas for the rest of my days," Geoff promised, and Henry's gaze lingered upon his face.

"You are my true son, Geoff. The others, they are the baseborn ones, the bastards."

Geoff was speechless. Swallowing with difficulty, he blinked back tears, which Henry and Ranulf tactfully pretended not to see. Looking from one to the other, Ranulf felt a deep and abiding gratitude that Harry's wounds no longer bled. God Willing, mayhap now they might begin to heal. "You asked me once if I thought Thomas was a saint," he said, smiling. "Who could have guessed that it would be Thomas himself who'd answer you?"

O NCE HE WAS SATISFIED that the English rebellion was quelled, Henry turned his attention to ending hostilities in France, and landed at Barfleur on August 8, exactly one month since he'd sailed for England. He'd brought back with him the Earls of Leicester and Chester and the unfortunate Scots king, and after depositing them safely at Falaise, he struck out for Rouen. By the night of August 10, he was within fifteen miles of the city, and ordered his men to make camp for the night, intending to enter Rouen on the morrow.

LIFTING A SMOLDERING OIL LAMP, Henry leaned over to illuminate a parchment map. "Take a look at this," he directed, and Rhys ap Gruffydd's son Hywel crossed the tent to study the map. Rhys had dispatched Hywel as a gesture of solidarity at the start of the rebellion, and since Henry now had one thousand of Rhys's Welshmen at his disposal, it made sense to put them under Hywel's command.

"This is Rouen, here. It is not an easy city to besiege, protected by the River Seine on one side and by hills on the other. I've been told that the French did not have enough men to surround the city, and they have concentrated upon the east. They are employing their soldiers in eight-hour shifts, so that they can continue bombarding Rouen day and night with their siege engines and crossbowmen. But because the townsmen still control the bridge to the west, they have continued to bring in supplies and need not fear being starved into submission."

"So we can march right into the town through the west gate," Hywel said, marveling at the ineptitude of the French commanders. "It sounds like a waste of time, effort, money, and men. What is the point of laying siege to a city unless they are cut off from reinforcements?"

"You'd have to take that up with Louis Capet," Henry said cheerfully. "As for me, I am just thankful that my foes are conducting this campaign with the military skills of a mother abbess. Look over here, Hywel. This area east of Rouen is heavily wooded. I well remember the havoc you Welsh wreaked upon my men on my last incursion into Wales. It was like fighting phantoms, forest demons who'd strike without warning, then fade back into the shadows ere we could retaliate. What I propose is turning your men loose upon our French friends. Can you circle around behind their lines and cut off their supply wagons?"

Hywel grinned. "I thought you were going to offer us a challenge. That will be too easy!"

Henry grinned, too. "I promise to find you something more perilous next time," he said, and then turned as one of his men ducked under the tent flap.

"My liege, a man has just ridden into camp, bold as you please, and asked to see you. He said to tell you—this is going to sound daft, but he said '*planta genesta.*'"

He sounded so puzzled that Henry burst out laughing. "I will see him straight-away," he said, and dismissed the other men in his tent, allowing only Willem to re-main as they awaited the mysterious stranger.

"I am not going to ask," Willem said at last, and Henry took pity on him, saying with a smile, "*Planta genesta* is the Latin name for the broom plant. My father liked to wear a sprig on his cap, and when I was thinking of a code word, that just came to mind."

"I take it I am about to meet one of your spies?"

"One of the best, Willem, one of the very best," Henry said, as a young man was ushered into the tent. He was as dark as a Saracen, with unfashionably long hair and slanted black eyes that laughed up at Henry as he knelt before the king. "Willem," Henry said, "meet . . . well, you may call him Luc." Gesturing for his visitor to rise, he pointed toward the table. "There is a flagon of wine; help yourself. Why are you not at the siege with Louis?"

Luc rose as lithely as a cat, and then strode over to pour himself some wine. "The French king heard an alarming rumor that you'd sailed for Normandy. I kindly volun-teered to ride to Barfleur and keep vigil, for it occurred to me that would be an easy way to pass on my report once you arrived. It was a surprise, and a pleasant one, to find you almost within hailing distance of the city walls. Your eerie ability to appear in a puff of smoke has saved me a two-day ride!"

"Glad to oblige," Henry said. "So Louis does not know for certes that I left En-gland? The way his agents serve him, it is a wonder he even knows about the sinking of the White Ship."

Luc grinned. "He is already out of sorts, sure that St Laurence is sorely offended with him. Wait till the morrow when he finds you in the city. He'll think he's died and gone to Hell!"

"We can only hope." Henry had been in the saddle since dawn and his injured leg was throbbing. Sitting on his bed, he swung the leg up and propped a pillow under it. "Why does Louis think he's affronted a saint? What did he do . . . hear Mass only twice in one day instead of his customary three times?"

"No, my liege. The saint has a greater grievance than that." Luc finished his wine, went to pour more. "Louis has always revered St Laurence, and so he proposed to the citizens of Rouen that both sides observe a truce in honor of the saint's day. They quickly agreed, and this morning they opened the gates and the townspeople began to venture forth. They were soon playing games and dancing, and some of the knights from the garrison staged a mock tourney, all within sight of the French army. Many of the younger men and women gathered by the riverbank and began to shout insults across the water. The Count of Flanders was enraged by their mockery, and he and a few other lords—the Counts of Dreux and Blois and Évreux—sought out the king and urged him to catch the townsmen off guard and launch a surprise attack."

Henry had lain back on the bed. Sitting upright at that, he said with a tight smile, "Let me guess what happened next. Louis was horrified by the very idea of such sacrilege, refused to consider breaking the truce, and then let himself be talked into it."

"You'd have made a fine prophet, my liege." Luc's smile held no more humor than Henry's. "That is exactly what happened."

"Obviously something went amiss, though, or Louis would not be back in camp, brooding over the wrong done St Laurence. Why did their surprise attack fail?"

"St Laurence was not pleased with their double-dealing. Two monks had gone up into the bell tower, which offered a clear view of the French camp. They saw the stealthy preparations under way, and began frantically ringing the bell. If not for their warning, Rouen might have been lost. As it was, the citizens fled back into the town, and by the time the French reached the walls with their scaling ladders, the gates were barred and men were ready for them. There was fierce hand-to-hand fighting on the walls, but the French were driven back. When Louis sent me off to watch for you, they were going at it like stags in rut, trading accusations and blame for the blunder."

"Louis seems to go stark, raving mad in August," Willem observed. "Last year it was Verneuil, and now this."

Henry nodded, but he was not fully listening. He opened his mouth, stopped, and then said abruptly, "What of my son? Did he approve this attack?"

"No, my lord king. He was not happy with it, argued that it was dishonorable to violate their own truce. His knights were disapproving, too, especially Will Marshal. They truly believe in the chivalric code, may God pity their innocent young souls. But Lord Hal's protest was brushed aside. They . . . they do not pay much heed to his opinions."

Henry scowled, taking umbrage that these men should dare to disrespect his son. The irrationality of it did not escape him, but that awareness did nothing to assuage his indignation. Hal had been ill served by those he had most reason to trust—his father-in-law, the French king, his maternal uncles, and his mother, above all, his mother.

Rousing himself, he expressed his thanks to Luc, suggesting that the young spy might want to claim his reward now rather than continuing his clandestine activities. He was not surprised when Luc declined, insisting that he was not at risk, that he'd tell the French king he was captured by Henry's men. Henry did not argue, for he'd encountered men like Luc before, men who thrived on danger, who needed it as others needed air and food. It was easier to understand the Porteclie de Mauzés, those who acted only out of self-interest. Going to a coffer, he drew out a pouch heavy with coins, and Luc smiled, tucking it safely away in his tunic before he accepted Willem's offer to find him a meal and a bed.

Henry bade them good night, pleased with Willem's action. The other man had learned to read his moods well, sensing that he was distracted and wanted time alone. Once they'd departed, Henry dropped to his knees, ignoring the discomfort of his painful thigh. His thoughts of Hal had sent his spirits into a downward spiral, forcing him to dwell upon memories and regrets that served for naught. Just as he'd prayed at Canterbury, "St Thomas, guard my realm," he lowered his head now, and whispered, "St Thomas, save my son."

T HE FRENCH KING had suffered a restless, wakeful night, and stayed abed the next morning, exhausted and disquieted and reluctant to face the day. He'd finally fallen asleep, only to have his dream disturbed by an insistent voice crying out, "My lord king!" Opening his eyes, he saw one of his squires bending over the bed. "Forgive me, but you must wake up, my liege!"

Louis sat up with a groan, smothering a yawn. Over his squire's shoulder, he could see other men crowding into the tent, recognized his sons-in-law, the Count of Blois and Hal, and behind them, several bishops and Flemish lords. They all looked so somber that he yearned to go back to sleep, not wanting to deal with the troubles they were about to thrust upon him. "What is it?" he asked irritably. "I was not to be disturbed. And what is that infernal noise?"

"Church bells," the Archbishop of Sens said, sounding just as vexed as Louis. "Every church bell in Rouen is pealing, chiming to welcome the English king into the city."

"He's here?" Louis rarely cursed, but those closest to the bed thought they heard him mutter something that sounded very much like an obscenity. Fully awake now, the French king winced at the joyful sound of the bells, knowing it was the death knell of his hopes to capture Rouen.

T HE DAY AFTER HE RODE INTO ROUEN, Henry sent his Welsh to harass the French supply lines. They were highly successful, capturing and destroying more than forty wagons loaded with food and wine. The following day, Henry took the offensive, opening the city gates and sending out men to fill in the defensive ditch that separated the foes, making it possible for a charge by his knights. When he led his army out of the city, the French scrambled to meet them, and in the clash that followed, the French took the worst of it; some were taken prisoner and the Count of

Flanders saw another of his brothers struck down; Peter, who'd renounced the bishopric of Cambrai after Matthew's death in order to become Count of Boulogne, was seriously wounded.

That night Louis sent the Archbishop of Sens and the Count of Blois to Henry, seeking a truce so he could withdraw his army to Malaunay, promising to meet with the English on the morrow. When Henry agreed, Louis pretended to set up camp at Malaunay, but under cover of darkness, he fled for the safety of French territory. He then requested a conference at Gisors on September 8, and once more, Henry agreed.

CHAPTER NINETEEN

✦

September 1174
Gisors, Norman Vexin

W HEN HE REACHED THE CONFERENCE elm at Gisors, Henry
saw that the French were already there. Louis was flanked by his bishops
and barons, while the Count of Flanders was standing apart with his own
men, and Henry wondered if there were cracks showing in their alliance. What interested him the most, though, was that Hal and Geoffrey had also distanced themselves
from the French king. He reined in before Louis, who waited for him to dismount, and
looked perplexed when he did not.

"Welcome, my lord king," Louis said once it was apparent that Henry was not going to speak first. "It is our hope that we may agree to a truce in order to put an end to
this unfortunate war."

Henry was staring at the sons he'd not seen in a year. Hal looked no different, cutting a handsome figure in a crimson tunic decorated with gold thread and a fur-
trimmed mantle casually thrown over his shoulder. He did not meet Henry's eyes,
glancing away when he realized his father was watching him. Geoffrey had experienced an impressive growth spurt, was taller than Henry remembered, but he was still

some inches shorter than Hal and Richard. He was more composed than his elder brother, returning Henry's gaze with a respectful nod of acknowledgment.

Henry swung back to the French king. "Where is Richard?"

Louis smiled sympathetically, one father to another. "Alas, Richard is balking at taking part in the council. When we summoned him, he refused to come. He is young and hotheaded, as were we all at his age." Stepping forward, he gestured expansively. "Shall you dismount so that we may talk?"

"If Richard is not here, what is there to talk about?"

Louis did his best to ignore Henry's brusque tone. "Whilst Richard's absence is regrettable, it need not prevent us from reaching an accommodation. Come, and we shall discuss it further."

"I think not," Henry said tersely, and the Count of Flanders strode over, casting Louis a glance of poorly concealed impatience.

"We are willing to agree to a truce that specifically excludes Richard. You may deal with him as you see fit; that is no concern of ours."

"I see." Henry looked from one to the other, then back at his sons. "I will grant you a truce of three weeks. We shall meet again at Michaelmas. I will notify you where the council is to be held."

When they realized that he was about to depart, Louis and Philip exchanged troubled looks, and the Fleming said sharply, "Wait, my lord! We need to talk over the terms of peace."

Henry pricked his stallion with his spurs and the animal leaped forward. As Philip jumped out of the way, he glanced over his shoulder. "You will learn my terms at Michaelmas." His men followed, and Willem soon spurred his horse to ride at Henry's side.

"What now?" he asked. "Do we go into Poitou to rein Richard in?"

"Yes." Henry looked over at the other man, and then slowly shook his head. "Richard will long remember this birthday."

"What do you mean?"

"Today," Henry said, "Richard turned seventeen."

Richard and his men were encamped by the River Vienne southeast of Poitiers. Morale was low, for they'd been retreating steadily from the Angevin forces under Maurice de Craon; they did not have sufficient numbers to meet Henry's commander on the field. Dusk was beginning to darken the sky as Raoul de Faye stormed out of Richard's tent. The head of his household knights came quickly to his side, but when Raoul angrily shook his head, the man asked no questions.

"Come and eat, my lord," he said instead, gesturing toward an open fire, where a group of men were clustered around a large pot. Raoul shook his head again, for his latest quarrel with Richard had taken away his appetite. But the air was redolent with the enticing aroma of venison stew, and he was about to change his mind when a sudden shout heralded the arrival of riders.

To Raoul's vast relief, the lead horseman was a familiar figure, and he hastened over to bid Saldebreuil de Sanzay welcome. Once greetings had been exchanged and Saldebreuil's men sent off to share the supper, Raoul grasped the constable's arm and drew him aside.

"Thank God you are here! Mayhap you can talk some sense into Richard. I've been unable to convince him that we must surrender. We never recovered from our losses in Saintes, and our numbers have been dwindling daily. It was bad enough when we were running from de Craon. But our scouts report that the English king has now joined the hunt, too, is encamped less than ten miles away. Richard still refuses to yield, though. That boy could teach a mule about stubbornness!"

"Take me to him," Saldebreuil said, once Raoul had run out of breath. "I have news he needs to hear." And he fell in step beside Raoul as the two men headed toward Richard's tent.

Richard was alone, staring down at a crudely drawn map of Poitou as he grimly plotted out lines of retreat. He glanced up with a surprised smile that quickly faded as he studied the constable's face. "I am not going to like what you've come to tell me, am I?"

"No, my lord Richard, you are not. I'd come to warn you that your lord father is on your trail. It seems you know that already. But you do not know what happened at Gisors a fortnight ago."

"That craven council of theirs?" Richard said scornfully. "What of it?"

"Your brothers and the French king and the Count of Flanders have served you up as a scapegoat to the English king. They struck a truce with Henry that excludes you. In other words, lad, you are on your own, can expect no aid from your so-called allies."

Richard's intake of breath was sharp enough to be audible. Raoul indulged in a flare of temper, calling Henry various colorful names that were not flattering, calling Louis even worse. Saldebreuil waited patiently until he was done, and then limped across the tent, coming to a halt in front of Eleanor's son.

"It is over, Richard," he said softly. "It is time to go to your father and seek his forgiveness."

Richard reacted as if he'd been stung, recoiling violently. "No! I will not do that. I will never abandon my mother!"

"Listen to us, Richard," Raoul entreated. "Eleanor is my niece and I love her dearly. But there is nothing more you can do for her. The war is lost."

"No!"

Saldebreuil reached out and caught Richard's arm in a grip too tight to shake off. His voice, though, was kind, even gentle, as he said, "You can no longer hope to save your mother. Now you must save yourself. She would expect no less from you. Do you truly believe she'd want you to sacrifice yourself for her sake?"

Richard's mouth contorted, and he jerked free of the older man's hold. "Rot in Hell!" he cried. "All of you can rot in Hell!"

Raoul started after him as he plunged out of the tent, but halted when Saldebreuil said, "No, Raoul. He needs time. Let him go."

RICHARD'S FLIGHT FROM HIS TENT had not stopped there. So great was his need to get away that he did not even wait for his stallion to be saddled, instead took the horse of one of their scouts, leaving the man staring after him in astonishment. Once he was out of the camp, he gave the horse its head and urged it on, racing the wind and his own doubts. Common sense told him that Saldebreuil and Raoul were right, but he still saw surrender as shameful, as a betrayal of the person he loved most in the world. How could he do that to her? He knew she was relying upon him to gain her freedom. If he gave up, what hope would she have?

He diverted some of his pain into rage, dredging up memories of the worst curses he'd ever heard his father utter. The French king was a fainthearted, misbegotten weasel, not worthy to wear a crown. The Count of Flanders was a self-seeker of the worst sort, one who'd pawn his honor for the mere promise of profit. The French lords were spineless lackeys, the Flemings no better. His brothers were beneath contempt, Hal a swaggering, empty-headed puppet and Geoffrey a backstabbing sneak. He could almost believe they were foundlings, for how else explain their treachery?

And now what? He was cornered, trapped with no way out. He'd gone up against the Aquilon, the North Wind, and had been found wanting. What mercy could he expect from his father? He'd be publicly humiliated, shamed, tethered like a lady's pet spaniel. He was a man grown, but his father would never see that. The years would go by and nothing would change. Aquitaine would not be his as long as his father drew breath. And his mother would grow old in an English prison, her exile ended only by death.

Twilight had given way to full night, but he hadn't noticed. It was not until he saw the glow of campfires in the distance that he realized how much time had passed and how far he'd ridden. Halting his mount, he gazed down at those flickering fires in his father's camp. During the course of this wild, wretched ride, he'd swung back and forth between anger, defiance, and despair, spitting out curses and blinking back tears that he blamed on the wind's edge, whispering prayers only God could hear. But he understood now where the Almighty had been leading him.

For an endless time, he sat there, absently patting the neck of his lathered mount as he watched the soldiers move about below him. And then, before he could repent of it, he spurred the horse down the hill. Sentries rode out to block his advance, alarmed by the sudden appearance of this lone youth in their midst. Richard reined in his stallion before them. "I am Richard, Duke of Aquitaine and Count of Poitou," he said in a loud, clear voice. "I am here to see my lord father, the king."

RICHARD WAS USHERED into Henry's tent by startled guards. He had a quick glimpse of the men—his father, the Earl of Essex, Maurice de Craon, and Richard du Hommet, the constable of Normandy—all of them looking no less astonished than the guards. At the last moment, his courage failed him, and he looked away, not wanting to watch their triumphant faces as he humbled himself. Fumbling with the belt of his scabbard, he unbuckled his sword. It was his prized possession, a gift from his mother on that day two years ago when he'd been invested as Duke of Aquitaine, fashioned by the best bladesmith in Bordeaux, with a thirty-inch double-edged blade, an enameled pommel, inlaid with silver for that was thought to prevent blunting, engraved in Latin with the words *In Nomine Domini*, the ultimate symbol of knighthood. He'd called it Joyeuse, said to have been the name of Charlemagne's celebrated sword, which flashed lighting in the heat of battle. He'd never expected to surrender it, and giving it up now was as painful as any physical wound.

Coming forward, he carefully placed the sword and scabbard on the ground, then sank to his knees before his father. "I am here to seek your forgiveness, my liege," he said hoarsely. "You may do with me as you will." To his horror, tears filled his eyes, and he angrily swiped at them with the sleeve of his tunic before nerving himself to look up at Henry. To his amazement, he could see tears shimmering in his father's eyes, too. Henry reached down, holding out his hand.

"Of course you are forgiven," he said, and when Richard took his hand, he was raised to his feet and then gathered to the older man in a tight embrace.

RICHARD WAS NOT SURE what he'd expected, but not this warm welcome, this genuine and manifest joy. His father's companions seemed to share it, too, treating him as if his was the return of the Prodigal Son, not the surrender of a beaten rebel. Wine was brought out, and then food, venison like the meal being served back in his own camp. Richard held his plate awkwardly, not sure if he could swallow a morsel. "I ought to send word to my men," he said hesitantly. "Raoul de Faye and Saldebreuil de Sanzay are there, amongst others. Need I . . . need I fear that they will be punished for my sins?"

Henry reached for another piece of bread, unable to remember when he'd been so hungry. "No," he said, "I mean to issue a general pardon for all who took part in the rebellion."

Richard's shoulders slumped, so great was his relief. "Thank you," he mumbled, for that seemed expected of him. All around him, the other men were laughing and talking, gesturing with their wine cups, and his sense of unreality grew ever stronger. Could it truly be this easy?

"We will return to Poitiers on the morrow," Henry declared, "and ride into the city together so that all may see peace has been restored. And at Michaelmas, we will meet your brothers and the French king, put all this foolishness behind us." He shifted so that he could look directly into Richard's face. "I mean to do right by you and your brothers. The provisions will not be as lavish as the terms I offered last year, but I think you will be pleased."

"Thank you," Richard said again, the words coming automatically to his lips with a calm that belied his inner turmoil. He knew it would be wise to keep silent, to do nothing to threaten this rare moment of harmony. But he could not do that. "May I ask you a question?"

Henry nodded. "Ask," he said, with a slight smile, and Richard drew a deep, bracing breath.

"You have forgiven me for taking up arms against you. You have said that you do not mean to imprison or disinherit the others who joined the rebellion. You have been more generous than I dared hope. But there is this I must know. Can you not find it in your heart to forgive my mother?"

The mood in the tent was transformed as soon as the words had left his mouth. He saw the other men stiffen in the way he'd seen people react when caught out in a storm, listening uneasily to the rumble of thunder and scanning the skies as lightning flashed overhead.

Henry did not speak for a time, struggling against the tide of raw emotion unleashed by the mere mention of Eleanor's name. He'd not wanted to make Joanna choose between them, for she was a child, an innocent who could not be blamed for loving unwisely. He'd not intended to extend that privilege to his sons, for surely they'd forfeited that right by swallowing her poison so willingly. But as he looked now at Richard, he realized that it would not be that simple, that easy. He saw emotions in

Richard's face as conflicted as his own—fear and defiance and confusion and love, love for the woman who'd betrayed him so cruelly. He was going to have to learn to live with that, with Richard's misplaced loyalty, at least until the boy came to see the truth about his mother.

"That took courage," he said at last, "and you've earned an honest answer . . . this one time. I will not speak of this again, Richard. I know this is not what you want to hear. But it cannot be helped. No, lad. I cannot forgive your mother. Not now, not ever."

On september 29, Henry met the French king on the riverbank of Montlouis-sur-Loire, not far from Tours. The day was overcast and dark clouds were gathering ominously along the horizon. Henry and Richard arrived at the same time as the French, and after an awkward exchange of greetings, they moved into the village churchyard so they could take shelter in the church if the storm broke.

"Before we discuss terms for peace," Louis said earnestly, "your sons wish to express their remorse and grief that it ever came to this."

Henry frowned, not sure if he could long endure Louis at his most sanctimonious and self-righteous. As if he were a Good Samaritan, who wanted only to heal this lamentable family feud! But Hal and Geoffrey had taken their cue and were coming forward to kneel respectfully before him. Hal's distress seemed genuine; Henry could not help wondering, though, what he regretted most—that he'd rebelled or that he'd lost. He did not want to let such suspicions mar their reconciliation, and he did his best to put any doubts aside as Hal and then Geoffrey expressed their sorrow, their contrition, and their resolve to make amends, to be the dutiful, loving sons that he deserved.

When their penance was done, Henry played his part and offered them absolution, raising them up for the formal kiss of peace and then quick, paternal hugs. "What's past is past," he said, "and it is forgiven."

Beaming, Louis then embraced Hal and Geoffrey, too, but when he took a step in Richard's direction, he was warned off by the expression on the youth's face, and contented himself with declaring his joy that this breach was mended, quoting from Scriptures to prove his point. *Honor thy father, as the Lord thy God hath commanded thee; that thy days may be prolonged.* And if some noticed that he'd diplomatically edited the Holy Writ by excising any mention of *thy mother,* none were tactless enough to comment upon it.

Hal and Geoffrey now offered strained greetings to Richard, who was even more laconic in reply. Hal then took Henry aside, seeking a moment alone. Withdrawing into the cemetery that bordered the churchyard, they walked among the wooden crosses and flat gravestones as Henry waited, with rare patience, for his son to speak.

"Not the most auspicious of settings, is it?" Hal said wryly, gesturing toward the moss-covered grave markers. "Making peace in a burial ground is like getting wed in a whorehouse. But I do want there to be peace between us, Papa. That I swear to you upon the surety of my soul."

Henry was as moved by the tears in Hal's eyes as he was by his words, and he felt a surge of gratitude that the Almighty and St Thomas had given him this second chance, an opportunity to make things right with his sons. "I also want that, Hal," he said, and when they embraced, he truly believed that they'd made a new beginning. From the way Hal's eyes were shining, he could see that Hal believed it, too.

"As much as I enjoy watching Louis wriggling on the hook," he said, "we'd best rejoin the others so I can end the suspense about my intentions."

Hal was one of those anxiously awaiting Henry's judgment, for all knew this was not a genuine peace conference. As the victor, the English king would be the man dictating the terms of that peace, and they would have to swallow his brew, however bitter they found it. He could only hope that his father would be lenient as he followed Henry back into the churchyard.

Henry wasted no time on preliminaries. "I mean to issue a general pardon to all those who took part in the rebellion," he said, before adding a proviso. "There are four exceptions, however, four men who will not be included in the pardon: the Scots king, the Earl of Leicester, the Earl of Chester, and the Breton lord, Raoul de Fougères. They will have to bargain for their freedom, and only after I feel they can be trusted to honor their oaths."

There were murmurings of relief, for all who owed homage to Henry had been well aware that he could have charged them with treason. Hal edged over toward Will Marshal to murmur sotto voce, "See, I told you that there was no cause for concern. I knew my father would not punish you for being loyal to me."

Will hadn't been so certain of that, and he was savoring his reprieve. Pray God that he'd never again be forced to choose between his king and his young lord. "We were lucky, my lord," he said softly, "so very lucky."

Hal thought that remained to be seen, for his father had yet to announce what provisions he'd make for his sons. "The first thing I want to do is send for Marguerite. I am sure she was well treated, but my bed has been cold without her. I am not used to sleeping alone."

Will was not fooled by the flippancy, for he knew how upset Hal had been by his wife's gilded captivity. Hal was still talking about Marguerite, and Will nudged the younger man, saying, "Your lord father is about to speak again."

Henry waited until the audience fell silent, until he was sure all eyes were upon him. "Last year I offered what I felt to be generous terms to settle this conflict. Sadly, they were rejected. Circumstances have changed since then," he said dryly, unable to resist reminding Louis and the Count of Flanders of the respective reality of their positions. "This was a costly war." How costly he was not going to admit to these men—more than twenty percent of his yearly revenues had gone toward the protection of his crown and kingdom. "Alas, I can no longer offer the same terms that I did last September."

Addressing his sons directly now, he said, "I think, though, that you will not be displeased with what I am offering. I realize now that I was remiss in not providing incomes commensurate with your titles." That was an argument he'd often had with Eleanor, a memory he hastily pushed away. "My lord king," he said to Hal, "I will be endowing you with two castles in Normandy and an annual income of fifteen thousand Angevin pounds, to be spent as you choose."

Hal swallowed, thinking of how much more he'd been offered last year at Gisors: half the crown revenues of England or Normandy, plus four English castles or six strongholds in their continental domains. Reminding himself then, that this was still a very generous offer from the victor to the vanquished, he smiled and made a graceful acknowledgment of his good fortune and his gratitude.

"I have already discussed this with my son Richard," Henry continued. "He is to receive two unfortified castles in Poitou and half of my revenues from that province. To my son Geoffrey, I offer half of the income of Brittany, and all of it once he weds the Lady Constance."

Richard and Geoffrey expressed their appreciation in appropriately formal terms, and Henry smiled to see the three of them standing together, thinking that this was the first step toward the restoration of his fractured family. "Now . . . there is the matter of my youngest son's inheritance. I regret to report that I have recently received very sad news from England. Alice of Maurienne, my son John's betrothed, was taken sick last month and the doctors were unable to save her. We gave orders for a funeral befitting her high birth, distributed alms to Christ's poor in her name, and this sweet child of God will not lack for prayers that she may soon depart Purgatory for the glory of Life Everlasting."

The men had not heard of the little girl's death, and they were quick to offer conventional expressions of sympathy, with many repetitions of "May God assoil her." There was little surprise, though, for all knew how fragile life was in those early years of childhood. Some considered it remarkable that Eleanor had given birth to ten children in the course of two marriages and only had to bury one.

Hal felt a quick stab of pity for the little girl, thinking how sad it was to die so young, so far from her family and homeland. That was followed by great relief as he realized that Alice's death rendered John's marriage settlement moot, which meant there was no longer any need to surrender his castles at Chinon, Mirebeau, and Loudun, the proximate cause of the rebellion. But he felt then a twinge of shame that he could find reason for rejoicing in the death of a child.

"Naturally," Henry continued, "I hope to make another favorable marital alliance for John. I have decided, however, that he ought to have lands of his own. I am therefore giving him the English castles of Nottingham and Marlborough, as well as five castles in Normandy, Anjou, Touraine, and Maine. This will require, of course, the consent of my eldest son, but I am confident that he will find it acceptable now that we have restored harmony in our family and our domains."

Hal's gasp was loud enough for Geoffrey to jab him warningly in the ribs. That reminder alone would not have been enough. But his gaze happened to alight upon his brother Richard, who was watching him with malicious satisfaction. Richard's smirk acted as a lifeline to pull him back from defiant disaster. "If it pleases my lord father," he mumbled, "it pleases me."

Henry had not expected any other response. "Ere we commit these terms to writing, I think it advisable to renew acts of homage. As for my sons, I will gladly accept homage from Richard and Geoffrey, but I waive this act from my eldest son, in recognition of his rank as a crowned king." He'd thought that Hal would be very pleased by this boon, this public recognition of their status as peers. Hal showed no enthusiasm, though; he was staring at the ground, his face hidden by a sweep of fair hair.

Turning his eyes away from his son, Henry looked coolly at the Count of Flanders. "I believe, my lord, that you have a charter to relinquish, one that gave you a claim to my castle at Dover and the county of Kent."

After receiving Count Philip's assurances that it would be forthcoming, Henry decided then to give them food for thought—an example of what he could have demanded had he been vindictive or vengeful. "From here, I expect to return to Falaise to continue negotiations with the Scots king. I am willing to grant his freedom, but after such savage raids against my English subjects, I understandably feel the need to demand proof of his future good will. He will not be released from confinement until he acknowledges himself as a liegeman of the English Crown and agrees that the Scottish Church shall be subordinate to the Church of England. I shall require also that the Scots earls and barons do homage to me against all other men, and if King William should default in his fealty to me, his liege lord, the Scots lords and bishops will hold to me against the King of the Scots, and in such an event, the Scots bishops shall place

Scotland under Interdict until the Scots king repents of his disloyalty. Lastly, to guarantee the safety of my borders, I will take possession of the Scots castles at Roxburgh, Berwick, Jedburgh, Edinburgh, and Sterling, with the costs of garrisoning them to be paid by the Scots treasury."

There was utter silence when he was done speaking, as his adversaries pondered the sad fate of the Scots king and the fearful consequences of defying the man who was King of England, Duke of Normandy and Aquitaine, Count of Anjou, Poitou, Touraine, and Maine, Lord of Ireland and Wales, liege lord of Brittany, now restored to the good graces of the Church and the favor of St Thomas of Blessed Memory.

After this chilling revelation of what could have been, Henry was soon surrounded by men eager to show their good will, and it was not long before he found himself cornered by the French king, no less eager to mend fences and banish the hounds of war. Hal had backed away from the chaos, and after a moment's hesitation, he walked over to his brother.

"Richard . . . did you speak to him about Maman?"

Richard scowled, accurately interpreting Hal's words to mean he would not be raising that dangerous topic himself. "Of course I did!"

"And . . . ?" When Richard slowly shook his head, Hal bit his lip, and for a brief moment, their hostility forgotten, they looked at each other in perplexity and mutual misery.

S ALISBURY PLAIN WAS A VAST MARSH, fed by six rivers, a barren, windswept area of chalk hills and grassy downs. On a promontory north of the River Avon, a castle had been erected in the eleventh century, unusual in that it shared the precincts with a cathedral. The inner bailey contained the keep, several towers, and a palace built by a Bishop of Salisbury for the use of Henry's grandfather. The cathedral was situated in the western half of the outer bailey, with the bishop's palace, buildings for the canons, and three cemeteries.

Eleanor had never passed much time at Sarum Castle; both she and Henry preferred Clarendon Palace just four miles distant, she for its greater luxury and Henry for its hunting park. So her spirits had plummeted at her first sight of the stark stone keep rising up against a bleak Wiltshire sky. Few areas in England were so desolate. The winds were constant, so brutal that the first cathedral had been destroyed in a gale only five days after its consecration. The canons complained that the winds drowned out the sounds of the Divine Office, and they suffered from the joint evil and vision maladies caused by the blinding glare of the sun upon the chalk hills. As she'd ridden through the gatehouse into the inner bailey of the castle, Eleanor was morbidly certain that Sarum would be the death of her.

It was a great surprise, therefore, to discover that she actually preferred Sarum to Falaise. She'd dreaded being penned up in one of the cheerless, cold chambers of the great keep or, even worse, in Herlewin's Tower along the north inner wall. But she'd been escorted to the royal palace and taken up to the private quarters on the second floor. She had a fireplace here, and access to a privy chamber, and she was even able to attend Mass through a private entrance in St Nicholas's Chapel. Best of all, she was permitted to walk in the inner courtyard, to pick flowers in the garden if she chose. She thought she understood why she was no longer being guarded so zealously. The castle at Sarum was escape-proof, so secure that she could be given a few more liberties.

She learned that she was in the custody of a man she knew, Ralph Fitz Stephen, one of the king's chamberlains and sheriff of Gloucestershire. She'd had only one awkwardly polite encounter with him since her arrival, for he was rarely at Sarum. It was the constable of the castle, Robert de Lucy, who was responsible for her daily care, and he'd treated her with distant but impeccable courtesy. She knew her neighbor, too, Jocelin de Bohun, the Bishop of Salisbury, who dwelled on the western side of the outer bailey, but he'd so far paid her no visits. This was not a surprise, for he was not the most resolute of men, and wary of incurring the king's disfavor. He'd sided with Henry over Becket, most likely because he feared the king even more than the archbishop. His loyalty had come at a great cost, for he'd been excommunicated twice by the irate archbishop, and he was destined to be remembered mainly as the man who'd offended a saint. So Eleanor had no expectations of aid from that quarter.

Although she'd found no cause for complaint in her treatment by the constable, the chaplain, servants, or guards, she'd so far had no luck in cultivating another Perrin, and until an unexpected event in mid-August, she'd known nothing of what was occurring in the world beyond the walls of Sarum. This changed, however, when she was granted the privilege of having a visitor.

The man ushered into her chamber was also familiar to her, Reginald Fitz Jocelin, the Bishop-elect of Bath, a cleric who'd been unwillingly caught up in the Becket conflict through no fault of his own. Reginald had a dubious background, for he was the son of Bishop Jocelin. His father had doted upon him, naming him as his archdeacon and thus setting him upon the path toward a church career. He'd been for a time in Becket's household, but that had ended badly when he'd been lured away by the chance to serve the king. Becket had never forgiven him, bitterly assailing him as "that bastard son of a priest, born of a harlot," and some felt that the archbishop's increasing animosity toward Jocelin was actually rooted in his anger with the son.

Eleanor never knew what prompted the visit by Bishop Reginald; he'd offered no explanations. She could only surmise that he was, in his way, striking a blow at Becket, for he'd said enough to indicate that his rancorous memories of the man did not lend themselves to an easy acceptance of the archbishop's sainthood. But she cared little for his motives. What mattered was that, under the guise of offering spiritual solace, he'd opened a window briefly to the world. From him, she learned the astonishing news of Henry's penance at Canterbury, and the equally astonishing results. He'd not stayed long, but when he left, she knew that the rebellion in England was dead and her only hopes rested with her sons and the French king, then besieging Rouen. As disheartening as it was to learn of her husband's triumphs, she still preferred knowing bad news to not knowing any news at all.

E LEANOR WAS NOT HAVING A GOOD DAY. The weather could not be faulted; it was a sun-splashed, mild October morning. But she'd begun keeping track of her time at Sarum by marking the wall with charcoal, and she'd suddenly realized that this was Joanna's ninth birthday. She was sure that Marguerite would make much of her, sure that she'd not lack for either affection or attention. It was hard, though, missing yet another milestone in one of her children's lives, even harder not to know how many more would be denied her.

She was sitting in the window-seat, watching a small bird flit from bush to bush in the courtyard below, morosely trying to make sense of Bishop Reginald's story of her husband's dramatic mea culpa at Becket's tomb. That sounded so unlike Harry that it baffled her. Whatever had possessed him to humble himself like that? Her first impulse had been to assume it was a cynical, political ploy, a way to gain the Church's good will and keep the rebels from appropriating Becket for their own ends. But he already had the support of the Pope and the English bishops. And he could easily have performed a public penance that did not involve baring his back to the lash. Could he truly have been that desperate? If so, mayhap Ranulf was right; mayhap she did not know him as well as she'd thought she had.

Her musings were interrupted by the arrival in her lap of a small whirlwind. As she started, the kitten leaped down and scampered away, but soon returned and began to stalk the hem of her gown. Eleanor could not help smiling at its antics. She'd not really expected to take the cat with her into English exile. But Joanna was very single-minded; she'd carried the kitten onboard ship with her, and presented it to her mother in a travel basket as Eleanor made ready to depart for Salisbury. Eleanor was still dubious, assuming it would run away or her new gaoler would confiscate it once she reached Sarum. The constable had not even lifted an eyebrow, though, at the sight of the cat, and had ordered a servant to provide the queen with a box of dirt as if that was an everyday occurrence. Nor had the kitten absconded. To the contrary, it seemed quite content to share Eleanor's confinement, and within a fortnight, Eleanor was startled to realize how much this little ball of fur had begun to matter to her.

She was luring the kitten closer with the fringed end of her belt when a knock sounded and Sir Ralph Fitz Stephen entered. He greeted her courteously, explaining that he'd returned to Sarum the preceding night, too late to pay his respects. "I wanted to ask if there is anything you need, Madame?"

Eleanor did her best to conceal her surprise, for in nigh on a year, no one had asked that before. With nothing to lose, she said nonchalantly, "As a matter of fact, there is, Sir Ralph. Bishop Jocelin is known to have an excellent library. Time hangs heavy on my hands these days. Would it be possible for me to borrow some of his books?"

To her astonishment, he agreed at once. "I am sure he will be pleased to be of service. I will send a man to the bishop's palace this very afternoon."

"Thank you," she murmured, not wanting him to see how much that meant to her. Books! They would be such a blessing, a way to maintain her sanity. Rolling the dice again, she wondered aloud if the bishop would mind if she made some specific requests, and once again, she won.

"I cannot imagine why he would object, Madame."

"You are very kind, Sir Ralph." Very kind, indeed. Why? As best she could see it, he had nothing to gain and quite a bit to lose by coddling his royal prisoner. Why would he risk angering Harry?

"I have received a message from the lord king," he said, almost as if he'd read her mind. "He has instructed me to provide you with a handmaiden, Madame. If it meets with your approval, I thought I would see if I could find someone suitable in the village."

"God in Heaven," she whispered. "He has won. That is it. He has won and so he can afford to spare me a few crumbs from his table." When he did not answer, she said, with sudden vehemence, "Tell me the truth! I am entitled to that much, surely."

"Yes, my lady, you are right. The king has prevailed over his enemies, won a great victory. After he routed the French from Rouen, they sought a truce. Both sides met near Tours and signed a peace treaty at Michaelmas. The king was very magnanimous to the rebels, Madame, forbore to punish them as severely as he could have done. He provided most generously for the lord princes, your sons, and they have fully reconciled. The young king is to get a stipend of fifteen thousand Angevin pounds a year. Lord Richard is to be given half the revenues of Poitou, and Lord Geoffrey may draw upon the resources of Brittany. The king also issued a general pardon for all the rebels, save only the Scots king, the Earls of Chester and Leicester, and a Breton lord, Raoul de Fougères."

Eleanor's mouth had gone dry. "And what of me?"

She had her answer in the look he gave her now, one of unmistakable pity. "I am sorry, Madame," he said, "but there was no mention made of you in the treaty."

"I see . . ." Her voice sounded strange even to her own ears, flat and toneless. He must have said something before he withdrew, but she did not hear it. Once she was alone, she moved like one sleepwalking to the bed, sank down upon it. *I'll never forgive you, never. Look upon the sun. You'll not be seeing it again. The king provided generously for your sons and they have fully reconciled. I'll never forgive you. Never.*

CHAPTER TWENTY

✦

February 1175
Le Mans, Anjou

O N THE DAY AFTER CANDLEMAS, Richard and Geoffrey once again
did homage to their father; Hal was still exempted because of his status as a
crowned king. Afterward a lavish feast was planned, but before the meal and the
entertainment began, Henry summoned his sons to the castle solar. They entered to
find him already waiting for them.

"Come in, lads," he said cheerfully. "Ere we go back to the great hall, I want to tell
you of my plans for this coming year."

They exchanged guarded glances, for experience had taught them that they were
not always in accord with his plans. He was standing by the hearth and they quickly
joined him by the fire, for the chamber was chill and damp, with drafts seeking entry
at the shuttered windows and winter cold seeping in from every crack and fissure.

"It is time you started to earn your keep," Henry said with a smile. "No more
lolling about like pampered princelings." His gaze lingered fondly for a moment on his
second son, for Richard had come to full manhood in the past year; at seventeen, he
was taller than most grown men, even taller now than Hal. "Come the morrow, you're

off to Poitou. My scouts tell me that the Poitevin barons are champing at the bit again. I want you to rein them in."

To Richard, that sounded almost too good to be true. "I'll have a free hand to restore order?" he asked warily, and when Henry said that he would, he grinned. "Do I have to wait till the morrow? I could be ready to leave within two hours."

Henry grinned, too, remembering how eager he'd been at Richard's age to prove himself. "Tomorrow will be soon enough." He turned then toward Geoffrey, saying, "And you're to go into Brittany, lad, to deal with Eudo de Porhoët and the rest of those Breton bandits. Roland de Dinan will accompany you. I know his loyalty has been suspect in the past, but that is only to be expected of a Breton lord; they play at rebellion the way other men play at dice. He has been steadfast for the past nine years, which counts as an eternity in Brittany. I can trust him with your safety, and you'll learn much from him."

Geoffrey glanced from Henry to Richard, back to his father. "Why do I need a wet-nurse if Richard does not?"

"I'd not call Roland a wet-nurse to his face, lad; he'd not like it. And the reason you need more guidance than Richard is simple. He's a twelvemonth older than you and passed much of last year on his own in Poitou, where by all accounts he acquitted himself well."

Richard's face flushed with pleasure, but almost at once he felt a twinge of guilt. How could he take pride in his father's praise as long as his mother remained entombed at Sarum?

Geoffrey was not satisfied with his father's response, but unlike his brothers, he never wasted time or energy in arguments he was sure to lose, and he subsided with a shrug and a neutral "As you wish."

Hal had been a silent observer until now. No longer able to conceal his impatience, he interrupted when Henry began to expand upon the unreliability of the Bretons. "What of me?"

"You may be sure I've not forgotten you, lad," Henry assured him. "You'll be spending the coming year as a king in training. I have to venture into Anjou, but I expect to be back in Normandy within a few weeks. Then we will take ship for England, you and I."

Hal struggled to hide his dismay. "Together?" he said glumly, his hopes dashed. He'd known that his father was planning to return to England and, when he listened as Richard and Geoffrey were given authority and commands, his own expectations had soared. Why should he not be entrusted with Normandy? Or at the least, Anjou. Instead, he was to be his father's shadow, at his beck and call day and night, with no more independence than an indentured apprentice. Where was the fairness in that?

"This time together will give us a chance for a new beginning, Hal, whilst being a learning experience for you," Henry said, with such enthusiasm that Hal mustered up an unconvincing smile, and tried to ignore his brothers, who were laughing at him behind Henry's back. Let them mock all they wanted, for the last laugh would still be his. He was the one who was king, even if it did seem like an empty honor more often than not.

THE EARL OF ESSEX reached the coastal city of Caen in late March, and headed for the ducal castle. He was at once ushered into the king's solar, where Henry was occupied in confirming to Montebourg Abbey the chapel of St Maglorius on the Isle of Sark. He looked up with a smile as Willem entered, then reached for his great seal. A number of men had gathered to witness the charter, but once it was done, they exited the chamber, leaving Henry with a handful of his most trusted inner circle: the Archbishop of Rouen; Maurice de Craon, his English justiciar; Richard de Lucy, his Norman constable; Richard du Hommet; the abbot of Mont St Michel; his natural son Geoff; and the newly arrived Willem, returning from a diplomatic mission to the court of the Count of Flanders.

Willem had just begun his report, though, when they were interrupted by a message from Henry's eldest son, presently at Rouen. Henry at once ordered the man to be admitted, explaining to Willem that he and Hal would soon be sailing for England. He was somewhat surprised by the identity of the messenger, for Hal's letter was delivered by his vice-chancellor, Adam de Churchedune, not the sort of errand normally undertaken by men of rank.

"Take a seat, Adam," he said, for the cleric was not a young man, and then broke Hal's seal, began to read his missive. Almost at once, he looked up, his expression so blank that the other men knew at once something was very wrong. "Hal refuses to accompany me to England," he said, and he sounded so shocked that the normally even-tempered Earl of Essex felt a stab of hot rage, fury that the king's ungrateful whelp was once more giving his father grief.

"I do not understand," Henry confessed. "When we parted last month, all was well between us. What new grudge can he be nursing now?"

"Does it matter?" Willem said. "You've been more than patient with him, my liege. If it were me, I'd command him to come to Caen straightaway and nip this nonsense in the bud." As Willem glanced around, he saw that his words were well received by the other men; several were nodding in agreement and Geoff was muttering under his breath, too outraged by his brother's antics for circumspection. But Hal's chancellor was shaking his head emphatically.

"My lord king, that would be a great mistake." Leaning forward, he said earnestly, "I offered to take Lord Hal's message myself so that I might speak with you in confidence."

None of the others were surprised by this revelation; they'd taken it for granted that Henry would have put men he could trust in Hal's household, men whose loyalty would be to the sire, not the son. Henry looked down again at Hal's letter, so terse and succinct, so brusque and defiant. Glancing up at the chancellor, he said, "I hope to God you can explain this, Adam," too shaken to pretend he was not angry, perplexed, and hurt by Hal's latest transgression. "I thought we'd put all this lunacy behind us last September."

"My liege . . . it grieves me to say this, but the young king, your son, is as constant as wax. I do not doubt that he has a good heart. He is easily swayed, though, swings like a weathercock in a high wind, and of late he has been listening to the wrong men again, to those who wish you ill. They have planted a poisonous seed in his mind, warning him that you want to lure him to England so that you may then imprison him like the queen."

Henry was stunned. "And he believed that?"

Adam nodded somberly. "Alas, he did, my lord. They played skillfully upon his doubts, his resentments, and stirred up his fears by suggesting that there was something sinister in your decision not to demand homage from him. They argued that homage is an act of mutual obligation, claimed that you did not want to accept his homage because you did not want to be held accountable as his liege lord, proof that you must be plotting treachery once he was in England and utterly in your power."

"That is ludicrous! I waived homage to honor Hal."

"I know that, my liege. But now you see why I say it would be a mistake to command his presence at Caen. That would only confirm his suspicions, convince him that his so-called friends had spoken true."

Henry slumped down in his seat, suddenly as weary as if he'd spent a full day on the hunt. "What would you suggest?" he said at last, and when the chancellor urged gentle persuasion, words of reassurance rather than rage, he agreed to take that approach. But he felt defeated even before he began. Christ on the Cross, were they to start the madness all over again?

WOLVES WERE USUALLY HUNTED only from September's Nativity of Our Lady to March's Annunciation. But upon Henry's arrival at his hunting lodge, the villagers of Bures asked him to track down and slay a lone wolf that had been killing their sheep. He set out early the next morning. His lymer hounds had no luck in picking up the rogue wolf's scent, though, and men, horses, and dogs returned tired and disappointed at day's end, where he found Hal and Marguerite were waiting for him.

Hal greeted him effusively, apologized for the "misunderstanding," and announced that they were ready to depart for England whenever he wished. Greatly relieved that Adam's "gentle persuasion" had worked, Henry welcomed his son and daughter-in-law warmly, thankful that they'd avoided a confrontation. The lodge was neither large nor spacious, ill suited to accommodate the retinues of two kings and a queen, but Henry's servants did their best to provide a more elaborate meal than Henry would otherwise have expected, and after the dining was done, Hal held court in the great hall, laughing and jesting and charming with his usual ease, basking in the attention he was attracting. He did not notice when his father withdrew, ceding him center stage.

Henry slipped out of a side door, stood for a time staring up at the starlit April sky. His initial pleasure had slowly ebbed away as the evening wore on, leaving him with an edgy sense of unease. Was this to be the pattern for years to come? Hal would balk, be coaxed into compliance, and all would be well—until the next time he took offense. How could the thinking of his own son be so alien to him? How had they ever gotten to this road that led nowhere?

It was a mild night and others were outside, too. As he was recognized, several men would have approached him, but he waved them off impatiently. But then he saw one man he did want to speak with, and he moved to intercept William Marshal as he ambled from the direction of the latrines.

"Marshal," he said, stepping from the shadows into the knight's path. Beckoning, he led the younger man away from their audience of eager eavesdroppers. Will followed, but his stiff posture and ducked head conveyed his discomfort as clearly as words could have done. He showed no surprise when Henry launched into a low-voiced, angry reprimand, for he'd been anticipating his sovereign's displeasure.

"I expected better from you, Will. You are one of the few men of Hal's household who has a grain of common sense and a speaking acquaintance with honor. Why have you failed so dismally to protect my son?"

"My liege . . . what would you have me say? I told you at Avranches that I could not spy upon him."

"I am not asking that of you," Henry snapped. "But I do expect you to give him the benefit of your maturity and your good judgment, and I see precious little evidence of that. When his legion of lackeys and drones and leeches seek to poison his mind against me, what do you do? Do you stay silent? Or do you join in with the rest of the baying hounds?"

"Sire, that is not fair! I would never speak against you to the young king. I have always encouraged him to mend this rift between you. But mine is not the only voice he heeds."

That was not what Henry wanted to hear. He needed to believe there was at least one rational voice to counsel his son, for his own words seemed to be falling upon deaf ears. "Then what good are you to me?" he said harshly, and turned on his heel before Will could respond, heading back toward the great hall. Will trailed unhappily after him, but knew better than to try to plead his case when the king was in one of his tempers.

Hal was encircled by his knights, and they were applauding and cheering so enthusiastically that Henry wondered sardonically if he'd just ordered another wine-keg broken open. Gesturing to Will, he said, "Tell the 'young king' that the old one wants to speak with him upon the dais."

Hal soon sauntered in his direction, an arm draped around Marguerite's waist, his face flushed with wine, his eyes bright with laughter. "You wanted me, Papa?"

"I am going to my own chamber, will leave the festivities to your keeping. Enjoy yourselves, but remember that men bed down in the hall at night, so if you carouse till dawn, they'll get no sleep."

Hal promised to keep that in mind, then turned as one of his knights approached, fervently expressing his eternal gratitude and loyalty. Hal sent him off with a laugh and a quip, then explained for Henry's benefit that Giles had suffered a stroke of bad luck; his palfrey had gone lame on the ride to Bures and the village farrier had given a dread diagnosis, that the horse had foundered and must be put down. "Giles has barely two deniers to rub together, and a tightfisted father who'd see him mounted on a goat ere he'd help out. So I offered him one of the horses in my stable. He's a good lad, is Giles, so why not?"

"Why not, indeed?" Henry agreed dryly, for he knew that he'd end up getting the bill for the stallion Hal would buy to replace the one he'd so magnanimously bestowed on Giles. But he reminded himself that generosity was a virtue, lauded in a prince, and he asked Hal if he'd like to join the hunt on the morrow for the elusive, sheep-killing wolf.

"I'd like nothing better! I'd ask a favor of you, though—that I be given the wolf's pelt to make a mantle."

Henry blinked in surprise. "Why? You know how difficult it is to get rid of the stink of wolf."

Hal grinned and dropped his voice conspiratorially. "You know Adam d'Yque-beuf," he said, naming one of the most sycophantic and fawning of his knights. "He's not a bad sort, but sometimes I think that if my boots got muddied, he'd offer to lick them clean."

Henry understood, for that was always a risk of kingship; a crown too often drew the servile and obsequious as well as the capable and confident. "So you are going to give that poor sod a fur cloak that is likely to reek to high heaven," he said, "knowing he'd wear it day and night if it came from you." Hal laughed and Marguerite giggled even as she pretended to disapprove of his mischief-making, but Hal looked thoughtful when Henry then pointed out that since d'Yquebeuf was so often in his company, he'd be exposed to the rank wolf smell, too. Before bidding them good night, he offered Hal one final boon, seeking to ease his mind by removing any doubts about the dual obligations of homage, and told his son that he would receive Hal's homage ere they sailed for England. But he was taken aback by his son's reaction. Hal's face shadowed and he glanced away, no longer meeting his father's eyes.

A PILE OF CORRESPONDENCE had been heaped on the table in his bedchamber, and Henry had planned to tackle it before he went to bed. But he was too restless to concentrate, and instead of summoning his scribe, he began to root through a coffer for something to read; the recipient of an excellent education, he never traveled without books. The first one he picked up was Wace's *Roman de Brut*, a history in verse of the English people. Wace had dedicated it to Eleanor, though, and that reminder was enough for him to put it aside. He flipped through Geoffrey of Monmouth's *Historia Regum Britanniae* next, a mythic history of the English kings and the legend of King Arthur, and eventually settled upon *Commentarii de Bello Gallico*. But even Caesar's own account of the conquest of Gaul could not long hold his attention, and he sent one of his squires to fetch his son.

H AL DID NOT LOOK PLEASED to be dragged away from the revelries in the hall, and did not seem reassured when Henry dismissed his squires so they could speak in private. "Help yourself to wine," Henry said, and Hal quickly drained a cup, almost as if he needed to fortify himself for this interview. For a fleeting moment, Henry was assailed by a treacherous memory from his past, the day he'd awakened his wine-besotted father to confide that he would be marrying Eleanor as soon as she could shed the French king.

Geoffrey had cursed him freely and loudly for this unwelcome invasion of his bedchamber, and when Henry had laughed and said he had a great favor to ask, he'd grumbled, "Quit whilst you're ahead, Harry, whilst you're still in my will." Henry's news had sobered him, of course, and he was soon marveling that "Marriage to Eleanor could make you master of Europe one day . . . Christ Jesus, Harry, Caesar might well envy you!" He'd later warned Henry, though, that he should save his passion for his concubines, not his wife, offering the cynical counsel that "the best marriages are those based upon detached good will or benign indifference. But unfortunately for you, the one emotion you will never feel for Eleanor of Aquitaine is indifference."

The memory was troubling. Any remembrance of Eleanor was painful, especially recollections of those early years. But recalling the easy camaraderie and barbed banter he'd enjoyed with his father, he also felt a deep sense of loss, of regret and bafflement that he did not have the same close relationship with his own sons. Where had he gone wrong?

"Papa?" Hal was regarding him in perplexity. "Why did you summon me? You pulled me away from a game of hazard when I was winning!"

"Hal . . . I know that others sought to convince you I had a nefarious motive in not demanding homage from you as I did your brothers. You need not look so surprised, lad; nothing travels faster than gossip. I daresay at least half of these boon companions of yours are in the pay of the French king, and I expected no better from them. But I never imagined that you'd be taken in by such slander. Jesu, lad, how could you believe that of me?"

Hal had stiffened, but by the time Henry was done speaking, he'd been disarmed by the naked pain in his father's voice. Hal hated discord and quarrels, could not understand people like his brother Richard, who seemed to thrive on strife and controversy. He truly wanted to be at peace with his father, truly regretted their constant clashes of will. "I am sorry, Papa," he said, as contritely as he could. "I ought not to have doubted you. It will not happen again."

"Hal, words are cheap and easily offered. Actions are what count. And when I told you tonight that you'd do homage after all, I saw the expression on your face. You liked it not. Whatever I do, it seems to displease you. If I do not demand homage, you see that as some sort of devious scheme. If I do, your royal dignity is affronted. God's Bones, lad, what do you want from me?"

Hal looked at him unhappily. "I guess I . . . I want your respect."

"Respect cannot be demanded or given, Hal. It must be earned. There are wounds still to be healed. But this I can assure you, that I love you as my life. Surely you believe that?"

"Yes . . . I do. And I love you, too," Hal added quickly, even though there were times when he was no longer sure that was true.

"Then why . . . why in Christ's Name are we always at odds like this? Why can you not come to me when you have a grievance instead of letting it fester? Why do you pay more heed to that fool on the French throne than your own father?"

"Louis listened to me, said what I needed to hear. I ought not to have had such faith in his good will. I know that now; things were never the same after that shameful trick he pulled at Verneuil. But . . ." Hal hesitated, pinioning his lower lip with even, white teeth. "How honest can I be, Papa?"

"Speak your mind," Henry said. "I'll not get angry."

Hal smiled faintly. "Can I have that in writing?" He rose suddenly, went to the table to pour another cup of wine, and finished half of it before he could nerve himself to take his father at his word. "I said I love you, Papa. But . . . but I am not sure I can trust you."

Henry drew a sharp breath. This from the stripling who'd played him for such a fool at Chinon! That betrayal lay between them like an imperfectly healed scar, for they'd never discussed it, prevented first by circumstances and then by caution. But he'd promised to hold his temper and so he said only, "Why not?"

"Because . . . because I know the king will always prevail over the man, over the father."

Henry started to speak, stopped himself. "That may be true," he said at last. "But all that I am doing, I do for you, Hal! I want only to secure for you a peaceful and prosperous kingdom. Nothing matters more to me than that. Why must we be at crosspurposes about this? Our interests are one and the same. Why can you not see that?"

Hal had never been one for the unexpressed thought, rarely curbed a jest in the interest of prudence or even good manners. He almost made a dark joke now about the flaw in his father's grand scheme—that the only way two kings could contentedly share power was if one of them was dead. But he sensed that Henry would find no humor in the gibe, for there was too much truth in it for comfort. He studied Henry's face intently, wondering how honest he could be. Dare he confess his resentment that his father meant to bestow his English castles upon that unwanted afterthought, Johnny? When there were sons to spare in most great families, one would be destined for the Church. Why would Papa not pack the little tadpole off to a monastery? Or if he was bound and determined to reward the boy beyond his station in life, let him look to Richard's lands or Geoffrey's.

All of this remained unsaid, though, for he was not a fool, knew better than to trust his father's assurance that there'd be no anger, no recriminations. If he dared to defy Papa's will, he'd be tossing a torch into a hayrick. It had always been so. Nothing had changed.

"In the future," he promised, "I will come to you first with my grievances," and the evening ended upon a note that satisfied neither father nor son.

CHAPTER TWENTY-ONE

November 1175
Sarum, England

*T*HAT YEAR WAS NOT A GOOD ONE for England. The weather was severe, and there were outbreaks of plague and famine in the outlying areas. The summer was hot and dry, withering crops in the field, and autumn was cold and rain-sodden. November had been a month of gale-force winds and black ice, and winter was promising to be particularly harsh on the exposed marshlands of Salisbury Plain.

Eleanor was curled up on the settle with a book and a blanket. She was not reading, though, her thoughts wandering far from the page open on her lap. Edith, her maid, was sitting by the hearth as she mended one of Eleanor's gowns, humming a cheerful little song as she stitched. Cleo, her cat, was stalking prey in the floor rushes; Eleanor preferred not to know what was being hunted. The rain had ceased earlier in the day, but the wind still sought entry at the shuttered windows, rattling the latches and testing the hinges. Although it was not yet midday, the chamber held enough shadows for night, poorly lit by an oil lamp and several tallow candles that sputtered and filled the air with smoke and the pungent odor of burning fat. Eleanor had never used any candles but the expensive ones made of beeswax, and she wrinkled her nose at the smell, wondering how the queen's allowance of a penny a day for lamp oil was being spent now.

The cat froze in the rushes, ears flattening, and then darted under the bed. Eleanor had learned to take her cues from the little creature, and listened for the sound of footsteps approaching her door. There was soon a discreet knock, and she said, "Enter," grimly amused by the charade they enacted every day. Her door was no longer locked as at Falaise, but it was mockery to pretend she still retained the right to refuse admittance to her chamber. It was too early for dinner, and she closed her book, hoping it would not be that tiresome Father Ivo, the castle chaplain. She'd have been more amenable to his attempts to save her soul if he'd been a better source for news, but either he knew nothing of the world beyond his chapel or he was that rarity, a man of God who truly knew how to practice the cardinal virtue of prudence. At least when Bishop Jocelin had finally gotten around to paying a call, he'd spiced up his sermon with a dose of gossip.

"Madame." An elderly servant poked his head into the room. "You have a visitor," he announced lugubriously; Eleanor was convinced that if he ever smiled, his face would crack. But when he stepped aside to admit her guest, she jumped to her feet so swiftly that the book fell, forgotten, to the floor.

"Rhiannon! Is it truly you?" In two quick steps, she was at the Welshwoman's side, taking her arm to guide her into the room. "There is a coffer just to your right, but the settle is straight ahead." Once they were safely seated, she leaned back to marvel at this unexpected appearance of Ranulf's wife. "You are my first visitor who has not taken holy vows," she said, and laughed. "How did you gain entry? Ah, of course, Ranulf. They'd not gainsay the king's uncle."

Rhiannon started to remove her mantle, then changed her mind when she realized how chilly it was in the chamber. "No, Ranulf did not accompany me. It was actually Emma who got me permission to see you." And she launched into a surprisingly accurate impression of Emma at her most imperious. "'I am the sister of the king, consort of the Prince of Gwynedd. How dare you question my authority?' In no time at all, they were wilting before her like flowers in the noonday sun."

Eleanor was thoroughly confused by now. "Emma? Harry's sister? What in the world—"

"You do not know?" Rhiannon exclaimed, as always turning her head unerringly toward the sound of Eleanor's voice. "But how could you? The king married Emma off to Prince Davydd last year. Ranulf and I are attending the king's Christmas Court at Windsor, and when she learned of our plan, Emma asked to accompany us. It is a bit awkward, what with her husband and mine loathing each other! But we could hardly refuse her, for she is Ranulf's niece, after all. And it turned out to be bread cast upon the waters, for when we reached Clarendon and I found out it was only four miles from Sarum, she was willing to come with me after Ranulf . . ."

She let the words trail off, but Eleanor had no trouble finishing the sentence for her. "After Ranulf refused," she said, and smiled to show it did not matter before remembering that smiles were wasted upon Rhiannon. "That was kind of Emma, for I am delighted to see you. But . . . but why are you this far south? If Harry is holding his Christmas Court at Windsor, why are you so deep in Wiltshire?"

Rhiannon did not answer right away, alerting Eleanor that the answer would not be welcome. "The king is at Winchester now," she said. "We will be catching up with him there, and then going on together to Windsor."

Eleanor fell silent. Sarum was only about twenty-five miles from Winchester. Bishop Jocelin had told her that Hal had returned with Henry to England, so this was the closest she'd been to one of her sons in more than two years. Why had Hal not tried to see her? Richard would have, even if it meant scaling the castle walls in the dead of night. Rhiannon was looking troubled, and she roused herself, saying lightly, "Of course you are not really riding all the way from Wales to visit with Harry, are you? Your son Morgan is still in his household, no?"

Rhiannon laughed. "You've caught us out," she admitted. "Morgan is the lure—" She stopped suddenly, head cocked to the side. "What was that noise? Are we alone?"

"No, not *exactly*. That was Edith, my maid. We can speak freely in front of her, for she speaks no French, only English." Eleanor's smile was wry. "She is useful at times, but as a companion, she leaves much to be desired. I have wine, Rhiannon. Would you . . ." Getting a polite refusal, she leaned over and covered the other woman's hand with her own. "Tell me of my children."

Rhiannon did. Joanna was still at Devizes with Constance and Alys, but she was sure the girl would be at Windsor for the Christmas Court, and so would John. Hal and Marguerite would be there, too, of course. Richard and Geoffrey would be holding their own courts, in Poitou and Brittany. They had both enjoyed considerable success in the field, she reported, knowing how proud Eleanor would be. Richard had captured the rebel stronghold of Castillon-sur-Agen that past August after a two-month siege, and the Countess of Chester had written to Ranulf that Geoffrey had Eudo de Porhoët on the run.

"The Countess of Chester," Eleanor said softly. "Is she well?" And when Rhiannon affirmed it, she forced herself to ask, even though she dreaded the answer. "What of her son? Is Hugh still being held prisoner?"

"No," Rhiannon said. "He was freed last year, in October, I believe, although his lands have not been restored to him yet."

"*Gratia Dei*," Eleanor whispered, closing her eyes for a moment, and Rhiannon, who was as perceptive as her husband, squeezed her hand affectionately.

"I do have some sad news, though," she said. "Ranulf's brother died in July."

"Rainald? I am sorry to hear that," Eleanor said, and she was; she'd always had a liking for Henry's cheery, brash uncle. "Was he long ill?"

"No, it was sudden. He'd been with the king at Woodstock a fortnight earlier, and seemed quite well. He was no longer young, of course."

"None of us are," Eleanor said with a sigh. "So . . . my sons have truly been forgiven, are back in Harry's good graces?" And she felt both relief and a prickling of resentment when Rhiannon assured her that family peace had indeed been restored. "Rhiannon, I will never forget your kindness in coming to see me, especially since you had to defy Ranulf to do it. I hope to God I have not caused harm to your marriage."

"You need not worry, my lady," Rhiannon said with a quick smile. "It is true that Ranulf was not pleased with me. But he knows full well that Welshwomen are not as submissive and docile as our English sisters. We have minds of our own. And I was not going to let him stop me from visiting you. You spoke of my 'kindness.' Well, I am only repaying yours to me, during those months when I was stranded at your court whilst our husbands were chasing about France."

"Ah, yes," Eleanor said. "I remember. I was with child—Geoffrey—so that was seventeen years ago. When we got word that Harry's brother Geoff had died of a sudden, Harry and Ranulf hastened over to Rouen to comfort Maude. They were supposed to return within a fortnight, but it was nigh on four months ere Ranulf came back to England and another month after that ere I was reunited with Harry for our Christmas Court . . ."

She was quiet for a time, remembering. The men had trooped into the solar at Winchester Castle, muddied and boisterous and jubilant after a day's good hunting. For a moment, she thought she could actually hear echoes of their raucous laughter on the wind. Henry had pulled her into his lap as he told Ranulf of Thomas Becket's recent, spectacular entry into Paris, vastly amused by his chancellor's flair for the dramatic. When she'd asked for a cushion for her aching back, he'd obliged with a grin, saying to the others, "Imagine how she'd order me around if I were not a king."

Rhiannon was sorry she'd reminded the queen of a time when her marriage was a source of joy, not misery. Hoping to distract Eleanor from memories that served only to hurt, she said hastily, "I was so homesick for Wales, missing Ranulf and feeling like a stranger in an alien land. If you'd not been so good to me, I truly do not know how I would have endured those wretched months."

"Your visit today eclipses any kindnesses I may have shown you," Eleanor assured her. "Rhiannon . . . may I ask you about your blindness? But if you'd rather not talk about it—"

"Other people are the ones who have difficulty speaking of it, not me."

"You were not born blind, were you?" Eleanor asked, hoping that her memory was not playing her false.

"No, I was not. I lost the sight in one eye when I was eight after I was hit by an ice-encrusted snowball. But within a year, I lost the sight in my other eye, too. My father consulted every physician in Wales, and they all said the same. They did not know why my other eye should also fail, but it was often the case with such injuries, and nothing could be done. My mother would have wrapped me in soft wool, coddled me till her last breath, but my father, bless him, would have none of that. He insisted that I 'defy the dark,' live my life as if I were still sighted. I learned to play a harp, to sew and do household chores, even to ride a horse, finding ways to compensate for my lack of sight. It was not easy, but I was so lucky, my lady, that my father was so stubborn!" A fleeting smile touched her lips. "The blind are often hidden away from the world, as if they are a cause for shame."

Eleanor had listened intently, and was quiet for a few moments. "I've met few people as calm, as contented as you, Rhiannon. You always seemed to me like a serene small island in a turbulent sea. I often wondered how you'd achieved that sense of peace, given how severely you'd been tested by the Almighty."

By now Rhiannon had grasped which way the wind was blowing. "Acceptance of life's setbacks is never easy, my lady. For me, the hardest time came when I reached marriageable age, when I realized that few men would be willing to take a blind wife. But my father never let me wallow in self-pity, and his own life was so beset with tragedy that he'd earned the right to speak on the subject."

Eleanor knew very little of Rhiannon's father, save that he'd been crippled some years ago when he'd been trampled by a runaway horse. "What losses did your father suffer?"

"His brothers and sisters had all died ere their time. He found great contentment in marriage to my mother, but he lost her, too, and of the six children she'd borne him, three were stillborn or died in the cradle. Only my brother Cadell, my sister Eleri, and I survived childhood. Cadell died at twenty, thrown from his horse, and when my father wed again, his new wife proved barren, but he was too fond of her to put her aside, even though he no longer had a male heir and his lands could have been forfeit to his prince when he died."

Eleanor agreed that Rhodri ap Rhys had been visited far more than he ought by the Grim Reaper. Thinking the man might better have been named Job than Rhodri, she said, "So how did he cope?"

"He dealt with his disappointments as he'd dealt with his blind daughter, by seeking to change what could be changed and accepting what could not. He taught me to acknowledge my mistakes, to learn from them, and then put them aside. He never let me forget that the morrow might bring greater glory than yesterday's ills, for none of us know the Divine Plan of Our Saviour. In that, we are all blind, and see through a glass, darkly."

Rhiannon smiled again, a smile that spilled sunlight into the dimly lit chamber. "And indeed, good did come with the bad. Ranulf came back to us, filling the hole left in our hearts by Cadell's death. When we least expected it, my father found a male heir to save his lands and I found joy beyond imagining. And Ranulf . . . he found what he most needed, a way to heal, to escape a past weighted down with regrets and remorse and guilt. Not a day passes that I do not thank the Almighty for His Blessings, but not a day passes that I do not thank my father, too, for teaching me that there is a time for every purpose under the heaven and the greatest gift we can offer Our Lord God is to pray with a loving, humble heart, 'Not what I will, but what Thou wilt.'"

Eleanor's eyes searched the other woman's face, but she felt letdown, hoping for more than that. "You make it sound so simple," she said, and Rhiannon shook her head so vehemently that her veil swung from side to side.

"Oh, no," she said. "It is not simple at all. Indeed, it may be the most difficult task you ever undertake in this life, my lady. But think upon this. What other choices have you?"

I F ELEANOR HAD BEEN SURPRISED by Rhiannon's unexpected visit, she was dumbfounded by the identity of her next visitor. On a cold, overcast day in late December, that same mournful servant announced the arrival of the Lady Emma, sister of the English king.

E MMA HAD TAKEN one disapproving glance at Eleanor's accommodations and sent the plump, moon-faced Edith to the great hall. "The wench does understand the word for 'wine'?" she asked, seating herself beside Eleanor with a rustle of silken skirts. "Or is she likely to come back with verjuice or buttermilk?"

"No, 'wine' was one of the first words I taught her," Eleanor said with a smile. "Whatever are you doing here in Wiltshire, Emma? Rhiannon said you were attending Harry's Christmas Court at Windsor."

"I was, but I chose to leave earlier than I'd first planned. It was not as entertaining as I'd hoped."

Eleanor studied her sister-in-law with curious, speculative eyes. They'd always gotten along well enough, although they'd never been confidantes; the twenty-five-year gap in their ages had not been conducive to greater intimacy. She'd always thought Emma was one of the most beautiful women she'd ever seen; like Hal, she'd inherited Geoffrey le Bel's striking good looks. She was fashionably fair, with cornflower-blue eyes and sunlit flaxen hair hidden now by wimple and veil, blessed with good bones, deep dimples, and an ethereal, delicate appearance that led people, especially men, to miss the steel in her spine. Now she busied herself in placing a cushion behind her back before saying nonchalantly,

"I brought you a New Year's gift, a tame magpie in a wicker cage. Alas, though, a clumsy servant let it escape."

"I thank you for the thought," Eleanor said, although she was not disappointed, for she did not fancy keeping a captive bird as a pet, unable to soar into the sky as God intended. "But if you are returning to Wales, surely Sarum is greatly out of your way?"

"It would be, if I were going back to Wales. But I intend to take ship at Southampton by week's end, assuming the winds are favorable. I want to visit my son."

Eleanor remembered that Emma had a small son, born of her first marriage. As the young Lord of Laval, he'd not been able to accompany her into Wales, yet another reason for Emma to begrudge her marriage to Davydd ab Owain. "I am gladdened to see you," she said, "but I'll admit to some surprise. Most people seem to fear that the king's disfavor is contagious."

Emma's shoulders twitched in a graceful shrug. "I doubt that Rhiannon had much gossip to share with you, whereas I have enough scandals and rumors and idle talk to entertain you for months to come. Consider it my good deed for the year."

They were interrupted then by Edith's return, carefully balancing a tray with wine cups and wafers. She was a good-hearted girl, and beamed when Eleanor thanked her in her own tongue. Motivated as much by boredom as anything else, Eleanor had begun to learn a few phrases of English; on her bad days, she feared that she might be fluent in English by the time her captivity ended, either by release or death.

"I am assuming that you are as innocent of recent happenings as a cloistered nun," Emma declared, taking a swallow of wine and grimacing at the taste. "Harry's son Geoff is now the Bishop of Lincoln, as the Holy Father approved his election, and he was formally welcomed into his city in August. But Harry then decided that he should continue with his schooling ere he is actually consecrated and will be sending him to Tours for further study, much to Geoff's relief."

Eleanor had always had a good relationship with Geoff, but she was sure that was one more casualty of the rebellion, as badly ruptured as her friendship with Ranulf. She thought it a pity that her husband had not found a destiny for his son that was a more comfortable fit, but she refrained from commenting, not wanting to risk alienating Emma with criticism of her brother.

"I imagine Rhiannon told you of Rainald's death, and that Richard and Geoffrey had some success against rebels in Poitou and Brittany. It looks as if marriage negotiations for Joanna are on again, and the King of Sicily is sending envoys to the English court in the spring."

Eleanor frowned, saying nothing. She'd approved of the match, which would give Joanna a crown and a husband likely to treat her well, but now she could think only that if her daughter were sent off to Sicily, she might never see the girl again.

"As for the Clifford slut, Harry makes no secret that she shares his bed, but he has so far refrained from flaunting her at court. When he needs a woman to grace his table or act as hostess, he relies upon Marguerite, most likely in a vain attempt to mollify Hal."

Rosamund Clifford was the least of Eleanor's troubles. "'A vain attempt,'" she echoed. "Are you saying that Harry and Hal are at odds again? It was my understanding that they'd made peace and all was well between them."

"On the surface, it is," Emma said, pausing to sip more wine. "They were together day and night this year past, riding the length and breadth of England as they dealt with the duties of kingship. They made a pilgrimage to Canterbury to give thanks to St Thomas, held forest courts in Nottingham and York, forced the Earl of Gloucester to yield Bristol Castle, met with the Welsh princes this summer, then traveled north to receive the allegiance of the Scots king and his barons. I suspect Harry is trying to keep Hal so busy that he does not have time to collect new grievances, but if so, it is not working as well as he'd hoped."

Eleanor thought it interesting that Emma had dismissed her husband with that casual phrase, "the Welsh princes," but she was far more intrigued by the possibility of dissention between father and son. "What are Hal's grievances?"

"The usual complaints—not enough money, not enough time to himself, not enough authority of his own. As long as they are yoked together, Hal is going to be utterly overshadowed by his sire, and he likes it not. Lately he seems to be looking for reasons to disagree with his father, although he does have the right of it in their squabble about the forest courts. But I find it hard to believe that he is truly so concerned with the injustice of it, think he is just using the issue as a way to assert his independence."

"What do you mean, 'the injustice of it'?" Eleanor asked, and Emma smiled, thinking that she sounded more like the prideful Duchess of Aquitaine at that moment than a royal prisoner resigned to her fate.

"During the rebellion, Harry had proclaimed free hunting in the royal forests. But he's had a change of heart, and he is now amercing stiff fines against those who took him at his word. Even his justiciar protested, producing the royal writ authorizing such trespasses. Harry would not be dissuaded, though, and ordered both barons and clerics into his court as he traveled around the country. Not a popular move for certes, one that has stirred up resentment against him."

"He must be in great need of money," Eleanor said thoughtfully, "to resort to such drastic measures. The cost of putting down the rebellion must have been higher than he'd anticipated."

"I daresay you're right," Emma agreed. "But I think he also sees it as a way to re-assert the authority of the Crown, reminding his subjects and vassals that the lax days of the past are gone for good. He has always been strong-willed, but he is less amenable to compromise now than he once was, less concerned about the fairness of his decisions. His seizure of the earldom of Cornwall is a good example of that."

"Rainald's earldom?" Eleanor paused for a moment to recall the late earl's family circumstances. He'd claimed the vast earldom through his wife, a great heiress who'd also been unstable of mind. They'd had three daughters and a sickly son, who'd not survived his father, leaving him with a natural son, Rico, who was barred from inher-itance by his out-of-wedlock birth. But even lacking a male heir, the earldom should have been divided among his daughters and their husbands.

"That does not sound like Harry," she said. "God knows, he could be stubborn once he made up his mind, but he was rarely arbitrary, and the only time he was truly unjust was when he exiled Becket's kin and household in a fit of fury."

Emma shrugged again. "Well, if he has indeed changed for the worse, you must bear some of the responsibility for that, no?"

She'd half-expected Eleanor to flare up, and was surprised when the other woman nodded. "Yes, I suppose I must."

"Good heavens," she said, faintly mocking but without real malice, "has captivity caused you to examine your conscience, Sister?"

This time it was Eleanor's turn to shrug. "It helps to pass the time," she said com-posedly and, as their eyes met, Emma was suddenly glad that she'd followed this inex-plicable impulse and detoured to Sarum.

"I promised you scandal, too," she said. "But alas, it is not one you'll take pleasure in, for it involves your niece, your sister Petronilla's elder daughter."

"Isabelle? What has happened?"

"It seems she took those troubadours' tales about courtly love too much to heart, or at least her husband thought so. Flanders was apparently not fertile ground for no-tions of romance and besotted swains and unrequited love. Philip caught Isabelle with one of his knights in compromising circumstances. She swore that they were not lovers, as did the man, but Philip was not convinced. He ordered the knight to be beaten nigh onto death with a mace, then hung by his heels over a cesspit until he suffocated."

"Jesu," Eleanor breathed. "What did he do to Isabelle?"

"Well, he would not end the marriage, for then he'd lose her inheritance, Vermandois. So he somehow 'persuaded' her to assign her rights to him." Emma dropped all pretense of insouciance and said, with a hard edge now to her voice, "Better we not know how he managed that."

"Indeed," Eleanor said, just as grimly. "God help the girl. It does not matter if she was guilty of adultery or not, does it? The mere appearance of impropriety was enough to damn her."

Emma nodded, and they both fell silent for a time, contemplating the bleak future of Isabelle of Vermandois and the sad fate of her alleged lover. "I never thought I'd say this," Eleanor said finally, "but I am glad that my sister is dead. She'd be half mad with fear for her daughter, whilst knowing there was little she could do."

Emma decided to overlook the unsatisfactory quality of the wine and drained her cup. "There is something else you need to know, Eleanor. Last month, Harry met with Cardinal Ugo Pierleoni, a papal legate he'd invited to England."

"Harry sought the cardinal out?" Eleanor was astonished, for no papal legate had set foot on English soil during the twenty-one years of her husband's reign. It did not take her long to guess why Henry wanted to consult a papal legate, and she said, with a thin smile, "So he wants to see if the Pope would be agreeable to the dissolution of his marriage."

"Well, ostensibly the cardinal's mission was to settle the interminable feuding between the Sees of York and Canterbury, but I think you can safely assume that the question of your marriage came up in conversation."

"He'd have no trouble finding grounds for annulment," Eleanor conceded. "Louis and I made use of that reliable pretext, consanguinity, and Harry could invoke it, too, for we are actually more closely related by blood than Louis and I were. Or if he wanted to break new ground, I suppose he could raise the specter of treason. But then he'd find himself in the very same predicament that faced Louis. Once our marriage was ended, he'd lose any claim to Aquitaine. Somehow I cannot envision Harry being quite as trusting as Louis, bidding me farewell to return to my own duchy, knowing how happy the French king would be to come to my defense, how eager to fulfill his obligations as my liege lord."

"I agree," Emma said. "However much Harry might want to rid himself of you, he'd not be willing to yield up Aquitaine, either to you or Richard. It is a tangled coil for certes, a Gordian knot. But this I know. If there is a man capable of escaping that maze, it is my brother."

"Yes," Eleanor said reluctantly, "you may well be right. At least I will not be taken by surprise now. Thank you, Emma, for the warning."

"You are welcome." Emma rose without haste, smoothing her skirt and adjusting her wimple. "There is one more matter," she said, "one more good deed I can do for you. Rhiannon told me about the milkmaid." Her gaze flicked toward the oblivious Edith, an expression of disdain turning down that lovely mouth. "I think I can do us both a good turn, for one of my ladies-in-waiting has been pining away in Wales. I'd send her back to Normandy, but she has no family there. She's thrice a widow, but barren, and she is too proud to impose upon cousins. Why not speak with her? If she suits you, I'll be spared her sulks and complaints, and at the least, you'll have an attendant who speaks French."

"Would she be willing? It could be argued that serving me is a form of captivity in and of itself. Since she's not taken vows, I assume the quiet of the cloister holds no appeal for her."

Emma's smile was dismissive. "Trust me, she'll thank God fasting for the chance to escape from Wales."

Eleanor let her reach the door before she spoke again. "Emma . . . I have to ask, if only out of curiosity. Why did you come to see me? Why did you warn me that Harry is pondering an annulment?"

Emma paused, silent for so long that Eleanor decided she was not going to answer. "Let's just say," she said, "that it was a gesture of good will, one unhappy wife to another."

A MARIA DE TORIGNY was a still-handsome woman in her forties, with wide-set dark eyes, strong but comely features, and more curves than were fashionable. She bore Eleanor's scrutiny with equanimity, and answered readily enough when she was asked of her history. Yes, she was indeed kin to the abbot of Mont St Michel, a second cousin, she believed. And yes, she had been wed three times and thrice widowed, first as a lass to a neighbor old enough to be her grandfather, then to a Norman knight, and lastly to the steward of the Breton lord, André de Vitré, adding that she'd entered the service of the Lady Emma after her last husband's death.

"And you have no wish to try matrimony a fourth time?" Eleanor queried, both curious and wanting to be sure Amaria could be content in the seclusion of Sarum.

"It would take a brave man to take me to wife, given my sad marital history. To be widowed twice is not so out of the ordinary, but when you lose a third husband, people start to take notice," Amaria said, so matter-of-factly that Eleanor almost missed it, the faintest gleam of very dry humor.

"And you have no close kin?"

"Yes . . . I do, Madame," Amaria corrected, sounding surprised. "I have several brothers and a sister who is a nun at Fontevrault Abbey, and of course, my Laval cousins."

"I must have misheard the Lady Emma," Eleanor said, "for I thought she said that you had no children or family back in Normandy."

"The Lady Emma misspoke. I bore my second husband two babes, one who died when we overlay her in our bed and one who was stillborn. And the Laval cousins I mentioned are kin to Lady Emma's late husband."

Eleanor was quiet for a moment, assessing what she'd so far learned. This was a strong woman, strong enough to have buried two children and three husbands and survived. Yet there was something that did not ring true about the entire matter. Emma was not particularly interested in the personal lives of others, and may well have forgotten that Amaria had lost two babies in infancy, assuming that she'd even known. But how could she have forgotten that Amaria was kin to her husband?

"You are wondering what pieces are missing from this puzzle," Amaria said unexpectedly. "May I speak candidly, Madame?"

"I wish you would."

"The truth is that the Lady Emma had her own reasons for her offer to you. I have been with her for a year and a half now, and I think I have worn out my welcome. But I am her late husband's cousin, and so she would not want to dismiss me out of hand. If I entered your service, my lady, my family back in Laval would feel that she'd done right by me. It is true you are in disgrace, but you are still the Queen of England, and that would not fail to impress my brothers."

"What have you done to displease Emma?" Eleanor asked, although she thought she already knew the answer to that.

"I have my share of failings, Madame, as do we all. But the one that seems to vex the Lady Emma the most is my unfortunate habit of speaking my mind too forthrightly. I've never learned the art of dissembling, and it seems that is highly valued in a lady's maid. Apparently too much candor can become tedious, or so Lady Emma tells me."

"I suspected as much," Eleanor said, suppressing a smile. Any woman who'd tell a queen to her face that she was "in disgrace" would not flourish in the artificial, mannered society of the highborn. The "art of dissembling" was more than a virtue in the corridors of power; it was a survival skill.

Amaria was watching her intently. "I suppose I've ruined my chances," she said, sounding resigned but not apologetic. "I did not think it was likely you'd take me on, in truth. Thank you, my lady."

As she started to rise, Eleanor waved her back. "You are too hasty, Lady Amaria. As it happens, I think you'll do very well."

"Truly?" Amaria hid neither her surprise nor her pleasure. "I'd never have wagered on that outcome, my lady!" she said and grinned. "If my outspokenness did not put you off, I feared you might be suspicious, wondering if this was not a plot concocted by Lady Emma and the king to place a spy in your household."

Eleanor laughed outright. "The thought did cross my mind. But I could see no profit in it. You see, Amaria, the victor rarely bothers to spy upon the vanquished." She rose then, indicating the interview was over. "You may tell the Lady Emma that I will be pleased to have you join my household, such as it is."

Amaria had gotten to her feet as soon as Eleanor rose. "You will not be sorry, my lady. Well, at least I hope not," she amended and curtsied before moving toward the door. There she paused. "Madame . . . I would not pretend to know the king's mind, have only seen him briefly. But at Windsor he seemed surprisingly tense and troubled for a man you call the 'victor.'" And then, fearing she'd overstepped her bounds before she'd even entered Eleanor's service, she curtsied again and backed out the door.

Eleanor sat down again on the settle. There was some satisfaction in the image conjured up by Amaria's words. As wretched as she was, she wanted Harry to be miserable, too. And yet, she was aware of an underlying sense of sadness. Theirs may have been the first war in which there were no winners, only losers.

CHAPTER TWENTY-TWO

✦

February 1176
Woodstock, England

*M*ELIORA WATCHED FROM a distance as the king emerged into the manor bailey. He did not look happy, and her spirits sank; it must not have gone well with Rosamund. She waited until he'd entered the great hall before making her way to the royal bedchamber. There she found Rosamund huddled on the bed, weeping as if she'd never stop.

"Ah, lamb . . ." Scrambling up onto the bed, she gathered the younger woman into her arms. "The king would not agree, then?"

"No . . ." Rosamund looked up, blue eyes swollen to slits, her face streaked with tears. "I tried so hard to make him understand, Meliora. I told him how much I wanted to retire to the nunnery at Godstow, that I could no longer live in a state of sin. But he became very distraught. He asked if I still loved him, and of course, I had to say that I did and I do. He insisted that was what mattered, and we could find a way to ease my mind. He said he could not bear to lose me—"

She sobbed again, seemed to have so much trouble catching her breath that an alarmed Meliora slid off the bed and brought her a cup of wine, urging her to drink. Rosamund obediently took a swallow, and then wiped her face with her sleeve. "Tell me what to do, Meliora. I cannot bear to cause him such pain, but this is the kindest way . . . I know that. If I cannot convince him of this, though . . ."

Meliora found herself blinking back tears of her own. "You may have to tell him the truth, lamb," she said softly. But as she expected, Rosamund shook her head vehemently.

"No! I will not do that to him. I will not make him watch me die!"

Meliora did not know what to say, and rocked Rosamund in her arms until her sobs subsided and eventually she fell into an exhausted sleep. Only then did she get her mantle and leave the chamber.

Outside, she halted in confusion, unsure what to do next. She considered the idea of going to the king herself, but not for long. She could not betray Rosamund's confidence. Nor had she the courage to confront the king, to argue without the one weapon that might sway him. Who in Christendom did?

An icy rain had fallen earlier in the day. It was dry now, but the bailey was still muddy and windswept as she started toward the chapel, intending to beseech the Almighty to aid His daughter Rosamund in her time of travail. She'd only gone a few steps, though, before she came to an abrupt halt, staring at the man who'd just exited the great hall. The Lord God had answered her prayers, for there *was* one at Woodstock with the courage to tell the king what he did not want to hear, and the moral authority to prevail without revealing Rosamund's illness.

"My lord bishop!" As Roger turned, she hastened toward him, would have sunk to her knees in the mud before him had he not stopped her. "I am Dame Meliora, Your Grace, handmaiden to the Lady Rosamund. Can you spare a few moments for me? It is a matter of the greatest urgency—the state of my lady's immortal soul."

"WHY DID YOU INSIST upon dragging me out to the springs, Roger?" Henry cast a pessimistic glance at the overcast sky. "We're likely to have to swim back to the manor."

Roger decided they'd come far enough and slowed his steps. "I wanted to speak with you in privacy," he said, "with no fear of prying eyes or pricked ears."

"About what?"

"Sin."

Henry's brows shot upward. "You do remember, Cousin, that you are not my confessor?"

"I am not jesting, Harry. This is too grave a matter for that. I need to speak with you about the Lady Rosamund Clifford."

"Indeed?" Henry's voice had hardened; Roger could see the tightening of the muscles along his jaw. "Rosamund is none of your concern, my lord bishop."

"Harry . . . you must let her go."

"She spoke to you about this . . . about Godstow?" Henry sounded incredulous and then, defiant. "As I said, this is none of your concern. Let it be, Roger."

"I cannot do that, my lord king, for the stakes are too high. If you love her—and I think you do—that is why you must let her withdraw to the nunnery at Godstow priory."

"I do love her," Henry said, "and that is why I will not let her go. This is but a whim of hers, a fancy that will pass. I know her, Roger. You do not."

Roger was silent, marshaling his arguments, regretting his promise to Meliora that he'd say nothing of Rosamund's suspicions, the recurring pain in her breast. Henry was scowling, but Roger took heart from the fact that he'd not stalked away in a royal rage. He hoped that meant his cousin was not as free of misgivings as he claimed. "I am willing to risk your anger," he said quietly, "for royal favor means little when balanced against eternal damnation. It is my concern for her immortal soul that bids me be so bold with you. She gave up much for your sake, Cousin . . . her maidenhead, her honor, marriage, and motherhood. Would you have her give up her chances of salvation, too?"

"Damn you," Henry said, low voiced. He'd backed against a nearby oak, a massive tree barren of leaves, gnarled and ancient. "Damn you," he said again, even as his shoulders slumped and the color drained from his face.

THE BENEDICTINE NUNNERY of St Mary and St John the Baptist had been founded in the year of Henry's birth. Situated on an island between two streams of the River Thames just north of Oxford, it had always been a haven for Rosamund; she'd been educated there and still had a deep and abiding love for the convent and the nuns who'd schooled her in her youth. Standing in the familiar priory precincts to bid farewell to the king, Rosamund experienced a sense of utter unreality. Was this a dream or had her long love affair with Harry been one?

They had exchanged their private farewell the night before at Woodstock, and so they were formal now in the presence of Prioress Edith and the other nuns. Henry kissed her hand and she made a respectful curtsy, even though she knew that the nuns were well aware of their scandalous liaison.

"I have to attend a great council with the papal legate next month in London," Henry murmured, too softly for any ears but Rosamund's, "and then I'll be holding my Easter Court at Winchester. I will stop to see you on the way."

"Go with God, my lord," she whispered, seeing him through a blur of tears.

"COME," Prioress Edith said briskly as soon as Henry and his men had departed. "We have prepared a guest house for you."

Rosamund was honored that the prioress herself had chosen to escort them. She'd known they would make her welcome; the king's favor would be a great blessing for the priory. But she was touched to find so many of the nuns waiting for her at her new lodgings. As her anxiety about her reception had increased, the pragmatic Meliora had pointed out that she'd been very generous with the convent since becoming the king's mistress. To Rosamund, that counted for little against the shame of adultery. So far, though, she'd encountered no hostility or disdain, neither overt nor implied. Nuns who had taught her in her youth greeted her warmly as a former pupil, not as a wanton seeking redemption.

Seeing the exhaustion etched into Rosamund's face and posture, the prioress sent the other nuns off to their duties, leaving Rosamund alone with Meliora. The older woman hovered nearby, not wanting to smother her with too much attention, too much solicitude. It was not easy, though, for she'd learned to love Rosamund as one of her own daughters.

"You will consult with the infirmarian this afternoon, dearest?"

"I will, Meliora," Rosamund promised dutifully. She sat on the bed, watching as Meliora set about unpacking their coffers, still feeling as if she were sleepwalking. She could feel the tears welling up in her eyes again as she thought of her last night with Henry. His pain was so much harder to bear than her own. Rising abruptly, she announced she was going for a walk, slipping out before Meliora could protest.

Prioress Edith had said dinner was served in the guest hall, and the position of the sun told her that noon was nigh. There were several widows living at the nunnery, and she could imagine they'd be avidly curious about the king's concubine. She had no appetite, was never hungry these days, and she decided to forgo the meal, not yet ready to face an audience. Instead, she headed for the church.

Inside, all was serene, shadowed, and still. Nothing had changed; it was like going back in time. Moving into the nave, she approached the high altar. Kneeling, she began to pray for her royal lover, that he would not grieve for her too much. She'd expected to fall apart once she was alone, giving way then to the heartbreak she'd been stifling for his sake. But her tears soon dried, and as she prayed, she realized that some of her sorrow was easing. There was comfort in these familiar surroundings; there was comfort in the invocations of childhood. This was the first time in years that she'd been able to bare her soul to the Almighty without being in a state of sin. Her confessor had never been able to absolve her, for they both knew she'd continue sleeping with the king. Now she could repent without reservations. She could accept the penance laid upon her, could atone for her transgressions, and die in a state of grace. And kneeling there in the church of Godstow priory, she rediscovered what she'd long ago lost and thought forever denied her—the promise of inner peace.

A KEEN MARCH WIND was gusting and winter's chill still lingered, even though Easter was less than a fortnight away. Eleanor did not mind the mercurial weather, though, so pleased was she to be riding in the open air under a sky the color of bluebells. Her mare seemed to have been infected with her high spirits and was fighting the bit, eager to run. Glancing over at Amaria, mounted on a more docile gelding, Eleanor was tempted to challenge her to race. Thinking of Sir Ralph's panicked reaction should his royal prisoner suddenly gallop off into the distance, she laughed aloud.

Amaria smiled at the sound of that laughter. She did not know what awaited them. Sir Ralph had told them only that he'd received orders to move the queen from Sarum to Winchester. But it was enough for her that the queen was so happy on the journey, however it ended. Amaria was convinced that the queen found confinement so oppressive because she'd always enjoyed far more freedom than most women. She was a wild bird caught in a net, unlike her tamer sisters bred in captivity. At the very least, Winchester would offer novelty, a change from the predictable dreariness of days that were indistinguishable one from the other.

It was dusk before they saw the walls of Winchester in the distance. As they approached the Westgate, Amaria glanced toward the adjoining castle and cried out at the sight of the banner flapping in the March wind. "My lady, look! The king is here!"

Eleanor did not share Amaria's surprise. She'd quickly concluded that this trek to Winchester was connected to her husband's annulment plans. Why else would Sir Ralph have said she'd not be returning to Sarum? What was Harry up to now? Well, she'd soon see. She was not as nervous about this meeting as she'd been before their confrontation at Falaise, for she had more than two years of experience as his prisoner to draw upon now, knew where he'd set the boundaries for himself. She need not fear physical punishment or abuse, or even deprivation to any great extent. He might even free her for the sake of their children if he could find a way to clip her wings or blunt her talons. That was such a mixed metaphor that she could not help laughing again, but it was as apt as it was incongruous. If she saw herself as a caged dove, Harry saw her in far more predatory terms, as a bird of prey.

By the time they passed into the outer bailey of Winchester's great castle, the sky was the shade of lavender. Dismounting first, Sir Ralph hastened over to assist Eleanor from her mare, and she hoped her next gaoler would be as conscientious. She'd learned that courtesy mattered the most to those with no right to demand it.

"Maman!" The cry rang out across the bailey, as clear as a harp chord. Eleanor spun around at the sound, just in time to catch her daughter to her in a close embrace. Joanna was hugging her so tightly that her mantle brooch was being pressed into her skin, but she did not care, any more than she'd cared about the driving rain when they'd been reunited at Barfleur. This reunion was different from the first one, though, for it was not being held under her husband's glowering, baleful gaze. Henry was nowhere to be seen.

Eleanor noted with ironic amusement that she had not been put in the Queen's Chamber, but she had no complaints about her lodgings. The room was freshly painted, hung with decorative wall hangings to shut out the cold, the floor covered with fragrant rushes, and the candles were made of costly beeswax, not the malodorous tallow. "Thank you, dearest," she said warmly, for she was sure this was Joanna's doing. "The chamber is a fine one."

Joanna was sprawled on the bed, playing with her mother's cat as it cautiously ventured from its travel basket. She glanced over her shoulder with a smile. "Tell me what else you want, Maman, and I will persuade Papa to get it for you."

"You sound very sure of yourself, Regina," Eleanor teased, with a smile of her own, and Joanna's throat constricted, for it had been a long time since she'd heard that affectionate pet name, bestowed upon her by her brothers when talk had first begun of marriage to the King of Sicily. She could no longer remember who had first used it, Hal or Richard, but it brought back memories of those days when her parents were not at war with each other and her family was still intact.

"Papa rarely says nay to me," she admitted. "And he is being even more generous now, for the King of Sicily is sending envoys to the court this spring, and if all goes as planned, I could sail for Sicily ere the year is done."

"So that is why I am at Winchester?"

Joanna nodded. "I told him that nothing mattered more to me than having you with me ere I wed. I explained," she added with a grin, "that a girl needs her mother at such a time."

She was a confident, clever child, but a child, nonetheless, only in her eleventh year, and soon to be a wife. Eleanor had accepted the practice, for it was all she knew. Confinement had caused her to question many of the tenets she'd once taken for granted, though, and regret caught at her heart now as she thought of sending Joanna off to an alien land, an unknown husband, a fate to be determined by factors beyond her parents' control.

Sitting cross-legged on the bed, Joanna had lured the cat into her lap, pronouncing herself satisfied with the name Eleanor had chosen, Cleopatra, in recognition of the little creature's haughty elegance and queenly will. "Did I tell you, Maman, that I got my first letter?" She sounded so proud, as if this were a milestone toward adulthood, and Eleanor felt another protective pang, wishing she could keep this fledgling in the nest for a little longer.

"It was from Tilda," Joanna revealed, obviously flattered that her elder sister had thought she was old enough to receive her own correspondence. "She wrote to Papa, too. She had another baby, a second son, who has been named Lothair." The sound of that odd German name sent her into a fit of giggles, but she soon grew serious again. "Tilda is distraught by what has happened to our family, Maman. She says she does not understand. I do not know what to tell her, for I do not understand, either."

"Ah, child . . ." Eleanor sat beside her on the bed, put an arm around the girl's shoulders. It occurred to her, then, that Joanna had yet to mention Hal, an odd omission unless he was no longer at his father's court. "What of your brother? Will Hal be permitted to see me, too?"

"Hal is gone, Maman. He has been very restless of late and none too happy. He decided he wanted to go on pilgrimage to the shrine at Santiago de Compostela. Papa was loath to consent, did not seem to think that was a good idea at all. But Hal persisted; he can be very stubborn, you know. And at last Papa compromised, agreed to let him go to Normandy for a time. Hal and Marguerite left a few days ago for Porchester. Such a shame you missed him, for I know how dearly he'd have loved to see you."

"Indeed, a shame," Eleanor said, very dryly. If Joanna thought Hal's absence was due to coincidence, well and good. She knew better.

JOANNA APPEARED IN ELEANOR'S BEDCHAMBER early the next morning, reluctantly leaving later only for dinner in the great hall. Eleanor was served her meal in her own chamber, although she had to admit the quality of the Lenten food was no less than what was being served at the high table in the hall. It was clear to her that Henry did not want to give Joanna any cause for complaint about her mother's treatment, and she grudgingly gave him credit for putting their daughter's wishes above his own. She'd dressed that morning in the best of her gowns, for she was anticipating a royal summons, and it was not long in coming. Once dinner was done, the castellan came to escort her to the king.

THE SOLAR WAS STILL SHUTTERED, for the day held none of the longed-for warmth of spring. It was well lit, though, with oil lamps and a large iron candelabrum. Henry was alone, walking back and forth before the fireplace. This was the first time she'd seen him in almost two years, and she was startled by the change in his appearance. Although his ceaseless activity had kept him fit, he'd always had a powerful, stocky build. He was noticeably thinner now, his face so drawn that it almost looked gaunt, and his closely cropped reddish hair was showing traces of grey. She suspected that these past months had been no kinder to her, but the fashionable wimple framed her face in a flattering way, concealing any signs of aging, and her own grey hairs were covered by the graceful folds of her veil.

They regarded each other in silence for a few moments, Eleanor content to let him set the pace. "If you'll have a seat," he said coolly, "we have matters to discuss."

Eleanor sat in the chair he'd indicated, noting that he'd provided wine for them both; so this was to be a duel conducted with civility. As he took a seat across the table from her, she said, as if they were resuming an interrupted conversation, "So will you accept the King of Sicily for our Joanna?"

Taken by surprise, he said, "Yes, I think so. I'll put his proposal before my council in London, but I do not expect any objections to be raised. It will be a good match for her, one she seems content with."

"Yes, she does," Eleanor agreed, claiming a small victory by compelling him to acknowledge that she still had the right to voice her opinions about their daughter's future. "What dowry is he proposing to give her?"

"The same that was discussed when the issue of marriage was first raised. He will grant her the county of St Angelo, the cities of Liponti and Viesta, and various castles and towns." Henry was not comfortable with the direction their discussion had taken; this could have been any idle, intimate conversation between husband and wife. "We need to talk about the future," he said abruptly, retreating into his public persona—the dispassionate king, detached and distant.

That was a part Eleanor had often played herself, but she had no intention now of submerging the woman in the queen. Whether he liked it or not, he'd have to deal with his wife. Smiling, she raised her cup and took a sip of wine. "How is the annulment progressing?"

She had to admire his control; only the narrowing of his eyes told her that her thrust had hit home. "I expect," he said, very evenly, "that you are as eager as I am to end this mockery of a marriage. If only for the sake of our children, we need a resolution, a way to put the past behind us and move on."

"I am certainly in favor of that," Eleanor said lightly; to her surprise, she was beginning to enjoy herself. "But there is that awkward little problem—Aquitaine. We both want it, and I actually have a blood right to it, a right the French king would be only too happy to recognize. If you set me free, I can promise to be guided by you in all matters of importance, to be good." Her smile came and went so fast that he could not be sure he'd seen it. "Could you trust me, though?"

Henry took the bait. "I'd sooner trust in the honor of the lowest Southwark whore," he snapped. He at once regretted the flare of temper; he'd sworn that he'd not let her provoke him, not like that wretched morning at Falaise. "You want your freedom, and I am willing to grant it to you—under certain conditions. Do you care to hear them?"

"I am waiting breathlessly," she assured him. "What is the price I must pay?"

"I will never let you loose in Aquitaine again. That big a fool I am not."

"That was not one of Louis's better decisions, was it? Even if it did rebound to your benefit. So what do you propose, then? Do not leave me in suspense, I entreat you."

"You agree to the annulment. You agree, too, to relinquish your rights to Aquitaine."

"And what do I get from that Devil's deal? I am free to do what . . . to beg my bread by the side of the road? You'll have to do better than that, my lord husband."

"You did not let me finish," he said coldly. "You take the veil and enter Fontevrault abbey—as its abbess. It is one of the most renowned abbeys in Christendom, one of the few where the abbess rules over monks as well as nuns. You could have a very comfortable life, with enough authority and influence to satisfy even a former duchess. I would retain my overlordship over the duchy, but Richard's status as heir would not be affected. He would still be recognized as the Count of Poitou and eventual ruler of Aquitaine. I think it is a reasonable solution, far more than you deserve if truth be told. You get your freedom and enormous prestige as the abbess of a great abbey. I get peace of mind. And Richard still gets Aquitaine, which is what you always wanted."

Eleanor leaned back in her chair. For a moment, her face was noncommittal; he had no idea what she was thinking. And then she startled him by clapping aloud. "Ah, well done, Harry! I knew you'd find a way once you put your mind to it. An ideal solution, for certes. You no longer need fear that I am becoming too friendly with Louis or Philip of Flanders. You can still meddle in Aquitaine whenever you get the urge, and you can continue to spend my money, of course, whilst keeping Richard on a tight rein, for an heir and a duke are not quite one and the same—as you learned to your cost with Hal. Best of all, Fontevrault is in Anjou, so you can make sure that I'd not do more plotting than praying."

Henry found her flippancy very irritating. There was too much at stake to yield to it, though. "As I said, it will be beneficial to us both. Moreover, it will please our children if we reach an accord. Do you need time to consider this? I would think the advantages would be too obvious to require much thought, but if you—"

"No, that is kind of you, but quite unnecessary. I do not need any time to consider. My answer is no."

Henry was on his feet so fast that his chair toppled over into the floor rushes. "May I ask why?" he said, measuring each word with deadly calm.

Eleanor smiled. "I do not think I have the vocation for the religious life, Harry. I'd not make a very good nun."

"I was doing you a courtesy by asking, Madame. Your consent is but a formality."

"That is not what the Church says. You cannot force me to take holy vows."

"Do you care to wager your freedom on that? I offered to make you the abbess of the richest abbey in my domains. It can just as easily be an impoverished Irish convent, so remote and secluded that not even God could find you!"

"Do you truly think it would be as easy as that to make me disappear? I am not just your unwanted wife. I am the Duchess of Aquitaine." She stood now, too, took her time in positioning her mantle about her shoulders. "You need not see me out, dearest. I am sorry to disappoint your little trifle, but surely she could not have been so stupid to think you'd marry her once you were rid of me." She was taken aback when he went ashen. She'd intended only a glancing blow, had not meant to hit a vital organ.

"Get out," he said tonelessly, and the very lack of emotion in his voice was what she found most disquieting. She moved toward the door, keeping her eyes upon him all the while, pausing outside in the pentise to catch her breath. The silence from the solar was ominous. It was with relief, therefore, that she heard the sudden, sharp thud, the sound of his wine cup striking the door behind her. Only then did she walk away, a faint smile playing about her mouth.

I T T O O K W I L L E M some time to track Henry down, finally finding him in the stable, examining his new white palfrey. Henry had told him he'd be broaching the subject of Fontevrault Abbey with Eleanor that afternoon, and he wanted to make sure it had gone well. He could not imagine why it would not, but if all women were capricious, creatures of impulse, Harry's disgraced queen was downright perverse and, even as a prisoner, dangerous. One look at Henry's grim profile was enough to give him his answer.

"She balked?" he asked in astonishment.

"She said she does not think she'd make a very good nun." Hours later, Henry was still seething. "The bitch all but dared me to force her into a nunnery. As God is my witness, Willem, I swear I—"

"My liege," Willem said warningly, for he'd seen what Henry had not, the appearance of Joanna in the doorway of the stable.

"There you are, Papa. I've been looking everywhere for you," she chided, hurrying toward the stall, where she paused to admire his new stallion. "He is a beauty, Papa. May I name him for you?"

Henry did not think that was a good idea; he'd heard some of the names that Joanna bestowed upon her pets. But he found it almost impossible to deny her anything these days; she'd become even more precious now that he was so close to losing her. "If you insist, lass," he said, making an effort to swallow his anger. "Do not embarrass him, though, by giving him a name better suited to a mare."

"Horses are not embarrassed . . . are they?" Momentarily distracted, she pondered that for a moment. "You are just teasing me. Papa . . . did you speak with Maman yet about becoming the abbess of Fontevrault?"

"I did, Joanna. She refused the offer."

Willem blinked; he hadn't known that Henry had discussed this with his daughter. But when he saw the look of disappointment that crossed her face, he understood. That was shrewd, he thought, getting the lass on Harry's side. It was to be expected that she'd like the idea. From a child's perspective, it must seem like the perfect solution. Her mother would no longer be a prisoner; instead would rule an important abbey. It would have to be easier for the girl to leave England for her new life in Sicily if she could believe that her mother was beginning a new life, too.

"I'll talk to her," Joanna said. "Mayhap I can get her to change her mind . . ." She frowned, lost in thought, and then smiled. "I know who could persuade her, Papa! Hal could."

"Hal is most likely in Normandy by now," Henry reminded her, but she was shaking her head.

"No, he is still at Porchester. I heard men talking in the hall at dinner. They said the winds were still blowing the wrong way, allowing ships to sail from Normandy but keeping Porchester's ships in port. Hal is very unhappy with Maman's confinement. I think it would ease his mind greatly if she became the abbess. And he can be most convincing when he wants to be, Papa."

Willem stayed silent, curious to see how Henry got out of the trap. But to his surprise, Henry seemed to be giving it consideration, telling Joanna that she might be right. He restrained himself until after the little girl had gotten bored and wandered off, and then said, "Are you serious about summoning Hal back to talk to the queen?"

"It is not a bad notion," Henry conceded. "I cannot keep them apart forever, however much I'd like to, Willem. He has asked me twice if he may visit her, and sooner or later I must agree or he'll not forgive me. Jesu, how that lad can cherish a grievance! And I think Joanna is right. He probably would favor the idea."

"Yes," Willem said, "he probably would." Leaving unsaid the rest of his thought: that Hal was always one for the easy way. He'd likely be relieved if he did not have to fret about his mother's welfare. He glanced at Henry as the other man reached for a brush and began to curry his horse, wondering if he'd also seen that flaw in his son's character. Most likely he had; that would explain why he so often watched Hal with such troubled eyes.

B Y THE FIRST SATURDAY IN APRIL, Winchester was overflowing with highborn guests, barons and princes of the Church come to pay honor to their king and the King of Kings upon the solemn festival of Easter. With the Archbishop of Canterbury, the Bishops of Winchester, Exeter, Bath, and Ely present, the castle cooks were already anticipating the end of Lent, planning the great feast they would serve the king and his guests once Eastertide began.

Henry was enjoying a frank political discussion with the Bishops of Ely and Bath, for he need not weigh his words with either man; Geoffrey Ridel and Reginald Fitz Jocelin had been his agents before being rewarded for their loyalty with mitres. From the corner of his eye, he saw that his daughter had sidled up onto the dais and seated herself in his high-backed chair, obviously practicing for the day when she, too, would wear a crown, and he felt a surge of affectionate pride soured by anxiety. Ten suddenly seemed such a tender age, and Sicily at the back of beyond. Seeing the direction of his gaze, the bishops smiled, willing to indulge the father until the king turned his attention back to them. It was then that the steward hastened into the hall, headed straight for Henry.

"My liege, the young king has just ridden in," he announced. He hesitated then, and decided to let Lord Hal be the one to tell him the rest of the news, for he suspected the king would not be pleased; this development could only complicate his tenuous truce with the queen.

Hal had never learned the royal skill of dissembling in public, and as he strode into the hall, he seemed to trail storm clouds in his wake. Henry had known he'd be disgruntled at being summoned back to Winchester like this, for he'd fear that his Normandy jaunt was imperiled. He knew, too, that once Hal learned the reason for his return, he'd be flattered that his father had sought his aid and delighted to see his mother. But as he looked at his son's handsome, sullen face, Henry could not suppress a sigh. Why did he have to work so hard to keep the lad in a good humor? As a boy, Hal had been sunny-natured and full of fun, given to pranks but not tantrums. How had he changed so much in such a few short years?

"My lord king," Hal said, giving a formal salutation appropriate to their distinguished audience. But then Joanna squeezed through the encircling guests to greet him with a pert "Brother, you're back!" Hal abandoned protocol and gathered her into a fond embrace; Joanna's brothers had always vied with one another to see who could spoil her the most.

"Where is Marguerite?" Henry asked, coming forward to welcome his son.

"She stayed behind at Porchester. That made more sense, as I assumed I would not be long at Winchester," Hal said, delivering a veiled warning as well as an explanation, letting his father know that he was still set upon departing England. "You once told me you were stranded at Barfleur for six weeks, awaiting favorable winds, my lord father. I do not know how you endured the wait; we've been bored unto death in Porchester!"

"You'll want to send for her," Joanna predicted, "when you hear the reason for your return. We have a special surprise for you!"

"Do you now, imp?" Hal grinned down at his little sister. "As it happens, I have a surprise, too. Guess who landed yesterday at Southampton?"

Henry felt a sudden premonition. Before he could confirm his suspicions, the door banged open and his sons Richard and Geoffrey entered the hall. They started toward him, looking far more pleased to be at Winchester than Hal. But Joanna was faster. With a gleeful cry of "Richard!" she met him in mid-hall. Henry could only watch as the scene played itself out to its inevitable conclusion.

"Maman is here!" Joanna gasped, so excited she was almost hyperventilating. "Here in Winchester!"

Hal looked dumbfounded, Geoffrey no less surprised. Richard grasped Joanna's arm, demanding, "Where? Show me!"

"Come on," she said, and they headed for the door. Hal and Geoffrey caught up with them in a few strides. Acutely aware of the utter silence in the hall, Henry followed after them, halting in the doorway. Richard and Hal and Joanna were strung out across the bailey, running as if their very lives depended upon speed. Geoffrey trailed in the rear, his a more measured pace. And as he watched them, Henry could hear again, with haunting clarity, his wife's bitter taunt. *You've already lost what you value almost as much as your kingdom. You've lost your sons.*

CHAPTER TWENTY-THREE

✦

April 1176
Winchester, England

J N HER GIRLHOOD, Eleanor had learned to play the harp, for that
was considered a social requisite for young women of high birth. She
had not continued with the lessons, though, and so she was quite pleased to
learn that Amaria was an accomplished harpist. After a word to Joanna, a harp was delivered to her chamber, and she was watching intently as Amaria played a plaintive
melody.

"Wait, let me see you play that chord again," she said, for she'd determined to revive her rusty musical skills during this enforced idleness. Amaria was comply-
ing when the door was thrust open without warning and her sons burst into the
chamber.

"Splendor of God," she whispered, not believing her own senses until she was being embraced by Richard and then Hal, then Richard again, as Geoffrey and Joanna
waited impatiently for their turn, and Amaria, who had a secret sentimental vein she'd
so far hidden from Eleanor, smiled through tears as she watched her lady's reunion
with her sons.

✦

Wɪᴛʜ ᴛʜᴇ ɪɴɴᴏᴄᴇɴᴛ ꜱᴇʟꜰ-ᴀʙꜱᴏʀᴘᴛɪᴏɴ of the young, they'd asked few questions so far about their mother's confinement. Instead, Richard and Hal were vying for her attention, each one seeking to impress her with his exploits and adventures in these past two years. Richard had the advantage here, for he had military deeds to brag about, and Hal had only accounts of forest court sessions and diplomatic missions, which even he would concede lacked the panache or verve of castle sieges and raids. That did not stop him from seeking to regain control of the conversation every time Richard paused for breath. Joanna was just as rapt an audience as Eleanor, but Amaria noticed that Geoffrey had soon stopped competing with his brothers and was slouched in the window-seat, conceding them center stage.

Feeling Amaria's gaze upon him, he smiled and said softly, "Rather like watching two dogs fighting over a bone, no?" That so eerily echoed her own thoughts that she gave him a surprised smile, although later she would think the comment was too cynical for a lad of seventeen.

Richard was dwelling again upon his triumph at Castillon, assuring his mother that "Arnald de Bonville sang a very different tune the day he surrendered than when the siege began. He'd claimed it could hold out till Judgment Day, but that came much sooner than he'd expected!"

Hal heaved an audible sigh, and shifted in his seat, stretching his legs out so Joanna could lean against him. He wondered how long his brother was going to hold forth about the capture of one paltry castle; he made it sound like the most significant military accomplishment since the days of Caesar. He suddenly remembered, then, that he had news of a sensational nature to share, news Richard wasn't likely to have heard yet, and he wasted no time in cutting Richard off in mid-sentence.

"I have astonishing news, Maman, concerning that Clifford harlot. She has withdrawn from court and our father's bed and entered the nunnery at Godstow!"

As he'd hoped, that ended any interest in his younger brother's boasting. They were all staring at him, exclaiming in surprise; even Richard looked interested in this dramatic revelation.

"Are you sure, Hal?" Eleanor asked doubtfully, for that did not seem very likely to her.

"I swear it is so, Maman. Last month Papa escorted her from his manor at Woodstock to Godstow, where he made a generous contribution to the nunnery. It has been the talk of the court ever since. No one seems to know why, though. Some think Papa was growing tired of her, others that she was ailing. I've heard people insist that she was stricken with guilt and wanted to repent for sinning as Papa's concubine. But I've also heard it claimed that she is with child, and hopes to have the babe in secret. The truth is that no one knows the real reason, for no one has been brave enough to ask our father. And yes," he conceded with a wry grin, "that includes me, too!"

"Has she taken vòws?" And when Hal admitted he did not know, Eleanor fell silent to ponder this amazing bit of news. She did not have any great animosity toward the girl, for she knew how beguiling her husband could be when he put his mind to it. She knew, too, that it would be no easy thing to refuse the king. Her anger had always been aimed more at Henry than Rosamund, not for the infidelity itself but for the emotional attachment that she'd seen as a betrayal far more than any sins of the flesh. It was then that she remembered the strange way he'd reacted to her barb about Rosamund earlier in the week. Whatever the reason for Rosamund's nunnery retreat, it was not because Harry had tired of her. A man does not grieve for a woman who no longer holds his affections.

Just then a timid knock announced a servant with a message for the "young lords." He'd been sent by the steward, he explained, to remind them that the hour was growing short and the Easter Eve feast was soon to start. Eleanor's sons rose reluctantly, surprised when she remained seated. It was left to Joanna to tell them that she'd been eating her meals here in her own chamber, not in the hall with their highborn guests.

"That is absurd!" Hal said indignantly, as Richard snatched up his mother's mantle and held it out. Eleanor took it without hesitation, and then linked her arm in Hal's as he made a gallant's bow. Richard glowered at Hal, but recovered quickly and made Joanna laugh when he asked for the honor of escorting her in the exaggerated, courtly style made popular by jongleurs and troubadours. That left Geoffrey to offer his arm to Amaria, which he did with that quick smile of secret amusement.

Amaria was nervous, though, as they emerged into the bailey and headed for the great hall. She'd heard so many stories of the king's notorious tempers, had no wish to witness one firsthand. The odd intimacy of their circumstances had encouraged a bonding that would not normally take place between a queen and her attendants. In the few months since she'd entered Eleanor's service, Amaria had come to see them as allies, even friends, and she had no desire to return to the Welsh court of the discontented Lady Emma and her unscrupulous braggart of a husband. But it occurred to her that King Henry might well look around for safer targets for his rage, turn upon her the fury he could not turn upon his queen.

Catching the hesitation in her step, Geoffrey gave her a curious glance, and she decided to take him into her confidence, saying quietly, "My lord, we both know the king will like it not when the queen enters with the young king. Do you think he will react with anger or make a scene?"

"No, Dame Amaria, I do not," Geoffrey said at once. "Most likely he suspects this will happen. But even if he is truly taken by surprise, he will save face by acting as if this were planned. To do otherwise would be to admit before all his bishops and barons that my mother outwitted him." He seemed to read her mind then, for he added, "Nor will he dismiss you in disgrace. In fairness to him, he has never been one to chase after scapegoats, prefers to hunt more challenging quarry."

"You've eased my mind, kind sir," Amaria said playfully, and hoped that he knew his father better than Henry seemed to know his sons.

Their arrival stopped all conversation, created just the sort of commotion that they'd hoped it would. As the highborn guests forgot their dignity and crowded closer to gape at Henry's rebel queen, Henry himself seemed to take Eleanor's dramatic appearance in stride, and came down the steps of the dais to meet her.

"Madame," he said composedly, kissing her hand and then taking her arm to escort her to the high table. Eleanor played her part with no less aplomb, pausing to acknowledge the greetings of her husband's guests as they made their way toward the dais. Henry's self-control never faltered, but the arm she held was as hard and unyielding as granite. Once she was seated beside him, she did her best to hide her jubilation behind a demure demeanor. But after their wineglasses had been filled, she could not resist a gentle gibe.

Raising her cup, she favored Henry with her most loving smile, as she murmured, "I trust I've no need of a food taster?"

The smile he gave her in return was not in the least loving. "Poison is your weapon of choice, not mine, Madame," he shot back, just as softly. "Though it is true that you prefer to poison minds rather than wine."

Her smile did not waver, and she clicked her cup lightly against his as all eyes in the hall fastened avidly upon them. But she had the uncomfortable feeling that he'd gotten the last word in that exchange.

THE TAVERN WAS LOCATED in Goldstret in the goldsmiths' quarter, close by St Clement's Church. Richard had been waiting long enough for his simmering impatience to reach the boiling point. He was fidgeting restlessly, drumming his fingers on the scarred, wax-splattered table, waving away a serving maid who'd approached to see if he wanted more wine. Finally the door was shoved open and his brothers swaggered in. Geoffrey was accompanied only by a squire, but Hal had his usual entourage of household knights, and they made such a noisy entrance that all heads turned in their direction.

"What took you so long?" Richard demanded as soon as they approached his table. "I told you by Compline!"

"Blame Sir Bountiful here," Geoffrey said, pointing his thumb at Hal. "He had to stop and give alms to every beggar within a half-mile of the castle, even chasing one across the street to press coins upon him."

"Charity is a virtue," Hal responded, jostling Geoffrey good-naturedly, "but then you'd not know much about virtues, would you?"

"Sit down," Richard said quickly, before Geoffrey could retort in kind. "We need to talk." Hal's knights were milling about nearby, and he added, "Alone," with a pointed glance toward the other men.

Hal dismissed them with an airy "You heard my little brother. Go off and debauch yourselves. I'll pay for your wine, but not for your whores. There you're on your own." As they grinned and obeyed, he looked around at the other tavern patrons and said, "Ah, why not? I'll buy drinks for everyone!"

His generosity won him enthusiastic cheers from all but his brothers and the tavern keeper. Richard saw Hal's magnanimous gesture as shameless grandstanding, and Geoffrey laughed out loud at the look of horror on the tavern owner's face. Pulling up a stool to the table, he said, "The poor sot knows he has a better chance of sprouting wings than collecting so much as a farthing."

"That is not so," Hal protested. "I always pay my debts . . . eventually." He and Geoffrey both laughed, and looked vexed when Richard waved the serving maid away again.

"I did not ask you here to drink this swill. We need to talk about Fontevrault Abbey. Maman says that—"

"I already know all about it," Hal interrupted, with a hint of smugness. "Papa told me last night."

"Well, no one bothered to enlighten me," Geoffrey said testily, "so suppose one of you lets me in on the secret."

Richard looked around to make sure the other customers had gone back to their drinking and gambling. "He wants Maman to agree to an annulment and then retire to Fontevrault Abbey—as its abbess."

"As bribes go, that is not a bad one," Geoffrey allowed, and Hal grinned, saying that was his thinking, too.

Richard glared at his brothers. "She does not want to enter a nunnery!"

Hal shrugged. "Is she sure of that? It is a generous offer, would give her far more influence than she is enjoying these days. Maman could make of it what she wanted.

We're not talking about life as a recluse or an anchoress, for pity's sake. She'd be abbess of Fontevrault, and there are queens who might well envy that."

"Is your hearing faulty? I said she does not want to do it, Hal!"

Hal returned Richard's scowl in full measure, and Geoffrey could see another of their squabbles brewing. Before Hal could respond, he said sharply, "Enough!"

They looked at him in surprise, and he glanced over his shoulder to see if they'd attracted attention. "As usual, Hal, you see only what is right in front of your nose. As for you, Richard, even when you're right, you're right for all the wrong reasons. Neither one of you has fully considered the consequences of this annulment."

Temporarily united in their irritation with Geoffrey, they launched a joint attack, Hal insisting that he understood the situation quite well and Richard wanting to know what he meant by the "wrong reasons."

"Keep your voices down," Geoffrey warned. "Tell me this. How old is Papa?"

"I do not know," Richard said snappishly. "Forty-two?"

"No, forty-three," Hal corrected, remembering Chinon and his father's March birthday. "What of it?"

"To us, that seems as old as God. But it is not. He could easily wed again and have sons with his new queen. Think about that for a moment."

Hal was already shaking his head. "He would never disinherit me!"

Richard did not look so sure. "You truly think we could be put at risk, Geoff?"

"I do not know," Geoffrey admitted. "But I am not willing to take that chance. Are you? Look how he has begun to dote upon Johnny, even giving him the earldom of his uncle Rainald. I am just saying that if he had a few more sons, we could become superfluous. At the very least, it would give him a formidable club to hold over our heads. Now if you both have utter faith in his good will, there is no cause for concern. So . . . do you?"

Neither Hal nor Richard answered him, but words were not needed. They regarded one another in silence, in a rare moment of mutual understanding and total accord.

Henry glanced toward his scribe. "Are you ready, Simon? Write as follows:

"To William, by the Grace of God, the illustrious King of Sicily, the Duke of Apulia, and the Prince of Capua, Henry, by the same grace, King of England, Duke of Normandy and Aquitaine, and Count of Anjou, greetings and the enjoyment of health. Inasmuch as we expect that—"

He got no further, for it was then that his sons sought admittance to his bedchamber. Henry immediately gave them permission to enter and dismissed his scribe, telling him they'd resume on the morrow. When they asked if they could speak with him alone, he readily agreed, surprised to see them together, for he was unhappily aware that they rarely sought out one another's company.

As soon as the other men had exited the chamber, Henry bade his sons help themselves to the flagon of night wine on a side table, saying with a smile, "It is good that you are all here, for I have plans to share with you. Richard, you requested further aid in subduing the Poitevin rebels, and you wanted the same for Brittany, Geoffrey. Your requests are granted. You will be provided with the funds that you need ere you depart Winchester." His gaze shifted then to his eldest son. "I know you have been restless of late, Hal. I daresay that was behind your sudden desire to go on pilgrimage. So I am sending you back to Poitou with Richard, to assist him in restoring peace in that troublesome land."

Hal was very pleased, Richard less so, for he'd wanted men and money, not to be saddled with his brother. He joined Hal in expressing his gratitude, though, thinking that Hal would soon lose interest in the drudgery and tedium of a siege and go off in pursuit of pleasure. Hal was reconsidering the timing of their mission, not wanting to jeopardize his new command, and as soon as Henry's back was turned, he mouthed a message to his brothers that they ought to delay discussing Fontevrault.

Richard and Geoffrey would have none of that, though, neither one trusting Hal to remain resolute if their father's inducements were sweetened enough. "We have come to talk with you about our mother and your intent to make her abbess of Fontevrault," Richard said, so abruptly that his brothers both winced. "It is only fair that I tell you at the outset that I am adamantly opposed to this scheme."

Henry had been about to pour wine. At that, he swung about with a frown. Before he could speak, Geoffrey hastily interceded. "Actually, it is a sound plan, fair to both you and Maman, and if she were willing, I'd gladly support it. Alas, she is not, as you know. And since it concerns her most directly, we have to be guided by her wishes in this."

Henry studied his younger sons, and then looked toward Hal. "What of you, Hal? Do your brothers speak for you, too?"

Hal bridled. "I can speak for myself. But I happen to agree with them."

"Do you? Passing strange, for you seemed much more receptive to the idea when we discussed it last night."

"Yes, that is true. But once I had a chance to think about it, I changed my mind." Hal smiled snidely. "The way you changed your mind about the forest laws."

Henry was quiet for so long that his sons began to shift uneasily. "I understand," he said at last, "and I will give your opinions the consideration they merit."

E LEANOR WAS HOLDING UP A MIRROR while Amaria brushed her hair. Even in the candlelight, she could see the sprinkling of silver, and she grimaced, remembering how she'd once taken her beauty for granted, not realizing what a potent weapon it had been until it was slipping from her grasp. "Should I bother to hide the grey?" she wondered aloud, and Amaria at once volunteered to go into Winchester to purchase the needed ingredients.

"I cannot count all the sermons I've heard priests give over the years," Amaria said with a grin, "railing at female vanity and the sinful use of dyes and face paints. But women will always do whatever they can to hold the years at bay and to make themselves look attractive to men."

"Why go to all that trouble, though?" Eleanor mused. "After all, none but you can see the grey. It is not as if my husband is going to be demanding his conjugal rights any time soon, and I cannot say that I have plans to take a lover."

Amaria chuckled. "Women rarely plan to take a lover. It just happens."

"Not for queens. The one essential for love affairs is privacy, and royal palaces have even less privacy than nunneries."

Amaria had heard, of course, of the scandalous stories of the queen's youth, and would have loved to know the truth of them. She would not have blamed Eleanor for cuckolding the French king, thinking that he deserved horns if any husband did. Outspoken though she might be, she was not foolhardy, and that was not a question she'd have dared to ask. Instead, she decided to broach a subject that had been causing her some unease of mind.

"Madame . . . you do not think the king would truly force you into taking holy vows, do you?"

"He might if he thought he could get away with it," Eleanor said, sounding much too nonchalant for Amaria's liking. "But whatever Harry's failings, slowness of wit is not amongst them. He knows his grand scheme would work only if I agree to cooperate." Glancing over her shoulder at Amaria, she smiled coolly. "I am not as quick to gamble as I once was, though, so I told Richard to appeal to the Archbishop of Rouen on my behalf."

Amaria sighed with relief. "I am so glad to hear that," she admitted, and then spun around with a gasp as the door banged open. She backed away hastily as Henry stormed into the chamber. He was in such an obvious rage that her first instinct was to flee, but she was reluctant to leave Eleanor alone with him for that very reason, and so she stealthily retreated into the shadows, trying to make herself as inconspicuous as possible.

She need not have bothered; Henry never even noticed her, so focused was he upon the object of his anger—his infuriating, conniving wife. Setting down the mirror, she regarded him with provocative calm, saying, "Do come in, my lord husband," as if he were the one in the wrong.

"I thought you'd like to know that your latest scheme was highly successful. Your sons gallantly rode to your rescue tonight, proclaiming themselves your champions. It is a wonder you did not give them tokens of your favor to flaunt, so that all would know they were your knights."

"However little you like it, Harry, they *are* my sons. Is it truly so surprising that they are protective of me?"

"What did you tell them precisely? That I was going to load you down with chains and haul you off to a nunnery in the dead of night?"

"As a matter of fact, I did not mention your threat."

"You expect me to believe that? As if you'd pass up any chance to portray me as the knave and you as the innocent, sacrificial lamb, the damsel in distress!"

"I did not tell them because I did not take your threat seriously. I know how you rave and rant when you lose your temper. I also know that once you cool down, you rarely if ever carry these threats out, so I saw no reason to share them with our sons, not unless you forced me to it. More strife is the last thing our family needs."

"St Eleanor of Aquitaine," he mocked, "so wise and forbearing. It is rather difficult, though, to reconcile that angelic image with the woman who urged my sons to rebel against me!"

"That was a mistake."

He stared at her in disbelief. "A mistake? You destroyed our family and you call it a 'mistake'?"

"Yes, damn you, a mistake! Are you going to tell me that you've never made a mistake, Harry?"

"No," he growled, "I made a great one on May 18 in God's Year 1152." And with that, he turned and stalked out, slamming the door resoundingly behind him.

Amaria leaned weakly against the wall for a moment. To her surprise, the queen did not seem as distraught as she ought to have been after such a blazing row. Deciding, though, that they both needed wine, she went over without being asked and poured two cups.

Bringing one back to Eleanor, she made an attempt to sound blasé as she said, "May I ask what happened on May 18 in 1152, my lady?"

"Harry and I were wed in Poitiers." Eleanor took a swallow of the wine before saying, "Usually he could never remember our anniversary."

Amaria did not know what to say, so she busied herself hunting in the floor rushes for the brush, which she'd dropped when Henry barged into the chamber. Eleanor drank in silence, seemingly lost in her own thoughts. When their eyes met, though, she smiled, a smile that somehow managed to be wry and rueful and bleak, all at the same time.

"Harry and I have more in common than quick tempers," she said. "We rarely make mistakes, but when we do, they tend to be spectacular."

Amaria could not argue with that, not when she considered the consequences of those mistakes. The queen's rebellion had cost her dearly, might mean imprisonment for the rest of her days. The king's rash, angry words had resulted in a martyr's death upon the floor of Canterbury cathedral. She could only hope that the king's decision to crown his son would not prove to be a mistake of the same magnitude, for all their sakes.

CHAPTER TWENTY-FOUR

July 1176
Poitiers, Poitou

*J*HE BISHOP'S CLERKS smiled at the sight of the two men walking in the gardens, for they were a study in contrasts. John aux Bellesmains, Bishop of Poitiers, was a tall, willowy, and elegant figure, towering over the diminutive John of Salisbury. Their history went back more than twenty years, begun in those distant days when they and Thomas Becket had been clerks together in the household of Archbishop Theobald of Canterbury. John aux Bellesmains had been elevated to his bishopric at the same time as Thomas, and now John of Salisbury would have his own See, too, having been elected by the chapter of Chartres on July 22. He was on his way to Sens for consecration, but he'd detoured to Poitiers to see his old friend, and on this muggy afternoon in late July, they were making up for lost time, sharing confidences both personal and political as the sun rose higher in the sky and the city sweltered under the summer heat.

Once they'd seated themselves in the shade and accepted wine and fruit from the bishop's attentive servants, John of Salisbury raised his cup in a mock salute. "To your military exploits, my lord bishop. You are a man of many talents, for certes. You did remember to use a mace, though, and not a sword?"

Salisbury was indulging in some canonical humor, for warlike bishops had been known to carry a mace into battle as a means of avoiding the stricture against priests shedding blood, on the dubious grounds that Scriptures said nothing against battering an enemy's brains into mush. His companion smiled, somewhat sheepishly, for he'd never expected to garner military acclaim. "Actually," he said, "all I did was raise the local levy, providing the men for the defense of Poitou when the rebels sought to take advantage of Count Richard's absence in England. I did not take the field against them, so credit for the victory at Barbezieux must go to Richard's second-in-command, Theobald Chabot."

"I know," Salisbury admitted with a grin. "I could not resist teasing you, old friend. How goes the rebellion? I'd heard that the king sent Richard and his brother Hal back to Poitou with enough gold to hire half the routiers in Hell."

"Richard has been very successful since his return; he's clearly inherited his father's flair for command. After winning a battle near Bouteville, he took the Viscount of Limoges's castle at Aixe, then the city of Limoges itself. He is currently laying siege to Angoulême, where the Counts of Angoulême and the Viscounts of Ventador, Limoges, and Chabenais have taken shelter. When the castle falls, he'll have captured all of the main rebels in one fell swoop. Not bad for a lad not yet nineteen."

Salisbury was not acquainted with Richard. He did know Hal, though, from his days in Becket's household, and asked now, "And Hal? Surely he deserves some of the praise, too."

Bishop John smiled thinly. "I'd not suggest that in Richard's hearing. Hal went off to Paris to visit his father-in-law, did not even make an appearance in Poitou until midsummer. He finally joined Richard in besieging the castle at Châteauneuf-sur-Charente, but once the castle was taken, he lost interest. He's been holding court here in Poitiers for the past fortnight."

Salisbury knew his friend well enough to catch the unspoken echoes of disapprobation. Since the bishop would hardly fault Hal for not displaying enough warlike fervor or bloodlust, he assumed there was more involved than Hal's lack of enthusiasm for siege warfare. "I've not seen Hal since last year, when he and the king made a pilgrimage to Canterbury. Thomas was always fond of the lad. It hurt him when Hal refused to see him in those last weeks of his life. What has he been doing in Poitiers to incur your disapproval?"

"What he does best," Bishop John said dryly, "which is charming every man, woman, and child who happen to cross his path. The Poitevin barons not in actual rebellion have been drawn to Poitiers like dogs to vomit. They have been fawning over Hal as if he were the blessed Archangel Michael, telling him how much they wish he were their liege lord rather than Richard."

Salisbury's jaw dropped. "Are you saying Hal is seeking to subvert his brother's vassals?"

"He'd insist he has no such intention, but he does nothing to discourage such seditious talk. I cannot tell if he truly wants to undermine Richard's authority in Poitou, or if he merely enjoys hearing his brother belittled. Either way, it does not bode well for the future."

"No, it does not," Salisbury agreed, and then sought to lighten the conversation by sharing the latest gossip from England. The Bishop of St David's had died that past May, and there were rumors that the malcontent Earl of Norfolk had died in the Holy Land, where he'd gone to expiate his many sins. The Almighty truly worked in mysterious ways, he observed, for few men deserved such a sanctified death less than Hugh Bigod, but then he made John laugh by saying cheerfully that at least the miscreant earl's stay in Purgatory would surely last an aeon or two.

"My lord bishop." One of John's servants was coming up the garden walkway. "The queen has just arrived, Your Grace, and asks to see you straightaway."

"By all means. Have her join us here in the gardens, Milo, and see that refreshments are brought out." As the man retreated, Bishop John glanced toward Salisbury with a smile. "I wonder if a time will ever come when we hear the words 'the queen' and do not think of Eleanor."

Salisbury knew Eleanor, too, although not as well as Poitiers's bishop. "Not in our lifetimes," he predicted, watching with alert interest the young woman just entering the gardens.

Noting that Marguerite's attendants had lagged behind, the two men exchanged thoughtful looks, for that indicated her visit was not a routine social call. "Madame, this is an unexpected pleasure," Bishop John said, hastening to meet her. "May I introduce an old friend, John, the Bishop-elect of Chartres."

Marguerite's eyes flicked uneasily to Salisbury's cherubic face, then back to Bishop John. "Your Grace, I have an urgent matter to discuss. May I rely upon your utter discretion, and that of your friend?"

"Of course. Whatever you tell us will be kept as secret as anything we'd hear in the confessional."

Marguerite let them seat her upon a wooden bench. "Do you know Adam de Churchedune, my husband's vice-chancellor?"

The bishop nodded. "I believe he was a clerk to the prior of Beverley ere joining the young king's household. What of him, my lady?"

"It seems he has been serving two masters, my husband and his father. He was caught trying to send a confidential message to King Henry in England." Marguerite dropped her eyes to the hands clenched in her lap. "Adam was concerned that my husband had taken up with what he called 'highly suspect company.' He particularly objected to the presence of the de Lusignans and several lords who'd taken part in the last rebellion against King Henry, men whom he suspected of aiding and abetting what he called 'the current crop of rebels.' It . . . it was not a letter that portrayed my husband in a favorable light."

"Ah . . . I see. And the young king is irate?"

"More than that, Your Grace. I have never seen him so angry. He says that Adam has betrayed him, and he is set upon punishing him severely for his lack of loyalty. He and his household knights are trying Adam for treason even as we speak, and I greatly fear that he may well do something he'd regret for the rest of his life."

"Has he forgotten that Adam de Churchedune is a cleric, and not subject to the king's courts?" Bishop John spoke calmly, although his composure was belied by the sudden taut line of his jaw. "Surely there were men there who dared to remind your husband of that salient fact?"

"Yes, several spoke up, including Baldwin de Bethune and Will Marshal. But my husband is listening to others, to men who are urging him to make an example of Adam. They have made it sound as if my husband's honor, his very manhood, is at stake . . ." Marguerite's voice faded away, and when she looked up at the bishops, tears were brimming in the corners of her eyes. "Your Grace, you were the only one I could think of, the only one who might stop this madness ere it goes too far. When I left, they were clamoring for the death penalty!" Despite the summer sun, she shivered. "I may not know much of political matters, not like Queen Eleanor, but even I know how outraged the Holy Father would be, how angry King Henry would be. I entreat you, my lord bishop, do what you can, for poor Adam's sake and for my husband's sake, too."

As they were admitted to the royal palace, John gave his companion a searching look. "Are you sure you want to accompany me? This could get very ugly."

Salisbury nodded emphatically. "You know I was a witness to Thomas's slaying. You may not know that I was amongst those who ran from his killers. The monks and his clerks fled, leaving him alone to face those brutes. Only one man, a monk who did not even know him, dared to come to his aid, and he paid a grievous price for his courage, had his arm all but severed."

"Thomas would not have wanted others to die with him. Did he not warn the killers that they were not to harm any of his people?"

"He may not have asked it of me, but I asked it of myself, and was found wanting. I swore upon the Rood that it would not happen again."

"*Deus vult*," the other man said quietly, and then turned to a hovering servant. "Take us to the king," he commanded, in a tone that would brook no refusal. They were led across the courtyard toward the great hall, where a large crowd had gathered under the open windows, jockeying for position, putting the bishops in mind of those eager multitudes who would turn out for a public hanging. Their own attendants cleared a path, aided by shouts of "Make way for the bishop!"

Inside, they were hit by a blast of hot, humid air. So many men had squeezed into the hall that they were trampling on one another's feet, elbows jabbing into ribs, necks craning toward the dais. Bishop John moved forward with a ruthless will that would not be denied; the much smaller Salisbury slid into the space he created and followed, feeling, with an incongruous flash of humor, like a little skiff bobbing in the wake of a war galley.

Hal was seated on the dais, surrounded by knights and barons of Poitou. He looked very handsome and very regal, his good looks enhanced by his anger, giving him high color and a smoldering intensity that riveted all eyes upon him. Most of the men seemed to share his agitation; they looked either indignant or excited or both. The bishop did find a few somber faces, but not many. He wasted no time scanning the spectators, his gaze searching out the man at the center of this storm, the unfortunate Adam de Churchedune.

Adam had the stunned expression of a man unable to understand what was happening to him, the dazed disbelief of one realizing he was going to drown within reach of shore. "My lord," he pleaded, "I am truly sorry if I have offended you, for that was never my intent. But you do not want to do this—"

"Yes," Hal cut in, "I do! Your treachery deserves nothing less. The sentence of death stands."

"That is a grim jest," the Bishop of Poitiers said loudly, "but I assume it is a jest, nevertheless, for you cannot pass a death sentence upon this man."

All heads swiveled in his direction. Adam spun around, stretching out his arms toward the bishop like a man grabbing for a lifeline. "Your Grace, I beg you to help me!"

Hal's reaction was no less dramatic. He jumped to his feet, stood watching as the bishop moved toward the dais, his head high, his shoulders squared, feet planted apart, every line of his body communicating tension and defiance. "My lord bishop," he said curtly. "What are you doing here?"

"Apparently stopping you from making a grave mistake, my lord king," the bishop said, with equal coldness, and as hostile murmurings swept the hall, Salisbury felt a sinking feeling in the pit of his stomach. Why had John taken such a harsh approach? Would they not have been better served by more conciliatory tactics?

"With all due respect, my lord bishop, you do not know what is occurring here, what this man has done. He has betrayed me, has been spying upon me and reporting back to my father! What could be more despicable than treachery like that?"

"I am not here to defend what he has done, my liege," the bishop said, and Adam seemed to shrink before their eyes as the hope stirred by John's appearance was snatched away.

Hal was momentarily thrown off balance. "Well," he said, "I am glad to hear that."

John had reached the dais by now. "Whether he is guilty of a betrayal is not the issue. It would seem to me that this is a matter best taken up with your lord father, but again, that is beyond my purview. My only concern is with the punishment you are threatening to inflict upon him. As I said, that cannot be."

Hal began to bluster again. "That is not for you to say!"

"Yes, it is. Adam de Churchedune is not subject to the jurisdiction of your court. He is in minor orders and can be judged only by Holy Church."

Hal scowled. "He is not a priest, has never taken holy vows!"

"That is irrelevant. The Church's position has always been quite clear upon this subject. It matters not if a man is in minor orders or if he be one of the Pope's own cardinals. In either case, he is to be judged by the Church and only the Church."

The mutterings were becoming louder now, the antagonism needing only a spark to burst into flame. Salisbury moved over to stand beside his friend, wondering if the Church was to get two new martyrs. Hal knew the sentiment in the hall was with him, and that realization was both encouraging and daunting. "I say he is to be judged here and now and by me, the liege lord he wronged! Go home, my lord bishop. You are not needed here."

John looked around the hall, his gaze so piercing that not all of the men could meet his eyes. "Have you forgotten that bloodstained floor at Canterbury Cathedral?" he demanded. "St Thomas died for the very principle that you would violate. His quarrel with the king began because he would not agree to let clerics be judged in royal courts. Do you truly think that I could stand aside whilst you defy the Church and defame the blessed martyr's holy memory? I tell you that you shall not harm this man," he said, thrusting his arm toward Adam in a gesture reminiscent of an Old Testament prophet. "If it is God's Will that I die in his defense, so be it."

The image he'd called up of the archbishop's mangled and bleeding body had a sobering effect upon the men. Even those most eager to see Adam suffer for his sins were starting to have second thoughts. Salisbury took heart from the sudden silence and decided it was time for the voice of reason to balance his friend's splendid defiance. Approaching the dais, he addressed Hal with all the polite persuasion at his command. "My liege, I remember you well from your time in Archbishop Thomas's

household. You are a good son of the Church, would not want to bring upon yourself
the shame and infamy that engulfed your lord father after the archbishop's murder."

One of the de Lusignans saw that Hal's resolve was weakening, and shoved his
way toward the young king. "Do not heed them, sire. Your House has a proud tradition of holding your ground against the Church's encroachments. Remember what
befell an arrogant Bishop of Séez who dared to defy your grandfather, Count Geoffrey
of blessed memory. The count's men deprived him of what no priest needs—his
manhood."

But he'd gone too far. Hal did not want to be associated with so brutal a deed. "My
grandfather denied that they were acting upon his orders," he said, turning some of his
frustration and thwarted fury upon the de Lusignan agitator. "Will Marshal always
warned me that you de Lusignans were an untrustworthy lot. I ought to have paid
more heed to him."

The de Lusignans were as known for their fiery tempers as for their sharp double-
dealing, and the man gave Hal a look now that was murderous. But Marshal had
shouldered his way over to Hal's side, and he did not want to be challenged to a duel
by combat, for Will's lethal skills and enduring grudge against the de Lusignan clan
would make him a very deadly foe, indeed.

Hal glanced at Will, appreciating his silent support and remembering that Will
had argued against this from the beginning. Wishing he'd listened, he came down the
steps of the dais, putting a swagger in his step as he halted before the Bishop of
Poitiers. "I like it not," he said coolly, "but I will spare that wretch out of the respect I
have for you, my lord bishop."

Adam's gasp was almost a sob. He sank to his knees like a man whose body no
longer had the strength to support him, his breath wheezing like a broken bellows. Salisbury reached over and put a hand on that heaving shoulder, giving it a reassuring
squeeze. But the Bishop of Poitiers had yet to take his eyes from Hal.

"Do I have your word upon that, my lord king?"

There were more resentful mutterings at that. Hal's brows drew together, his
mouth tightening. But the bishop continued to look at him expectantly, challengingly,
and at last he gave a grudging promise that he would not seek to execute Adam for his
treachery. Glaring at the quaking figure of his vice-chancellor, he warned, "I will not
forget, though. Nor will I forgive."

I T WAS ONE OF THOSE RARE, perfect summer days, splashed with
golden sun, cooled by errant breezes, the sky the brilliant shade of blue more often
seen in September than mid-August. The gardens at Winchester were in full bloom,

and Eleanor and Amaria were enjoying the fragrant scents, the flight of gossamer-winged butterflies, and the antics of the spaniel that was Henry's recent gift to Joanna.

"Melusine!" Amaria called, seeking to stop the puppy from digging in a raised flower bed of scarlet peonies. When the little dog ignored her warning, she bent down and scooped it up into her arms, where it began to chew contentedly upon the lacings of her gown. "What an odd name for a dog. What made your daughter choose it, Madame?"

"Melusine was the name of the Demon Countess of Anjou," Eleanor said, smiling. "Her husband was very happy with her, but he became suspicious when she rarely attended Mass and always left before the consecration of the Host. So one day he ordered four of his knights to step upon her mantle and hold her there. Whereupon she gave a fearful scream, revealed herself to be the Devil's daughter, and flew out a window, never to be seen again. Harry has such interesting ancestors."

"Speaking of the Devil," Amaria said with a grin. "Is that not your lord husband amongst those riders who've just passed through the gatehouse?"

Eleanor was not surprised by Henry's arrival, for Joanna had told her that he'd arranged to hold a church council at Winchester in order to spend time with her before she departed for Sicily. Eleanor was surprised, though, by what Henry did once he'd dismounted. After glancing across the bailey toward the gardens, he handed his reins to a groom and walked in her direction.

As he entered the garden gate, Amaria took Melusine and discreetly withdrew out of earshot. Eleanor seated herself on a turf bench and watched him approach. Coming to a halt a few feet away, he gestured toward Amaria and the puppy. "Is that the dog I sent Joanna?"

Eleanor nodded. "It was love at first sight. Guess what she named it? Melusine."

Henry's mouth curved at the corners. "I knew it was a mistake to tell her that story. Where is she? Inside at her lessons?"

"No, she went into the city. It seems that one of the nuns of St Mary's speaks Tuscan, and has agreed to teach her a few phrases. I explained that each region of Italy has its own dialect and what they speak in Tuscany might not be understood in Sicily, but you know Joanna once she gets an idea into her head."

"You did remind her that William is of Norman descent and his first language is French?"

"I did. But she has her mind set upon being able to 'speak to my people,' as she puts it."

Henry's smile was touched with sadness. "I hope the Sicilians appreciate how lucky they are." He hesitated and then sat beside her on the bench. "Is she nervous about the marriage?"

"Of course she is, even though she'd never admit it. She did confess to some unease, though, when the Bishops of Troye and Capua arrived at Winchester to make sure she was pretty enough to satisfy their king."

Henry felt a flicker of resentment even now. "I never heard of such a thing," he said indignantly. "Royal marriages are matters of statecraft, a means of forging alliances. Yet William would have his men inspect Joanna as if she were a prize filly! He is fortunate I did not end the negotiations then and there."

"I assured Joanna she had no cause for concern, and indeed, they were bedazzled by her. In truth, though, I can understand William's concern. He may be allying with England, but he'll be living with a flesh-and-blood woman. Is it so surprising that he'd prefer a pleasing bedmate? He is said to be quite handsome himself, so he and Joanna ought to have beautiful children."

Henry could think of few subjects less appealing than envisioning his ten-year-old daughter as a man's bedmate, and he was irked with Eleanor for discussing it so nonchalantly. "Joanna is a child herself," he said sharply. "I just pray to God that her husband remembers that."

Eleanor understood then. This was the father here in the garden with her, not the king. "Harry . . . Joanna will become his wife, but not his bedmate, not yet. You know that the Church frowns upon consummation of the marriage until the girl reaches a more suitable age, at the very least until she has her flux."

"That sounds well and good—in theory. But how can we be sure that it prevails in practice?"

"We cannot," she said, with unsettling candor. "But from what we know of William, he does not sound like a man who'd enjoy deflowering a little girl. We have to remember that we judged him to be a worthy husband for Joanna. We should remember, too, that self-interest encourages men to follow the Church's teachings in this matter. A very young wife is more likely to die in childbirth, and the babe, too. Princes and kings know that, and do not want to put their heirs or their alliances at needless risk."

"I know, I know," he said impatiently, before admitting, "The husbands of our older girls seem to have taken their ages into account."

For a moment, they thought of their absent daughters. Tilda had been wed at age eleven to the Duke of Saxony and Bavaria, a man more than twenty-seven years her senior, a man older than her own father. She'd become a mother three times already, but she'd not had her first child until she was sixteen. Her sister, named after Eleanor, but known now by the Spanish Leonora, had wed the King of Castile at an even younger age than Tilda or Joanna; she'd been just nine. She was only in her fifteenth year now, and so far, they'd heard nothing of any pregnancies.

Eleanor was astonished that they were actually having a conversation that was not only civil, but easy and unforced, even intimate. "We have to trust him, Harry, to do right by Joanna." Unable to resist adding playfully, "After all, he is called William the Good. Surely that is a cause for reassurance?"

"He's called that because his father was known as William the Bad," Henry said, with a faint glimmer of sardonic humor. "It is just that . . . that Joanna is so fair . . ."

"Ah, I see. You fear that he might be tempted by her beauty, tempted enough to ignore the reality—that she is still a child."

"Are you saying it never happens?" he challenged. "I'd wager that Louis consummated the marriage on your wedding night, and you were all of . . . what, thirteen?"

Eleanor blinked in surprise. "Well, yes," she conceded. "How did you know?"

"For God's sake, woman, no man would sleep chastely in your bed, not even a born monk like Louis!"

He was on his feet now, beginning to pace as she watched him in amused amazement. "Careful, Harry, that sounds suspiciously like a compliment." She was at once sorry for the gibe, not wanting to spoil this unlikely rapport.

He shot her a sharp look, but surprised her again by not stalking off. Was he that troubled by Joanna's marriage? Or had he something else on his mind? She decided to take advantage of the fact that they were still talking, see if she could extract some information from him about their sons. "I hear that Richard has been very successful since he returned to Poitou," she said, waiting to see if he'd respond.

"Yes, he has done well. I had a message from him just four days ago, telling me that he'd taken Angoulême and was sending the captive counts to me for judgment."

Eleanor was delighted; she hadn't known that Richard's triumph had been so sweeping. "We have a son to be proud of," she said, and their eyes met and held for a heartbeat or two before he glanced away.

"You have not heard, though, about Hal's latest lunacy."

"No," she said cautiously. "What has he done?"

"He caught his vice-chancellor, Adam de Churchedune, sending me a warning that he was consorting with rebels and riffraff, and he flew into a wild rage, lost all reason."

Ah, Harry, what did you expect? But the words never left her lips, for she very much wanted to hear what had happened. If he felt the need to discuss it with her, it must truly be dreadful. "What did he do?"

"He charged Adam with treason and sentenced him to death."

Eleanor's eyes widened; she'd not been braced for a blow like this. "Holy Mother Mary," she whispered. "Are you telling me he executed a man of God?"

"No, but that was due only to the fortuitous arrival of the Bishop of Poitiers. He faced Hal and his lackeys down, and God bless him for it. Hal reluctantly agreed not to proceed with the death sentence." Henry paused, gazing up at the sky as if searching for answers, slowly shaking his head. "But once the bishop had gone, he took a harsh vengeance upon Adam. He had the poor man whipped naked through the streets of Poitiers, preceded by a herald who proclaimed that this would be the fate of all who betrayed the trust of their lord. He then had Adam cast into prison."

"Christ Jesus. Is he still confined? Can you not intervene on his behalf?"

"I did as soon as I learned what happened. I arranged to have him released and taken to a monastery in England."

Henry stopped pacing, running a hand absently through his unruly hair, as she'd seen him do so many times over the years. But then he turned back toward her, with narrowed eyes and set mouth. "Well? Is this not when you charge to Hal's defense, make excuses for what he's done, and place all the blame squarely at my feet?"

"No . . . his actions cannot be excused or justified, mayhap only understood."

He gave a bleak laugh. "I would to God I did understand! I tell you, Eleanor, I am at my wit's end with the lad. I could almost believe him possessed. At least that would explain his folly. I am at a loss what to do next. I tried keeping him with me last year, tried to get him interested in governing, to no avail. So then I gave him the freedom he demanded, sent him into Poitou to aid Richard. And this is how he repays me!"

"Ah, Harry . . . I do not know what to tell you. Hal has gone so far astray that I am not sure we can get him back onto the right road."

"Would you even bother to try? Why not just sit back and enjoy the blood-letting? This is what you were aiming for when you urged our sons to rebel, was it not?"

She was taken aback by his sudden flare of hostility; she'd been lulled into unwariness by the genuine give-and-take of their conversation. "God, no," she said softly. "I never wanted that."

"You say that with such sincerity. Almost enough to make me believe you— almost." He reached out, grasped her arm, and pulled her to her feet. "You do not get to shrug your shoulders and wish me well. This is as much your doing as mine. At the least, you can try to repair the damage you've done. You owe me that much and you owe it to Hal."

His fingers were digging into her arm, but she did not protest, for she did not think he was aware of it. "I would if I could, and that is God's truth, Harry. But I do not know how to heal Hal's wounds, to heal any of our wounds."

He looked down into her face, and then abruptly released her and stepped back. "So what then? We just watch as Hal gallops headlong for the cliff's edge? What am I supposed to do, Eleanor? How do I reach him?"

She found herself blinking back tears. "You must let him go, Harry. Even if he goes over that cliff, you have to set him free."

"What does that mean? Set him free to do what?"

"To make his own mistakes, no matter how costly. I know that would not be easy for you, but you have no choice, not any longer. You made Hal a king, and now we must live with it."

"'Live with it'?" he echoed incredulously. "Is that what you'd have told Adam de Churchedune?"

"I regret what happened to Adam de Churchedune as much as you do. But if you'd not set him to spy upon Hal—"

"Here it comes! I am only surprised it took you so long. Hal nearly executes a man, nearly causes a dangerous rupture with the Church, and of course it is somehow all my fault!"

"I did not say that! But surely you must see now that you made a mistake, that putting a spy in Hal's household was not the approach to take."

"What I see is that I was right to worry about him, that I was right to think he needs supervision, that he is not to be trusted with a king's authority or with men's lives!" Henry was flushed, bitterly disappointed that this was her response, that he'd turned to her in his despair and she'd used it as a weapon against him. "I should have known better," he said and, swinging about on his heel, he strode from the garden, not looking back.

On September 8, Joanna sailed from Southampton for Barfleur, accompanied by her uncle Hamelin, the Archbishops of Rouen and Canterbury, and the Bishops of Ely, Évreux, and Bayeux. Henry had provided for her so extravagantly that it took seven ships to transport her and her party. Upon her arrival in Normandy, she was met by her brother Hal, who escorted her into Poitou, where Richard was waiting. He accompanied her through Aquitaine to the port of St Gilles, where she was formally turned over to the Bishop of Siracusa, and bade farewell to her brother, uncle, and most of the English prelates. On November 9, she sailed for Sicily.

CHAPTER TWENTY-FIVE

✦

December 1176
Nottingham, England

A STORM WAS THREATENING and the Bishop of Worcester and his companions were relieved to reach Nottingham's great castle before it broke. They hastened to dismount in the middle bailey, glad to turn their mounts over to waiting servants. Upon being told that the king was in the great hall, they headed in that direction. Roger noticed, though, that his sister's steps were lagging, and gave her a curious glance.

"You are not nervous, Maud?"

"Now why ever would I be nervous?" she said tartly.

"Well, I can understand your unease," he commiserated, "especially after the dire fate of the Poitevin rebels."

Maud came to an abrupt halt. "'Dire fate'? I thought Harry pardoned them!" Realizing then that she was the victim of brotherly humor, she jabbed Roger in the ribs with her elbow. "Very amusing."

"I thought so," he said cheerfully. "You are being foolish to worry, Sister. Harry has been remarkably merciful to rebels, forbearing to charge them with treason as he well could have done. Instead, he chose to follow the teachings of Our Saviour and offer forgiveness."

Not to Eleanor, Maud thought, knowing that the queen was celebrating Christmas alone at Winchester. Her anger toward her former friend had cooled, mitigated by her son's reprieve and her sense of fair play; she did not think it right that Eleanor alone should be the one to suffer for that ill-advised rebellion. She said nothing, though, knowing that Roger did not share her sympathies, and followed him into the hall.

It was overflowing with highborn guests and princes of the Church, all eager to display their loyalty and enjoy the splendors of the king's Christmas Court. Henry was upon the dais, but not seated, a hardship on his less energetic subjects since they could not sit unless he did. He turned as Roger ushered Maud toward him, and for an uneasy moment, she could not tell what her reception would be. But then he said, "Welcome, Cousin Maud," and gathered her into a quick embrace.

Maud had not feared being penalized for her son's treason, for Roger had been able to convince Henry that she'd played no part in it. She had feared, though, that their friendship might have been irretrievably damaged, and she was greatly relieved to find it was not so. "I wanted to thank you again," she said warmly, "for the kindness you've shown Hugh. He told me that he has been fully restored to favor, and you even plan to entrust him with a mission to Ireland in the spring."

"Some people might argue that sending a man to Ireland is hardly a mark of royal favor," Henry said dryly. "You owe me no thanks, Cousin. What's past is past."

Maud didn't agree, but she knew he did not like profuse expressions of gratitude and after a few moments of idle talk, she graciously excused herself so that she could discover where she and her ladies were being lodged. Roger stayed on the dais with Henry, asking who else was expected at Nottingham.

"The Bishop of Norwich is due any day now from Sicily: I'd sent him ahead of Joanna to convey gifts and good will to William. I got word this week that she will be celebrating Christmas in Naples, for the poor lass was so seasick during the voyage that it was decided she needed time ashore to regain her strength." Henry, who was never seasick, sounded both sympathetic and bemused. "Once she feels up to it, they will resume the journey to Sicily, but they'll be traveling by land to make it easier for her."

Henry waved away a servant who was offering wine, but Roger snared a cup. "Willem is here, though not for long. He has taken the cross and plans to accompany the Count of Flanders to the Holy Land come the spring. Hamelin is here, and Johnny, of course, and Geoffrey, too. But Richard is in Bordeaux, and Hal and Marguerite are holding their Christmas Court in Normandy at Argentan. Oh, and Geoff just arrived yesterday," Henry said, and when Roger asked how Geoff's studies were progressing in Tours, he grinned. "Well enough, he says. I can only hope he is spending more time in the university library than in the town taverns!"

Roger grinned, too; he'd done his own studies at Tours and he remembered the secular attractions quite vividly. Seeing that they were relatively alone, none within immediate earshot, he said quietly, "How is the Lady Rosamund faring?"

"I have not seen her since October, when I stopped at Godstow on my way from Windsor to meet the Scots king at Feckenham. She looked very frail to me, Roger, although she insists she is well and in good spirits." Henry paused. "It is not easy to admit, but she seems content there, at peace."

"I am glad to hear that," Roger said; he'd spared more than a few prayers in the past nine months for the soul of Rosamund Clifford, a sinner who'd repented before it was too late. "I hear you are holding a council at Northampton next month. Shall I attend?"

"I think you'll want to, Cousin. Amongst other matters, I plan to restore their lands to your nephew Hugh and his irksome ally, the Earl of Leicester. Saving a few strategic castles, of course."

"That is good news, indeed! Maud will be delighted. Why did you not tell her that earlier?"

Henry shrugged. "You know how women are. She'd have squealed and kissed me. You are not going to do that, are you?"

"No, although of course I'd want to," Roger said gravely, paying Henry back in his own coin, which he acknowledged with another grin. Roger was debating whether he ought to make any mention of Hal and his outrageous treatment of a man of God when Henry was informed that a messenger had just ridden in from the nunnery at Godstow.

"Send him in," Henry ordered, before saying to Roger, "How is that for timing, Cousin?" He recognized the man being escorted toward the dais, one of Prioress Edith's servants who'd delivered letters from Rosamund in the past. He'd always had an excellent memory for names and faces and it stood him in good stead now, recalling that the courier was called Edwin.

"You need not hurry back to Godstow, Edwin," he said expansively. "You might as well linger for a few days and enjoy the festivities. I expect that—"

He cut himself off so abruptly that Roger turned in his direction. Henry read faces well and the man approaching was a study in utter misery. Kneeling before Henry, he mutely held out his letter, never meeting the king's eyes. Henry glanced down at the seal; it was not Rosamund's, belonged to the prioress. He froze, making no attempt to take the letter.

Roger glanced from one to the other and then reached for it himself. Surprised by the depth of sadness he felt, he looked at his cousin in silent sympathy, waiting until Henry could bring himself to take that letter and get confirmation of what he already knew.

So far his stay at Nottingham had been a great disappointment to John. He'd been looking forward to it eagerly, for his tenth birthday would occur two days after Christmas. Best of all, his father had told him that Nottingham Castle was his.

He hadn't been sure what to expect, but it seemed to him that the Lord of Nottingham would be the center of attention, or at least the object of more deference than he usually received. That did not happen. His father remained the focal point of all eyes, and any leftover honors were claimed by his brother Geoffrey, newly returned from a successful campaign in Brittany. Once more John was overlooked, forgotten.

Worse was to come. Yesterday his father had gotten bad news. John did not know what it was, for he'd not dared to ask. He'd tried to eavesdrop on other people's conversations, thinking they might know, but they would fall silent as soon as they caught sight of him. He feared that his father would not be in the mood for celebrating the Christmas revelries, much less his birthday. He'd been promised a surprise, but now he wondered if his father would even remember.

Nottingham had been a huge letdown. What he found most disquieting, though, was his father's withdrawal. He'd made few public appearances and when he did, he was remote and aloof. John's world had suffered such dramatic upheavals in the past three years that he often felt as if he were a leaf borne on the wind. He'd not liked the abbey of Fontevrault very much, but at least it was familiar and there he felt safe. John never felt safe anymore. Too much had changed, too fast. His mother and father had gone to war, his brothers all siding with her. After that, she was in disgrace, a prisoner whom he'd not seen in more than three years. If a queen could fall so far, anyone could. She'd been a glamorous stranger to him, but he'd been proud that she was his mother, and he missed her even though he did not understand how he could miss someone he'd seen so infrequently.

He did not miss Richard and Geoffrey; he'd not spent much time with them and when he did, they'd teased him mercilessly. Hal had been kind to him once, on those rare occasions when they met, tousling his hair and calling him "Sprout" but not in a mean way; a few times he'd even played with John. That had all changed since his fight with their father. Now when he saw Hal, his brother was brusque, dismissive like Geoffrey and Richard. Hal seemed angry with him, but he did not know what he'd done.

Joanna had been more than his companion at Fontevrault. She'd been his rock, but now she'd gone away and he might never see her again. Without Joanna, he had only his father, and ever since his father had gotten his bad news, he'd been there and yet he was not there. John could not explain it, could only sense it, and it frightened him. His feelings for his father were complicated. He was very proud to be the son of Henry Fitz Empress. But he never felt that comfortable with Henry. He'd watched his father's fits of rage, watched other men cower before him. He'd never yelled at John, but John was always afraid that he would. Joanna was the only member of his family with whom he felt completely at ease, and he missed her very much.

He'd been wandering about all morning like a lost soul, trying to find some way to entertain himself. In late morning, he'd ventured up to his father's chamber in a tower of the inner bailey, but he'd lost his nerve at the last moment and started back down the stairs. It was dark and the stone steps were slick, well worn by countless feet, for this part of the castle was over a hundred years old. John was carefully making his way down when he heard the voices below him. It was a man and a woman, and he caught his breath when he recognized the male voice. It was his brother Geoffrey. He could guess what they were doing by the way they were laughing, but he had no idea who the woman was. She could be a serving maid of the castle or a maid servant of one of the guests or a lady's handmaiden or even a lady, he supposed; most of the barons had brought their wives and they'd all brought large entourages. He hesitated, not sure what to do next. If Geoffrey caught him, he'd get his ears boxed for certes. But the temptation to eavesdrop was irresistible, a chance to learn more about the things men did with women and mayhap even their father's bad news, for Geoffrey must surely know.

The girl giggled, saying breathlessly that they must stop, for someone could come along at any moment. Geoffrey murmured something too softly for John to hear, then suggested they go to his chamber where they could be assured of privacy. She protested that she could not risk it, startling John when she mentioned her husband. It had to be someplace safe, she insisted, and after mentioning several places and then rejecting them as too dangerous, she announced in triumphant tones that she knew where they could meet—in the stables when the grooms went to their midday meal in the hall. Geoffrey seemed less than enthusiastic, pointing out that it would be colder than a witch's teat and he'd likely freeze the body part she was most interested in, but she laughed huskily and murmured she'd warm him up soon enough. There was more laughing, low and intimate, and then John heard their footsteps descending, fading away. He'd sank down upon the steps, but now he came quietly to his feet, his eyes shining, for an idea had come to him, a daring idea that was as appealing as it was scary.

Before he could think better of it, John trudged through the snow of the outer bailey to the stables and waited until no grooms were about to clamber up the ladder into the loft. There he burrowed deep into the hay, making himself a secure, hidden nest. He thought it most likely that Geoffrey and the girl would choose to come up into the loft, too, but even if they stayed below in one of the empty stalls, he'd still be able to watch. He knew what a risk he was taking, shivered to think of his brother's anger if he were found spying on them. But he could not resist this chance to watch while they did it, whatever it was that men and women did. He had a fairly good idea, having watched dogs humping, but imagining was not the same as actually seeing for himself. The thought even crossed his mind that this might be something to hold over his brother's head, that if ever Geoffrey threatened to give him a thrashing, he could make a threat of his own, mentioning the girl Geoffrey had been groping in the stairwell, the one with a husband.

It was warmer beneath the hay than he'd expected, and he began to feel so comfortable that he was soon yawning. The night's storm had awakened him well before daybreak and he'd been unable to go back to sleep, listening to the eerie wailing of the wind and thinking it sounded like a pack of hungry wolves. Curling up like a cat, he yawned again, feeling drowsy. He hoped they'd come soon.

He must have fallen asleep after that, for he awoke with a start, not remembering for a moment where he was. It all came back to him, though, when he heard their voices. Peering from his hideaway, he could barely make out their figures, for the loft was filled with shadows, as dark as night in the far corners. As he listened, he realized that they'd already done it, and he felt a sharp pang of disappointment, angry with himself for sleeping through it. He could not go anywhere, though, until they did, so he settled down to wait, consoling himself with the thought that they might do it again.

"See . . . this was not such a bad idea," the girl murmured, and Geoffrey agreed that she'd more than kept her word, had kindled enough heat to burn the barn down. She giggled and they talked for a while of matters that John found very boring, mainly of people he did not know. He was dozing again when he heard the girl mention "the queen" and his eyes snapped open.

"Is she as beautiful as men say?"

"Well," Geoffrey said, sounding as if he were yawning, "now she is old, of course. But yes, when she was young, she was very beautiful. I remember her coming into the nursery to bid us good night. Her skirts would rustle and she always smelled so good, even better than fresh-baked bread."

"Were you often with her when you were young?"

"A fair amount of the time. Boys stay in their mother's care only till they are seven or so, and after that, we did not see her as much, of course. Obviously she could not travel with all of us, but she usually had a couple of us wherever she went. God knows, we saw more of her than our father."

"Fathers are never underfoot, are they? Mine only noticed his children when one of us got into trouble, and then he would roar and rant, but he never hit me or my sisters. My brothers now—that was another story. He would thrash them till they were as raw as uncooked beef. And my mother was just as strict; she had the makings of a fine lady abbess, God's truth. Were your parents strict with you and your brothers, Geoffrey?"

He laughed softly. "Lord, no! We got away with holy hell. Our father was rarely around and when he was, he could always be coaxed into giving us whatever we wanted. I suppose he was loath to discipline us when he saw us so seldom. Our mother was not as easy to fool, but she did not care much if we got up to mischief. Oh, she'd scold us if we were caught in the act, but her heart was not in it, we could tell. What I most remember is that she was fun. She'd chase fireflies in the garden with us or let us bring our dogs into bed at night and when we fell out of trees, she would shrug and say it was lucky she had sons to spare, could afford to lose one or two. No, she was not like other mothers."

He laughed again. "I remember one time when Richard and I found a snake. We were trying to decide what to do with it, and I do not recall which one of us had the idea, but we ended up smuggling it into our mother's bed. Then we hid outside her chamber that night, waiting to hear all the shrieking and carrying on. We were not sure she'd scream, but we figured her ladies would. We heard nothing at all, though, and crept back to our bed, very disappointed. Not a word was said about it the next day, either, so we decided the snake must have escaped. We'd forgotten all about it by that night—until we climbed into bed and found something warm and slick and slithery under the covers with us!"

The girl joined in his laughter. John stifled a laugh himself, thinking of his brothers yelling and bolting from the bed in panic. Geoffrey was telling her that they decided to play her game and say nothing about it the next day, but as soon as they'd met her eyes, all three of them had begun to laugh helplessly, while everyone else watched in bafflement, not knowing what the joke was. But after a while, it no longer seemed as funny to John. It occurred to him that he did not have any memories to match Richard's and Geoffrey's, no recollections of playing games with their mother or sharing jests or having her sit up with him at night after he'd caught poison oak, as Geoffrey was relating now. Why not? Why was it different for him?

When Geoffrey and the girl finally departed, John waited till it was safe to venture out and scrambled down the ladder just as two of the grooms sauntered into the stables. They looked surprised and he knew they wanted to ask what he was doing up there, but he raised his chin and, reminding himself that this was his loft, he walked past them as if he'd not seen them. He was at a loss what to do next. He'd missed dinner, and he wondered if anyone had noticed his absence. Once he was back in the middle bailey, he decided to go to the kitchen and get something to tide him over till supper that evening. But then he happened to glance across the bailey toward the chapel and he had another idea, even better than his notion to spy on Geoffrey.

Last night he'd heard his cousin Morgan and two other boys in the royal household discussing the magical properties of holy water. According to them, it was supposed to burn sinners if it was splashed upon them, and they were eager to make the test. They'd decided to try it out upon a culprit in the town's pillory, but their scheme had been thwarted when a priest caught them trying to dip water out of the chapel font. If he could obtain a vial of holy water, they'd be sure to be impressed. They were all several years older than he was, so that would be quite a coup. Darting into the kitchen, he snatched a clay cup when no one was watching, then hurried toward the chapel.

At least it was not as dark here as up in the loft, for candles burned in wall sconces and on the High Altar. Best of all, there was no sign of the chaplain. Hoping that his luck had changed for the better, John approached the stone font and filled the cup to the brim. But then he paused. What if they did not believe this was holy water? It was John's experience that the world was not a trusting place and they were likely to be skeptical of his claim, especially since he'd succeeded where they'd failed. After pondering the problem, he moved quietly up the aisle toward the High Altar. There were two silver chalices upon it. If he put the holy water in one of them, they could not doubt him. But taking a church chalice was not the same as filching a kitchen cup. What if there was a hue and cry over its disappearance? Well, he could return it afterward. Anyway, how could it be stealing if it was his to begin with?

He poured the water from the cup into one of the chalices and smiled, pleased with his handiwork. It was then that the door to the chapel swung open. He ducked down behind the High Altar, holding his breath. Footsteps were echoing up the aisle of the nave; risking a glance, he caught a glimpse of a priest's cassock. To his relief, the footsteps soon receded, but he decided to stay where he was until he was sure the priest was not loitering outside.

Sitting cross-legged on the floor, he stuck his finger in the chalice, relieved when the water did not burn. A pity he could not figure out a way to spill it on Geoffrey. He was surely a sinner, guilty of adultery and fornication this very day. To John, those were the least of his sins. Having brothers so much older than he had been a trial, for when they were not ignoring him, they were amusing themselves by playing pranks on him and making him feel foolish. His most vivid Christmas memory was of such an episode. He'd been very young, four, he thought. It was one of those rare times when he'd been summoned from Fontevrault with Joanna to his father's Christmas Court at Bures. It was only a hunting lodge and there was not enough room to accommodate so many people. Both of his parents were short-tempered and edgy, not showing any taste for the revelries; years later, he would realize that this was the infamous Christmas Court when his father flew into such a rage and doomed Thomas Becket with a few ill-chosen words. At the time, though, he'd known only that no one seemed to be paying him much mind.

He had dim memories of playing with Joanna in the great hall, chasing each other around and being scolded by their mother. But the memory he'd have liked to forget continued to burn brightly in the back of his brain. He'd been disappointed to find that Hal was in England. He was still drawn to Richard and Geoffrey, though, for at thirteen and twelve, they seemed very grown-up to him, and so he'd trailed after them, much to their annoyance. One day he'd followed them into the village cemetery, where he'd fallen into an open grave and was trapped there for what had seemed like hours. They'd later sworn that they'd not heard him crying for help, but he had never believed them. After that, he no longer tried to be included, avoided them whenever he could.

He'd just risen, intent upon sneaking out, when the door opened again. He dropped down again, so hastily that he spilled some of the holy water upon his mantle. The priest was back. He did not enter, though, saying, "I will remain outside, my lord, make sure that you are not disturbed." Footsteps now sounded, a heavier tread than the priest's, and John peeked from behind the altar cloth, saw to his horror that it was his father.

Henry moved toward the High Altar, and John shivered, for they were now separated only by a length of embroidered cloth. His father had knelt, began to pray. John caught random words, but not enough to make sense, for his Latin studies were not that advanced. He stayed very still, hoping Henry would soon go away. He made no move to leave, though, murmured a name, "Rosamund," and John stiffened, for he knew that was his father's leman. He risked another look, saw that Henry had buried his head in his hands, and was stunned to realize that his father was weeping. The sight frightened him. He'd never imagined grown men cried, and for certes, not his father, not the king. Knowing that this was a scene no one was supposed to see, he panicked and decided to creep toward the sacristy, where there were more places to hide. If he were very quiet, his father ought not to hear him. But his fear made him clumsy, and as he rose to a half-crouch, the chalice slipped from his grasp, tumbled onto the tiles with a sound loud enough to be heard in Heaven.

Henry's head came up sharply. Outraged that even here in God's House he could not have privacy to grieve for Rosamund, he got swiftly to his feet and strode toward the High Altar. "Who is there? How dare you spy upon me!"

He was shocked to find his youngest son huddled behind the altar, his eyes enormous in the white blur of his face, Eleanor's eyes, although he'd never seen in them what he now saw in John's—sheer terror. "Johnny?"

"I am sorry," the boy mumbled, "so sorry . . . I was not spying, I was not!"

"I know, Johnny, I know. It is all right, lad. I am not angry, not with you. You just took me by surprise." Henry was appalled to see how the boy was trembling. Christ Jesus, was he afraid of his own father? Kneeling so that he could look into John's eyes, he said, "I am sorry I yelled at you, lad."

John did not know what to say, so he kept silent, for he'd learned silence was usually the safest way.

"I had grievous news yesterday," Henry said softly. "One very dear to me has died. I'd been deluding myself, refusing to admit how ill she really was. Grown men ought to know better, but we can be as foolish as children that way. As if denying what we fear will somehow make it any less true . . ."

John had not thought his father feared anything on God's Earth. "I am sorry," he said again, feeling as if the very ground were shifting under his feet.

"There is nothing to be sorry for, Johnny. I am glad that you are here."

John blinked. "You are?"

"Yes," Henry said, and gathered the boy into his arms. "I was feeling very alone today. I needed to be reminded that it is not so, that I have you, I still have a son . . ."

John did not move, even though his father was holding him so tightly that it hurt. His cheek was scratched by Henry's beard, and he inhaled the scent of wine and sweat and horses. He still did not know what to say, but his father did not seem to require any words. Getting to his feet, he held out his hand. John took it and followed him from the chapel.

CHAPTER TWENTY-SIX

June 1177
Paris, France

ARGUERITE'S BEDCHAMBER was shadowed and still, although outside the morning sun was bathing Paris in blinding white light. As Hal entered, one of his wife's attendants rose from her seat by the bed and came to meet him. Most of her ladies were high-spirited, pretty girls, but Agace was well into her forties, for she'd been with the young queen since the latter's childhood, and they often seemed like mother and daughter to Hal. He was thankful that she'd been with Marguerite during her delivery, and he was heartened now by her vigil, sure that no evil would befall Marguerite as long as the formidable Agace was on guard.

"How is she this morn?" he asked softly, and smiled when she assured him that Marguerite had passed a peaceful night. "Our lad," he said, "is doing well, too. His wet-nurse said she got him to take a little more milk, and that is surely a good sign, no?"

Agace regarded him somberly, wondering if he was truly so oblivious of his son's danger. Marguerite's labor had been long and difficult and at one point, they'd been terrified that her life was bleeding away. She'd finally given birth to one of the smallest babies Agace had ever seen, his skin so red he seemed badly sunburned. She'd been so sure he was stillborn that she burst into tears. The midwife had breathed life into his little lungs, but she was not sanguine about his chances of survival, telling Agace privately that the baby had many battles ahead of him. Three days had passed since his birth, and Agace saw no great improvement in his condition. No one had told Marguerite of their fears, but Agace knew she shared them. Each time she cradled her son, she seemed spellbound by his every breath, mesmerized by the feeble sound of his heartbeat.

The midwife had been far more candid with Hal than Marguerite. To no avail, Agace now realized. He could not face the fact that his son might die, and so it was not going to happen. Hal's reality was whatever he wanted it to be. She felt honor-bound to warn him, nonetheless, that he ought to be braced for the worst, as it was not for mortal men to understand the mysterious workings of the Almighty. "My lord, the midwife said that babies born early are—"

"Hal?" Marguerite's voice came sleepily from the bed, and he hastened to her side, Agace and her forebodings forgotten.

"I am right here, my heart." Leaning over, he kissed her gently. "I have something for the new mother," he said, producing an object swathed in silk. Marguerite unwrapped it to reveal an ivory box and, inside, a delicate opal ring set in gold filigree. Sliding it onto her finger, Hal kissed her again. "Opals are said to be lucky."

She smiled, praying that he was right, for their son needed all the luck he could get. "How is he this morn?"

"Fine. All agree he is a handsome little lad, bearing a strong resemblance to his father. Except that he is as bald as an egg, of course!"

"Go and fetch him for me, Agace," Marguerite said, and the older woman was happy to obey. She did not have far to go, for Marguerite had insisted that the baby's cradle be placed in the antechamber; she would have had it beside her bed if Hal and Agace had not objected, fearing that a newborn's wailing would rob her of the sleep she so desperately needed. She had reluctantly acquiesced, but now she said resolutely, "I am going to keep him with me tonight. I feel much stronger, Hal, and it will ease my mind to have him close at hand."

Through the open doorway, they heard Agace's voice and the answering murmur of the wet-nurse. "If you insist," Hal agreed, pretending to admire her new ring so he could press a kiss into the palm of her hand. "He does not cry much, is a very good baby so far, no trouble at all . . . once again taking after his sire."

The scream was like the slash of a sword, splintering their last moment of peace into an infinity of pain. It was followed at once by another choked cry and then, weeping. Hal swung toward the sound, his expression one of denial and disbelief. But Marguerite knew better, and she began to sob.

E LEANOR AND AMARIA WERE PLAYING a desultory game of chess, for it was too hot to concentrate. They'd opened the windows of their bedchamber in hopes of attracting an evening breeze, but the air still simmered with the day's heat, offering no relief. Muted sounds came drifting in, the arrival of late riders, a barking dog, the tolling of distant church bells. Eleanor glanced again at the chessboard and then sat back with a sigh. "Let's keep this till the morrow, Amaria."

Smothering a yawn, Amaria rose and stretched. "Shall I pour you some wine, Madame?" Eleanor nodded and then they both turned, hearing the sounds of footsteps in the stairwell. There was a soft knock and the door swung open, almost simultaneously.

"Harry?" Eleanor stared at her husband in surprise. "What are you doing back in Winchester?"

As Henry stepped forward into the circle of light cast by the candles, Eleanor frowned, thinking he looked exhausted, shadows lurking like bruises under his eyes, his mouth so tautly drawn that she could not imagine those lips ever curving in a smile. "Dame Amaria," he said politely, "I need to speak with my wife in private." And Eleanor was suddenly frightened.

Once Amaria had departed, Henry moved toward Eleanor and seated himself across the table from her. He seemed to be favoring his left leg, and she said, "You've hurt yourself."

"It's nothing, an old injury that has flared up again." He did not speak for several moments, but she did not urge him, sure that she did not want to hear whatever he'd come to tell her. "There is no easy way to say this," he said at last. "On June 19 in Paris, Marguerite gave birth to a son. The baby came before his time, was too frail. He only lived for three days."

Eleanor's eyes filled with tears. "Oh, Harry . . . those poor children. A wound like that will never heal . . ."

"I know."

She dried her cheeks with the back of her hand. "I will want to write to them."

He nodded, and for a time there was only silence. When he got to his feet, he moved as slowly as an old man, and she realized that his pain was physical, too; his limp was much more pronounced now. "Thank you for telling me," she said, and he nodded again.

He hobbled to the door, and then paused, searching for words of comfort even though he knew there were none. "He was baptized ere he died. At least there is that. They'll know his innocent soul has gone straight to God's embrace."

"What was he named?"

He seemed reluctant to answer, and when he finally murmured, "William," she understood why. That had been the name of their firstborn, the son who'd died two months before his third birthday. Their eyes met and held, and for an anguished moment, they were grieving—not for the grandson they'd never seen—but for the son whose death had left such a ragged, gaping hole in their lives, the son whose death seemed even more tragic as the years went by and Hal's follies mounted. What if their Will had lived, if he and not Hal had been the heir? That was not a question either of them had ever asked aloud, but it was one that occurred to them both on those nights when sleep wouldn't come and they lay awake in the dark, trying to understand how things had gone so terribly wrong for their family.

AFTER LEAVING WINCHESTER, Henry passed a week at Stanstede in Sussex, waiting for a favorable wind to cross to Normandy. During this time, he gave the church at Wicumbe to the Godstow nunnery in Rosamund's memory, and he learned that the French king had gotten a papal legate to threaten an Interdict against his domains unless he stopped delaying the marriage of his son Richard to Louis's daughter Alys. But his leg injury was not healing as he'd hoped, and he returned to Winchester until his health improved.

THE SUMMER HEAT WAVE CONTINUED; August was even hotter than July. Eleanor and Amaria had taken a wooden embroidery frame out into a secluded corner of the gardens, and they were frowning over their handiwork. "Let me show you again how to make a couched stitch, Madame," Amaria said, hiding her surprise that the queen handled a needle so clumsily; she had assumed that everything came easily to Eleanor.

"Let me try." Eleanor knotted a length of silk thread, did her best to imitate Amaria, and stabbed her thumb with the needle. "Damnation!"

Neither one had heard the soft footsteps and they were startled now by laughter. Amaria turned to find they were being watched by a slender woman about Eleanor's age, fashionably dressed in a sapphire-colored bliaut, girdled at the hip with a jeweled belt. Her dark eyes agleam with amusement, she sauntered forward, saying, "I never thought I'd see Eleanor of Aquitaine with a needle in her hand."

Amaria was startled by the familiarity, but when she glanced at Eleanor, she saw that while the queen was surprised by this stranger's appearance, she was also pleased. "Shall I fetch a thimble, my lady?" she said, assuming that if Eleanor did not want time alone with the other woman, she'd say so. When she didn't, Amaria made a tactful withdrawal.

"Do sit down," Eleanor said, gesturing toward the other end of the bench. "What are you doing here, Maud?"

Maud sat. "I was disquieted to hear that Harry had delayed his return to Normandy. I'd never known him even to acknowledge a physical infirmity, much less change his plans because of one, and I feared that he must be at death's door."

"No, but he has been in enough pain to make him loath to ride a horse, much less make a Channel crossing."

"What ails him?"

"He did not tell you?"

"You know how difficult it is to pry an answer out of Harry. He muttered some foolishness about taking one misstep too many. Did he have an accident and if so, why did I not hear about it?"

"Because," Eleanor said, "it happened three years ago, when he was kicked in the thigh by an unruly horse."

"Ah, yes, I remember that." Maud was not surprised that Henry should be troubled by an old wound, for that often happened in their world. Poor Harry, she thought. It must be an infection of the bone. "I am so sorry about Hal's baby, Eleanor."

"Thank you," Eleanor said simply, acknowledging Maud's sympathy at the same time that she indicated the hurt was still too fresh to probe. "Does Harry know you are here with me?" she asked, with just the hint of a challenge.

Maud took it up without hesitation. "Yes, he does. I got his permission ere I sought you out." Answering the question that Eleanor had not asked, she said, "Had he refused, I would have respected his wishes."

That was a diplomatic declaration of loyalty, a discreet warning that she would not be putting herself or her family at risk for Eleanor's sake. Eleanor did not blame her, though. "I am gladdened to see you, Maud," she said, and smiled. "You've always had an ear for choice gossip, and I hope you've a scandal or two to share."

"A few. But you must be hungry for word of your children. Shall I begin with them?"

"Actually, Harry has been good this past year about keeping me informed of family matters. He notified me when Joanna came ashore at Naples, and when she reached Palermo at Candlemas, he sent me an account of her spectacular entry into the city. It was night and there were so many torches flaring that the city seemed on fire. Joanna was mounted on a white palfrey, clad in her best robes, with her hair loose about her shoulders, a magnet for every eye. She and William were wed less than a fortnight after her arrival, and that same day she was crowned by the Archbishop of Palermo."

Maud knew her own daughter would have been overwhelmed by such splendor and ceremony, but Joanna was made of stronger stuff and she suspected that Eleanor's daughter would have enjoyed being the center of attention, the brightest star in the firmament. She hoped that the fates would be kind to Joanna, that she would find contentment in her new life and her new island home.

"Harry has also informed me whenever Richard or Geoffrey have won a victory over Poitevin or Breton rebels," Eleanor continued, "and he even kept me apprised of John's prospects, telling me that he plans to make John Lord of Ireland, and letting me know last summer when he plight-trothed John to your brother William's daughter Avisa."

"So you know of that, too? Harry is certainly determined to make sure that none ever call John 'Lackland' again." The proposed marriage could make John Earl of Gloucester one day since William did not have any male heirs. But the earl did have two other daughters, and Maud knew their husbands were very disgruntled by the marriage settlement, for under normal circumstances, the earldom would have been divided between all three daughters. The Viscount of Limoges had been so outraged when Henry refused to allow Rainald's earldom of Cornwall to pass to his wife and her sisters that he'd been in rebellion ever since. Maud hoped that the earldom of Gloucester would not prove to be as disruptive. She hoped, too, that John appreciated how lucky he was; few youngest sons were so lavishly provided for.

"Well," she said lightly, "I did promise you some good gossip. I'm sure you've heard that Hugh Bigod died on pilgrimage—proof that the Almighty has a sense of humor—and his son Roger is feuding fiercely with his stepmother, Hugh's widow. There are rumors that Louis is considering wedding his youngest daughter, Agnes, to the Emperor of Byzantium's son. The Earl of Essex is in the Holy Land with the Count of Flanders, and Harry's sister Emma is in Wales with child."

Eleanor wondered if Emma had welcomed the news of her pregnancy. The pressure to produce a male heir could be intense, as she well remembered from her years with Louis. But a child also sealed her fate; a barren wife could hope for the dissolution of her marriage. "All that is interesting, Maud, but hardly scandalous or shocking."

"This next story is both. One of your vassals, the Count of La Marche, suspected his wife of infidelity. He repudiated her and had her supposed lover put to death, on Easter, of all holy days. But his only son died suddenly soon thereafter, and he is said to be in despair, stricken as much by guilt as by grief. It seems his 'proof' of adultery was not as conclusive as he first thought, and now he fears that God took his son as punishment for executing an innocent man." She paused then, almost imperceptibly. "And Rosamund Clifford died last December at Godstow nunnery."

"Ah," Eleanor said, "I see." That explained the mystery, then, why she'd withdrawn from the court. "Harry has not been very lucky of late, has he?"

"I'd say not," Maud agreed. Noting Eleanor's apparent indifference to Rosamund, she wondered if she should make any mention of Harry's latest leman, and decided to be circumspect for once.

Eleanor seemed to have read her mind, though. "So tell me, Maud . . . who is Harry swiving these days? Somehow I doubt that he's been living like a monk just because Rosamund wanted to live her last days as a nun."

Maud grinned. "No, not Harry. He's had bedmates, of course, this past year. And I've heard talk that he's taken up with the daughter of the Lord of Conches, but her name escapes me at the moment."

"Most likely it escapes Harry, too," Eleanor said, but she sounded cynically amused, not bitter.

Maud studied the other woman thoughtfully. "I must say that you seem to be faring much better than I'd have expected."

"Better than I'd have expected, too," Eleanor admitted. "The first two years were the hardest, and not just because I was so cut off from the rest of the world. I still had hope, then, you see, and hope can be both a blessing and a curse. But it has been much easier for me at Winchester. It helped greatly to be able to spend so much time with Joanna last summer, and to see my sons again, of course. And, as you can tell, Harry is a more gentle gaoler these days. We had one dreadful storm at Falaise and several lesser tempests after that, but lately the weather has been almost peaceful . . . almost."

"Yes, I can see that Harry's wounds are not quite as raw. But neither are yours, and that surprises me. You are still his prisoner, after all."

"Good of you to point that out," Eleanor said dryly. "Trust me, I am not likely to forget." Rising, she said, "Come, walk with me." They moved from the sun into the shade, halting under the spreading branches of a medlar tree. "When Emma came to visit me," Eleanor said after a silence, "she expressed surprise that I seemed to have been examining my conscience, and I told her that it helped to pass the time. Time is a prisoner's worst enemy, Maud. Suddenly there are so many empty hours to fill, endless days to get through. So, yes, I have been thinking a great deal about my past and my future. I even came to understand why Harry and I misunderstood each other so fatally."

"And what did you decide?"

"Harry has always seen me, first and foremost, as his wife. But I have always seen myself, first and foremost, as the Duchess of Aquitaine."

Maud had reached that same conclusion, but she hadn't expected Eleanor to see it, too. "So if you had it to do over again . . . ?"

"I would have paid more heed to your sound advice," Eleanor said with a slight smile. "And I would have listened more to the mother, less to the duchess. I did not realize how grievously Joanna would be hurt, and I should have. Nor is Joanna the only one to suffer for our family mistakes and misjudgments. I am sure my older daughters have been sorely troubled, too."

"And John," Maud said, thinking of the wary little boy she'd seen at the Nottingham Christmas Court.

"Yes, and John," Eleanor agreed. "Say what you will of us, Maud, Harry and I do nothing by halves. I still think that I was in the right and he was in the wrong. You cannot treat a mettlesome destrier the way you would a plodding sumpter horse, not without goading it to defiance or utterly breaking its spirit, and I fear that the mistakes he has made and continues to make with our sons will haunt him till the end of his days. But when I look back upon the scorched, barren battlefield that our marriage has become, I can take no pride in being right."

Maud had cocked her head, regarding Eleanor with something almost like awe. "By God," she said, "you truly have changed!"

"No . . . not yet," Eleanor said, with another ghostly smile. "But I am trying."

ELEANOR WAS SURPRISED when Henry did not appear for dinner in the great hall, for it was filled with highborn guests, including three bishops. Taking his steward aside after the meal, she got from him a reluctant admission that the king's leg was worse. As she and Amaria made their way back to her chamber, she came to a sudden halt, sent Amaria on ahead, and impulsively headed for Henry's bedchamber.

The antechamber was crowded, as always, but Henry's brother Hamelin was guarding access to the inner sanctum, and he reacted to Eleanor's entrance with outrage, barring the door with his own body.

"Oh, for the love of God, Hamelin," Eleanor snapped, "stop acting like a damned fool and let me by."

"Indeed, I will not. The king is ailing, and he does not need to be vexed by unwelcome visitors, especially those who might prove injurious to his health!"

"I do not have time for this nonsense!" Over Hamelin's shoulder, she could catch a glimpse of her husband, and called out, "Harry, will you tell this dolt to admit me?"

To her annoyance, he took his time in thinking it over. "Let her pass, Hamelin," he said at last. "I promise to be on my guard."

When Hamelin grudgingly gave way, she swept by him disdainfully, then slammed the door in his face. "Thank you, my lord husband," she said, with sarcasm that Henry pretended to take at face value.

"Glad to be of service. You must miss being able to order men around." Moving to the table, he poured wine for himself. "Why are you here, Eleanor?"

"I want to talk to you."

"My lucky day," he muttered, but he poured a second cup for her.

"If I promise to be on my best behavior," she said, "can we conduct this conversation sitting down?" When he hesitated, she scowled at him, a scowl he'd seen hundreds of times over the years. "Jesu, Harry, must you be so stubborn? Does your doctor have to tie you to a chair to get you off that bad leg?"

He threw up his hands in mock surrender. "No, he just has to set you on me." Limping across the chamber, he sat down heavily upon his bed.

Eleanor followed with their wine cups. Pulling a chair closer to the bed, she studied him critically. "Your fever has returned, else you'd not look so flushed. Harry, how do you expect to heal if you will not get the rest you need?"

"Enough," he said impatiently. She noticed, though, that he settled back against the pillows with a sigh of relief. "So . . . what do you want to talk about?"

"I heard something very interesting in the hall today—that you and Louis are locking horns again, this time over Richard's marriage to Alys. And no, it was not Maud who told me; I overheard your justiciar talking with Ralf de Glanville. Is it true that you are facing the threat of an Interdict?"

"Not a serious one. Louis complained last year to the Pope that I was unduly delaying the marriage. To placate him, the Pope agreed to send a legate with a papal bull that would lay my lands under Interdict, but he gave the legate no instructions to publish it, for the Holy See does not want another breach with England. Louis has been making such a pest of himself, though, that the legate insisted that I meet with them to discuss the matter—which I'll gladly do if this blasted leg ever heals."

"When you meet them, what then? I know you're not keen on the marriage."

"Why should I be? You think I want to hand another son over to Louis, trussed up like a Martinmas stoat? That worked out so well with Hal, after all. And the girl brings no marriage portion to speak of. I must have been mad to agree to the betrothal."

Eleanor knew why he had, of course. He'd been eager to get Louis to acknowledge his sons as his heirs, Hal for England and Normandy and Anjou, Richard for Aquitaine, and Geoffrey for Brittany. She'd often thought it was ironic that one of his purest impulses—his desire to protect the succession for Hal—had been such an unmitigated disaster. "So what will you tell Louis and the legate?"

"That I am quite willing to have the marriage take place—once Louis fulfills his side of the bargain and turns over the dowries he promised—the French Vexin for Marguerite and the city of Bourges for Alys."

Eleanor's eyes widened at the sheer audacity of the demand. "Harry, Louis did turn over the Norman Vexin to you, and we both know he never promised Bourges for Alys."

"The Norman Vexin was mine by rights; why would I settle for that? And I am sure Louis would have offered Bourges if it had occurred to him at the time. What father would want his daughter to go to her marriage bed as a pauper?"

"Louis would sooner give you every drop of blood in his body ere he'd surrender Bourges. So what are you really after?"

He shrugged. "You tell me."

"Very well. Clearly, you are seeking to put Louis on the defensive. If he backs off from insisting upon the marriage, you are then free to look for a more profitable bride for Richard. If he agrees to provide a dowry, you still win. My guess is that you are simply trying to make the problem go away, mayhap beguile Louis into making a peace that will allow you to meddle in the Auvergne and Berry, where you and the French have competing claims."

Henry had forgotten how sharp she could be, had forgotten how much he'd once enjoyed talking to her about the stratagems, subterfuges, and feints that were such an important part of a king's arsenal. Reluctant to admit that she'd read him so easily, he did not reply.

Eleanor sipped her wine while she mulled over the implications of this latest clash between Henry and Louis. "What does Richard think of all this? Since Alys is his betrothed, I assume you did mention it to him?"

He surprised her then by saying, "As it happens, I did. We talked about this ere he returned to Poitou last summer. He showed very little interest in the subject, was much more interested in discussing the aid I'd provide against the Poitevin rebels."

That rang true to Eleanor. She knew Richard had never indicated the slightest desire to wed Alys; she doubted that he'd ever given much thought to the girl at all. "So you are saying that Richard is indifferent, cares little whether he weds her or not."

"That sums it up rather well. For certes, he is not burning to take a wife. Unlike Geoffrey, who keeps dropping hints heavier than anvils, reminding me that he is in his nineteenth year now and Constance is sixteen, more than old enough for the holy state of matrimony."

That rang true, too, for Richard had nothing to gain by wedding Alys and Geoffrey had a great deal to gain by wedding Constance. Their marriage would validate his claim to Brittany, and he'd no longer be dependent upon Henry's good will, would have power of his own. Eleanor suspected that the very reasons which made the marriage so attracttive to Geoffrey were why Henry seemed in no hurry for it to happen. But that was a worry for a later time, and more Geoffrey's concern than hers. The hardest part of confinement was accepting the fact that she could no longer influence the course of events or even the interactions in her own family.

"It sounds," she said, "as if you have the situation well in hand."

He shot her a suspicious look. "And that sounds as if you are actually supporting me in this."

"Why would I not? I agree that we can do better for Richard than Alys, and I'd like nothing better than to see Louis discomfited and humbled. He proved to be an even worse ally than he was a husband."

"As you ought to have known," he pointed out, and she acknowledged the truth of that with a rueful smile. He had propped himself up on his elbow and was regarding her so impassively that she realized she had not the slightest idea what he was thinking. "So," he said, after a brief silence, "you'd raise no objections if I disavowed the plight-troth. But what if Richard truly wanted to wed the girl?"

"In that case, I would fight for the marriage till my last breath," she murmured and saw that she'd finally managed to startle him.

"Your honesty is commendable, if rather reckless, for you've hardly reassured me of your good faith should I set you free."

"Could you ever trust me again, Harry?"

He did not even pause for breath. "No, never."

"Exactly," she said. "So what would be the point of telling you what I thought you'd want to hear? I know marriage is not usually fertile ground for the truth, but mayhap a little truth-telling might have helped us avoid some of the grief of recent years."

He was openly skeptical. "Are you saying that you're going to forswear lies from now on, speak only God's truth? I'll believe that when unicorns roam the English countryside."

"Go ahead," she challenged, "ask me a question, then. But I ought to warn you that the rules of the game apply to you, too."

He considered it, but she knew he was never one to refuse a challenge. "Very well. Do you regret the rebellion?"

"You can do better than that, Harry. Of course I do. Ask me something less obvious."

"What do you regret? That you set my sons against me? Or that you lost?"

"Better," she conceded. "Both. Now . . . your turn. Answer me honestly. If I'd demanded that you put Rosamund Clifford aside, would you have done so?"

"No."

"And if I'd asked it of you?"

That gave him pause. "I am not sure," he admitted. "I just do not know, Eleanor."

"Fair enough. Your turn."

She'd expected a question about Rosamund, for she knew he still thought jealousy was at the root of their estrangement. But what he asked was far more dangerous. "That day at Falaise . . . why did you not seek my forgiveness?"

She exhaled a soft breath. "Ah, Harry, we are getting into deep waters here."

"An honest answer. Your rules, remember."

"Very well. I did not want your forgiveness, not then."

"And now?"

"Yes, I would ask your forgiveness now. But only if you asked mine in return."

"Are we back to Rosamund again?" he said wearily. "So if I said I was sorry for taking her to my bed, that would have satisfied you? That would have been enough?"

"Indeed not! If you truly think I would rebel because you had a sugar-sop on the side, you do not know me at all and you never have."

He frowned, but kept to the rules of the game, saying honestly, "Then I do not understand. But whatever answer you offer for your betrayal, it can neither explain nor justify your treachery. You were my wife. You owed loyalty to me above all others."

"Obviously I did not see it like that," she said coolly. "And if you'd wanted a meek little dormouse for a wife, you ought to have married your Rosamund. You cannot have it both ways, Harry. You wanted Aquitaine, enough to overlook that I was nine years older than you and had not given Louis a son and had a reputation that was frayed around the edges. You used my lands as a stepping-stone to the English throne. It seems hypocritical to bemoan the fact that I was not and would never be a docile, gentle creature without an independent thought in her head. You knew what you were getting with me. I was never one for sailing under false colors."

"Yes, I wanted Aquitaine. But I also wanted you, and you know it. Do not make our marriage sound like such a one-sided bargain. You got what you wanted, too, Madame. I gave you a crown, and a better life than ever you'd had with Louis Capet. And you repaid me with the worst sort of betrayal. My sons would never have rebelled against me if not for you!"

"And you wonder why I did not seek your forgiveness? Because you blamed me for all and yourself for nothing! The mistakes were always mine, never yours. And nothing has changed, has it? You still see yourself as the innocent one, the victim. Well, I have just one last question for you, my lord husband. Come December, it will begin my fifth year as your prisoner. When you are forced to face the fact that *our* sons are still chafing under your stranglehold, what then? Who will you blame when they rebel again, Harry? And they will, for you seem utterly unable to learn from your mistakes!"

Henry started to swing off the bed, grimaced in pain, and fell back against the pillows. "I want you gone from this chamber, would to God I could have you gone from my life!"

Infuriated at being dismissed as if she were a servant, Eleanor got to her feet without haste, defiantly taking her time. "I never thought I'd be saying this, but you are a fool, Harry Fitz Empress, as much of a fool as Louis. You are the one who is alienating our sons, not me. I said you could not learn from your mistakes. Worse than that, you cannot even acknowledge them!"

"I'll acknowledge one mistake right now. I ought to have pressured the Pope to annul our marriage, ought to have insisted that I would no longer tolerate you as my wife or queen. Had I done that, you'd be cloistered in some remote Irish nunnery today and I'd be rid of you for good!"

Eleanor strode to the door, then turned back to face him. "You are not only blind to the truth about our sons. You are equally blind to the truth about us. We've been wed for twenty-five years, have shared a bed for more than twenty of those years. I bore you eight children and we buried one together. We've schemed and fought and loved until we are so entangled in hearts and minds that there is no way to set us free. God help us both, Harry, for we will never be rid of each other. Not even death will do that." And confident that she'd had the final word for once, she walked out and closed the door quietly behind her.

CHAPTER TWENTY-SEVEN

✦

August 1178
Winchester, England

*E*LEANOR WAS PLAYING THE HARP and Amaria working on her embroidery when Turold sought admittance to their chamber. Surprised by his appearance, for it was not mealtime, Eleanor gave him an encouraging smile. Although the youth had been at the castle only a fortnight, she felt confident that she could mold him into another Perrin, for he was cheerful, innocently cheeky, and always eager to please.

Turold was panting; he'd taken the stairs three at a time. "Madame," he gasped, "men just rode into the bailey, and a groom said one of them is your son!"

Eleanor came hastily to her feet. "Which one?"

Turold flushed. "I forgot to ask," he said. "I wanted to tell you straight away . . ."

He looked so crestfallen that Eleanor hid a smile. "It does not matter, Turold. I'll know soon enough."

Reassured, Turold promised to find out more, and bolted from the chamber. Amaria lay down her sewing and moved to Eleanor's side. "Who do you think it might be, my lady?"

"I am not sure, Amaria. As far as I know, John is the only one presently in England, and we can safely say it will not be him."

They did not have long to wait. Soon there were footsteps, followed by a perfunctory knock, and then Eleanor's third son entered. "Geoffrey!" Eleanor came quickly toward him, the warmth of her greeting fueled by a twinge of guilt; her initial reaction had been a muted sense of disappointment that it was not Richard.

"Sorry," Geoffrey murmured, "it is only me," and she gave him a startled look of appraisal; did he have second sight?

"You are more than enough," she insisted and embraced him affectionately. "This is a delightful surprise. I had no idea that you were back in England."

Geoffrey kissed her on the cheek and then sauntered over to kiss Amaria's hand with a gallant flourish that would have done Hal credit. "Papa and I crossed from Normandy last month," he explained as he moved to the table and poured wine for them. "He knighted me on Sunday at Woodstock."

Accepting a cup, Eleanor studied him carefully. "You do not seem all that pleased about it."

"A man hungering for meat is not likely to be satisfied with bread." Geoffrey sprawled in the window-seat with the boneless abandon of youth. "I asked him again to let me wed Constance. Instead, he gave me a knighthood."

She was clearly being invited to join in his criticism, but she resisted the temptation; it would serve none of their interests to prolong their family's strife. "Well . . . I grant you that a knighthood is not worth a duchy. But you've the right to half the revenues of Brittany, no?"

"No, not the 'right,'" Geoffrey corrected her quickly, "the privilege. And privileges, as we know, Maman, can be revoked at any time." He paused expectantly, and when his mother did not comment, he heaved a theatrical sigh. "Hal and I have a wager going; how many more years can he postpone the wedding? I just hope that when he finally relents, I am not too old to totter to the altar."

Eleanor decided it would be best to change the subject, for she truly did not want to worsen Henry's estrangement from his sons. Winchester's castellan had kept her informed about much of the political happenings in Henry's domains, for he'd assumed that her greater visibility meant she was no longer in such deep disgrace. She knew, therefore, that Henry and Louis had forged another tentative truce when they'd met with the papal legate; both kings had pledged to take the cross, and Henry had grudgingly agreed that Richard and Alys would eventually be wed, although he'd refused to commit himself to a specific date. But she'd not seen Henry for almost a year, and she took the opportunity now to interrogate Geoffrey about family matters.

"How is your father faring these days? Does his bad leg continue to pain him?"

"He said nothing about it and is no longer limping, so I'd say he's well enough. His temper is as quick to kindle as it ever was, though, and he is starting to go grey. I think he is beginning to feel his years, for he's been fretting that his hair is thinning and he's taken to cutting it even shorter than usual."

Geoffrey grinned at that, for he was still a month from his twentieth birthday and had a handsome head of luxuriant brownish-blond hair. Eleanor was not as amused, for she, too, was feeling her years. "And what of your brothers?"

"I did not see John. Ralf de Glanville—the one who captured the Scots king, remember—has taken charge of his education. Richard is off spilling blood somewhere in Poitou, and Hal is chasing after glory on the tournament circuit. In fact, I will be joining him upon my return to Normandy, for why should he have all the fun? Brittany is reasonably quiet at the moment, so I might as well enjoy the peace whilst it lasts."

Eleanor knew, of course, about Hal's abiding passion for tourneys. "I thought that he had not been very successful?"

"At first, he was not. But Will Marshal noticed a ruse that the Count of Flanders was employing at tournaments. He would hold back from the first assault, wait until the other participants were milling about in small groups, wearied, battered, and bruised. Then he and his men would rush in and take advantage of the confusion, sweeping all before them. Marshal confided this to Hal, who adopted the same tactics, and since then, he has been winning more often than not."

"Then why was Harry grumbling so about the expenses of Hal's tourneys? If he is winning, Hal must be reaping a goodly profit from the ransoms and captured horses."

Geoffrey laughed. "True enough, but Hal's spending could put a drunken sailor to shame. He outfits his knights in the very best armor and weapons, using his largesse to lure skilled fighters into his service, and he buys the finest horses, of course, and he loves to lavish gifts upon Marguerite, and he never refuses a friend, and his alms-giving is open-handed, and—"

Eleanor held up her hand, laughing, too. "Enough! Do you have any other family news for me?"

"Indeed, I do. Tilda had another son last year. They named the poor lad Otto, but that is not as bad as the name they burdened his brother with—Lothair!"

Eleanor felt a pang, remembering how Joanna had laughed, too, at Lothair's name; the last she'd heard, Joanna was faring well in her new land and her new life, but Sicily seemed so far away.

Geoffrey was regarding her with an enigmatic expression. "I am not sure if I ought to tell you this, Maman. Papa has sired another bastard. Ida de Tosny, the Lord of Conches's daughter, gave birth to a son last year."

Eleanor's shrug of unconcern was not feigned. "I am pleased to hear that he has acknowledged the child as his. Not all men do, sad to say. What name did Harry bestow on the baby?" But when he told her it was William, her indifference ebbed away, replaced by a prickle of resentful anger. Why must Harry choose the name of her dead son? Their Will had been cheated of so much—a long and healthy life, a king's crown, love and lust and sons of his own. He ought not to have to share his name with one of Harry's by-blows.

Geoffrey got to his feet and stretched. "I am loath to go, Maman, but I hope to reach Southampton by dark. I've been told the winds are favorable, and I want to take advantage of them ere they shift. There is something else, though, that you need to know. It concerns your vassal, the Count of La Marche."

Eleanor already knew what he was about to tell her, for Maud had shared the story of the count's scandal. Not wanting to deprive Geoffrey of the pleasure of relating such lurid gossip, she smiled innocently. "What has Audebert done now?"

"He thought he had reason to suspect his wife of infidelity. With his usual rashness, he acted upon the suspicion without waiting for proof. The wife was cast off, and the unfortunate lover was put to death. But then his son and heir died of a sudden, and the count began to fear the Almighty was punishing him for slaying an innocent man. He plunged into a deep melancholy, vowing to do all he could to make amends and regain God's Grace."

"Somehow I doubt that involved taking back his wronged wife," Eleanor said tartly. "Has he taken to sackcloth and ashes, forsaken the world for the serenity of the cloister?"

She was being sarcastic, but to her surprise, Geoffrey nodded. "Close, Maman, close. He decided to take the cross, to expiate his sins by a hallowed death in the Holy Land. But ere he departed on his pilgrimage of atonement, he sold the county of La Marche to Papa for fifteen thousand Angevin livres."

"He did *what*?"

Eleanor had not raised her voice, but there was something in her tone that attracted the attention of Amaria, who'd retreated across the chamber to give them the semblance of privacy. One glance at the queen's glittering green eyes, burning all the more brightly against the sudden pallor of her face, and Amaria jumped to her feet in alarm. "Madame, are you ill? What is wrong?"

Eleanor did not appear to hear her. "Count Audebert," Geoffrey said, "is the vassal of the Duchess of Aquitaine, liegeman of my lady mother and my brother Richard. At least he was until my father snatched La Marche from under their noses."

Eleanor was on her feet now, too, stalking to the window and back before whirling to face Geoffrey again in a flurry of silken skirts. "Does Richard know this?"

"He knows. Papa struck this deal last December, boasted of it to Richard, Hal, and me when we gathered for his Christmas Court at Angers. He was right pleased with the bargain he'd made, and well he should be, for La Marche must be worth three times what he paid for it."

"His pleasure be damned! What did he say to Richard about his piracy?"

"Oh, he explained it as too good a deal to pass up, and assured Richard that there was no need for concern, that he could still consider La Marche as part and parcel of Aquitaine." Geoffrey had been fighting back a smile, but at that it broke free. "Richard found that very reassuring."

Eleanor said something under her breath, but Amaria did not catch it, for she did not speak the *lengua romana* of the queen's homeland. She needed no translation, though, not after looking at the other woman's face. "Might not the king have spoken the truth?" she ventured cautiously, wanting to offer comfort but well aware of the shakiness of her footing. "Mayhap he truly does mean to pass it on to Richard?"

Again, it was left to Geoffrey to respond. "Mayhap he does, Dame Amaria. But just like my marriage to the Lady Constance, La Marche's fate depends now upon my lord father's whim, upon his mood at any given moment, and as we well know, his moods can shift faster than those Channel winds I need to catch."

Moving to his mother's side, he kissed Eleanor in farewell. "I must be off, Maman. Have you any words of advice for me? Any suggestions how to stay in Papa's good graces and mayhap even pry my bride from his talons?"

"Yes," Eleanor said, "as it happens, I do, Geoffrey. You need never doubt that your father loves you and your brothers. But never make the mistake of believing you can trust him."

"My thoughts exactly," he said and, smiling, made his departure.

To ELEANOR'S JOYFUL AMAZEMENT, Henry chose to hold his Christmas Court that year at Winchester. Richard had remained in Poitou, where he was planning an unusual winter campaign, but Hal, Marguerite, Geoffrey, and John were there, as were Roger and Maud. Even Ranulf and Rhiannon had made the long trip from Wales in order to visit with Morgan. What followed was Eleanor's best Christmas since Chinon six years ago.

HENRY SHOOK HIS HEAD when he was offered more wine and then glanced inquiringly at his wife. "Madame?"

"No, my lord, I have had enough," she said blandly. They were sharing dishes as was customary, and Henry was conscientious about making sure that Eleanor received the best portions, for men were expected to look after their female dinner-mates. Good manners demanded as much, and Henry had taken care to treat Eleanor with impeccable courtesy at the Christmas Court. She in turn had been no less polite, showing deference and decorum whenever they met in public. There had been no private encounters, and she was content that there were not, for what would it serve to raise the issue of La Marche with him? If he'd not heeded her when their passion had burned at white-heat, he was not going to listen now that their marriage lay in smoldering ruins.

E LEANOR HAD BEEN BOTHERED by a headache all afternoon, but she was determined not to miss any of the festivities. She'd taken an herbal remedy and was now returning to the solar, where an informal gathering was in progress; unlike the feasts held in the great hall, this one was confined to family and friends.

When she re-entered the solar, she was not surprised to find that Hal was still the center of attention. Slipping into her chair next to Henry, she discovered that Hal was no longer passing on gossip from the French court, but was entertaining with some of his experiences on the tournament field.

"The tourney was held this past spring along the Norman border between the towns of Anet and Sorel. Knights had come from all over, from Flanders and Brittany and Anjou and Poitou and Champagne. Even from England," Hal added, with a mischievous look in his father's direction, for Henry's disapproval of tournaments was well known; he considered them a waste of time and a threat to public order.

Hal had been talking so long that his throat had gone dry and he paused to accept a fresh wine cup from Will Marshal. "The tourney was held on the level ground by the River Eure. Two of the French companies had already clashed and were fighting when we came upon the scene. We hit them with such force that they soon gave way and then fled the field. Our men chased after them, so eagerly that they left me behind! Only Will stayed by my side," Hal said, with a fond glance toward the knight, who smiled and sought to appear modest and unassuming, with limited success; he was understandably proud of his prowess.

"Will and I followed after the others, riding downhill into Anet. The knights, both the hunted and the hunters, had already raced through the town, but the French lord, Simon de Neauphle, was still there, with three hundred foot soldiers he'd ordered to protect the lists. They saw us at the same time that we saw them, and Will, bless him, declared, 'There is nothing for it but to charge them.' And so we did."

That provoked an admiring murmur from his audience. Hal grinned disarmingly. "I know, we were quite mad. But damned if they did not scatter like a flock of chickens! I was glad enough just to avoid capture, but Will saw his chance and snatched the bridle of Simon de Neauphle's horse—his favorite method of capturing enemy knights.

"So we galloped through the town, towing Simon along behind us, for without his reins, he had no control of his mount. But then we happened to pass under a low-hanging gutter and Simon grabbed it, as neat a trick as I've ever seen. Poor Will never looked back, so he did not know he'd lost his prisoner, not until it was too late."

"And of course you never thought to warn me," Will complained mildly, and Hal grinned again.

"Hellfire, Will, I was laughing too much to talk, laughing so much I damned near fell off my own horse!" Throwing an arm around the knight's shoulders, he acknowledged that "Will was a good sport about it, though, laughed as heartily as any of us afterward."

Hal was about to launch into another tournament tale, but just then a servant entered with a platter of wafers, some filled with cheese, others with honey. Henry and Eleanor watched with amusement as Hal and Geoffrey and their friends pounced upon the platter and gobbled up the wafers like starving wolves. Rising, Eleanor crossed to her daughter-in-law and gave Marguerite a quick hug. The young woman smiled, but she seemed very fragile to Eleanor, as if she might be bruised by a breath, and Eleanor's heart ached for her.

Across the solar, Maud and Rhiannon were talking quietly together, and when Eleanor's eyes caught Maud's, the countess sent her a silent message. Curious, she strolled over to see what Maud wanted.

"We need to talk to you," Maud said, and steered Eleanor and Rhiannon toward a window seat. "Rhiannon and Ranulf are fretful about their son. Morgan is old enough now for the next stage of his education, and Hal has kindly offered to take the lad into his household."

Eleanor glanced from one woman to the other. "And . . . ?"

Rhiannon looked so unhappy that Maud realized it was up to her. "Rhiannon is loath to speak frankly. Fortunately, I've never had that problem. The truth, Eleanor, is that Ranulf and Rhiannon are not sure that this is best for their son. Morgan is at an impressionable age and easily influenced, especially by someone as charming and beguiling as Hal. See for yourself," she said, jerking her head toward Morgan.

Eleanor's gaze came to rest upon Rhiannon's son. He was a handsome youngster, with his father's dark eyes and his mother's thick chestnut hair, and he was listening to his cousin Hal as raptly as a young novice monk eager to pledge himself to the greater glory of God.

"I see," Eleanor said. Her first reaction was displeasure, a mother's indignation that Maud and Rhiannon should dare to disparage her son, to imply that Hal's flaws were a cause for concern. But it soon passed. She owed Rhiannon a great deal, for the Welshwoman had given her support when she most needed it. She owed her an honest answer, and as much as it grieved her to admit it, she knew in her heart that her eldest son was not the best role model for a lad like Morgan. She loved Hal, but she was not blind to his faults. He was good-hearted, generous, engaging, and dashing. He was also irresponsible, impulsive, fickle, and malleable.

"It might not be for the best," she said at last, "to place Morgan in Hal's household. He is not likely to give Morgan the supervision a lad of his tender years needs. What a pity Richard is not here. He took Rico, Rainald's natural son, as one of his squires last year, and I am sure he'd have been willing to take Morgan under his wing, too."

No one spoke, for Rhiannon was dismayed that Eleanor had confirmed her misgivings; she'd hoped for reassurance. And Maud had the heretical thought that Morgan would be no better off with Richard than he would with Hal. No one would ever accuse Richard of being flighty or irresolute. But he was gaining a reputation for recklessness, for the sort of mad courage that other men found so irresistible and mothers of squires found so alarming. She was not about to say that to Eleanor, though, and so she said instead that her son Hugh would be happy to accept Morgan into his household, but she feared that the lad was so bedazzled by Hal that he'd see the Earl of Chester as a great letdown.

Eleanor considered the problem, and then smiled. "I have the solution. I'll ask Geoffrey to accept Morgan as one of his squires. He takes part in enough tournaments to satisfy Morgan's craving for excitement, and he's proving himself to be a capable commander in his campaigns against the Breton rebels."

Rhiannon was vastly relieved. "That would be so good of you, my lady! How can I ever thank you?"

"It is my pleasure," Eleanor said, and indeed it was, for this was the first time in five years that she'd been able to do a favor for a friend, to dispense the patronage and largesse that was expected of those who wielded royal authority.

Rhiannon soon excused herself, and a few moments later, she had joined Ranulf and was murmuring in his ear. Eleanor smiled when Ranulf glanced in her direction. While Rhiannon and Maud had embraced her warmly during this Christmas Court, she'd gotten only cool civility from Ranulf and Roger. She knew Ranulf would feel honor-bound to thank her for placing his son in Geoffrey's household, and she was looking forward to gaining the upper hand, however petty it might be. Maud had remained by her side, but now she gave an audible sigh, and Eleanor saw that her gaze had fastened upon her son Hugh, in animated discussion with Willem, who'd recently returned from his pilgrimage to the Holy Land.

"I'd better rein him in ere he gets sloppy drunk and makes a fool of himself," Maud said grimly, and Eleanor realized that Hugh had been drinking a lot since his arrival at Winchester.

"Is he developing too much of a fondness for wine?" she asked quietly, and Maud shook her head.

"Only when he's in the king's presence. You've not noticed that he gets as nervous as a treed cat around Harry?"

As the countess went off to take charge of her wayward son, Eleanor felt an envious itch, wishing that she could be as pragmatic about motherhood as Maud. The other woman had long ago made a clear-eyed, unsentimental assessment of her eldest son, accepting his weaknesses but loving him wholeheartedly anyway. That was no easy feat, for affection and expectations invariably colored most parental appraisals of their offspring. Eleanor hoped she was able to see her sons as they truly were, but all she could be sure of was that she saw them more realistically than her husband did.

Some of her earlier high spirits had faded, and she suspected it was because she'd been forced to pass a judgment upon her eldest son, weighing Hal in the balance and finding him wanting. As her eyes lingered upon his golden head, she sought to assure herself that it was not too late for him. Jesu, he was not yet twenty-four. Surely he had time to sort himself out.

She was intending to speak to Geoffrey about his cousin Morgan when her eye was caught by a movement in one of the window-seats. With casual nonchalance, she began her approach, not wanting to scare her quarry off, and she slid into the window-seat beside her son before John could retreat.

"I have not seen much of you this week, John." Thinking that was an understatement; her youngest had been as elusive as a ghost during the Christmas Court so far.

The boy sprang to his feet, reluctantly reclaiming his seat only when she gestured for him to sit. "Madame."

Eleanor took this opportunity to study him. He was just a few days from his twelfth birthday, but looked younger, for he was undersized. Henry was of average height, although he'd always appeared larger due to his powerful build. Both Hal and Richard were taller than he, Geoffrey shorter. Unless he sprouted up like a weed in the next few years, she thought John would likely be closer to Geoffrey's height than his other brothers. It was disconcerting to see her own eyes in that thin little face. This was a child of her womb, so why did he seem like such a stranger?

She decided not to waste time with superficial chatter, for such a chance might not come again. "It occurred to me," she said, "that you and I have never talked about the rebellion or my part in it." When he did not respond, she prodded gently. "Surely you've talked about it with your father."

"Yes . . . he said it was all your fault," he said, slanting her an oblique glance through surprisingly thick lashes, and she thought she caught a glimmer of humor.

"Most of Christendom agrees with him," she conceded lightly. "But I thought you might have questions that only I could answer. Ask whatever you want, John, and I will try to be as honest as I can."

John gnawed his lower lip, and she saw his eyes dart across the solar, where his father was talking with Hal and Marguerite. "I do have a question," he said, just when she was about to give up hope of cracking that turtle's shell. "Did you . . . did you really put a snake in Richard and Geoffrey's bed?"

Eleanor blinked in surprise. "I was not expecting that query," she confessed. "So they told you about that, did they? Alas, I must plead guilty. In my defense, I can say only that your brothers were born hellions. Lord, the trouble they could get into!" Smiling at John, she said, "I will make a deal with you, lad. If I tell you about some of their more hair-raising mischief-making, will you promise not to try any of these tricks yourself?"

John ducked his head, his face hidden by a tumble of unruly dark hair. But then he shot from his seat as if fired from a crossbow. "I am sorry, Madame. I think my lord father has need of me." And before she could protest, he fled.

Eleanor watched as he threaded his way among their guests, finally surfacing at Henry's side. Henry stopped in mid-sentence, slipped an affectionate arm around the boy's shoulders before he resumed his conversation with Hal. Marguerite also gave John a welcoming smile. But Eleanor could not help noticing how brusquely Hal treated his younger brother, barely according John a nod, and she frowned. It was true that John's castles in England and Normandy had come at Hal's expense, but it was not fair to blame the lad for that. It was not John's fault that his mere presence conjured up unpleasant memories for Hal.

Her frown deepened, for she was suddenly thinking of her own unpleasant memories, those connected with John's birth. Warned by her sister, she'd made a foolhardy winter crossing of the Channel, stubbornly set upon determining if the gossip was true, if Harry had really dared to install Rosamund Clifford openly at their Woodstock manor. She'd been feeling ungainly and clumsy in the late stages of a difficult pregnancy, feeling every one of her forty-two years, only to come face-to-face with a radiant young girl, young enough to be her daughter. She'd told herself it was her pride that was bruised, not her heart, and during those pain-filled hours as she struggled to give birth, she'd vowed that she would not die so Harry's child might live. John had finally been brought into the world as the midnight hour drew nigh, a small, feeble shadow of the robust, sun-kissed children who'd come before him.

"Eleanor?" She was so focused upon the awful night of John's birth that she started at the sound of Maud's voice, and the other woman said with a smile, "I did not mean to startle you so. You have such an odd look upon your face. Are you all right?"

"I was just thinking that you may have been right, Maud."

"Must you sound so surprised by that? I am always right. About what?"

Shaking off the past, Eleanor returned Maud's smile. "That I may have changed, after all."

CHAPTER TWENTY-EIGHT

✦

May 1179
Taillebourg, Aquitaine

ERCHED ON A STEEP CRAG overlooking the River Charente, the castle of Taillebourg seemed to be scraping the clouds, so high above the valley was it. Protected on three sides by sheer cliffs, its one accessible approach was so well defended that none had ever dared to lay siege to it, for its fortifications boasted no less than three deep ditches and triple walls. Within those bastions nestled a small town, now filled with the inhabitants of the nearby villages, who'd taken shelter there as word spread of an advancing army. Despite the crowding, their mood was calm, for the town and castle were well provisioned with enough supplies to endure a long siege.

The castle garrison was even more confident than the townspeople and villagers, for more than a thousand men patrolled those battlements and ramparts, answerable to one of the greatest barons of Aquitaine, Geoffrey de Rançon, and none doubted that their lord was more than a match for the Angevin king's cub. Richard had laid siege to de Rançon's stronghold at Pons early in the new year, and made so little progress that after three months, he'd given up and gone looking for easier prey. He'd had better luck than he had at Pons, taking five castles in less than a month. But Pons still held

out defiantly and Taillebourg was even more formidable, so safe that de Rançon himself had chosen to defy Richard from within its redoubtable defenses. Upon being told
by his scouts of Richard's approach, Geoffrey de Rançon had laughed and his knights
began to wager how long it would be until the foolhardy stripling crept away with his
tail between his legs.

RICHARD HAD RIDDEN AHEAD of his army with a handful of his
household knights, and as they gazed upon the rebel lord's rock-hewn citadel, their
spirits plummeted and their cockiness ebbed away. As they exchanged glances, the
same thought was in all their minds: that Taillebourg made Pons seem as exposed as a
nunnery. Only Richard and his young squire Rico were not disheartened, for Rico was
convinced that Richard could walk on water if he put his mind to it, and Richard
would not admit that failure was possible, not even to himself. He knew he'd been
damaged by his inability to take Pons, and he knew, too, that he needed a dramatic victory if he hoped to prevail over de Rançon and the Count of Angoulême and their allies. There was no way on God's green earth that he would slink back to England and
confess defeat to his father. No, if he could not take Taillebourg, then better he die in
the attempt. At least there was honor in that.

Noticing that his squire had drawn up beside him, he glanced at the youth with a
sidelong smile. "Well, what do you say, Rico? Shall we give it a go?"

Rico's eyes were shining. "Indeed, my lord!" The past year had been the best one
of Rico's young life. He knew his half sisters and their husbands were embittered by
the king's refusal to let them lay claim to Rainald's earldom, but Rico had always
known it would never pass to him, the son born out of wedlock, and so he'd been indifferent to its disposition. He'd jumped at the chance to learn the arts of war from
Richard, and reality had exceeded all of his expectations. He was utterly convinced
that his twenty-one-year-old cousin was the most valiant man ever to draw breath and
would soon bring these disloyal, contemptible rebels to heel.

While the knights shared Rico's appreciation of Richard's courage, they did not
have his starry-eyed faith, and could muster up no enthusiasm for an assault upon
Taillebourg. They would not be getting a vote, though, and so they girded themselves
for the worst as Richard turned back toward them.

Glancing at Théodore Chabot, the captain of his routiers, Richard wasted no time
declaring what he wanted done. "Send men out to forage," he instructed Chabot.
"Check every barn and chicken roost and be sure to search the woods, for that's where
the peasants will have hidden their livestock."

"It will be done, my lord," Chabot said matter-of-factly; the knights thought he'd have sounded as imperturbable if Richard had ordered him to make a lone assault upon the castle walls. Guillaume de Forz and André de Chauvigny were young Poitevin lords who'd been with Richard since his ill-fated rebellion, and it never occurred to either of them to question his decision, for it had long been a joke between them that it would be easier to teach Richard to fly than it would to get him to back down once he'd made up his mind. They'd expected his order to forage, for armies lived off the land. It was what came next that troubled them. How could Taillebourg be taken?

"After we gather whatever food we can find," André said, with a brave attempt to sound as nonchalant as if they were discussing a day's hawking, "what then?"

Richard knew they were uneasy, but he did not fault them for it. Although he did not understand the fear that surged through other men's veins, he asked only that they not give in to it, for he'd come to realize that few shared his utter contempt for danger or death. "Then," he said, "we show them what Hell is like."

C HEVAUCHÉE WAS THE TERM USED for the most common tactic of warfare—the ravaging of an enemy's lands. But the people of Taillebourg had never seen a raid as deadly or destructive as the one launched by Richard that May. Church bells sounded the alarm as his routiers spread out across the countryside. Those who'd not already taken refuge in Taillebourg fled in panic; the slow and the old and the ill were cut down like sheaves of wheat. The sky was soon smudged with dense black clouds as villages, barns, and manors were put to the torch. Cattle were butchered for Richard's men, and those not needed were still slaughtered to deny them to his enemies. Oxen were slain and ploughs broken. Fruit trees were uprooted and crops were burned in the field. Vineyards were trampled. Wells were salted. Horses were taken, sheep gutted, chickens either eaten or killed. The horrified townsmen and villagers watched helplessly as their world went up in flames.

T HE FIRES WERE STILL BURNING when Richard brought up his siege engines and began to bombard the town. Mangonels launched heavy rocks and stones and even the carcasses of dead animals, the men working in eight-hour shifts so that the assault continued both day and night. From the castle battlements, Geoffrey de Rançon and his men seethed with rage, vowing vengeance, but panic was spreading in the town as people realized that withstanding the siege would not bring victory. When Richard gave up and retreated, nothing would be left to them but scorched fields, the bloated bodies of their slain livestock, and the fearful specter of famine.

Richard had set up their camp so close to the town that dust from the battered walls was soon coating their tents, and when his knights grumbled that the nonstop bombardment was robbing them of sleep, he smiled grimly. "It will not be long," he assured them, "until they take the bait."

On May 8, the castle garrison sallied forth in a dawn attack. Such surprise assaults were often successful, but Richard had been expecting this one, sure that de Rançon would not be able to resist their tempting proximity. The fighting that followed was brutal, with Richard in the very thick of it, and his men were so inspired and emboldened by his utter fearlessness that they soon had the garrison retreating back toward the town.

This was the moment Richard had been waiting for. "Now!" he shouted. "After them!" And as de Rançon's knights plunged through the town gates, Richard and his men fought their way in, too. A wild melee broke out as the garrison fled for the safety of the castle. Geoffrey de Rançon and many of his knights were able to reach it, but Richard and his men were hot on their heels, and they saw at once that they'd never be able to hold the bailey. They raced for their last refuge, the stone keep, flinging a torch onto the wooden stairs just as their pursuers got there, and tumbled, bruised and bleeding, into the hall. All of the windows were tightly shuttered, so they were half blinded as they escaped from sunlight into shadows. Blinking owlishly in the semi-gloom of the hall, they slumped against the walls, collapsed in the floor rushes, and for a time the only sound was the harsh gasping of men fighting to get enough air into their laboring lungs. Stunned by how swiftly the tide had turned against them, de Rançon buried his head in his hands and wept.

The soldiers who had not made it into the keep were quickly struck down, and Richard dispatched men to patrol the castle ramparts and the town walls. Leaning against the inner bailey well to catch his breath, he gratefully accepted a bucket from a grinning routier, yanked off his helmet, and poured it over his head. The water quickly turned pink as it splattered onto the ground, but none of the blood was his. It was here that Theobald Chabot found him.

"Can my lads have their sport now?" he asked, and when Richard nodded, he raised his arm high, signaling to one of his sergeants that the town was theirs for the taking. His men jubilantly claimed their reward; plunder was mother's milk to the battle-seasoned routiers who lived and died by the sword. Smoke was soon spiraling up from the narrow, unpaved streets, and the sounds of their city's suffering were not long in reaching the miserable men trapped within the dark, sweltering keep, reminding them what their fate would be if they tried to hold out. A town or castle taken by storm was fair game, for by their stubborn resistance, the besieged forfeited the right to be treated with leniency and could be slain without violating chivalric codes of honor.

Squires were not supposed to take part in actual fighting, and it took Rico a while to make his way into the town. He found he had to step over bodies in the street, had to keep jumping aside to avoid being trampled by celebrating bands of routiers as they surged from looted taverns in search of more wine. Men bumped into him as they emerged from ransacked shops and houses, their arms filled with booty, while others were on the prowl for bedmates, willing or otherwise. Again and again he heard a dog's barking become shrill yipping and then, silence. Goods were raining down from open windows, caught by laughing passersby. Whores, painted and powdered, had emerged from their bolt holes to mingle with the soldiers in the streets. Rico saw sights that shocked him to the marrow of his bones, had to watch his footing lest he step into puddles of congealing blood. But by the time he reached the castle, he was no longer flinching every time he heard a screaming woman or a wailing child.

Richard was conferring with several of his knights as they appraised the keep defenses. Rico waited patiently till his lord had time for him, noting that his sword needed a good cleaning and so did the tunic he'd worn over his hauberk, for it was soiled and torn; even his lord's boots had bloodstains on them. He'd have much to do.

Noticing the boy at last, Richard beckoned him over. "You are looking a little greensick, Cousin," he joked. "If you are going to spew, try not to aim in my direction."

He was surprised when Rico did not laugh or at least acknowledge the jest. Rico had proven to be an excellent squire, in great part because he was so eager to please, but also because he was so invariably cheerful. But now Rico was looking at him very somberly, like a sinner about to confess to his priest.

"I have never seen a captured town before," he confided hesitantly. "I guess . . . guess I did not know how bloody war can be, my lord."

Richard considered what the boy had said, and then nodded in agreement. "Yes, war can be bloody and brutal and disquieting, Rico. But there is also a . . . a kind of glory in it."

Rico did not understand, but he nodded, too, for if Richard said it, it must be so.

H ENRY HAD SENT WILLEM to the Flemish court for negotiations with the Count of Flanders, and he was unable to return until June. Taking ship at Wissant, he landed at Dover, and then began the tedious task of chasing down the king. He finally found Henry at his Woodstock manor.

As he entered the great hall, Willem saw that most of the men and some of the women were clustered at one end. He knew Hal was spending some time at his father's court, and he assumed that the young king was the attraction. He was surprised, therefore, to notice Hal standing on the dais, his arms folded across his chest. Wondering who was stealing Hal's thunder, Willem took a closer look and when he caught a glimpse of a reddish-gold head, he understood, both the commotion and Hal's obvious discontent. The hero of Taillebourg was here, and Hal's tournament victories had been put in the shade by Richard's dramatic capture of a castle said to be impregnable.

Joining Henry upon the dais, he was warmly welcomed by the king and courteously by Hal. Henry was beaming every time he looked over at Richard, and wasted no time in bragging of his exploits, telling Willem that Geoffrey de Rançon had surrendered two days after Richard took the town. "He also yielded Pons, and ten days later, Count Vulgrin ended his rebellion and surrendered his castles at Angoulême and Montignac. A number of our highborn rebels were so shaken by Richard's conquests that they have taken the cross, and are making plans to leave for the Holy Land as soon as they can get away." Henry grinned. "Aquitaine has not been so peaceful in years!"

Seeing how much pleasure Richard's triumph was giving his father, Willem was happy to indulge his paternal pride, and began to ask questions, thus giving Henry the opportunity to discuss the fall of Taillebourg at length. He was still in mid-cry when Hal quietly withdrew, first from the dais and then from the hall, but few noticed.

"It was an amazing feat, Willem," Henry concluded enthusiastically. "I do not know anyone who could have done better, even me! And the lad is only twenty-one; think what a commander he'll make once he gains more experience." Willem agreed, finding it easy to echo Henry's praise, for no soldier could fail to be impressed by Richard's triumph. Henry added that Geoffrey had been successful in Brittany, too, if not quite on such a spectacular scale, forcing that habitual rebel, Guihomar de Léon, to surrender all his strongholds. But he soon returned to praising Richard, and when Willem asked how he planned to reward the young man, he laughed.

"I am giving him Aquitaine. God knows he earned it."

Willem was impressed, knowing how reluctant Henry was to relinquish authority. "He must have been overwhelmed," he said, and Henry's pleasure lost some of its luster.

"He was not as joyful as I would have expected," he admitted. "When I told him that from now on, he could govern the duchy as he chose, he thanked me as calmly as if I'd just offered him a new saddle." His eyes rested for a mystified moment upon the tall figure of his second son. "I confess, Willem," he said quietly, "that I do not understand the lad, never have if truth be told. He keeps his own counsel, has learned to guard his thoughts. As his king, I find that commendable, for no ruler should be as easily read as . . . well, as Hal is. But as his father, I do wish he were more forthcoming, at least with me."

After a moment, though, he shook his head, and began to question Willem about his mission to the Flemish court. Willem had just begun his report when there was a sudden stir in the hall. Curious, he paused, and was taken aback to see the queen coming through the open doorway.

Henry caught his questioning look and shrugged. "Richard wanted her here," he said simply, and Willem thought it was encouraging that the king was learning to pick his battles with his sons. But then Henry said, "Actually, what he'd asked for was her freedom, and there is no way I could have granted that wish. So it would have been churlish to deny him her presence at revelries in his honor. I've tried to be a good sport about it, Willem, even bought her a gilded scarlet saddle and new robes for the occasion. I cannot say, though, that I am pleased to have her here."

Willem understood why. The change in Richard's demeanor was startling. Where before he'd been detached, even aloof, he was now displaying considerable animation as he conversed and laughed with his mother. Henry made no comment, but he kept his eyes upon them even as Willem completed his account of his meeting with Count Philip. By then Richard had noticed Willem's presence and was heading in their direction, his mother pacing serenely beside him, her hand resting lightly but possessively upon his arm.

Once greetings had been exchanged, Willem made ready to hear Richard's first-hand account of Taillebourg's fall. Richard had other matters upon his mind, though. "I've not had a chance to talk with you since your return from the Holy Land, and I am eager to hear all about your experiences there. You were one of the victors at Ramlah, no? Is it true that your siege of Harenc was interrupted by the arrival of Saladin himself? What do you think of his military prowess? Did you get to Jerusalem—"

Willem flung up his hand in mock surrender, and let Richard lead him away to continue his interrogation. Henry and Eleanor found themselves alone for the first time since her arrival at Woodstock. After an awkward moment, Henry took refuge in courtesy and escorted her toward their chairs upon the dais. Richard and Willem had moved to a window-seat to continue their discussion of Holy Land warfare, and they were soon surrounded by a large throng, for Richard was exercising the sort of magnetic appeal that had previously been Hal's alone. Henry watched his son for a few moments more, wishing that Richard could be like that with him—enthused and unguarded. Glancing toward his wife, he said, "What were you saying that Richard found so amusing?"

His brusque tone made it sound more like an accusation than an inquiry. Eleanor ignored the undercurrents and said composedly, "Ah, that. I told Richard that I was particularly gratified to see Taillebourg Castle reduced to rubble, for Louis and I spent the first night of our marriage there."

Henry gave her a sharp look, but decided he did not want to talk of wedding nights with Eleanor; that was too intimate for his liking. It vexed him that she insisted upon displaying a wife's familiarity instead of a rebel's contrition. "You like to accuse me of never learning from my mistakes," he said. "But Louis does not even learn from other men's mistakes. Did you hear that he is planning to have Philippe crowned in August on Ascension Day?"

"No, I had not heard that," Eleanor said. "I cannot say it surprises me, though. Louis always had a talent for taking a bad situation and making it worse."

"To be fair, he did have some misgivings about the idea after observing how well it worked with Hal. But he has decided to go ahead with it, mayhap because he has been ailing this past year. It will be interesting to see how it goes," Henry commented, in a masterly understatement.

Eleanor regarded him pensively. "I saw Hal out in the bailey," she said. "He looked out of sorts and, sad to say, was making no attempt to hide his discontent. I fear that he is not handling Richard's newfound fame very well."

"No, he is not," Henry said, and sighed. "Hal and Richard show all the good will of Cain and Abel. And for that matter, Richard and Geoffrey are not much better."

Eleanor's eyes narrowed; was he saying the dissension between their sons was Richard's fault? But as he continued, she saw that was not what he was implying. "I confess to being baffled by their constant squabbling and strife, Eleanor. It is true I never got along with my brother Geoff, but that was mainly his doing. Will and I were always very close."

"I know," she said, remembering how grief-stricken he'd been by Will's sudden death at twenty-seven. "I was only six when my brother died, so I do not have many memories of him. I probably considered him a pest, as big sisters are wont to do. But Petronilla and I were confidantes and allies—even partners in crime—as far back as I can remember. Somehow, though, our sons have managed to reach manhood without any true sense of brotherly affection or loyalty, and I do not know what to do about it."

"Neither do I," Henry admitted, frowning as he saw the corners of her mouth curving upward. "What possible amusement can you find in this?"

"Not amusement exactly. It just occurred to me that we have finally found some common ground to agree upon, Harry, and what is it? Our failings as parents!"

Henry shared her sense of the ridiculous and when their eyes met, they were soon both laughing, laughter that stopped abruptly when they realized that this was the first time they'd laughed together in more than seven years.

CHAPTER TWENTY-NINE

August 1179
Woods near Compiègne, France

T FIRST PHILIPPE WAS ANGRY—with his horse for bolting and with his companions for taking so long to find him. He'd been calling out until his voice was hoarse, but the only sounds he heard were the normal noises of the forest. He was getting hungry and tired and, as the afternoon wore on, increasingly uneasy. The prospect of being lost in the woods at night was a daunting one. This was the first time in Philippe's fourteen years that he'd ever been utterly alone, and he liked it not at all.

He was scratched from brambles and overhanging branches, bothered by swarms of gnats and other insects, as miserable as he'd ever been in his entire life. When his mount suddenly shied and he banged his elbow painfully against a gnarled oak, he lost his temper altogether. He did not enjoy riding, had always viewed horses with dislike and distrust, and this particular horse was to blame for all of his troubles today. Giving in to his rage, he jabbed it in the sides with his spurs at the same time that he brought his whip down upon its withers. The gelding snorted and reared up suddenly. Philippe dropped his spear and clung to the mane as he tried to maintain his seat. But the horse began to buck, and the boy lost his grip and his stirrups, went sailing over its head into a wild blackberry bush.

Like his father, Philippe rarely cursed; the strongest oath he normally used was "By the Lance of St James!" But as he sought to extricate himself, he was muttering an obscenity, one that could have come from the mouth of the English king or any of his sons. When he finally fought free of the thorns and briars and saw that the wretched horse was nowhere in sight, he had to bite his lip to keep further profanities from spewing out into the humid August air. As bad as being lost was, being lost and on foot was far worse.

Philippe rooted around in the undergrowth until he'd recovered his spear. They'd been hunting boar and had not seen one all day. But now it seemed to him that boars lurked in every thicket, behind every felled tree, and he gripped the weapon so tightly that his knuckles turned white. He shouted again, listened in vain for a response and then, hunching his shoulders, began to trudge along the path.

The tree branches intertwined, forming an opaque, green canopy over his head, and he went for long stretches without seeing the sky. He was slow to realize, therefore, that the light was ebbing. With the awareness that the sun would soon be setting, he suffered his first surge of fear. His second came when he tripped over an exposed root and nearly landed on a snake, and his next when he heard an owl's prey in its death throes, unseen in the twilight dusk. But it was the distant howl of a wolf that sent him into panicked flight. He ran until he stumbled and fell flat, hitting the ground with enough force to bruise his ribs and drive all the breath from his lungs. The shock of it enabled him to regain control of himself. Realizing it was madness to keep racing around in the darkness, he crawled over to the closest tree, curled up next to its trunk, and prepared to endure an interminable night.

He was sure he'd never be able to sleep, but he finally dozed, and jerked upright just before sunrise. During the night, fog had drifted in and the trees were wreathed in patches of pale vapor, blotting out the sun. Shivering in the damp dawn air, he struggled to his feet, every muscle in his body cramping in protest, took a deep breath, and yelled for help. He thought he heard an answering shout, but he did not trust his own senses. His next cry brought another echo, though, louder this time.

"I am here! Over here!" He could hear running footsteps now, and then a huge, hulking figure was looming out of the mist, a giant with bare, muscled arms, hands like hams, a blackened, smudged face, and an axe dangling by his side, the ogre of Philippe's boyhood night terrors. Shrinking back against the tree, he gasped, "Stay away from me! I am Philippe Capet, the king's son! Keep away!"

HENRY WAS BACK AT WOODSTOCK; it had always been one of his favorite manors and it gave him comfort to visit the nearby nunnery of Godstow, where
he lavished largesse upon the priory and prayed for Rosamund's soul. He'd held a
council meeting that afternoon, a productive session in which they discussed a wide
range of topics: the coming Christmas visit of the King of Scotland, the feasibility of
issuing a new coinage, a report upon his recent judicial reform in which he'd divided
the realm into four circuits, and the need to fill the justiciarship now that Richard de
Lucy had resigned the post because of ill health. The council was done but Henry and
a few others still lingered in the solar.

As all of them were men who stood high in Henry's favor, the talk was more relaxed and informal; they'd been idly discussing the Lateran Council held in Rome that
spring. One of the canons had banned "those abominable jousts and fairs, which are
commonly called tournaments," but Henry and his companions agreed that the
Church prohibition would not likely be heeded. Nor did they expect the Lateran
Council's excommunication of routiers to discourage rulers from hiring them.

Henry candidly admitted that he'd continue to make use of routiers when the
need arose. "Though it could be argued that routiers are actually more dangerous
when they are not employed. My son Richard kept his routiers under tight rein, but
once he came to England in June and they were no longer being paid, they sacked Bordeaux."

Getting to his feet and beginning to pace, Henry stopped the others from rising,
too, for Gilbert Foliot and the Bishop of Winchester were no longer young. "I received
two interesting communications from the French court this week," he said, and these
men knew him well enough to understand that there was something highly unusual
about those "interesting communications."

"One came from the French king," Henry continued, "and the other from . . .
well, let's just say a well-placed source at Louis's court. Louis has had to postpone his
son's coronation. Philippe was hunting in the royal forest near Compiègne and somehow he became separated from his companions. He spent the night alone in the
woods and was finally found the next morning by a charcoal burner. But my 'source'
tells me that the charcoal burner must have had a fearsome visage for his appearance
scared Philippe so badly that he took ill soon after his rescue."

The men exchanged grins and several laughed outright. Henry shared their
amusement; royal heirs were not supposed to be so delicate. "At that age, any of my
hellions would have considered a night alone in the woods a grand adventure. But
we know Philippe is as high-strung as a lass. The humor of his mishap soon soured,

though, for within a day he was burning up with fever, and they are now fearing for his life."

They were no longer laughing; if Philippe died, the repercussions would be felt throughout Christendom. Louis's own health was said to be failing. If he died soon after his son, there could be a vicious struggle for his crown. His two sons-in-law, the Counts of Champagne and Blois, would be sure to make claims on behalf of their wives, his daughters with Eleanor, Marie and Alix. Some would look to Marguerite, too, even though she was a younger daughter, for there were bound to be French barons who would eagerly embrace the idea of having the easygoing, pleasure-loving Hal as their king, just as there were Poitevin lords who'd prefer Hal to his more martial brother, Richard.

"Marie is the eldest, of course," Willem said thoughtfully, "but that might not count for much, what with her husband now in the Holy Land. My money would be on Thibault of Blois . . . unless you seriously back your son and the Lady Marguerite, my liege."

Henry knew this was the question in all of their minds, but only Willem was bold enough to voice it. Thinking that Hal had yet to show he could rule one kingdom, much less two, he said, "You are getting the cart before the horse, Willem. Let's not be so quick to bury Louis's son. I said I'd heard from Louis as well as from my spy. He has been half out of his mind with fear." Adding fairly, "As any father would be. But it seems that St Thomas came to him in a dream and told him that if he made a pilgrimage to Canterbury, Philippe would recover. Needless to say, when he suggested this to his council, they were greatly dismayed and dismissed it out of hand."

Henry's smile was sardonic. "My spy tells me they lectured Louis that it would be utter madness to enter the lion's den of his own free will. The lion, I suppose, is me, which might be considered a perverse sort of compliment. Be that as it may, Philippe's condition continued to worsen, and Thomas paid Louis two more nightly visits. After the third dream, he did what he ought to have done from the first—found a king's backbone and told his council that he meant to make a Canterbury pilgrimage, their misgivings be damned. And so he has written to me, earnestly entreating me to issue a safe conduct so that he may come to England and pray for St Thomas to spare his son."

There was a moment of astonished silence and, then, incredulous laughter. "For some reason," Willem said dryly, "a verse of Scriptures comes to mind: *He that diggeth a pit shall fall into it,*" and Hamelin gleefully recited a proverb to the effect that revenge was a dish best eaten cold.

Henry smiled. "I've always believed that the best way to deal with temptation was to yield to it. So it came as a surprise to discover that it is not actually that difficult to tell Satan to get behind me. An interesting lesson to learn so late in life, no?"

Hamelin's mouth dropped open. "Harry, surely you are not saying that you might give Louis a safe conduct!"

"Yes, I am," Henry said, and saw that Hamelin was not the only one to be gaping at him. He had not expected to have to defend his decision, but he said, with rare patience, "It is too easy to put myself into Louis's shoes. If one of my sons were on his deathbed, I would bargain with Lucifer if I thought that would save him. It is not the French king that I am accommodating, Hamelin. It is a grieving father."

O N AUGUST 22, Louis landed at Dover, where Henry was waiting to welcome him and to escort him to Canterbury. It was the first time that a French monarch had ever set foot on English soil.

H ENRY LED WILLEM into the cloisters of the cathedral. He'd sent Willem to France with the safe conduct, and this was the first time they'd had to talk since Willem had returned to England with Louis and the Count of Flanders. It was a beautiful evening, that twilight hour in which stars were just beginning to glimmer in the sky and the clouds still reflected the dying glow of the setting sun. Both men paused to breathe in the sweet clover-scented air, listening as a passing bell chimed somewhere in town, signaling that a parishioner had gone home to God. Henry came often to Canterbury in the years since he'd done penance at the archbishop's tomb, and he was always surprised that this place, the scene of sacrilege and murder, could seem like such a peaceful haven, that the cathedral he'd entered in such despair and dread could now be soothing to his soul.

"I am on a rescue mission," he confided to Willem. "Louis's physicians begged me to coax him into ending his penance. They fear that he may become ill himself if he passes a second night fasting and praying. I promised to do what I could, for it would be rather awkward if he were to die whilst he was an honored guest of the English Crown."

Willem agreed that Louis was too frail for severe mortification of the flesh, and for a moment, Henry remembered what he'd been told of Thomas Becket's self-abasement in the last years of his life, baring his back thrice daily for scourging, wearing a lice-infested hairshirt and braies, spending hours on his knees or prone upon the stone floor as he offered up his prayers to the Almighty. Even now, five years after he and Thomas had made their peace in that shadowed, silent crypt, Henry found it difficult to reconcile the holy martyr with the worldly chancellor who'd been his friend.

"Ere I go chasing after Louis," he said, "there is something I want to discuss with you, Willem. I learned this morning that the Count of Aumale died on Monday."

It was never comforting to hear of the passing of a man who was close in age to them, and Willem instinctively sought to distance them from the dead count, saying, "He was not in the best of health, was he? I seem to recall that he was called Guillaume le Gros, at least behind his back!"

"He was on the stout side," Henry allowed. "But it is not his sin of gluttony I want to talk about. He had no son, and his estates will pass to his daughter, Hawise. It is my intention to give the girl to you, Willem."

Willem was rarely taken by surprise, but he was now. Kings were usually loath to give up the wardship of an heiress, for that gave them control of her revenues and eventual marriage. "I am honored by your trust in me. I will be greatly pleased to have the lass as my ward, will do right by her, you may be sure."

"I am not offering you her wardship, Willem. I am giving her to you in marriage," Henry said, amused to see that he'd managed to render the courtly, urbane earl quite speechless for once.

Willem was overwhelmed. As Earl of Essex, he need never have to beg his bread by the side of the road, but his was not the wealthiest of earldoms. Guillaume of Aumale had held extensive lands in Yorkshire and other shires as well as his estates in Normandy. Henry was offering him a great heiress as casually as if he were proffering a benefice to an improvident priest.

"Harry! How can I ever thank you?"

"I'm sure I'll think of something," Henry joked, before saying, quite seriously, "Kings are not denied much in this life. But their friendships are as scarce as hen's teeth, which is one reason why we rely so often upon kinsmen—though that obviously has its drawbacks, too. I've been luckier than most, for I've had two men I could call 'friend,' you and Thomas." Unable to resist teasing, "Let's hope that our friendship ends better than mine and Thomas's did."

They laughed and embraced, and Henry then went off in search of Louis, in good spirits, delighted to be able to reward Willem's loyalty as lavishly as he deserved. Entering the Martyr's Door into the choir, he descended the steps into the crypt. There he found the French king, prostrating himself upon the tiles before St Thomas's tomb, attended by one of his physicians, the archbishop, the new prior, and several monks.

As soon as Louis's prayer was done, Prior Alan impressed Henry by taking the initiative. Coming forward before the French king could begin another invocation, he said quietly, "My liege, King Henry is here."

Louis glanced up, squinting in the dim light, and Henry was struck anew by how feeble he looked. Louis was twelve years his senior, which put him in his late fifties, but if Henry had not known that, he'd have assumed that the French king had easily reached his biblical three score years and ten. Even allowing for the stress of Philippe's illness, Louis seemed to be carrying the weight of the world upon his stooped shoulders.

Reaching out his hand, Henry helped the other man to rise. "You have been keeping this vigil since your arrival yesterday. For a day and a night now, you have done nothing but fast and pray. St Thomas will not take it amiss if you get a few hours sleep."

Louis would have demurred, but Henry did not give him the chance. "What did Thomas say to you in those dreams? I assume you remember?"

"Of course I do! He said, 'Our Lord Jesus Christ sends me as your servant, Thomas the Martyr of Canterbury, in order that you should go to Canterbury, if your son is to recover.'"

"As I suspected. He said not a word about your sacrificing your life for your son's. You'll do Philippe no good by dying at Canterbury. If you'll not rest for your own sake, do it for mine, Louis. Spare me the embarrassment of having to explain to the rest of Christendom that the first French king to visit English shores did not make it home alive."

Henry had long ago concluded that Louis did not have a humorous bone in his body. But the French king was still able to recognize humor in others, and he mustered up a wan smile. "You are right," he admitted. "I am indeed bone-weary and in need of sleep." Looking vastly relieved, his physician started toward him before he could change his mind. But he held up his hand, and slipping his arm in Henry's, drew him aside. Henry did not resist, startled by how heavily Louis was leaning upon him for support.

"You have been very kind, Harry. But I must impose upon your kindness by seeking yet another favor from you. I would ask that you add your prayers to mine, that you entreat the Blessed Martyr to save my son. St Thomas showed himself willing to perform a miracle on your behalf, so I think yours would be the voice he'd be most likely to heed."

Henry managed to keep his face impassive, and he would later consider that a remarkable accomplishment. "I will pray to St Thomas for your son," he promised the French king, after taking a moment to savor the irony of Louis's request, and watched, bemused, as the older man let his physician lead him from the crypt.

Archbishop Richard and the others accompanied Louis, but one of the monks lingered behind. "Should you wish some time for private prayer, my liege?"

"Yes, Brother Bertram, I would," Henry confirmed, for this had become his practice upon his visits to Canterbury. He waited until the monk's footsteps receded before walking over to the martyr's tomb. "Well, I suppose you heard that, Thomas," he said breezily, for that is what his talks with Thomas were, conversations rather than prayers. He'd discovered that he could unburden himself to the dead far easier than he could with the living. The Thomas he confided in was the friend he'd lost to the Church, somehow restored to him by his anguish in this crypt and the victory at Alnwick, a miracle so manifest that not even the French king could doubt it.

"I hope that you'll show mercy to Louis. If you could snatch a king and scatter a fleet, curing a skinny, skittish whelp like Philippe ought to be child's play. And yes, Thomas, I daresay you're marveling at how magnanimous I've become in my old age. You need not fret, for I have no yearning for sainthood, am not poaching in your woods."

Henry cocked his head, half listening for a response. "I admit it—my own interests are invested in Philippe's recovery. Louis does not look as if he is long for this world, and I'd rather my son face a stripling like Philippe than Henri of Champagne or Thibault of Blois. Christ help him, Thomas, for either one of them would eat Hal alive."

There was a relief in being able to confess his doubts about his eldest's capacity for kingship. In the past few years, he'd occasionally asked Thomas for guidance, entreated him to show Hal the way home, to restore the laughing, fair-haired lad of cherished memory, not the sullen, erratic stranger he'd become. But tonight his prayers were only for Philippe Capet, and he said softly, "I never thought I'd pity that fool on the French throne, Thomas. Fathers and sons . . . mayhap you were wise to choose the Church."

He paused then, for he'd caught the sound of sandals on the crypt stairs. "My lord king, may I approach?" Brother Bertram hovered in the doorway, loath to intrude upon his sovereign's prayers. "Your son has just ridden in, my liege, and is asking to see you straightaway. Is it your wish that I send him down?"

"Of course." The monk retreated before Henry could ask the identity of this son, and as he waited, he entertained himself by trying to guess which one it might be. Not Johnny. Not Richard, either, for it would not even occur to him to ask for permission; he'd just sweep on into the crypt. Nor would Hal have sought permission. His innate good manners had succumbed to a more pressing need—to show the world that he was a king in deed as well as name, his father's equal in all matters. So that left one of his Geoffreys, he concluded, and was pleased to be proven right a few moments later when Geoff came into view.

"What a welcome surprise, Geoff! When did you get back to England?" Struck by a sudden ominous thought, he did not wait for his son's reply. "You are not bringing word that Philippe has died?" And when Geoff shook his head, he sighed with relief.

"Thank God for that. I do not see myself as craven, but I would not want to be the one to tell Louis that his son was dead."

"I came straight from Tours, did not even know Philippe was ailing until I landed at Southampton. It was good of you, Papa, to let the French king make this pilgrimage. When I think of all he did to turn your sons against you, I would not have been so generous."

"Not all of my sons, Geoff—not you," Henry said fondly. But as he studied the young man, he felt a prickle of unease. "You may not be bearing sad tidings about Philippe, lad, but you've come to tell me something I'd rather not hear."

Geoff blinked. "How did you guess? Can you read my mind?"

"No, but I can read your face. What is it, Geoff?"

"My news is indeed sad, Papa. On August 9, the Bishop of Worcester died at Tours."

Henry sucked in his breath. "Roger? God in Heaven . . ." He turned aside as he fought to get his emotions under control, and then sat down heavily upon the closest seat, which happened to be the archbishop's tomb. Geoff took an anxious step forward, remembering that St Thomas had punished a young boy for falling asleep against his shrine. But he decided then that the martyr was willing to allow his father liberties that he'd deny to other men, and came forward, dropping his hand to Henry's shoulder in a mute gesture of comfort.

"Tell me," Henry said huskily, "how he died."

"The Archbishop of Tours was accompanying Roger to Rome for the Lateran Council, but he fell ill in Paris and had to turn back," Geoff said dutifully, for he'd been rehearsing this speech since he left Tours. "Upon his return from Rome, Roger journeyed to Tours to see how the archbishop was faring. He became ill himself soon after his arrival and died at the abbey of Marmoutier not long afterward. He was buried with great honors in the abbey church of St Martin."

"One of the world's bright lights has gone out," Henry said, after a long silence. "My cousin was a good man and a brave one. He alone dared to tell me that I was not blameless for Thomas's murder, for he was never intimidated by my temper or my rank."

"I remember your telling me of the time you and he quarreled on the road over Thomas and over Hal's coronation. You said that when you shouted at him, he shouted right back, and when some of your courtiers sought to curry favor with you by denouncing him, you flew into a rage, saying 'Do you think, you villains, that if I say what I please to my cousin, you and the rest can insult him?' And you and Roger then rode off in perfect harmony."

Henry nodded. "I remember that day well. I remember, too, another time that we quarreled because of Thomas. He'd excommunicated my chancellor, Geoffrey Ridel, and of course that meant other Christians could not consort with him. When Roger encountered Ridel during Mass, he turned around and walked out. I was angry that he was heeding Thomas and not me. I lost my temper, Geoff, and ordered him from my domains. Another man would have tried to make peace, to beg my pardon. Roger said his foot was already in the stirrup and stalked off. I soon calmed down and sent a messenger to recall him. But damned if he would come! It took three messages ere he'd deign to return and I had to make sure that Geoffrey Ridel did not come into his presence for the remainder of his stay."

Henry smiled sadly. "I often thought that it was a pity he'd not been my uncle Robert's eldest son instead of his youngest, for he'd have made a far better Earl of Gloucester than that boneheaded William. But then, that would have been a great loss to the Church."

Henry had dropped his head into his hands. When he looked up, Geoff saw that his eyes were wet. "Did I ever tell you my favorite story about my cousin, lad? Roger was on his way to see me when he came upon two wretches being held outside under armed guard. He always had a cat's curiosity and stopped to see what was happening. He was told that these men had gotten drunk in an Eastcheap tavern and uttered words insulting to the king. They had sobered up by now and were scared out of their wits. Roger told them to deny nothing, to admit what they'd said and plead for mercy."

Geoff had never heard this story, and he said, "What happened then?"

Henry grinned. "They were brought before me and freely confessed that they'd called me 'evil tempered' and a 'miser' who wanted to tax Londoners of their last drop of blood. Whilst I was considering this, one of them added, 'And that was nothing to what we would have said if the wine had not run out.' Of course I laughed, and then sent them on their way. Roger later denied that he'd put words in their mouth, but that sounded so like him that I never believed it."

Geoff grinned, too. "That does sound like Cousin Roger," he said, chiming in with a story of his own about the bishop's dagger-sharp humor, and they stayed for a time in the cathedral crypt, mourning Roger the way he would have wanted—laughing through tears.

PHILIPPE RECOVERED FROM HIS ILLNESS and was crowned at Rheims by his uncle the Archbishop on All Saints' Day. Henry's three oldest sons attended the coronation. Hal carried the crown for his young brother-in-law and then held it steady for Philippe during the ceremony once he realized it was too heavy for the boy. But Louis could not attend. He'd suffered a stroke soon after his return to France, one which left him unable to speak and partially paralyzed.

CHAPTER THIRTY

❦

April 1180
Reading, England

PON LEARNING THAT GEOFFREY would be returning to
England that spring, Ranulf and Rhiannon decided to make the long
journey from Wales, for they'd not seen Morgan in more than a year.
Since Henry published his itinerary a month in advance, they knew he'd be at Reading, and arrived at the Cluniac abbey of St Mary and St John the Evangelist on an
overcast afternoon in early April.

Ranulf rose early the next morning, as was his habit, choosing to let his wife sleep
in, for it had been an arduous trip for them both; he was sixty-one now and Rhiannon
only a few years younger, and he knew the day would be coming when they'd not be
able to chase after their son or the king like this. Upon his entry into the guest hall, he
was delighted to be told that Hal and Geoffrey had arrived late the night before, after
he and Rhiannon had retired, and instead of breaking his fast, he went in search of
his son.

He had no luck until he found Will Marshal in affable conversation with Abbot
Joseph. Morgan was with the king, they told him; he had offered to show his young
kinsman their family tombs, for not only was the abbey's founder, Henry's grandfa-

ther of blessed memory, buried here, so was the son who'd died at age three, and more recently, the Earl of Cornwall. Ranulf headed for the gatehouse that connected the north and south garths, and entered the church. Not finding Henry and Morgan within, he lingered long enough to say a prayer at his brother Rainald's tomb, thinking that the most burdensome aspect of aging was that a man had to bury so many of his friends and loved ones.

Exiting via a side door into the cloisters, he came upon his son and nephew. They were laughing together in one of the carrels, tossing a coin back and forth. At the sight of his father, Morgan hastened over to enfold Ranulf in a boisterous embrace; the latter was startled to realize that Morgan was now the taller of the two.

"The king has been telling me about the new silver penny," Morgan exclaimed, with the enthusiasm that was a large part of his charm; he was invariably curious about all things, great and small. He showed his father the coin, with a short cross on one side and on the reverse, the king's crowned head, under the inscription *Henricus Rex*. "This is one of the first to be struck, as they are not to be exchanged for the old coins until Martinmas. He says I can keep it, too, so I'll have the only one in England for the next seven months!"

He paused, then, to glance questioningly back at Henry. "It seems like a lot of work and trouble, my lord. Why not just continue using the old coins?"

"Over time, they become debased, Morgan," Henry explained. "Knaves file the edges off the coins and melt the clippings down to make counterfeit coins, so they are not worth as much. Sometimes, too, the moneyers who operate the mints cheat, mixing the silver with cheaper metals when they make the pennies. Coin clipping is a serious offense, and those caught pay dearly for it, but greed can entice men into all sorts of lunacy."

Ranulf inspected the new penny; since no Welsh princes minted their own money, these coins would be circulating in Wales, too. "I appreciate your tutoring Morgan in money matters, Harry," he joked, unable to resist teasing his son. "Judging from the way he spends, he needs all the lessons he can get."

"All of today's youth are money-mad," Henry said cheerfully. "Compared to my lads, though, Morgan is as frugal as a Cistercian monk."

Morgan smiled dutifully, for he knew he was expected to acknowledge adult humor, no matter how lame, and Ranulf felt a surge of pride in his son's good manners. When he suggested that Morgan go to the guest house and greet his mother, the youth still remembered to excuse himself politely before he went dashing off to find Rhiannon.

"He is growing up so quickly," Ranulf said, his the bittersweet satisfaction of a father recognizing that his son is fast approaching the borders of manhood.

"Be thankful for it, Uncle. Lads his age are vulnerable to so much—their own foolhardy impulses and, even worse, the calculating flattery of men eager to take advantage of their youth and inexperience."

Ranulf assumed Henry was thinking of his own wayward sons, and made a sympathetic murmur of agreement, all the while hoping that Morgan would show better judgment than his royal cousins. But then Henry said that Philippe's youthful mistakes were likely to haunt him well into his manhood if something was not done, and Ranulf realized that he was speaking of the fourteen-year-old French king, not Hal and his brothers.

"I did not know about the French unrest," Ranulf said, "until we stopped in Chester to ask Maud to accompany us. The only news that had trickled into Wales was of Louis's apoplectic seizure and Philippe's lavish coronation."

"I wish you could have persuaded Maud to come with you."

"She took Roger's loss very hard," Ranulf said quietly, and Henry nodded somberly, saying that they all had.

Ranulf still found it difficult to talk of Roger's death, and nudged the conversation back to the subject of the French turmoil. "Maud told us that Philip of Flanders has been hovering over young Philippe like a hungry hawk, and Philippe has stopped listening to anyone else, including his mother and his uncles. Is it truly as bad as that?"

"Worse," Henry said, and as they began to stroll along the cloisters walkway, he told Ranulf about the troubles at the French court. "Philippe is ruling as if his father were already dead, with the ever-helpful Philip there as guide and tutor. His first act was to dismiss all of Louis's councilors and replace them with men of his choosing— or Philip's, depending upon whom you believe. The lad is now in Flanders with Philip, waiting until Lent is over so that he may marry Isabelle of Hainault, Philip's ten-year-old niece."

Ranulf whistled. "How did Adèle and her brothers react to that?"

"About as well as you'd expect. Adèle was so disquieted that she began to fortify her dower lands. When Philippe heard that, he gave orders to seize her lands, and she felt threatened enough to flee to her brother Thibault in Blois."

"Jesu," Ranulf whispered. How could a family tear itself apart like this? Had the French learned nothing from Harry's feuding with his sons? "Poor Louis . . ."

"Wait until you hear the rest, Ranulf. Hal and Geoffrey brought with them a truly amazing letter, from the French queen Adèle and her brothers, the Archbishop of Rheims and the Counts of Blois and Sancerre, entreating me to come to their aid."

Ranulf was dumbfounded. The houses of Blois and Anjou had been enemies even before Stephen of Blois had stolen the English crown from Henry's mother. That they should now be seeking to ally with England's king against their own son, nephew, and sovereign seemed utterly incomprehensible to him.

Henry read his thoughts easily enough, and smiled grimly. "I know, Uncle. The world has gone mad. I realized that as I stood in the crypt of Canterbury Cathedral and listened to the French king beg *me* to intercede with Thomas. After that, I did not think anything would surprise me. But I was wrong."

Ranulf shook his head slowly. "What will you do, Harry?"

"Damned if I know."

ABBOT JOSEPH HAD TURNED OVER his private quarters to the king, and Henry and Geoffrey were seated in the abbot's bedchamber, listening as Hal raged about the shameful way Louis was being treated.

"They even took away Louis's chancery seal, Papa, so that he could not revoke any of Philippe's acts! It is outrageous enough to dishonor an anointed king like that, but the man is Philippe's father. How can he be such an ungrateful wretch?"

Henry was beginning to think that he was the only one still able to recognize or appreciate irony. But he noticed then that the corner of Geoffrey's mouth was twitching, and it reassured him that at least one of his sons could see the madness of this moment. As their eyes met, Geoffrey smiled and shrugged, and to Henry, that rueful acknowledgment meant more than the formal public apologies he'd gotten from his sons at Michaelmas 1174.

"Marguerite is distraught," Hal confided. "In truth, the blame does not lie as much with Philippe as it does with the Count of Flanders. He has the boy doing his bidding as if Philippe were one of his lackeys instead of the King of France. It is pitiful, like watching a fly caught in a spider's web!"

Henry had rarely seen his son so irate, and he wondered how much of Hal's indignation was on Marguerite's behalf, for he did not think Hal was all that fond of his father-in-law. "You both have the advantage of me," he said, "for you know Philippe better than I do. Tell me more about him. What sort of man is he likely to become?"

"An annoying one," Geoffrey drawled, and Hal grinned.

"Geoff's assessment is not kind," he said, "but accurate. Of course, in fairness to Philippe, he is young yet, so there is still hope. If I did not know he was fourteen, though, I'd swear he was forty, for he is so very serious and earnest about everything. And he can be a bit of a prig. Not only does he not curse, he has actually forbidden swearing in public, and anyone who does must pay a fine of twenty sous! He is the only person I've ever met—male or female—who is uneasy around horses. He has shown no interest whatsoever in tournaments or music or jongleurs, which baffles me exceedingly. And he does not seem affectionate by nature, at least not with his sisters. For certes, he has never shown much warmth to Marguerite, and Marie thinks he is a horse's arse."

Henry had never met Eleanor's eldest daughter, but he decided he'd like her. "You are not painting a very appealing picture of the lad, Hal."

"I suppose I am not," Hal conceded. "He does have his good qualities. He is clever enough and well mannered and pious, and he does not seem to hold grudges. But he is also very naïve. Putting his trust in Philip proves that, and so does the nonsense he believes about the Jews. Do you know what he told me, Papa? That the Jews meet secretly in caves beneath Paris where they sacrifice Christian children!"

Henry blinked. It had been his experience that only the uneducated believed the stories of ritual murder periodically raised against the Jews. "I'd heard that he had the Paris synagogues raided and seized all their property. Is that why he did it?"

"Part of the reason," Geoffrey commented. "He also has a good eye for profit, and he told me he plans to cancel all the debts that Christians owe to Jewish moneylenders, whilst reserving to the Crown one-fifth of the amount. He assured me, though, that he will be calculating the sum on the debt principal only, not wanting to benefit by usury."

"You are making him sound like a hypocrite," Hal protested, "and in this I do believe he is sincere, that he well and truly hates the Jews. His father always protected them, even protesting to the Holy Father when the last Lateran Council forbade Jews to hire Christian servants. Philippe is very critical of Louis's leniency, and he does not look kindly upon your policy toward the Jews either, Papa. He told me he disapproved greatly of your decision to allow English Jews to be buried in other towns than London."

"I daresay I can live with Philippe's disapproval," Henry said. "The Jews often serve as bankers of the Crown, and Louis understood that. Philippe will learn that lesson the hard—"

"Be that as it may," Hal interrupted, "you must find a way to free Philippe from Philip's baneful influence, Papa. I promised Marguerite that we'd do what we could for her father." He'd moved to the open window and, catching sight of several of his knights crossing the garth, he found a reason to excuse himself, and was soon striding out into the sunlight, calling to Will Marshal and Peter Fitz Guy.

Henry was pleased when Geoffrey remained, for he wanted to get his younger son's views of the French crisis. "You did not say that much," he observed, and Geoffrey smiled, saying that few men could compete with Hal or Richard in laying claim to a conversation.

"It did surprise me," Henry admitted, "to hear Hal speak so harshly of Philip of Flanders. I'd not go so far as to say Hal idolized the man, but he did seem rather fond of the ground upon which he walked. So this is quite a reversal."

Geoffrey was laughing. "Have you ever known a spurned lover to take rejection well? Philip spent years cultivating Hal's good will. For certes, he did not pay for Hal's tournament expenses out of the goodness of his heart. Hal's nose is out of joint because Philip has dropped him like a hot coal in favor of a more promising prospect, young Philippe."

Henry frowned, for he did not want to see Hal's outrage as personal pique; that implied Hal's sense of justice was only engaged when his self-interest was. Why was it that his sons were so critical of one another? "Do you agree with Hal's appraisal of Philippe?"

"Yes . . . up to a point. I think Hal is too quick to put all the blame on Philip. Philippe may be callow, and God knows he lacks Hal's style or Richard's swagger. But he is no man's fool and no man's puppet. He knows his own mind, Papa. I do not believe he'd have heeded Philip unless he also believed that his uncles exercised too much influence at Louis's court. Paris is rife with rumors that Philippe means to take the seneschalship away from Thibault and bestow it instead upon Philip. But if there is any truth in that, it would be like ridding your woods of foxes by bringing in a pack of wolves."

Henry leaned back in his seat, his expression pensive. "Men have always observed how closely Hal resembles my father, and he does have the same coloring and features. But I think you are the one who is most like him."

Geoffrey glanced up with a surprised smile. "I take that as a compliment."

"You should, for I've known few men as shrewd or as astute as my father. It is not too much to say I owe him my kingship. It is true that my blood claim came from my mother, but if my father had not won Normandy at the point of a sword, I may not have been able to win the English crown. Because he did take Normandy and then turned it over to me, Stephen's barons were forced to choose between their English and Norman estates, and his support began to bleed away."

"At the very least, I doubt Maman would have agreed to wed you if you were not already Duke of Normandy and not merely the Count of Anjou's heir," Geoffrey said daringly, and was both pleased and relieved when Henry laughed.

"You've got my father's sense of humor, too, lad. He always had a feel for the vitals."

As far back as he could remember, Geoffrey had looked at his world with oddly dispassionate eyes; sometimes he felt as if he were watching someone else's life. He knew that he was about to make a mistake, but he'd never before experienced a mo-

ment of emotional intimacy like this with his father, and he could not help himself.
"You were not yet seventeen when he handed Normandy over to you."

Henry stiffened, for he knew where this was going. "That ground has been
ploughed over and over again, lad."

"But I need to know, to understand. Your father could have held on to Normandy
until you were of age, and few would have blamed him. Why can you not do the same
for me and my brothers?"

"Because—" Henry broke off and shook his head. "Let it be, Geoffrey."

Geoffrey couldn't. "Papa, I need to know!"

"Because—because I cannot trust you and your brothers the way my father could
trust me!" The bitter words were no sooner out of Henry's mouth than he wished
he could call them back. "I did not want to say that," he said at last, "but you kept
pushing . . ."

"I wanted an honest answer," Geoffrey said slowly, "and you gave me one. I've no
cause for complaint." But even as he sought to make light of it, he was shaken, for he'd
recognized a truth that did not bode well for the future. The wound inflicted upon his
father by their rebellion had not healed, would never heal. And that meant his father
would never be willing to share power, not until he drew his last mortal breath.

P HILIPPE'S RELATIONSHIP with his family and nobles continued to de-
teriorate, as more and more of his barons became alarmed at the influence wielded
by the Count of Flanders. Philippe had announced plans to have his new queen
crowned with him that June on Whitsunday. But Philip advised him to have the coronation performed earlier so that none could hinder it, and Philippe and Isabelle were
secretly crowned by the Archbishop of Sens at the abbey of St-Denis on Ascension
Day. As French kings were traditionally crowned only by the Archbishop of Rheims,
Philippe's uncle was outraged by the slight, and war seemed more and more likely until Henry persuaded the young French king and the count to meet him near Gisors in
late June.

T HE DAY WAS HOT and despite the shade offered by the tree known as the
peace elm, the men were soon sweating. Henry found himself reminded of the many
times he and Louis had assembled here in past years. It seemed strange to see Louis's
place taken by this fledgling. Philippe was still two months shy of his fifteenth birthday, still in that awkward gangling stage, his pallor hinting at his serious illness last

summer, his face framed by a halo of tousled brown hair, bristling like a hedgehog's quills. Henry could see little of Louis in the boy.

Henry's patience was fast fraying, for he'd made what he considered a very fair offer, agreeing to make peace with Philippe upon the same terms that he and Louis had accepted three years earlier at Ivry. He knew he'd surprised them, for he was known to take ruthless advantage of an adversary's weaknesses and Philippe's vulnerabilities would have been obvious to a blind man. They were quite willing to avoid hostilities with England, but they were balking at one of his conditions—that Philippe reconcile with his mother, Queen Adèle, and her brothers.

Philippe was letting Philip do most of the talking, but he was watching Henry intently, taking in every word, every gesture. Unlike his father, his face was not a window to his soul, and Henry noted approvingly that it was impossible to know what he was thinking, for that was a valuable skill in a king, one Hal had so far failed to master, much to his disappointment. Glancing up at the sun, he measured the passing time, and then said in an abrupt change of tone:

"I think it will be in all our interests if we speak frankly, cast aside the ambiguous, elusive language of statecraft. I need not point out, my lord Philippe, that you may be facing the Devil dogs of rebellion and war if an accommodation is not reached with me and your royal kinsmen. That would not be an auspicious way to begin your reign. And you take the risk that I may not always be feeling so benevolent. The time might well come when I can no longer resist the temptation to profit at the expense of your youth and family troubles."

Philippe's eyes flickered, but he showed no other reaction. Philip was scowling openly. "Is that meant as a threat?"

"A threat, a warning, call it what you will," Henry said, and then, like the others, he was turning to watch the approaching riders. As they drew nearer, it became evident that one of them was a woman, and when Philippe's face suddenly flamed with color, Henry hid a smile, knowing that the young king had recognized his mother. Sauntering over, he gallantly helped the French queen to dismount.

Adèle of Blois had been only fifteen when she'd wed Louis, and twenty years later, she was still a strikingly handsome woman. Moving toward her son, she made a graceful curtsy. "My lord king." And when she added, "My son," Philippe no longer looked like the ruler of a great realm, more like an errant youngster whose sins were about to be made public.

"I thought it was time," Henry said blandly, "for mother and son to talk face-to-face, without intermediaries or mediators." Draping his arm around Philip's shoulders, he suggested that they go for a walk in order to give the French king and queen some privacy. The Flemish count's body was rigid, resistant, but Henry was not to be denied, and Philip reluctantly let himself be led away once he realized that it would take physical force to disengage the English king's grip.

"Let's get out of the sun," Henry said amiably, "so we can talk candidly." Moving into the shadows of a leafy willow tree, he leaned comfortably against the trunk as he regarded the Count of Flanders. "I cannot say I blame you, Cousin. A gyrfalcon coming across a newborn lamb alone and unprotected will want to make a meal of it. But once the gyrfalcon realizes that the flock's ram is close at hand, it flies off in search of easier prey."

"Very amusing," Philip said coldly. "You are enjoying this."

"Actually, I am. There are times when the exercise of power can be very gratifying, Philip."

"I am Philippe's godfather and, now, his uncle by marriage. That gives me the right to offer him advice and counsel and comfort."

"Need I remind you that your mother and my father were sister and brother? That makes us first cousins, but that would hardly give me the right to meddle in Flemish affairs, would it?"

"I know what I can get from Philippe. What can I get from you, *Cousin?*"

"We once had an agreement under which I paid you a yearly fief-rent of one thousand pounds in return for the service of five hundred of your knights. I am willing to renew that agreement."

Philip considered the offer. "Why should I settle for that when I can obtain so much more?"

"Enough about offers and profits and benefits, *Cousin.* Let's speak instead of debts, of what is owed." There was no longer any amusement in Henry's voice. "For years you did all you could to estrange me from my eldest son. You owe me a blood debt, my lord count, but until now I have made no effort to collect it. You might want to think about that, think about it long and hard."

Philip was ten years Henry's junior, had effectively ruled Flanders since he was Philippe's age. Renowned for his knightly prowess on the battlefield and in the tournament, he was not a man who was easily intimidated. But he was also a realist, one who'd always known when it was time to fish and time to cut bait.

Correctly interpreting his silence, Henry said, "I think we understand each other. Shall we go back and see how the family reunion is going?"

Emerging from the willow's screen, they walked without speaking for several moments. They were soon close enough to see that Philippe and Adèle had drawn apart from the others and were conferring quietly together, their faces earnest and intent. Seeing the last of his hopes fluttering away on the wind, Philip came to a sudden halt.

"At least you can tell me why you are doing this for Louis's son. I am entitled to that much."

Henry had stopped, too. "Because," he said, "there were none to do this for *my* sons."

L̥ouis capet, seventh of that name to rule France, died on September 18 of that year at Barbeau, the Cistercian abbey he'd founded, and Philippe's reign officially began.

CHAPTER THIRTY-ONE

✦

July 1181
Winchester, England

*E*LEANOR HAD JUST FINISHED dictating a letter to a scribe. "Thank you, Edwin," she said, and as he departed, she exchanged a look of amused understanding with Amaria, both of them sharing the same thought: that her circumstances had definitely taken a turn for the better. She was permitted to write and even to receive letters now, although she was sure that they were read before being dispatched or delivered. Henry had named Ralf de Glanville as his new justiciar, and she was technically in his custody, although Ralph Fitz Stephen continued in his role as her warden. She'd confided in Amaria that she suspected de Glanville was interpreting the rules of confinement as generously as possible, for he'd struck her as a highly capable man with an eye for the main chance, one too shrewd to make an enemy of their future king's mother.

"I was writing to my daughter in Castile," she told Amaria. "Not yet twenty and already the mother of two. My grandchildren are certainly getting singular names: Berengaria and Sancho, Richenza, Lothair, and Otto." She wondered if there'd ever be an Eleanor. Hal would name a daughter after her if Harry was dead, but would he dare do so whilst his father lived? Richard would, and Geoffrey . . . mayhap; her third son remained the one she found hardest to read.

"We may as well go down to the great hall," she said, "for the dinner hour is fast approaching." Amaria was helping her adjust her wimple when they heard footsteps in the stairwell, and a moment later, the Countess of Chester was announced.

Eleanor's delighted smile faded at the sight of her friend's face. "Maud? What is wrong?"

Maud's eyes filled with tears. "My son . . . Eleanor, my son is dead."

"D RINK THIS, DEAREST," Eleanor urged. "Amaria fetched it from the buttery just for you." She'd held the other woman as Maud wept, knowing there were no words to ease so great a grief. When Maud felt like talking, she listened; when she did not, Eleanor kept silent, and gradually the story emerged. Hugh had taken ill soon after Easter and his condition steadily worsened. He died a fortnight ago at his manor in Staffordshire, only in his thirty-fourth year, leaving a young widow, an eleven-year-old son, and four daughters. Death came for them all in God's Time, but Eleanor thought it was harder to accept when it came in a man's prime. Parents should not outlive their children.

"I've done my share of mourning." Maud's sobs had subsided, but tears still streaked her cheeks. "I lost my parents and my husband, though widowhood was a blessing of sorts. Then Roger was taken, as were all of my brothers except Will, the worst of the lot. Until now I thought my greatest heartbreak was my son Richard, that he never lived to manhood. But now Hugh is gone, too, and all I have left is my daughter."

"Not so. You have Hugh's children. And Bertrada, for you've often said she is more like a daughter than a daughter-in-law. She is going to need you, Maud, with five children to raise on her own."

"Hugh had a fine crop of bastards, too," Maud said, smiling sadly, "four that he acknowledged as his. He'd want me to make sure they were taken care of . . . Ah, Eleanor, how have you done it? How have you survived nigh on eight years of confinement without going mad with grief or rage or sheer boredom? Teach me how, dear friend, teach me to accept God's Will as you have done."

"It is an ongoing struggle, Maud. Too often I have days in which my captivity seems to be Harry's will, not the Almighty's. But I persevere, for as a wise Welshwoman once pointed out, what other choice have I?"

"What choice do any of us have?" Maud acknowledged, and they talked for a while of her son, finding comfort in memories of happier times. They spoke, too, of

Eleanor's first husband. Eleanor admitted that she prayed for Louis's soul, which convinced Maud that she had indeed learned to let go of many of her earthly grudges. Eleanor also shared sad news of her own, that her daughter Marie had been widowed that February. The Count of Champagne had been captured in the Holy Land and although the Emperor of Byzantium ransomed him, his health had suffered in captivity and he'd died on his way home to France.

"Enough," Maud cried at last. "No more talk of death or regrets or unhealed wounds. Tell me something cheerful, something hopeful, even if you have to make it up!"

"As it happens," Eleanor said, with a sudden smile as luminous as her eyes, "I do have good news—a letter from my daughter Joanna. She is with child." And Maud discovered that she could take solace from that, from this reassuring proof that the circle of life was eternal and her son Hugh would live on in his children until the day that they'd be reunited at God's Throne.

As MORGAN AND HIS ELDER BROTHER walked along the quays of the Rouen waterfront, they were attracting glances from passersby, and Bleddyn finally noticed. "These Norman maidens are bold ones," he joked, "for they are definitely looking you over, lad."

Morgan grinned. "I'll not deny that women find me irresistible, but you're the one drawing all the attention. They are not accustomed to seeing men with mustaches but no beards, are doubtless wondering what odd and alien land you come from."

"Passing strange that you should say that, Morgan, for I find the sight of your beard to be just as odd. Who knew you were old enough to shave?"

"Clearly your memory is failing in your old age," Morgan shot back, "if you've forgotten that I turned seventeen in February." As much as he was enjoying this brotherly banter, he was somewhat surprised by it, too. Bleddyn was almost thirteen years his elder and they'd never before bandied jests and gibes as equals, so he was particularly pleased that his brother was no longer treating him like a fledgling newly fallen from the nest.

When Bleddyn had first sought him out at the castle, he'd gone cold with fear, terrified that he was bringing word of a family tragedy. To his vast relief, Bleddyn assured him that their parents were quite well; he was here with the Lady Emma, who had stopped in Rouen on her way to visit her young son at Laval. Morgan had been astonished to learn that Bleddyn was now serving Emma's husband, given the long-standing hostility between Davydd ab Owain and their father.

Bleddyn had laughed at his surprise, assuring him that Davydd was actively pursuing friendly relations with the English Crown and Ranulf's status as the king's favorite uncle mattered more than his past friendship with Davydd's slain brother Hywel. Nor did he see any difference between his serving the Prince of North Wales and Morgan's serving the English king's son, he'd pointed out dryly. And Morgan had conceded defeat, stopped bedeviling Bleddyn about the loathsome Davydd, and took him out to see the city of Rouen.

So far he'd shown Bleddyn the marketplace, the partially completed cathedral, the archbishop's palace, and the belfry tower from which two alert monks had spotted the French king's sneak attack and rang the great bell "Rouvel" in time to alert the citizens and stave off attack until Henry could come to their rescue. Bleddyn did not have any particular interest in Norman towns, but he was willing to indulge his young brother and listened patiently as Morgan bragged about the leper hospital Henry had built five years ago and the stone bridge paid for by his mother, the Empress Maude, and the fact that Rouen had once been a Roman outpost known as Rotomagus. But when Morgan suggested that they visit the tomb of William the Bastard in the Abbey of St Ouen, Bleddyn balked, and expressed his desire to find a tavern, the sooner the better.

"Thank God!" Morgan exclaimed. "I could not take you to the most interesting neighborhoods, for I doubt your wife would appreciate that, so I had to make do with the marketplace and the churches." Coming to a halt, he glanced around, and then took Bleddyn's arm. "There is an excellent tavern up ahead, but it is too close to the River Renelle and the tanners' quarter; as good as their wine is, it cannot compete with the stench. I know another place, though, a bit on the shabby side, but it'll do us well enough." And he led his brother into a maze of alleys, showing such an intimate knowledge of the less reputable areas of the city that Bleddyn realized his little brother was indeed growing up.

Once they were seated at a corner table with two henaps of red wine, Morgan brought Bleddyn up to date on the latest political news. The king had expected to cross the Channel after Easter, but then Philip of Flanders had besieged a French castle. He'd met the Flemish count and the young French king at Gisors again, managed to persuade Philip to withdraw his forces, and was now on his way to Cherbourg with the Scots king, where he planned to sail for England, just missing the Lady Emma by a few days.

Bleddyn doubted that the Lady Emma was heartbroken by that, for time had not reconciled her to living in Wales. "So what is this I hear about a great row between the king and your lord? Since Geoffrey has been given permission to wed the Breton heiress, what other grievances does he have?"

"They made peace ere the king departed Rouen, but Geoffrey has good reasons for his discontent." Morgan took a swallow of wine, then lowered his voice even though they were speaking in Welsh. "I am guessing you are not that familiar with

Breton affairs," he said, and laughed when Bleddyn insisted that Brittany claimed his last thought upon retiring at night and his first upon awakening in the morning.

"Well, Breton history is complicated, so bear with me. The king initially supported Constance's father, Conan, in his fight for the duchy with his stepfather. But Conan could not keep the peace and, as his liege lord, Cousin Harry finally grew tired of putting out Breton fires. So fifteen years ago, he forced Conan to abdicate and betrothed Constance to Geoffrey, although he did allow Conan to keep his vast English estates. You're probably wondering why he had English lands. It is because his father was the Earl of Richmond; his claim to Brittany came through his mother. When Conan died five years later, the Honour of Richmond then became part of Constance's inheritance."

Bleddyn's eyes were glazing over, but he nodded attentively, and Morgan continued. "Then there is the county of Nantes. It was once ruled by the Breton dukes but twenty-some years ago, the people rebelled and offered it to Cousin Harry's brother Geoffrey. But he died suddenly two years later, and both Conan and Harry claimed Nantes, Conan because it had once been ruled by his uncle and Harry because he was his brother's legal heir. Not surprisingly, the king won that dispute."

Bleddyn was beginning to see which way the wind was blowing, for it was his experience that Welsh and English rulers shared the same vices—a hunger for more than they already had. "So the bone of contention between Henry and Geoffrey is either Nantes or Richmond, depending upon which one the king is holding back."

"I think Geoffrey expected that much, knowing his father as he does. But he was not expecting Cousin Harry to hold on to both of them, for that is two-thirds of Constance's inheritance. Geoffrey does not often lose his temper, but when he learned that he'd get neither Nantes nor Richmond, he flew into a rage. It availed him naught, though, for the king remained adamant, and eventually they patched up their quarrel. But . . ." He let his words trail off, busied himself in finishing his wine.

Bleddyn thought that Morgan was bound to be torn in his loyalties, and said encouragingly, "Think of me as your confessor. Your secrets will be safe with me, for who am I going to tell—Welsh sheep?"

Morgan did need to discuss this, and he smiled gratefully at his brother. "The king has been very good to me, Bleddyn. I did not see him all that often, of course, but he always took an interest in my education, always made me feel welcome. It is different, though, with Geoffrey. As his squire, I see him every day, and he treats me as his cousin, not just as a retainer. It troubled me greatly to see him so distraught over this. I'd never seen him so angry before. He even said . . ."

"What did he say, Morgan?"

"He said that much of the blame lay with his grandmother, the Empress Maude.

He claimed that she taught Cousin Harry to treat men the way a wild hawk was tamed, by offering it meat and then snatching it away ere the hawk could eat."

"Well, that method is said to work with hawks, making them more obedient and biddable. Whether it works as well with sons remains to be seen." Bleddyn set his henap down, barely touched. "Listen, lad, I was not entirely candid with you earlier. I offered to be part of Lady Emma's escort, and I did so because I wanted the chance to talk with you about your future."

Morgan was flattered, but puzzled, too. "I daresay you have a wealth of advice to share with me; big brothers always do. But you could not entrust it to a letter?"

"No, it needed to be done in person. Morgan, I have misgivings about the path you're following. I know what it is like to be the proverbial fish out of water, neither fully Welsh nor truly English. When I was nineteen, I chose the Welsh way, cast aside Gilbert Fitz Ranulf and became Bleddyn ap Ranulf. You were too young to remember, but it caused serious dissension between our father and me. As he saw it, I was rejecting his heritage, rejecting him. We eventually made our peace, but I hurt him, and I was sorry for it. It was the only path for me, though, and I've never regretted it."

Morgan was genuinely bewildered. "I am glad of that. But what does this have to do with me?"

"It is not easy for us, lad, to be stranded between two worlds. The sad truth is that we can never feel completely comfortable in either world. You are three-quarters Welsh and one-quarter Norman-French. I want you to be sure you are making the right choice, taking the road that is right for you, and I fear that you are letting yourself be borne along by the wind, your decisions made by chance or convenience. You need to think seriously about what you want from this life, not what Papa wants for you, what *you* want, Morgan."

Morgan was astonished. "Papa is not forcing me to this, Bleddyn. I like being at the English court, and I have never felt as if I were stranded between two worlds. That is your truth, not mine. I consider myself blessed to have both Norman and Welsh blood flowing through my veins, have never seen it as a burden."

Bleddyn was equally astonished, for it had not occurred to him that his brother might not share his confusion, his conflicted sense of identity. "Are you sure, lad?" And when Morgan swore he was, the older man could only shake his head in rueful bafflement. "Well, now I feel like a fool. Here I was, rushing off to save my little brother from pirates, only to find that he fancies being a pirate himself!"

Morgan burst out laughing. "Our cousin Harry has been called many things in his life, but I think it is safe to say that you are the first to brand him as a pirate." He set himself, then, to dispelling his brother's discomfort, joking and teasing until Bleddyn was laughing, too. He was warmed by this dramatic display of family love and loyalty, and he found himself feeling sorry for his royal cousins, who knew nothing of brotherly solidarity. But afterward, when he marveled how he and Bleddyn could drink from the same cup and yet find the taste so very different, he finally began to understand why the king and his sons seemed unable to reach common ground, no matter how they tried.

CONSTANCE'S WEDDING was just as unpleasant as she'd always expected it to be. In fact, it was even worse, for she'd never anticipated that her mother would not be in attendance. Widowed by the death of Constance's father ten years ago, her mother Margaret had wed an English baron three years later. Constance had been glad of the remarriage, for it was so much easier to see her mother once they both dwelled on the English side of the Channel. But now Margaret's English residency worked to her daughter's disadvantage, for when Constance was summoned to Rouen on such short notice and told that she was to marry Geoffrey as soon as possible, there was no time for Margaret to make the trip, too.

Constance had only one small consolation, that her wedding was not taking place in Normandy. When she learned that the English king was not going to ease his grasp on either Nantes or the Honour of Richmond, her long-smoldering resentment had flared into outright fury. She did not trust herself to sit beside Henry at her wedding feast, exchanging pleasantries with the man who'd ruined her father and now sought to rob her of her rightful inheritance, and the thought of him being present at the bedding-down revelries was even more distasteful to her. In desperation, she had asked Geoffrey if they could be married in Brittany, and to her amazement, he readily agreed. Even more surprising to her, so did his father. It was only later that she realized why they were willing to be so accommodating—because the wedding itself was meaningless to them. They cared only for the legal rights that Geoffrey would acquire once he made her his wife.

She'd suggested that the wedding be held in the castle of one of her most loyal barons, André de Vitré, only to learn that André had recently left on pilgrimage to the Holy Land. Before she could despair, though, Geoffrey brought her remarkable news: Raoul de Fougères was willing to act as host. Knowing that Raoul shared her loathing for the English Crown, she was morbidly curious as to how they'd compelled his cooperation.

And so it was that Geoffrey and Constance exchanged vows on the porch of St Leonard's Church in Fougères, for weddings were commonly held in public to guarantee as many witnesses as possible to the union. After they entered the church for the

Mass conducted by the Bishop of Rennes, they were then escorted through the steep streets of the town and back to the great hall of the castle, which had only recently risen from the ashes of a crushing defeat; fifteen years earlier, Henry had captured the supposedly invincible stronghold and razed it to the ground.

The day had been one of humid August heat, and even as twilight slowly trickled into the river valley, the sun's warmth still lingered, turning the hall into a sweltering cauldron. Constance was pleased to find that it was essentially an all-Breton affair, for she'd been given no voice in the hasty preparations.

André de Vitré was absent, of course, but his wife, Matilda de Mayenne, was present, as were the most prominent of the Breton barons. No less than three bishops were in attendance, as were the abbot of Holy Trinity and Robert de Torigny, the venerable abbot of Mont St Michel. Geoffrey's mentor, Roland de Dinan, had been invited, as were a number of men who'd been familiar presences at Constance's father's court, and Constance was relieved that no needless slights had been offered, for her Breton lords were as touchy and high-tempered as their more notorious neighbors in Poitou. When she learned that the wedding guest list was Geoffrey's doing, she grudgingly gave him credit where due, even though she was not inclined to look kindly upon her new husband. The most favorable thing she could say about him was that at least he was not Richard or Hal.

However he'd been coerced into it, Raoul de Fougères had spared neither expense nor effort, and the great hall was richly decorated, with fresh rushes upon the floor, white linen tablecloths draped over the trestle tables, and cinnamon and cloves burned to combat the ripe smells of summer and sweat and spilled wine, for the wedding guests were happily doing their best to drain Raoul's wine kegs dry. So was her groom; when he'd given her the kiss of peace at the conclusion of the Mass, Geoffrey had already tasted of wine, which was one more grievance to hold against him, for Constance did not dare to follow his example. Too much wine might loosen her tongue, and that was not a risk she was willing to take. She was yoked to this man for the rest of her earthly days, and it would be the height of folly to antagonize him from the very outset of their marriage.

She did her best to play the role that had been forced upon her, smiling and accepting congratulations and demurely turning her cheek for the bridal kisses pressed upon her by the increasingly inebriated male guests. Afterward, there was dancing and entertainment by a rising young troubadour star, Bertran de Born, who interspersed his own songs with the bawdy poetry of Geoffrey's great-grandfather, Count William of Aquitaine. The verses were explicit enough to cause the bishops some discomfort, but Constance kept a smile upon her face even as she felt her cheeks growing hot. She was not prudish, not easily shocked, but she still had the bedding-down revelries to get through, and was in no mood to appreciate ribald lyrics or the drunken cheering of the men who'd soon be crowding around her marriage bed.

Eventually the interminable evening came to an end, and she and Geoffrey were escorted across the bailey to their bridal chamber in the northwest tower. They knelt by the bed for the bishop's blessing, were sprinkled with holy water as he prayed that their marriage would be fruitful and find favor in the eyes of the Lord. Clerics often reminded newlyweds that they ought not to consummate their marriage that first night, spending it instead in prayer and meditation. But the Bishop of Rennes was a realist and omitted an admonishment that he knew was so rarely heeded. The men then trooped out noisily so that Constance could be made ready for her husband.

The women guests clustered around the bride, helping her to undress, brushing out her long, dark hair, and dousing her in so much perfume that she had a coughing fit. At last they departed, leaving her alone with her two handmaidens, Juvette and Blanche, and Enora, her childhood nurse. This was not unusual; she knew that both Marguerite and Alys were still served by women who'd tended to them in their cradles. But she assumed that the French king's sisters were fond of their longtime companions, and she found Enora to be a vexing, foolish creature, prone to fluttering about and clucking like a mother hen. She'd promised herself that once she was the Duchess of Brittany, she'd send the old woman to live in her mother's household, but for now she had to grit her teeth as Enora prattled on about how beautiful she looked and how lucky she was, for Lord Geoffrey was quite good-looking, even if not as spectacularly handsome as his brother, the young king. Constance thought that she was attractive enough, but she well knew she was not a great beauty. Nor did she much care if Geoffrey had a fair face. All that truly mattered was that he was the spawn of her enemy, the English king.

Her women exited when the men returned, their arrival heralded by raucous singing and shouting and the lewd jests that were such an inevitable part of wedding festivities. Shielded behind the bed hangings, Constance lay very still. She refused to admit she was nervous, for she was no child. She was twenty, after all, and she knew what to expect in the marriage bed. But her breathing quickened as the humor grew cruder, jokes about castles under siege and broken blades and the best way to mount a skittish mare and ride her bareback. Rolling over, she clasped the pillow over her head, so tightly that she could no longer hear their laughter.

She was startled, therefore, by a sudden burst of cursing, followed by thumping noises. Good God, were the fools brawling in her bedchamber? It certainly sounded like it, for voices were raised and there was a scuffling sound, more swearing. Sitting up, she scowled and reached for the bed curtains, her first instinct to give the culprits a right sharp scolding, but she thought better of it just in time. Geoffrey seemed to have the trouble well in hand, for it sounded as if he were ejecting the mischief-makers from the chamber, with some help from the more sober members of the wedding party. He got rid of them so fast, in fact, that she was taken by surprise when the bed hangings were suddenly yanked open.

Her husband was standing there, clad only in his linen shirt and braies, holding out a brimming wine cup. When she realized he was offering it to her, she shook her head, saying primly, "No thank you. I am not thirsty."

He ignored her refusal and pressed the cup into her hand. "I've never seen a woman more in need of a drink, darling. This is a special wine I had brought in from my mother's lands in Poitou. I think you'll like it once you try it."

Constance was beginning to bristle, not caring for his flippant tone in the least. "Why would you think I need a drink? I assure you that it is not so. I am not at all nervous, am quite prepared to do my duty as your wife."

"I daresay you are. And nothing stirs a man's lust more than the prospect of deflowering a woman resigned to 'doing her duty.' Who could resist a temptation like that?"

Constance's brows slanted down. She'd submit to his caresses, but if he thought she'd submit to his mockery, too, he was about to learn otherwise. "If your lust is lacking, there's always greed. Just close your eyes and think of Brittany's riches whilst you bed me." She was sitting upright in the bed, her hands clutching the sheet as if it were a shield against his anger. But to her astonishment, he gave a shout of laughter, and her own anger was diluted now by bewilderment. She'd been betrothed to Geoffrey since she was five and he was eight. Nevertheless, she was realizing that this half-dressed man was a stranger; she did not know him at all.

"Hellfire, I forgot to lock the door!" Careless of his near nudity, he strode across the room and slid the bolt into place. "Better safe than sorry. Sometimes drunken guests think it is a great joke to burst in upon the wedding couple at the most inopportune moment."

Constance took a sip of the wine, discovered that he was right; she did like it. "What was all that squabbling about earlier?"

"Oh, that. Men playing the fool, which doubtless does not surprise you any, since you seem to hold such a high opinion of my sex. Juhel and Hervé got into a shoving match, but Gérard and I separated them ere any blood was shed."

She knew that Juhel was Raoul de Fougères's son, and Hervé was one of the Breton knights in Geoffrey's retinue. She'd been surprised to note that almost all of his household knights were Bretons like Hervé; the Frenchman Gérard de Fournival was one of the few exceptions. "I was pleased to see so many influential lords amongst our guests—Reginald Boterel, Roland de Dinan and his adopted son, Alan de Rohan, even the de Moulton twins. You forgot nary a one."

He'd moved to the table, was reaching for a small coffer. But at that, he gave her a lazy smile over his shoulder. "Must you sound so surprised? I've spent most of the last six years in Brittany. I'd have to be feeble-minded if I could not learn who mattered in all that time. Ah, here it is."

Coming back to the bed, he held out a small package. "Your bride's gift, darling."

Constance undid the linen wrapping, and shook out an oval-shaped object of silver gilt. She recognized it at once, and thought that Geoffrey had not wasted any time in having his ducal seal made up. But as she held it up to the light, she saw that it bore the image of a female figure, mantled in a long cloak, holding a lily in one hand and a bird in the other. She stopped breathing for a moment, but she still did not believe it, not until she read the engraved legend: *Constancia Dvccissa Britannie, Comitissa Richenvndie.* "This is for me?"

"Well, I'd hate to think the image looks like me. For mine, I used the same design as your father did, just changing the name. Would you believe I never had my own seal until now? My lord father did not think I had need of one."

Constance dampened down her rising excitement; did he think to win her over with an empty gesture? "So now I will have a seal to confirm your acts. How convenient."

The bed shifted as he sat down upon it. "And to validate your own acts. Governing Brittany is likely to be as great a challenge as taming those lunatics in Poitou, and it will take us both to keep your Breton barons from running roughshod over the chancery."

She was silent for several moments as she considered the implications of what he'd just said, absently sipping wine as she ran her fingers over the name carved into the seal mold. "What chancery?" she said cautiously. "It was abolished when my father abdicated."

"And I plan to restore it straightaway. In fact, I intend to revive the ducal government as it was under your father. Some of my father's innovations are worth retaining, such as creating the office of seneschal for each of the Breton counties. But I know I can improve upon—"

"Stop," Constance begged, for the unreality of this conversation was affecting her as much as the wine. Did he mean any of this? But what did he have to gain by lying to her?

He cocked his head, regarding her quizzically, and then he grinned. "I know, strange talk for our wedding night. It is just that I've been waiting so long, and now we can start putting all these ideas into practice—at long last!"

Constance took another bracing swallow of wine, surprised to discover that her cup was almost empty. Geoffrey reached over, took the cup from her lax fingers, and padded barefoot over to the table to refill it. Watching as he came back to the bed, she said suspiciously, "Are you trying to get me drunk?"

Settling down beside her again, he passed her the cup. "If I were?"

"It would be a waste of wine. You do not have to seduce me, Geoffrey. I'm your wife now."

"Yes, you are," he said amiably. "But what if I want more than that?"

She drank some more wine to cover her confusion. "What?"

"An ally." He saw that she did not understand, and sighed. He rarely second-guessed himself, but he started to do so now, wondering if it would have been wiser to have waited until he'd won her trust. Her cup was tipping precariously and he grabbed it before she could spill wine over them both. "I think you've had enough, darling."

She thought so, too, for she was feeling light-headed. It was a strange sensation; she'd never even been tipsy before, never willing to relinquish control. "What did you mean about us being allies?"

"I just think it would be a shame if we did not join forces, for we want the same things."

"Somehow I doubt that, Geoffrey."

"Shall I tell you what your priorities are, Constance? You want to keep Brittany strong and prosperous, and to protect it from your predatory neighbors—the French cub, my brother Richard, and my esteemed sire. Oh, yes, and to provide an heir, preferably two. Did I leave anything out?" When she slowly shook her head, he said, "Well, those are my priorities, too, which is why it makes sense for us to unite."

"I do not know that I can believe you," she confessed, vaguely aware that the wine was subverting her sense of caution. "You seem to be saying that you'd put Brittany's interests above those of your father, and why would you do that?"

"Because our interests are not identical, even if he seems to think so. I am his third son, and Brittany is all I—we—have."

She wondered if it was the flickering candle flames, for his eyes seemed to change color, sometimes decidedly blue and at others very grey. "Prove it to me, then," she challenged. "Tell me how you got Raoul de Fougères to agree to hold the wedding here."

"I am sorry, darling, but I have no sordid secrets to reveal. Raoul was quite willing to do it, needed no persuasion or extortion from me."

She felt a sharp throb of disappointment. She'd almost let herself be taken in by his honeyed tongue and easy smile. "I am not a fool, Geoffrey! Raoul hates the English king."

"I daresay he does," he said calmly. "But I am the Duke of Brittany." While she was thinking that over, he pulled his shirt over his head, and she found herself paying sudden rapt attention to his bare torso; the candlelight caught the golden glints in his chest hairs, played upon the ripple of muscles as he slid next to her. "I am going to tell you something that no one else knows yet," he murmured, so close now that his breath was warm against her cheek. "I am going to dismiss Roland de Dinan, for he is my father's man, not mine. Then I intend to create a new office—Seneschal of Brittany—and once I do, I am offering it to Raoul."

"Why?" she whispered. They were lying together in the bed now, and she was faintly surprised to find that her arms had slipped up around his neck, that she was holding on to him as if he alone could anchor her to the earth.

"As I told you, darling, because I seek allies wherever I can find them."

Constance had never felt so relaxed, so comfortable in her own body. If this was what wine did, she'd been missing out on a lot. "I would suggest, then, that you begin looking in your bed."

"An excellent suggestion," he said, and raised up on his elbow to shed his braies.

She moved over to make it easier for him. "Why did you not take all your clothes off ere this?"

"We were interrupted by that brawl," he reminded her. "And then I thought it best to wait after that, not wanting to overwhelm you with my male magnificence right away." When she laughed, he said, "Thank God, you do have a sense of humor!"

"Of course I do!" she said, but her indignation was soon forgotten, for he'd begun to kiss her throat. Her inhibitions and her wariness had been dramatically diminished by the excellent wine of Aquitaine and Geoffrey's intriguing candor, and she delighted him by proving to be an apt pupil, quite unlike the bride he'd feared to be burdened with, the indifferent, inert virgin passively resigned to her fate. This woman was warm and willing and eager to follow his guidance, and he experienced far more pleasure than he'd expected to find in her bed. Afterward, he assured her drowsily that it would get better, but she said she had no complaints and then gave him a promising sign that their marriage would be a successful one, for she showed no inclination to talk as so many of his other bedmates did. Instead, she curled up against his back and went to sleep.

She awoke the next morning just before dawn, with a dull headache, a dry mouth, and total recall of the extraordinary events of her wedding night. Propping herself up on her elbow, she studied the man beside her. He looked younger in his sleep, less guarded, and she realized that the flighty Enora was right, after all; her new husband was easy on the eye. Best of all, he was quick-witted and clever and ambitious. *We will make effective partners. We will be good for Brittany and good for each other, and who would ever have imagined it?*

The sheet had slipped, only partially covering him, and she smiled at the sight of his early-morning erection, then slid over until their bodies were touching. Still half-asleep, he responded at once to the soft female curves nestled against him, and they were soon entwined together in a carnal embrace. She suspected that he'd begun making love to her without fully realizing who she was, but she was not bothered by that. She may have gone to her marriage bed a maiden, but she was no wide-eyed, convent-bred innocent. She fully expected Geoffrey to stray, for that was the way of their world. She felt confident, though, that he would never shame her by flaunting a concubine the way his father had flaunted Rosamund Clifford. He was too shrewd to make a mistake like that. And as she gave herself up to the moment, to the sheer physical sensations that he was stirring with hot kisses and intimate caresses, she discovered that he'd been right; it did get better.

Henry HAD SAILED FOR ENGLAND in the belief that he'd patched up a peace between Philip of Flanders and the young French king. It was to be short-lived. Adèle and her brother the Archbishop of Rheims had been reconciled with Philippe because of Henry's efforts, but her other brothers, Thibault of Blois and Étienne, Count of Sancerre, were still disaffected. In an act of utter cynicism, they allied themselves with their former enemy, Philip, against their nephew. They were soon joined by the Count of Burgundy, the Counts of Hainault and Namur, and Philippe's half sister Marie, regent for her fifteen-year-old son, the new Count of Champagne. Étienne was the first to strike, occupying Saint-Brisson-sur-Loire and then doing homage for it to the Flemish count. The hostile coalition was soon threatening Philippe's precarious hold on power, and he appealed urgently to the English king for help. Once again Henry proved to be Philippe's salvation, providing military aid under the command of his own sons.

Eleanor WAS JUBILANT when she learned that Henry would be holding his Christmas Court that year at Winchester, for her last two Christmases had been lonely ones, with the royal court at Nottingham and then Angers. But Henry was back in England after more than fifteen months on the other side of the Channel, and her spirits soared at the prospect of seeing one or more of her sons. She was to be disappointed, though. Richard had remained in Poitou, Hal and Marguerite were visiting her brother the French king, and Geoffrey and Constance were holding their first Christmas Court in Rennes.

Henry's son Geoff had accompanied him, as had John, but Geoff could barely bring himself to be civil to Eleanor, and John was her phantom son, vanishing with breathtaking speed every time she got within ten feet of him. Somewhat to her surprise, though, Henry was on his best behavior, so attentive that she did not have time to dwell upon her discontent. They enjoyed a pleasant supper as Henry told her what he knew of Constance and Geoffrey's wedding, revealed that Geoff had resigned as Bishop-elect of Lincoln, confessing that he did not think himself fit for such a high office, and was now Henry's chancellor, and disclosed that Richard's betrothed, Alys, would soon be residing at Winchester, as she'd complained life was too lonely and dull at Devizes Castle.

Henry also reported that Richard had a tumultuous summer. He'd angered the citizens of Limoges by insisting that the city walls be torn down, and then found himself embroiled in strife with the brothers of the Count of Angoulême. Count Vulgrin had died unexpectedly in June, leaving only a small daughter, and Richard claimed her wardship and then announced that she would inherit Angoulême, which did not sit well with the count's kinsmen.

"I would think not!" Eleanor was taken aback, for primogeniture was not the custom in Aquitaine and Vulgrin's brothers would have expected to share his inheritance. It sounded as if Richard had poked a stick into a hive, not the best way to obtain honey.

"Richard chased them out of Angoulême, and they took refuge with their half brother Aimar in Limoges. They've been joined by the Count of Périgord and several of his neighbors and will be plotting mischief in the coming year. This is why Richard did not join us in Winchester, for I know he wanted to see you."

Eleanor looked at him with surprise and some misgivings. Why was he being so kind to her tonight? When he proceeded to do his best to reassure her about the fledgling rebellion Richard was facing, lavishly praising their son's military skills, she began to feel more and more uneasy. It had been a long time since he'd shown such solicitude for her peace of mind. What was he up to now? "Is it true that you sent our sons to Philippe's aid last month?"

He smiled slightly. "So you heard about that, did you? Philip's Flemings sacked Noyon, captured Clermont and Senlis, and actually got within fifteen miles of Paris. By then I was back in England, so I dispatched Hal and Richard and Geoffrey, and they were quite successful, soon had Philip and his allies on the run."

Eleanor gazed at him in bemusement. Three times he'd acted to salvage Philippe's budding kingship, twice intervening personally to stave off disaster, and now this latest rescue. *Name of God, Harry, why can you not be as generous to your own sons as you are to Louis's son?* The question never left her lips, though. She knew it would only destroy their newfound camaraderie, for hers would be the last voice that he'd ever heed when it came to their children.

Henry stayed by her side after the meal was done, chatting so easily that she saw they were being watched—and gossiped about—by virtually every guest in the hall, gossip that doubtless reached spectacular levels when Henry accompanied her once she was ready to leave the festivities.

Ice crunched underfoot as they walked across the bailey. Eleanor glanced over her shoulder at their footprints in the snow, not sure how he'd come to be escorting her back to her chamber. She let Henry keep up the conversation, for her mind was racing as she tried to anticipate him, to guess what his latest scheme was. When Henry actually offered an offhand apology for Geoff's rudeness, she was convinced that something was in the wind, and decided to put her suspicions to the test.

"I am not troubled by Geoff's ill will, Harry. I would be grateful, though, if you had a word with John on my behalf. I tried all evening to speak with him, to no avail. Can you assure him that the sky will not collapse if he exchanges a few civil words with me?"

"I suppose I could. But you have our other lads dancing to your tune quite happily. Surely you can spare me one son, Eleanor?"

She stopped abruptly and studied him. There was just enough moonlight to catch the glimmer of a smile. "I think we need to talk. Let's go into the garden where we can be alone." He didn't object and they crossed the bailey in silence, opened the wicker gate, and entered the gardens.

As she'd expected, none were about at that hour. Stopping by a bench, Henry cleared snow from it with the corner of his mantle, for he only wore gloves when hunting. He stayed on his feet, though, after seating Eleanor. "You are right," he said in a low voice. "We do need to talk."

She'd thought that he had political intrigue in mind and needed her cooperation. Now, though, she felt a chill go up her spine, utterly unrelated to the winter weather. "Is this about one of our children? It is not good, is it?"

"No, it is not. You know that there has long been tension and suspicion between the Holy Roman Emperor and our Tilda's husband. It has now gotten much worse. Heinrich has been banished in disgrace, compelled to leave Germany. As soon as I learned about this, I sent Willem to the emperor to argue on Heinrich's behalf. The most he could gain, though, was the reduction of Heinrich's exile from seven years to three. So he will be taking refuge at my court in the coming year, and Tilda and their children will accompany him."

"That is indeed sad," Eleanor agreed, but in truth, she was somewhat relieved, for she'd feared more grievous news than that. At least Tilda and Heinrich were well, in no physical danger. "It is good that they have a shelter from this storm, a place where they will be safe and welcome until the emperor can be placated and coaxed into ending the banishment. And I confess that it will be wonderful to have Tilda back, and to see our grandchildren at last." When he did not reply, she said sharply, "I will be able to see them, Harry?"

"Of course." ✦

For the first time, Eleanor realized how cold it was in the garden. Rising, she shook snow from her mantle, smiling as a memory suddenly surfaced. "Do you remember the time we were pelting each other with snowballs, and your mother caught us at it? She was horrified that we were acting in such an unseemly way. Where was that . . . Rouen or Caen?"

"Rouen, I think." He sounded distracted, as if he had other matters on his mind, and she decided it was time to bring this surprising evening to an end while they were still on such amicable terms. But when she suggested that they go indoors, he made no move to leave. "Eleanor . . . there is more. I ought to have told you at once, but I was too craven, wanted to put it off as long as I could . . ."

"You are the least craven man in Christendom," she said, but her voice was no longer steady, for her fear had come flooding back. "What . . . what is it?"

"I had grievous news this week from Sicily. Joanna gave birth to a son, but he came too early. He only lived long enough to be baptized."

"Oh, no, no . . ." This was not the first time that Death had claimed a grandchild. Marguerite and Hal were still mourning for their infant son, and just that autumn, Eleanor had learned that the baby born earlier in the year to her daughter Leonora had been found dead in his cradle. But Joanna's heartbreak was harder for her to bear. Joanna was just sixteen. Why had God done this to her?

Turning away blindly, she would have stumbled and fallen if Henry had not reached out swiftly to catch her. Putting his arm around her shaking shoulders, he drew her to him, and she wept against his chest, wept for Joanna and her baby son, wept for herself, too, for her husband and their sons, for their accursed ill luck and their deplorable blunders, for all the evil that had overtaken their family.

CHAPTER THIRTY-TWO

May 1182
Winchester, England

THE SPRING HAD BEEN ONE of incessant rains and unrelenting bad news. It began when Eleanor learned that her sister Petronilla's elder daughter had died just before Easter. Eleanor had told Amaria about Isabelle's sad story. She'd been wed to Philip of Flanders at a very young age and their marriage had soured when she'd been unable to give him an heir. Six years ago Philip had accused her of adultery, had her suspected lover beaten to death, and compelled her to give him control of her inheritance—the French province of Vermandois.

Isabelle's untimely death had greater significance, therefore, than merely the end of her misery, for neither Eleanor nor Amaria doubted that Philip had made her life a living hell. Now that she was dead, Vermandois should have passed to her younger sister, Alienor. But Alienor's rights were ignored as Vermandois became one more bone of contention between the Count of Flanders and the young French king, both of whom claimed that rich county. Eleanor was infuriated that her niece had been treated so shabbily. She could not help Alienor, though, and that only added to her discontent.

Eleanor was still fuming over her impotence when news came from Poitou that Richard was facing a formidable coalition of rebel lords—the disinherited Taillefer brothers of Angoulême, their half brother Aimar, Viscount of Limoges, the Count of Périgord, and the Viscounts of Ventadour, Comborn, and Turenne. Richard had, as usual, chosen to strike first and attacked the Count of Périgord's castle of Puy-St-Front in Périgueux, but he did not have enough men with him to hold it, and to Amaria's troubled eyes, Eleanor seemed to age years in the span of days, her face pallid and drawn, her appetite gone, her sleep sporadic. If Amaria had doubted Eleanor's partiality for her second son, those doubts were dispelled as she witnessed the depths of the queen's fear. For better or worse, Richard was closest to Eleanor's heart, and now she could do nothing as he faced the most serious threat yet to his authority in Aquitaine.

That morning they learned that Ralf de Glanville had ridden in the night before, and Eleanor made haste to seek him out, for the justiciar had accompanied Henry to Normandy and he would be likely to have the latest word about the rebellion. As she waited for Eleanor to return, Amaria paced nervously, unable to sit still for long. To distract herself, she even tried to pet the cat, and she'd never cared for felines, considering them to be vexing, odd creatures. But Cleo haughtily rebuffed her overtures, and she resumed her pacing, wondering how she could comfort Eleanor if evil had befallen her favorite son.

When Eleanor finally came back to their chamber, though, Amaria knew at once that the news was good. For the first time in weeks, there was color in the queen's cheeks and her eyes had lost that glazed, inward look. After instructing Amaria to pour them some wine, she sat down in the window-seat and shared what she'd learned.

"Would you believe that Harry is still acting as Philippe's guardian angel?" she marveled. "Ralf said he met Philip and Philippe at Senlis and patched up yet another peace between Flanders and France. He then headed south, summoning the rebels to meet him at the abbey of Grandmont in Whitsun week. He told Ralf that if he could not end their rebellion by peaceful means, he would then take the field with Richard against them. Richard actually requested his support, which shows how precarious his position had become; my son does not easily ask for help. Harry told Ralf to assure me that there was no further need for concern. He'd summoned Geoffrey to Grandmont, too, and he said that if the war continued, Hal would also join them in punishing the rebels."

"Madame, that is wonderful news!"

"Yes, Amaria, it is. It was a long time coming, but at last the men in my family will be fighting on the same side!"

The count of Périgord had retaken his castle at Puy-St-Front after Richard's April seizure of the fortress, and in June, Richard, his father, and his brother Geoffrey set about recapturing it. The siege was going so well that Richard expected the count would soon surrender. But as of the first day of July, Hal had yet to put in an appearance.

Richard and Theobald Chabot, one of his mercenary captains, were inspecting Puy-St-Front's defenses for weaknesses, venturing so close to the castle walls that his knights and his squire Rico were alarmed, for he was now within range of Count Élie's bowmen. Richard was disdainful of the danger, studying the battlements intently. "If we were to shift the mangonels," he said, "aim them at this corner tower—"

"My lord duke!" One of his soldiers was approaching at a run, for Richard's men knew that he expected his commands to be carried out with dispatch; in that, he was truly his father's son. "The young king has just ridden into camp, and with a goodly force of knights and men-at-arms."

"Has he, indeed?" Not for the first time, Richard found himself thinking that Hal had an uncanny talent for arriving just as a siege was winding down. "I suppose, then, that I ought to bid him welcome."

Hal and his knights had already dismounted, and he was conversing easily with their father and Geoffrey, looking immaculate and well groomed and rested in the midst of the begrimed, sweaty, weary men who'd been besieging the castle for nigh on a month. As Richard shouldered his way toward Hal, the throng parted to let him pass, and Henry turned with a smile, pleased that his sons had come together like this, the first time that all three of them had gone to war under his command.

The smile left Henry's face, though, with Richard's first words. "Thank God Almighty, for now victory is assured. Once the rebels learn that the young king is here at last, they will surely be clamoring to surrender."

It could conceivably have been meant as a joke—if not for the razor edged tone of Richard's voice. Henry looked taken aback, Geoffrey interested, and Richard's knights amused. Hal's knights took it for what it was—a mortal insult—and angry murmurings swept through their ranks. But Hal appeared unperturbed. Smiling at his younger brother, he said pleasantly, "Given how heavy-handed you are with your liegemen, Little Brother, rebellions like this will be a common occurrence. Since we'll have to be riding to your rescue so often in years to come, it seemed wiser to pace myself."

The glitter in Richard's eyes did not bode well for a peaceful resolution, and Henry hastily stepped between them. "Enough," he said, low-voiced. "Will you make a spectacle of yourselves in front of the entire camp?" Others came to his aid, then, seeking to draw Richard aside, offering to show Hal where his men would be setting up their tents, and the moment passed. Henry did not move, though, not until Willem came to his side. "God grant me patience," he said softly, pitching his words for the earl's ears only. "Whatever that was, it was not the usual brotherly rivalry. *That* I can understand. But this . . . this was lethal, Willem."

And since Willem agreed with Henry, he could think of nothing to say and they stood in silence for a time, watching as men sought to keep the king's sons as far from each other as possible.

R EBELLIONS WERE NOT FOUGHT to the death, and when they realized that they'd been outmaneuvered and outfought, Viscount Aimar and Count Élie sued for peace. Aimar was compelled to offer two of his sons as hostages, and Henry, Hal, and Geoffrey accompanied Aimar to Limoges, where peace terms were sworn in St Augustine's abbey. Richard remained in Périgueux to supervise the destruction of Puy-St-Front's walls. With only Aimar's Taillefer half brothers in Angoulême still in defiance of Richard, the revolt sputtered to an end.

L IMOGES WAS, LIKE NOTTINGHAM, two separate cities, one clustered around the bishop's palace by the River Vienne and the other spread out on the hillside around the viscount's castle and the great abbey of St Martial, where Henry and his sons chose to stay.

The day after the peace terms were accepted, Henry and his sons celebrated with a hunt in the viscount's woods. By the time Geoffrey returned to his guest chamber, Compline was chiming. His squires, Morgan and Jehan, had just helped him to change his muddied hunting tunic when his brother Hal made an unexpected appearance. Both surprised and curious, Geoffrey sent his squires down to the guest hall so they could talk in privacy. He assumed Hal had a specific purpose in mind, for while they had never had a serious falling out, they were not confidants or even boon companions.

Hal seemed in no hurry, though, to get to the point, and began to discuss the day's hunt. But Geoffrey alone of his family had learned the art of patience, and he lounged at ease on the bed, sharing Hal's wineskin as he waited for his brother to reveal his intent.

"So . . ." Hal said, sprawling on the bed beside him as if they were still youngsters without a care in the world, "how do you like being married?"

"Well enough."

Hal doubted that, for he'd always found Constance to be as prickly as a hedgehog. "I'd wager your lady is not as easy to content as my Marguerite. Take the advice of a seasoned husband; gifts do wonders for marital harmony, the more frequently the better!"

"You may be right. Constance did seem quite pleased with the barony of Tréguier." Taking note of his brother's blank look, Geoffrey explained, "Tréguier was held by Constance's father, but when he died, our father gave it to Conan's uncle. The uncle died earlier this year, and I reclaimed it in Constance's name."

Propped up on his elbow, Geoffrey grinned, saying his wife had been very grateful, and Hal regarded him in surprise, for that sly smile was easy enough to interpret. So the demure, dignified Constance was a hell-cat in bed! Who would ever have guessed it? Flipping the wineskin to Geoffrey, he said, "So . . . you've had no luck in getting Papa to hand over Richmond or Nantes?"

"No," Geoffrey said tersely, but then made an effort to sound more positive. "At least he has given me a free hand in governing the rest of Brittany."

Hal was looking at him pensively, no longer smiling. "I wonder," he said, "if you and Richard realize how lucky you both are."

Geoffrey was in no mood for one of Hal's self-pitying rants. "Need I remind you that a king takes precedence over a duke—even a king in waiting?"

"Yes, but would either of you truly trade places with me? I think not. Anyway, that was not what I meant. You are lucky because the two of you are not as emotionally entangled with Papa as I am. It is easier for you."

Geoffrey sat upright on the bed. "What do you mean?"

"Give me the wineskin back and I'll tell you." Making a deft one-handed catch, Hal took a swig before saying, "Let's suppose that another Great Flood engulfs the world on the morrow, and the Almighty selects Richard to be the new Noah, only He tells Richard to fill his ark with family, not creatures of the earth. What would Richard do?"

"How would I know?"

"You know. The only person Richard loves is Maman. He'd take her onboard and leave the rest of us to drown."

"I'll grant you that," Geoffrey said, after a moment's reflection, "though he might also take Joanna. But what of me? Are you saying my ark would be empty, too, except for Maman?"

"No, you'd take us all along. Well, not Richard; he'd better hope he could swim.

But you'd warn the rest of us of the coming Flood. We'd only have so many chances, though, to catch the ark. If one of us had used up his chances, you'd sail off without a backward glance. I cannot say for certes when you left Papa stranded on the shore, but most likely it happened last year when he kept control of Nantes and the Honour of Richmond."

Hal had not often surprised Geoffrey, but he'd done so now. He'd not thought Hal was that insightful. Looking at his brother through new eyes, he said, "And who would occupy your ark, Hal? Would you find room for Papa?"

Hal shrugged and then sighed. "It depends on the day. That is why I say you and Richard are the lucky ones."

Geoffrey was finding this conversation intriguing, but he wasn't sure it was wise to venture into such uncharted terrain. He'd never before talked openly about his own ambivalent feelings for their father. "As interesting as this is, Hal, I doubt that you sought me out to talk of arks. What really brought you here?"

"You're right. I do have something in mind. One reason I took so long to reach Puy-St-Front was that I was meeting with some of Richard's rebellious barons. On St Martial's feast day, I was in Limoges, where the viscount and the people welcomed me warmly and then—"

"Save your breath, Brother. I am not interested in another rebellion against Papa. I did that once before, and it did not turn out so well."

"I agree with you, Geoff. Papa is not the target. Richard is."

Geoffrey rose, crossed the chamber, and slid the bolt into place. Coming back to the bed, he stood looking down at his brother. "What have you gotten yourself into now, Hal?"

"Over the past few years, I've come to know quite a few of the Poitevin lords. If truth be told, they've sought me out. Richard has done the impossible—gotten that lot of mules and malcontents to unite in a common cause. They grudgingly respect his battle skills, but when he tried to change local laws of inheritance, that was too much for them to swallow. They do not want him as their duke, have promised to transfer their allegiance to me if I am willing to help them overthrow him. I thought you might be interested in joining us."

"What would I gain by that?"

"Apart from the great satisfaction in seeing Richard brought down?" Hal's grin was so contagious that Geoffrey could not help returning it. "I'd make it worth your while, Geoff. One of these days I will actually become king, for not even Papa can live forever, and when I do, I'll hand over Richmond and Nantes to you straightaway."

"Mayhap you would, but Papa could live another twenty years. Who's to say that

I cannot coax him into dealing with me fairly whilst he is still alive? He has never re-fused me outright, keeps saying that he'll give them to me in time."

"If you still believe in Papa's good faith, you probably believe in mermaids and dragons, too. I am willing to offer more than future gains. Once I am in control of Aquitaine, I'll no longer be dependent upon Papa's whims, his meager acts of charity. There will be lucrative wardships and marriages at my disposal, and who better to share them with than my brother? And Poitou is a land of many castles, a number of which are located close to the borders of Brittany. What would make more sense than to turn some of these castles over to you?"

"I will not deny it is a tempting offer," Geoffrey said slowly, "for I do not fancy having Richard as my neighbor, constantly watching Brittany with hungry eyes. But it is a risky proposal, too. Are you so sure we could bring Richard down?"

"His delusions of grandeur notwithstanding, Richard is not Caesar or Charle-magne. Nor would we lack for allies. Virtually all of the barons of Aquitaine would come in with us, even the wily de Lusignans. They see this as a matter of their survival. And we could expect aid from my brother-in-law, too. After all that Papa had done for him, I was hesitant about broaching the subject with Philippe. I need not have wor-ried, though. Indeed, I was surprised how willing he was to join us."

That did not surprise Geoffrey at all. "So you are saying you'd have the backing of all the lords of Aquitaine, and the backing, too, of the French king. Are you not for-getting someone?"

"I do not think so. The Count of Toulouse would never be able to resist an op-portunity like this, and mayhap even the—"

"What about our father?"

"What about him? We would be striking at Richard, not him."

"And you think he'd stand aside, do nothing as Richard went down?"

"Why not? I know full well he loves me better than Richard. Papa might even be relieved to be rid of him. You cannot tell me that a man as full of ungodly suspicions as our father does not worry about Brother Richard's trustworthiness. Surely he knows how much Richard resents him for keeping Maman captive all these years." Hal got to his feet, too, reached out and put his hand on Geoffrey's arm. "So . . . what say you?"

"I will think about it."

"You can give me no better answer than that?"

"As I said, I will think about it. But this you must bear in mind, Hal. This cannot be a halfhearted effort. There can be no eleventh-hour regrets. If you are serious about this, you must commit to it . . . and you must prepare for all possible consequences. In other words, you cannot take it for granted that Papa would not rush to Richard's rescue. If you do this, you must be willing to fight Papa, too, if it comes to that."

Hal had no such misgivings, sure that if their father were forced to choose between him and Richard, he'd be the chosen one. He did not want to lose Geoffrey, though, by pushing too hard, too soon. Geoffrey would be an invaluable ally, for he had a cool head, was quick-witted, and could dip into the royal coffers of Brittany to hire the routiers they would need. "Fair enough," he said. "Think about it. Just do not wait too long. Opportunities like this do not come along that often."

Geoffrey knew he was right. The trouble was that opportunities and pitfalls could not always be easily or clearly distinguished, one from the other. He would talk to Constance, he decided, although he already knew what she would say, for they were very much alike, born gamblers willing to take great risks if the rewards were equally great. And the rewards Hal was offering were very great, indeed.

THE DUCHESS OF SAXONY AND BAVARIA was standing with her brothers on the battlements of Chinon Castle, where she discovered that they were right: the view was indeed breathtaking. Below them lay the narrow, crooked streets and blue slate roofs of the village, and beyond was the silvery expanse of the River Vienne, shimmering against a deep blue September sky.

"How lovely," Tilda said admiringly, and then laughed when Hal gallantly turned her comment into a compliment, pretending to think she was referring to herself. She was indeed ravishing, he assured her solemnly, but it was not seemly for her to call attention to her own beauty. Better she wait modestly until others noticed it, as they undoubtedly would.

"You have not changed a whit," she said, playfully and untruthfully, for nothing was as she'd remembered it. She'd last seen her father's domains fifteen years ago, when she'd been sent off to wed the man known as Heinrich der Löwe—Henry the Lion. She'd been only eleven, twenty-seven years younger than her new husband, a man renowned for his courage, military prowess, temper, and lack of tact, but it was obvious to her brothers that there was genuine respect and affection between Heinrich and Tilda, and they were glad that she'd found contentment in Germany. They were still getting accustomed to the Tilda of today, for this poised young woman of twenty-six was very different from the fragile, shy sister who still flitted through their childhood memories of yesterday. They were surprised by how much she'd grown; she was almost tall enough to look Richard and Hal straight in the eye, noticeably taller than her husband, and the slender, sylphlike girl had ripened into a beauty, so much so that they felt uncomfortable taking notice of the voluptuous curves motherhood had given her.

Tilda found their new selves to be no less startling. Hal had been twelve when they'd last met, Richard ten, and Geoffrey nine, and she had to make a conscious effort to associate those boisterous boys with these worldly, grown men of twenty-seven, twenty-five, and twenty-four. But she'd expected that she'd find strangers in their skins. What she'd not expected was to find her father was a stranger, too.

She'd remembered him as a veritable whirlwind, remembered a hoarse, raspy voice that could shout down the heavens or purr intimately in her mother's ear, remembered coppery curly hair and sunbursts of pure energy, a giant who towered above other mortal men, a force of nature as dazzling and daunting as heat lightning in a summer sky. What she found at Chinon was a man of forty-nine who was not aging well, a man not much taller than her husband, with too many grey hairs, a stiff leg that throbbed when the weather changed, and hooded eyes etched in wrinkles that no longer looked like laugh lines. Heinrich had cautioned her to tread with care, fearful that too many questions about her mother might jeopardize Henry's favor, a risk they could not afford to take. But as she gazed into her father's face, she'd realized that the story of his ruined marriage and betrayals was writ plain for all to see, and her heart ached for him, for the mother sequestered in England, and for the little girl she'd once been, the child secure in the innocent belief that their family was, and would always be, favored by God.

A burst of laughter drew their eyes toward the middle bailey of the castle, where Henry and Heinrich were walking in the gardens. They'd just been joined by Tilda's three children—Richenza, Otto, and Heinrich—and five-year-old Otto was shrieking with delight as Henry swung him up into the air. The sight of her father taking such joy in his grandchildren brought a smile to Tilda's face, but it was tinged with sadness, for they'd been forced to leave their third son behind in Brunswick; Lothair's health was too frail for him to make the difficult journey from Saxony to Normandy. No matter how often Tilda told herself that she'd had no choice but to put the needs of her husband and other children before Lothair's, she continued to have dreams in which her absent son cried out for her at night. The separation was even harder because he was only eight, and she did not know if the emperor would keep his word and permit them to return in three years. Lothair could grow up without her. That fear gave her even greater sympathy for her mother, who'd been made to disappear from her children's lives as if by some malign spell, one cast by her own husband.

"Tell me the truth," she said, blue eyes moving from face to face. "How is Maman truly faring in confinement?"

Her brothers exchanged glances, and Hal said, lowering his voice instinctively even though they were not within their father's hearing, "Surely you talked to Papa about her. What did he tell you?"

"He insisted she was living in comfort and contentment, and then hastily changed the subject. He has spent more time discussing the French king's expulsion of the Jews from his realm and telling me about the new outbreak of war in Jerusalem between King Baldwin and the Saracen prince Saladin than he has talking about Maman. And when I asked why she could not cross over to Normandy to be with us at his Christmas Court, I never did get an answer from him."

"And you will not," Richard said sharply, "for the man is impossible to pin down even with a forked stick. If there is any justice, he will come back in his next life as a snake or an eel."

Hal looked at his brother with dislike he made no attempt to conceal. The three of them had agreed to put the best face upon their mother's plight and to speak well of their father in Tilda's hearing, not wanting to make her exile any harder than it already was. He should have known that Richard would not hold to the bargain. "Hopefully in your next life, you'll come back as a mute!"

Richard's eyes narrowed. "A pity you were not born a woman in this life, Little King of Lesser Land, for you seek only to please and to be admired by all. You'd have made a right fine whore."

Tilda gasped. She did not understand why he'd called Hal "Little King of Lesser Land," although she recognized it as a grave insult. Geoffrey did understand and bit back a grin; Richard was quoting from a song by the troubadour Bertran de Born, who'd mocked Hal for not displaying more martial fervor.

Hal flushed, but he lashed back at once, saying with all the contempt at his command, "And a pity you were not lowborn in this life, that the blood of kings keeps you from following your heart's desire. You are never happier than when you are up to your knees in blood and guts and gore. Clearly the Almighty meant you to be a butcher."

Hal knew his retort had missed its mark as soon as the words left his mouth, even before Richard laughed at him. "When men fight, they bleed and sometimes they die, for war is not as pretty or fanciful as your tourney games. War is real, so little wonder you like it not."

"Rot in Hell!" Hal spat, but Geoffrey decided to intercede before things got totally out of hand, and interrupted Hal in mid-curse.

"We're attracting an audience," he warned, nodding toward the bailey below, and the others saw that he was right. As their voices had risen, men were beginning to look upward, including Henry and Heinrich. When her husband beckoned to her, Tilda was only too happy to comply, for she'd been shaken by what she'd just witnessed. Geoffrey escorted her down to the gardens, but she could not forget that ugly scene up on the battlements and came to a sudden stop while her husband and Henry were still out of earshot.

"They sounded as if they hate each other, Geoffrey. How did it ever get to this?"

"Blame the Demon Countess of Anjou," he said flippantly. "If we're the Devil's spawn as our enemies claim, we are only being true to our nature. But it is not only Hal and Richard, sweeting. If I were drowning, Brother Richard would throw me a lifeline with an anchor attached to it, and in all honesty, I'd do as much for him."

Tilda stared at him. She did not know this man, did not know any of them. What had happened to her family? And standing there in the warm, sunlit bailey, she shivered, suddenly sorry that she'd ever come home.

THAT AUTUMN HAL made another demand for territory of his own, insisting that Henry give him Normandy. When Henry refused, Hal withdrew to Paris in a rage and announced he was taking the cross and going to the Holy Land to fight the infidels. Henry entreated him in vain to reconsider. He did not agree to return to his father's court until Henry promised to increase his allowance to a generous one hundred Angevin pounds a day with an additional ten pounds a day for Marguerite and to pay for the cost of maintaining one hundred knights in Hal's household for a year.

Henry had decided to hold his Christmas Court that year at Caen and spared no expense to make it a memorable occasion—as an official welcome for his daughter and her husband and proof that the tattered family loyalty of the Angevins was once more intact and flying high. Heinrich had gone on pilgrimage to the Spanish shrine of Santiago de Compostela while Tilda remained in her father's care, but he returned in time for the December festivities. So did Hal and Marguerite. Only John and Eleanor were absent, both of them left behind in England.

CHAPTER THIRTY-THREE

December 1182
Caen, Normandy

AN ICY RAIN HAD BEEN ASSAILING the riverside city of Caen since midday, but the king's solar that evening was a cheerful scene, shutters barred against the storm, a hungry fire in the hearth. Henry's Christmas Court had drawn princes of the Church, barons and their ladies, and more than a thousand knights. The gathering in the solar was an informal one, though, for Henry was determined to spend some time with his family in as much privacy as a king could reasonably expect.

Richard was due to arrive any day, but the others were all present: Tilda and her husband, Geoffrey and Constance, Hal and Marguerite. If any thoughts were spared for Eleanor, the ghost at the feast, they were not expressed aloud and Henry was in a mellow mood, delighted to have his daughter back, relieved to have lured Hal away from the Paris court and his too-helpful young brother-in-law. It was one more worry for Henry that the seventeen-year-old French king had begun to show greater steadiness of purpose and will than Hal, who was fully ten years Philippe's elder.

Tilda was comfortably ensconced on the settle, with her father on one side and her husband on the other. Hal and Marguerite were together in a window-seat and

Constance was seated in a high-backed chair, with Geoffrey lounging on cushions at her feet. Henry's grandchildren had just been ushered out of the solar, reluctantly sent off to their beds, and the echoes of their carefree laughter seemed to linger pleasantly in the air. Marveling at the resilience of the very young, who were able to take even exile in stride, Henry found himself hoping that their stay at his court would be an extended one. It had been a long time since he'd been able to enjoy the simple pleasures of parenthood.

"Have you talked to Richenza about a name change?" he asked his daughter and Tilda gave him a shy, sideways smile.

"Yes, Papa, we have. We explained that Richenza is a foreign-sounding name to Norman or English ears and highborn brides often take names more familiar to their husbands' subjects, like my sister Leonora. Richenza seemed comfortable enough with the idea, but wanted to choose her own name. Fortunately, she does not have Joanna's fertile imagination, and she decided she'd like to be called Matilda, after me."

Henry was pleased that his mother's name was being kept alive in a new generation; Matilda was the Latin form of Maude. Hal and Marguerite expressed their approval of Richenza's new name, but Constance mused aloud whether Richenza's brother Otto would change his foreign-sounding name, too, and Henry gave his daughter-in-law a tight smile, sure that she was amusing herself at his expense. He was very fond of Marguerite and he'd done his best to like Constance, too, but she did not make it easy, putting him in mind of Eleanor on her worst behavior. She was adept at delivering pinprick wounds with a smile, planting her barbs with a specious air of innocence. He was not going to let his son's caustic wife ruin the Christmas revelries, though. He could only hope that Geoffrey thought Brittany was worth her peevish tempers.

He'd begun to question Tilda and Heinrich about the son they'd had to leave in Brunswick when a servant entered with welcome word: his son Richard had just ridden into the castle bailey. Richard made his appearance soon afterward, for he'd not bothered to change from his travel clothes and his boots were still caked with mud. He greeted his father and Heinrich with rather formal courtesy, kissed his sister on the cheek, and gave courtly kisses to his sisters-in-law. But he acknowledged his brothers with a flat, toneless "Hal" and "Geoffrey," greetings they returned with equal terseness, the tension so palpable that even Henry, blind believer in family unity, could not help noticing.

He had no time to fret about it, though, for Richard at once revealed what was on his mind. "I do not understand," he said, "why my mother was excluded from the Christmas festivities."

Henry stiffened. These arguments about Eleanor had been occurring with more and more frequency, but this was the first time that Richard had thrown down the gauntlet before others. His son did not even wait for his response, saying curtly, "You know how much she wants to see Tilda and her grandchildren. How can you justify keeping her away?"

Henry was sorely tempted to remind his troublesome son that he did not have to justify himself to anyone, one of the prerogatives of kingship. But because he wanted to extinguish this quarrel as quickly as possible, he said only, "It is neither the time nor the place for this discussion, Richard."

Richard would not be distracted, though, knowing his father was a past master at such evasive tactics. Instead, he sought allies and turned toward his sister. "Tilda has not seen our mother in fifteen years. You think she was not disappointed by this arbitrary decision of yours?"

Tilda's husband closed his hand over hers, giving a warning squeeze. She understood his concern; her father had been extremely generous to them, providing a lavish allowance while continuing his efforts to shorten the length of their exile. But Richard was right; she wanted to see her mother very much, and her father's vague promises had done little to fill that void.

"I admit I am eager for Maman to meet your grandchildren, Papa," she ventured, in a vain attempt to satisfy her husband, her father, and her own conscience.

"And it shall happen, Tilda," Henry said, in a much softer tone of voice than he'd used with Richard. "I promised you that we will arrange for your return to England this spring, at which time you may visit with your mother to your heart's content." Still smarting over Richard's "arbitrary" accusation, he regarded his son coolly. "You seem to have forgotten how perilous Channel crossings can be. Even in good weather, it is dangerous. It's less than seven years since your brother Hal's chamberlain and three hundred souls drowned when their ship went down off the French coast. Did you truly want your mother to risk a crossing in December, of all months?"

Richard started to speak, stopped himself, and Henry felt a satisfying moment of triumph, for even this stubborn son of his could not refute the truth. December crossings were dangerous, and they all knew it. But it was then that Constance chose to dip her oar into troubled waters, saying in the painstakingly polite tones of one earnestly seeking information, "But ought that not to have been a decision for the queen to make? She may have considered the risk worth taking."

Henry drew upon a lifetime of self-control to say calmly to his daughter-in-law, "Forgive me for speaking bluntly, my dear, but this is not truly your concern, is it?"

Constance always knew when a strategic retreat was called for, and she withdrew from the field. But Henry's rebuke now drew Geoffrey into the fray. "Surely you'd agree that it is *my* concern, Papa. I am no happier about Maman's absence than Richard. And my wife is right—you should have offered her the choice."

"Whether that be true or not, the fact remains that it is done and cannot be undone. I do not see any point, therefore, in continuing this discussion."

"I expected you to say that." Richard strode forward, stopping in front of his father. "And you're right. It is too late to redeem my mother's Christmas. But the time is past due to discuss her continuing confinement. She is about to begin her tenth year as your prisoner, and for what reason?"

Henry got to his feet, not liking the way Richard loomed over him when he was seated. "Enough, Richard. Let it be."

"You've forgiven all the others who took part in the rebellion. You welcomed that French fool Louis to Canterbury, whilst knowing that he bore as much blame as anyone for the revolt. You pardoned the rebel lords, even that dolt Leicester, a man who drew his sword upon you, for Christ's sake! You ought to have sent the bastard to the block, but instead you restored his lands. The only one who continues to suffer for her past sins is my mother, and I want to know why. I want you to tell me here and now why you refuse to set her free!"

"I'd be interested in hearing that answer myself," Geoffrey interjected, and Hal now chimed in, too, saying that he also wanted to know.

Henry looked from one to the other, saw that they were all allied against him in this, and that knowledge was as bitter as gall. "I told you once before that I would not discuss my wife with you, Richard, and nothing has changed. I would suggest that you apologize to your sister for your bad manners and that for the remainder of the Christmas Court, you remember this. If you will not accord me the respect due your father, then by God, you'll give it to your king. Now this conversation is done, and I'll say no more on it."

For a long moment, he stared down his sons, daring them to protest. They did not, but their silence was shrouded in hostility and he knew it. Bidding good night to Tilda, Heinrich, and Marguerite, he left the solar without looking back.

By the time Henry reached the bottom of the stairwell, he'd still not decided whether he'd return to the great hall or withdraw to his own chamber. But when he opened the door, he came to a halt, for the storm had intensified and rain was coming down sideways. He'd left his mantle behind in the solar and, after his dramatic departure, he did not want to go back for it. Sheltered from the worst of the wind, he gazed out across the deserted bailey, thinking that this bleak sight was a good match for his mood.

He particularly resented the accusation that he meant to keep Tilda and Eleanor apart. As if he'd be that cruel! The perilous Channel crossing had definitely been a factor in his decision; why else would he not have summoned Johnny to join them? And if he'd wanted to enjoy one Christmas without having to share his daughter with Eleanor, what of it? He was entitled to that much.

Tilda's coming had forced him to face a painful truth—that his children sided with Eleanor. He thought he understood why their sons continued to agitate for her release; they had to feel guilty that she'd paid so high a price for their rebellion. And he'd not blamed Joanna for failing to comprehend the enormity of Eleanor's offense, for she was just a child. But Tilda was a woman grown, and he'd expected better from her. Heinrich saw the truth of it. What greater sin could a wife commit than to turn upon her own husband? Why was Tilda so willing to forgive it?

The answer seemed all too obvious. His children loved their mother in a way that they did not love him. Assuming that they loved him at all. He doubted that Richard did, could find nothing in his second son's eyes but resentment and reproach. Since wedding that Breton bitch, Geoffrey had grown more distant, more guarded. And Hal was . . . Hal. More and more, his eldest son was beginning to remind him of the man who'd stolen his mother's crown—Stephen, so charming and good-hearted and courageous, so utterly inept at the mastery of other men. Thank Christ for Johnny. There were times when it was only the thought of his youngest son that kept him from utter despair.

The rain had yet to slacken off, and it occurred to him that, just as he was trapped by the storm, he was trapped by his own family, by his inability to give his sons an honest answer to Richard's angry question. But how could he tell them that their mother's continuing confinement was their fault? The truth was that he'd have freed Eleanor long ago if only he could trust them. He still did not fully comprehend why she'd rebelled, but he no longer doubted the sincerity of her regrets. Nor did he still believe that she'd throw herself at once into plots and conspiracies if he set her free. He did not fear, as he once had, that she'd do all in her power to revenge herself upon him. But he never doubted that if one of their sons rebelled again, she'd draw upon the considerable resources of Aquitaine on behalf of that son, offering her unqualified support. Especially if that son was Richard.

He'd never underestimated his wife's shrewdness or her cunning or her ability to dissemble, to beguile others into doing her bidding. He'd valued her for those very qualities—until she'd turned them against him. But even if she'd made it safely to Paris nine years ago, her presence would not have tipped the balance in their favor, for men like Louis and Philip of Flanders would never have heeded the advice of a woman.

Henry laughed suddenly, mirthlessly. Any man who thought women were the weaker vessels had never met his mother—or his queen. Thank God Almighty that she'd not been able to take the field against him. But now she had Richard, the son who was most like him, the son who loved him not. He remained confident that he would prevail if Richard ever rebelled again. But Richard would pose a greater challenge than any foe he'd fought, and he was too pragmatic to deny it. Until Richard and his brothers proved that they could be truly trusted, the way a man ought to be able to trust his sons, how could he risk letting Eleanor go? And yet, how could he say that to Richard or Geoffrey or Hal? How could he confess that he still harbored such doubts and misgivings about their loyalty? He could only ask the Almighty and St Thomas to show his sons the error of their ways, to pray that they saw the light ere it was too late.

Raised voices came to his ears now, muffled in the winding stairwell. Either his sons were squabbling again or making ready to depart. He looked out dubiously into the wet, gloomy night, remembering when he'd been utterly indifferent to such storms, when his body had not yet begun to show the results of so many years of hard riding and careless confidence in his own invincibility. Shivering as he stepped out into the rain, he could take no comfort from the irony of it—that he and his exiled wife were sharing the same wretched Christmas.

THE LAST MONTHS of God's Year 1182 were among the most miserable of Will Marshal's life. Without the favor of his lord, the young king, he felt like a ship gone adrift, lacking moorings or direction. Because the other knights of Hal's mesnie did not know why they'd fallen out, speculation ran rampant and Will found himself the target of gossip and innuendo, vulnerable to the malice of his enemies. And enemies he had, for his privileged position in Hal's household and his spectacular tournament successes had long provoked the envy and jealousy of lesser knights. Too proud to acknowledge the talk, Will did his best to ignore the whispers and stares, but his heaviest burden was that he could not confide in his friends, could not reveal the cause of the young king's displeasure—not without betraying Hal's confidence.

Will was accustomed to being Hal's confidant, basking in their friendship even though he knew it had cost him the good will of the old king; Henry blamed him for failing to curb Hal's whims and reckless spending. Will did not think that was fair, but he accepted that kings were often unfair and there was naught to be done about it. What he could not accept was the sudden change in his status. Hal no longer sought his advice, no longer wanted his companionship. It was as if the last twelve years had never been.

It had begun that autumn when Will noticed Hal's preoccupation, his moodiness. He'd always believed that his duties involved more than protecting Hal from an enemy's lance, a foe's sword thrust; he was often called upon to protect Hal from himself. He'd encouraged Hal to reveal the source of his distraction, and finally it had all come spilling out—the blandishments of the Poitevin lords, his hunger for lands of his own, and his loathing for his brother Richard. Will had been appalled once he realized Hal was entangling himself in such a lethal spider's web, and he'd spoken out forthrightly against it, with a blunt candor that kings did not often hear. Hal had been furious and ever since their quarrel, he'd kept Will at a distance. Will did not even know if he still intended to follow through with this folly. In his despair, he'd considered approaching the queen, but he'd soon abandoned that idea; Marguerite was not cast in the same mold as her mother-in-law. All he could do was to wait—for Hal's temper to cool, for his common sense to reassert itself. What he would do if neither happened, he did not know.

It was not until his friends came to him on a rain-sodden December night at Caen that Will learned what was being said behind his back—that he was guilty of far worse than arrogance or pride, that he was seeking to cuckold his lord, to seduce Hal's lovely young queen. Accustomed as he was to the spite and jealousy that thrived in the artificial atmosphere of a royal court, he was dumbfounded by such baneful rancor, for he was being accused of the greatest crime a man could commit against his liege lord.

Baldwin de Bethune, Simon de Marisco, and Peter de Preaux had agonized over warning him of the stories being circulated, at last deciding that it was more dangerous for him not to know. They watched Will now with sympathetic eyes, bracing themselves for the questions to come.

"How did you find this out?" he asked at last, and they explained that the conspirators had tried to win over one of Hal's friends, Raoul de Hamars, hoping that he'd take the tale to Hal. But Raoul had scoffed at the story, and instead of warning Hal, he'd chosen to warn Will's friends.

"At least all are not willing to believe the worst of me. Who are these men who slander me so foully?"

They were reluctant to say, fearing an even greater scandal, but Will was insistent and they were forced to reveal that the ringleaders were Adam d'Yquebeuf and Sir Thomas de Coulonces. Just as they'd feared, Will at once announced his intention of challenging them to combat, vowing to clear his name—and the queen's—with the power of his strong right arm.

"You cannot do that, Will! If you proclaim yourself innocent of adultery, you'd be spreading the scandal even farther, making sure that all who'd not heard the rumors now know of them. That would do you no good, would shame the queen—and the king."

Will's shoulders slumped, for he realized Baldwin was right. Surely Hal could not know of this. If he had, would he not have acted? Would he not have punished the men who'd dared to slander his queen? But Will discovered that he still had to ask. Looking from one face to the other, he finally blurted it out. "Does Lord Hal know of these rumors?"

None of them seemed in a hurry to answer him. "We are not sure," Simon admitted. "Raoul de Hamars agreed to find out more, and reported that after he'd refused to pass the story on, they got one of Lord Hal's pages drunk and convinced him it was his duty to tell the king. Supposedly Hal laughed it off, forcing them to take more drastic action, and they then came to him, swearing on their honor that it was so."

Seeing Will's look of dismay, Baldwin said hastily, "We do not know if that truly happened. It is only what Raoul was told when he went out drinking with Thomas de Coulonces."

Will fell silent. He'd assumed that Hal's coldness was due to their quarrel, to his disapproval of Hal's grand schemes for claiming Aquitaine. But what if he'd been wrong? What if Hal had heard these vile accusations and believed them?

"What will you do?" Simon asked, and Will could only shrug.

"I do not know . . . yet."

T HE CASTLE CHAPLAIN accompanied Hal into the church of St George, and Hal feared that he'd continue to hover, but he excused himself at once, promising to make sure the king would not be disturbed during his prayers.

"Thank you, Father Matthew," Hal said with a smile, sighing with relief when he was finally alone, for that was a rarity in his life; even more than his father, he seemed to be a magnet for all eyes. Usually he enjoyed such attention, but this Christmas Court at Caen was different and he longed to escape the constant scrutiny, to have time to himself without any demands being made upon him. Realizing that a church ought to be a good place to find solitude, he'd decided to take refuge there, although he did intend to pray, too; he was in God's House, after all.

Hal had always loved Christmas. Not this year. Part of the reason for his discontent was being thrown into such close proximity with Richard. His brother's glowering presence made it impossible for him to ignore his misgivings, reminding him that he had to make a decision soon. Did he commit himself irrevocably to the rebels in Aquitaine or did he step back from the cliff's edge? The trouble was that he did not truly know what he wanted to do. Well, he knew he wanted Aquitaine, but he was not sure he wanted to fight to the death for it. And after his talk with Geoffrey, he'd realized how naïve he'd been, how shortsighted. How could he have been so certain that their father would stand aside whilst two of his sons destroyed the third?

For that was what it would come to—Richard's destruction. Only death could make his brother accept the loss of Aquitaine. And would Maman forgive him for that? She'd always had an inexplicable fondness for Richard. No, it would not be as easy as he'd first thought. He did not want to alienate or hurt his mother, nor did he want to fight his father again. But how could he walk away from such an opportunity? If he held Aquitaine, he'd no longer be answerable to his father for every denier he spent; he'd finally have enough money to reward his liegemen, to attract the best knights to his banner, to buy a stallion without fretting about Papa's dour disapproval, to indulge Marguerite as she deserved.

That was why he'd again asked his father for Normandy, for it would be the perfect solution to his dilemma, giving him his own duchy without any of the risks that taking Aquitaine entailed. But of course Papa had balked. When had he ever listened to reason? And now the vultures were circling for certes. Aimar of Limoges had turned up in Caen, ostensibly to prove he was honoring the summer's peace, but in reality, to remind Hal of his commitment to the rebels. He'd even brought news that Richard had obligingly given them the ideal excuse for attacking Aquitaine; he'd begun to build a castle at Clairvaux, in an area that was under the sway of the Counts of Anjou. Hal was not surprised that Richard should be poaching in his woods. He was surprised, though, that he was not better pleased about it, for, as Aimar had been quick to point out, he was now the wronged one, justified in protecting his own domains. But because Richard had given him a legitimate grievance, he felt even more pressured to take action. Soon all of Christendom would know of Richard's encroachment into Anjou, thanks to that impudent poet. According to Geoff, Bertran de Born had written one of his mocking verses about Clairvaux, claiming it shone so brightly that the young king could not help but see it.

It seemed to Hal that the fates were conspiring to force him into making a decision ere he was ready, and he yearned for another opinion, one dispassionate and dependable. But he, who'd always had friends beyond counting, had no trusted confidant when he most needed one. He could not consult Geoff, for his brother would be scornful of his inability to make up his mind. In that, Geoff was like Richard, both of them strangers to doubts or forebodings. None of his knights could be relied upon, either. They'd tell him what they thought he wanted to hear or they'd be unable to keep such a secret and blab it all over creation.

Nor could he turn to the two people he most trusted, his wife and Will Marshal. He'd hinted to Marguerite of his intentions, and mere hints had been enough to alarm her greatly. No, he could not confide in Marguerite and that created problems, too, for she wanted him to take her to the holy shrine of Our Lady at Rocamadour in southern Aquitaine once the winter weather broke. She'd learned that barren women often conceived after making a pilgrimage to Rocamadour, and she'd been both hurt and bewildered by his refusal. Nor could he explain that Aquitaine might well be at war by the spring.

And Will had let him down badly, acting for all the world as if he were about to commit high treason in attacking Richard. At the time that he most needed Will's support, the knight had lectured him about his duty to his father and liege lord, droned on about fidelity and sworn vows and nonsense like that. It was particularly infuriating because Will knew how shabbily Papa treated him, knew, too, what a swine Richard could be. Hal's tempers rarely lasted long; he'd never been one for holding grudges. But so great was his disappointment that he'd found it difficult to forgive Will. Then, just when he'd decided to let Will back into his good graces, those idiots had come to him with their absurd accusations.

He had been outraged, both by their suspicions and the terrible timing. Here he was about to make the most important decision of his entire life, and he was supposed to deal with tawdry gossip like this? He'd ordered them from his chamber after warning them not to repeat such vile rumors. But somehow he found himself blaming Will, too, for his unwitting part in this farce. All he wanted was enough time to consider all his options without being dragged into his household's petty squabbles or being nagged by his wife about that damnable pilgrimage. Was that so much to ask?

Apparently so, for he'd yet to find a peaceful moment at Caen, not with Marguerite sulking and Aimar lurking and Will acting put-upon and Geoff wanting to lay plans and Richard strutting around as if he were the incarnation of Roland and poor Tilda grieving over Maman's absence and his father refusing to heed any voice but his own. He was sorry he'd let himself be talked out of going to the Holy Land. At least there it would be simple enough—fight the infidels and protect the sacred city of Jerusalem from Saladin and his Saracen hordes.

By now Hal had convinced himself that few men had suffered the burdens he was expected to bear. A pity he could not stay here in the hushed quiet of the church, for it seemed a world away from the chaos and turmoil of his life. It occurred to him then to ask the Almighty for guidance, and he wondered why he hadn't thought of that before. Feeling more cheerful, he approached the high altar, knelt, and prayed for a sign, for some manifestation of God's Will, so that he would know what the Lord wanted him to do. He was just getting to his feet when a clamor erupted outside, the door slammed, and his brother Richard stalked into the church, trailed by the flustered priest.

"My liege, I am sorry!" the priest stammered. "I told the lord duke that you were at your prayers, but he would not wait."

"Do not distress yourself, Father Matthew. The lord duke is not known for his good manners. In fact, they are so deplorable that some suspect he was raised by wolves."

"Whereas you are the veritable soul of courtesy," Richard jeered. "You'd be sure to ask ere you borrowed a man's dagger to stab him in the back, and I daresay you'd wipe it clean afterward."

"What are you babbling about now, Richard?"

"Did you think I would not find out? I know about your treacherous double-dealing with my vassals, know about your visit to Limoges this summer. You gave the monks a banner for their abbey, one with *Henricus Rex* inscribed in gold thread. What else did you give them, Hal—a promise that you'd be a far more benevolent liege lord than me?"

"I'd hardly have to tell them that," Hal said coolly, "as anyone with eyes to see knows it already. I've even heard it said that Fulk Nerra would have been a more benevolent lord than you. Is this what you are whining about, my visit to Limoges? Need I remind you that Limoges is on the way to Périgueux? You might as well complain that I stopped in St-Denis on a journey to Paris!"

"My lords . . ." the priest began timidly, but they ignored him utterly, glaring at each other with such hostility that he was thankful swords were not worn at the Christmas Court.

"Your conspicuous sojourn in Limoges was only the beginning of the trail," Richard snapped. "I assumed that you'd conspire as carelessly as you do everything else and, indeed, you covered your tracks very sloppily. You've been meeting with malcontent lords from the Limousin and Poitou for some time now, offering a sympathetic ear for their complaints and—"

"That is my great crime—feeling sorry for your ill-used barons? I freely admit to it. I feel sorry for anyone who has to suffer your foul tempers, Little Brother. But that hardly constitutes proof of conspiracy and rebellion."

"Ere I'm done, I'll have enough proof to convince even your wife. And when I do, I'll make a formal protest to our father. If he gives me no satisfaction—and I rather hope he does not—I will deal with you myself, and you'll not find me as forgiving as he is. You can wager the surety of your soul on that."

"As entertaining as your rants always are, I have no more time to waste with you." Hal started to brush past his brother, but Richard grabbed his arm.

"We are not done here!"

Hal swung around and brought the stiffened edge of his hand down upon Richard's wrist, breaking his brother's hold. Richard lunged forward just as the priest desperately flung himself between them. Both of the king's sons were much taller than he, and he found himself crushed between them, his nose buried in Richard's mantle, unable to see their faces but feeling such tension in their bodies that he was terrified there'd be blood shed in his church, for he'd remembered that they'd be carrying eating knives.

"My lords, please . . ." he pleaded, but they were exchanging curses, calling each other names so vile that he doubted they'd even heard him. They did hear, though, the astonished exclamation from the direction of the door, and they stepped back, allowing Father Matthew to breathe again as they confronted two of their father's most distinguished guests, the Archbishops of Canterbury and Dublin.

The Archbishop of Canterbury was a mild-mannered individual, utterly unlike his predecessor, the fiery Thomas Becket, not one who'd be eager to rebuke the king's sons. Fortunately for Father Matthew, the Archbishop of Dublin was made of sterner stuff. "What sort of outrageous behavior is this?" he demanded, striding down the nave so swiftly that his cope billowed out behind him, giving him the appearance of a ship under full sail. "Would you spill blood in God's House? For shame, my lords, for shame!"

Hal recovered his poise first, patting the priest apologetically on the shoulder as he moved to greet the prelates. "You are quite right, my lord archbishop. There is no excuse for our bad behavior, and I beg your pardon. I will be sure to confess this transgression to my chaplain so that he may impose a suitable penance."

Watching as his brother pacified the archbishops, Richard shook his head in disgust. He knew he should keep silent, but he'd been watching Hal perform these conjuring tricks as long as he could remember, and as Hal started up the aisle with the clerics, his bitterness spilled over. "You could rob a man blind in broad daylight and then somehow make it seem as if he were the one at fault. But if you meddle again in Aquitaine, all your smiles and pretty compliments will not save you. Nothing will!"

Hal could recognize an opportunity when he was presented with one, and he paused at the door, then turned without haste, and looked back at his furious brother. "You put me in mind, Richard, of a cuckolded husband bewailing his wife's infidelity, when he is the one who drove her into another man's arms." And confident that he'd gotten the last word, he departed the church with the archbishops, leaving Richard standing by the high altar, fuming, but vowing that Hal would not get away with his treachery, not this time.

ON THE DAY AFTER CHRISTMAS, Henry was obliged to hold a hearing to adjudicate a bizarre incident that had happened during the Christmas feast. As a silver basin of scented water was borne to the king's table so that he and his guests might wash their hands before the meal began, William de Tancarville, a highborn Norman baron, had rushed forward, forcibly seized the basin, and insisted upon carrying it to Henry himself, refusing afterward to surrender the basin to Henry's indignant chamberlain. De Tancarville did not lack for enemies, and protests were made, resulting in the next day's session. Henry had no liking for de Tancarville, for the baron had been one of the first to defect to Hal in the rebellion of 1173, but he accepted the man's passionate defense: that as the hereditary chamberlain of Normandy, it was his sole privilege to attend his duke on ceremonial occasions.

While Hal had been amused by the fracas in the hall, he was fidgeting and squirming in his seat as he listened to de Tancarville proclaim his right to retain custody of the silver basin, for it had occurred to him that Richard might see this as the ideal forum to charge him with subverting his rule in Aquitaine. He was reasonably confident that Richard did not have convincing evidence yet, but his brother might well choose to make a public scene after their confrontation in St George's chapel. He was relieved, therefore, when the proceedings were finally concluded, and Richard's window of opportunity slammed shut. But before Henry or any of the lords could withdraw, Will Marshal strode toward the center of the hall and declared, "My lord king" in a clear, carrying voice.

Henry sat down again reluctantly, wondering why he could not enjoy one peaceful Christmas without any drama or strife. But then he saw that the king being approached was Hal, and he settled back to watch, as did the rest of the men in the hall.

"Sire, hear me." Will was very nervous, more uneasy than he'd ever been before a tournament or a battle, but when he spoke, his voice revealed none of his inner turmoil. "I have been unjustly accused of a vicious and vile act of treason. I am here to defend myself before you and your noble father and these assembled lords and barons. Have the men who accused me come forward and agree to meet me in combat. I will fight three of them in turn, and if I am defeated in any contest, I am willing to forfeit my life, for I would not want to live if I could not clear my name."

As soon as Will stopped speaking, the hall was utterly still. Hal could feel every eye upon him, and he felt a sudden flare of anger, resentment that Will should pick this inopportune moment to make his overwrought, theatrical challenge. Will made it sound as if he were not in control of his own household knights. His father was watching him with an enigmatic expression, and Geoffrey looked puzzled, but Richard was smiling faintly, and that smile was enough to arouse all of Hal's suspicions. Had Richard put Will up to this? They'd always been too friendly for his liking. For that matter, Will was de Tancarville's cousin. Could that odd event have been deliberately staged to give Will this chance to appear before the king's court? If he allowed the trial by combat, this would drag on for three days, delaying their departure from Caen. Was that what Richard had in mind? Was he seeking time to produce witnesses, a Poitevin baron that he'd coerced into making a confession?

"I do not know what you are talking about, Marshal," he said sharply, "and I will not have my household disrupted with petty personal quarrels. There will be no trial by combat. Now let that be an end to it."

Will looked at him gravely, and to Hal's discomfort, he felt heat rising in his face under that unblinking regard. Pushing back his chair, he got to his feet, and that seemed to break the spell. But instead of withdrawing, Will turned and knelt before Henry.

"Sire, I can no longer remain at court. I beg you to grant me safe conduct through your domains." Henry was glad to do so, wishing he could rid himself of all of Hal's knights, and Will bowed stiffly, then departed the hall, holding his head high and paying no heed to the buzz of questions and conjecture that swirled in his wake.

WILL MARSHAL'S ACTIONS had created a furor, and for the rest of the evening, there was no other topic of conversation, for Will was a star on the tournament circuit, and all thought it odd that Hal would have parted with such a redoubtable knight. Most of the men did not know what Will had been accused of, for the rumors had not spread much beyond Hal's household. Shaken by Will's challenge, for none of them wanted to meet him on the field, the conspirators kept quiet, doing their best not to call attention to themselves. The paucity of facts did not discourage gossip, though, and it seemed to Hal that there was not a soul in Caen who did not have a theory about Will's fall from favor, and every last one of them was eager to expound upon it at great length.

Hal discovered now that there was a drawback to the sort of popularity he'd long enjoyed. He was well liked by virtually everyone and greatly admired for his tournament successes, but men felt free to approach him with a familiarity they'd not have dared to show his father or Richard. Much to his annoyance, he found himself having to deflect obtrusive questions, avid curiosity, and speculation that he considered both unseemly and presumptuous. Pride kept him from making an early departure from the hall, but when he was finally able to withdraw to his own chambers, he was weary and thoroughly out of sorts.

But in his bedchamber, Hal found that an unpleasant evening was about to get much worse. Marguerite had excused herself after they'd eaten, pleading a headache, but she was still fully dressed, and her face was so pale and drawn that he felt a pang of guilt, for he'd been so consumed with his own troubles that he'd not had a thought to spare for her.

"Sweetheart, you do not look well at all. Shall I send Benoit to summon a doctor?" Glancing around the chamber, he noticed for the first time that neither his squires nor Marguerite's ladies were in attendance. "Where did the lads wander off to?"

"I dismissed them." Marguerite startled Hal by crossing the chamber and sliding the bolt into place. She stayed by the door, arms folded tightly across her breasts. "I must know, Hal. Do you believe that gossip about Will Marshal and me?"

Hal was shocked. "Jesu, you heard that?"

"Agace came to me, believing—correctly—that I needed to know. It did not occur to me that you credited it, though—not until today."

"Sweetheart, of course I do not believe it!" He moved swiftly to her side, but when he put his arm around her, her body remained rigid in his embrace. "Never for a moment did I think there might be any truth to it. I swear that to you, Marguerite, upon the soul of our dead son, may God assoil him."

He could feel some of the tension go out of her shoulders, but when she gazed up into his face, her blue eyes were still shadowed with anxiety and uncertainty. "You do believe, though, that Will made improper advances to me. And he did not, Hal, that I swear, too, upon our son."

"Marguerite, there is no need for this. I know Will would never betray me like that."

Then why did you let him leave your court in disgrace? Marguerite did not voice the question, even though it burned on her tongue. Instead, she allowed herself to take a moment of comfort in her husband's arms, clinging to him as her refuge in a world gone mad.

Hal kissed the tear tracks on her cheeks, murmuring love words and endearments. But after a time, he said, "Sweetheart, why did you not come to me about this? I never dreamed that you'd heard these vile rumors. Why did you not tell me?"

"Because I know you've been troubled and uneasy in your mind about something and I did not want to add to your worries," she said, surprising herself by how readily the lie came to her lips. In truth, she'd been waiting for him to take action, to banish the culprits from his court, and she still did not understand why he'd not done that.

"Hal . . . if you believe Will to be innocent of these charges, why are you still so displeased with him? What has he done that you cannot forgive?"

"It is not important," he insisted, and he sought to stop further questions with kisses. But for once, she was not as compliant. Stepping back, she searched his face intently and then repeated her question. Hal was momentarily at a loss. He did not like lying outright to her, considered that a more serious marital offense than lies of omission.

"Tell me," she pleaded. "We promised there'd be no secrets between us, not like your parents. It has long been obvious to me that something is wrong, and I've been waiting for you to confide in me. I can wait no longer, Hal. I want to know now, tonight."

He was both surprised and amused by her sudden assertiveness. But he was touched, too, and he realized that he did need to talk about his concerns. At least with Marguerite, he could rely upon her utter loyalty. Leading her over to the bed, he sat down with her, and after a brief hesitation, he began to speak. There was a relief in being able to speak candidly about his ambivalence, and he ended up telling her more than he'd initially intended. By the time he was done, she knew it all—the conspiracy with the lords of the Limousin and Poitou, the dazzling prospects offered by the capture of Aquitaine, his overtures to Geoffrey and her brother, Philippe, his temptations and his misgivings, even his chapel altercation with Richard.

"So," he concluded, "now you know." He waited expectantly, but she stayed silent, and her head was lowered, hiding her face from him. "Marguerite?"

"What do you want me to say?" When she glanced up at last, her eyes reminded him of the way Will had gazed at him in the hall, the silent reproach of a dog unable to understand why it had just been kicked. "Why, Hal, why must you risk so much?"

"Because there is so much to gain!" He was on his feet now, needing to move as he sought to deal with his disappointment. "You sound just like Will, but I expected better of you, Marguerite. You're my wife, and if I cannot rely upon your heartfelt support, then I am truly alone midst my enemies!"

"Of course I support you! It is just that . . . that I fear for you, too, beloved."

Her eyes were shimmering with tears, and he was quick to take her in his arms. They clung together with an urgency that revealed their shared misery more than words could have done, for they'd failed each other and on some level, they both understood that—Hal let down by her tepid response, Marguerite horrified by his intrigues and planned betrayals. Hastily shedding their clothes, they fell into bed. Their lovemaking was intense, ironically given an impassioned edginess by the very fears they were trying to escape. Afterward, Hal had no trouble sliding into an exhausted, sated sleep. Marguerite was not so lucky.

She lost track of the time, but she heard Hal's squires enter and bed down, heard church bells pealing in the distance, heard dogs barking, all the familiar sounds of night. But there was nothing familiar about her world, not anymore. She gently stroked Hal's tousled fair hair, and he murmured her name in his sleep, instinctively reaching out for her warmth and softness. Her throat was so tight that it hurt, for she was determined to choke back her tears. Oh, my beautiful boy, what have you done? She had no memories of a life without Hal. She still loved him dearly, would love him until she drew her last breath. But it was as if their roles had reversed, for she suddenly felt so much older and wiser than he. Watching him sleep, she found herself wondering if the Almighty, in His Infinite Wisdom, had taken her son because her husband would always be as he was now, a charming child adrift upon stormy seas.

A PALLID WINTER DAWN had not yet dispersed the night shadows, and a few stars still glimmered along the horizon. Because it was so early, the castle was not yet astir, and Will's leavetaking was witnessed only by a small group of friends and a few sleepy-eyed guards. Baldwin de Bethune and Simon de Morisco were doing their best to act hearty and jovial, making bad jokes and pretending that this morn was no different from any number of past departures. Will appreciated the effort, just as he appreciated their attempts to reassure him that his future still shone brightly, that Christendom was full of lords eager to snap him up like a starving trout. The practical part of his nature knew that they were right; he'd have no trouble finding a place in another great household. But that knowledge did not blunt the sharp edges of his newfound awareness—that he was thirty-five years old, with no lands or wife, cast aside by the man who'd been his friend, his liege lord, his lodestar.

He was not going alone, accompanied by his squire, Eustace de Bertrimont, and a few fellow knights who'd pledged themselves to his banner when it was flying high and were unwilling to abandon him now that his luck had soured. As he looked about at these loyal men, he could not help remembering how proud he'd been the first time he'd fought in a tournament as a knight banneret, leading his own company of men. That had been at Lagny, the tourney held after the young French king's coronation. Was that truly only two years past? It felt like a lifetime ago.

When his eyes began to burn, he awkwardly embraced his friends, submitted to their equally clumsy hugs, and swung up into the saddle. With their farewells echoing in his ears, he and his small party rode toward the gatehouse and out onto the drawbridge. The dawn continued to lighten, and a brisk wind sent clouds scudding across the sky. It would be a good day for travel. Spurring his stallion, he settled into an easy canter, not allowing himself to look back, keeping his eyes on the road ahead.

CHAPTER THIRTY-FOUR

January 1183
Le Mans, Anjou

AL NO LONGER HAD QUALMS about going ahead with the conspiracy. When he'd asked the Almighty for a divine sign, he'd not expected what he'd gotten. But the wrathful chapel altercation with his brother had dispelled his doubts. Aquitaine was worth fighting for, and Richard deserved to be defeated and shamed if any man did. Their father had to believe that Richard was the one in the wrong, though, if they hoped to keep him out of it, and so Hal was grateful for his brother's fiery, impulsive nature. If Richard had been more calculating, he'd have said nothing until he'd assembled his proof and then set up an ambush. As it was, Hal had the opportunity to plan his own response, and by the time the confrontation came, he was ready for it.

Summoned to Henry's bedchamber, he found his father and Richard waiting for him. Richard was leaning against the wall, arms folded across his chest, looking both defiant and expectant. Henry shared none of his son's anticipation; he looked tired and troubled. "Come in, Hal," he said. "Your brother has made some grave accusations against you. For all our sakes, I hope he is mistaken. These charges are too serious, though, to be dismissed out of hand. I thought it best that we discuss this matter in private. But if there is truth to his claims . . ."

Richard shot Henry a resentful glance. Could the old man make it any plainer how eager he was to believe Hal's denials? "Hal has been conspiring with my vassals against me," he said coldly, for he was determined to be matter-of-fact, not to let Hal bait him into losing his temper. "I do not know who was the instigator, whether he came to them with honeyed promises of a lenient lordship or whether they sought him out first. It does not really matter, does it? What does is that they have engaged in treason, scheming to depose me as Duke of Aquitaine and put Hal in my stead."

Hal regarded him calmly. "Have you any proof of this, Richard?"

"Yes, I do have proof," Richard said, with a smile like an unsheathed dagger. "I have a witness, one of the household knights of Viscount Aimar of Limoges. He is willing to testify that his lord met with you on numerous occasions, that you have been conspiring together to stir up a rebellion against me, and that you have involved others in your plot—including Joffroi de Lusignan, and those habitual rebels, the Taillefer brothers. So . . . deny it if you dare!"

After Richard accosted him in the chapel at Caen, Hal had been dreading this moment of reckoning. But now he found that he was actually enjoying himself, so confident was he of the stratagem he'd devised during those bleak days at the Christmas Court. "You are right, Papa. These are indeed serious charges, and I welcome the chance to respond to them. But not here. I want it done in public, before witnesses of unimpeachable probity, so that Richard cannot twist my words to suit his own ends."

Hal stifled a smile, gratified by the startled reactions of his father and brother. Sounding highly skeptical, Richard demanded to know when this would take place, and Hal did grin openly then, thinking that if suspicions were fuel, Richard would be a flaming torch. "The sooner the better," he said agreeably. "This afternoon, if it pleases you."

"It pleases me," Richard said grimly, and Henry looked from one to the other in utter dismay, singed by the heat of the hostility burning between them.

THE CASTLE'S GREAT HALL was the site for the drama Hal was about to stage. The royal family and the most honored of their guests had been ushered onto the dais. Henry was flanked by the Archbishops of Canterbury and Dublin. Geoffrey, Constance, Richard, Marguerite, Heinrich, and Tilda were seated nearby, and behind them stood Henry's natural son and chancellor, Geoff, the Bishop of Le Mans, and several of Henry's trusted advisors, including Willem and Maurice de Craon.

Catching Marguerite's eye, Hal winked, and she smiled, if rather wanly. He was amused to see that his father and brothers had retreated behind their inscrutable court masks, a clear indication that they were curious and uneasy, unsure of his intentions. That was exactly how he wanted them to be—slightly off balance. He was sorry that he'd not been able to warn Geoffrey beforehand, but it could not be helped. Glancing about the hall, he let the suspense build until all eyes were upon him, and then he raised his hand for silence.

He felt that rush of excitement that he imagined a player must feel the first time he stepped onto a stage and took command; he'd always thought that acting must be great fun. "Those who wish me ill have been spreading rumors about my loyalties." Ostensibly speaking to Henry, he was also playing to the audience, and many of them noticed that his eyes had lingered upon his brother Richard when he spoke of "those who wish me ill." Richard certainly did, and his mouth set in a hard, thin line.

"These accusations are baseless," Hal declared. "I would not have you harbor any doubts about that, sire." Taking the cue, his chaplain came forward, knelt before him, and held out a book bound in fine calfskin, beautifully illuminated in gold leaf, borrowed that day from the Bishop of Le Mans. Putting his hand upon the book, Hal said solemnly, "I swear upon the Holy Gospels that my fidelity to you is as true and steadfast as my faith in Christ the Redeemer. I further vow that I will be loyal to you, my liege, for all the days of my life, and show you the honor and obedience due you as my father and my king."

It was hard for Hal to read his father's expression, but the scornful twist of Richard's mouth needed no translation. *Let him smirk; the hellspawn was about to get the surprise of his life.* "I realize that oaths can be broken," he continued, thinking that his father had broken more than his share of them. "But I want there to be perfect trust between us from now on, and to prove my sincerity, I shall be utterly honest with you, my lord father. My brother Richard has accused me of plotting with his liegemen against him. I do not deny it. I did indeed enter into a pact with the disaffected barons of Poitou and the Limousin."

The stunned expression on Richard's face was quickly followed by one of triumphant wariness. Geoffrey simply looked horrified. But Henry had blanched, like a man bleeding from an internal wound. Hal ignored the murmur sweeping through the audience, and kept his eyes upon his father's face.

"I am sure that none here are surprised by the anger and resolve of the lord duke's barons. They have chafed for years under his heavy-handed rule, charging that he tramples their cherished traditions into the dust, that he makes free with their women, and imposes his will by force and violence. How could I not sympathize with legitimate grievances like that? But it was not sympathy that drove me into this conspiracy. It was his treachery. He has fortified a castle at Clairvaux, which lies within the holdings of the Count of Anjou—and all know it. Can you imagine his outrage, my lord father, if I'd intruded into Poitou and dared to put up a castle in his domains? It was this threat to the sovereignty of Anjou that stirred me to action, for I would not willingly cede so much as a shovelful of Angevin dirt to the Duke of Aquitaine!"

There was so much commotion in the hall now that Hal had to raise his voice to be heard over the clamor. "My only regret is that I did not come to you first, my liege, as soon as I learned of his perfidy. I ask you now to take the castle at Clairvaux from my brother and keep it in your own hands, so that peace may be restored to our family."

HAL WAS PLEASED with the outcome of his dramatic declaration, for all had gone as he'd expected. Richard was infuriated. Henry's attention had been diverted from Hal's wrongdoing to his brother's encroachment into Anjou. He'd impressed people, particularly the clerics, by his willingness to swear upon the Holy Gospels. His own knights were inspired by his boldness, and Richard's men were suddenly on the defensive. He did feel a prickle of remorse that Marguerite was so proud of his candor, knowing she believed that the conspiracy was now part of the past, but he assured himself that he'd make her understand when the time came.

The only surprise was that Geoffrey had not sought him out afterward for an explanation. He'd have liked to think that Geoffrey had instinctively understood what he was doing, but that unguarded, shocked expression on his brother's face argued otherwise, and as the evening wore on, he went looking for the Breton duke, to no avail. It was only when he found Geoffrey's squires, Jehan and Morgan, flirting in a window-seat with the castellan's fetching daughter that he learned Geoffrey and Constance had departed some time ago.

HAL STILL MARVELED that his brother seemed to enjoy such a satisfying sex life with the prideful, sharp-tongued Constance, but he could imagine no other reason for their abrupt withdrawal from the hall. After bounding up the stairs to their private chamber, he made sure to knock loudly on the door and waited until he heard Geoffrey call out, "Enter."

He was half expecting to find them in bed, but they were still fully dressed, seated together by the hearth. Smiling, he greeted his sister-in-law warmly before asking if he could borrow her husband for a brief time.

"You may speak freely in front of Constance."

Hal blinked, for he could not imagine trusting Constance the way he trusted Marguerite. He had no real interest in his brother's marriage, though. "As you will," he said affably. "I thought you might have some questions for me."

"Did you, indeed?" Geoffrey's eyes had always been changeable, but now they were as grey as flint and just as welcoming. "Unfortunately, they're questions I ought to have asked you last summer at Limoges. You were so busy instructing me how Richard and I would captain our arks that we never got around to discussing your own views on seamanship. A pity, for it would have been useful to know that you were a believer in lightening the load when you ran into rough waters. At the very least, it would have prepared me when you chose to push our allies over the side. I can only wonder why you did not throw me overboard, too—unless you're saving me for a particularly severe storm."

Hal was genuinely shocked by the accusation and, then, offended. "Jesus God, Geoff, I'd never do that! You're my brother."

"So is Richard," Constance pointed out coolly, and Hal gave her the sort of vexed look that she was accustomed to receiving from his father.

"I can understand that you are unhappy with me, Geoff," he said, striving to sound apologetic even though he thought Geoffrey was being needlessly contentious. "I ought to have alerted you to what was coming. But I had no time, truly I did not. You know about my chapel quarrel with Richard. I had to find a way to deflect his accusations. As for 'pushing our allies over the side,' that is absurd. Richard already knew they were conniving against him. Nor did I mention any names."

Geoffrey and Constance exchanged a meaningful glance, one that spoke volumes without a word being said. "Richard *suspected* they were conniving against him," Geoffrey pointed out, "but he did not know for certes—not until you helpfully made a public confession. Do you truly think Aimar and the others will be pleased with the work you've done this day?"

Hal shrugged. "It does not matter whether they are pleased or not. They'll still be keen to ally with me, for where else can they go?"

Geoffrey was silent for a moment. "I cannot decide," he said slowly, "whether you're a complete fool or an utter cynic."

"Look, Geoff, we had to put Richard in the wrong. Well, I've done that and quite adroitly, I think. Now the pressure will be on him to yield that accursed castle. In all honesty, can you envision him doing that?"

Geoffrey was still frowning, but he had to shake his head at that. "No, I cannot," he admitted.

"Exactly! And when he balks, we both know Papa's temper will catch fire, as it always does when his will is thwarted. I've proven my good faith by confessing freely to my part in the plot. Now it will be up to Richard to prove his, and when he refuses, he'll become the legitimate target for our father's wrath. Once Papa is publicly defied like that, how likely is it that he'd go racing to Richard's rescue?"

"Not likely," Geoffrey had to agree. "You do make a plausible argument, I'll grant you that."

"Of course I do. I'd given this careful thought," Hal insisted, apparently unaware he'd just contradicted his earlier claim—that he'd not had time to consult Geoffrey. "As for Aimar and the others, leave them to me. I'll smooth their ruffled feathers easily enough." Crossing to Constance's side, he kissed her hand with a flourish, and departed with a jaunty bounce in his step, a smile lingering at the corners of his mouth.

It was quiet for a time after he'd gone. Constance was the first to break the silence. "You cannot ever trust that man, Geoffrey."

"I know. But then I trust no one, darling."

She arched a brow, but did not make the obvious response, the one that most women would have asked, and because she did not, he amended his statement. "Except for you, of course."

"You'd have to say that," she pointed out, and when their eyes met, they both laughed.

RICHARD HAD COME in grudging answer to the king's summons, but he was in no conciliatory mood, unable to understand how his father kept allowing himself to be taken in by Hal's act. "You may as well save your breath," he warned, "for I will not give Clairvaux up."

Henry had been expecting just such a response. "Why did you decide to fortify the castle at Clairvaux?"

Richard was surprised by the reasonableness of that question. "It is not as clear-cut as Hal pretends it to be," he said, less truculently. "Clairvaux was once part of Poitou. It is not as if I started building a castle in the heart of Angers."

"I have a map of Anjou burned into my brain, know where Clairvaux is." Henry's tone was mild enough to take any sting from his words. "But why Clairvaux? Why do you think you need a castle there?"

It was not an accusation; Henry sounded as if he truly wanted to know. "The work at Clairvaux was not done with Hal in mind, at least not directly. Clairvaux is just six miles from Châtellerault, and as you know, Châtellerault controls the crossing of the Vienne on the Poitiers road."

Henry nodded thoughtfully. "But the present Viscount of Châtellerault is your cousin; his father Hugh was Eleanor's uncle."

"And you think our shared blood will guarantee Guillaume's loyalty? The way blood binds me and Hal?"

Henry acknowledged the accuracy of Richard's thrust with a bleak smile. "So you have reason to doubt Guillaume's fidelity. Fair enough. But would it not have made life easier for us all if you'd come to me first, explained why you wanted to fortify Clairvaux? As it is, you gave Hal the perfect excuse for heeding the siren songs of your malcontent barons."

Richard had not expected his father to see that Clairvaux was as much a pretext as it was a grievance. "It would have been more prudent," he conceded, and then flashed a sudden smile. "But prudence is not one of my more conspicuous virtues, is it?"

"No, I cannot say that it is," Henry agreed dryly. But there were worse vices than a lack of prudence, far worse.

"You do not sound as if you hold me much to blame," Richard said cautiously, for he had little experience with this evenhanded sort of justice; as far back as he could remember, his father had favored Hal.

"I do not. I am not saying you are an innocent, mind you. But your sins in no way justify what your brother has done."

To Richard, that admission was sweet balm for a wound he'd never have acknowledged. They were standing by the fireplace, and he gazed for a time into the shivering, shooting flames. "But you still want me to give over Clairvaux."

"Yes, Richard, I do."

Richard almost said it was not fair. He did not want to sound like a spoiled, pampered lordling, though, did not want to sound like Hal. If his father's maltreatment of their mother was his most grievous sin, crowning Hal was surely his most idiotic one. Bertran de Born had accompanied Richard to court, and the troubadour had been quick to lambaste Hal's public confession, calling him the "King of Fools." His mockery changed nothing, though. Hal was God's Anointed, and Richard knew he had to deal with that, however little he liked it. Tonight he suspected that his father did not much like it, either, and there was some comfort in that realization, for much of his resentment had been fueled by Henry's failure to see Hal as Richard saw him.

"I will never turn it over to Hal," he warned, and Henry nodded.

"I would not ask that of you, promise to keep it in my hands. I will even consult with you ere I choose a castellan."

"Well, I trust you more than Hal," Richard said, a joke that was too bitter for humor. "But if I surrender Clairvaux—even to you—Hal wins."

"Does he?" Henry asked blandly, and his son looked at him with an emotion that he'd rarely felt for his father, one of reluctant admiration. Papa was right. What pleasure would Hal take from a "win" like that? Without Clairvaux, he'd have no pretense for further plotting. The more Richard thought about it, the more he could see the irony of such a solution. He'd still have to sacrifice some pride, and that would not be easy. But the look on Hal's face when he understood he'd been outfoxed might well be worth it.

"I'll give it over to you—and only to you. But you're just putting a bandage upon a festering belly wound, Papa, and I think you know that."

Henry did, but he was not yet willing to admit it, not even to himself. "For now," he said wearily, "I'll be content enough if I can stop the bleeding."

H ENRY KNEW THAT THE SURRENDER of Clairvaux was a temporary solution to a problem that threatened not only the peace of his realm but even the survival of his empire. He'd always envisioned a federation of loosely linked self-governing states, with Hal reigning over England, Normandy, and Anjou, Richard over Aquitaine, and Geoffrey over Brittany, each one following the customs of his own domains, but bound by a common interest, a mutual commitment to a dynasty capable of dominating all the great Houses of Europe. This was to be his legacy. But in those early days of January, he was forced to face a troubling truth—that upon his death, his sons might well turn upon one another, tearing apart all that he'd labored and fought for and attracting a multitude of enemies drawn by the scent of blood.

This was the greatest threat he'd ever faced, for it came from within. But, as was his way, once he acknowledged the problem, he set about finding a means to resolve it. One of his greatest strengths had always been his ability to remain dispassionate; only in his clash with Thomas Becket had that ability failed him, with tragic consequences. Now, though, he found himself caught up in the same sort of emotional turmoil, unable to judge his sons as a king, not a father. His awareness of this weakness eroded some of his innate self-confidence, and for one of the few times in his life, he sought validation and support from others.

There had never been many allowed into his trusted inner circle, and death and distance had whittled the number down even further. His parents were dead. So were his brother Will and his greatly mourned cousin Roger. Thomas Becket had been elevated from king's confidant to holy martyr. Ranulf was in Wales, and Eleanor banished from his bed and to the outer edges of his heart. He'd always assumed that he'd have his sons as allies once they were grown, but that fire had burned down to ashes and smoldering cinders, giving off neither heat nor light. And so he reached out now to the only ones whose loyalty was neither suspect nor tainted by past betrayals, and confided in his friend Willem and his son Geoff.

They listened in sympathetic silence as he unburdened his heart, confessed to his fears that his family's unity was broken beyond repair, and at last admitted that the son he'd loved the best was the one who'd inflicted the deepest wounds. Hal's bright luster was dimming, and he could no longer deny his doubts about the sort of king his eldest would be. How was he to rout the demons let loose at Caen? How was he to patch together a peace between his sons that would not die with him?

Pacing restlessly in his bedchamber at Le Mans, the room in which he'd taken his first breath nigh on fifty years ago, he told them that he'd convinced Richard to surrender Clairvaux. But if he could not reconcile Richard and his rebel barons, he feared that Hal would be tempted again to taste that forbidden fruit, and there would be no shortage of serpents to beguile him. As for Richard, he was a fine soldier and showed promise of becoming a brilliant battle commander, but he'd yet to learn that there were times when he could win more by concessions than by threats and intimidation. So it was his intent, Henry explained, to summon Richard's disgruntled lords to a peace council at Mirebeau, where he hoped to address their grievances and persuade Richard that compromise and flexibility were also arrows in an archer's quiver.

Neither Willem nor Geoff saw much chance of success in these plans, for they were convinced the barons of Aquitaine were as changeable as the shifting sands, and trusting Henry's sons was like toting water in a sieve. They would never have admitted that to Henry, though, and so they nodded and made appropriate responses indicating agreement and optimism. And when he told them that he also meant to have his sons renew their oaths of allegiance to him and to enter into a compact of perpetual peace with one another, they struggled to hide an emotion that Henry had rarely if ever invoked in others—a sorrowful sense of pity. But they did not know how to heal Henry's ailing family any more than he did, and so they could only hope—as he did—that a solemn oath could avert the coming calamity.

After they'd gone, Henry slumped into a chair, stretching his legs toward the fire. If he'd been on the other side of the Channel, he'd have called for a horse and ridden for Winchester. It was not that he expected Eleanor to have the answers that eluded him. But only the mother of their sons could understand the depths of his despair. He'd been sleeping poorly since Hal's dramatic confession, and he must have dozed for a time, for he jerked upright in his seat to find Geoffrey leaning over him.

"Let me get you some wine, Papa," he said. "I was about to knock when I heard you cry out. A bad dream, I suppose." Handing Henry a wine cup, he stepped back. "Can you spare some moments for me?"

"Of course." Henry drank, then set the cup down in the floor rushes. "Would you be willing to do homage again to your brother if I asked it of you?"

"Why not?" Geoffrey said, sounding puzzled. "As Duke of Normandy, Hal is the liege lord for Brittany, so why would I object?"

"Why, indeed," Henry murmured. At least one of his sons was amenable to reason.

"I am going to need your help, Geoffrey, in settling this feud between your brothers. Richard has agreed to yield Clairvaux, but we both know that will not be the end of it."

Geoffrey's eyes had widened. "Did he, by God?" he said softly. "That is a surprise."

"Mayhap if you talked to them . . ."

"I doubt that they'd heed me, but I'm willing to try, of course, if you wish it."

"Good lad." Henry roused himself to ask Geoffrey if he wanted wine, too, and then leaned back in the chair, closing his eyes. He could not remember the last time he'd been so bone-tired. It seemed so long since he'd awakened each morning eager for what the day would bring. When had the joy begun to seep from his life? When had his losses begun to loom so large?

"Papa, I came here to talk with you about the Honour of Richmond. Constance and I will have been wed two years come August, so we have been patient. But how much longer must we wait for what is rightfully ours? If you'd rather give me Nantes, that is your choice. But Richmond or Nantes, one or the other. I can see no reason why you'd continue to withhold them. It is a matter of fairness if nothing else."

Henry opened his eyes reluctantly. Geoffrey had been handsomely provided for, given a great heiress and a duchy. How many third sons could say that? But no matter how much he gave them, his sons always wanted more. And if he handed Richmond over to Geoffrey now, that would only add to Hal's discontent, only strengthen his belief that his brothers were reaping benefits that had been denied to him.

"I will endow you with the Honour of Richmond, but not just yet. This would not be the best time to do that, not whilst Hal and Richard are at each other's throats. Once I've resolved their differences, I will give consideration to your request. Till then, you must be patient. It is not as if you need the incomes from Richmond, after all. The revenues of Brittany are more than sufficient to provide you and Constance with all the comforts you could ever need. I daresay Hal would thank God fasting for your resources."

Henry saw the shadow that crossed his son's face, and sighed. "I promise you that I will give you both Richmond and Nantes, when the time is right." Getting stiffly to his feet, he looked longingly at his bed. As weary as he was, mayhap tonight he'd be able to sleep through till dawn. "Can you summon my squires, lad? I sent them off so I could speak with Willem and Geoff."

"I'll see to it."

Geoffrey had not moved, though, and Henry gave him a quizzical look over his shoulder. "Was there something else you wanted to discuss with me? Besides Richmond?"

"No," Geoffrey said. "We're done."

CHAPTER THIRTY-FIVE

January 1183
Angers, Anjou

AL WAS HAVING A RUN OF LUCK. He seemed unable to lose, winning every throw of the dice. He was usually elated when he won at raffle, but on this cold, wet afternoon, he was finding it difficult to focus upon the game. His thoughts kept straying to other matters. He was still brooding over his brother's improbable decision to surrender Clairvaux Castle; he would have wagered the surety of his soul that the old man would never be able to coerce or coax Richard into cooperating. And now what? Without Clairvaux, there was no reason for rebelling, at least none that his father would accept.

"If I surrender unconditionally," his friend Raoul de Farci pleaded playfully, "can we switch over to hazard?"

Hal didn't care which game they played, and Raoul quickly removed the third dice before he could change his mind. He had no opportunity to cast the remaining dice, though, for Hal's brother had materialized at the table, and was insisting that Hal come with him. The other men were not happy at forfeiting the chance to recoup their losses, but Geoffrey was not to be denied, and they could only watch glumly as Hal was spirited away.

Hal followed his brother out into the bailey with poor grace. He did not see why he must be the one to inspect Geoffrey's lame stallion; their father had forgotten more about healing horses than he'd ever known. But he could not muster up the energy to object. It was sleeting again, and he felt damp and chilled by the time they entered the stables. Several grooms throwing dice scrambled to their feet, looking discomfited. When Geoffrey flipped a few coins their way and suggested they warm up with mulled wine, they did not argue and eagerly abandoned their duties. Hal was standing by one of the stalls, regarding Geoffrey's stallion and looking perplexed.

"If this horse is lame, he is hiding it remarkably well. What is this about, Geoff?"

"Well, either I needed to talk with you out of earshot of eavesdroppers or I just fancied a stroll over to the stables." Geoffrey glanced around to make sure they were alone. "I saw Papa this morn. He wants us to enter into a compact of perpetual peace and swear to abide by his disposition of his domains. Then he asked me again if I was willing to do homage to you for Brittany."

None of this was news to Hal, and none of it seemed worth freezing his butt over. "So?"

Even in the subdued stable lighting, Geoffrey's eyes shone like silver. "He is also going to ask Richard to do homage to you for Aquitaine."

Hal's jaw dropped. "I am not Richard's liege lord! He owes allegiance for Aquitaine to the French king."

Geoffrey had often marveled at Hal's fondness for belaboring the obvious. "I know, and you may be damned sure that so does Brother Richard."

"Richard will never agree, never!" Hal burst out laughing. "And when he refuses ever so rudely, Papa will be so wroth with him that my minor sins will be forgotten. Geoff, this is a gift from God. How else explain it—unless the old man has gone stark raving mad?"

"He is not mad," Geoffrey said, "just desperate," and he frowned, for however much he told himself that his father did not deserve it, he still felt an unwelcome flicker of pity.

Richard stared at his father in shock. "You cannot be serious?" As suspicious as he so often was of Henry's schemes, he'd never expected this. "I will never agree to so outrageous a demand. Hal and I stand as equals. Just as he lays legitimate claim to your crown and lands, so do I lay claim to my mother's inheritance. I owe him nothing for Aquitaine, and I owe you nothing either!"

Henry had known how difficult it would be to gain Richard's consent, and he was prepared to be as patient as needed. "Will you listen first whilst I explain my reasoning, why I want you to—"

"No, I will not! Aquitaine is my mother's and it is mine, and I will never give that lazy, idle drone any rights over it. I have been unable to gain my mother's freedom, but I can safeguard the independence of her homeland, and by God, I will!"

"You can at least hear me out—" But Richard was already heading for the door, and when Henry started after him, his son slammed it resoundingly in his face.

Richard was conferring with the most trusted of his household knights, for he and André de Chauvigny were cousins, André's mother being Eleanor's aunt. So tense was the atmosphere in the chamber that they jumped like startled cats when a knock sounded at the door.

"I am seeing no one, Rico," Richard instructed his squire, and the youth hurried to do his bidding. As soon as he'd opened the door, though, he spun around to face Richard, his eyes as round as moons.

"My lord," he stammered, "it . . . it is the king!"

Richard was impressed that his father had been the one to seek him out, but he was not about to show it. Folding his arms across his chest, he regarded Henry stonily. André did not share his sangfroid and quickly found excuses to leave, with Rico right behind him.

"Richard, we need to talk."

"No, we do not. There is nothing you can say that I care to hear."

"Do you not even want to know why I would ask that of you?"

"I already know why—because you'd go to any lengths to secure my idiot brother's feeble hold on power!"

Henry shook his head vehemently. "No, you are wrong. I am trying to protect you, not Hal."

Richard was so obviously taken aback that Henry seized his chance, and said quickly, "An act of homage is a double-bladed sword. Yes, it would impose obligations upon you, but it would do the same for Hal. As your liege-lord, he would be honor-bound to respect your rule in Aquitaine, would no longer feel so free to conspire with your vassals. He would owe you protection, and you could hold him to that."

Richard wondered if his father really believed Hal could be fettered by an oath. "I am quite capable of defeating Hal on my own. Indeed, I would welcome the opportunity."

"Do not hold your brother too cheaply, Richard. Once I am dead, he will have the resources of England, Normandy, and Anjou to draw upon, money to hire more routiers than you could hope to count. Nor would he lack for allies in Aquitaine; you've seen to that."

"Let him do his best," Richard said, with such bitter bravado that Henry took a step toward him, yearning to shake some sense into this stubborn son of his.

"I am trying to help you, lad! Why will you not let me?"

He sounded so sincere that Richard almost believed him. "Assuming your intentions are good," he said, with less hostility, "it changes nothing. I will never agree to do homage to Hal. Aquitaine is mine."

"For how long? Christ Jesus, can you not see the danger you'd be facing? And not just Aquitaine would be at risk. If you and your brother lunge for each other's throats as soon as I draw my last breath, what do you think will happen to my empire? My life's work would be undone in a matter of months if you and Hal cannot make peace. Our enemies would be drawn by the scent of blood, and who do you think they'd choose to side with? They'd flock to Hal the way wolves go after a crippled deer, and after they helped take you down, they'd turn on him. Can you not see the truth in what I am saying? I can think of no other way to rein Hal in, to safeguard my legacy, and to keep our family from being ripped asunder."

"I do not blame you for fearing a future in which Hal is king. His reign will make Stephen's look like a golden age. But the survival of your empire is not my responsibility. I am the Duke of Aquitaine, not the King of England. As for our family, it is too late. That ship has already run aground."

"No, you're wrong, Richard. It is not too late. I will not accept that."

"Delude yourself if you will. It is no longer my concern."

Henry drew a labored breath. "What must I do to get you to agree?"

"You have nothing I want."

"Are you so sure of that?"

Richard's eyes narrowed. "What are you saying, that you'd be willing to free my mother?"

Henry had been braced for this. "If that is the price I must pay for your cooperation, yes. I will release Eleanor after you do homage to Hal."

"No, I'll do homage after you release her."

They stared at each other, having reached the end of the road once again. But this impasse was to be different than their others. Instead of storming out, Henry sat down wearily in the closest seat. "Do you remember asking me at Caen why I would not release Eleanor?"

"Why—are you going to answer me now?" And to Richard's amazement, his father nodded.

"I am not seeking to punish her. In all honesty, I doubt that I could ever fully forgive her betrayal. But ten years have passed, and we've made our peace. Even you cannot deny that her life is much more comfortable than it once was. She has her own chamberlain again, her own servants. Despite your suspicions, I have no intention of keeping Tilda from her. I let Joanna see her, did I not? And the wound was still bleeding then."

Richard was searching Henry's face intently. His voice was drained of rage; even those defensive echoes seemed to come more from force of habit than genuine indignation. "Why, then? Why have you not set her free?"

"Because . . . because I no longer fear she'd conspire against me, but I do believe she'd do so for your sake, or for your brothers if one of you rebelled again."

That was such a simple answer, one that made sense to Richard, and he wondered why it had not occurred to him. Picking up a stool, he carried it over, and seated himself next to Henry. "Maman has always had an appreciation for irony, but this is a jest worthy of Lucifer himself. She told me once that much of your troubles could be traced to the fact that you saw her as your queen and she saw herself as the Duchess of Aquitaine. You could not have picked a worse time, Papa, to come around to her point of view."

At that hint of grim humor, Henry's head came up sharply. He'd not truly expected Richard to understand, had fallen back upon utter honesty because he had no more weapons at hand. He saw now, though, that this son was capable of the sort of dispassionate analysis that had been the cornerstone of his own success, and that was a revelation.

Richard was discovering that he felt more kindly toward his father now that he knew his mother's confinement had not been rooted in vengefulness. It was even a perverse sort of compliment, he supposed, that Papa had recognized what a formidable adversary she'd be, even if she were a woman. But she was a woman with a man's brain and a man's daring and she ruled a duchy richer than the domains of the French king. "We are going to have to do something that does not come easily to either of us, then," he said wryly. "We are going to have to trust each other."

Henry exhaled a deep breath; he'd almost forgotten to breathe. For the first time he saw in Richard what his wife had seen, and it was a bittersweet moment, this realization that his second son would have made a far better king than Hal. "You will do homage to your brother, then?" he said cautiously. "Here at Angers, on the morrow?"

The younger man's mouth tightened, but he gave a terse nod. "If you will give the order on the morrow to set my mother free."

"I will," Henry said, and Richard studied him pensively, at last able to see the man in the masterful king and the flawed father. It was a pity, he thought, that they'd not been able to talk like this until now—when it was too late. Hal would not honor an oath of homage. Even if he meant well, he'd fall victim to the blandishments of others, let himself be talked into treason again. My beloved brother, the male whore. And now, God help him, but Papa is starting to see it, too. But if agreeing would gain Maman's freedom and buy him time to make ready for Hal's future aggression, he would not begrudge the price—or so he tried to convince himself.

CONSTANCE WAS SEATED on a bench in her bedchamber while Juvette unfastened her braids. When Geoffrey entered, he seemed in good spirits, teasing Juvette, snatching up an ivory comb so he could brush out his wife's long, dark hair, claiming he'd never understood why troubadours lavished such praise on day, when any man of discernment found true beauty in the night. Juvette giggled, for she was a brunette, too, and Constance marveled how her husband managed to turn sensible girls into simpering sheep with a smile and a few polished gallantries. When Geoffrey deftly steered Juvette toward the door, though, Constance's interest sharpened. If he wanted more privacy than their curtained bed provided, either he had something confidential to tell her or he had one of his erotic games in mind. Lacking imagination herself, she'd come to value this attribute in her husband.

As soon as they were alone, she turned to look up into his face. One glance was all she needed, for by now she'd learned to see past the mask he showed the rest of the world. "What is wrong, Geoffrey?"

He'd already bolted the door once Juvette departed. "I am beginning to believe my father puts Merlin to shame. If my suspicions are right, he could turn dross into gold. I think he has somehow convinced Richard to do homage to Hal."

Constance was astonished. "That is not possible . . . is it?"

"You tell me. Richard was planning to leave Angers at first light, but he changed his mind of a sudden—after my father made a surprise visit to his private chamber. And they were later seen in the hall, conversing together with remarkable amiability given the outrageous demand he'd made of Richard."

Constance did not ask how he knew so much of Richard's plans, for Geoffrey believed that knowledge was power and he paid well enough to attract reliable agents. "I fear you may be right. Richard must have come to terms with your father, for nothing else explains his behavior. It makes no sense, though. Why would Richard ever agree?"

Geoffrey shrugged. "Witchcraft, threats, a staggeringly rich bribe—who knows? But if I've guessed rightly, the rebellion has breathed its last gasp. Which means our best chance of gaining Nantes or Richmond has given up the ghost, too."

Constance gnawed her lower lip, a habit she reverted to under stress. She and Geoffrey had agreed, after considerable deliberation, that their only hope of claiming the rest of her rightful inheritance depended upon Hal's alliance with the rebels. If he won control of Aquitaine, he'd reward them with the promised Poitevin castles now and Richmond and Nantes once he became king; given the lavish way he'd been willing to compensate his allies during the last revolt, they had no worries that he'd renege upon the deal. And if he lost, it was still possible that they could win, for the unrest might give them the leverage they needed to pressure Henry into giving up Richmond at least.

"And if the rebellion sputters out like a quenched candle," Geoffrey said morosely, "we'll actually lose more than Hal. Those routiers I hired did not come cheap, and if I have to cut them loose, they're likely to do what masterless men usually do, and plunder the Breton countryside the way Richard's dismissed routiers sacked Bordeaux a few years back."

Constance frowned at this reminder of their financial investment in the rebellion, for she was thrifty by nature. "Let's assume the worst and you're right about Richard. Why does that mean the rebellion is dead? Why not just delayed until a more opportune time?"

"Because Hal is ruled by whim, and who knows what he'll decide to do six months or a year from now. And because if Richard really does homage, he will earn himself unlimited credit with my father for the foreseeable future. Which means that Papa is likely to turn a blind eye to Richard's border incursions."

As they were convinced that Richard was too predatory a neighbor for comfort, this was a prospect that they both found daunting. Constance chewed on her lower lip again, thinking that Richard's next Clairvaux Castle could well be on Breton soil. "Well," she said, "then we have to make sure that Richard does not do homage to Hal." They'd dissected Hal's failings with merciless honesty, but they'd not really discussed Richard's weaknesses. "You know Richard better than I do, Geoffrey. Where is he most vulnerable to attack?"

"At one time, I'd have said his temper, but he is showing signs of learning self-control. So I would say his hubris."

"I already know you had a fine education, so you need not flaunt it. What is hubris?"

"Pride," he said, "vainglory, arrogance, vanity, all terms that can fairly be applied to Brother Richard."

Constance nodded thoughtfully. "So we have a man who is prideful and hot-tempered. Surely you can find a way to turn those traits against him?"

He was silent for some moments, and then he smiled. "Yes," he said, "I think I do know a way."

BEFORE A DISTINGUISHED AUDIENCE of bishops, barons, and high-born lords, Geoffrey did homage to his brother for Brittany, and then it was Richard's turn. Making little attempt to hide his aversion, he came forward, fixed Hal with a baleful hawk's stare, and knelt in the floor rushes. Before he could speak, Hal held up his hand for silence, and beckoned to his chaplain. The man hastened over, cradling a silver-gift reliquary as if it contained the Host itself. Hal accepted it with equal solemnity, although as his eyes met his co-conspirator's, he winked. Geoffrey winced, thinking that if this was Hal's idea of circumspection, God have mercy upon them all.

Smiling down at his glowering brother, Hal seemed in no hurry for the ceremony to begin, and Henry frowned, for he was taking too much obvious pleasure in Richard's submission. All eyes were upon his sons, and Henry could see the bafflement on many faces; from the moment he'd announced that Richard would do public homage to Hal, there'd been no other topic of conversation at Angers, for none could figure out how he'd gotten Richard to agree to this. Wanting to get it over as soon as possible, exasperated by behavior he saw as juvenile and petty, Henry shot his eldest son a warning look, making up his mind then and there to return Clairvaux Castle to Richard's custody, and if Hal liked it not, what of it?

Taking his cue at last, Hal again signaled unnecessarily for quiet. "An act of homage is not to be entered into lightly," he said gravely. "Whilst I am gladdened that my brother, the Duke of Aquitaine, has offered to do so, I regret that I cannot accept his oath without some misgivings."

Richard stiffened, Henry took an involuntary step forward, and a low buzz swept the hall. Hal let the suspense build for a few moments longer, noticing that his brother's eyes had fastened suspiciously upon the reliquary. Holding it up as if it were an actor's prop, he said loudly, "As sorry as I am to say it, I cannot trust the lord duke's sworn word without additional validation. Therefore, I would have him swear homage to me upon these blessed holy relics so that there will be no doubts as to his good faith."

Bedlam ensued, even more chaotic than Hal had hoped. Cat-quick, Richard was on his feet, his face flushed with incredulous fury, his lips peeled back in a snarl that went unheard in the confusion. Henry looked no less dumbfounded, staring at Hal in disbelief and, then, utter outrage. Quarrels were breaking out across the hall, as Richard's followers began to exchange insults and threats with Hal's household knights. Watching from the sidelines, Geoffrey kept his face carefully impassive, but inwardly, he was relishing the moment, a master puppeteer who'd succeeded even beyond his expectations.

Richard had leaped onto the dais, was telling Hal in no uncertain terms exactly what he could do with those holy relics, and if his suggestion was anatomically impossible, it was nonetheless an eloquent declaration of his mood at the moment. By then Henry had reached them and, as Richard cursed his brother to Hell for all eternity, he grabbed Hal in a grip that would leave bruises. "Have you lost your bloody mind? Come with me—now!"

Hal was not pleased to have his dignity disparaged like this, but Henry's fingers had clamped onto his wrist like talons, and he decided against attempting to break free, not wanting to be seen physically brawling with his father in public. As Henry pulled Hal toward the stairwell, Richard turned on his heel and made a dramatic departure, slamming out of the hall as people scattered out of his way and his men made haste to follow.

Constance moved to Geoffrey's side with a low, throaty "well done" meant only for his ears. They were soon joined by several of the bishops, and when they entreated him to act as peacemaker between Henry and Hal, he graciously agreed to do what he could in the interest of family harmony.

As he mounted the steps, Geoffrey could hear the yelling, only slightly muffled by the closed door. Entering without knocking, he found his father and brother glaring at each other, both shouting at once, neither listening. Geoffrey closed the door, and then leaned back against it to watch. Henry was as angry as he'd ever seen him, giving off as much heat as a flaming torch, berating Hal bitterly for his lunacy, his irresponsible, selfish blundering, saying all that he'd kept bottled up for years. Hal was more in control, but he was angry, too, defending himself by casting as much blame as possible upon Richard.

His chest heaving, his blood pounding in his ears, Henry at last exhausted even his hoard of invectives. Once his rage no longer burned so hotly, his suspicions began to flare up. "With that insulting demand, you alienated Richard to the point where he's not likely to ever agree to do homage again. Is that what you had in mind, Hal—to cripple my efforts to make peace between you?"

"Of course not!" Hal exclaimed indignantly, and Geoffrey decided it was time to intervene, not wanting to give their father a chance to dwell upon those suspicions.

"Hal is not alone in his mistrust of Richard, Papa," he said, moving to step between them. "I share it, too. I daresay you do not want to hear this, but we know Richard better than you do, and he has given us reason, time and time again, to doubt his good will, to suspect his good faith. Hal's method may have been lacking in subtlety, but he was only trying to protect himself, hoping that a sacred oath might be more binding upon Richard than the one he intended to make."

Henry was inclined to give Geoffrey more credence at that moment than Hal. But their treacherous, ravening Richard did not resemble the man he'd bargained with last night. "Whatever your suspicions, Hal, you could not have handled it worse. I am not even sure I can repair the damage you've done this day."

When Hal would have argued further, Henry cut him short. "We've said enough," he said curtly. "Better that we discuss this later, once our tempers have had time to cool." And turning away, he left the chamber, left them alone together, hoping that Geoffrey might be able to convince Hal that compromise was an important aspect of statecraft. He'd spoken the truth when he'd confessed that he did not know if Richard could be placated, knew only that he dreaded trying. Could he truly blame Richard if he suspected collusion, if he'd concluded that he'd been led into an ambush?

Retreating to his own chamber, he pondered the best way to heal this ugly breach between his sons. He could think of only one way to convince Richard of his good faith, and while it would not be easy for him to do, his son had spoken true yesterday. They had to trust each other. If he still held to his part of the bargain and ordered Eleanor's release, that should convince Richard that he'd known nothing of Hal's duplicity.

Deciding that once again he must be the one to come to Richard, he rose tiredly from the bed, limping slightly for his bad leg was sensitive to wet weather. The bailey was muddy, but at least the rain had eased up. Catching sight of his steward, he called the man over; it might be best to avoid any surprises, to give Richard warning that he was on his way. When he instructed the man to carry this message to his son, though, the steward flushed in dismay.

"I am sorry, my liege," he mumbled, looking anywhere but at Henry's face. "I thought sure someone would have told you . . . The lord duke is gone. He and his men rode out immediately after the . . . the altercation in the hall. He did not even take the time to pack, left his clothes behind in his chamber."

H AL ESCORTED MARGUERITE to her mare, assisted her to mount. She was pale, but her eyes were dry. She'd shed her tears already in the privacy of their bedchamber as she'd argued against being sent to her brother's court in Paris. She did not want to go. She could not counter Hal's contention that it was too dangerous for her to remain as long as war might be looming. She'd had no answer for him when he'd reminded her how she'd been caught by Henry at Poitiers and held in honorable confinement for several months. She still did not want to go, for she did not trust Hal's protestations of innocence. She suspected that he was still conspiring with the rebel lords against Richard, and she had a terrifying premonition that if they were parted now, she might never see him again.

He'd laughed away her fears, assuring her that she had no cause for concern, that even if Richard forced a war, he'd be in no danger. Holding her hand in his, he pressed a kiss into her palm and promised that he'd soon join her in Paris. She mustered up a brave, farewell smile, trying very hard to believe him.

Constance was no happier than Marguerite. She'd quarreled with Geoffrey for days, to no avail, for he was stubbornly set upon having her accompany Marguerite to Paris. She'd preferred to return to Rennes, but he insisted that she'd be safer in France in the event the war went badly for them. She'd finally stopped arguing, although she had no intention of humoring him. Once they were well away from Angers, she meant to inform her escort that there'd been a change of plans and they'd be heading back to Brittany.

Standing in the castle bailey with Geoffrey, she found herself reluctant to mount her mare, reluctant to leave. She realized that her reluctance was illogical; she could not very well ride to war with him. Yet she continued to linger, delaying her departure with needless questions and last-minute admonitions. It was disconcerting to recognize the real reason for her disquiet—fear for his safety. She was not accustomed to worrying about someone else's welfare, and did not like the sensation in the least. Nor did she want to sound foolish by urging him to take care. Instead she wrapped her arms around his neck and gave him a kiss that was not at all wifely, breathing in his ear a promise to celebrate his victory with a game of the novice nun and the lecherous monk.

Geoffrey laughed, said with an incentive like that, how could he possibly lose, and helped her up into the saddle. Henry had come out to bid his daughters-in-law a safe journey, and he joined Geoffrey as the women's escort mounted and they headed off. Hal went back indoors, but Geoffrey remained in the bailey to watch their departure.

So did Henry. He looked drawn and tired, for he'd not been sleeping well. He'd sent an urgent message after Richard, but so far there'd been no reply. He knew, though, that Richard would have to come to Mirebeau for the peace conference with the rebels of Poitou and the Limousin, and he hoped, then, that he'd be able to give Richard the reassurances he clearly needed. How he would reconcile Richard and Hal, he did not yet know, but he told himself that he could only take one step at a time. For now, he had to concentrate upon making peace between Richard and his defiant barons, and with that in mind, he drew Geoffrey aside.

"I want you to go to Limoges on my behalf. Do whatever it takes, but convince Viscount Aimar and the others that they must meet with me at Mirebeau. Assure them that I will hear their grievances and Richard and I will work out some sort of accord. Can you do that for me, Geoffrey?"

His son looked startled, but then he smiled. "I can do that," he said.

CHAPTER THIRTY-SIX

January 1183
Angers, Anjou

*H*ENRY WALKED TO THE HEARTH and thrust a parchment into the fire, wrinkling his nose as an acrid smell of burning sheepskin filled the chamber. When he'd been unable to dictate the letter to his scribe, he'd dismissed the man and tried to write it himself, to no avail. The words just would not come. How could he tell Eleanor that the curse of Cain had afflicted their two eldest sons? He wanted to believe that he'd be able to patch up a peace between Hal and Richard, but for once his innate optimism and boundless self-confidence were guttering like candles in the wind. The survival of his empire had been predicated upon the premise of family solidarity. He'd envisioned Hal as ruling over a loose federation, ably supported by his brothers in Aquitaine and Brittany. He'd expected that they would be allies, never enemies.

No, he could not burden Eleanor with such knowledge. At least he could take action, do what he could to mend the breach. She could only grieve and blame herself— just as he was blaming himself. As suspicious as he still was of her influence over their sons, he knew this was not her doing; she would never have deliberately tried to set

Hal and Richard at odds. Better that she not know. He'd reluctantly sent Tilda an oblique warning, for she and Heinrich had settled in at Domfront Castle in Normandy, and they'd likely hear of the confrontation at Angers. With luck, though, the Channel might keep gossip and rumor from reaching Eleanor's ears, at least until he'd been able to repair these fraying brotherly bonds.

He was watching the parchment burn when Willem and Geoff were escorted into the solar, and some of his edginess eased in their familiar presence. Thank God Almighty that there were still a few men whom he could trust. They were discussing his plans for the Mirebeau council when Hal joined them, and he entered enthusiastically into the conversation, criticizing the various Limousin barons as if these same men had not been his conspirators only a few months past. Henry watched his performance without comment, wondering how this stranger had gained possession of his son's body. He refused to believe that Hal had always been this shallow and self-centered, could only assume that he'd somehow missed the warning signs that Hal was losing his way. He refused, too, to look too far into the future. A man who'd always been one for long-range planning, now he took one day at a time. Today he must reconcile his sons and then reconcile Richard and his barons. Tomorrow . . . tomorrow he would figure out how to keep Hal from heeding the seductive whispers of the serpent and taking another taste of the forbidden fruit.

They were interrupted briefly when a servant entered and murmured a few words for Henry's ear alone. His gaze fastening upon his son, he knew Hal would soon be seeking entertainment elsewhere, and he gave the man a low-voiced directive with that in mind. As he'd predicted, it was not long before Hal lost interest and found an excuse to depart, but it gave Henry no satisfaction that he was now able to read the younger man so accurately. He wished that, like Eleanor, he could have remained in blissful ignorance of his eldest son's failings, both as a man and as a king.

Once Hal had gone, Henry moved over to warm himself by the fire before telling Geoff and Willem that his best agent had arrived and was about to be ushered up to the solar. "I told Matthew to wait until my son went back to the great hall," he said, and shook his head when they offered to leave. "No, there is no need to go. You've met him already, Willem, and it is time that you did, too, Geoff."

A memory stirred for Willem. "I remember. The young man who was spying upon the French king for you. His name was . . . Luc, no?"

"Well, that is the name he was using," Henry said, with a faint smile. "He has not been at the French court for well over a twelvemonth, though. His mother was born in the Limousin, and after she was widowed, she chose to return to her family in Limoges. She took ill last year, and Luc hastened to Limoges to look after her until she recovered. He'd intended to return to Philippe's service, but when he discovered that one of his cousins was a household knight of Viscount Aimar's, he thought that might be a better place to fish than Paris and arranged to be taken on, too."

Henry smiled again. "I suspect he was finding life rather dull at Philippe's court, whereas the Limousin was bound to be a fertile ground for intrigue and rebellion, which is mother's milk to him. I am surprised that he did not discover Hal's plotting, for he misses little and my son plays at conspiracy as if it were a game of camp-ball. I can only assume that Aimar was more careful."

Geoff looked away lest his father see his anger, for he knew his was an expressive face. He did not have a forgiving nature, as he'd be the first to admit, and he'd never forgiven his half brothers or the queen for their betrayal. He was an admirer of Richard's battle skills and he thought that Geoffrey was showing a deft touch in his dealings with the Breton lords, but he had no use whatsoever for Hal, was one of the few at court who was utterly immune to the young king's charm.

When Luc was escorted into the chamber, Willem had to remind himself that nigh on nine years had passed, for the younger man seemed to have kept time at bay; he looked much as he had when Willem had last seen him, on the road to Rouen. He still put Willem in mind of a wolf masquerading as a domestic dog, sleek and supple and dangerous.

Stepping forward, Luc knelt at the king's feet. Henry's welcoming smile faded as he got his first look at Luc's face. His agent was so somber that he knew at once something was very wrong. Gesturing for Luc to rise, he braced himself for yet more bad news. "What have you come to tell me?"

"What I wish could have been done by someone else, my liege," Luc said in a low voice, and when his dark eyes locked with Henry's grey ones, the older man was chilled by what he saw in them—pity. "My lord king, there is no easy way to say it. Your son has betrayed you."

Henry's relief was so great that he laughed aloud. "You need not tread so carefully, Luc. I already know of my son's scheming with the Viscount of Limoges and the others. The young king made a full and public confession at my Caen Christmas Court."

Luc sighed and then shook his head. "You do not understand, my liege. I am not speaking of the young king, but of your other son, the Duke of Brittany."

Henry was incredulous and, then, enraged. "That is a lie!"

Luc faced his anger without flinching. "My lord king, do you truly believe I would give you such grief if I were not sure? I ask you only to hear me out."

Henry was regretting his flare of temper. Luc had earned better than that. He was mistaken—obviously—but he was not lying. "Speak, then," he said. "I will listen."

"The lord duke arrived in Limoges last week," Luc began, and Henry could not help interrupting.

"I know that, Luc. I sent Geoffrey to Limoges, instructing him to persuade Aimar and the other barons to meet me next month at Mirebeau. So there is nothing suspicious about his presence there."

"I know his peace mission was the public reason given for his arrival in Limoges. But what troubled me from the first was that Aimar and the others welcomed Lord Geoffrey more like an ally than a mediator. I had no proof, nothing to go on but my instincts. They've served me well in the past, though, and so I kept my eyes open and my ears pricked. The duke is a cautious man, not one to boast of his shifting alliances, but I got lucky. I happened to overhear him instructing a courier, and so I trailed inconspicuously after them into the stables. He gave the man a sealed letter, told him that it must be delivered to Lord Raoul de Fougères without delay and warned him of the urgency of his undertaking."

"I do not find it strange that he'd be sending a message to one of his Breton barons," Henry said, but he was now sounding more defensive than defiant, for he, too, put a great deal of trust in Luc's instincts.

"It could well have been utterly innocent," Luc admitted. "I knew only that I wanted to get my hands upon that letter, and so when the courier rode out, I followed him. I did not expect to get a chance to steal it until that evening, but the fool stopped in a Limoges tavern on his way out of town, and put away enough wine to need to relieve himself in an alley nearby. I slipped in behind him and clouted him ere he even knew I was there."

Luc would normally have digressed from his account at this point, explaining there was a spot behind the ear that could render a man unconscious ere he hit the ground, for Henry was interested in esoteric facts like that. Now, though, he knew better, for the king's color was taking on a waxen hue. "I took his purse and ring, too, to make it look like a robbery, and I am sure that was how he explained it to the lord duke when he eventually woke up, doubtless conjuring up three or four brigands against whom he'd struggled fiercely."

When Henry said nothing, Luc reached into his tunic and withdrew a rolled parchment. "You'll recognize the lord duke's seal, sire. He tells Raoul de Fougères to dispatch the routiers they'd hired, saying war is imminent and he expects Lord Richard to take the offensive and strike first, so the sooner the routiers can reach the Limousin, the better."

Henry was still silent, but when Luc held out the letter, he took it. Glancing down at the elegant, slanting handwriting, he recognized it at once as his son's. Keeping his gaze upon that damning document, he said huskily, "You'll be well rewarded for this service, Luc, but that can wait. For now, you'll be wanting a meal. Tell my steward to see that you're fed and then to find you a bed, and a wench, if you want one."

"Thank you, sire," Luc murmured, and backed out of the solar. Geoff and Willem had sat frozen, finding it almost as hard as Henry to credit the spy's revelation. They exchanged troubled glances, neither knowing what to say. But as the door closed behind Luc, Henry raised his head.

"Find my son, Willem," he said. "Fetch him here straightaway."

"So you claim you knew nothing of Geoffrey's treachery?" Henry's eyes bore into Hal's, and there was such icy accusation in his voice that his eldest felt heat rising in his face.

"Jesu, of course I did not!" Hal insisted, with all the indignation he could muster. "Had I suspected Geoffrey was so vulnerable to Aimar's blandishments, I'd have come to you in private and argued against sending him to Limoges."

"How can I doubt you when you've always been so devoted to my interests?" Henry said, with sarcasm that cracked like a whip.

"Papa, I understand that your nerves are on the raw after getting such news. But it is not fair to blame me for what Geoffrey has done. We're not even that close. If he'd been planning this beforehand—and I doubt that he was— he'd hardly have confided in me, not when he was planning to usurp my place in the rebel plot. It is true that you addressed my grievance by taking Clairvaux from Richard." Hal paused and then smiled wryly. "But in all honesty, any peace between Richard and me is likely to last as long as a whore's chastity vow. Sooner or later, he'll start lusting after Angevin lands again. When he does, I'd like to be able to rally his barons to my side, and what better way to do that than to put forward my own claim to Aquitaine?"

There was a certain wayward logic in Hal's argument, something persuasive in his candid admission that he'd not ruled out making another try for Aquitaine if circumstances warranted it. Seeing Henry's hesitation, Hal swiftly pressed his advantage. "So why would I want to see Geoffrey as the new Duke of Aquitaine? If Geoffrey held both Brittany and Aquitaine, that would give him far too much power for my comfort. I trust Geoffrey more than Richard, but then I'd trust the Saracen chieftain Saladin more than Richard."

Henry turned to the table, poured a cup of wine, and let the liquid trickle down his throat. But he knew that all the wine in the world would not wash away the foul taste in his mouth. Sitting down in the closest chair, he looked from Geoff to Willem, then back to Hal. "Why do you think this was not premeditated?"

"Because I know how persuasive Aimar can be, Papa. If he seduced women the way he seduces allies, he'd have sired enough bastards to populate an entire city. In fairness to Aimar, he has just cause for loathing life under Richard's reign. It shows you how desperate they are that they turned to Geoffrey now that I am no longer available. And in fairness to Geoffrey, I daresay they bedazzled him with their promises; Aimar is good at that. He'd never expected more than Brittany, and that comes with a price—having to put up with Constance. How many younger sons would not have been tempted by the riches of Aquitaine?"

"You make a curious defense of your brother, Hal, by pleading his weakness and greed."

"Who amongst us is without sin, Papa? As far as I am concerned, much of the blame rests with Richard, for Geoffrey would not have gotten himself entangled with Aimar if Richard had not pushed them into rebellion." Hal was surprised to see how much his father seemed to have aged in a matter of hours, and he found himself wanting to offer some genuine consolation. Moving to Henry's side, he knelt by him so their eyes were level and said earnestly, "You ought not to take this too much to heart, Papa. You are not the target here—Richard is. I hope you'll bear that in mind and, for once, let him reap what he has sown."

Henry looked into Hal's eyes, saw sincerity and sympathy and an utter inability to understand that Geoffrey's double-dealing was putting their entire empire at risk. "I am glad we had this talk," he said wearily. "I want you to tell my council and court that Geoffrey has gone over to the rebels. They'll have to know . . ."

"I will do it now," Hal promised, getting lightly to his feet and letting his hand drop to Henry's shoulder in a gesture of comfort. Glancing toward the other men, he said, "Willem, Geoff? Do you want to come with me?" Again, that rueful smile surfaced. "I know how tattered my credibility is in some eyes, and none would doubt either of you."

When Willem rose, Geoff had no choice but to rise, too. Wishing he had the power to see into his brother's brain, he regarded Hal with poorly concealed antagonism. He was willing to admit that Hal's performance had been convincing, but that was the trouble; he suspected it was a performance. Henry gave no indication of wanting him to stay, and so he followed the others to the door. But then he looked back, and what he saw caused him to catch his breath as if he'd taken a blow, for, thinking himself alone, Henry had leaned forward and buried his face in his hands.

BY THE TIME HE FOUND WILLEM, Geoff was seething, so flushed and distraught that he looked as if he were at risk for an apoplectic fit. "Have you heard?"

he demanded. "Hal has offered to go to Limoges to coax Geoffrey into abandoning the rebels, and my father has agreed to let him!"

"I know," Willem said morosely, "but for God's sake, lower your voice, Geoff, or they'll be able to hear you in Saumur."

"I think my father has lost his mind," Geoff said, but in more circumspect tones. "How can he trust Hal on such a mission? Let's assume he is not already in this plot up to his neck, though that takes more faith than I have. How is he supposed to bring Geoffrey back to the fold? He has as much backbone as a hemp rope, and like as not, Geoffrey will talk him into joining the rebellion!"

"You do not have to convince me, Geoff. I agree with you."

"Then you must go to my father, make him see that this is a great mistake. I tried, but he'd not hear me. Mayhap if you voiced your concerns, too—"

"I already have, to no avail. He would not heed me either."

Geoff's breath hissed through his teeth, and his chest heaved as he sought to get his temper under control. "Why?" he asked simply, and Willem had no answer for him.

"I do not know," he confessed. "I remember the way Harry was ere he did penance at Canterbury. You were not with us, then, Geoff, but he sailed in a gale that the Devil himself would have shunned. It was almost as if he were leaving his fate up to the Almighty, leaving it to God to choose whether he prevailed or not. It may be that he is doing that again." Willem shook his head and repeated, "I just do not know."

None of that made any sense to Geoff. "What can we do?"

Willem's shoulders slumped. "We can pray that his trust in Hal is justified."

HAL CROSSED THE CHAMBER and embraced his father, which he'd not done in years. "You will not be sorry, Papa. I'll not let you down," he promised. "When all this is done, you'll have no reasons for regrets."

"Go with God, Hal," Henry said softly, not moving until the young king had departed the chamber. He went, then, to the window, flung the shutters open and, heedless of the cold, gazed down into the castle bailey. Hal soon emerged and started toward his men, who were already mounted. Catching sight of Willem and Geoff, he veered in their direction. Henry could not hear what was being said; he assumed Hal was bidding them farewell. Willem, ever the courtier, was responding courteously, but Geoff was glowering, looking rather like Richard in one of his rages. Henry knew they were distraught over his decision to let Hal go after Geoffrey. It was not something he could explain, though, for it was neither logical nor wise in light of Hal's past history. It was not the king who was setting Hal loose; it was the father. His head and heart were at war, and he could no longer endure the uncertainty. He had to know if his eldest son could be trusted, and this was the only way to find out. If Hal let him down, it could not be more painful than Geoffrey's betrayal, for he'd never seen that coming. At least there'd be no surprise if Hal confirmed his fears and betrayed him, too. Better he knew the worst, for then he could deal with it.

Hal was mounted now on a prancing grey stallion. Glancing up, he saw Henry and waved jauntily before riding out. Henry stayed at the window, not moving until long after Hal was no longer in sight.

F OR MONTHS, HAL'S EMOTIONS had been swinging back and forth like a pendulum in a high wind. Never had he felt so conflicted, so confused. Whenever Richard had the upper hand, he'd burned to bring his brother down, furious and frustrated that his chance for rebellion was slipping away. But whenever Richard had taken a misstep and fallen from their father's favor, he'd been beset by doubts, feeling as if he was being pressured into making a decision ere he was ready. He'd departed Angers in high spirits, confident and eager for what lay ahead. The trip had been long enough, though, for misgivings to creep back in, and as he approached Limoges, he felt more like a hostage to fortune than the commander of his own fate.

Limoges was actually two cities, the ville, which held the great abbey of St Martial and the viscount's castle, and the cité, site of the bishop's palace and cathedral. Each was enclosed within its own ramparts, and, as was so often the case, the rivalry between the ville and the cité was not good-natured. As they were coming from the north, Hal reached the ville first, and he drew rein once they neared the Montmeiller gate, saying a silent prayer that he'd made the right decision and asking the Almighty to send another sign that it was so.

The gates were open and they were close enough now to see the people thronging the narrow streets, waving and cheering. Hal and his men rode into a warm welcome, found themselves acclaimed as heroes by people eager to throw off Duke Richard's yoke. Hal was already popular in Limoges, for he'd always been generous with his spending and alms-giving, and now he was hailed as their savior, the man who would deliver them from Richard's harsh rule.

Hal's spirits soared and he acknowledged the acclaim with grace and a shower of coins. This was clearly a good omen, a portent of success to come, and he forgot the qualms that had been nagging at him in recent days. He hadn't been lying when he'd assured Henry that he'd have no reason for regrets, for he honestly believed that all of their problems would be resolved if only he could gain control of Aquitaine. The duchy's deep coffers would allow him to support his household in kingly style, no longer dependent upon Henry's miserly pension, and that would be bound to improve their relationship, eliminating the worst bone of contention between them. Once Richard was defeated, all would be well.

Ahead lay the viscount's castle, and he saw his brother and Aimar standing in the gateway, watching his triumphant procession. With banners streaming in the wind, escorted by the enthusiastic citizenry, Hal reined in before them, swung to the ground, and embraced Geoffrey, then Aimar.

"An imaginative touch," Geoffrey said dryly, looking to the conspicuous white flag of truce, and Hal grinned, sure that he was where he was meant to be, doing God's Work and soon to have the power that a king ought to wield.

CHAPTER THIRTY-SEVEN

February 1183
Gorre, Limousin

*T*HE VILLAGE WAS A SCENE of devastation. The houses that were not charred ruins had doors smashed in, their contents ransacked by men in search of booty. Some of the soldiers were sleeping in these cottages, finding them more comfortable than their tents, and the stench was rank, for routiers rarely bothered to dig latrines. A few bodies lay where they'd fallen, those villagers who'd not fled in time. Piles of entrails were strewn about, what was left of livestock butchered for food. The animals that were not needed by the camp cooks were dead, too, for one of the aims of a chevauchée was to wreak havoc upon an enemy's lands. Even the cemetery had not been spared, some of the graves dug up by men hoping to find that the more prosperous burghers had been buried with rings or other valuables.

Raymond Brunnus barely noticed the destruction, for it was too familiar a sight to register with him. In the two decades since he'd left his native Gascony in search of profit and adventure, he'd sold his sword to more lords than he could remember, taking naturally to the lawless life of a mercenary. When his nephew, William Arnald, had sent him a message that there were easy pickings in the Limousin and the Viscount of Limoges and the young English king were eager to hire routiers, he'd wasted no time in leading his men north. One of his scouts had reported that the viscount and his nephew's routiers were besieging a church in the village of Gorre, and he'd headed there instead of the viscount's city, arriving in mid-morning under an ashen February sky that warned of a coming storm.

Welcomed boisterously by his nephew, he listened without great interest as Arnald related how some of the Duke of Aquitaine's men had been ambushed, the survivors retreating into Gorre and taking shelter in the church. By the time they were discovered, they'd fortified the building, barricaded the windows and doors, and burned the external wooden stairway leading up into the bell tower. It was a substantial stone structure, could not be fired like the village houses, and they'd apparently gambled that the routiers would soon grow impatient and seek easier prey. That would have happened, too, Arnald admitted, had he not sent word to the viscount. Aimar had ridden the dozen miles from Limoges to see for himself, and once he learned these were Duke Richard's knights, he'd set men to building a massive, iron-tipped battering ram.

Raymond's interest quickened, for Viscount Aimar's personal involvement indicated rich ransoms were in the offing. "So there is someone inside whom Duke Richard will pay dearly to save, then?"

Arnald shook his head. "There'll be no ransoms." Seeing his uncle's lack of comprehension, he took it upon himself to inform the older man of recent developments in the war. "This is what happened. The Duke of Brittany sent for routiers he'd hired earlier in the year, and as they moved into Poitou, they burned and plundered on their way south. Duke Richard raced to head them off, and there have been numerous clashes. Whenever Richard caught any of his brother's men, he beheaded them right then and there."

While mass executions were not the norm, they were not unheard of, either, for routiers were considered expendable by both sides, even by the men who hired them, and they could be slain without fear of Church censure and with the enthusiastic support of the people they'd been victimizing. Raymond had long ago become inured to the hypocrisy of his highborn employers, seeing it as an occupational hazard. "Well, from what I've heard of Duke Richard, I cannot say that surprises me much."

"Ah, but he did not just slay Lord Geoffrey's routiers. He killed the knights, too."

"Whoa!" That was indeed a different kettle of fish. "The duke and viscount must have loved that."

"They were raving and ranting like madmen," Arnald confirmed, and as their eyes met, they shared a moment of grim humor, taking some satisfaction that for once the highborn faced the same risks as their lowborn hirelings. "So . . ." Arnald continued, "as soon as the viscount heard that some of Richard's knights were trapped in the church, he saw an opportunity for vengeance, though I daresay he'd put it more elegantly—as well-deserved retribution." Slapping his uncle fondly on the shoulder, he said, "Come on over and meet your new patron."

Raymond did not move. "Why the viscount? I'd heard the young king was paying more."

"Yes, he's been putting out word that men can make their fortune in his service, but that one has not two coins of his own to rub together. You'd do better with his brother, but Duke Geoffrey is off raiding into Poitou. So between the king and the viscount, go with Lord Aimar. You'll have a much better chance of collecting from him."

Nonpayment was not usually a problem for routiers; their lords knew that if they were cheated of their just due, they'd turn on their masters without qualm or compunction. Raymond believed, though, in keeping things as simple as possible, and he accepted his nephew's advice, saying, "Lead on, lad. Any chance we can fill our bellies ere the assault begins?"

Arnald cast an appraising eye toward the men working upon a huge tree trunk. "They do not have the wheels on it yet, so there ought to be time to eat. First things first, though. Let's see how much money you can squeeze out of the viscount!"

THE VISCOUNT OF LIMOGES had not always been at war with his Angevin overlords; he'd stayed neutral during the last rebellion of Henry's sons. But that all changed when his father-in-law, the Earl of Cornwall, died and Henry cheated his wife, Sarah, of her inheritance. For that was how he saw it. Henry himself had arranged Aimar's marriage, and that only exacerbated his grievance. As Rainald's legitimate son was dead and Rico born out of wedlock, Aimar had expected the earldom to pass to the old earl's daughters, with Sarah, the eldest, getting the lion's share. When Henry chose to bestow the earldom upon his son John, he'd turned the hitherto loyal Aimar into an embittered rebel. Until now, Aimar's animosity had been reserved for Henry and not his sons, but after Richard's brutal execution of Geoffrey's Breton knights, the viscount had sworn a blood-oath that this ruthless prince would never again rule over the Limousin.

Casting an eye toward the leaden skies, he hoped they'd be able to launch the final assault while there was still light. He did not doubt that the battering ram would be able to smash through the church's thick oaken door. It was likely, though, that the men would retreat up into the bell tower once that happened, and they could be difficult to dislodge from that refuge. He did not know what provisions they'd managed to bring in with them, but they had to be running low on food, for they'd been trapped in the church for nigh on a week. Well, if it came to that, they could always be starved into submission.

He'd just accepted a wineskin from one of his squires when a sudden, urgent shout turned all heads. One of their sentries was galloping toward the camp, yelling that riders were fast approaching. Knowing this seasoned soldier would not have been alarmed unless the riders posed a threat, Aimar whirled and ran for his horse, snatching up his helmet. Jamming it down upon his head, he fumbled with the chin cord as he swung up into the saddle. All around him, men were running and shouting, scrambling for weapons and horses. Whores almost inevitably turned up at an army encampment, and some of these women were screaming shrilly even before the riders came into view—clad in chain mail, swords drawn and lances leveled, mounted on horses caked in lather and dust. One glimpse was enough to tell Aimar that they were in for a fierce fight.

One of the lead knights drew Aimar's attention, for he was spurring ahead of his companions. Encountering a campfire, he jumped his stallion neatly over the flames instead of swerving around it, an act of horsemanship that the viscount could not help admiring, even at a moment like this. The knight had caught Arnald's eye, too. Darting forward, quick as a snake, he grabbed for the other man's leg. It was a daring maneuver, but if successful, was guaranteed to unhorse a man. Aimar had seen Arnald drag more than one foe from the saddle this way, for the routier was a big man, as well-muscled as a blacksmith.

What happened next stopped Aimar in his tracks. The knight under attack did not pull back as men usually did; instead he leaned in, and suddenly blood was spurting everywhere, a red haze before Aimar's eyes. Arnald reeled backward, his face contorted as he stared in shock at the stump where his hand had been. The knight's sword was already sweeping down again, a powerful blow that all but decapitated the routier.

Aimar heard the command to retreat and was surprised that the order was coming from his throat, for he'd not made a conscious decision to withdraw. But by then he'd recognized the knight bloodied with Arnald's blood, and his instincts for self-preservation had taken over. The awareness that they were facing Richard himself banished any desire for battle. He was no coward, but Richard was a lunatic. Would he be mad enough to execute a man of Aimar's rank? The viscount found that hard to believe, but he knew that men could get drunk on bloodlust and he preferred not to put Richard's sobriety to the test. Followed by those of his men lucky enough to have reached their horses, he spurred his mount toward the Limoges road, all of them riding as if the Devil were on their tails.

B Y THE TIME RICHARD RODE back into Gorre, the trapped knights had ventured out and were quenching their thirst at the village well, easing their hunger with the meal intended for their foes. Not all of Richard's men had followed him in pursuit of Aimar, and they'd rounded up close to a hundred prisoners, the rest of the routiers having been slain or escaped. André de Chauvigny grinned at the sight of his duke; he had a wineskin in one hand and bread in the other, and he waved the loaf over his head in a jubilant, joyful salute.

"I won a right goodly sum on you, my lord," he laughed. "I wagered two marks that you'd arrive in time."

That was indeed a handsome sum, for knights rarely earned more than a shilling a day. "How could you lose?" Richard pointed out. "You'd either win or you'd die, and in neither case would you have to pay the wager."

André laughed again. "Fortunately Alan is as thick as a plank, and he never worked that out." Coming forward as Richard slid from the saddle, he hovered by the younger man's side, overwhelmed by the intensity of his gratitude, but not knowing how to express it, for banter and mockery were the most common coins of their realm. "Your men said you'd ridden for nigh on two days and nights to reach us." Not having the words, he playfully offered the purloined wineskin and loaf, joking that all he had was at his lord duke's disposal.

Richard appreciated his cousin's insouciance, for he'd not have been comfortable with earnest protestations or lavish praise, not from André. "You look like you've been wallowing in a pigsty after an all-night carouse," he said, which was as near as he'd come to acknowledging the harrowing ordeal André and the others had endured— hungry, thirsty, and fearing they were doomed. "I came so close to overtaking that whoreson, André," he burst out, "so bloody close! I would have caught him, too, if my horse was not so winded and worn down . . ."

Some of the other rescued men had gathered around them by now, were beginning to offer their thanks with none of André's nonchalance, and Richard was glad to be interrupted by one of his knights. "My lord duke, what is your wish regarding the prisoners?"

Richard looked over at the routiers huddled on the ground, bound to one another by ropes, subdued and silent, all their bravado gone. He glanced around at the skeletal remains of Gorre, and his eyes took on the winter chill of the February sky. "We will take them with us to Aixe," he said, "where other brigands will learn from their sorry fate what befalls those who ravage my lands and my people."

U PON REACHING HIS CASTLE at Aixe, Richard made good on his promise to make an example of the captured routiers. Some were drowned in the River Vienne, others had their throats cut, and eighty men were blinded. Unlike his beheading of Geoffrey's knights, this ruthless, effective means of denying the routiers' future services to the rebel lords occasioned little comment. The prior of Vigeois Abbey even noted approvingly of the treatment meted out to these "sons of darkness."

E NTERING THE GREAT HALL at Aixe, André de Chauvigny soon spotted his duke and headed in Richard's direction. Richard was conferring quietly with one of his most trusted men, a grizzled serjeant who'd been in his service since he'd been invested with the duchy at age fourteen. He smiled as André approached, and once they were alone, he surprised his friend by confiding that he'd instructed the serjeant to escort his young son to Poitiers for safety's sake.

André knew Richard had an illegitimate son, but he knew nothing whatsoever about the child and even less about the child's mother; Richard was as close-mouthed as a clam about such matters. Agreeing that it was wise to bring the boy to Poitiers, he confessed then that "I do not even know the lad's name. What was he christened?"

"Philip." Richard hesitated and then offered up another rare nugget of private information, saying, "She wanted to name him after her father." His shoulders twitched in a why-not shrug. "I was not about to name him after mine."

André knew better than to pursue that further; Richard's troubled relationship with his father was as fraught with peril for the unwary as a walk across a thinly iced lake. He asked instead if the rumors were true that the Viscount of Turenne was bringing more routiers to join Aimar and the young king at Limoges. Richard confirmed it, and they began an intense discussion of the rebellion and Hal's prospects until they were interrupted by the arrival of one of Richard's knights, just back from a scouting foray.

He was not alone; his men were dragging a prisoner into the hall, a glum-looking man of middle years who was shoved forward to kneel at Richard's feet. "We saw him galloping along the Limoges road," the young knight explained breathlessly, "and I was curious why he was in such a tearing hurry. Most men who race the wind are either outlaws on the run or they're bearing urgent messages. So we stopped him, searched him, and discovered the reason for his haste. He is a courier for the French king, carrying a letter for your brother, the young king."

He beamed at Richard, his face aglow with triumph and pride, for all knew their duke put a high value upon men who were resourceful and quick-witted. Nor was he disappointed, for Richard responded with heartfelt praise. Delighted that he'd earned his lord's favor, he produced the royal letter with a flourish. "I did not think it was my place to read it. But I recognized the seal as King Philippe's, and after a little persuasion, our friend here admitted he was delivering it to your brother."

"Well done, Ancel." Richard quickly broke the seal and held the letter under a smoking rush-light. When he glanced up, his face was utterly without expression, as blank as a sepulcher's graven image, and André felt a frisson of disquiet shoot up his spine. "Summon my seneschal and the other members of my council," he instructed André in a voice that was toneless, so dispassionate that the other man's unease flamed into outright alarm.

RICHARD HAD NEVER SPENT much time at Aixe, a castle he'd taken from Viscount Aimar several years ago, and he'd expended little money on its upkeep. Lacking a solar, they had to gather in his bedchamber. Richard stood by the hearth, his eyes moving from face to face as if taking inventory of the men he trusted.

Robert de Montmirail was his new Seneschal of Poitou. Eleanor's uncles were not present, for Hugh had died seven years ago and Raoul de Faye was in ailing health. But Raoul's eldest son and namesake was there, as was Ourse de Freteval, his son-in-law. The Chauvignys were represented by André and his cousin Nicholas, who'd served Eleanor with such loyalty; as soon as he'd been released from his imprisonment at Loches, Nicholas had transferred his allegiance to Richard. Guillaume de Forz was, like André, a friend since boyhood, and Richard's cousin Rico had recently earned the accolade of knighthood.

After briefly telling them how he'd come into possession of the French king's letter, Richard wasted no time in breaking the bad news. "Philippe writes that he regrets he cannot come to fight alongside Hal in person. But he has sent a large band of Brabançon routiers to Limoges. Moreover, he assures Hal that his cousin Hugh, the Duke of Burgundy, is showing considerable interest in joining their alliance. And he claims that the Count of Toulouse is another one who is likely to throw in his lot with them, unable to resist this opportunity to bring me down."

There was a prolonged silence when he was done. As the men looked around at one another, it was obvious that they were sharing the same thoughts. Richard was already facing a formidable coalition: his brother the young king, his other brother the Duke of Brittany, Viscount Aimar, the Taillefer brothers of Angoulême, several de Lusignans, Elias, the Count of Périgord, the viscounts of Ventadour, Comborn, Turenne, and Castillon, the latter's brother Oliver, the castellan of Chalus, and Fulcand, Lord of Archiae, as well as several lesser lords who could, nevertheless, contribute men and money. Even with the Archangel Michael himself fighting on Richard's side, he could not hope to defeat so many rebel lords if they were backed by the French king, the Duke of Burgundy, and the Count of Toulouse. All of Richard's battlefield brilliance would avail him little against an army of that size.

But if they were in agreement as to what must be done, none of them were eager to try to convince Richard. The burden should have fallen upon his seneschal, but Robert de Montmirail had only recently been appointed to his post, and he prudently held his tongue. Neither Richard's friends nor his kinsmen wanted to risk their rapport with their young duke. It was finally Nicholas de Chauvigny who spoke up, as forthrightly as he'd done on the day he'd defied Porteclie de Mauzé for Eleanor's sake.

"My lord, you must seek the aid of your lord father, the king."

Richard's failure to flare up at the mere suggestion showed them that he'd already had the same thought, and his common sense was warring with his pride. They waited uneasily for his response, for with Richard, they could never be sure which one would prevail. "I do not see how I can do that," he admitted after a long silence. "My father and I are hardly on good terms these days. I left his court without his consent, and have ignored all the messages he's sent since then. And I would rather go down honorably in defeat than grovel and plead for his help."

André cleared his throat. "My lord, send me to the king," he said, utterly earnest for once. "I will not grovel on your behalf. You have my sworn word upon that. I will simply relate the facts, let the king make up his own mind. There is no dishonor in that."

Richard looked intently into his face, and then away. "Go, then," he said in a low voice. "Be sure you take a strong escort, though, for the roads to Angers are swarming with bandits, rebels, routiers, and masterless men seeking to take advantage of the unrest." His mouth twisted down. "Such is the evil that my brothers have let loose upon my duchy."

THE ENGLISH KING'S newest bedmate had raised some eyebrows, for she had a curly mane of flame-red hair, which had been thought unlucky since the time of Judas, and a crop of unfashionable freckles. But she also had an earthy sensuality, a merry laugh, and a good-natured tranquility that Henry found soothing. There was so little serenity in his life these days that he sought it out wherever he could find it.

She'd fallen asleep while waiting for him, awakening only when she'd reached out drowsily for his warmth and found his side of the bed cold and empty. Pulling the bed hangings aside, she sighed when she saw him seated by the hearth, still fully dressed, his sleepy squires struggling to stay awake should he have need of them. "My lord, are you never coming to bed?"

Henry glanced up at the sound of her voice. "Soon, Belle. Go back to sleep," he said, knowing that, bless her, she would. She was easily contented, utterly lacking in undercurrents, and he found that a strong part of her appeal. Rubbing his eyes, he looked down blearily at the pile of petitions in his lap. He was bone-tired, but he knew he'd not be able to sleep. His nights were always the same now. He'd lie awake for hours, unable to silence his inner voices, unsettled thoughts ricocheting around his brain until it was almost dawn, until his body's exhaustion would finally triumph over his mind's disquiet.

Rifling through the petitions randomly, he tried to focus upon the multitude of requests. The castellan at Loches had written to tell him of storm damage. His lazar house at Caen was also seeking aid. He'd always had a deep, visceral sympathy for lepers, had founded hospitals at Caen, Rouen, Le Mans, and now Angers, and it seemed that they all had unexpected expenses he must bear—roofs to be repaired, cisterns to be dug, fences to be mended. Even one of his proudest accomplishments—the great levee he'd built along a thirty-mile stretch in the Loire Valley to prevent seasonal flooding—was showing its age, in need of shoring up at Bourgueil. It was almost as if all of his life's work was crumbling at the same time.

Jesu! That last thought had him shaking his head in disgust. It was bad enough that he was wallowing in self-pity like this; must he be maudlin, too? Thrusting the petitions aside, he found himself staring into the dying fire. Why had he not heard from Hal by now? An eerie silence seemed to have settled over the Limousin; his scouts had little to report. When he got to his feet, his squires stirred, looking hopeful that he might be ready for bed. But he'd heard what they had not—a soft knock at the door.

It was his chamberlain, explaining apologetically that a courier had arrived with an urgent message from his son, and he'd reluctantly agreed to see if the king was still awake, warning the man that if not, he'd have to wait till morning.

Henry felt a vast, weary surge of relief. But his hopes were soon dashed, for the man being ushered in was one of Richard's household knights, not one of Hal's. Brushing his disappointment aside, he took solace that at least he was hearing from one of his recalcitrant sons. "André de Chauvigny, is it not?" he asked, in an impressive display of the memory that had always served him so well. "Are you kin to the Nicholas de Chauvigny who was one of my queen's men?"

"Indeed, sire. We are cousins." André came forward and sank to his knees in the floor rushes, as much to ease his aching body as to show proper reverence to the king, for he'd spared neither himself nor his horse in his haste to reach Angers. "My liege, there are matters that you need to know about." As concisely as possible, for he knew

Henry had no more patience than his duke, he related what they'd learned from the French king's letter, revealed the magnitude of the conspiracy confronting Richard.

Henry listened without interrupting, and when he was done, said only: "Are you so sure, then, that the young king is allied with the rebels?"

André paused, recognizing a pitfall when he saw one. "We have no reason to think otherwise, sire," he said cautiously.

Henry's expression was not easily read. Beckoning to the chamberlain, he said, "See that Sir André gets a bed for the night and whatever else he needs."

Realizing he'd just been dismissed, André got reluctantly to his feet. It took all of his self-control to do as he was bade, not to argue further on Richard's behalf. His discipline took him as far as the door, and there he could not help blurting out in despair, "My lord king . . . what will you do?"

"What do you think?" Henry said brusquely. "I am going to put out this fire ere it engulfs us all."

CHAPTER THIRTY-EIGHT

February 1183
Winchester, England

SOME OF THE PREROGATIVES of queenship had been restored to Eleanor in recent years, and she now had her own household, her own servants. When her chamberlain informed her that Lord Ranulf Fitz Roy and his son were asking if she'd see them, her brows arched in surprise. Was Ranulf finally thawing? But when he was ushered into her chamber, he greeted her with such brittle courtesy that she knew this wasn't the case. So what had brought him here?

"This is my eldest son, Bleddyn," Ranulf said, and Bleddyn bent over Eleanor's hand as if he were a polished courtier, welcoming the chance to study this controversial queen at such close range. Ranulf did not waste time in social pleasantries, at once revealed the reason for their unexpected presence at Winchester.

"My son and I are taking ship at Southampton, and as we approached Winchester, it occurred to me, Madame, that you might have the latest news from Aquitaine. It has been almost a fortnight since we got word of the rebellion, and much could have happened since—"

"Rebellion? What are you talking about, Ranulf?"

"You do not know?" he asked incredulously. This was a complication that he'd not foreseen. "The Lady Emma heard that war had broken out in the Limousin, and she was kind enough to pass word along to me, knowing that my son Morgan is serving as your son's squire."

Eleanor had rarely been so bewildered. What did Geoffrey have to do with the Limousin? Unless he'd come to Richard's aid? But that did not make sense, either, for why would that have sent Ranulf racing from Wales in such haste? "Did Viscount Aimar rebel again?" This was Harry's fault, damn him. Aimar had been a faithful vassal until he'd been denied Rainald's earldom.

"It is far worse than that, Madame. Your sons are at war with one another. Hal and Geoffrey have joined forces with the rebel barons against Richard. They aim for nothing less than to make Hal the Duke of Aquitaine, and my son is caught up in the midst of this madness!"

Eleanor stared at him blankly, as if she'd not been able to process what he'd just told her. It was the first time that Ranulf had ever seen her utterly at a loss. She swallowed with an effort, and her voice did not sound like Eleanor's at all, barely audible, with a noticeable quaver. "What . . . what of Harry? What is he doing about this?"

Ranulf shook his head. "I do not know. Emma's message made no mention of him."

She turned away, blindly, and he instinctively put out a hand in case she needed his support. Amaria had also hastened to her side, her eyes wide with horror. But then Eleanor said, "Get my mantle," in a very different tone, biting the command off so sharply that Amaria flinched away from the words as if they were weapons. Eleanor did not notice. She seemed to have forgotten Ranulf, too. Wrapping herself in her mantle, she moved swiftly toward the door, jerked it open, and plunged into the stairwell. Ranulf and his son exchanged glances, and then hurried after her.

RALPH FITZ STEPHEN LOOKED utterly miserable. "My lady, it was not my doing. I would never have kept this from you if I'd not been ordered to do so by the king."

The pupils of Eleanor's eyes had contracted to slits. "Did he, indeed?" she said softly. But the reckoning with Harry could wait. "Tell me what you know of this war between my sons."

He did, but he did not have much more information than Ranulf. The last he'd heard, Geoffrey had joined the rebels at Limoges, Hal had gone after him, and bloody fighting had broken out all across the duchy. He'd heard that the king was on his way, too, to Limoges, and there were rumors that the French king was coming to Hal's support. He was confident, though, that the king would quell the rebellion and reconcile her sons.

Eleanor dismissed his reassurances with an impatient shake of her head, and the rest of his words trickled away into the silence enveloping the hall. No one else ventured to speak, all eyes riveted upon the queen. "From now on," she said, "you will let me know as soon as you hear anything from Aquitaine, Sir Ralph—anything at all. Is that understood?"

He assured her that he understood, but over the years he'd grown protective of her, impressed by her courage. "Madame, if I may be so bold as to tell you what the lord king told me. He said that he meant to do all in his power to make peace between his sons, and that he hoped you would never need to know."

Eleanor was not mollified, saying icily, "He did not have the right to keep this from me." This was Eleanor at her most imperious, and none dared to argue with her. But it was, oddly enough, at this moment that Ranulf finally forgave her, for his father's fear had sharpened his perception and he saw beyond the queen's camouflage to the anguish underneath.

ANDRÉ DE CHAUVIGNY HAD BEEN EDGY and unsettled ever since they left Angers, for Henry had taken only his household knights, and André considered that an inadequate escort to ride into the lawless chaos that had descended upon Richard's duchy. Henry had brushed aside his misgivings so curtly that he decided his king and his duke were more alike than either one wanted to admit. He was vexed, too, that so many of Henry's men had elected not to wear their mail on the road. This was a common practice when speed was of the essence, and he was the only one clad in both hauberk and helmet.

They traveled fast, pushing their mounts and making no allowances for the winter weather, but André was accustomed to that from years of riding with Richard. Despite his qualms, they encountered no troubles on the road, and at dusk on the fourth day, they were within sight of Limoges. André was not happy about their destination, either, but he'd failed to convince Henry that it made more sense to rendezvous with Richard at Aixe before attempting to contact the young king and the rebels. He could only wonder which contributed more to the royal family's stubbornness—their Angevin blood or their high birth.

The gates of the ville were closed tight, a sign that the city was on a war footing, and Henry was displeased to see how much progress had been made in restoring the walls torn down at Richard's command two years ago. Aimar was becoming more than a nuisance, a burr under the saddle. His habitual rebellions were causing too much havoc in the Limousin. If there were any more intractable, troublesome vassals than Eleanor's barons, he hoped to God he never encountered them. They made the Welsh seem downright tame and docile.

As they approached, bells began to peal loudly. When one of Henry's men demanded entrance in the name of the king, there was no indication that he'd been heard, although they could see men's heads bobbing up in the embrasures. The church bells were still ringing, and they could hear men shouting, dogs barking. They drew closer, but before they could shout out again for admittance, they were met with a hail of arrows.

In the confusion, two men were thrown from their horses. Henry saw one of his knights take an arrow in the shoulder, and then he was rocked back in the saddle, slamming into the cantle. He felt no pain, just the impact, but Geoff was pointing and shouting, and he glanced down, saw the arrow shaft protruding from his mantle. They were all in retreat by now, and as soon as they'd gotten out of arrow range, the men clustered around Henry, the wounded knight temporarily forgotten.

"You've been hit," Geoff gasped, the soldier totally submerged for the moment in the son. Henry had already pulled his mantle back, and they all stared at the arrow caught in the metal links of his hauberk.

"I am not hurt," Henry insisted. "The point did not penetrate the mail. I may have a bad bruise, but the royal hide is not even scratched."

His attempt to make light of the hit did not convince the other men, for they knew that mail had no magical properties that would always deflect arrows; injuries depended upon such variables as the size of the arrowhead and the angle of the shot and simple luck. Moreover, some of them remembered that Henry had wavered about wearing a hauberk on the journey, prudence finally prevailing over comfort. Henry remembered that, too, but he took it as a sign of Divine Favor. This was not his closest call; when he'd been ambushed in the deep forests of Wales, an arrow had almost grazed his cheek. Still, though, it was a shocking assault upon the person of the king, upon God's Anointed, assuming it had been deliberate.

When Willem and André de Chauvigny insisted they must ride for Aixe, Henry did not protest. After tending to the injured knight as best they could, they detoured widely around Limoges and headed south to ford the River Vienne. And as he rode, Henry refused to let himself dwell upon that near-miss, for then he'd have had to confront questions he was not ready to face, questions about the complicity of his sons in those arrows raining down upon his men. Had it been an accident? Or an assassination attempt?

GEOFF HAD BEEN TAKEN ABACK by Richard's outraged reaction to their father's narrow escape. He found it difficult to dismiss his suspicions, though, and later could not resist commending his brother sarcastically upon his sudden filial devotion.

Richard liked Geoff no more thań Geoff liked him, and he gave the older man a suspicious look of his own. "What did you expect—that I'd not be angry if some damned fool nearly kills the king? If his aim had been a little better, we might have found ourselves facing calamity. The surest sign of the coming Apocalypse will be the day Hal gets to call himself a king in fact and not in name only." Catching the vexed expression on Geoff's face, he frowned. "What?"

"Our father was almost slain this afternoon, and you're just thankful that Hal will not be king? I swear the lot of you make Absalom look like a dutiful, loving son!"

"Why . . . because I spoke the truth? Sorry to disappoint you, but I am not a good liar. I could not hope to compete with Hal in that arena."

"I cannot argue with you there," Geoff conceded grudgingly. "The truth is not an utterly alien tongue to you, as it is to our brothers."

"Praise like that will turn my head, Geoff," Richard said, very dryly. "Hal is the worst offender, though. Geoffrey can lie as easily as he breathes, but at least he does not lie to himself. Hal usually gets entangled in his own webs, and that makes him truly dangerous."

Again, Geoff could find no fault with Richard's assessment of their brothers. "Do you think they deliberately ordered—" he began, only to be halted in mid-sentence by the stunned look on Richard's face. Following his gaze, Geoff turned and then he, too, gasped, for Hal had just entered the hall.

Henry had been seated on the dais, paying little heed to the men clustering around him, friends and sycophants alike trying their best to distract his thoughts from the day's troubling events. At the sight of his son, he jumped to his feet, although he remained where he was and let Hal come to him. Richard and Geoff were already in motion, too, and all three of them converged upon the dais at the same time.

"Are you unhurt, my liege?" Hal stopped on the steps, looking up searchingly into Henry's face. "I was horrified to hear of your mishap. It was an unfortunate misunderstanding. A fool watchman mistook your men for a raiding party from the cité and rang the alarm bell, crying out that the town was under attack. Thankfully one of my knights was on the castle walls and he recognized the royal banner. When I think what could have happened . . ." He grimaced, shaking his head. "You may be sure the bowman will be punished for his carelessness, and the watchman, too."

"I can spare you the trouble," Richard said laconically. "Send them to Aixe and we'll punish them for you."

Hal gave Richard a cool, dismissive glance. "How very kind of you to offer, Brother. But you've been known to discipline offenders with . . . an excess of zeal. I think it best that we deal with the culprits ourselves."

Richard dropped all pretense of civility and said with a snarl, "If you truly do punish that bowman, it will be because his aim was off!"

Hal flushed, looking genuinely angry. "You dare to accuse me of seeking my father's death?"

"And you dare to come here and insult us with your talk of 'accidents' and 'mishaps'? It is not wise to think all men are as dull-witted and foolhardy as you, *Brother*. Now I have another question for you. How do you plan to get back to your friends in Limoges?"

The knights who'd accompanied Hal took that as the threat it was meant to be and moved closer to the young king, hands now on sword hilts. "I'd sooner trust the good faith of an infidel Turk than yours," Hal jeered. "But I am here to speak with my lord father, and unlike you, he is a man of honor."

Now it was Richard's turn to sneer. "What would you know of honor? You're a joke, the King of Cockaigne, who's done naught but spend his sire's money and play the fool—"

"Enough!" Henry said suddenly, up till now a stricken witness to his family's fratricide. His eyes flicked from one to the other, and then, making up his mind, he beckoned to Hal. "I will hear what you have to say. Come with me," he commanded, and people hastened to clear a path as he stepped from the dais and headed for the door. Hal gestured to his knights to remain in the hall and then followed after his father.

Richard and Geoff watched them go. "That gibe about the 'King of Cockaigne' was clever," Geoff said at last, thinking that Hal was indeed meant to reign over that fabled land of milk and honey, never one in the real world. Richard did not reply, but as their eyes met, they silently acknowledged the start of an unlikely alliance.

THEY'D COME TO A HALT out in the bailey, snow crunching under their boots, chilled by a wind that had sprung up without warning, the damp, heavy air warning of rain before dawn.

"Papa, surely you cannot believe that arrow shot was anything but mischance!"

"What am I supposed to believe, Hal? You ask to be allowed to make peace with Geoffrey and the rebel barons, and then you disappear into blue smoke, with nary a word of your whereabouts or your intentions. When I reach Limoges, I find you dwelling comfortably in that den of thieves, and as I approach the gates, I come under attack. If you were not my flesh and blood—"

"But I am, and that makes all the difference in the world! What greater crime could there be than patricide? Yes, I was at Limoges, because that is where Geoffrey and the others are to be found. I have not abandoned my hopes of mending this rift between you and Geoffrey. I think I've been making headway, too. But Aimar and his allies are naturally doing their best to keep Geoffrey's resolve from wavering, so it may take more time. I've been assuring him that you are willing to forgive, will hold no grudges. That is true, is it not? I cannot act as your cat's-paw, Papa, cannot make promises to Geoffrey and the others if you do not mean to keep them."

"Of course I mean to keep them," Henry snapped, not sure how he'd ended up on the defensive. "I want no more strife in our family, Hal. But that peace must extend to you and your brothers. It is not enough that you all pledge fealty to me. You must somehow learn to live amicably with one another, however little love there is between you."

"Well, I get along with Geoffrey and Johnny. Two out of three is not so bad, is it?" Hal smiled then, saying quickly, "I ought not to be jesting about it, Papa, for I can see the pain it gives you. I know you are right. I just wish Brother Richard did not make it so damnably difficult!"

Henry studied his son's face, but the moon was obscured by clouds and the stars, too, were hidden. He'd always found it easy to detect lies and falsehoods, for all but the most practiced liars gave subtle signs that they were not telling the truth. It was a useful talent for a king, so why did it fail him when he needed it most? Why could he not tell when his sons were being truthful and when they were playing him false?

Putting Hal's veracity to the test, he demanded to know the identities of the other conspirators. Hal readily reeled off the names of prominent barons of the Limousin, including a few whose involvement had not been known to Henry. Raymond of Turenne was expected to arrive by next week, along with his son Boso and Bernart du Casnac, his son-in-law, he confided, and he wanted the chance to talk them out of throwing their lot in with Aimar, adding, "Now that you're here, that should make my task easier, for their grievances are with Richard, not you."

"So you want more time?"

"With so much at stake, Papa, I think it is worth my while to keep trying," Hal said earnestly, and Henry released a breath as soft as a sigh, making his choice, the only one he could.

"Go back, then," he said. "I will await word from you here."

HAL RETURNED TO LIMOGES in a surly mood, tersely reported that he'd achieved his objective, allaying Henry's suspicions and gaining them the time they needed to hire more routiers. But he'd then stalked off to his own quarters, and they could not help worrying that he was having second thoughts. Even Geoffrey was concerned, knowing how mercurial his brother could be, and after a hurried conference, they delegated several of their number to find out if Hal was indeed prey to misgivings.

In addition to Geoffrey, they selected one of Hal's closest friends, the Fleming Roger de Gaugi, and a man known for his battle prowess and his iron will, the head of the rapacious House of Lusignan, the Lord Joffroi. Hal did not look pleased to see them at his door, but he let them enter and sent his squire down to the buttery for wine. He then sprawled in the chair closest to the hearth and stared broodingly into the flames as if oblivious of their presence. There was something so deliberately dramatic about his pose, though, that Geoffrey was sure he was playing to his audience and could be coaxed into revealing what was troubling him.

And indeed, it only took a few probing questions to uncover the reason for Hal's discontent—guilt. Not that he'd admit it, but when he grumbled about Henry's trusting nature—a charge rarely if ever brought against the English king—Geoffrey found it easy enough to draw the natural conclusion. Hal felt remorseful that he'd taken advantage of their father's desperate need to believe in his innocence. Geoffrey did not begrudge Hal a twinge or two of conscience; he'd occasionally had them himself. But he had to be sure Hal did not mean to act upon those regrets, and he drew up a stool next to his brother.

"I know what you're feeling, Hal," he said, not altogether truthfully, for he was capable of unsentimental, pragmatic assessments that eluded his brother altogether. "You are not comfortable relying upon deception or guile. But we fight with what weapons we have at hand, and if we see an enemy's weakness, we'd be fools not to make use of it."

"I know," Hal admitted. His brother was right; he did not take naturally to deceit, preferred a more forthright, straightforward way. He was sorry he'd had to deceive his father, but why did he have to rush to Richard's rescue? Why could he not have stayed out of it? Was that so much to ask?

"It is only to be expected that you'd have some regrets," Geoffrey said, in the reassuring, sympathetic tone that had coaxed any number of skittish women into his bed. "But you cannot dwell upon these regrets, Hal. It is too late. That ship has sailed."

Roger and Joffroi had no idea what he was talking about, but Hal did, and he mustered up a wry smile. "You mean 'That ark has sailed,' do you not?" The shared memory was a bracing one, though, reminding him that they were in this together. "You need not fret," he assured his brother. "I am not losing heart. I just wish there'd been another way."

"So do I," Geoffrey said, with utter sincerity. Exchanging glances with the other men, Geoffrey saw that they agreed with him; the crisis had passed. He started to talk, then, about military matters—how many men they could expect from the French king, how long it would take them to finish replacing the city walls that Richard had destroyed, whether the Count of Toulouse could be lured into joining their alliance.

Hal stretched his long legs toward the fire, accepting a wine cup from his squire. In better spirits now, he told them about his ugly exchange with Richard. "I would barter the surety of my soul to bring that bastard down," he confessed, and when he glanced up, he was heartened to see that they were all united in their loathing for his arrogant churl of a brother.

Geoffrey had been hoping for such an opening. "Actually, there is something you can do, Hal, to make victory more likely. You can call William Marshal back into your service. For the life of me, I do not understand why you let so able a knight go. His battlefield judgment is solid, his courage unquestioned, and he handles a sword as well as any man I've ever seen. We need all the Marshals we can get."

Roger de Gaugi had been waiting for this chance, too, and quickly added his voice to Geoffrey's, urging Hal to bring Will Marshal back. Hal was not surprised by his praise, for he knew Roger and Will were good friends and had often partnered in tournaments. He took more notice when Joffroi de Lusignan also argued for the Marshal's recall, as there had long been bad blood between Will and the de Lusignans.

Acknowledging that now, the knight said bluntly that he knew Marshal loved him not. "He has always blamed me for the death of his uncle in that ambush, and I was never able to convince him that we'd wanted very much to take Salisbury alive. Our differences notwithstanding, I would be the first to welcome him back."

In truth, Hal wanted Will back, too. He'd begun to miss him almost as soon as Will had ridden off, and he'd toyed with the idea of recalling him. His pride had kept him from doing it, though, for he was not willing to risk the humiliation if Marshal balked at coming. The other men were presenting him with an opportunity now to reach out to Will while still saving his pride; if Will refused, he could always say that he'd never truly wanted him back, that he'd agreed only because his brother and friends had asked it of him.

"Very well," he said graciously, "if it means that much to you all, I'll take him back." And he did not object when Geoffrey at once sent for his chamberlain, not wanting Hal to change his mind during the night. When the man entered, Hal instructed him to go in search of Will Marshal and tell Will that "I am summoning him in good faith, confident that he'll not fail me."

CHAPTER THIRTY-NINE

March 1183
Limoges, Limousin

ENRY AND HIS MEN drew rein, gazing at the newly fortified walls of the ville. So their scout had been right when he'd reported that they had torn down more than half a dozen churches to get timber for the walls. Henry's mouth tightened; this was hardly an indication of the peaceful intentions Hal had avowed. No one spoke; he knew he'd been the only one to have doubted the scout's story, insisting upon seeing for himself.

"My lord king?" Maurice de Craon nudged his mount closer to Henry's. "Shall we continue on to the cité?"

Henry found himself torn between amusement and exasperation, for he well knew what Maurice was really saying. They'd been greatly relieved when he'd agreed to enter the cité rather than the ville, and they were worrying now that he might have changed his mind. "You need not fret, old friend," he said, with just a touch of sarcasm. "I daresay we'll get a warmer welcome at the bishop's palace than the viscount's castle."

The words were no sooner out of his mouth than it happened. His stallion was shifting restlessly and tossed its head up just in time to take an arrow in the neck, which pierced the carotid artery. Blood spurted wildly, all over Henry, the horse, and even Maurice de Craon. Henry's years of horsemanship now stood him in good stead, and as the animal's legs began to buckle, he flung himself from the saddle to escape the fate of the Scots king, who'd been pinned by his own mount when it was slain at Alnwick. His horrified men moved hastily to get between their blood-splattered king and the unseen bowman on the town walls, holding up their shields to deflect any more arrows. None came. There was only silence from the ville as Henry got to his feet, wiping blood from his face, and stared down at his dying mount.

RICHARD WAS EXHAUSTED and angry by the time he got back to Aixe that evening. He'd ridden south to investigate a report that routiers had been seen near Pierre-Buffière and found it was even worse than he'd feared. A large band of men led by one of the most notorious of the routier captains, a Basque known as Sancho of Savannac, had seized control of the citadel at Pierre-Buffière. This was another of Viscount Aimar's castles that had been taken away from him by Richard, and it was now back in rebel hands, for Richard knew that Sancho was in the hire of Aimar and the Viscount of Turenne. He'd not had enough men to challenge their occupation, could only watch from a safe distance and fume.

He was dismounting in the bailey at Aixe when he saw Geoff coming toward him. The look on his half brother's face warned him that he was not about to hear good news, and he listened grimly as Geoff gave him a succinct account of the latest attack upon their father. "He was not hurt, though?"

Geoff shook his head. "But that was by God's Grace, for if the stallion had not raised his head at that very moment, Papa would have taken the arrow in his chest."

Richard had not expected them to be so brazen, to make another attempt on Henry's life. But mayhap it was for the best if this latest treachery had opened his father's eyes to the truth. "What did he say about it? Surely he must know by now that Hal is less trustworthy than a hungry weasel."

"He has not spoken much about it, except to express his sorrow at losing such a fine horse. So I cannot say if he is still deluding himself or not. But you have not heard all of it, Richard. Who do you think just rode in, bold as you please? And this time Hal brought along his partner in crime!"

Richard swore, making use of one of Henry's favorite oaths. "Where are they?" And when Geoff said that Henry had taken them up to his bedchamber, he flung the reins of his stallion at the closest of his knights and headed for the keep.

Geoff hurried to keep pace. "What are you going to do?"

"I'd not miss this performance for all the gold in Montpellier!"

Reaching Henry's bedchamber, Geoff was about to knock on the door when Richard shoved it open, with enough force to slam it into the wall. "I hope the mummery has not started yet?"

Hal scowled at the sight of the intruders. It was Geoffrey, though, who seemed most eager for a confrontation. "You are looking surprisingly well, Richard. You must have found a very strong soap to wash all that blood off your hands."

"I make no apologies for what I did, and I will do it again if the need arises. When men invade my lands, they will pay with their lives, be they lowborn routiers or Breton knights. My only regret is that the truly guilty ones are likely to escape the reckoning they so richly deserve!"

Richard was easily the taller of the two, but Geoffrey stood his ground, and the look that passed between them was so virulent that both Henry and Geoff acted instinctively and stepped forward in case they needed to intercede physically. Henry had reached a milestone—his fiftieth birthday—that week, and he looked every single one of those years at the moment.

"Enough!" Henry said wearily. "I told Hal and Geoffrey that I'd hear them out. You are welcome to remain, Richard, and you, too, Geoff, but only if you keep your mouths shut. If you cannot do that, go."

A brief silence settled over the room, a truce that they all knew was not likely to last. Hal was the first to speak. Ignoring Richard and Geoff, he looked intently into Henry's face. "As we told you, Papa, I had no luck in finding the man who shot that arrow. None of them are willing to own up to it. Not surprising, I suppose. He's afraid and with good reason. I am so sorry, for this ought never to have happened. As soon as we learned of it, we came straightaway to assure you that it was mischance, no more than that." He glanced then toward his brother.

Geoffrey tore his gaze away from Richard, made a visible effort to focus himself. "Hal speaks true, Papa. That bowman was not acting on our orders."

Henry would have expected Richard to be the one to erupt first. Instead, it was Geoff. "Well, whose orders was he acting on?" he snapped. "You cannot convince me that he'd have dared to act on his own. So who told him to shoot the king?"

Henry started to speak, then stopped, for he wanted the answer to that question himself. Geoff took advantage of his father's hesitation and glared accusingly at his brothers. "Well?" he demanded. "Can either of you tell us in all honesty that none of your honorable allies would have given that command?"

"Yes, I can," Hal said with certainty at the same time that Geoffrey admitted, "No, I cannot." Hal stared at his younger brother in surprise.

"How can we?" Geoffrey gave Hal an impatient look. "The fact is that Papa's death would be very advantageous to a number of men. I make no accusations, have no reason to suspect any particular one of the lords now in Limoges. But neither can I say with utter certainty that such an order could not have been given."

"Well, I can," Hal repeated. "None of them would sully their honor with a crime like regicide. It was an accident, no more than that."

"The most convenient accident since William Rufus was slain in the hunting mishap that made his brother king," Richard muttered, and Hal glared at him before turning his attention back to Henry.

"Neither one of us would ever have done this, Papa. Surely you know that?"

Henry was not sure what he knew. "Is that why you came, Geoffrey? To tell me this was none of your doing?" And when his son inclined his head, he reached out suddenly and grasped the younger man's arm. Geoffrey stiffened, but did not pull away. Nor did he avert his gaze, meeting Henry's eyes unflinchingly.

"What of the rebellion? Hal says he has been seeking to win you back to your family, your natural loyalties. Have you heeded him? Are you willing to renounce this accursed alliance?"

"I have been thinking about it," Geoffrey said. "But I cannot abandon my allies without a backward glance. I would need to know that their grievances will be heard."

"I am willing to do that," Henry said, letting his hand slip from Geoffrey's arm. Richard drew an audible breath. "Well, I am not!"

"They want to meet with the king, not with you," Geoffrey said disdainfully, and for a moment, his eyes rested upon his brother's flushed face, silently promising Richard that there would indeed be a reckoning. "I will talk to Aimar and the others, tell them that you agree to a truce whilst they consider their choices," he told Henry, and startled them all, then, even Hal, when he made ready to depart.

"That is it?" Henry stared at his son. "That is all you have to say?"

Geoffrey paused, his hand on the door. "What would you have me say?"

"I would have you explain yourself! I would have you tell me why you would betray me like this, why you—"

"How could you possibly not know?"

"I do not," Henry insisted, and Geoffrey's control cracked.

"That you do not know, Papa, says it all," he said sharply, and left before Henry could respond.

Henry's frustration found expression in anger. "What is he talking about? What grievance could he have that justifies his betrayal?"

"You truly do not know, do you?" Hal marveled. "It is because of Richmond and

Nantes, Papa. Geoffrey and Constance feel that you cheated them out of two-thirds of her inheritance."

"That is the reason he rebelled? How could he be so foolish? I've always told him that I'd give him Nantes and Richmond when the time was right. He had only to be patient!"

Hal and Richard were looking at him with an oddly similar expression, one of amazement, for it was obvious to them that Henry was quite sincere, that he did not understand why Geoffrey might not trust his promises or be willing to wait indefinitely. Even Geoff was uncomfortable with his sire's inability to see any viewpoint but his own.

"I'd best catch up with Geoffrey ere he takes all our men and leaves me stranded here," Hal said with a quick smile. "But I think I know a way, Papa, to reassure you that Aimar and the townspeople are not utterly set on war. Suppose they offer up hostages for their good faith?"

When Henry agreed, Hal made his departure, too, making an ostentatious display of ignoring his brothers as he walked past them to the door. Richard at once started to follow, halting with obvious reluctance when Henry ordered him to wait there until Hal and Geoffrey had gone.

"Whilst you were ducking arrows at Limoges, my lord king," Richard said coolly, "some of Aimar's routiers retook the castle at Pierre-Buffière. Unless you want us to be trapped in Aixe under siege, we need to take action, and take it now."

"I have sent into Normandy and Anjou for my levies and for the routiers who've served me well in the past. They are better trained and better disciplined than the brigands hired by Aimar and Geoffrey, who're like to riot and go wild the first chance they get."

Richard agreed that his father's and his own routiers were superior soldiers to the men in the rebels' employ. He was heartened, too, that Henry was at last reacting as a king and not a foolish, overly fond father. "It is about time," he said, gruffly approving, and went off, then, in search of a late supper. Geoff would have lingered, but Henry clearly did not want him there, and so he, too, departed.

Alone at last, Henry slumped down in his seat and closed his eyes. Whenever he'd faced a crisis in the past, he'd known what he must do to prevail. Even when he was imperiled by the Becket scandal and then his family's first rebellion, he'd seen a way clear, a route that would lead him out of the morass and back onto solid ground. Now he saw no such escape. The best he could hope for would be to lure Geoffrey back to the fold and reconcile Richard with his angry barons. But that would be a short-term solution, slapping a bandage upon an ulcerating wound, one that oozed blood and pus and could prove mortal if it were allowed to fester.

RANULF AND BLEDDYN had been stuck in Southampton for several weeks, waiting for favorable winds. Then there had been a further delay as they tried to find men going south into a war zone, for it was too dangerous to venture into the lawless lands of Aquitaine without a good-sized escort. They did not reach Aixe, therefore, until late in Lent. Before they could seek Henry out, though, they were waylaid by Richard and Geoff and borne off to the great hall.

"I've ordered food for you," Geoff said as soon as they were seated. "But we need to talk with you ere you see our father. Your arrival is a blessing, Uncle Ranulf, for you're one of the few men that Papa may be willing to heed. You must convince him that Hal and Geoffrey cannot be trusted, that they are playing him for a fool."

"It would help if I knew what is going on," Ranulf said, somewhat testily, for these past weeks had been highly stressful. He'd not expected to be making urgent journeys like this at his age. "Where is Morgan? At the castle with Geoffrey?"

"The last we heard, Geoffrey is still in Limoges," Richard confirmed, "and I assume Morgan is with him. You're right to fear for the lad, Uncle, for he has fallen in with men who are no better than outlaws and cutthroats."

That was hardly what Ranulf had hoped to hear. But before he could press for more information, they were interrupted by the arrival of their food, an unappetizing Lenten meal of salted herring supplemented by a tastier dish of hulled wheat boiled in almond milk, commonly known as frumenty. Bleddyn was very hungry and tucked in, but Ranulf lost his appetite once Richard and Geoff satisfied his need to know "what is going on." He was shocked by Henry's two narrow escapes, although he was not as certain as they seemed to be that Henry had been deliberately targeted; it would take a bold man to strike down a king.

He was deeply troubled, too, to hear how Hal and Geoffrey had been taking advantage of Henry's trust; even allowing for Richard's bias, it sounded to him as if his nephew was indeed being "played for a fool." He prodded his knife into his herring without enthusiasm, thinking that none of this boded well for Morgan.

"You've not even heard the worst of it yet." Richard leaned forward, no longer remembering to keep his voice low. "Hal promised that they'd offer up hostages, and when Maurice de Craon went to fetch them, he and his men were fired upon! Then Hal had the gall to come back and once again avow that this was another of their many 'mishaps.'"

"Did Harry believe him?"

Geoff shrugged. "Who knows? He'll not even talk to us about it anymore. But the mere fact that he is still willing to listen to their lies is more than I can comprehend!"

"Geoff is right," Richard declared, loudly enough to turn heads in their direction. "I tell you, Uncle, it shames me to see him being duped like this. He's usually quick to suspect the worst, for certes where my mother is concerned. But now he keeps giving those double-dealing hellspawns the benefit of every doubt! It is enough to make me wonder if he is slipping into his dotage."

"It is not his brain that is leading him astray. It is his heart," Ranulf said, with such heat that the younger men looked at him in surprise. "Do you truly find it so strange that he'd not want to believe his sons could be conniving at his death? If either of you had sons of your own, you'd not be so quick to pass judgment on him!"

"I do have a son," Richard protested, earning him curious glances from Geoff and Bleddyn. But Ranulf was not mollified.

"And I'd wager he's too young to give you any grief yet. Just wait until he's old enough to balk, until he stops paying heed to a word you say, and then tell me that Harry is in his dotage!"

Bleddyn had begun to look uncomfortable, not sure whether Ranulf was drawing upon painful memories of their own estrangement. Richard and Geoff merely looked baffled. "Are you saying, then, that you'll not even try to talk some sense into him? For if you cannot convince him, Uncle, I do not know who can."

"Of course I will talk to him, Richard. I am simply saying that I understand, I understand all too well. But Harry is not my first concern. I am here to get my son Morgan out of this . . . this blood feud. Will the rebels honor a flag of truce?"

Geoff and Richard exchanged glances and then nodded. Richard could not resist a flash of mordant humor, though, saying sardonically that "I hope, though, that you have better luck with your flag of truce than my father had with his."

R ANULF STARED AT HIS SON in dismay. "You cannot stay here, Morgan! God only knows how this will all end, but I can safely say it will not end well. Your brother and I have come to take you back to Wales."

Morgan glanced toward his brother, his indignation showing clearly on his face. Bleddyn shrugged and gave him a sheepish smile, for unlike Ranulf, he'd been sure Morgan would refuse. He'd still chosen to accompany Ranulf on this perilous trip, if only to keep him safe. But he'd never expected them to succeed.

"Morgan, you are not being given a choice! I am not going to leave you in the midst of a civil war."

Morgan began to bridle, but the anguished expression on his father's face stilled his temper before it could fully ignite. "Papa," he said gently, "I am no longer a child. I was nineteen in February. Need I remind you that in Wales a lad reaches his legal majority at fourteen? I am old enough to make my own choices, and my choice is to remain with Cousin Geoffrey. He has been very good to me, has even promised to knight me himself and has offered me a place in his own household. Moreover, he has a just grievance against his father. How can I abandon him at a time like this?"

"Because he is fighting against his king, because that is treason, Morgan, and if you stay with him, it makes you guilty of treason, too."

Morgan felt as if they were speaking two different languages, neither one able to understand the other. "Papa . . . we do not see it like that. We are fighting for *our* king, fighting for Cousin Hal. He is God's Anointed just as much as Cousin Harry. So how can that be treason?"

Ranulf looked at his son in despair, seeing that he was not going to prevail. Making one last effort, he said, "I promised your mother that I'd bring you home. How am I supposed to tell her that you refused to come?"

"That was a low blow," Morgan said, sounding more reproachful than resentful, and Ranulf's shoulders slumped in defeat.

"I know," he admitted, and after that, there seemed nothing more to say.

ONE GLANCE AT RANULF'S FACE and Henry knew his mission had failed. Beckoning his uncle up onto the dais, he signaled to a passing servant for wine. "You look like a man greatly in need of a drink. It is one of the regrets of my life that I never learned how to drown my troubles in wine, but who knows? It might work for you."

Ranulf gratefully sank down in an empty chair. "I do not remember ever being so tired," he confided. "I must be getting old . . ."

"You *are* old," Henry pointed out, with the glimmer of a smile. "Hell and damnation, Uncle, we're both old, and getting older by the day."

Ranulf took a deep swallow of wine, then another. "Were we this stubborn and foolhardy when we were young?"

Henry was gazing down into his wine cup, as if it held the answers they sought. "So Morgan is still beguiled by my sons, chose them over you. My sympathies, Uncle. I can say in all honesty that I know exactly what you are feeling right now."

"Harry . . . whilst I was at the ville, I heard men talking in the hall. They were saying that Viscount Aimar had summoned all the townspeople to the church of St Pierre, where they were instructed to swear fealty to Hal." To Ranulf, this was the final nail in the coffin of Hal's credibility, and he was taken aback when Henry continued calmly to sip his wine. "You do not seem surprised," he said at last, and Henry regarded him in silence for a moment, then leaned over and clinked their wine cups together, with the saddest smile Ranulf had ever seen.

"Shall we drink," he said, "to the joys of fatherhood?"

W HEN RALPH FITZ STEPHEN was admitted to her chamber, Eleanor's eyes locked upon the letter in his hand. He did not keep her in suspense, hastened toward her and held it out. "This has just arrived for you, Madame, from your son."

Amaria wondered which son he meant, but Eleanor already knew even before she saw the familiar ducal seal of Aquitaine. It had been broken, of course, for her greater freedom did not include freedom from discreet surveillance. Snatching the letter, she moved toward an oil lamp and began to read.

Ralph Fitz Stephen withdrew, and Amaria wondered if she should leave, too, not sure if Eleanor would want to be alone or not. It depended, she supposed, upon the contents of that letter.

When Eleanor looked up, she eased the other woman's uncertainty by saying, "This is from my son Richard. I am thankful that he thought to write to me, but all his news is bad, Amaria. He says the French king has sent routiers to aid the rebels and they have done widespread damage, burning the town of St-Léonard-de-Noblat after stripping it bare, killing the men and carrying off the women. Périgord, Angoumois, and the Saintonge have all been overrun by the rebels. He admits that they'd be in dire straits if the rebel lords could control their men and launch concerted attacks. But fortunately their routiers lack discipline and are more interested in plundering and looting than in fighting a real war."

It sounded to Amaria as if Richard and Henry were already in dire straits, and she suspected that Eleanor thought so, too. The queen had that glazed, faraway look in her eyes again. Deciding to take her cues from her lady, she asked no questions, waiting to see if Eleanor wanted to confide in her, and after a time, the older woman began to speak again, her tones brittle and taut, sounding as if the muscles in her throat had constricted so painfully that the words had to fight their way free.

"Richard says that Hal and Geoffrey have done nothing but lie to Harry, that again and again he has offered them forgiveness, only to have them make a mockery of his trust. He says that Harry was twice shot at as he approached the city. That Hal promised hostages and then ambushed Harry's men when they came to get them. That he claimed to have taken the cross and threatened to depart for the Holy Land, but let himself be persuaded when Harry entreated him not to go. That when Harry sent two envoys to Geoffrey, his men attacked them, stabbing one and throwing the other off the bridge into the river. Neither Geoffrey nor Hal took any measures to punish their men for these breaches of the truce."

Eleanor related this litany of her sons' sins so matter-of-factly that Amaria found herself on the verge of tears, for she knew how much that dispassionate recital had cost the queen. She wanted to say how very sorry she was, but Eleanor's wounds were beyond her power to heal. "What are the king and Lord Richard doing to defeat the rebels, my lady?"

"Harry set up his camp at the cité and is besieging the ville, that part of Limoges controlled by the rebels. But Richard says it is not going well, that the weather has been wretched and they've been unable to seal off the ville completely. So Richard has gone south in pursuit of the routier bands, and he says they have been unwilling to face him on the field, have been fleeing instead of giving battle."

Amaria seized upon this last statement, so eager was she to offer Eleanor some slivers of hope. "Surely it is a promising sign, Madame, that the routiers are afraid to fight the duke. The king and Lord Richard are such brilliant battle commanders that they will soon have the rebels on the run, will crush them like King David smote the Philistines."

Eleanor understood that Amaria was only trying to comfort her and so she did not point out that two of her sons would be leading those "crushed rebels." Nor did she comment upon the eerie aptness of Amaria's choice of biblical verse, for King David had been betrayed by his best-loved son, the beautiful, beguiling Absalom, who'd stolen the hearts of the men of Israel.

"I want to go to the chapel," she said, and Amaria hurried to find her mantle. An icy sleet was falling for it had been a cold, wet spring, and as she crossed the bailey, Eleanor no longer fought back her tears, let them mingle with the raindrops upon her skin. What could she ask the Almighty? No matter who won this accursed war, she and Harry would lose.

CHAPTER FORTY

✦

April 1183
Limoges, Limousin

NOWN TO BE A STALWART SUPPORTER of the Duke of Aquitaine, the abbot of St Martial's had prudently taken refuge in a nearby town when Viscount Aimar rebelled again, leaving the abbey in the charge of his prior. That individual lacked the moral fortitude to deal with the latest crisis, and he'd gone in despair to one of their guests, Geoffroi de Breuil, for he was the prior of the abbey of Vigeois to the south of the city, had once been a monk himself at St Martial's, and had the necessary steel in his spine to stand up to the scandalous demands of the young English king.

Upon hearing the alarming news that Hal's soldiers had entered the abbey grounds and were making off with the silver plate, chalices, and jeweled reliquaries of St Martial's, Prior Geoffroi hastened to find the king, finally tracking Hal down in the cloisters. The scene that met his eyes was a dismal one: men joking and squabbling with one another, their arms full of booty, trailed by unhappy monks. Outraged by this violation of God's House, Prior Geoffroi cried out to Hal and was taken aback by the warmth of the younger man's welcome.

"Ah, it is Prior . . . Geoffroi, is it not? I met you at the viscount's castle last summer as I recall." Hal smiled benevolently at the prior, pleased that he'd been able to re-member the man's name, and Prior Geoffroi gaped at him in amazement, unable to treat this banditry as a social occasion.

"My lord king, may I speak with you in private? It is urgent, I assure you."

Hal's smile faded. But he thought a refusal would be rude and reluctantly fol-lowed the prior toward the Chapter House, hoping this was not going to be a lecture. It was not as if Prior Geoffroi's own abbey was being affected, after all.

Prior Geoffroi's trip to Limoges had been an impulsive one, motivated both by his fondness for his former abbey and his awareness that the prior would not be up to the challenge of keeping St Martial's safe in the abbot's absence. Now he realized why he was here; the Almighty had chosen him to stop this sacrilege.

"My lord, you cannot do this. No matter how much you need money, there is no justification for stealing from God."

Hal had not expected such a direct assault, not after the prior's timid, wavering protest. "I am not stealing from God!" he said indignantly. "Did Prior Gautier not tell you that I have promised to repay every last sou? This is a loan, no more than that, like the loan made to me by the good citizens of the ville."

Prior Geoffroi had heard about that "loan." Hal had extorted twenty thousand sous from the burghers of Limoges, who were intimidated by the continuing presence in the ville of so many swaggering, brawling routiers. "That matter is between you and the townsmen, my lord. What you do here today is between you and the Almighty, and I urge you to reconsider. There is still time to remedy this sin."

"It is hardly a sin," Hal said curtly, regretting the good manners that had gotten him into such an awkward predicament. "As I said, I have every intention of repaying the loan."

"It is not a 'loan' if it is not voluntary, my lord king. Moreover, your men are tak-ing more than money. They are carrying off valuable chalices and reliquaries that can-not be replaced."

Hal yearned to escape back into the cloisters. But Prior Geoffroi had positioned himself before the door, and Hal was loath to shove the prior out of the way; he was an elderly man and frail for all his bold talk. "Look . . . Prior Geoffroi, it is like this," he said, lowering his voice to increase the intimacy of his confession. "I do not want to do this, but I have no choice. Viscount Aimar and I agreed to hire all the routiers who sought us out, wanting to deny their services to my father and brother. But the cost has been higher than we expected. What can you do with a pack of hungry wolves except feed them?"

The prior was unmoved by his plight. "Why cannot Viscount Aimar pay your routiers? Or the Viscount of Turenne or Joffroi de Lusignan?"

"Because they do not have the money, either." Hal heard the impatient note creeping into his voice and drew a deep breath. "If my brother the Duke of Brittany were still at Limoges, I could have turned to him for aid. But he has gone north to protect the Breton borders. So you see, Prior Geoffroi, I must borrow from the abbey. I took measures to make sure that none of the monks or abbey guests would be molested, and I even ordered men to protect your library, for I know that St Martial's has a fine collection of books. And as I already said, I have sworn to repay the loan."

Hal could see no sign of softening in the chiseled granite of the older man's face, but he'd exhausted the last of his patience. "I had a chirograph drawn up, setting forth my promise to repay the abbey, as proof of my good faith." When Prior Geoffroi did not reach out for it, Hal thrust it into the prior's hands, saying brusquely, "Here is the abbey's half. Now I have no more time to spare for you, my lord prior. If you'll step aside . . ."

Prior Geoffroi hesitated, but then realized the foolishness of resistance, for Hal was half a foot taller and almost forty years younger. Grudgingly, he gave way, his fist tightening around the chirograph, for he knew its true worth. He could not help giving one final warning, though, as Hal brushed past him.

"Look to your soul, king of the English, for you've just put it in grave peril!" But Hal did not bother to reply, and once he was alone, the aged prior sank down upon the closest bench, his eyes stinging with angry tears.

Hal and Aimar's Taillefer half brothers had captured Angoulême with surprising ease. Leaving them to hold the castle and town, Hal decided to return to Limoges, to share his triumph with Aimar and the other rebel barons. His success was proof that the Almighty understood why he'd had to take the silver plate and treasures of St Martial's, and when his money started to run low, he made another forced "loan," this one from the monks at La Couronne just west of Angoulême, securing enough funds to hire Sancho of Savannac and his equally notorious partner Couraban. They'd left the Viscount of Turenne's service when he'd been unable to keep paying them, and Hal was looking forward to bedeviling Viscount Raymond—good-naturedly, of course—about it.

They reached Limoges in late afternoon. The gates were closed, and they could see men standing guard on the walls. One of Hal's knights rode up to demand entry in the name of the young king. To their surprise, the gates remained shut. When another shout for admittance brought no results, Hal spurred his stallion forward impatiently, identified himself to the sentries, and waited expectantly.

The gates did not open, though. Instead a shower of rocks rained down upon them from the walls. Several men and horses were struck and Hal's stallion reared up in fright and then bucked wildly; had he been a less skilled rider, he'd have gone sailing over its head. The hailstorm of stones continued, forcing them to retreat. And now Hal could hear the taunts and curses, the angry shouts of "We will not have this man to rule over us!"

H AL WAS GENUINELY SHOCKED to be turned away by the citizens of Limoges, and when Aimar sent out a messenger, he brought no words of comfort. The townspeople had been outraged by the plundering of St Martial's Abbey, the man reported, and the viscount had been unable to calm them down. It would be best if Hal did not try to enter the city again.

Hal and his men withdrew to Aimar's newly recovered castle at Pierre-Buffière, and used it as a base to burn crops and launch raids on neighboring towns. But the insult he'd received at Limoges continued to rankle, and as May dragged on, he became more and more discontented. He'd truly expected the war to be of short duration, and now they seemed likely to face a prolonged struggle. Once the wretched weather improved, Henry resumed the siege of Limoges, and Richard was in deadly pursuit of the roving bands of routiers that had been terrorizing the Saintonge and Poitou. Hal still expected them to win, but he was beginning to realize that victory could come at a much higher price than he'd wanted to pay.

He was soon thoroughly unhappy with his routier allies. They seemed far more interested in looting than in laying siege to castles, and he had little confidence in Sancho and Couraban's ability to control them. He found the routier captains to be as irksome and offensive as their men. Until now he'd never had many dealings with mercenaries, and he did not enjoy their company. The routiers were scornful of the chivalric code that had governed Hal's life and mocked the concept of knightly honor. They showed him none of the deference he was accustomed to receive from others, and he suspected that they did not respect him much either. Most vexing of all, they were draining his coffers, charging exorbitant fees for their services, and demanding to be compensated on a regular basis, unwilling to accept vouchers or promises of payment.

His disillusionment extended well beyond the routiers, though. He was annoyed with Geoffrey for racing off to defend Brittany. He'd argued that the struggle in the Limousin was critical to their success, but once Geoffrey got word that Henry's agent, Roland de Dinan, had occupied the ducal castle at Rennes, he'd turned a deaf ear to Hal's pleas, promising only that he'd return as soon as he could. Hal missed his brother more than he'd expected, aware that Geoffrey had a cooler head in a crisis than his own.

He was not pleased with Aimar, either, for allowing the citizens of the ville to rebuff a king, and he was having some doubts about the reliability of his other allies. His brother-in-law Philippe's routiers were wreaking havoc in the border regions, but he thought the French king ought to have put them under his command instead of turning them loose to ravage like mad dogs. He'd heard rumors that Joffroi de Lusignan's brothers were gaining a foothold in La Marche and there were reports, too, that the Count of Toulouse's son was raiding in Quercy and Cahors. Since the de Lusignans had vigorously opposed the sale of La Marche to Henry and Count Raimon had lost Cahors and Quercy during one of his wars with the English king, Hal could not help wondering if they were acting in his interests or their own.

But his greatest grievance was with his father, for he was sure that his war would already have been won if only Henry had stayed out of it. He did not understand why Henry must meddle in a dispute that did not involve him directly. But it was obvious by now that Henry was backing Richard with the full power of the English Crown. After weeks of offering an olive branch, he'd unsheathed his sword, giving the command to ravage Geoffrey's lands, calling upon his levies in Normandy and Anjou, bringing his mangonels and battering rams to Limoges in a far more serious siege of the ville. At Easter he'd ordered the arrest of the Earl and Countess of Leicester and other prominent participants in the rebellion of '73; he'd even included the Earl of Gloucester in his net, although there'd never been proof of his participation. And rumor had it that he'd asked the Church to issue sanctions against the rebels. No, this was not the war Hal had expected to fight.

O N MAY 23, Hal, his knights, and routiers seized control of Richard's castle at Aixe. Afterward, the men celebrated raucously in the great hall, but Hal did not share their pleasure, for he knew it to have been a hollow victory. Richard had left only a token garrison at Aixe, and Hal could not take pride in such a lopsided win. This was new for him—this clear-eyed assessment of their accomplishments—and he did not welcome it, thinking morosely that life had been more fun before he'd discovered this hitherto hidden sense of realism.

He had little appetite for their simple, soldiers' meal, was even less inclined to join in the revelries, and when a tipsy Couraban lurched over to offer the services of a buxom, drunken whore with hair the shade of beet juice, Hal's distaste was enough to drive him from the hall. As if he'd take a routier's leavings! He'd decided that Couraban was even more disreputable than his partner in crime, Sancho, for he'd finally learned the meaning of Couraban's odd name. He was, the brigand had boasted, a Saracen prince at the siege of Antioch. Hal could not begin to understand why a man would choose to call himself after a godless infidel. If he'd needed more proof that he was consorting with the dregs of their world, surely this was it.

He'd claimed the bedchamber he hoped was Richard's and flung himself down upon the bed without bothering to remove his muddied boots. He wished he'd thought to bring a flagon from the hall, but he could not muster the energy to go back for one and he had no idea where his squires were. It had not escaped his notice that his household knights had been making themselves scarce in recent days, waiting for his bad mood to pass. But the news he'd heard today was not likely to raise his spirits. One of their scouts had reported that Henry had summoned the Archbishop of Canterbury and numerous Norman bishops to Caen, where they were to pass sentence of excommunication upon the rebels.

Hal was stunned that his father would put him at risk for eternal damnation. An excommunicate who died without making amends would burn for aye in Hell. No matter how often he reminded himself that these excommunications were purely political, he still found the prospect chilling. How could Papa even consider that? How had they ever come to this?

His thoughts were so morbid and unpleasant that he welcomed a sudden rap on the door. Several of his knights trooped into the chamber, brandishing wine and dice, and Hal was touched by their attempt to cheer him up. At least he had good friends, by God. But he soon lapsed back into melancholy, for two of the men—Roger de Gaugi and Simon de Marisco—were also good friends of William Marshal, and of Hal's many disappointments that May, Will's betrayal was one of the sharpest.

He supposed that betrayal was too harsh a word for the knight's failure to answer his summons, but it hurt, nonetheless, that Will could let him down like this. For nigh on two months, he'd heard nothing from Ralph Fitz Godfrey, the man he'd sent after Will, and when he did get word, it was not encouraging. Fitz Godfrey reported that Will had accepted a position with the Count of Flanders and then left on pilgrimage to the Shrine of the Three Kings in Germany. Hal was stung that Will could so blithely offer his services to another lord, and this news did not endear Count Philip to him in the least; it was like poaching in a neighbor's woods. Eventually he'd gotten a second message that Fitz Godfrey had finally caught up with Will and he'd agreed to return. But Hal's jubilation soon soured once he read the rest of the letter. Will said he would come as soon as he could, but not before he obtained a safe conduct from Hal's father, the lord king, and with that in mind, he planned to visit the French court and ask for recommendations from King Philippe and the French bishops, hoping their good words would sway Henry in his favor.

To Hal, that meant he was not coming, for he was sure his father would never grant Will a safe conduct to fight against him. Why should he? No, this was a clever pretext, a way for Will to get credit for loyalty without putting himself at risk. But he was damned if he'd let Marshal cast a shadow over the rest of the night, and he called for wine, reached for the dice.

They were soon interrupted again, and this time the visitor was not as welcome as Hal's knights. He glanced up with a frown at the sight of Sancho of Savannac, offended that the routier should take the liberty of seeking him out in his own bedchamber. At least he'd left that drunken swine Couraban down in the hall.

"A word with you, my lord king, if I may," Sancho said, with a perfunctory politeness that grated on Hal's nerves. "I've been giving thought to our next target, and I've come up with an idea I think you'll fancy."

"You think so, do you?" Hal knew that not all routiers were lowborn; one of the usurper King Stephen's most trusted captains had claimed to be the bastard son of a Count of Flanders. But he had no doubts that Sancho and Couraban came from the gutter, and he valued their advice accordingly. He paid these men to bleed for him, not to think for him.

Sancho either did not notice his disapproval or was indifferent to it, for he sauntered forward without waiting to be asked. "I know you're running out of money again," he said, and Hal scowled. Whose fault was that? Every time he turned around, these accursed routiers had their palms out.

"So," Sancho continued, "why not pay a visit to Grandmont?"

Grandmont was a penitential religious order greatly favored by Henry. Its monks, known as "bons hommes" or "good men," lived lives of extreme austerity and deliberate poverty. Hal pointed that out now, asking sarcastically what the monks had that was worth taking?

Sancho grinned, showing teeth that explained his foul breath. "That is what they all say. The Cistercians claim to be as piss-poor as leprous beggars, but believe me, I've carried off enough from the White Monks to go on a monthlong drunk. Monks always have riches hidden away. Did your sire not give Grandmont a pyx of solid gold? Who knows what other treasures they have?"

"Yes, my *lord father* did give them such a pyx," Hal acknowledged, stressing the proper way to refer to a king even though he knew it would go right over Sancho's head. But he began to give serious consideration to the routier's proposal. It was not just the appeal of ready money, although God knows, he needed it. His father was

Grandmont's most illustrious patron. He'd been very generous to the monks, even re-building their church, and had expressed the wish to be buried at their Mother House. Striking at Grandmont would be a dramatic way to strike at his father, too, sending a message that he was not intimidated by those threats of excommunication. He almost asked his knights what they thought, but decided against it, for he'd begun to see that most of them told him only what they thought he'd want to hear. A pity Geoffrey was not here, for his advice could be counted upon.

They were all waiting, and Hal made up his mind, saying nonchalantly: "Why not? We'll visit the good monks on the morrow."

THE PYX HENRY HAD GIVEN GRANDMONT was a thing of beauty, made of beaten gold crafted in the shape of a dove. Even in the subdued light of the church, it seemed to shimmer in the dark as Hal approached the high altar. He was ir-ritated with his knights for balking at retrieving it, but they'd mumbled that it did contain the Host, after all, and it was obvious it would take a direct command to get one of them to fetch it. Sancho and Couraban were quite willing to do it, but Hal did not want the pyx to be sullied by their bloodied hands, and so he had no choice, had to get it himself. He felt a superstitious prickle along the back of his neck when he reached for it, and for a moment, it seemed as if the air itself had chilled. Telling him-self his imagination was overwrought and the Almighty would understand, he care-fully lifted the pyx and carried it from the church.

There he was confronted by Guillaume de Trahinac, the outraged prior, and his equally indignant monks. Garbed in coarse brown tunics with scapulars and hoods, they looked like Old Testament prophets to the uneasy knights, and several glanced toward the sky, almost as if expecting the prior to call down celestial thunderbolts upon their heads.

At the sight of the pyx, the prior stiffened, for he'd not really believed Hal would dare to take it. "Take heed," he said hoarsely. "Do you think that the Almighty does not see what you do here? Nothing in creation can hide from Him, and if a man sin against the Lord, who shall entreat for him?"

Hal hated the way churchmen were so quick to quote Scriptures, using God's Words to make their own paltry opinions seem more than they were. He turned to glare at the prior and saw that one of the routiers was swaggering toward the monks, clearly eager to end the argument. Hal was tempted to let him, for he'd enjoy seeing the sanctimonious prior knocked on his skinny butt. But then he sighed and ordered the man to stop. "I just saved you from a beating, Prior Guillaume," he said. "Look upon it as an act of unexpected mercy from an unrepentant sinner." His men laughed, but the monks were not cowed and continued to shout out dire warnings as they rode off. Hal stirred laughter again by feigning dismay that men of God should use such unseemly language, but he was glad when they were out of hearing range and the angry voices no longer echoed on the wind.

B Y THURSDAY, MAY 26, Hal and his men were fifty miles to the south, approaching the town of Uzerche. Hal had no one riding at his side, for his nerves were still on the raw and his knights were avoiding him again. Their plundering of the monastery at Grandmont had left a bitter aftertaste, and he'd had unpleasant dreams about the self-righteous monks and their arrant threats. Even his body seemed to be out of sorts, for he'd awakened that morning with a queasy stomach and loose bowels. All in all, it had been a week he wanted only to forget.

That changed, however, within an hour of their arrival at Uzerche. They'd stopped at the abbey of St Pierre, creating a panic until they convinced the monks that they meant only to pass the night there. Hal was so irked by the obvious anxiety of their hosts that he decided to forgo supper and withdrew to the abbot's chamber, hoping that a night's sleep would settle his stomach. But several of his knights soon burst into the chamber with the best news that he'd heard in weeks. His allies were here at long last. The Count of Toulouse and Hugh, the Duke of Burgundy, had just ridden into the abbey garth.

H AL DID FEEL BETTER the next day, and took it as a sign that his luck had changed. With all the men brought by Raimon and Hugh, they would now outnumber the forces of his father and brother. While there was some discussion of heading north to lift Henry's siege or hunt for Richard, no one was keen to fight a pitched battle, not even the routier captains, and they began drifting south, instead, raiding at random. In this almost aimless fashion, the first day of June found them approaching the famed abbey of Rocamadour.

Hal had never been to Rocamadour before, and like all visitors, he was awed by his first glimpse of the celebrated shrine, perched on a limestone cliff five hundred feet above a deep river gorge. A hamlet had sprung up on the lower level of the ridge, shabby taverns and shops selling wine, ale, cider, food, and the ubiquitous pilgrim badges. Higher up was a hospice, the basilica of St Sauveur, and the chapels of St Michel and Notre Dame. It was the latter that drew the pious and the ailing to such a remote, inaccessible site, for Rocamadour was one of the most popular shrines dedicated to the Blessed Virgin Mary, and on this hot summer day, they could see a trail of pilgrims straggling up the steep hill in the hope that they'd be the ones deemed worthy of Our Lady's miraculous cures.

Later, Hal was not sure who'd first broached the subject, but it was probably in all their minds—the awareness that Rocamadour offered much more lucrative spoils than Grandmont, which had been a decided disappointment, aside from Henry's gold pyx. The Duke of Burgundy quickly bowed out, joking that heights gave him nosebleeds, and when the Count of Toulouse also declined to participate, Rocamadour's fate hung for a time in the balance. Hal was astonished by Count Raimon's stance, for he had a reputation for being as grasping as any pirate and he'd certainly plundered his share of churches in the past. But when pressed, he argued that this was different, that Rocamadour was becoming renowned throughout Christendom.

"Granted that it is not the same as sacking Mont St Michel or the Holy Sepulcher in Jerusalem," he conceded. "But why stir up the Church needlessly? I have enough problems with them as it is."

Hal was envious of Duke Hugh and Count Raimon, men who had their own rich domains, their own resources, lords who were not impoverished kings, forced to such desperate measures by their humiliating lack of lands or money. Still, though, he was irresolute until Sancho and Couraban prodded him into action by implying that there was something shameful about his allies' refusal and reminding him how deeply he was in debt.

There was no question of taking horses up that imposing cliff; Hal doubted that even a mountain goat could have done it. The sun was scorching, and he was sweating and out of breath by the time they reached the summit, for his stomach ailment had not gone away, after all. Looking down at the serpentine windings of the river far below them, he felt suddenly light-headed and found himself wondering what strange path had led him to this place and this moment. By then the monks were hurrying toward them, looking to him like flapping crows in their black Benedictine garb, their faces so white and set that he knew they'd heard about St Martial's and Grandmont.

Rocamadour was different from the other plundered abbeys; here they had a larger audience than aggrieved monks. Throngs of pilgrims were staring at them in alarm, shrinking back when the routiers unsheathed swords. The monks blanched, too, at the sight of those naked blades, but they stood their ground, gathering around the man designated as their spokesman, a stooped, spare figure who leaned heavily upon a heavy, oaken cane. But the eyes sunken back in that furrowed, pockmarked face were blazing with an anger that was ageless.

"Go no farther," he declared, "if you value your immortal souls."

The routiers laughed at him and headed toward the church. But he was not ready to concede defeat and stepped boldly in front of Hal, holding up his hand as if to hold back the tides. "Thirteen years ago," he said in a surprisingly strong voice, "the English king came close to dying of a tertian fever. When he recovered, he and his queen made a pilgrimage to Our Lady of Rocamadour to express their gratitude for sparing his life. You are of their flesh; their blood courses through your veins. Should you dishonor them by this barbarous, evil deed, there can be no going back. Harken unto thy father that begat thee. Turn away from this unworthy undertaking ere you shame your noble father and bring down the awful wrath of God Almighty upon your head."

By now Hal was thoroughly tired of these dramatic, biblical scenes. Noble father? This withered old man had a droll sense of humor. "I will submit to divine judgment upon *Dies Irae* as all good Christians must, and when I face the Great Creator, at least it will not be with the blood of a martyred archbishop upon my hands," he snapped and shoved past the monk.

The chapel of Our Lady had been filled with pilgrims, but they were fleeing in panic before the routiers. Sancho grinned at Hal, holding up a hemp sack stuffed with silver plate, candlesticks, and chalices, all of which had proudly adorned the high altar. "We hit the mother lode this time," he announced gleefully. "You'll be able to hire a whole troop of routiers with what you're getting today."

"Need I remind you that this is a loan, not a treasure trove?" Hal said truculently, and then came to a halt, his eyes locking upon the Black Virgin. Carved of dark walnut, it dominated the chapel, conveying none of the mercy and grace associated with the gentle Mary. This was a stark, severe image, almost primitive in its austerity, as if harkening back to a time long lost in the mists of memory. That was such an odd, irreverent thought that Hal felt a sudden chill, much as he'd experienced in the church at Grandmont, and he abruptly abandoned his intention to offer the Mother of God a prayer of apology and explanation. Turning on his heel, he started to leave the chapel, signaling one of his knights to keep a sharp eye upon the routiers; they were not going to benefit personally from their plunder if he could help it.

He stopped, though, when Sancho called out, "Wait, my lord! Do you not want the sword of Roland?"

Hal spun around. He'd forgotten that the sword reputed to have been wielded by the legendary French hero was kept at Rocamadour. Retracing his steps, he took the weapon from Sancho, his fingers lingering upon the blade as if it were a holy relic. "Durandal," he said softly. "That is what he named it."

Sancho no more believed this was Roland's sword than he believed in the bona fides of all those fragments of the True Cross; he'd once taken part in a scheme to dupe gullible pilgrims into making offerings at a manger said to contain some of the holy straw that had cradled the Christ Child. This experience had convinced him that people were as simple as sheep, and he included Hal in the flock. He was in good spirits, though, for they were all going to profit handsomely from their haul at Roca-madour, and in truth, he felt a little sorry for this pampered young lordling. If a man was going to follow the brigand's road, he ought to enjoy it, and from what he could tell, Hal had less joy in his life than these shriveled, stiff-necked Black Monks.

"Why not take it?" he suggested, seeing how Hal was caressing the sword with his eyes. The lad might as well be hung for a goat as a sheep, he thought, and managed to keep himself from slapping Hal on the back when the young king unsheathed his own weapon, then reverently slid the celebrated sword of Roland into his scabbard.

THE WALLED TOWN OF MARTEL was only eight miles north of Roca-madour, and Hal heaved a sigh of relief when its seven towers finally came into view. His abdominal cramps had gotten more severe, and by the time they reached Martel, his bowels had become so loose that he'd had to make several quick stops by the side of the road. Colic and diarrhea were such common ailments, though, that the teasing he had to endure was offhand, and he was thankful for that; he'd always prided him-self on his sense of humor, but this spring it had definitely begun to unravel around the edges.

They were lodging in a fortified manor house in the center of town; known as the Maison Fabri, it was a substantial stone three-story building overlooking the market-place. Once Étienne de Fabri had escorted Hal up to the best bedchamber, he wasted no time in stripping off his hauberk and soiled clothes, then ordered a bath. He felt a little better once he was clean, but his stomach roiled at the mere thought of food, and he settled instead for wine flavored with comfrey root, a reliable remedy for his mal-ady. Lying back on the bed, he soon fell asleep.

When he awoke, he was momentarily disoriented, not remembering where he was. "God help me," he groaned, "if it is morning already," and his squires responded with laughter.

"Nay, my lord. Dawn is hours away. But you have a visitor."

Hal squinted up at them in disbelief. "There is only one person in the world I am that eager to see. So unless you've awakened me to welcome my queen, the pair of you will need to find a new lord on the morrow."

They greeted that sally with even louder laughter, and Hal sat up with another groan, thinking that he must teach his household to take his mock threats more seri-ously, but knowing he would not, for he'd realized very early in life that he'd much rather be loved than feared. "I am awake . . . I think. Just who is this distinguished guest worthy of disturbing my sleep?"

"Sir Baldwin de Bethune and Sir Hugh de Hamelincourt, my liege."

Hal smiled, for both knights were friends as well as liegemen, and it pleased him greatly that they had responded so promptly to his summons. "Well, send them in," he said and winked at his squire. "You've been reprieved, Benoit, need not seek a new lord, after all."

Benoit was beaming. "They were not traveling alone, my lord," he said, and nodded to the other squire, who swung the door open wide.

Hal caught his breath as Will Marshal entered the chamber, flanked by Baldwin and Hugh. Swinging his legs over the side of the bed, he started to get to his feet, and was startled when the room began to spin. He grabbed for the closest arm, and it was only after he'd straightened up that he saw it was Will's. The other men had discreetly withdrawn, leaving them alone.

"The sight of you gladdens my eyes," Hal said huskily, "indeed it does."

"Sit back on the bed, my liege. I was told you'd been ailing?"

"Nothing worth mentioning," Hal assured him, but took Will's advice and sat down again. "Germany must have agreed with you," he joked, "for you are looking sleek and well fed."

Will could not return the compliment, for Hal had lost so much weight that his cheekbones stood out in sharp prominence, making him look almost gaunt, and his fair skin was splotched with hectic color. "Let me get you some wine," he said and busied himself in pouring drinks for them both, using that time to disguise his concern.

"So . . ." Hal said happily, "you decided you did not need that safe conduct after all."

Will blinked in surprise. "I have one, my liege. Your lord father was good enough to grant it."

Hal's mouth dropped open. "You are serious? Jesus wept, if that is not just like my father! He has his bishops cast me out into eternal darkness and then he gives you permission to fight with me."

Will handed him a cup, his eyes searching Hal's face. "You were not excommunicated. The old king instructed the bishops to pass sentence upon all the men who'd stirred up dissension between the two of you, but he told them not to include you in the damnation."

"For true, Will?" Hal had not realized how nervous he was until that fear was suddenly lifted. "Well, I'll be damned," he said, and then grinned. "No, I guess now I will not! What about Geoffrey? Was he spared, too?"

"I do not know," Will admitted. Reaching into his tunic, he drew forth two sealed parchments. "The French king gave me this for you, my lord. And this one is from your lady, Queen Marguerite." His eyes met Hal's levelly, but Hal did not take up the challenge; he was the first to look away.

Hal could feel heat rising in his face, heat that had nothing to do with his fever. An awkward silence fell. What did Will want? An apology? Fair enough if it would mend this rift between them. "I am sorry," he said carefully, "for any misunderstandings we may have had. I want us to put the past behind us, Will, to start anew. Can we do that?"

This was, Will realized, as close to an apology as he was going to get. "Yes, my liege," he said quietly, "we can do that," and was rewarded with a radiant smile, the smile of the young lord he'd loved and tutored and protected for so many years.

Hal got to his feet again, somewhat unsteadily, and embraced the older man. "Welcome back, Will," he said, and laughed joyfully. "Welcome home."

H AL HAD RELUCTANTLY AGREED to spend the next day in bed, but that night he insisted upon joining the others in the great hall. A hunting party had been successful, and they were able to feast on venison, washing it down with prodigious amounts of wine. Hal merely pushed the meat around on his trencher, but he drained his wine cup often and discovered that it was as effective a restorative as comfrey root. The other men were drinking freely, too, and the atmosphere in the hall soon became boisterous and rowdy.

Will Marshal was one of the few who stayed completely sober. At Hal's insistence, he'd eaten with them at the high table, but once the dishes were cleared off and the tables removed, he slipped away and sat down inconspicuously in a window-seat, where he was soon joined by Peter Fitz Guy and Baldwin de Bethune. Without speaking, they watched the antics upon the dais, where Hal was bantering with Duke Hugh and Count Raimon. Hal was very animated, laughing often, making such expansive gestures with his wine cup that he was in danger of dousing the knights crowding around him.

"Is he drunk?" Baldwin sounded uncertain, for he could not remember ever seeing Hal totally in his cups.

"I think it is the fever more than the wine," Will said, low-voiced, and then frowned at a loud burst of profanity coming from a corner where the routiers were dicing.

Seeing the direction of his gaze, Peter dropped his voice, too. "We scraped the bottom of the barrel for that lot," he said grimly. "I tell you, Will, it grieves me to say this, but these past weeks I've felt as if I were riding with an outlaw band."

Will looked at him intently. "Why have you stayed, then, Peter?"

"For the same reason that you came back, old friend." After a moment, Peter said softly, "God help us all." Although he smiled, it was not a joke, and Will and Baldwin knew it.

WILL WAS UP EARLY the next morning, breaking his fast with a plentiful helping of soft cheese and sops of bread soaked in wine. He was soon surrounded by friends, and they began to tease him about his ravenous appetite, doing their best to act as if things were as they'd once been, back in those halcyon days when they'd been so proud to serve the young king, so proud to be known as his knights, and the world seemed full of such shining promise.

"My lord . . ." Hal's squire materialized at Will's elbow, asking for a private moment, and as soon as Will led him aside, Benoit blurted out that Hal had a bad night, not falling asleep until dawn was nigh.

"The doctor said I must give him a potion of comfrey root and costmary every two hours, but I have been unable to rouse him, and I do not know what to do. Should I let him sleep?"

Will knew what the boy really wanted—someone to assume a responsibility that was too heavy for such narrow shoulders. "I'll come up to his chamber with you and see how the king is faring this morn," he said, and Benoit's face glowed with the intensity of his relief. As they mounted the stairs, Will assured the squire that Hal was on the mend, and he was convincing for he believed it himself. Hal was young and healthy and there was no reason to think he would not soon recover.

The chamber was stifling, so hot that Will strode over to the window and flung the shutters wide. His nose wrinkling as he breathed in a fetid, rank odor, he crossed swiftly to the bed. The sheets were soaked in sweat and the stench grew stronger. "My lord, you must wake up," Will said firmly. When he got no response from the man in the bed, he touched Hal's shoulder and drew a sharp breath, for his skin was searing to the touch. "My liege . . . Hal!"

Hal mumbled incoherently, turning his head away from the light, and Will reached for the sheet, pulled it back. Benoit had followed him to the bed, and cried out at the sight of the blood and feces, his face twisting in horror. Will swung around quickly and grasped his arm.

"You must not panic, Benoit. I need you to keep your head. Do you understand me?" And when the boy nodded, he released his grip, saying as calmly as he could, "Good lad. Now I want you to fetch the doctor straightaway."

Benoit nodded again and fled. Will could hear the thudding of his feet on the stairs. Once he was sure that help was on the way, he leaned over the bed again. "The bloody flux," he whispered. "Ah, Hal . . ." But his throat had constricted, making further speech impossible.

CHAPTER FORTY-ONE

✦

June 1183
Martel, Limousin

*H*AL HAD BEEN BLESSED with bountiful good health as well as beauty and had only vague memories of childhood illnesses. He was dimly aware now that he was very sick. He'd drifted far from familiar shores, his dreams shot through with swirling hot colors and hazy forebodings. He wanted only to sleep, yet people would not let him alone. They kept poking and prodding him, swathing his body in cold compresses, trying to get him to swallow bitter-tasting liquids that he did not want to drink. He'd thrashed about in bed, seeking to evade these unwelcome ministrations, but they persevered and he was too weak to resist.

Delirium was not unlike drowning, for he was caught up in a riptide carrying him farther and farther from reality. And when he finally regained consciousness, he had to fight his way back to the surface, gasping for breath as he broke free of the feverish currents dragging him down. The light was unbearably bright, even after he filtered it through his lashes. Gradually the room came into focus. Two of his friends, Robert de Tresgoz and Peter Fitz Guy, were slumped on a bench by the bed, and his squire Benoit was seated cross-legged in the floor rushes; he wondered why they all looked so miserable. When he opened his mouth to ask them, though, the words that emerged from his throat were so slurred that even he could not understand them.

The sound was enough to jerk their heads up, and the next moment, they were gathered by the bed, all talking at once. They were not making much sense to Hal. Benoit kept murmuring "God's Grace" as if he had no other words, and Peter seemed to be blinking back tears. But Robert was acting the most strangely, wanting to know if Hal could recognize him. Hal thought that was a very odd question, for he'd known the Norman knight for most of his life. He opened his mouth again, meaning to assure Rob that he was too ugly to forget, but he was surprised to discover that speaking demanded more energy than he could muster. When he flinched away from the sunlight flooding the bed, one of them hurried to close the shutters, and the chamber was soon a scene of joyous confusion as other men crowded in.

Hal felt a great relief at the sight of Will, sure all would be well now that the Marshal was here. He was not as pleased to see the doctor, looming over the bed like an avenging angel, for he recognized the man as his chief tormentor, the one who'd kept pouring vile potions down his throat, who would not go away.

"God be praised, the fever is down," the doctor announced, but he sounded so triumphant that Hal thought he was claiming more credit than the Almighty for that benevolence. Doctors were like that, he knew. It was always their doing when a patient recovered and God's Will when he did not. He could not summon up the effort to tease the physician, though; since when did talking tire a man out so? He was finding it hard to stay awake, but he was loath to slip back into those disquieting dreams, and when his eyes met Will's, he silently entreated the older man to keep vigil whilst he slept. When Will brought a stool close to the bed and sat down, he smiled. Will had understood. Bless him, Will always understood.

WHEN HAL AWOKE HOURS LATER, he was disappointed that he was still as weak as a newborn cub. He must have been at death's door, for certes. He was astonished to learn that this was Sunday; he'd lost three full days of his life! He remembered some of it now—the sharp pains in his belly, the endless bouts of diarrhea, the nausea. No wonder he felt as flat as a loaf of unleavened bread. He'd have to be patient as he got his strength back, and patience came no easier to him than it did to the rest of his family.

His stomach was not ready to cooperate, though, and when they tried to feed him egg yolks mixed with cumin and pepper, he promptly vomited them up. He could not even keep wine down, and the doctor had to settle for mixing galingale and yarrow in spring water, then feeding it to Hal one small spoonful at a time. At least he was no longer passing clotted blood, doubtless because he had nothing left to void. But he sounded like a croaking crow and looked like a corpse waiting to be sewn into his shroud, complaints his friends were happy to agree with. He thought they were much too eager to regale him with accounts of his suffering, gleefully describing how he had been "sweating like a Southwark cut-purse caught by the Watch" and "spewing your guts out" and "shitting a river of blood."

When the doctor made ready to bleed him, that brought back another unpleasant memory, and he grumbled that "I dreamed I was stabbed by a lunatic with a knife, but it was really a leech with a lancet!" The knights all laughed, but the doctor ignored his protests and deftly opened a vein in his arm, explaining needlessly that it was done to drain away the noxious humors that caused fever.

Knowing full well that bloodletting was an approved method of treating numerous ailments, Hal thought the doctor sounded like a prideful buffoon, but it was probably not wise to vex a man with a blade in his hand and so he submitted grudgingly to the treatment, although he noticed that he seemed much more light-headed after the procedure.

The men around his bed were members of his inner circle; most had been with him since his coronation at age fifteen. His gaze flickered from one familiar face to another. Will and Baldwin de Bethune and Simon de Marisco and Roger de Gaugi and Robert de Tresgoz and Peter Fitz Guy. A man could not ask for better friends. He'd been told that they'd rarely left his side during the worst of the crisis. He wished he could thank them for their devotion, but knew they'd be flustered and discomfited if he did, for banter and sarcasm were the only languages spoken in their realm.

At the moment, they were harassing Rob, entertaining Hal with exaggerated accounts of Rob's erratic behavior in the last few days. It seemed that he'd recalled some folklore that a fever could be cured by the liver of a beaver, and he'd been flailing around on the riverbank as long as there was light, trying to catch one. When Hal asked if this was true, Rob confirmed it with a sheepish grin, insisting that beaver liver, if fried with onions, could heal the worst fever. He would have elaborated upon this miracle remedy if Will had not seen the greensick look on Hal's face and hastily cut him off.

Hal could bring up only yellowish bile, for he'd not been able to eat for days. His friends were clustering around him, offering wine and putting wet compresses on his forehead and rushing off to see if the doctor thought he ought to be bled again. "Go away," he groaned, "you're worse than a mother abbess with one novice nun," and they laughed uproariously, for these glimmers of humor were surely the best proof that the Almighty had heeded their prayers and not those of the vengeful monks.

✦

S UNDAY'S CELEBRATION CONTINUED into the next day, for Hal's al-
lies and routiers were just as pleased by his recovery as the knights who loved him. Will
lost track of all the toasts drunk to Hal's health, but he observed the hilarity with a
jaundiced eye, well aware that these men had a vested interest in the young king's well-
being. The more he saw at Martel, the more he understood Peter's bleak admission.
How had Hal ever come to this—leading an outlaw band of cutthroats and bandits?
And how was he going to convince Hal to renounce these false friends and return to
his proper allegiance?

Hal was no stronger on Monday, still could not eat without becoming nauseous,
and although he now had a constant thirst, he could only keep water down. But he was
quite lucid and his men took heart from that, assuring themselves that he'd soon be on
the mend. Will was not so sure and began to harbor doubts. Hal was young and had
been robust and vigorous. Shouldn't he have begun to regain some of his strength by
now? It frightened Will to see how feeble he was; the man able to wield a ten-foot lance
with lethal skill could not even hold a cup to his blistered lips.

Because of his own disquiet, Will soon picked up on the doctor's unease and
nerved himself to demand the truth. He was not prepared, though, for the grim response he got from the physician. Once they were safely away from eavesdroppers, the
doctor seemed relieved to share his fears. It was not just that the young king was showing no signs of improvement. His new symptoms were troubling, too. His skin and
mouth were very dry, and his thirst could not be quenched. His eyes were sunken back
in his head, and despite all the water he was drinking, his urine was scant and when it
did come, it was a dark yellow. Had Sir William noticed that he was no longer sweating? Will had not, and when he asked what that meant, the doctor muttered evasively
that it was never a good sign.

"Are you . . . are you saying that he will not recover?"

The physician no longer met his eyes. "That is in God's Hands, and not for me to
say." Will stared at him in horror, understanding that he'd just pronounced a death
sentence upon the young king.

H AL WAS FRUSTRATED that he was making so little progress. This was
Tuesday morn; ought he not to be regaining strength by now? He'd been dozing since
dawn, and each time he awoke, Will and Rob and Baldwin and Benoit were keeping
watch by his bed, standing guard against night demons and, quite likely, the routiers.

When he'd emerged from his delirium, Hal had been surprised to find an unfamiliar emerald ring upon his hand. Emeralds were said to have the power to vanquish fevers, they reminded him, and the Duke of Burgundy had kindly offered his own ring. It was a valuable piece of jewelry and Hal had jested with his knights, wondering how much they could sell it for. But he'd begun to fret that a routier might sneak into his chamber and steal it, and he decided that, if only for his peace of mind, they ought to return it to Hugh. He did not need it anymore, after all, for his fever had not spiked again, was more like a smoldering peat fire now than a roaring conflagration.

He watched his friends for several moments before they noticed he was awake. "If you are not a sad-looking lot," he mocked. "You'd think I was on my deathbed or that Richard had Martel under siege and we were running out of wine . . ."

He'd meant it as a joke, but there was nothing amusing about the reaction he got. His jape was met with a stricken silence, and suddenly they were looking everywhere but at his face. He stared at them incredulously. "I am not dying . . . am I?"

This time they responded with a flurry of frenzied denials, assuring him that of course he was not dying, what a foolish notion, he'd be up and about in no time at all. Hal was stunned, for he could see they were lying. Will alone had kept silent, but now he cried out sharply, "Enough! He deserves the truth."

When they would have protested, Will stared them down. "He has the right to know," he insisted. "He needs to know whilst there is still time to make amends."

They could see the pulse thudding in Hal's throat, hear the ragged edge to his breathing. "But . . . but I was getting better . . . You all said so . . ."

Will knew that Hal had always preferred an oblique approach to unpleasant truths. But he had no choice now, had to face it head-on. "We hoped you were, my liege. But you've been growing weaker and . . . and the doctor says your recovery is now in God's Hands."

Hal looked at him mutely and then turned his head away from them. "Go," he said hoarsely, "leave me be . . ."

They did not argue and fled in unseemly haste, none of them knowing what to say or how to comfort him. Will did not go far, though, for he knew that Hal, of all men, would never find solace in solitude. He waited what he hoped was a decent interval, time enough for Hal to absorb the blow, then knocked on the door and came back into the chamber.

"I will go if you wish it," he said, and when Hal didn't object, he approached the bed, dreading what he would see. Hal's spectacular tournament successes had overshadowed the fact that he was not as gifted a battle commander as Richard, or Geoffrey either, for that matter. He did not seem to have a head for strategy, to be able to anticipate the unforeseen or to adopt long-range plans. No one had ever questioned his courage, though. If he did not have Richard's reckless daring, few men did. Will had never seen him display fear, either at castle sieges or in the wild mêlées of the tourney, which could be as dangerous as battle skirmishes. But he'd never seen Hal look as he did now—eyes wide and staring, pupils so dilated that much of the blue had been swallowed up, filled with utter panic.

When he spoke, his voice was unsteady, almost inaudible. "God is punishing me for my sins, Will."

"Yes," Will said softly. "I fear he is, lad."

"I ought to have heeded the monks. They tried to warn me, but I would not listen. And now it is too late. Lucifer is here, waiting to claim my soul . . . Can you feel his presence, too?" Hal shivered. "I am damned and it is my own fault, Will—"

"Hal, no!" Will had to fight the urge to glance over his shoulder, half expecting to see diabolic red eyes glowing in the shadows. "It is not too late. The Almighty has not forsaken you, has given you a great mercy—time to repent and seek forgiveness."

Hal had a heartbeat of hope, but no more than that. "No . . ." he whispered. "They'd not forgive me. How could they?"

Will was momentarily puzzled, not sure who "they" were. But then he understood. Hal was speaking of his Divine Father in Heaven and his earthly father at Limoges. "Of course they'd forgive you, Hal. The mercy of the Almighty is everlasting and endureth forever. And the lord king has never ceased to love you. Why do you think he spared you from excommunication? Or granted me a safe conduct to come to you? Are those the actions of an unloving father?"

Hal desperately wanted to believe him. "But my sins are so grievous . . ."

"That does not matter, not if you are truly contrite." As complete as Will's education had been in military matters and the tenets of chivalry, he'd not learned to read or write. He'd never regretted that lack, not until now when he yearned to quote Scriptures that could assuage Hal's fear. Fortunately, even though he'd never been able to read the Holy Writ, he did have an excellent memory and could remember enough to paraphrase with reasonable accuracy. "The Lord God will not turn His Face away from you if you return to Him." Will forced a smile. "Holy Writ says there is great joy in Heaven over even one sinner who repents."

Tears welled in Hal's eyes. "When I thought that salvation would be denied me and that it was all my doing . . ." He shuddered, but he no longer sounded like a man sure he was doomed. "Fetch me a priest, Will, so I may be shriven."

Will managed another smile even as his own eyes filled with tears. "You need not settle for a priest, lad. You have a bishop at your beck and call. Bishop Gerald of Cahors rode in an hour ago. Shall I summon him now?"

"Please." Hal was suddenly terrified that he might die before he could confess his sins. But he still called Will back as he reached the door. "Will . . . I must see my father ere I die, must tell him how sorry I am . . ."

Will doubted that Henry would come, not after being shot at twice under flags of truce. But he was not going to rob Hal of the smallest sliver of hope, and he said, as confidently as he could, "We shall send a man to Limoges straightaway." Once he was out in the stairwell, though, he sagged against the wall, feeling as if his bones were suddenly made of sawdust, incapable of supporting his weight, much less his grief.

ALFONSO, the young king of Aragon, had arrived to assist Richard and Henry in fighting the Limousin rebels and his personal bête noire, the Count of Toulouse. Daylight held sway well into the evening on summer nights, and Richard took Alfonso to see Aixe, the castle now garrisoned by rebels.

"We'll lay siege to it on the morrow," he said, "and if they balk at surrender, God may pardon their sins, but I will not."

Alfonso smiled, thinking that Richard had changed little since their first meeting at Limoges, ten long years ago. He was still as decisive and confident as ever. "I can see," he joked, "why your men call you Richard Yea or Nay, for you're never one to dither at crossroads, are you?"

Richard glanced at him in surprise; he'd not known he'd been given that nickname. He was not displeased, though, thinking there were far worse things a man could be called. He'd begun to suggest unflattering nicknames for his elder brother— Sir Spendthrift and Lord Lies a Lot among the least insulting—when a scout sounded the alarm.

"A horseman is coming, my lord, riding like he's escaping from Hell!"

To Alfonso's amusement, Richard at once swung onto his stallion and rode out to intercept this mystery rider. He mounted with less haste and followed after his friend. By now the horseman was within recognition range and after a moment, Alfonso identified him as the old king's chancellor and natural son, whom he'd met just hours ago at the cité. Pebbles and dirt flew everywhere as Geoff reined in his mount. The animal was streaked with lather and Alfonso braced for bad news, knowing that Richard's brother would not push a horse like this unless the message he bore was urgent.

Richard had reached the same conclusion. "What has happened now?" he asked warily, for lately the war had not been going well. He'd chased Geoffrey's routiers out of Poitou into Brittany, but his duchy was still infested with these vermin, some hired by the French king and the rebel lords, others freelancing, and the arrival of the Duke of Burgundy and the Count of Toulouse threatened to tip the balance in their favor.

"You'll not believe Hal's latest knavery!" Richard was accustomed to Geoff waxing indignant about their brother, but he'd never seen him so outraged; he was literally shaking with the intensity of his emotions. "He sent a man to our father tonight, claiming that he is dying and pleading that Papa come to Martel and forgive him ere he does!"

Richard's jaw dropped, and his indrawn breath was audible enough for Alfonso to hear. Many considered it shocking and even sacrilegious that Henry dared to swear upon the Almighty, God's Bones being one of his favorite oaths. The holy body part that Richard now blurted out was so scandalous that Alfonso did not know whether to laugh or move out of range. It was obvious, though, that Richard's blasphemy was involuntary; he looked as if he'd been pole-axed.

"Every time I think that whoreson has gone as low as he can," Richard spat, "he finds a shovel and keeps digging!"

"You have not heard the worst of it yet. Papa wants to go to Martel!"

"Then he is not just in his dotage, he is stark, raving mad!"

Richard wasted no more time questioning his father's sanity, took off in a cloud of dust, with Geoff right behind him. By now Alfonso's men had caught up with him; they'd been alarmed to have their lord and the duke ride off like that. They were further puzzled to see Richard already disappearing in the distance, with his own knights scrambling to keep pace, but their king did not appear to be perturbed by these odd events. When they reined in and asked him if all was well, Alfonso assured them it was and then grinned.

"It seems we are returning to Limoges," he said. "It should be an interesting evening."

RICHARD FOUND THE SITUATION at the Bishop of Limoges's palace was not as dire as he'd feared, for he did not lack for allies. In fact, the one without allies was Henry; he was facing unanimous opposition from kinsmen, friends, barons, and bishops. Ranulf, Richard, and Geoff presented a united family front. Willem and Maurice de Craon and Rotrou, Count of Perche, were adamantly opposed to his going to Martel, too. The newly arrived Archbishop of Canterbury and the Bishops of Angers and Agen were also lined up against Henry. The only one holding his peace was Sebran Chabot, their host; he'd been embroiled in a contentious dispute with Henry and Richard upon his election to the bishopric of Limoges several years ago and thought the iced-over breach with his duke and king was too fragile to test.

As was his wont, Richard seized control and launched into a passionate assault upon Hal's tattered credibility. He demanded to hear this "dunghill of lies" with his own ears and Robert de Tresgoz was ushered back into the bishop's great hall. At the very sight of the Norman knight, Richard burst out into scornful laughter.

"Well, well, if it is not one of Hal's pet lapdogs! They'd have done better to send a priest, but after the raids on St Martial's, Grandmont, and Rocamadour, even Hal's own chaplain has likely taken to his heels."

Rob was enraged to be dismissed so disdainfully, but his anger was muted by exhaustion, for he'd covered more than seventy-five miles in less than two days. "I am speaking God's Truth," he insisted. "The young king was stricken with the bloody flux, and he is not expected to recover." But to his despair, he saw that his words were echoing into a void; no one was paying him any heed and he was ushered out again, knowing that he had failed Hal in his moment of greatest need.

Henry had lapsed into silence as the argument raged around him, no longer attempting to rebut the objections coming fast and furious from his two sons; with fine teamwork, Richard and Geoff were taking turns reminding him of that arrow deflected by his hauberk, the death of his stallion outside the walls of the ville, the ambush upon Maurice de Craon, the treacherous assault upon his envoys by Geoffrey's men, the lies, the betrayals, the numerous breaches of trust.

It was Henry's uncharacteristic reticence that attracted Ranulf's attention. When had Harry ever been passive in the face of defiance? Why was he even bothering to hear them out if he was set upon trusting his faithless son yet again? And then Ranulf understood. Harry was not free of doubts, either. Once more he found his head warring with his heart. And with that realization, Ranulf saw a path opening up through this maze.

"My liege, may I have a moment alone with you?" he asked, and while Richard and Geoff seemed reluctant to trust Henry out of their sight, the others took hope from this, for all knew that if any man could get through to the king, it would be his uncle. Henry seized upon the opportunity to escape his sons' hectoring and led Ranulf out into the garth.

Twilight was laying claim to the cité, and the sky was a deepening shade of lavender, spangled with stars and fleecy clouds the color of plums. It was such a beautiful summer evening that Ranulf and Henry walked in silence for several moments, as if reluctant to sully this hallowed peace with the feuding and bad faith of mortal men. Without speaking, they crossed the garth and, by common consent, entered a side door of the cathedral. It was empty save for a lone canon, who discreetly disappeared when Henry frowned in his direction. Pacing up the nave, they halted at last in front of the high altar, and only then did Henry look challengingly at the older man.

"You cannot tell me, Uncle, that you would not go to Morgan if you received such a message."

"Yes, I would go," Ranulf admitted, but refrained from pointing out that Morgan had never given him reason to distrust his word, for he knew that his nephew was painfully aware of his son's failings. "If you do go to Martel, we may have to sneak out in the middle of the night," he said, only half joking, for he could see Richard and Geoff locking Henry in his chamber rather than let him risk his life and his kingdom on Hal's word of honor.

"*We?* Take care with your pronouns, Ranulf, lest you find yourself accompanying me to Martel," Henry said dryly, and was surprised when his uncle smiled.

"I will go with you, Harry—if you answer one question. Can you honestly tell me that you have no doubts or suspicions about the truth of Hal's story?"

Several tall candles burned on the high altar, and Ranulf thought he caught the glimmer of tears in his nephew's eyes. Henry did not reply, and they both knew that was an answer in and of itself.

R ANULF HAD GONE BACK to the bishop's hall to tell the others that Henry would not be taking Hal's bait, not this time. Henry was never to know how long he remained alone in the church. Until this June evening at Limoges, he would have said that the most despairing, desperate moment of his life had been passed at Canterbury, kneeling before Thomas Becket's tomb. Now he knew better. Eventually one of the canons appeared, coming to a sudden stop as soon as he saw the motionless figure of the king. Before he could retreat, Henry beckoned him forward, giving a terse one-sentence command that sent the man hastening out into the night.

The Bishop of Agen did not keep Henry waiting long. "Sire? How may I be of service? Is it your wish that we pray together?"

Henry doubted that he had God's Ear these days, but he kept that blasphemous thought to himself. "I have another mission in mind for you, my lord bishop. I want you to ride to Martel at first light, see for yourself if my son is ailing. And if you find . . . if you find that it is true, tell him for me that he has my forgiveness, that he has my love."

The bishop inclined his head, feeling so much pity for the English king that he was momentarily mute. Henry didn't notice. Tugging at a ring on his finger, he pulled it free and pressed it into the bishop's hand. "Give him this. It was my grandfather's, passed on to me by my mother when I was invested as Duke of Normandy. Hal will recognize it as mine."

"It will be done, my lord king," the bishop said quietly. But as he withdrew, he was struck by a disconcerting thought. Whatever he found in Martel, he would be bringing grievous news back to the king. What would be worse—that Hal was truly on his deathbed or that once again he'd taken shameless advantage of his father's trust, exploiting his love to lure him into a lethal trap?

H AL CONTINUED TO GROW WEAKER, but his knights were convinced he would cling to life until he could make peace with his father, for now that he no longer feared eternal damnation, he was obsessed with righting the wrongs he'd done, especially to Henry. In a way, this was a mercy, for he was so concerned with making amends and making a "good death" that he'd not had time to mourn all that he was losing. A man who'd lived utterly for the pleasures of today with nary a thought for the morrow was now consumed with regrets, able to focus only upon his yearnings for salvation and forgiveness, and his friends prayed fervently that he would obtain both.

Will was not alone in thinking it unlikely that Henry would come, and as the hours slid by, they were finding it harder and harder to maintain a cheerful pose in Hal's presence, to keep his hopes alive even as his body wasted away. He was displaying a single-minded resolve that he'd never shown before; he'd worked out in his mind how long it should take Rob to reach Limoges and then to return with Henry, and when Friday dawned, his eagerness was painful for the other men to watch.

Rob arrived as Vespers was chiming in the town churches. So guilt-stricken did he feel that he'd been tempted to take his time on his return trip, rationalizing that he'd be sparing Hal great pain as well as himself. Was it not better for Hal to die still hoping for reconciliation than to know his father had not believed him? But he continued to spur his horse onward, driven by a sense of duty that was stronger even than his sorrow. When he dismounted before the Fabri manor, he was mobbed by the other knights. But after one look at his haggard face, they asked no questions. The king would not be coming. Did it matter why?

To their surprise and relief, Hal seemed to take the news better than they did. He listened without speaking as Rob stammered and stuttered and tried to put the best possible face upon Henry's refusal, and then he said softly, "It would have taken Merlin to make it happen, Rob. Do not blame yourself."

Will was not fooled, though, by Hal's composure, and when Hal then whispered for his ears alone, "I did not deserve his forgiveness," the older man could not bear it and, excusing himself, started for the stables, determined to ride to Limoges himself. When Baldwin and Peter learned of his intent, though, they were able to talk him out of it by pointing out that it was too late. Even if Will could somehow convince the king, Hal would be dead long before they could get back to Martel. For Will, it was the worst moment of a wretched week. He was naturally a man of action, and he was finding it intolerable to watch helplessly as the young king's earthly hours trickled away like sands in an hourglass. But he must be at Hal's deathbed, for it was the last service he could perform for his lord.

H AL HAD BEEN SINCERE when he said he did not deserve forgiveness; there could be few epiphanies as dramatic as one brought about by the awareness of impending death. But no matter how often he told himself that his punishment was just and fitting, he was anguished by his father's rejection. If the man he'd finally become in the last week of his life could try to accept Henry's judgment, the boy he'd always been cried out for mercy, needing his father to bring light into the encroaching darkness of his world, to say he understood and the slate of his misdeeds was wiped clean—just as he'd done time and time again.

When Will burst into the chamber and saw Hal lying so still, his eyes flew to the dying man's chest, holding his own breath until he reassured himself that Hal still breathed. Baldwin and Peter were keeping watch, and they started to warn him to be quiet, grateful that Hal seemed to be sleeping at last. Will ignored them and leaned over the bed. "My liege, a messenger has just ridden in, sent by your lord father!"

Hal's lashes flickered. "Truly?"

"It is Bertrand de Berceyras, the Bishop of Agen, and his escort, the Count of Perche." Will glanced at Simon and jerked his head toward the door. The knight hurried to open it and ushered the men into the chamber. They both came to an abrupt halt when Will shifted, giving them their first look at Hal. That was all it took to banish their suspicions, doubts, and misgivings.

Rotrou of Perche was particularly remorseful, for he'd been one of Hal's allies during the first rebellion, and when his eyes met Hal's, he flushed. Hal acknowledged their past with a wan smile. "Who'd have thought, Rotrou, that I'd get to Hell ere you did?" As the bishop approached, he said hastily, "That was a joke, my lord . . . and a bad one. Have . . . have you really come from my father?"

"Indeed, my liege." Bishop Bertrand was so shaken by Hal's shocking decline that he unfastened his own paternoster from his belt and placed it on the pillow next to Hal, then reached out and took the young king's hot, dry hand in his. "King Henry bade me tell you that he freely and gladly grants you full forgiveness for your sins, and that he has never ceased to love you."

Hal's lashes swept down, shadowing his cheeks like fans as tears seeped from the corners of his eyes. "Thank you," he whispered, although the bishop was not sure if it was meant for him, for Henry, or for the Almighty.

"I bring more than words," he said and, taking a small leather pouch from around his neck, he shook out a sapphire ring set in beaten gold. He started to tell Hal that this was Henry's ring, but saw there was no need, for Hal could not have shown more reverence if he'd produced a holy relic.

"He does forgive me, then!" he cried and gave the bishop such a dazzling smile that for a moment the ravages of his illness were forgotten and they could almost believe this was the young king of cherished memory, the golden boy more beautiful than a fallen angel, able to ensnare hearts with such dangerous ease. Then the illusion passed and they were looking at a man gaunt, hollow-eyed, suffering, and all too mortal. Too weak to do it himself, Hal looked entreatingly at the bishop, saying, "Please . . ."

When the bishop slid the ring onto his finger, he smiled again and closed his eyes. A hush settled over the chamber. The bishop directed an urgent low-voiced question to Will, and sighed with relief when Will assured him that Hal had been shriven by the Bishop of Cahors and that he'd made his last testament, for that was every Christian's duty.

Death seemed very close to them at that moment. But then Hal opened his eyes and said faintly, "I would send a letter . . . my father . . ." And that spurred them all into action. Within moments, pen, ink, and parchment had been found, and the bishop insisted upon taking them himself. "I've never had so exalted a scribe . . ." Hal whispered, and as the bishop bent forward to hear him, he tried to tell Bertrand what he wanted to say, but the words would not come and he looked at the older man imploringly.

"We could begin with a quote from Scriptures," the bishop suggested, and when Hal nodded, he paused to think of an appropriate verse. "*Remember not the sins of my youth, or my transgressions.* What would you say then, my lord?"

Will was holding a cup to Hal's lips. He swallowed with an effort, saying, "Tell him that I am so sorry for letting him down . . . that I was a bad son and a bad king . . ." Will tilted the cup for him again, and his voice steadied somewhat. "Tell him of my love. Entreat him to forgive my mother, not to blame her for my sins . . . Marguerite, ask him to provide liberally for my wife . . . And to pardon my allies, to blame no one but me . . . my brother, Viscount Aimar, and the good people of Limoges . . . I beg him to make restitution to the abbeys I plundered . . . I stole from God, am so sorry . . . ask him to provide for my knights . . . to make right my wrongs . . ."

Doubting that he had the strength to continue, the bishop said soothingly, "Very well done, my liege. I have it all, every word. It wants only your seal. I can say with certainty that your lord father will be proud you have shown such heartfelt repentance for your sins."

Hal was not through. "I want to be buried . . . at the Church of the Blessed Mary in Rouen. If only my father could pay my debts . . ." They thought he was done speaking then, but he added, so softly he could barely be heard, "So many regrets, so many . . ."

The bishop's vision was blurring with tears, and as he looked up, he saw that the other men were weeping, too. Will leaned over and gently pressed his lips to Hal's feverish forehead. At the touch, Hal's eyes opened again. "Will," he said drowsily, "so glad you came . . ." He seemed at peace for the first time, and Will sought to console himself with that. But then Hal's breath hissed through his teeth. "Jesu! Durandal . . ."

Will and Baldwin exchanged bewildered looks, having no idea what he was talking about. Peter did, though, and he said swiftly, "You need not fret, my lord king. We will see that it is returned, I promise."

Hal's lips twitched in what was almost a smile. "Good lad . . . I'd not want the Lord Roland to think me a thief . . ." His voice trailed off, his lashes fluttering down again, and after that there was quiet in the chamber, his knights wiping away their tears as they watched the shallow rise and fall of his chest, counting the breaths that were so tenuous each one seemed likely to be his last.

S ATURDAY WAS MARKET DAY in Martel, and Amand's tavern would usually be doing a brisk business. Not this Saturday. The locals were staying at home behind locked doors, almost as if the town had been invaded by a pack of hungry wolves. Amand supposed that, in a way, they had, for the young king's routiers were always on the prowl for prey. He had just decided to lock up and go home when the door banged open and some of those God-cursed coterels swaggered in. His stomach, delicate in the best of circumstances, lurched and he had to swallow the aftertaste of his morning's breakfast, but he managed a sickly smile and gave Modette a push when she did not move.

Glaring at him resentfully, she waited till Sancho and his companions seated themselves at a trestle table facing the door. When they ordered wine, Amand hurried over to pour from one of the large casks and sent the reluctant Modette back with four full henaps, praying that these dangerous customers would drink and depart without smashing up the place, maltreating Modette, and stealing his meager profits, but not expecting to be so lucky.

"Thank you, sweetheart," Sancho told the sullen serving maid, for flirting was an ingrained habit with him, even when he was in a sour mood, as he definitely was this noon. It was bad enough that the royal whelp was dying, but he was dying deeply in debt, and some of those deniers ought to have been theirs. Not only were they not going to be paid, but the war would likely sputter to a halt now that the rebels no longer had Hal to rally around. It had occurred to Sancho that with the dying king's knights so busy mourning his approaching death, it would be an opportune time to help himself to whatever was left of their Rocamadour booty. But that had occurred to Couraban, too, and the hellspawn had beaten him to it, riding off yesterday with the last of their abbey plunder.

The men with him were his trusted lieutenants, forming the core of a band he'd led for several years, and he could be more candid with them than with the rest of their company, so they were aware of their financial woes. They did not appear overly concerned, though, for they had confidence in Sancho's cunning and were sure he'd come up with something.

When Pere said as much, Sancho shrugged off the compliment, but he never took their support for granted. They were a motley lot, he supposed, for they did not even have a shared language. He and his cousin Ander were Basques, Pere was a Catalan, Gerhard a Fleming, and Jago . . . God alone knew what mongrel blood ran in that one's veins; most likely his own mother had not known. But what they had in common was stronger than their differences, for they were Ishmaels, condemned to live on the fringes of society, scorned even by the same lords who paid for their services. This hostility had forged a strong sense of solidarity, an us-versus-them mentality that often stood them in good stead. Sancho knew, though, that their loyalty depended upon his ability to produce, to keep their ventures profitable, and Hal's death was undeniably a setback.

A squeal from Modette interrupted his brooding. She'd brought more wine to their table and Gerhard's arm now snaked around her waist, pulling her down onto his lap. The other men paid her no heed as she squirmed to free herself, her eyes narrowing to slits when his hand groped under her skirt. Just then Ander entered the tavern, though, and she took advantage of Gerhard's momentary distraction to slip from his grasp, hastily putting distance between them as Amand looked on in dismay, fearing she'd expect him to speak up for her. Modette knew better, though, than to depend upon that frail reed, and impaling him with a contemptuous look, she began to back toward the door leading into their storeroom.

She had some good fortune then, in a life that had been singularly lacking in it. Ander brought news they found so interesting that she was forgotten, even by Gerhard. Pulling up a stool, Ander yelled to Amand for wine before saying, "Well, you missed quite a show, mates. I am surprised they did not charge admission, it was that good."

"I take it the royal whelp is not dead yet?"

"He is still clinging to life like a barnacle to a ship's hull. But to give the lad credit, he is going out in a blaze of glory. He began by confessing again, first in private to the bishops and then in public to anyone who cared to listen. I sidled in at the back, having never heard a royal confession. I have to say it was a great disappointment. He seems to have lived a very dull life, for he had no truly interesting sins to disavow, mainly boring misdeeds like betraying his old man and harrying monks and the like."

"You're being too hard on him, Ander," Jago protested. "Naturally you'd find his transgressions tiresome when compared to yours. You'll never find a priest corrupt enough or drunk enough to absolve you of *your* sins, but the rest of us do what we can."

Ander dug Jago in the ribs with his elbow, but Sancho put a stop to the horseplay before it could escalate. "That does not sound like much of a 'show' to me—a dying man confessing to tedious sins."

"Ah, but he was only getting started. Next he insisted that they garb him in a hairshirt. Damned if I know where they found one. That bunch does not seem likely to carry hairshirts in their saddle bags, do they?"

"They must have borrowed Gerhard's," Pere gibed, and the Fleming kicked him under the table, but missed and got Ander instead.

"Swine," Ander said, without heat. "I am not done yet, you cocksuckers. The fool then had them put a noose around his neck and pull him from his bed onto the floor and over to a bed of ashes he'd ordered them to make."

This was met with exclamations and expressions of disbelief, but Sancho came to his cousin's defense. "I believe it," he said. "Our young princeling has quite a liking for high drama. It would not be enough for him to repent. He'd have to be the most remorseful penitent since Cain wailed that his punishment was more than he could bear."

Gossip had it that Sancho was a renegade cleric and although he'd never confirmed it, the rumors persisted. This display of familiarity with Scriptures was too tempting an opportunity to resist and they began to heckle him with cries of "Father Sancho," while Ander appropriated Pere's henap and drained it in several gulps.

"Oh, and the Duke of Burgundy is making ready to depart," he said casually, for he knew this was hardly newsworthy. The Count of Toulouse had ridden off the day before, and they'd known it was only a matter of time before Burgundy abandoned the sinking ship, too.

But for Sancho, this information was quite interesting. He'd been playing around with an idea, not sure if it was feasible. But it would require Burgundy's departure for it to work. He wondered if he ought to confide in the others, then decided no, not yet. He'd take a little more time to think it over and then give them the good news that their prospects were not quite as bleak as they thought.

H AL'S FRIENDS KNEW he must be in acute discomfort, lying on the hard floor in a bed of ashes and cinders, and they were both awed and proud of him for making such a spectacular gesture of atonement. As the hours dragged by, he dozed fitfully, occasionally murmuring in his sleep. Once Will thought he said his wife's name, but he couldn't be sure. He was sitting cross-legged in the floor rushes by Hal's side, with Peter and Rob keeping vigil nearby. Baldwin was slumped in the window-seat and Simon was trying vainly to console Benoit; the boy was huddled in Hal's bed, his eyes so swollen with tears that he could barely see. Étienne de Fabri appeared from time to time, offering drinks and food that the knights always refused, for it did not seem right that they should enjoy what Hal was denying himself.

Hal stirred when bells chimed for None somewhere in the town, and Will at once leaned over to dribble a few drops of water upon his lips, the only liquid Hal would accept. As their eyes met, the corner of Hal's mouth curved. "Sorry . . ." he whispered, "to take so scandalously . . . long to die. Geoff would say I'd be late . . . for my own funeral . . ."

That was too much for Rob and, choking back a sob, he fled. The others were ashamed to admit they, too, yearned to bolt, for the very air seemed oppressive, so saturated with sorrow that they felt as if they were breathing in tears. Seeing that Hal wanted to speak again, Will moved closer to catch his words.

"So much to regret . . . especially that I am . . . am making Richard king." Hal tried to smile. "Could say it . . . it is killing me . . ."

"That is a very bad joke," Will said thickly. Hal's death would have repercussions that would echo from one end of the Angevin empire to the other, but he was not ready to think about that yet. For now the world had shrunk to the confines of this bedchamber, and time could be measured only by the faint beats of Hal's heart.

When Hal drew a ragged breath, Will braced himself for the death rattle. But the younger man's eyes were suddenly filled with urgency. "Cloak . . ." he mumbled, "fetch it . . ."

The men looked at one another in confusion. It was only when Hal said "cross" that they understood. Peter and Baldwin rooted around frantically in a coffer of his clothes until they found what he wanted, the mantle sewn with a blood-red crusader's cross. They handed it to Will and he knelt, draped it around Hal like a blanket. Hal's eyes traced the outlines of that crimson cross and he felt a surge of shame. He'd taken the cross so lightly, had sworn to go to the Holy Land more to vex his father than to honor the Almighty, and it seemed symbolic to him of a misspent life, yet another regret to take to his grave.

After a few moments, he indicated he wanted Will to remove the cloak. "Will . . . I entreat you . . . pay my debt to God . . . take it to the Holy Sepulcher for me . . ."

He'd just asked Will to make a pilgrimage on his behalf to Jerusalem, but the knight did not hesitate. "I would be honored, my liege, and shall do it gladly."

A smile flitted across Hal's lips. Summoning up the last of his strength, he moved his hand so that he could see the sapphire ring upon his finger, blessed token of his father's forgiveness. "Remember me . . ." he said, as softly as a breath, and after that he did not speak again.

THE MAN WHO WOULD BE KNOWN to history as the young king died at twilight on Saturday, the eleventh of June, on the festival of the blessed St Barnabas the Apostle. But the drama surrounding his death was just beginning.

CHAPTER FORTY-TWO

June 1183
Martel, Limousin

ILL STUMBLED DOWN TO the great hall the next morning feeling as if he was coming off a three-day drunk. He'd slept badly, could not get rid of a sour taste in his mouth, and for once his celebrated appetite was flagging. He forced himself to eat some cheese and bread, though, for he knew it would be a long, difficult day. When the other knights came over to join him, he saw that they looked no better than he felt—their eyes bloodshot and bleary, their faces either abnormally pallid or oddly flushed—and it occurred to him that men could indeed get drunk on grief.

He was not surprised when they told him that the Bishop of Agen and Count Rotrou had departed, for a king's death was like a sunset, and even his most loyal subjects would instinctively have their eyes already on the eastern horizon, anticipating the coming dawn. He was sorry to hear it, though, for he suspected they were in dire need of money, and they could have asked the bishop or the count for a loan. Peter and Rob soon confirmed his suspicions, reporting that Couraban had stolen the last of the spoils taken from Rocamadour, and they'd be lucky if they could scrape up enough to distribute the traditional alms expected when a highborn lord died.

Will could not regret the loss, for to use such ill-gotten gains for a noble purpose was still sacrilege in his uncompromising eyes. "We need to make plans," he said, knowing that the burden of dealing with Hal's death was going to fall squarely upon his shoulders. "I think we ought to take Hal to the monks at Grandmont. They can make his body ready for burial. After the king is notified, we can then take him to Rouen as he wished."

It made sense to turn to the monks, and if they took a grim satisfaction in undertaking funeral preparations for the man who'd plundered their monastery, they'd earned that right. The knights were looking at Will with puzzlement, though, voiced by Simon when he repeated, "Notify the king? Surely the Bishop of Agen will do that?"

Will marveled at the naïveté of the question, and Baldwin gave a derisive snort, saying, "Oh, yes, I am sure he'll not spare his horse to be the first to tell the king. 'Sire, I know I did my best to convince you that your son was lying, but it seems I was mistaken. Sorry, he really was ill, after all. And . . . well, he died.'"

Baldwin had just made a very effective argument for the bishop's taking as long as possible to reach Limoges. No one volunteered to bear the news to the old king, though, and Will sighed. He was no more eager than any of them to face Henry, but he feared this duty would end up in his lap, too.

"Master de Fabri will know who can best do what . . . what must be done ere we leave Martel," he said bleakly. He did not even want to think about the mutilation of Hal's body—the removal of his eyes, brains, and entrails, the use of salt and spices to delay putrefaction long enough to reach Rouen. He knew the Church dwelt upon the corrupt nature of mortal flesh so that all good Christians would remember that nothing mattered but their eternal souls. That body above-stairs looked too much like the young king he'd served, though, for him to view it as just a husk to be discarded now that it was no longer needed.

Wishing fervently for enough wine to drown all memories of this week of horrors, Will got slowly to his feet, saying, "We'd best see about—" He stopped abruptly, then, at the sight of the men swaggering into the hall. Why were Sancho de Savannac and his cutthroats still here? That made no sense, and he did not like it, did not like it at all.

"Good morrow," Sancho said cheerfully. He was accompanied by his chief henchmen, but as he approached, Will saw more of the routiers entering the hall behind him. Will had hung his scabbard on the back of a chair, and a quick scrutiny of his companions showed that most of them were not armed yet, either.

Acknowledging the outlaw tersely, Will started to move past him, saying that he had much to do. He was not surprised when Sancho barred his way. "You can spare a few moments for me, Sir William. We have a pressing matter to discuss. The young king, may God assoil him, died deeply in debt, alas, owing us a large sum of money."

"You profited handsomely from your service to the king," Rob said harshly. From the corner of his eye, Will saw that he and Baldwin were on their feet, too. Several of Étienne de Fabri's servants had been moving about the hall, but they now showed the heightened awareness of prey animals and made an inconspicuous, speedy withdrawal.

"Not as handsomely as we were promised." In answering Rob, Sancho kept his gaze unblinkingly upon Will. "But I am a reasonable man, do not want to add to your burdens in the midst of your mourning. I am willing to settle for a smaller amount. Pay us one hundred marks and we'll consider the debt paid in full."

There were indignant exclamations from the knights. Will shrugged. "You might as well ask for a thousand marks. We do not even have the money between us to pay for a Requiem Mass."

"That is a pity," Sancho said, shaking his head in feigned regret. "I suppose there is only one fair way to handle this, then. You will remain as our guest, Sir William, whilst your friends raise the money. Once it is paid, off you go with our blessings."

Will studied the routiers with narrowed eyes, not liking the odds. Sancho's cousin Ander and his lackeys Jago, Pere, and Gerhart had begun to fan out purposefully, hands on sword hilts. Even more troubling, other routiers had continued to saunter into the hall. Simon, always hot-headed, did not help matters then by calling Sancho a "lowborn churl" and declaring that they'd never agree to such brazen extortion.

Sancho's smile was toothy, mocking, and sharp with menace. "Now, lad, let's not be hasty. We know that you're all redoubtable knights, celebrated on the tournament circuit. You ought to keep in mind, though, that we've bloodied our swords a time or two ourselves. And you might want to do a head count whilst you're at it."

Will was glad to see Baldwin and Roger were restraining Simon from doing anything mad. He'd made a quick assessment of their chances, concluding that resistance was not an option. They'd have to bluff Sancho into backing down.

"How does it serve your purposes," he said coolly, "if we all end up dead?"

Sancho seemed amused by his challenge and Will realized that this was not a man who acted rashly or impulsively; he'd given careful thought to this ambush. "That would make it difficult to collect a ransom from you," he agreed. "So we came up with a second plan should you balk at cooperating. If we cannot claim the renowned Marshal as surety for this debt, we will have to look elsewhere. Fortunately for us, there is always the royal corpse."

The rest of his words were drowned out in an enraged roar of defiance coming from virtually every knight's throat. Sancho seemed unperturbed by their fury, continuing as if he'd not been interrupted. "I daresay the old king will pay dear to get his beloved son's body back for a proper burial. He might even offer more than a hundred marks."

Will waited until he was sure his fury was under control. "Yes, he'd pay . . . and then he'd track you down to the ends of the earth, into the gates of Hell if need be."

Sancho's smile did not waver. "Yes, he'd likely hold a grudge. That is why I'd rather do this the easier way—by offering you our hospitality, Sir William. It is up to you, of course. But you'd best make up your mind soon. It is a hot summer's day and it will not be long ere the royal corpse is too ripe to travel anywhere."

Will glanced toward his friends, saw that Baldwin and Peter had reached the same grim conclusion that he had. "My first duty is to the young king," he said, the calm voice belied by the fists tightly clenched at his sides. "I must escort his body to the monks at Grandmont. I will agree, though, to return and offer myself up as your hostage once this has been done. You have my sworn word on that."

Ander, Jago, and Gerhart howled with laughter, their mirth stopping abruptly when Sancho nodded. "As I said, I am a reasonable man. And you are known to be an honorable one. We have a deal."

The other knights gathered around Will, appalled, yet understanding they had no choice; even Simon could see that. But Sancho's men were now the ones to be incredulous and angry. Lapsing into their thieves' cant, a jumble of the *lengua romana* of Aquitaine seasoned with Basque and Catalan that enabled them to communicate privately in public, they began to protest vociferously. Sancho shouted them down.

"Enough! When have I not known what I was doing? I admit there are precious few men I'd trust to keep such a promise. The Marshal is one of them, mayhap the only one. This is a man who values his honor more than his life. Now you can argue whether that is an admirable virtue or a fatal character flaw," he said with a grin. "But what matters is that it gets us our hundred marks. Who knows, I might even be willing to spare a few deniers to buy candles for the royal whelp's soul!"

HENRY HAD NEVER SUFFERED from ragged nerves, had always been at his best in a crisis. In the days following Hal's message, though, he felt as if he were unraveling. He had more trouble than usual sleeping, had no interest in food, and most troubling of all, he was finding it difficult to concentrate. His thoughts were as skittish as unbroken horses, darting hither and yon as if he no longer had control of his own brain. Ostensibly, he was laying siege to the ville; in reality, his mind was roaming far afield.

Why had he not heard from Bishop Bertrand or Rotrou by now? They'd had more than enough time to get to Martel and then return to Limoges. What did their ominous silence mean? That Hal was truly ailing? Or had they ridden into a trap? Were they being held prisoner whilst Hal waited to see if the bait would be taken?

"My liege!" Geoff was bearing down upon him again and Henry strove for patience; who knew that sons could be worse than mothers? For certes, he'd never gotten such wearisome, constant solicitude from his other lads.

"You are hovering again, Geoff," he warned, and Geoff acknowledged the truth of the charge with an abashed grin.

"I am being a pest, I know," he conceded, for he'd already been chiding Henry about venturing within arrow range and nagging him about taking a midday meal. "I was just going to suggest that you seek shelter from the sun. Your nose is turning red!"

"So is yours," Henry pointed out, for Geoff had inherited his fair, freckled skin. Actually he was amenable to the idea, for the heat was unrelenting. By the Rood, how he loathed the Limousin! The spring had been miserably wet and cold, and now the summer was hellishly hot. So when Geoff gestured toward a nearby peasant's hut, he followed willingly, ducking through the low doorway into a small, gloomy cottage that reeked of onions and cabbage and sweat. Straightening up, he found himself face-to-face with the fearful occupants, a bony, spare man of indeterminate years and his toil-worn wife.

Henry had a rudimentary knowledge of Eleanor's *lengua romana,* for he'd always had an excellent ear for languages; only Welsh had proved to be impenetrable. He summoned up enough of it now to assure the frightened couple that they'd not be harmed, and his gentle words and the promise of a few coins did much to allay their unease. He sat cross-legged, then, on the hard dirt floor, his body admitting what his pride could not—that he was tired down to the very marrow of his bones.

Ranulf soon joined them; he was another mother hen, Henry thought wryly. But he did not come empty-handed. He had several wineskins, giving Henry the one diluted with water and tossing the other to Geoff.

"Make yourself comfortable," Henry invited, and Ranulf accepted the invitation, lowering himself stiffly to the floor beside his nephew, muttering that he'd likely need help getting up again. There were times when Henry felt that his fifty years were weighing him down like an anchor, but he was a stripling next to his uncle, for Ranulf would be sixty-five that November. Because he did not see the older man that often, the changes wrought by aging were more noticeable to him; Ranulf's hair was now pure silver and his shoulders were stooped, his stride slowed by a touch of the joint evil. The essential core of the man was still intact, though—the impish humor and courage and awkward habit of truth-telling—qualities that Henry appreciated even more now than in his youth.

"Is Bleddyn still balking at returning to Wales without you?" he asked, and Ranulf nodded, with a grimace that was part vexation and part pride.

"He is missing his wife and bairns, but he still insists that he'll wait so we can return together. He is a stubborn one, is Bleddyn. And though he'll not admit it, his real reason for staying is that he thinks I'm too feeble and aged to get home safely by myself!"

Henry cocked a brow in Geoff's direction, and his eldest had the grace to blush. Just then Willem entered the hut, saying, "So this is where you've all gotten off to! A monk from Grandmont has arrived, my liege, is asking to see you. Shall I send him into your audience chamber here?"

"I'll see him," Henry said, thinking that the monk had likely come about their stolen pyx; to their great relief, he'd promised that he'd replace it. Of all Hal's outrages in recent weeks, the plundering of Grandmont was the one that rankled the most, for Henry had taken it just as his son had intended—as a personal affront.

He was getting to his feet when a brown-clad form blocked the light from the door. As the man stooped to enter and then straightened up, Henry was startled to see a familiar face. "Guillaume . . . is that you?" And the heat of high summer notwithstanding, he went cold, for the prior of Grandmont would not be the one to bear a mundane message. His presence here was a message in and of itself. Henry's mouth was suddenly so dry that he did not even have enough saliva to spit. "All of you," he managed to croak, "out!"

They obeyed at once, Ranulf halting only long enough to shepherd the peasants ahead of him. He thought, too, to close the door behind them, and the hut was plunged into darkness. Henry welcomed it, for instincts honed as sharp as any sword blade were warning that he'd have need of its camouflaging kindness. The prior took several steps forward, would have knelt if Henry had not stopped him. "I do not bring good news, sire," he said softly.

Henry closed his eyes, never wanted to have to open them again. "My son . . ." he whispered, but he could go no further, struck by superstitious dread that to say it aloud would banish any splinters of hope, would indeed make it so.

"The young king is dead, my liege, stricken by fever and the bloody flux." The prior knew those were just symptoms of Hal's death; the real cause was the Vengeance of God for his wanton acts of sacrilege. He saw no need to salt the king's wounds by saying so, though, and instead continued quietly, telling Henry that Hal's knights had arrived at Grandmont that morn, bearing the body of their lord and the sorrowful story of his last days. After a few moments, he realized that Henry was not listening. "Shall I go, sire?"

Henry nodded, but cried out as the prior reached the door. "Wait! Wh . . . when?"

"On Saturday eve, my lord," the prior said sadly, and Henry shut his eyes again.

On Saturday. There had been time. If only he'd believed, he could have been at Hal's deathbed. If he'd not given in to his damnable doubts and suspicions, he'd have been there when his son needed him the most. The sound of a closing door told him that he was alone, and he sank to his knees, but prayers would not come. He prostrated himself on the floor of the hut, just as he'd once done upon the cold tiles before Becket's tomb, pressing his cheek into the dirt, hearing no other sound in the world but the wild hammering of his heart.

As WORD SPREAD, men began to gather near the hut. It was a subdued crowd, conversing only in hushed murmurs, and since Henry was not in sight, they were watching his advisors and confidants, for it was well known that the king would have gone to Martel if his counselors had not talked him out of it. But the latter were oblivious to the stares and speculation, for they could focus upon nothing except the man in that cottage.

Geoff, Ranulf, Willem, and Maurice de Craon were standing together, not speaking, each one alone with his regrets. After the prior had emerged from the hut, they'd heard only one cry, a lament that raised the hairs on the back of their necks, for it was a wail of pure pain and utter despair. After that, though, there had been silence, and somehow they found that more chilling than weeping or cursing or raging would have been.

RICHARD WAS TRYING OUT a relatively new siege engine at Aixe. Called a trebuchet, it had a long arm pivoting on an axle. The shorter end of the arm held the counterweight, and the longer end, called the verge, was being winched down to the ground so they could load heavy stones into its sling. Once it was ready, the engineers waited for the duke's signal and then released the trigger. As the counterweight plummeted down, the verge shot upward and rocks rained down upon the walls of the castle. The soldiers let out a cheer, and Richard turned to Alfonso with a delighted grin, looking like a boy who'd just been given a surprise present.

"It has a much greater range than the mangonels," he marveled, "and is more accurate, too. If those fools don't surrender soon, we'll bring the castle walls down about their ears!"

Alfonso agreed, equally impressed with the deadly potential of this new weapon. Thinking he'd love to test it against the Count of Toulouse, he followed after Richard as the duke paced around the trebuchet, inspecting it from every angle.

"Good work, Guy," he told a soldier, who beamed at the praise. Men were scurrying about, making ready to reload, and Richard watched intently, his brow furrowed in thought. When Alfonso caught up with him, he murmured, almost as if talking to himself, "I wonder . . . if we shortened the sling, would that increase the arc of the stone's flight? If so, it would cover greater distance, might even hit the keep itself."

When he looked questioningly at Alfonso, the Aragonese king smiled and agreed, although he had no clear idea what Richard was talking about. It was enough for him that the trebuchet worked; unlike Richard, he felt no need to understand how and why it did. But if Richard thought so, he was probably correct; at twenty-five, the duke was well on the way to becoming a master of the art of war.

"Are we within crossbow range?" Alfonso asked suddenly, for he'd noticed that Richard seemed remarkably casual about matters of personal safety. When his friend mocked his caution, he reminded Richard amiably that his son and heir was only nine years old, too young to rule in his own right. "So if I were killed at Aixe, it would cause no end of trouble in Aragon. Whereas if you, my lord duke, were to take a fatal arrow in the chest, your brother the young king would be happy to step into your shoes."

Richard's knights were taken aback, but Richard was amused, not offended, by Alfonso's irreverence, and laughed. "Dukes may be expendable in Aragon, but here in Aquitaine, the duke's death matters more than the loss of any king. As for the 'young king,' he'll never see the day dawn when he . . ." He stopped in mid-sentence, and Alfonso, following his gaze, saw that riders were being escorted into the encampment.

"Is that not your brother, the chancellor?"

Richard nodded. "And to judge by the doleful look on his face, he is bringing yet more bad news. I am beginning to think my father ought to have christened him Jonah rather than Geoffrey."

Geoff and his men had dismounted by the time Richard and Alfonso reached them. At close range, Geoff's agitation was even more obvious and Richard braced himself for yet more bad news. He greeted his brother brusquely, then said, "Well, what have you come to tell me that I will not want to hear?"

"It is not bad news for you. It might even be good news for England, too, but it is the worst possible news our father could have gotten."

Richard stared at him. "Are you saying . . . You mean Hal was actually telling the truth for once?"

"Yes, he was. He died on Saturday at Martel."

There were gasps and exclamations from those who'd heard. Alfonso made the sign of the cross. Richard was dumbfounded, for he'd had no doubts whatsoever that Hal had been lying through his teeth. He took a moment to absorb it, and then scowled. "Splendor of God! We're all in the soup, then, and me most of all. When he starts doling out blame, I'm likely to get the lion's share."

Geoff glared at him. "You have never understood our father, have you? He is not a man to seek scapegoats. When we tried to apologize for giving him such faulty advice, he would not hear it, saying 'I am not Louis Capet.' He has taken all the blame upon himself for not going to Martel, and when we argued that it was the only decision under the circumstances, he just looked at us with hollow, empty eyes."

Alfonso was becoming aware of an undercurrent of excitement surging through the camp. As word passed from one man to another, they were elated, understanding what this would mean for their duke. They were struggling to act sober and respectful, knowing it was not seemly to gloat over Hal's death, but most could not contain their glee. Glancing at Richard, Alfonso saw that the full implications of Hal's death had not yet registered with him; he'd reacted instinctively as a son and a brother. He kept his eyes upon his friend's face, and he would later tell his queen that he'd seen the exact moment when Richard realized that not only had he won his war, he was now the heir to the English crown. Geoff was still chiding him on Henry's behalf; he was no longer listening. His expression gave away nothing, but Alfonso was close enough to catch the hint of a smile curving the corners of his mouth.

HENRY HAD LEARNED OF his son's death on Tuesday afternoon. It was now Wednesday night and he was utterly exhausted, for he'd slept no more than four or five hours in that time. And when he had fallen asleep, he'd been tormented by remorseful dreams of Hal that gave him neither peace nor rest. As the hours dragged on, he'd told his squires to go to bed; in the shadowed chamber, he could barely make them out, sprawled on pallets in the corner. As tired as he was, he was not yet ready to plunge into the nightmare cauldron of his dreams, and he remained sitting in a window-seat, doing his best to keep the past at bay.

When a discreet knock sounded, he chose to answer the door himself, much to the surprise of the bishop's servant. He blinked and then said, speaking in the overly solicitous voice that people used to address the mortally ill, "My lord . . . Sir William Marshal has just ridden in. Since you are still awake, do you wish to see him? Or shall I tell him to wait till the morrow?"

Henry had known this moment would come, when he'd have to listen to a first-person account of his son's suffering. "I will see him," he said and tried to brace himself for the ordeal.

WILL'S MUSCLES WERE CRAMPING, and he was grateful when Henry gestured for him to rise and told him to find a seat. Fetching a stool, he sat down beside the king, keeping his gaze lowered, for it seemed somehow indecent to look upon another man's raw, naked pain. He had been dreading this meeting as much as Henry, but it had to be done. A reckoning had to be made. After waiting several moments for questions that did not come, he realized the reason for Henry's reticence—fear that he was about to hear a story that would haunt him for the rest of his life. Who could blame him for assuming Hal had died as fecklessly and carelessly as he'd lived?

"You may be proud of his last days, my liege," he said firmly, "for he showed courage, dignity, and grace, dying as a good Christian, as a great lord ought to die, setting an example for us all."

Henry searched his face intently, but he did not think Marshal would lie to him. "Tell me," he said, and Will did, thankful that he'd not joined Hal until the last week of his life and need not speak of those rash actions that the young king had so regretted at the end. He related, instead, the story of the reckless, selfish boy who'd not become a man until it was almost too late. He had to stop occasionally to collect himself, for he was finding that retelling it was like reliving it, and he was not surprised to see tears silently streaking Henry's face as he listened. How much worse it could have been, though, if Hal had not repented and been shriven whilst there was still time!

"We did not know what to do with your ring, sire," he concluded, "at last decided we ought to return it to you. But it was remarkable, for none of us could remove it from your son's finger. It was as if even in death he could not bear to part with it."

Henry swallowed with difficulty. "May God grant him salvation," he whispered, but it no longer seemed such a forlorn hope, not after what he'd just heard about Hal's remorse, regrets, and contrition. "There is one last duty you can perform for him, Marshal. I want you to escort his funeral cortege to Rouen."

"My liege . . . I would that I could, but that is not possible." And when Henry frowned, Will hastily told him of Hal's final debts and the pledge he'd been forced to make to the Basque routier, Sancho de Savannac.

"My son cost me greatly," Henry said when he was done, "but I would that he'd lived to cost me more. This is not your debt, Marshal. I will take care of it."

"Thank you, sire." Will reached then for the pouch dangling from his belt and drew forth Hal's deathbed letter. "This is for you, my lord king, dictated by your son to the Bishop of Agen."

Henry stared at that rolled parchment with dread. Will understood. As painful as it would be to read his son's last words, it might help to cauterize the wound, though. He waited patiently until Henry took the letter, assuming their conversation was over then. But Henry made no move to dismiss him.

Henry was gazing down at the unbroken seal, recognizing it as Hal's. He'd also used the sapphire ring to seal the letter, and that brought a lump to Henry's throat.

Looking up after a long silence, he said, "I wronged you, Marshal, blaming you unfairly for his mistakes and his sins. I see now that yours was the only level head in his
mesnie. Once you were gone, he foundered like a ship without a rudder. I thank you
for returning to him when you did, for I do not doubt that you helped to steer him
back onto the path to deliverance."

"I could not have done so if you'd not granted me that safe conduct, sire," Will
said and rose, taking this as his cue to depart.

"After you take my son to Rouen, come back to me, Will. You are a good and honorable man, and I would have you join my household knights."

Will gasped. He'd hoped that Henry would offer to assume responsibility for
Hal's debt to Sancho, but his expectations had gone no further than that. He'd resigned himself to the loss of royal favor, to a far different life from the one he'd enjoyed
during his years with Hal. "My liege, you do me great honor. I would gladly serve you
as I served your son. There is yet one more trust that I must discharge on his behalf,
though. He felt great shame for having taken the cross so lightly, and he asked me to act
in his stead, to deliver his crusader's cloak to the Holy Sepulcher in Jerusalem."

"And you agreed, of course," Henry said, with a faint smile, his first in more than
a week. "Go, then, with my blessings. Tell my chancellor how much you will need for
your pilgrimage and he will issue letters of credit. And upon your return, a place will
be waiting for you."

"Thank you, my liege." Will waited, sensing that there was something still to
be said.

"I would rather my son had triumphed over me than Death had triumphed over
him," Henry said, very softly, and Will did not doubt him. They regarded each other
without need of words, two very different men united in their shared sorrow for the
king's son.

CONSTANCE HAD BEEN BACK at the ducal castle in Rennes for only two
days and she was still busy cataloguing all the damage done when Roland de Dinan
had seized it on behalf of the English king. Trailed by a scribe clutching a wax tablet
and bone stylus, she was inspecting the storerooms. As she tallied up their losses, she
was seething, infuriated that so much would have to be replaced. Their flour was gone,
as were the salted herring, cod, and mackerel, the dried figs and dates, even the five
bushels of salt she'd purchased that spring.

"They were like a swarm of God-cursed locusts!" she fumed. "They stripped the
hall and bedchambers bare, stole our grey fur coverlet that had been a wedding gift

from the Bishop of Rennes, even looted several pounds of wax. I'm surprised they did not steal the grease used for cartwheel axles."

Her butler murmured his agreement, and the clerk scribbled hastily to keep up with her torrent of words. Her ladies, Juvette and Blanche, exchanged knowing looks, for they understood that her foul mood was not explained entirely by the sorry state of the castle. Duke Geoffrey had returned to the war after recovering Rennes and staging punitive raids into Roland de Dinan's lands at Becherel, and Constance had hoped that he'd left her with child. This morning she'd found out it was not so, much to her disappointment.

The butler now led the way toward the buttery, where Constance knew their greatest losses lay. Any of the tuns of wine not drained dry by de Dinan's men would have been carried off when he'd retreated, leaving a garrison behind to guard his prize. She'd heard that they had not put up much resistance when Geoffrey had besieged the castle, loath to fight against their duke. Constance could take some solace from that, yet more proof of Geoffrey's acceptance by her Breton lords. He'd managed to overcome a huge liability—that he was the English king's son—with uncanny ease. Of course she knew his campaign to win them over had begun well before their marriage; he'd laid the groundwork during those years when he was acting as his father's deputy in Brittany, forging bonds with men like Raoul de Fougères and Reginald de Boterel that would stand him in good stead once he no longer relied upon Henry for his standing in Brittany.

Constance still marveled at the vast difference between the reality of her marriage and her bleak expectations. She would have scoffed at the romantic idea of soul mates. Nevertheless, they had reached a remarkable understanding with surprising speed, discovering that they shared the same aspirations and ambitions, the same innate skepticism and gambler's instincts, with, as an added bonus, the pleasure they found in their marriage bed. They'd be wed two years in August, with only one serious quarrel in all that time. Geoffrey had been furious to learn that she had countermanded him and returned to Brittany instead of seeking safety at the French court. Constance had been forced to apologize, which did not come easily to her, but Geoffrey had right on his side—she had indeed been put at risk by the seizure of the ducal castle, and she'd had to concede that her capture would have been disastrous.

The buttery was a total loss; they'd even taken the keg of verjuice. "I hope my lord husband burned de Dinan's manor to the ground," she said angrily. "If it were up to me, I'd have sown salt into his fields, the Judas."

Her butler thought that was not entirely fair to Roland de Dinan, who'd been given the stark choice of offending his patron, the English king, or his duke and duchess. He was not crazed enough to offer a defense of the disgraced baron, though, and sought to console Constance by revealing that some of the wine had no longer been drinkable; wine rarely remained potable for more than a year, for if it was exposed to the air, it developed an acid, unpleasant taste.

That did cheer Constance somewhat; she hoped that the marauders had ended up as sick as dogs. She was turning to check the details on her scribe's tablet when Juvette rushed into the buttery. "Madame! The lord duke has just ridden into the bailey!"

Constance froze. Geoffrey's unexpected return could only mean something had gone very wrong. Had he gotten word of a coming attack upon Brittany? "He is not injured?"

"Oh, no, Madame. I could see no signs that he's been wounded. But . . . he and his men look very grim. I fear he brings bad news."

So did Constance. Normally she would have hastened out to greet him, but she decided now that a private reunion might be better and she said abruptly, "Leave me, all of you. Tell the duke that I await him in the buttery."

It seemed like forever to her before Geoffrey came through the doorway. Even in such subdued lighting, she could see that he was bone-white, the skin tightly drawn around his eyes, his mouth set in a thin, taut line. He closed the door, then leaned back against it. "Hal is dead."

"Dear God!" Constance's shock held her motionless for a moment and then she moved swiftly toward him. "How? Surely not even Richard would dare to kill a king!"

"It was not Richard's doing. He . . . he died at Martel of the bloody flux." Geoffrey sounded numb and she could easily understand why, for when they'd attempted to envision all the possible drawbacks to this war, it had never occurred to either of them that Hal might die. He was twenty-eight, in excellent health, and shielded from the ordinary dangers of the battlefield by his highborn status. Who could have imagined he'd be struck down by an infection of the bowels?

"Was he shriven ere he died?"

"Yes, thank God for that mercy. He made a very good end, for certes a dramatic one." Geoffrey meant to sound sardonic, sounded sad, instead. They'd never been very close, and his boyhood admiration for the dashing elder brother had faded once he'd begun to assess Hal with adult eyes. But he'd discovered, somewhat to his surprise, that he mourned Hal both as a brother and as an ally. "If I had not agreed to join him, he might still be alive. His war was made possible by Breton money—"

"No, Geoffrey! You did not coax Hal into rebellion. I'll not let you blame yourself. In his entire life, Hal never did anything that he did not want to do. Even if we had stayed out of it, it would have changed nothing. Aimar and the other barons were set upon rebellion and Hal . . . well, he could resist anything but temptation. He would still have—" She got no further, for Geoffrey kissed her.

"Thank you for that, darling."

"For what?" she asked, puzzled but pleased.

"For your use of pronouns." Seeing her lack of comprehension, he kissed her again. "For saying 'we.' I thought you might blame me for this, for entangling Brittany in a war we can no longer win."

"We made the decision together, Geoffrey. If we lose, we'll do that together, too."

Geoffrey was touched by this display of loyalty. He and Constance were still learning about each other, and he had not been sure how she'd react. He had no qualms about lying if it furthered his own interests. He did not want to lie to Constance, though, and he needed to be sure she understood what they were facing. "Fortune's Wheel has spun with a vengeance, Constance. It is not just that the rebellion is lost and we have no choice but to submit to my father and hope he is in a forgiving mood. It is—"

She reached up, stopped his words by putting her fingers to his lips. "I am not a child, Geoffrey. I understand what Hal's death means for England and for Brittany. But whatever comes, we will deal with it. What other choice do we have?"

He slid his arm around her waist, drew her in against him. "Have I ever told you," he murmured, "that I consider myself a lucky man?"

She was dismayed to find herself blinking back tears, and she turned her face into his shoulder so he'd not see, saying briskly, "Of course you are lucky. You are the Duke of Brittany, after all."

After a few moments, he said, "I want to found a chaplaincy in Hal's memory," and she agreed that would be a good thing to do. By mutual consent, they did not speak of the future and what it held for them—when they'd be accountable, not to an indulgent father, but to a soldier king who bore them a deadly grudge.

A GACE LOOKED UP as the door opened and Judith entered. Crossing the chamber, she murmured a few words in the older woman's ear. Agace got stiffly to her feet and approached the bed. "My lamb?" There was no response. Bending over, she gently stroked the tumbled fair hair spilling over the pillow. "Your lord brother is here again, asking to see you. Do you feel up to it?"

Marguerite shook her head.

"Are you sure, dearest?"

Marguerite kept her eyes tightly shut, but her lips moved and Agace leaned closer to catch the whispered words. "I do not want to see him . . ."

Agace and Judith exchanged troubled glances. Their young queen could not hide forever from the world. Eventually she would have to pick up the shattered pieces of her life and accept her loss. But if she needed more time, Agace was going to see that she got it. "Rest now, my lamb. I will send him away," she promised, and left Judith to watch over their mistress while she was gone. Judith sat down in the chair Agace had vacated, grateful that she would not be the one to deal with the French king. Philippe had always treated her with courtesy. He made her uneasy, though, for reasons she could not have articulated, and she understood why Marguerite did not turn to him for comfort. Her lady had a loving heart and a generous nature, whereas there was something bloodless and sly about her brother.

AGACE DID NOT LIKE Philippe any more than Judith did, and as she looked into his pale blue eyes, so oddly ageless in such a young face, she felt a throb of despair, knowing that Marguerite's fate was now in his hands. Hers had been a long and eventful life, though, and she knew better than to antagonize a king, especially this one. Greeting him with exaggerated deference, she told him regretfully that the queen had finally fallen asleep after yet another wakeful, wretched night. As she'd hoped, Philippe quickly told her not to disturb Marguerite, just to tell her of his visit.

Philippe was grateful for the reprieve. A sense of duty compelled him to check on his sister, but he did not know how to comfort her and their few encounters since learning of Hal's death had been awkward and uncomfortable. What was he supposed to say to a woman who'd done little but weep all week long?

After returning to the great hall, he was too restless to stay and strode out into the royal gardens at the west end of the island. If the Île was the heart of Paris, home to both his palace and the great cathedral of Notre Dame, the Seine was its main artery, and even at dusk, the quays were still busy, ships from Rouen unloading below the Grand Pont and those coming downriver docking at the Grève, formerly the site of the weekly Paris market but now where local vintners sold their wares.

This change was Philippe's doing, for he had established a new market at a more convenient location and erected two large sheds so merchants could do their haggling indoors. While he'd denied Parisians the right to form a commune, he did have a keen interest in civic improvements, and ambitious plans that went far beyond the indoor market at Les Halles; he hoped in time to build a defensive wall around the city and to pave the main streets. He did not have the funds for such projects yet, but Philippe believed in long-range planning and he was willing to wait for what he wanted.

Resting his elbows upon the stone garden wall, Philippe looked out upon his city as it was gradually cloaked in the soft shades of a summer eve. He was trying to be patient with Marguerite, but he feared that, if left to her own devices, she'd do nothing but weep and wallow in her grief. He wished there was some sensible female he could consult. But his mother had never shown any sympathy for the daughters of Louis's earlier marriages, his own queen was a child of thirteen, and Marguerite's mother was long dead, her sister Alys in England. He sighed, thinking that sisters were more trouble than they were worth.

His half sisters Alix and Marie were strangers, and Marie had openly allied herself with the Count of Flanders against him. There was his full sister, Agnes, a child bride caught up in a bloody coup in Constantinople, her fate uncertain.

And then there was the vexing problem that was his half sister Alys. She had been betrothed to Richard for fourteen years, and Philippe was offended that the wedding had not yet taken place. Henry kept offering excuses, but nothing changed—except that Alys got older. She was already twenty-two, for pity's sake! Philippe knew Richard had never been keen to marry Alys, and he couldn't really blame him since she had no marriage portion. He suspected that Henry and Richard were in collusion, looking elsewhere for a more profitable marital alliance while keeping Alys off the marriage market, thus preventing him from making any advantageous alliances by wedding Alys to someone else. It had been irksome, and was unfair to Alys, but Philippe had not seen it as a priority problem, for he'd assumed that Hal would become king sooner than later. From Philippe's vantage point, Henry's fifty years was a vast age, indeed; how much longer could he live? And once Hal was king, he'd have ordered Richard to marry Alys, whether he liked it or not.

Philippe's thoughts had come full circle, for he was back to Marguerite and the inopportune death of his brother-in-law. Hal's loss was a great blow to Philippe, for he'd predicated his plans upon having an amiable, pleasure-loving prince on the English throne. Instead, he'd have to deal with Richard, who was as unlike Hal as any two men could be. How could he be so unlucky?

Well, one step at a time. The immediate concern was recovering Marguerite's marriage portion from the English king. Sure that Henry would sooner cut off his arm than return the Vexin, Philippe frowned thoughtfully. If Henry held on to the Vexin, that would make Philippe the laughingstock of Christendom, the boy-king who was no match for the wily veteran on the English throne. An idea was glimmering in the back of his brain and he waited for it to come into focus. What if he could make it worth Richard's while to marry Alys? Suppose he offered the Vexin as Alys's dowry? That would save face, and would also give him leverage, for he could make the agreement contingent upon the marriage. And who knows, it might even stir up discord between Henry and Richard.

The wind had picked up and thunder echoed in the distance. Philippe considered it prudent to seek shelter, and he signaled to his waiting bodyguards. He must give this idea more thought, but it seemed promising. And as he exited the garden, he smiled, thinking that if he could marry Alys off to Richard, he could then concentrate upon finding a new husband for Marguerite. She was still of child-bearing age, with a pretty face and a docile nature, a queen with the blood of French kings in her veins. There'd be no shortage of princes interested in such a bargain bride.

THE ENGLISH QUEEN WAS back at Sarum, and Amaria was pleased by the move, welcoming any change in the predictable ebb and flow of daily life. On this sun-splashed June afternoon, she was enjoying the hustle and bustle of market day, held on the open ground below the castle's East Gate. Accompanied by a servant to tote her purchases, she'd spent several pleasant hours browsing among the booths, buying needles and thread, a vial of rosewater, scarlet ribbons, almond oil, the hazel- nuts that her queen liked, and several jars of honey. It was wonderful to have enough money for impulse and luxury buys; Amaria was very appreciative of the queen's rise in status. In good spirits, she bought candied quince from a vendor and included the delighted young servant in her generosity.

Some of her cheer began to dissipate as they headed back toward the castle, for the queen's chamber was no happy place these days. Eleanor had lost so much weight that her face looked drawn and pinched, and Amaria had to urge her to eat. Her days were long and her nights were worse. Amaria ached, too, feeling her pain and fear, and sympathizing with her rage. Had she been free, she'd have sailed for her homeland weeks ago, recklessly plunging into the very midst of war as she sought to end this frat- ricidal strife between her sons. Because she remained tethered to her husband's will, she unleashed much of her frustration and fury upon his absent head, speaking of him with more bitterness than Amaria had heard from her in years. Amaria did what she could, provided an audience for her rants and prayed earnestly that the king would soon restore peace to his domains and his family. Other than that, they could only wait for word from the Limousin.

She paused to exchange greetings with some of the townsmen streaming back into the castle; she'd discovered, to her amusement, that she was a source of consider- able interest to the inhabitants of Sarum—the person closest to that legendary being, Eleanor of Aquitaine. They soon parted ways, the villagers heading off toward the homes nestled under the castle walls and Amaria and her young helper continuing in the direction of the keep and royal palace.

As soon as they passed through the gatehouse into the inner bailey, Amaria sensed that something was wrong. The courtyard was usually like a hive for humans, with servants and soldiers and visitors milling about in raucous confusion, dogs getting underfoot and chickens squawking and horses eager to reach the stables and their waiting feed. Now, though, an eerie silence greeted Amaria. A few people were out and about, but they were also acting oddly, clustered together in small knots and conversing in the hushed tones usually heard only in church.

The boy felt it, too, glancing around uneasily as if he expected to find the castle under attack at any moment. Just then one of the maidservants spotted them. "Dame Amaria, we've been looking all over for you! It is just terrible . . . The queen's son is dead! He was stricken—"

But Amaria was no longer listening. Lifting up her skirts, she began to run.

SHE ARRIVED, panting and flushed, in the queen's chamber only to find it empty. For a moment, she stood, irresolute, and then realized that Eleanor might be in the chapel of St Nicholas. It was accessible from the royal apartments, but she paused for a moment before she entered, trying to collect her thoughts. She was not truly surprised, for she'd long feared that this would happen. Men might laud Duke Richard for his utter fearlessness, but not the women who loved him.

As she'd expected, she found Eleanor in the chapel, standing by one of the windows. Her face was partly in shadow, one cheek dappled with the deep rose hues of the panes above her head for the sun was setting the stained glass afire. She turned at the sound of footsteps upon the tiles, and Amaria bit back a cry, for the queen could have been a stranger. She seemed to have aged years in just a few hours, and Amaria had never seen her look as she did now—vulnerable, frail, and defeated.

"My lady, I am so sorry!" Amaria's words ended in a stifled sob as she came to a halt, stretching out her hand in a tentative gesture of comfort that fell short, her fingers just brushing the sleeve of Eleanor's gown.

"I wanted to pray for his salvation," Eleanor said dully, "but I do not think the Almighty is listening to me, not anymore . . ."

Amaria was momentarily mute, for she'd never known such despair herself; even when she'd lost her own babies, she'd not lost her belief in God's Mercy. She looked at the queen, her eyes blurring with tears. But she had to ask, had to know the worst if she had any hope of consoling this stricken woman. "Madame . . . was he shriven?" And when Eleanor nodded, she leaned against the wall, weak with relief. "God be praised! Surely that . . . that must be of some comfort, my lady. So often men die in battle without confessing their sins beforehand, and Duke Richard was . . ." She stopped then, for Eleanor was looking at her blankly.

Eleanor felt as if her brain was no longer working as it ought, and it took a moment or so until she understood the meaning of Amaria's words. "It is not Richard. It is Hal."

Amaria was astounded. Richard's death would have made more sense, for he gambled with his own mortality on a daily basis. But Hal? He'd seemed to be one of Heaven's favorites, blessed and beloved, not a man whose life would be cut short with such fearful finality. "H—how?"

Eleanor shook her head, not yet able to talk about it, just as she was not ready to think about the political consequences, what Hal's death would mean to Richard. For now she was a mother whose child had been cruelly taken from her and nothing else mattered. Her shoulders slumping, she leaned her forehead against the sun-burnished stained glass, closing her eyes against the glare.

"My poor Hal," she whispered. "He so wanted to be a king and he was never more than a pawn . . ."

CHAPTER FORTY-THREE

✦

July 1183
Sarum, England

*T*HE QUEEN'S NIGHTS had been so troubled that Amaria had gone to see the village apothecary, and after consulting him, purportedly for her own sleeplessness, she purchased a sleeping draught of henbane and black poppy. She returned to the castle with a lighter step, for it helped immeasurably to know the Countess of Chester was there. Maud was familiar with the blighted, desolate landscape of grief. She, too, had suffered the loss of a son. And she could be candid with the queen in a way that Amaria could not. Amaria thought she could already see an improvement in Eleanor's spirits and she blessed the countess for being such a loyal friend.

As she entered the queen's chamber, she found Eleanor seated by the open window, reading a letter, and Maud playing with the cat. Maud smiled at Amaria, beckoned her over, and related that the queen had just gotten a letter from the Duchess of Saxony. "It is bound to comfort her," she said softly, "hearing from her daughter." Amaria was not so sure; what if Tilda had more bad news to disclose? Cleo was curled up contentedly in Maud's lap and, lulled by her benign demeanor, Amaria ventured to pet her, only to have the feline flatten her ears and spit. Maud told her not to take it personally, explaining that cats were given to whims and unpredictable behavior, but to Amaria, she sounded faintly smug, the way people who never got seasick commiserated with those who did.

Glancing up from the letter, Eleanor said, "My daughter writes that Viscount Aimar surrendered his castle a fortnight ago. Harry razed it to the ground and Aimar was compelled to forswear further revolts, but Tilda thinks he got off lightly. The other rebels have gone to ground, too." For a moment, her eyes held Maud's and the same thought was in both their minds: that the rebellion had died when Hal drew his last breath. Eleanor swallowed with a visible effort and lowered her gaze to the letter. But then she stiffened in disbelief. "God in Heaven!"

When she looked up again, she was shaking her head in amazement. "Tilda says that as Will Marshal and Hal's knights carried his bier north, crowds gathered by the roadside to watch, weeping and mourning. A leper and a woman suffering from hemorrhages claimed to be cured after touching his bier." They were equally astonished, and she held up her hand to forestall questions. "Wait, there is more. When the funeral cortege halted at the monastery of St Savin, people said they could see a beam of light shining down upon the church. And as they approached Le Mans, a cross was seen in the sky and another beam of light enveloped the bier. The citizens of Le Mans were convinced they'd seen a miracle, and they seized Hal's body, insisting that he be buried in their city. Will and the knights protested, to no avail, and he was interred in their cathedral next to Harry's father."

The other women were dumbfounded. Naturally they believed in saints and miracles, but neither one could envision Hal as a saint. Could they say so forthrightly, though, to his mother?

Eleanor had resumed reading, continuing to shake her head at the contents of the letter. "Tilda says the townspeople of Rouen were outraged, threatening war with Le Mans if Hal's body were not re-interred and buried in their cathedral as he wished, and to keep the peace, Harry has had to order it done." Looking up, she said with a sad smile, "Hal would have been amused by the furor, and even more amused to hear himself proclaimed a saint. His ambitions never rose higher than a kingship."

Amaria was emboldened to confess that she did not understand any of it. She got her answer from Maud as the countess said dryly, "Saints are valuable commodities, Dame Amaria. Holy relics attract pilgrims. And saints are even more useful for political purposes. Cousin Harry could contend with his rebellious archbishop, but he had no chance whatsoever against the Holy Martyr."

Turning her attention again to the letter, Eleanor drew a hissing breath. "Do you remember the Archdeacon of Welles, Maud? Harry sent him to me with word of Hal's death, knowing that he had always been sympathetic to my plight. It seems the good archdeacon is one of those promoting Hal's sanctity. According to him, I already knew of my son's death, for I'd had a dream in which he wore two crowns, and I told Archdeacon Thomas that these dual crowns could only mean eternal bliss and everlasting joy. The archdeacon has been commending me in his sermons for 'fathoming the mystery' of my dream and for accepting Hal's death with such discernment and strength."

Amaria was now thoroughly confused, but not Maud, who said with a frown, "You'd best write to Harry and assure him that the archdeacon has a vivid imagination. If you wish, I will write to him, too, and tell him that I was present when you first learned of the archdeacon's claims."

"That is not needed, Maud, but I thank you. Harry will know without being told that I would not have said this." Seeing Amaria's bewilderment, Eleanor said, with a thin smile, "Harry's foes learned well from Archbishop Thomas's martyrdom. If they can convince people that Hal was a saint, that puts Harry in a very poor light, indeed. And whilst I admit that there have been times when that would have given me great satisfaction, if Harry is tarnished by this . . . this foolishness, then so is Richard. And Harry knows I would do nothing to undermine Richard's authority in Aquitaine." *He has enough troubles there as it is.* But this thought remained unspoken, for not even to Maud would Eleanor confess her misgivings about her second son's heavy-handed rule over the turbulent, defiant barons of her duchy.

Going back to her daughter's letter, she smiled again, only this one was genuine. "At last, some good news! Tilda says that Geoffrey has been summoned to meet Harry and Richard at Angers. God Willing, we can restore family harmony, although how long it will last . . ."

Maud was surprised that Eleanor seemed so eager to see Geoffrey forgiven, for she'd assumed that the queen would have been very wroth with him for the part he'd played in the assault upon her favorite son. Striving for tact, she said, "You bear Geoffrey no grudge, then?"

Eleanor's smile disappeared as if it had never been. "I am not happy with him. Nothing is more important, though, than bringing peace to our family and our domains. I have lost one son this summer, and I will be damned if I will lose another."

H ENRY WAS STANDING upon the dais in the great hall at Angers, conversing with the bishop and several of his barons. Losing interest, Richard drifted over to an open window. He was growing impatient, for they'd been waiting since noon for his errant brother to make his appearance. One of the castle dogs had followed him and he was roughhousing with the hound when Geoff joined him. Their alliance of expediency still endured, for both men had been equally outraged by the claims of sainthood being made on Hal's behalf. They began to discuss the latest developments now, for Geoff had just learned that Robert de Neubourg, the dean of Rouen Cathedral, had been the one making the loudest demands for the recovery of Hal's body.

"I think the dean is intent upon feathering his own nest," he said darkly. "All know his uncle Rotrou's ailment is likely to be mortal, and all know, too, that he is keen to succeed Rotrou as the next Archbishop of Rouen. What better way to court votes from the canons than by securing a 'saint' for their cathedral?"

Richard wondered why Geoff sounded so indignant, for he took it for granted that men acted out of self-interest. "Well, you did not think he truly believed in Hal's holiness, did you? The only ones who could swallow that fable are madmen, drunks, and gullible ceorls. At least they were not such fools in my duchy. There were no 'grieving crowds' lining the roads in the Limousin or Poitou. That lunacy did not start until they'd crossed into Anjou."

"It is hard to see a man as saintly when you've been watching him plundering your abbeys and terrorizing your clerics," Geoff agreed, but Richard was no longer listening. Nudging his brother, he gestured and, turning toward the window, Geoff saw that Geoffrey had just ridden into the bailey. "Will you look at that?" he said in surprise, for Geoffrey was not only accompanied by his duchess, but it appeared as if half the barons in Brittany were in his entourage. Geoff had not expected that, for Geoffrey had never shown Hal's partiality for pageantry and spectacle.

Richard was surprised, too. "The milksop! Does he hope to hide behind his wife's skirts?"

"No, he has something more subtle in mind." Neither of them had heard Henry's approach, and they both jumped at the unexpected sound of his voice. Kneeling on the window-seat to get a better view, he said, "He is a clever lad, Geoffrey. He is reminding us that he is Duke of Brittany by right of his wife, that he owes nothing to me. And the presence of his Breton lords testifies to the widespread support he enjoys amongst his barons—in case I should be rash enough to contemplate trying to divest him of the duchy."

Geoff and Richard exchanged looks of mutual aggravation, for their father sounded almost admiring of Geoffrey's political acumen. They'd already concluded that Henry was not likely to punish his son more harshly than he had the Viscount of Limoges, but it was still exasperating to get confirmation of their qualms. "Uprooting Geoffrey from Brittany sounds like a fine idea to me," Richard said acerbically, although he knew that had never been an option.

Henry didn't reply, watching as Geoffrey helped Constance to dismount. His attention was drawn then to a minor commotion on the edge of the crowd. Ranulf and Bleddyn had shouldered their way through the bystanders and were thumping Morgan on the back, bantering and laughing, showing such pleasure in their reunion that Henry felt a sharp pang of envy. Why could his relations with his sons not be as simple, as easy?

CONSTANCE GAVE GEOFFREY'S HAND a quick squeeze, and then he began that long walk toward the dais where his father and brother awaited him. He was determined to show no emotion, not willing to give Richard that satisfaction. Unfastening his scabbard, he put his sword upon the steps and then knelt. "My lord king, I am here to seek your pardon for the part I played in the rebellion. I offer no excuses for my actions, can only hope that you find it in your heart to forgive me."

Henry wondered how often he'd have to play out this farce with one of his sons. They always said the right things, showed the proper contrition. But their words rang hollow, and when he looked into their eyes, he saw strangers. He found he had no stomach for yet another of these public mock-capitulations and got abruptly to his feet. "Come with me," he said brusquely, and without waiting to make sure Geoffrey was obeying, he strode from the hall.

THEY FACED EACH OTHER in the castle solar, a chamber shadowy and stifling, for Henry had jerked the shutters into place, not wanting to risk eavesdroppers gathering below the window. Leaning back against a table, he regarded his son in baffled anger. Geoffrey's betrayal had been more painful than Hal's, for he'd never seen it coming. By that spring, he'd had few illusions left about his eldest, but he'd honestly thought Geoffrey was trustworthy. Finding that it was not so had been a severe blow, both to the king and the father. "You realize," he said at last, "that if you'd not thrown in with Hal, it is likely he'd not have been able to rebel."

He left the rest of the sentence unsaid, but Geoffrey found it easy enough to finish the thought. "And Hal might still be alive. So I am to atone for Hal's sins as well as my own. Who else am I to answer for? The French king? The Viscount of Limoges?" Geoffrey knew he was in no position to offer defiance, but that implied accusation had stung, all the more so because the same thought had crossed his own mind. He braced himself for Henry's fury. To his surprise, though, it did not come.

Henry looked at him in silence and then astonished him by saying quietly, "That was not fair of me. I do not blame you for Hal's death, nor would he want me to. It may not have happened until he was on his deathbed, but at the last he accepted full responsibility for his actions, took all the guilt for the rebellion upon himself." There was a dull, throbbing pain behind his right eye, and his bad leg had begun to ache. He shifted so that more of his weight rested against the table, keeping his eyes upon his son's face. "I do not want to hear your apologies or promises of future loyalty, Geoffrey. We both know how little such words mean. What I do want from you is honesty. You may speak your mind without fear of consequences. I want—I need—to know why."

Geoffrey blinked in amazement. "Jesus God, Papa, you know why!"

"No, I do not."

"How could you not know? Because you refused to grant us Richmond and Nantes."

"That may be the pretext, but it was not the cause. You knew it was only a matter of time until they came into your hands, for I'd promised them to you. Why were you not willing to wait?"

Despite Henry's demand for utter candor, Geoffrey knew he could not tell his father that his promises were dross, as unsubstantial as cobwebs and smoke. He compromised by offering as much truth as he dared. "Nantes is the heart of Brittany and the Honour of Richmond belonged by rights to Constance's father. When he died, it should have passed to her, and all know it. Have you never thought that by holding on to these lands, you diminish me in my wife's eyes? And the eyes of her barons?"

Henry was not sure how Geoffrey had managed to back him into a corner. "That is nonsense! Your barons know it is a delay, not a denial. Even after your recent treachery, I am not saying these lands are forfeit, although few would blame me if I did. But I cannot help feeling grateful that I held on to them, for if you'd had control of Nantes, that would have enabled you to launch attacks directly into Poitou. My giving you Nantes might well have made it possible for you to win your rebellion."

Geoffrey stared at him. "Christ, Papa, if you'd given me Nantes, I would never have rebelled," he said wearily, and after that, there seemed nothing more to say.

TILDA SMILED AT THE SIGHT meeting her eyes: her ten-year-old son, Heinrich, manfully struggling to pull a bow-stave back, with some unobtrusive help from his grandfather. "Suppose we find you a smaller bow on the morrow," Henry suggested tactfully, "and then we can have a real lesson."

"Will you shoot it one more time?" Heinrich entreated, and Henry obligingly showed the boy the proper stance and how to nock the arrow—"always on the left side of the stave." Drawing the bowstring back, he loosed the arrow, and Heinrich gave a jubilant shout when it flew across the garden and thudded into the trunk of a chestnut tree. "Can you do that again?"

"No, dearest, he cannot," Tilda intervened, "for it is past your bedtime."

"But it is still light out, Mama!"

"Heinrich, you know full well that it stays light in August until long past Compline," Tilda reminded him, but he continued to argue until Henry weighed in on Tilda's side. Conceding defeat, then, he made a reluctant retreat as the adults hid their smiles until he was out of view. "It is kind of you, Papa, to offer to tutor Heinrich in the use of a bow. He has always wanted to learn, but my husband told him it was not worth mastering since the bow is a weapon for the lowborn, the routier."

"He is right about that," Henry agreed. "No man of good birth would go into battle with a bow. But the lad needs to know how to shoot it if he ever expects to bring down a deer."

Tilda's husband did not share Henry's passion for the hunt. She had no intention of telling him that, however, for Heinrich's lack of enthusiasm would be beyond his ken. Deciding to take advantage of this rare time alone with her father, she linked her arm in his and steered him toward the closest bench. "May I ask you a question, Papa?"

"Of course, sweetheart," he said quickly, but she caught the flicker of a smile as he added, "I cannot promise to answer it, though, not until I hear what it is."

"You need not worry," she assured him with a smile of her own. "I will not ask anything awkward or embarrassing." In other words, she thought, nothing about her mother. "I am puzzled by something you did last month. I understand why you insisted that Geoffrey surrender control to you of his Breton castles. But why did you demand the same of Richard? He . . . he was not happy, saw it as an affront to his pride."

"Believe me, lass, I know. Richard is never one to suffer in silence." Henry was quiet for a moment, deciding how much to tell her. "I was not trying to demean Richard, Tilda. But I've become increasingly concerned about the hostility between Richard and his barons. God knows, they are no easy lot to govern and you can rarely go wrong suspecting the worst of Eleanor's Poitevins. Richard is too quick, though, to apply the whip and spurs. Passing strange, for he is a superb horseman, but he rides men too hard, and I have not been able to get him to see that."

Tilda had heard her husband voice the same opinion. She did not see, though, how it helped matters to put Henry's men in command of Richard's castles. "Mayhap it would ease Richard's resentment if you made a formal announcement that he is to be your heir?"

Henry was amused by her fishing expedition and decided to let her hook one. "As it happens, lass, I plan to do just that next month."

Tilda was glad to hear it, for she was troubled by her family's discord. She'd been deeply shocked by the rebellion, and she could take little comfort from the peace that followed Hal's death, for she feared it was not likely to last. Heinrich had warned her not to mediate between her father and brothers, saying it would serve for naught and might jeopardize their own position at Henry's court. Tilda was usually willing to defer to his wishes, but she would have ignored his admonition if she'd thought she might succeed. She knew, though, that she'd be wasting her breath, that neither her father nor her brothers were willing or able to see any side but their own.

"Papa . . . I have a favor to ask of you. I would like you to give me permission to go to England." Before he could respond, she reached over and touched his arm in silent supplication. "Please, hear me out. I want my children to meet their grandmother. Surely that is not so much to ask?"

"No, of course it is not. But there is no need."

Tilda felt a rare stab of anger. Why were the men in her family so stubborn? "You did promise me, Papa, that I could see Maman. How much longer must I wait?"

"You misunderstood me, Tilda. I meant that there is no need to go to England. I have sent word to Ralf de Glanville to make arrangements to bring Eleanor to Rouen."

"Truly? Papa, thank you!" Tilda flung her arms around his neck, and he laughed, wondering why daughters were so much easier to content than sons.

"Truly, lass. She ought to be here by Michaelmas."

AMARIA LOOKED UP from her embroidery as the queen came into their chamber. She knew at once that Ralph Fitz Stephen must have given Eleanor good news, for there was becoming color in her cheeks and her eyes were filled with light.

"You will never guess what Sir Ralph told me. How would you fancy a sea voyage, Amaria?"

"Madame?"

"My husband has summoned me to join our family in Rouen. Who says the Age of Miracles is past?"

"My lady, that is wonderful!"

"I will be able to see my daughter and grandchildren at long last, to spend time with Richard, to pray at Hal's tomb, and to escape this wretched, wet isle, at least for a while! It has always amazed me that I've been able to avoid the joint evil, for it is like living underwater in England," Eleanor said, and laughed.

"Your son's plea must have touched your husband's heart, Madame. Did you not tell me that his last wish was for the king to forgive you?"

"So Tilda said in her letter." Eleanor sat down in the window-seat as Amaria hastened over to pour wine for them both. Clinking their cups playfully together, they drank to "a quick departure and calm sailing." But after a time, Eleanor set her cup down and when Amaria glanced over, she saw that the queen was no longer smiling.

"Madame, is something amiss?"

"I am not sure, Amaria. I find myself wondering," Eleanor said, "what he is up to now?"

CHAPTER FORTY-FOUR

✦

September 1183
Rouen, Normandy

S THEY APPROACHED THE DOOR of the great cathedral, Henry's step slowed and Eleanor gave him an inquiring look. "I am sorry," he said, very softly, "but I cannot do this."

"I understand," she said, just as softly, and then, for the benefit of their audience, "I just had an idea, my lord. Whilst I go inside, you can go over to the palace to see Archbishop Rotrou, and we will meet you there afterward."

Robert de Neubourg had stopped when he realized they were no longer following him. "I think that is an excellent suggestion, my liege. I am sure a visit from you would cheer my uncle greatly, for he grows weaker by the day, poor soul."

Henry found something ghoulish about the dean's preoccupation with his uncle's health; he suspected Robert was far more concerned with the looming church vacancy than with Rotrou's mortality. All that mattered to him now, though, was escaping what he was not yet ready to do—pay a visit to his son's tomb. Seizing upon Eleanor's subterfuge, he gave her a grateful smile, declaring that he would go straightaway to see Archbishop Rotrou, and was soon striding off, with most of his entourage hurrying to keep pace.

The others stayed with Eleanor and Tilda, following as the dean escorted them into the cathedral. They found excuses to remain behind in the nave, though, knowing that the queen would want privacy while she prayed at her son's tomb. Holding a lantern aloft, the dean led the way down the stairs, keeping up a running commentary about the large crowds coming to the young king's sepulcher. "Shall I ask one of the canons to clear the crypt of pilgrims so you may pray in peace, Madame?"

When Eleanor agreed, he beckoned to the young canon standing vigil by the door. After exchanging a few words, he turned back to the queen and her daughter. "The pilgrims have already been removed, Madame, for your sons are within and they wanted time alone with the young king."

Eleanor was so startled that she almost slipped on the worn stone steps. Richard and Geoffrey together? She very much wanted to believe they could resolve their differences at Hal's tomb, but that did not seem likely to her, not knowing her sons as she did. Robert trailed after her as she continued down the stairs and would have entered with her had Tilda not intervened, diplomatically suggesting that the dean show her around the cathedral whilst the queen prayed. He looked disappointed, not wanting to miss the queen's reunion with her sons, but the Duchess of Saxony was smiling at him expectantly, and he yielded as graciously as he could, casting one last wistful glance over his shoulder at the queen as the canon opened the door for her.

The undercroft was lit by wall torches, but Eleanor still wished she'd thought to ask the dean for his lantern. Candles flamed around Hal's tomb, and she could make out Geoffrey's figure, kneeling in prayer. She did not see Richard, though. As she stepped forward, movement caught her eye, and she found herself facing her youngest son. She'd not seen John for almost two years, and those had been eventful years for him. He'd grown quite a bit, although he was obviously not going to be as tall as his brothers. His body had taken on the unmistakable signs of adolescence, and if he was not yet ready to flaunt a beard, he did look as if he had to shave now and then. Her son at sixteen.

In the past, he'd been as elusive as a wood sprite. She was surprised, therefore, when he came toward her instead of retreating back into the shadows. "Madame," he said formally, showing he'd mastered his lessons in courtesy and manners. But then he flashed a sudden, impish grin. "I am John, your son."

He had eyes like a fox, Eleanor thought, golden and alert and wary. "I am not likely to forget you, John," she said dryly. "I was present at your birth, after all. If I looked surprised, it is because I thought you were still in England."

"I reached Rouen three days ago. My father did not mention that he'd summoned me?" He still smiled, but she saw that it rankled to think he'd been forgotten.

"I only arrived this afternoon, so Harry has not had time to tell me much of anything. I did not even unpack yet, wanted to come here first."

They'd been speaking quietly, so as not to disturb Geoffrey's prayers. But he'd still heard the murmur of voices and turned toward the sound. At the sight of his mother, conflicting emotions chased across his face—both pleasure and unease.

John glanced from Eleanor to Geoffrey, back to Eleanor again. "I am sure I can find some mischief to get into," he said, and headed for the stairs. Pleasantly surprised by his sensitivity, Eleanor thanked him and then approached Geoffrey.

"Maman . . . it gladdens me to see you. I suppose you cannot say the same, though."

"I'll not deny that I was wroth with you and Hal. I thought the pair of you had more sense than to get entangled with Aimar and my malcontent barons."

Geoffrey was running his hand over the cold marble of his brother's sepulcher. "I am truly sorry, Maman."

"Sorry that you rebelled, Geoffrey? Or that you lost?"

"Both," he admitted, and was taken aback when she smiled.

"I was remembering," she said, "that when your father asked me that question, I gave that very same answer."

Geoffrey expelled his breath slowly. "I was afraid you'd blame me for Hal's death."

"It is enough that we answer for our own sins without being held to account for the sins of others. I understand your frustration over Harry's refusal to grant you Richmond and Nantes, I truly do. But your grievance was with your father, not with Richard. What you and Hal did was no better than banditry."

Geoffrey looked down at Hal's tomb. "I would gladly undo it if only I could, Maman."

"I know," she said and she did, for who knew more about vain regrets than she? Crossing the space between them, she held out her hand. He was quick to grasp it and she drew him to her. Holding him close, she found her eyes stinging. If only she could have embraced Hal like this, too!

Geoffrey kissed her on the cheek, then stepped back, looking past her toward the stairs. "Shall we speak louder for your benefit, Johnny?"

John looked abashed at being caught eavesdropping so openly. "I guess you would not believe I'd stopped to remove a pebble from my shoe?"

This time, with their eyes unwaveringly upon him, he really did depart. Once she was sure he had gone, Eleanor said pensively, "Passing strange that I must admit this about my own son, but I do not know John at all."

"None of us do, Maman, and that includes Papa. He cherishes this image of Johnny as his only loyal son, obedient and affectionate and trustworthy. Whether that is the real Johnny or not remains to be seen."

Eleanor was struck by Geoffrey's perception—and by his cynicism. Had she and Harry taught him that? Most likely they had. Kissing her hand with a playful flourish, Geoffrey said, "I'd best keep an eye on Johnny. I will await you up in the nave, Maman."

Grateful that he was giving her this time alone with Hal, she crossed to his tomb and, kneeling upon the hard tile floor, she began to pray for the soul of her son.

WHEN HE WAS UPSET OR ANGRY, Richard paced like Henry, and as he strode up and down her chamber, Eleanor thought she could have been looking at her husband in his youth. Richard was taller, but otherwise they had the same powerful build, the same vibrant coloring, and for certes, the same fiery temper. So far Richard had turned their reunion into a recital of his paternal grievances, and she was disappointed but not entirely surprised. She'd hoped that fighting the rebels together might have brought them closer, although without any real expectations of it being so, for they were too much alike to dwell in harmony for long. She thought it was a blessing that Richard would have his own sphere of power in Aquitaine, that unlike Hal, he'd not be dependent upon his father's largesse. Belatedly becoming aware that Richard had stopped speaking, she looked up to find her son regarding her reproachfully.

"Are you even listening to me, Maman?"

"Of course I am," she assured him, not altogether truthfully. "You were telling me about the troubadour, Bertran de Born."

"As I was saying, Bertran boasted that his castle at Autafort was impregnable, but Alfonso and I took it in just seven days. I then gave it to his brother and sent him to my father for judgment, where he beguiled Papa by professing great sorrow over Hal's death and writing a planh lamenting his loss. So what does Papa do? He not only pardons the man, but he restores Autafort Castle to him!"

He sounded so indignant that Eleanor hid a smile. "You must bear in mind, Richard, that your father's wound is still raw and bleeding. Is it truly so surprising that he'd show mercy to a man who shares his grief?"

Richard would never be able to fathom the widespread mourning over Hal's death, seeing it as one last trick that his brother had managed to play on him from the grave. Resisting the temptation to remind his mother that the "grief-stricken" troubadour had once dubbed Hal the "Little King of Lesser Land," he said, "I do not deny that Papa is still grieving. But how do you explain his action in demanding that I return control of my Poitevin castles to him?"

"That is indeed another matter," she conceded, "and I intend to speak with him about it. I may not be able to get him to change his mind, but at least I can learn what his reasoning was."

Richard was sure he already knew the answer—that his father did not trust him. He'd debated sharing his suspicions with his mother, not wanting to cast a shadow over her release. But he saw now that she needed to know the truth, and he crossed to her side, kneeling so he could look intently into her face.

"Has Papa told you that he has forgiven you because Hal asked it of him?" When she shook her head, he warned, "He will. And when he does, Maman, do not believe it. The real reason he has sent for you is to thwart the French king. In addition to demanding that Papa return the French Vexin to him, Philippe is claiming that Hal assigned certain other lands to Marguerite as her dowry. Papa denied it, insisting that these lands were yours and as you'd assigned them to Hal only for his lifetime, they now revert back to you, not Marguerite. So you see, Maman, he has an ulterior motive in—" He stopped in astonishment, for his mother had begun to laugh.

"Dearest, I have been married to that man for more than thirty years. Do you truly think I do not know all the twists and turns of that formidable brain of his? Of course he has an ulterior motive. He always has an ulterior motive, usually two or three. Why did he summon me from England? I daresay you're right about Marguerite's dower lands. But he likely did it, too, because Hal asked it of him, and to please Tilda, and possibly even to please you." Eleanor laughed again, thinking how shocked he'd be if she were to confide that she'd always found her husband's sharp, subtle intelligence to be as much of an aphrodisiac as his muscular strength or boundless energy.

Richard had gotten to his feet and was studying her in obvious bafflement. "How can you be so tolerant of his intrigues and scheming? He has taken away ten years of your life, Maman, yet you do not talk about him as if he is your enemy, and I do not understand why."

"Because he is also my husband, Richard, and that complicates matters more than you know. We are both encumbered by our history and by all that we've shared over the years, good and bad." It occurred to Eleanor that this was the first time she and Richard were having a conversation that was adult to adult, not mother to son. "This means that we can never truly be free of each other, however much we may wish it."

"You make marriage sound like a mysterious malady that has no cure, Maman. If that is so, I am glad I've been spared it."

"Well, eventually you'll have to risk it," she said with a grin, "for you'll need an heir for your duchy and your kingdom." He grinned, too, and she realized that he was still coming to terms with the momentous change wrought by Hal's death. "Speaking of marriage," she continued, "I gather you have no great desire to marry the French king's sister Alys?"

He shrugged. "What would I gain by it? The girl has no marriage portion to speak of. If Papa were one for getting in his cups, I'd wonder if he'd been sober the day he made that deal with Louis, for it was a poor bargain indeed."

"His primary concern then was in getting the French to recognize Hal as his heir and you and Geoffrey as the future rulers of Aquitaine and Brittany. But if it is not to be Alys, you ought to be considering other matches, dearest. Have you discussed this with Harry?"

"We've been rather busy in recent months, Maman. He did once mention the daughter of the Holy Roman Emperor. A pity Alfonso has no eligible female relatives. Of course he is already an ally, so it would make more sense to look further afield, mayhap to Navarre."

Eleanor looked at him fondly, very pleased to see the drift of his thoughts. If he was considering Aragon or Navarre, both Houses hostile to Count Raimon, that meant he was thinking ahead to the day when he could reassert their claim to Toulouse. "Yes, Navarre is certainly a possibility," she agreed, as she settled down to enjoy a simple pleasure other mothers could take for granted, but one which had been long denied her—mulling over potential brides for her son.

HENRY HAD GATHERED HIS FAMILY together on Michaelmas Eve, and there was an air of anticipation, for all expected him to reveal when he would formally recognize Richard as his heir. There should have been no suspense in such a straightforward announcement. But knowing Henry's penchant for eleventh-hour surprises, both Eleanor and Richard were on edge, and as the queen glanced around the chamber, she thought that Geoffrey and Constance seemed rather tense, too. Only Geoff, Heinrich, and Tilda appeared utterly at ease. Remembering John then, she located him in one of the window-seats, sipping wine as he watched the others, and she felt a small dart of regret that he seemed so solitary, always on the outside looking in. She'd concluded years ago that she and Henry had made some great mistakes with their older sons, failing to foster any sense of solidarity or family unity, and she could not help thinking now that they'd gone astray with John, too. It was too late for Hal, but was there time to repair the damage done with the others?

Sensing that his audience was growing restive, Henry moved to the center of the solar. He'd not been looking forward to this, sure that he'd encounter initial opposition from Richard and Eleanor. Now, though, he realized that his reluctance had deeper roots, that he was loath to bestow upon another what had always been Hal's. He recognized the illogic of it, for he knew that Richard would be a better king than Hal. At least his brain knew it, but his heart was another matter. There was an awful finality about the declaration, as if he were throwing one last shovel of dirt upon his son's grave.

He'd never had much patience for sentimentality, though, especially his own. "I am sure that what I am about to say will come as no surprise," he said, determined to get this over with as quickly as possible. "I intend to convene a great council and announce to the lords of the realm that Richard will be king upon my death."

Richard was not sure what response was expected of him, and he wondered why things always had to be so awkward with his father. To say "Thank you" seemed inappropriate, but it also seemed ungracious to say nothing at all. "I will do my best to meet your expectations. I'll not let you or my mother down," he said, sending a smile winging Eleanor's way. She smiled back, and he was grateful that she could be here for this moment.

"I am sure that you will be a good king," Henry said, with a smile of his own. "It is a bittersweet bequest I am giving you, though. You'll have a vast, unquiet empire to rule. Aquitaine alone would be enough for any man, for your mother's barons are as perverse and faithless a lot as can be found in all of Christendom. But you'll also have to govern an island kingdom, as well as Normandy, Anjou, Touraine, and Maine."

"Enough to keep me busy for certes," Richard agreed, not sure where his father was going with this. Neither was Eleanor, and she was watching Henry with a small frown creasing her forehead.

"After giving the matter much thought," Henry continued, "I think I have come up with a way to ease your burdens whilst still safeguarding your borders. I fear that Aquitaine is going to take up so much of your time and energy that you'll run the risk of neglecting your other domains. You'll have a far more successful reign if you relinquish the governance of Aquitaine to your brother Johnny."

For Richard, the shock was so intense that the impact was actually physical. Feeling as if he'd just been punched in the stomach, he found himself struggling for breath. *Why did Maman not warn me?* But one glance at his mother, white-faced and stunned, told him that she'd been ambushed, too. He cut his gaze sharply then toward Geoffrey, suspecting his brother's fine hand in this duplicity. Geoffrey and Constance were obviously dumbfounded, though. As Richard's eyes met Eleanor's again, she sent him a mute, urgent message, shaking her head almost imperceptibly. He understood her warning, but he was not sure he was capable of responding as she wanted, so great was his outrage.

He got help then from an unexpected source, his youngest brother. John had been caught by surprise, too, inhaling the wine he'd been about to swallow, which brought on a sudden coughing fit. Henry crossed to his side and thumped him helpfully on the back, joking, "It is not as bad as all that, lad. It could be worse—I could be sending you to Ireland!"

John was flushed, partly from his coughing and partly from embarrassment. But his eyes were glowing as he looked up at his father. "Aquitaine for me? Truly?"

"Truly," Henry said with a smile and then looked expectantly at his eldest son.

By now Richard was in control of himself again. "I must differ with you, Papa," he murmured, "for I'd say this most definitely qualifies as a surprise!"

Henry was encouraged by that wry response, for he'd not been sure how Richard would take the proposal. As little as he liked to admit it, the workings of this son's brain were a mystery to him. "It will change nothing," he said swiftly, "other than sparing you the vexation of daily dealings with those lunatic southerners. You will still be the liege lord of the duchy, and Johnny will, of course, do homage to you for it, just as Geoffrey will do homage to you for Brittany once you are king."

So far this was going better than Henry had expected, for there'd been no overt protests from Eleanor either. But he knew she was clever enough to see that Aquitaine's importance had diminished considerably with Hal's death. To a man about to inherit an empire, her duchy was merely one demesne amongst many, a part of Richard's legacy instead of the whole. Richard must expand his horizons, and his mother could help him greatly in making that transition, in learning to think like a king, not a duke.

"I do not want to do anything rash," Richard said, "so I will need time to consider it. You have opened my eyes tonight, though, for the idea had never occurred to me before. I will have to consult with my barons, of course, the sooner the better. News like this cannot be kept secret for long, and they need to hear it from me, not from rumors or gossip."

Henry glanced over at John's rapt, upturned face. Richard was right; there was not a sixteen-year-old boy alive who could keep news like this to himself. "Do you think your barons will be receptive to the idea?"

"I think they are likely to respond favorably." Why wouldn't they? Exchanging a battle-seasoned soldier for a green stripling who's never even bloodied his sword? God's Legs, they'd not be able to believe their good luck! And the old man knows it, too, damn him. He knows full well that they'd thank God fasting for a chance like this. Does he think I am as big a fool as his precious Hal?

Richard met his father's eyes, his gaze steady. "They might balk, though, if they felt that we were trying to shove this down their throats. They have to believe they have the right to say yea or nay, whether they do or not."

Henry could not fault his son's reasoning; none were touchier about their honor than those mulish, overweening troublemakers who kept Aquitaine in a constant state of turmoil. He would have liked to resolve it here and now, but he was pragmatic enough to see that it had to be done Richard's way. No more than his vassals, Richard could not think this was being shoved down *his* throat. As it was, his son was being more responsive than Henry had dared hope, confirming his suspicions that Richard might welcome being unyoked from that seditious, querulous land now that he no longer needed it. And for the first time in years, Henry let himself think that they truly could restore their fragmented family harmony. They'd always see the mended cracks, of course, but what did that matter if the center held?

He turned his gaze, then, upon his wife, his eyes locking challengingly with hers. "Have you nothing to say about this, Eleanor? It would truly be a historic event to find you at a loss for words."

"Richard is quite capable of speaking for himself," she said coolly. "If he is content with this, then so am I. After all, John is my son, too."

For the first time since Hal's death, Henry experienced a surge of genuine joy. His spirits soaring, he ushered the others from the solar, declaring that they had reason for celebration. Geoffrey and Constance were the last to follow him. Geoffrey was feeling almost light-headed, dazzled by how fast Fortune's Wheel could spin. This was not yet the time to discuss the evening's events with Constance, but as his eyes met hers, he saw his own excitement reflected in their dark depths, and he marveled how well they understood each other, for the same thought was in both their minds. *This changes everything!*

AFTER THE EVENING MEAL WAS DONE, the trestle tables were removed from the hall and dancing began. Henry had given Eleanor the place of honor beside him on the dais, trumpeting their reconciliation with this public display of marital amity. It was also, Eleanor thought, an effective way to make sure she and Richard had no time alone. She did not doubt that her husband would have both of them under discreet surveillance, but his spies would be disappointed. Richard was not going to fall into that trap, would make sure to keep his distance until his departure on the morrow. She'd never been as proud of him as in the solar, watching him match wits with Henry, showing he could dissemble as convincingly as his sire.

As she thought back over the past few hours, she could feel her rage beginning to flare again, and she swiftly dampened it down, thankful that she'd had years of practice in learning patience, in learning to congeal dangerous furies in ice. There would be time later to indulge her wrath. Glancing at Henry through downcast lashes, she

seethed in silence, still astounded that he would dare to meddle in her duchy so bla-
tantly, dare to disinherit the son who'd been consecrated before men and God in
solemn ceremonies at Poitiers and Limoges.

Becoming aware of Henry's scrutiny, she raised an eyebrow in query, and he
shifted in his seat so that they could converse quietly, without fear of eavesdroppers. "I
continue to marvel," he said, "at our accord this evening. It seems you can still surprise
me after all these years, for I never knew you had such an accommodating nature."

Even if she'd not caught his sarcasm, she'd have known better than to overplay her
compliance; he'd never believe it if she was too docile or biddable. "I suppose it was
too much to hope," she said tartly, "that you'd have consulted me beforehand. What
possible interest could I have, after all, in the succession to Aquitaine?"

"I should have talked with you first," he conceded, but she was not mollified by
that almost-apology, for words were cheap, especially his words. Leaning closer, he
said earnestly, "I do not want you to think I did this to disparage or diminish Richard
in any way. That was never my intent. His kingship is far more likely to flourish if he
is not burdened with Aquitaine, for he will never be able to pacify your barons."

Eleanor studied him with narrowed eyes. "What are you saying, Harry? That
Richard has been a failure as Duke of Aquitaine?"

"Yes, I am saying that," he admitted. "But hear me out. He has made mistakes that
cannot be undone, has been too heavy-handed in his dealings with them. Look what
happened when he arbitrarily tried to change the inheritance customs in Angoulême.
He stirred up a rebellion that continues to smolder even today. I am not saying it was
all his fault; he is young and still learning and they are vexing enough to try a saint's
patience. But he got off to such a bad start with them that there is no going back. There
is too much bad blood there, and they are not ones for forgiving and forgetting."

Eleanor looked at him in disbelief. How could he be so logical, so practical, and
so utterly wrong? How could he banish all emotion from the equation? There was
truth in what he said, but did he never realize that Richard was deeply attached to
Aquitaine? That he'd been raised from the cradle with the expectation that he would
rule the duchy one day? That he'd spent the past eight years fighting and bleeding and
struggling to put down rebellions and restore peace? These questions went unasked, of
course, for she already knew the answers. He'd taken none of that into consideration,
for he viewed their sons as pieces on a chessboard, to be moved hither and yon at his
whims.

"Far be it from me to be a naysayer," she said, "but if a brilliant battle commander
like Richard cannot end their rebellions, how do you expect John to do so? You do not
think he is rather young to be tossed into the lion's den?"

"He'll be seventeen in December," he parried, "and I was ruling Normandy at that age. I understand that he'll make mistakes, that he'll need more experienced guidance, and I am willing to step in when needed."

Yes, she thought grimly, I daresay you are. You'd turn John into a puppet prince, as you could not do with Richard. "I do have one concern," she said. "What happens after Richard abdicates in John's favor? What are you prepared to do for him, Harry? For the past eight years, he has governed Aquitaine. If you take that away, what do you give him in return? He's not one to amuse himself on the tournament circuit like Hal. I would suggest that you turn Normandy or Anjou over to him. That would enable you to make use of his abilities and give him the purpose that he needs, for he'll never be one to embrace an idle life of pleasure—no more than you would."

"You make a valid point, Eleanor. I will give it some careful thought, for certes."

I am sure you will, she jeered silently, knowing he'd never give up Normandy or Anjou to Richard. He could no more relinquish any of his power than he could fly. No, if he had his way, he'd keep Richard dancing attendance at his court, with no revenues or authority of his own. But this time you will not win, Harry. I will not let you unman Richard as you did Hal.

RICHARD DEPARTED THE NEXT DAY, ostensibly to consult with his barons. In the week that followed, Eleanor spent as much time as possible with Tilda and her grandchildren, for she did not know how Henry would react to their son's defiance. While Richard was beyond his reprisal, she was not, and he might well send her back to England straightaway. She also sought out Geoffrey and John, determined to make the most of her relative freedom, but did her best to avoid her husband whenever possible, for the tentative rapprochement they'd reached in the past few years had gone up in smoke in the solar of Rouen's ducal castle.

AMARIA LED A SERVING MAID up the stairwell to the queen's chamber. As she opened the door, she smiled at the sight before her. Eleanor and Tilda were playing a game of dice with John and Tilda's young son Heinrich. They welcomed her boisterously when they saw that the serving maid carried a platter of cheese wafers and cups of cider. As Amaria passed them around, Heinrich boasted that "Uncle Johnny" had taught them a game called hazard.

"Hazard?" Amaria pretended to be shocked, to Heinrich's delight. "But that is a game played in taverns and alehouses!"

"I know," the boy grinned, "and we've been winning!"

"Indeed they have," Eleanor agreed, with mock severity, pointing toward a pile of coins in the center of the table. "If I had a suspicious mind, I might wonder if some sleight of hand could be involved."

Heinrich laughed and John smiled. "I seem to be on a winning streak these days," he said cheerfully. "Are the Dukes of Aquitaine always lucky, my lady mother?"

Eleanor felt a pang of resentful regret that her husband had entangled John in his scheme. Her youngest was still very much a stranger to her; after these few days in his company, she could say only that he was clever and guarded and had inherited his share of the family's sardonic humor. But she did know he'd been bedazzled by the prospect of gaining Aquitaine and he was in for a great disappointment.

They played another game of hazard, and John and Heinrich won again. They were still whooping and slapping hands when the door slammed open with enough force to startle them all. Henry came to an abrupt halt, for he'd been expecting to find Eleanor alone. Tilda and Heinrich welcomed him happily, but John flushed and jumped to his feet as if he'd been caught in a misdeed. Eleanor returned his gaze calmly and her sangfroid confirmed Henry's suspicions.

After greeting them with strained affability, he explained that "I am sorry to interrupt your game, but I need to speak privately now with your mother and grandmother." Eleanor made a playful grimace at "Grandmother," to Heinrich's amusement, and her nonchalance added more fuel to the flames of Henry's rage. So she saw this as a joke, did she?

Heinrich was reluctant to end their fun, but Tilda had picked up on the tension in the chamber and she ushered her son out, with a troubled backward glance at her parents. John was already gone; he'd faded away as inconspicuously as that woodland fox. Amaria hesitated, not departing until Eleanor gave her a smile and a nod.

Eleanor helped herself, then, to more cider. "I take it you've heard from Richard?"

"Yes, I heard. He sent word that he will never relinquish Aquitaine, not as long as he draws breath. But you already knew that, did you not?"

"Of course."

"I should have known this was your doing!"

"And how did I manage that? I am sure your spies told you that I was not alone with Richard from the time you sprang your 'surprise' until his departure the next morning. Did we communicate in code by thumping on the walls of our chambers? Smuggled secret messages to each other? Mayhap used Heinrich as our go-between?"

He was disconcerted by her defiance; it had been years since her claws had flashed like that. "If you did not plan this with Richard, how did you know he'd refuse?"

"How could you not know? By the Rood, Harry, how can you be so blind about your own sons?"

"I told you my reasons for wanting this. You seemed to think they made sense last week!"

"Yes, they made perfect political sense. But Richard's love for Aquitaine is not political. It is visceral, in his blood and his bones. You might as well ask him to tear out his heart and give it over to you!"

"That is arrant nonsense! He'd still be liege lord of Aquitaine, would be losing nothing and gaining much. God's Bones, woman, you are the blind one! Can you honestly say that you are pleased with his rule of the duchy? That you do not think he has antagonized his barons needlessly and spread the seeds of rebellion with his own hand?"

"I do not deny that he has made mistakes. But he is the Duke of Aquitaine, not an errant child. You cannot step in and slap his hand when you think he has blundered. For God's sake, Harry, let him go! Your love for our sons is strangling them. Why can you not see that?"

"Why can you not see that I have to act for the good of our empire? I cannot just stand aside whilst our sons put my life's work at risk. Aquitaine would be a constant thorn in Richard's side, and turning it over to Johnny would benefit them both. A duchy is a small price to pay for a kingdom, and it troubles me greatly that Richard seems unable to understand that. If his judgment is so faulty—"

"Oh, enough!" Eleanor was on her feet, glaring at him across the table as if it were a battlefield. "You are such a hypocrite!"

His eyes darkened to a storm-sea grey. "And how is that?" he asked, his voice dangerously soft.

"You refuse to understand why Richard is unwilling to give up Aquitaine, but you are no less unwilling to surrender control of Normandy or Anjou. If you'd turned either one over to Hal, he'd never have rebelled. But you could not do that, could you?"

"Because I could not trust him to govern himself, much less a duchy!"

"I see. So you have it in mind to rule from the grave? Please, enlighten me—how exactly do you plan to do that?"

But Henry had heard nothing after her gibe about Hal. "So what are you saying?" he demanded hotly. "Are you blaming me for Hal's death? You think I drove him to rebellion?"

She heard the anguish underlying his rage, and her own fury ebbed away, leaving her sickened and shaken by the wreckage they'd made of their marriage and their world. "No," she said wearily, "of course I do not blame you for Hal's death, Harry. I did my part, too, as did Geoffrey and Richard and Hal himself. Hal most of all, for he was a man grown, a man who made his own choices and, to his credit, recognized that at the end . . ."

Henry's throat had constricted, for thoughts of Hal's last hours were still more than he could bear. "He died alone," he said huskily, "and it need not have been like that . . ."

"He was not alone, Harry. Will Marshal and his friends were with him—"

"But I was not!" He swung away, keeping his back to her as he fought to regain control of his emotions. "Hal wrote me a letter on his deathbed," he said, after a heavy silence. "Would you like to read it?"

Eleanor blinked in surprise. "Yes, I would, very much."

He nodded and then surprised her further by turning toward the door. "Harry, wait!"

When he faced her again, she was shocked by how ravaged he looked. "What do you intend to do about Richard?"

After coming together as grieving parents, she'd hoped they could come together, too, to repair the tattered father-son bond before it was beyond salvaging. But he looked at her expressionlessly, his eyes as veiled and opaque as John's. "I have not changed my mind," he said. "I still think Richard needs to relinquish control of Aquitaine, and I will do all in my power to bring that about."

The sound of the closing door seemed to echo in the empty chamber, reminding Eleanor of a wretched memory—standing in that chamber at Loches Castle and listening as the key turned in the lock. She sank down upon a coffer, was staring blankly into space when Amaria entered. With a soft cry of alarm, she crossed the floor and knelt at Eleanor's feet. "My lady? Are you ill?"

"That is not the man I married, Amaria. The man I knew was stubborn, yes, but he was flexible, too, capable of altering his course when need be. And he never let his suspicions get the better of him. Now . . . now he can neither trust nor compromise, God help us all."

Amaria was not sure what to say, so she stayed quiet. And as she watched the older woman, she saw Eleanor's despair drain away, to be replaced by an indomitable resolve. "For a long time, Amaria, I've blamed myself for those changes in Harry's nature. I'd not realized what a deep wound I was inflicting when I chose to rebel, never imagined that it would take so long to heal. Today I saw that it is never going to heal. I am done with feeling guilty, though. No more. If he wants to cherish his grievances instead of his sons, so be it." She raised her chin, her eyes taking on a hard, green glitter. "But as God is my witness, I will not let him take Aquitaine from Richard."

IN THE DAYS THAT FOLLOWED, Henry's court was not a happy place. Constance yearned to be back in Brittany, but she would not leave without Geoffrey and his father seemed set upon keeping his younger sons close for the foreseeable future. When the oppressive atmosphere at Rouen became too much for her, she made a brief pilgrimage to Chartres, proud possessor of the Sancta Camisa, the chemise said to be worn by the Blessed Mary as she gave birth to the Holy Christ Child. There she was welcomed by the bishop, prayed in the great cathedral, made offerings to the Mother of God, and was soon ready to return to Rouen, her spirit nourished and her faith renewed, for the Queen of Heaven had heard her prayers.

Upon her arrival at the ducal castle, she sent a servant to let Geoffrey know of her return and retreated to their bedchamber with her ladies. Juvette and Blanche had assisted her in washing away the grime of the road, and she was wrapped in a new silk robe as they brushed out her hair when Geoffrey burst into the chamber. Swooping her up into his arms, he kissed her exuberantly, then sent Juvette and Blanche away, giggling, when he declared slyly that he could see to all of his wife's needs. Watching as he barred the door, shutting out the rest of the world, Constance felt a throb of pure and perfect happiness, thinking that she would not want to be anywhere but here, to be anyone but the duchess of this laughing man with tawny hair and shining eyes.

"I have something to tell you," she said at the same time that he said those very same words, and they looked at each other in surprised amusement.

"My news first," he insisted, "for I've been waiting days to tell you. If I'd not expected you back so soon, I'd have ridden to Chartres myself to fetch you home."

She smiled at his boyish glee, for she was one of the few who ever saw that side of him. "You first then," she agreed. "I take it your news is good since you look so pleased with yourself."

"Yes, it is good news," he confirmed, before tumbling her backward onto their bed. Reaching for a handful of her hair, he inhaled its fresh, fragrant scent. "I ought to make you guess what it is, but you'd take too long, and I cannot keep it to myself for a moment longer." Kissing her throat, he propped himself up on an elbow, so close that she could feel the warmth of his breath upon her skin. "My lord father, that steadfast soul of consistency, has given us the Honour of Richmond."

"Geoffrey!" Flinging her arms around his neck, she showered his face with haphazard kisses. "That is truly amazing, downright miraculous!" But then she sat up, her brows slanting into a suspicious frown. "Why?"

Laughing, he pulled her back down beside him again. "That's my girl. Why, indeed? Naturally he would not tell me why he'd decided to do it now, and he utterly ignored the oddity and the irony of it, that he'd be rewarding a rebel with the very lands he rebelled over! Somehow I doubt that this was a belated birthday present. Here's another irony for you, darling. We most likely owe a debt of gratitude to Brother Richard."

"Yes, that makes sense. He is furious with Richard now, so it is to be expected that he's looking for allies, mayhap even seeing you in a new and appealing light. It is about time," she said indignantly, and then, "What of Nantes?"

He gave another peal of laughter and kissed her until they both were breathless. "He is continuing to dangle Nantes as bait, whilst still promising that it will be ours at a later date. And you know what, Constance? I think I almost believe him. As long as Richard continues to be his endearing, obstinate self, I'm going to look better and better to Papa."

Constance had a sudden, dazzling thought. Could Henry become so angry with Richard that he'd consider making Geoffrey his heir? She said nothing, though, not wanting to jinx them by saying it aloud. That was a dream to be held close, not to be shared with anyone yet, not even Geoffrey. He had slipped her robe off her shoulders and she squirmed out of his embrace, knowing that once she was naked, it would be quite a while before she could tell him her secret.

"Wait," she protested when he tugged at her belt. "You have not heard my news yet."

"Tell me, then, woman, and quickly, for my attention is beginning to wander."

"So are your hands," she chided. Sitting up again, she regarded him with a smile that was confident, serene, and triumphant, all in one. "I am with child, Geoffrey."

She was not disappointed by his response. He drew a sharp, audible breath, his eyes filling with light, and this time when he kissed her, it was with a tenderness he'd not shown before. Her mother had often told her that there was a special bond between a man and a woman who brought a child together into the world, and as she gave herself up to his lovemaking, her last coherent thought was, *Maman was right.* As they lay entwined together afterward, they both were sure their future was blessed, and it would never have occurred to them that Henry and Eleanor had once believed that, too.

In DECEMBER, Henry met the young French king at Gisors. Philippe relinquished his claim to Marguerite's dowry in exchange for Henry's promise to pay her two thousand seven hundred Angevin pounds annually for the rest of her life. Gisors and the Norman Vexin were to become Alys's marriage portion, and it was further agreed that she'd wed whichever of Henry's sons whom he chose, a not-so-subtle warning to Richard that he was not an only child. In return, Henry finally did homage to the French king for "all his holdings across the water."

CHAPTER FORTY-FIVE

April 1184
Le Mans, Anjou

GEOFFREY WAS NOT a willing guest at his father's Easter Court. He'd rather have been back at Rennes with Constance, for he was more excited about the coming birth of their child than he'd expected. Naturally the birth of an heir would elevate his status in Brittany. But he was not dwelling upon the political ramifications; more and more he found himself thinking of matters that were purely personal. He was concerned about Constance's health, although her pregnancy had been uneventful so far. He spent a lot of time thinking about baby names. And he vowed that he'd be a better father than his own.

A light rain was falling as he crossed the inner bailey of the royal palace. Two of Richard's knights were loitering by the stables, and they gave him an unfriendly stare as he passed by. It was some consolation to Geoffrey that, as discontented as he was to be here, Richard must be even more miserable. He'd love to know how their father had lured Richard to Le Mans, suspecting that his brother had asked for an insulting pledge of safe conduct. However it had been done, it was an exercise in futility. The tension between the two of them was combustible enough to burst into flame at any moment, and their animosity had spilled over to infect the rest of the Easter Court.

Geoffrey had broken up two fights between his men and Richard's, and he'd even seen evidence of bad blood between Richard's knights and their brother John's household.

Since he was not directly involved in this clash of wills, Geoffrey might have sat back and enjoyed the drama—had it not been for his mother and sister. It was obvious to him that Eleanor and Tilda were deeply troubled by this latest family contretemps, and their unhappiness bothered him, for he could see no quick resolution. He could see no resolution at all.

As Geoffrey entered the great hall, he noticed a boisterous dice game over by the center hearth. Several of his knights were playing, and when Gérard de Fournival waved and beckoned, he started in that direction. But he halted when he saw his youngest brother sitting alone in a window-seat and, on impulse, he veered toward John instead.

"You look even more bored than me," he said. "You want to join the dice game?" When John hesitated, he wondered if the boy had enough money to play. He had a title now—Count of Mortain—but Geoffrey was sure he had no income of his own yet. Geoffrey himself had not gained financial independence until he was finally allowed to wed Constance. John was betrothed to a rich heiress, his cousin Avisa of Gloucester, and the Earl of Gloucester's unexpected death just four months ago made the girl an even greater marital prize. Geoffrey was sure, though, that Henry would not let John claim that prize until cobwebs were collecting on the marriage contract. Their father could be lavish with his gifts, generous with his largesse. But it was a golden yoke, for it kept them beholden, always on a tight leash.

"If you're short, Johnny, I can make you a loan," he offered, and John's hazel eyes darkened with suspicion.

"Why would you want to do that?"

"Why not?"

"Why are you being so friendly of a sudden, Geoffrey? Since when are you willing to do me favors?"

"Ah . . . I see. You are nursing a grudge for my past sins."

He sounded amused, and John did not like it. "I do not have a single pleasant childhood memory of you or Richard, not even one!" His outburst was unplanned, but he found satisfaction now in being able to speak up for his younger self, at long last.

"How could you? We had to adhere to the code, after all."

"What code?"

"The one that sets out the rules for treating little brothers, of course. They are to be bedeviled without mercy, made the butt of every joke. It was just your bad luck that you had no one younger to pick on, in turn."

"My bad luck, indeed," John said coolly, remembering those hours he'd spent in that open grave, remembering his pleas for help that Geoffrey and Richard had claimed never to have heard.

Geoffrey was regarding him pensively. "Now that I look back upon it, all those jokes and pranks that we played on you . . ." He paused significantly. "I have to tell you, Johnny, they were fun."

Lulled into expecting an apology, John stiffened in surprise, but after a moment, he could not help laughing. "Come on, lad," Geoffrey said with a grin. "Let's go shoot some dice." They had just started across the hall, though, when John stopped suddenly, directing Geoffrey's attention toward the door behind the dais.

Tilda saw her brothers at the same time and came toward them, so hastily that they knew something was amiss. "Geoffrey, thank God you're here! Richard and Papa are having a terrible argument, their worst one yet, and if it is not stopped, I fear they may even come to blows!"

"I'd pay to see that," Geoffrey said before he could think better of it, and his sister stared at him in disbelief.

"I am beginning to think all of you have gone stark, raving mad! Maman and I could hear their shouting, and she went in to make peace. But by the sound of it, she's had no luck. Now are you going to help me or not?"

Geoffrey was not keen about getting into the crossfire, especially since he was sure his intervention would be meaningless. He did not have the heart to disappoint Tilda, though, for not only had her husband gone back to Mainz in hopes of obtaining a pardon from the Holy Roman Emperor, but she'd recently revealed that she was pregnant. "Of course I will help," he said, with far more confidence than he was feeling, and then glanced over at John, who'd once more been overlooked. Having spent much of his own life overshadowed by Hal and Richard, Geoffrey was motivated to say, "Come on, Johnny. I'll likely need all the help I can get."

"I would not miss it for the world," John said, with utter sincerity. He did not understand why Henry could not just order Richard to yield up Aquitaine, for he was the king, after all. He'd initially been sure it would be quickly resolved, but during the course of the Easter Court, he'd begun to fear that Henry might be the one to back down, not Richard. He'd never taken his father's talk of an Irish kingdom for him very seriously, for he could not envision himself ruling over that strange, wild isle on the western edge of the world. But Aquitaine was different; it was real, one of the richest duchies in Christendom, a land of milk and honey. He'd not even dreamed it might be his, not until that Michaelmas Eve in Rouen, but now he could not bear to think it might be snatched away. Richard was to be king, no longer needed it. Why was he being so selfish?

They found that Tilda had not exaggerated, hearing the angry voices while they were still in the stairwell. Geoffrey did not bother knocking, shoved the door open, with Tilda and John at his heels. Henry and Richard were confining themselves to verbal violence, at least so far. If Eleanor had interceded in hopes of mediating, she'd soon become a combatant herself, to judge from the way she was berating Henry. He and Richard were stalking each other like the big cats Geoffrey had once seen at the Tower of London, and he found himself thinking that this scene was true to form for his family, with everyone shouting and no one listening. Eleanor glanced in their direction, but the men were so intent upon their confrontation that they never even noticed the new arrivals—not until Geoffrey turned and slammed the door resoundingly.

"They can hear all the cursing and bellowing down in the hall," he said, "and they've started to wager which one of you will draw first blood. I came up to see whom I should put my money on."

That was not the sort of help Tilda had in mind, and she frowned at Geoffrey's levity. But it worked, for neither Richard nor Henry liked the idea of entertaining others with their quarrel.

"We are done here," Henry said, glaring at his eldest son, before adding an ominous warning, "for now."

Not at all intimidated, Richard glowered back, and started for the door. But then he stopped, unwilling to be dismissed so curtly. "I'll gladly go," he said defiantly, "and I'll not be coming back. The next time you want to threaten and rant, you can come to me in Aquitaine."

John, watching in dismay, saw his great chance slipping through his fingers, and he swung around to demand of his father, "Papa, does this mean Richard has bested you and Aquitaine is lost?"

Eleanor winced, Geoffrey rolled his eyes, and Henry gave his youngest a look John had never gotten from him before. "My life would have been much more peaceful if I'd had only daughters," he snapped. "As for Aquitaine, it is yours if you can take it."

Richard had halted when John protested. Now he looked the youth up and down very deliberately, and then he laughed. Geoffrey was astonished that his father had actually said that, for surely one Becket moment was enough for any man's lifetime. Clearly, Eleanor's thoughts had taken the same track, for she said scathingly, "Very good, Harry. It is always heartening to see that you've learned from your past mistakes."

But it was Tilda's reaction that overrode the others, for she cried, "Stop it!" in such pain that all heads turned in her direction. "I cannot bear any more, cannot watch my family being torn apart like this!"

There was a sudden, abashed silence and then alarm as Tilda seemed to falter. She looked so stricken that Geoffrey hastily grabbed her arm so he could hold her upright if necessary. Eleanor and Henry were immediately at her side, united, for that moment at least, in their concern for their distraught, pregnant daughter. She let them guide her toward the closest chair and the next few moments were hectic as Henry and Eleanor hovered over her, Richard hurried to get her wine, and Geoffrey asked if he could fetch one of her women. He was feeling remorseful, sorry he had not spared her this stressful scene by insisting she remain below in the hall, and his relief was considerable when she turned so the others could not see and winked. He at once entered cheerfully into the conspiracy, lamenting how pale and shaken she seemed and doing all he could to keep the focus upon Tilda, and away from their latest family conflagration.

John alone had not gone to Tilda's aid. He stood apart, as if he were watching a play, hearing only the echoes of Richard's scornful laughter and his father's dismissive words. *It is yours if you can take it.*

J UNE HAD BEEN A COOL, rainy month, but with the approach of July, the Breton summer finally put in an appearance. Constance had spent the morning dealing with tedious correspondence, and felt she deserved a respite for her diligence, so after dismissing her scribe, she headed for the nursery. Hearing the murmur of voices, she paused in the doorway, smiling at the sight meeting her eyes: her husband and Morna, the wet-nurse, hanging over the cradle, agreeing that they'd never seen a more beautiful baby.

"You just say that because she looks like you, Geoffrey," she said, and he glanced up with a grin.

"I do not deny I'm a handsome devil," he said, "but I think she looks more like you. She has your eyes."

Morna giggled at that, for she'd already explained to Geoffrey that it was too early to tell the baby's eye color. The infant had begun to whimper, and she reached for the child, but Geoffrey forestalled her.

"No, let me," he insisted and showed some skill in gathering his daughter up into his arms.

As Morna discreetly withdrew to give them some private time with their infant, Constance joined Geoffrey by the cradle. She loved her child with a fierce intensity that she'd not expected, but she'd still been greatly disappointed that their firstborn was not a son, and she had been both relieved and surprised that Geoffrey seemed so content with a daughter. It was true that females could inherit the duchy, as she herself had done. She'd observed, though, that most men were set upon sons. Watching as he rocked their baby, she could not help asking, yet again, "You truly were not letdown that I birthed a girl?"

"Look at her eyelashes," he marveled, "just like golden fans. I am beginning to think I'll have to swear a blood oath to satisfy you. How could any man be disappointed in this perfect little pearl? I'll not deny that I might become concerned if you give me four or five girls in a row, but I am not going to fret until then. We have time on our side, after all, and if it means I must pay more visits to your bed, well, I am willing to make the sacrifice."

"How noble," she said dryly, but once again he'd said what she needed to hear. He was right, for at twenty-three and twenty-five, they had all the time in the world. "I'm not sure I'd want to visit the birthing chamber as often as your mother, though," she confided. "Two with Louis and then eight with your father—the woman is truly a force of nature!"

"She definitely had a surfeit of sons," he agreed. The baby had begun to fuss, so he handed her over to Constance; he liked to watch as his pragmatic, commonsense wife melted as soon as she held that tiny bundle in her arms. Sitting down, Constance cradled their daughter, calling her "Aenor," the Breton form of Eleanor.

"I have to confess," Geoffrey said, "that I was surprised when you were so willing to name her after my mother. I'd thought for certes that I'd have to coax you into it."

Constance thought it was more than a fair trade-off, a reward he'd earned after responding so graciously to the birth of a daughter. "Well, I'll admit that I have never had any great interest in pleasing your mother," she allowed, "but I've always had a very healthy interest in vexing your father and calling our daughter Eleanor was virtually assured to do that."

As their eyes met over Aenor's head, they both laughed. Just then a knock sounded on the door and a servant entered to announce the arrival of Geoffrey's brother.

Geoffrey was taken aback. "Does he have an army with him?" When the puzzled servant said no, he glanced over at Constance with a shrug. "Then it cannot be Richard." He did not think that John or Geoff were likely to come all the way to Brittany for a family visit, either, and he wondered if his father had a bastard they didn't know about. The servant had departed before he could ask the identity of this mystery visitor, and he and Constance were unable to satisfy their curiosity until John was eventually ushered into the nursery.

Geoffrey stepped forward to bid him welcome, unable to resist joking, "In the neighborhood, were you?"

John smiled as if there was nothing out of the ordinary about his visit, and greeted his sister-in-law with his newfound gallantry, complimenting both her and

Aenor lavishly even though he thought all babies looked the same. Some of his urbanity slipped, however, when Geoffrey mischievously asked if he'd like to hold his niece. Reacting like the typical adolescent, he hastily shook his head. "No, I might drop her."

Almost as if she were reacting to his rejection, Aenor startled John by beginning to wail, making a surprising amount of noise for such a small creature. Morna hastened back into the chamber, took the baby from Constance, and retreated across the nursery to satisfy her hungry little charge. Much to Geoffrey's amusement, John seemed unable to take his eyes off Morna's exposed white bosom. Remembering what it was like to be seventeen and utterly obsessed with the female body, he took pity on his bedazzled young brother and suggested that Morna continue feeding Aenor in the antechamber. Feeling very benevolent at the moment, he even refrained from teasing John about his obvious distraction, instead asked for the latest family news.

As it happened, John had quite a bit of news to relate. Their mother was in England again, sent back by their father after his Easter Court. Henry had spent the spring seeking to bring about a truce between the French king Philippe and the Count of Flanders, and once he succeeded, he sailed for England in mid-June. Tilda and her children soon followed. Upon their arrival, he'd made his customary visit to the shrine of St Thomas at Canterbury, while Tilda continued on to Winchester as she wanted Eleanor with her in the birthing chamber.

"Maman was very pleased that you named your daughter after her," he reported, "but Papa not so much."

"Really?" Geoffrey said blandly, managing to sound surprised. His curiosity was getting the better of him by now, though, and he decided to nudge the conversation in the right direction. "Why did you not accompany Papa to England, Johnny?"

"I told him that I wanted to visit my estates in Mortain." John leaned forward, keeping his eyes intently upon his brother's face. "If you have some free time this summer, Geoffrey, I thought we might pay a visit to Richard in Poitou."

Constance frowned, but Geoffrey had been expecting an answer like this. "Did you, lad? Who do you have in mind to accompany us? Some of my knights and routiers hired with Breton gold?"

"You have the money; I do not," John said matter-of-factly. But then his eagerness surged to the surface. "He told us to do it, Geoffrey, said Aquitaine was mine if I could take it. So why not? I'll make it worth your while; will give you all the Poitevin castles that Hal promised you. And it is in your interests to overthrow Richard, for I'd make a far better neighbor, would not be constantly testing the borders between Brittany and Poitou. Nor would we lack for allies. Richard's barons loathe him, so why would they not rally to me as they did to Hal?"

"Hal was a king," Constance pointed out, "so they could claim they were not truly in rebellion."

"From what I've heard of lords like Viscount Aimar and the de Lusignans," John countered, "I doubt that any of them lose sleep at night about legal niceties like that," and Geoffrey began to laugh.

"Bless you, Johnny, you're proof that blood breeds true," he declared, and Constance felt a prickle of foreboding.

"Then we have a deal?"

"Not so fast, lad. I'll give it some thought, but I'm not ready to commit myself to another war just yet. Why not go back to the great hall and see if my steward has gotten your chamber ready for you?" Getting to his feet, Geoffrey deftly steered his brother toward the door, and once he was alone with his wife, he said playfully, "What is the name of the maidservant with the red hair and freckles? I doubt that Johnny will want to sleep alone tonight and that lusty little wench would like nothing better than to warm a prince's bed."

Constance had no interest in her brother-in-law's sleeping arrangements. "You are going to do it," she said slowly. "Good God, Geoffrey, why? Do you hate Richard so much?"

"There is no love lost between us," he conceded, "but can you truly see me fighting a war merely to settle a grudge?"

"No, I cannot. So why do it?"

"Darling, what else can I do? When opportunity falls into a man's lap like a ripe peach, he'd be a fool not to taste it. It is not as if I am corrupting an innocent, after all. Johnny came to me."

"That begs the question. What do you gain by joining with him against Richard?"

He could tell from her tone that she was fast losing patience and, no longer teasing, he crossed to her side, gently propelling her to her feet. "I think we'd have a good chance of winning. Richard's barons are not vanquished, are merely biding their time. I think Johnny is right and they would join with us against Richard. And who would you rather have as a neighbor, my little brother or Thor, the pagan god of war? By Richard's calculations, we owe him a blood debt and it is just a matter of time until he seeks to collect it. So it makes sense to strike first, does it not?"

"And what of your father? What do you expect him to do whilst you invade Aquitaine? Do you truly think he'd forgive two rebellions in less than a twelvemonth?"

"Ah, but this time I believe he'd stay out of it, Constance. When he told Johnny to 'take' Aquitaine, I think he meant it. He may not admit it, even to himself, but that was a cry from the heart. I think he'd secretly be relieved if we could get Aquitaine away from Richard. He loved Hal to distraction and seems genuinely fond of Johnny, but he knows full well that Richard loves him not, and he knows, too, that as long as Richard holds Aquitaine, his defiance will continue. So why would he not welcome our efforts to give him what he wants—the duchy for Johnny?"

"But what if you're wrong?"

He shrugged. "It seems a risk worth taking."

"That is what I do not understand, Geoffrey. I do not see what we gain from this, unless you have it in mind to then claim Aquitaine from Johnny?"

"No, that would indeed bring Papa into the fray," he said with a wry smile. "I'll settle for some Poitevin castles, a more peaceful border region, and the chance for future benefits."

"Ah, I knew it! Tell me about these 'future benefits.' What scheme are you hatching now?"

"No scheme, Constance. I merely want to give my father the chance to consider all of his options. It has to have occurred to him that I'd make a better king than Richard. I've proven myself to be an able battle commander, and I've done in Brittany what Richard has failed to do in Aquitaine—I've reconciled the barons to my rule. But he cannot disinherit Richard as long as he holds Aquitaine, for he knows it would mean unending rebellion. Richard would never accept it, not if he had the means of waging war. If he loses his duchy, he loses, too, his income to hire routiers and wreak havoc." He slid his fingers under her chin, tilted her face up to his as he murmured, "Tell me, darling, that a kingdom is not worth the risk."

She could not, of course. She wanted him to be the English king as much as he did. She wanted the power and security that only a crown could bestow, wanted it for Geoffrey and herself, for her Breton homeland, and above all, for Aenor and their children not yet born.

CHAPTER FORTY-SIX

✦

September 1184
Winchester, England

*Y*OUR SON IS SO SWEET, Tilda. May I hold him?"

"Of course, Alys," Tilda said with a smile and surrendered her baby to the younger woman. She was making a special effort to be friendly because of her discomfort in Alys's presence. She felt that her father and Richard had treated the French princess rather shabbily, cold-bloodedly using her as a pawn in their high-stakes diplomatic maneuvering. Her mother's attitude seemed callous to Tilda, too. Eleanor was obviously in no position to influence Alys's fate, but she'd shown a marked lack of sympathy for the girl in her conversations with Tilda, her only concern how Alys's fortunes affected Richard. Tilda's husband liked to tease her that she was too tenderhearted for her own good, and she supposed there was truth in that. She could not help pitying Alys, though.

As she glanced from Alys to her twelve-year-old daughter, Tilda found herself worrying what the future held in store for Richenza. Alys was not the only highborn bride to be treated as a commodity, after all. Alys's half sister Agnes had found only grief in Byzantium. And then there was the still-grieving Marguerite, being used by her brother for bait as he fished for allies.

Tilda had heard people claim that a nuptial curse hung over the French House of Capet. Louis had certainly been shipwrecked in matrimonial seas, surviving a turbulent union to Eleanor, losing his second wife in childbirth, and not gaining the son he so desperately wanted until he'd sired four daughters and given up all hope. His sister Constance had been unhappily wed to two abusive husbands, and his nineteen-year-old son, Philippe, had already weathered one marital crisis.

Earlier in the year Philippe had attempted to repudiate Isabelle of Hainaut, the niece of his onetime ally turned enemy, the Count of Flanders, claiming that she had failed to give him an heir, an unfair accusation in light of her extreme youth; she'd been ten at the time of their marriage and was now only fourteen. Isabelle had outmaneuvered him, though, taking to the streets of Senlis as a penitent.

Barefoot and clad only in her chemise, she'd made a pilgrimage from church to church, attracting huge, sympathetic crowds as she prayed aloud to God to forgive her sins and protect her from the king's evil counselors. The citizens had rioted in her favor, and when the flustered Philippe offered to find her a highborn second husband, she had responded, "Sire, it does not please God for a mortal man to lie in the bed in which you have lain." Facing the disapproval of his subjects and the likely opposition of the Church, his pride assuaged by his young wife's artful flattery, Philippe had relented and agreed to take her back. But Tilda still felt sorry for Isabelle, and hoped when her daughter was wed that she'd be treated more kindly than Philippe's queen.

Alys laughed, not at all disturbed when Tilda's infant son burped and spit up on the bodice of her gown. "You are so lucky," she said wistfully. "He is such a beautiful baby." Glancing over the child's head toward Tilda, she hesitated before saying, "I was sorry to hear that your husband had no success during his trip to Germany."

"It was a disappointment," Tilda conceded. "But we remain hopeful. My father met the Archbishop of Cologne at Canterbury last month and entertained him lavishly in London. The archbishop had long been one of my husband's fiercest foes, but my father got them together during the archbishop's visit and brought about their reconciliation."

The archbishop had suggested that Henry send an embassy to the Pope and ask him to mediate on Heinrich's behalf with the emperor, but Tilda was not about to reveal something so politically sensitive to Alys. Nor was she going to tell Alys the real reason for the archbishop's presence in England. His had been a diplomatic mission disguised as a pilgrimage; talks were under way for a marriage between Richard and the emperor's daughter Agnes. Tilda hoped that the marriage would come to pass, for at least that would free Alys from her political purgatory. But she did not know Alys at all, and it could be that the young woman really wanted to wed Richard, especially now that he was a future king, so it seemed wisest to say nothing.

Tilda's daughter was cooing over her baby brother with a motherly air that brought a smile to Tilda's lips. Richenza—Tilda found it hard to remember that she was now called Matilda—and Alys were taking turns extolling little Wilhelm's manifold virtues when Eleanor's abrupt entrance put a halt to their cheery conversation. Her greeting to Alys was so curt that the younger woman flushed and Tilda felt a prickle of resentment on her behalf. But then she took a closer look at her mother's ashen face.

"Alys, would you mind taking Wilhelm back to the nursery? My daughter will show you the way." Catching the eye of Gertrud, her attendant, Tilda nodded her head and the woman rose and followed the others out. Turning back to her mother, then, Tilda was alarmed to find that Eleanor had sank down upon a coffer, almost as if she no longer had the strength to hold herself erect. "Maman . . . what is it? What is wrong?"

"It is happening all over again."

Tilda had never heard her mother sound so vulnerable, so . . . old. "What is happening? I do not understand."

"Your brothers are at war with one another. Only this time it is Geoffrey and John against Richard."

"God in Heaven!" Tilda stared at Eleanor in horror. "You mean . . . they took Papa's angry words seriously?"

"So it would seem." Eleanor rubbed her temples with her fingers; she had a throbbing headache, and when she closed her eyes, she could see white light pulsing against her lids. "I am so tired," she confessed, "so very tired of all this, Tilda. It never seems to end . . ."

Tilda leaped to her feet, much too swiftly for a woman who'd given birth so recently. Crossing to Eleanor's side, she sat down beside her on the coffer and reached for her hand. "Maman, I know how painful this must be for you . . ." Her voice faltered, for in truth, she did not. She could not even imagine a world in which her own sons were set upon destroying one another. Could there be any worse grief for a parent than that? "You must not despair, Maman. Papa will not let this happen. He will stop the bloodshed, find a way to end their lunatic rivalry and make peace between them. He'll make this right, you'll see."

What if he does not want to make it right? The words hovered on Eleanor's lips, but she bit them back. She was not about to burden Tilda with her fears. If she could keep from voicing them, though, she could not keep them from taking root, could not banish them from the back of her brain. What if Harry's "angry words" had come from the heart? What if he meant what he said?

GEOFF WAS IN LONDON when he heard of his family's latest crisis. He was soon in the saddle, riding for Windsor in such haste that he covered the thirty-five miles at a pace one of Henry's royal couriers might have envied and reached the river-side castle that evening. Admitted into the middle bailey, he ran into Willem, who grimly confirmed that the rumors were true. "Thank God you're here, Geoff. You'll know how to comfort him."

Once he was escorted up to his father's chamber, though, Geoff was not so sure of that. Henry was seated by the hearth, staring into the flames as his squires tiptoed around in nervous silence. Recognizing his son's footsteps, he glanced over his shoulder. "You heard, then."

Geoff found a stool and brought it over to sit beside his father. "For a long time, I've suspected that my brothers are possessed."

"I would that it were true," Henry said, his voice so low that Geoff barely heard him. "At least then I'd have an answer for this family madness." They sat in silence for a time, the only sound the crackling in the hearth. Henry stretched his feet toward the fire, wondering why he was so much more sensitive to the cold as he aged. For most of his life, he'd never paid any heed to the weather, but in the past few years he'd begun to see his own body as the enemy, for on any given day he had more random pains and aches than he used to suffer in the course of a year. He did not want to think of fifty-one as old, though his muscles, bones, and sinew seemed to be telling him otherwise. Looking at Geoff from the corner of his eye, he said reluctantly, "I may have played a part in this latest outbreak."

"What do you mean, Papa?"

Henry sighed heavily. "During one of our quarrels at my Easter Court, I lost my temper and told Johnny that Aquitaine was his if he could take it from Richard. Do you think that . . . that they could have taken me seriously? Surely they must have known that I did not mean it?"

This was the first that Geoff had heard of his father's rash outburst, and he blinked in surprise. But he did not hesitate, saying stoutly, "Of course they knew you did not mean it, Papa! Anyone with half a brain would have known you were just speaking out of frustration. You must not blame yourself for their folly."

"I expected better of Johnny, though. Of course he is still young . . ." Henry said, with another sigh.

Geoff did not think John's age was an excuse, for he was just three months from his eighteenth birthday. But if his father wanted to harbor these comforting delusions about his youngest, then Geoff would not be the one to gainsay him. "What will you do?"

"I am going to order them to cease hostilities and summon them to England to answer for themselves."

"What will you do if they defy you?" Geoff asked, for he considered that a distinct possibility, but he was taken aback by the raw candor of his father's reply.

"I do not want to think about that," Henry admitted, for he found none of his choices palatable. If he stood aside and did nothing, his sons could tear his empire apart. He had limited control over Richard and Geoffrey, neither of whom were financially dependent upon him as Hal had been. But as angry as he was with them, he did not want to make war against his own flesh and blood. He'd already lost his eldest, his best-loved son. How much more would the Almighty ask of him?

A LIGHT NOVEMBER SNOW was falling as Eleanor, her daughter, and her son-in-law reached the palace at Westminster. The journey had not been a long one, for they'd been staying at Berkhampstead, which was much closer to London than Winchester. Eleanor was still very tired, and thoroughly chilled, too, for the day had been one of blustery winds. She did not summon servants to prepare her bath yet, as eager as she was to soak in warm, scented water. Henry had greeted them briefly upon their arrival, but she was expecting him to pay her a private visit.

He did not keep her waiting. Watching impatiently as servants stoked the fire in the hearth and piled fur-lined coverlets upon the bed, he seized his first opportunity to dismiss them, including Amaria. As soon as they were alone, he crossed the chamber to face Eleanor; she could not help noticing that he was favoring his bad leg again.

"I have summoned our sons to London. Johnny has already landed at Dover and Richard and Geoffrey ought to arrive by week's end. I intend to reconcile them, to put an end to this infernal rivalry once and for all, and I expect you to assist me in this endeavor."

"Of course."

"You are not always so biddable," he said suspiciously, and she gave him a tight smile.

"When our interests converge, I am always 'biddable,' Harry, and I want to end this strife as much as you do."

"See that you keep that in mind," he said brusquely and turned toward the door.

Eleanor waited until he'd reached it before she spoke again. "I will do all I can to make peace between them, however hollow it may be. But I will do nothing, Harry, to help you take Aquitaine away from Richard, and you forget that at your cost."

He'd paused and was regarding her impassively, but his eyes were as frigid and foreboding as the slate-colored November sky. "I can only put out one fire at a time," he said and left without waiting for her response.

IN ADDITION TO HIS DAUGHTER AND SON-IN-LAW, Henry was entertaining the Count of Flanders and numerous English bishops, having convened a council to discuss the selection of a new archbishop of Canterbury. But his first priority that November was bringing his rebellious sons back into the fold. With that in mind, he waited until all three of them had arrived at Westminster and then summoned them to a private reckoning at the Tower of London.

GEOFFREY WAS THE LAST TO ARRIVE, and he took his time climbing the stairs to the upper floor of the White Tower, knowing the coming confrontation would be an unpleasant one. As he was ushered into the great hall, he at once became the avid object of all eyes. To his relief, he was directed toward the private royal chamber that adjoined the hall; at least this was not going to be a public ordeal.

They were waiting for him: his parents and his brothers, Richard, John, and Geoff. Richard shot him a look that would have been deadly had it been launched from a bow, Geoff was glaring, and John seemed relieved to see him. Eleanor's expression was unrevealing, warning Geoffrey that he was facing the queen, not the mother. Henry's court mask was in place, too, but he seethed with restless, edgy energy, unable to stay still for long, not understanding why he, who'd always found the mastery of other men so easy, should be so hobbled when it came to controlling his own sons.

"Come in, Geoffrey," he said coldly. "It has been suggested to me that the lot of you are possessed. Others think that you must be secretly in the service of the French king, for no one benefits more than Philippe from our family bloodletting. As for myself, I do not know what to believe, for I can no more explain your inexplicable behavior than I can walk upon water. So I'd truly like to hear you speak for yourselves. Tell me why you are seeking to do what none of my enemies could, why you are so set upon following in the footsteps of Cain."

Geoffrey was silent, able to recognize a rhetorical question when he heard one. His brothers were not as prudent. "But you told me to take Aquitaine!" John protested. "I thought that was what you wanted, Papa!"

Richard was almost as quick as John. "I have nothing to apologize for. I was the one wronged, was merely defending myself!"

Henry dealt with Richard first. "The trouble is, Richard, that you always show what Hal called 'an excess of zeal' in dealing with your enemies. You were hardly defending your borders when you raided deep into Brittany."

The blatant unfairness of that took Richard's breath away. That was how warfare was conducted, as his father well knew, being an astute practitioner of the art himself—when at all possible, carry the war to the enemy. But Henry had already turned his attention toward John.

"That is not the best defense to make, Johnny, for it raises troubling doubts about your judgment and common sense. It was obvious that my words were spoken in anger, not to be taken seriously."

Geoffrey wondered if he'd said that, too, about the knights who'd been motivated by one of his fits of temper to murder an archbishop in his own cathedral. But he had no time to appreciate the irony of it, for he was now the one in the line of fire.

"At least Johnny has his youth and inexperience to explain away his misdeeds. That cannot be said for you, Geoffrey. In fact, I see your sins as twofold. Not only did you make war upon your brother, but you dragged Johnny into it, too. I expected better of you."

Geoffrey prided himself upon his inner discipline, but this tested his self-control to the utmost. He could not help glancing toward John, disappointed although not truly surprised when his younger brother kept quiet. John flushed as their eyes met, but his pang of guilt was more easily overcome than his instincts for self-preservation. He'd never understood how his brothers could defy their father so boldly, envying them their swagger and their apparent indifference to Henry's anger. He'd been blessed—or cursed—with a vivid imagination, and when he thought of his life, he envisioned a turbulent sea, with the only land the small, unstable island of his father's favor, an isle that could disappear under the waves in any storm.

"Well, Geoffrey?" Henry demanded. "Have you nothing to say?"

Eleanor had long ago mastered that skill so useful to kings, the ability to read others as a monk read his Psalter, a faculty also useful to prisoners, and she caught the warning signs—the jut of Geoffrey's chin, the clenched muscles along his jawline. Deciding it was time to intervene, she said coolly, "I have something to say. I, too, expected better of you, Geoffrey, and I am very disappointed in you. But John is not a child and is old enough to answer for his own mistakes."

That earned her a grateful look from Geoffrey, a sullen one from John, and a mistrustful one from Henry, who claimed control of the conversation again. "This is how it will be. I have convened a council for this week; the archbishopric of Canterbury has been vacant since April and it is time to select a successor. At that council I am going to have the three of you make a public avowal of peace, swear not to take up arms against one another again, and give none any reason to doubt the truth of your reconciliation."

Neither Geoffrey nor John raised any objections, but Richard was shaking his head in disbelief. "And that is it? They attacked my lands without provocation or justification and they are not to be punished for it? Where is the justice in that?"

"The sooner we put this embarrassment behind us, the better," Henry said impatiently. "The last thing I want to do is to drag this farce out any longer than need be. All of you are to do as you're bidden for once with no further arguments. And heed me well on this. It is not to happen again—ever. Now it is done and let that be the end of it."

No one spoke up, but they all knew this was not "the end of it," even Henry.

CONSTANCE HAD BEEN WILLING to accompany Geoffrey to London, but he'd insisted that she remain in Brittany with their child, saying that there was no reason they both should have to endure his father's recriminations and he might well be kept in England for the foreseeable future. But to her surprise, she'd gotten a message from him in mid-December, summoning her to meet him in Rouen. The winter was mild enough for her to bring their seven-month-old daughter, and she arrived in high spirits, pleased that they'd be able to celebrate Aenor's first Christmas together and bringing Geoffrey a gift sure to delight him—word that she was pregnant again. He reacted as she'd expected and they celebrated the news in bed. Afterward, they had food sent up to their chamber and enjoyed a private supper for two.

"THIS IS DELICIOUS, GEOFFREY." Constance's expectations had been low, for it was an ember fast day, but the castle's cooks had prepared a savory blanc manger made with almond milk, rice, and pike instead of chicken. "Give me another helping . . . and I am not being a glutton. After all, I am eating for two now."

"To judge by the way you've made that pike disappear, you could be carrying twins." Reaching under the covers, he slid his hand across her abdomen. "Though as flat as your belly is, it is hard to imagine you swollen up like a melon."

"Thank you for the compliment . . . I think. It is early in the pregnancy yet; my midwife says he'll most likely be born in the summer."

"He'll be born? So the midwife also told you that you're carrying a boy? Did she happen to mention what color eyes he'll have?"

"Tease me all you like, but I know it will be a son. I just know. Indeed, since we already have Aenor, I hope I birth only boys from now on."

"Why? It can be argued that a ruler with too many sons is no better off than the one without any. I'd say my family history proves there can be too much of a good thing."

"I like to think we'll raise our sons better than your parents did, Geoffrey. Surely it cannot be that difficult to foster affection between siblings."

"Even amongst the spawn of the Demon Countess of Anjou?"

"You are entirely too proud of your fire-and-brimstone heritage," she said with mock severity, but when he grinned, she could not help grinning back. "I'd rather have sons because daughters are more vulnerable to the vagaries of fate. Once she is married off, a girl is utterly dependent upon the whims of her husband. I remember all too well how it was for me—suddenly uprooted from my family and the only world I knew, sent off to be raised in the household of the man responsible for ruining my father. I'd not want that for a daughter of mine, and since girls are born to be pawns, better to have only sons."

"But I was given no more say in our marriage than you were, Constance," he protested. "Sons, too, are expected to wed for their family's benefit."

"It is not the same, Geoffrey. In the eyes of the Church and the law, a wife is subject to her husband's will, and if he maltreats her, what remedy has she? I would not want a daughter of mine to find herself a pampered hostage like Alys or humiliated like Philippe's queen."

Geoffrey had never given much thought to the plight of highborn brides, but he discovered now that it was very troubling to imagine Aenor in an alien land, under a stranger's control. "My sisters seem content enough, though. So if we take care in choosing the husbands for our daughters, surely we can avoid some of those pitfalls," he said, while silently vowing that Aenor would not be wed until she was at least twenty.

"I hope so," Constance agreed, without much conviction. She had revealed more of herself than she'd intended, for she was not accustomed to sharing her most intimate thoughts. Lying in bed with her husband, though, she found it surprisingly easy to speak with such candor, and she realized how much she'd come to trust him in the three years since their marriage. Marveling at the unlikely turns her life had taken, she reached over to snatch a slice of bread from his plate, for she was still ravenous. "I was so eager to tell you of my pregnancy that we did not discuss why you're in Rouen. How did you manage to slip your father's tether?"

Geoffrey set their tray down in the floor rushes, keeping a dish of dried figs for Constance to munch on. "Make yourself comfortable, darling, for this is quite a story. My father raged at us as expected, and somehow I found myself shouldering the blame for Johnny, too. I am sorry to report that my little brother practices Hal's kind of seamanship. Whilst he did not exactly push me out of his ark, neither did he throw me a lifeline."

"What penalties did your father impose upon you?"

"This is where it gets interesting—none. We all had to swear to uphold the peace in a public ceremony, but that was it. Richard almost had a seizure, he was so wroth."

"I can well imagine," she said dryly. "What of Aquitaine? Does your father still intend to claim it for John?"

"I think he has reluctantly concluded that Richard will hold on to Aquitaine until his dying breath, for he has begun to talk again of Ireland for Johnny. The lad seems to be of two minds about his prospects, eager for his first taste of freedom, but greatly disappointed that it shall not be Aquitaine. Understandable, for governing the Irish is like herding cats."

"So Richard has won . . ." Constance had known this for some time; Henry's intervention had made it inevitable. She still felt a keen regret, though, for the dream was not an easy one to relinquish. It would have been a great thing, to be wife and mother to kings. Nothing could have protected her family more than a crown.

"That remains to be seen."

"What do you mean, Geoffrey? You said that your father could not consider changing the succession as long as Richard holds Aquitaine."

"I know, but I am no longer so sure of that. Listen to the rest of my account and then judge for yourself. My father next turned his attention to the vacant See at Canterbury. He wanted the monks to elect Baldwin, the Bishop of Worcester, but they balked. So he sent Johnny and me to Canterbury to make the monks see reason." He smiled at the look of astonishment on his wife's face. "An odd choice, no? Failed rebels one day, royal agents the next. I thought Richard was going to choke on his outrage, God's Truth!"

"And did you succeed in this mission?"

"I did, and my father was very pleased, Richard less so. I said 'I' and not 'we,' for Johnny was more interested in entertaining two Canterbury sisters, not exactly whores but not nuns either, and as alike as two peas in a pod."

"Are you saying that you are back in your father's favor, Geoffrey?"

"Well . . . I am here in Rouen at my father's behest. He sent me to Normandy to govern it in his name."

"Geoffrey!" Constance was gazing at him with wide, dazzled eyes. "Then he must truly be thinking of choosing you, not Richard, as his heir!"

"One step at a time," he cautioned. "I think he is giving serious consideration to naming me as Duke of Normandy. And Richard certainly thinks so, judging by the threats he made to me. Who knows? He may well be the first man who gave up a kingdom in favor of a duchy."

Constance was deceived neither by his nonchalance nor by his jesting. He might not admit it, but he'd dropped his defenses, for the first time seeing their dream as more than a beguiling chimera, a bewitching illusion shimmering always on the horizon. Now it was taking on shape and substance, might actually be within their grasp.

"If your father has the sense to choose you over Richard," she declared, "then I am prepared to forgive him for all the wrongs he's done me and mine." Geoffrey burst out laughing, and while she did not understand why he found that so humorous, she was glad to share his laughter, glad to embrace his hopes for the glittering future that suddenly seemed within their reach.

HENRY AND ELEANOR celebrated their thirtieth Christmas Court at Windsor. He then moved on to Winchester, leaving Eleanor at Windsor with Tilda, Heinrich, and their children. It was there that the Archdeacon of Lisieux found him, bringing welcome news from Rome. The Pope had brought about a reconciliation between Heinrich and the Emperor Frederick. Delighted, Henry summoned Eleanor and his daughter and son-in-law to Winchester so they could celebrate his success and the end of their exile.

Henry also began to make plans to send John to Ireland and finally gave Richard permission to return to Aquitaine. Without even waiting for the spring thaw, Richard declared war against his brother and launched punitive raids into Brittany. Once more the Angevin empire was riven to its core by internecine hostilities.

CHAPTER FORTY-SEVEN

✦

May 1185
Winchester, England

*J*HE COUNTESS OF CHESTER was content to watch the festivities from a window-seat, for she was tired and feeling her years on this early May evening. She'd brought her grandson to Winchester to meet her cousin the king, only to learn that Henry had changed his plans because of Richard's assault upon Geoffrey's lands in Brittany. He'd hurriedly taken ship at Dover, celebrating his Easter Court at Rouen with the Patriarch of Jerusalem as he pondered how to deal with Richard's latest defiance. While Maud welcomed the opportunity to visit with Eleanor and Tilda, she was not looking forward to making a Channel crossing in pursuit of Henry.

"I am getting too old for all this to and fro, Randolph," she said, wryly amused when her grandson took her words at face value and apologized solemnly for taking her away from home and hearth. Noticing that he was glancing wistfully across the hall, where a jongleur was entertaining with some adroit sleight of hand, she relieved him of the duties imposed by blood and courtesy, and watched with a smile as he headed over to get a closer look at the conjuring tricks.

"My lady?" Turning at the sound of a soft voice, Maud found herself gazing up into the face of a young woman, one who looked somewhat familiar. Accepting the wine cup proffered by the girl, Maud recognized her in time to pretend that she'd known the identity of the French princess all along, thanking Alys and inviting her to sit in the window-seat.

"Is that your son Hugh's boy?"

Maud nodded. "I am taking Randolph to confer with the king about his future. He has been in wardship since Hugh's death, of course, but he is fifteen now and we need to begin making plans for when he reaches his majority. The earldom of Chester is a great inheritance and a great responsibility. Fortunately, I think the lad will be up to the challenge." Unlike his father, she thought sadly, may God assoil him.

Alys politely agreed that Randolph seemed quite mature for his age, and they passed the next few minutes in inconsequential conversation as the younger woman nerved herself to reveal the reason she'd sought out the countess. Maud was telling her that the April earthquake had done great damage to Lincoln Cathedral when Alys decided she could wait no longer. "Madame, you are known to speak your mind freely. I am hoping that you'll not be offended if I, too, speak forthrightly."

Maud did not like the sound of that. She felt that Alys had legitimate grievances, but she was, above all, a realist, and she knew there was nothing she could do about it. "Speak my mind, do I?" she said. "I've never heard my lack of tact described so delicately."

"I am not asking you to betray any confidences," Alys said hastily. "It is just that I know so little about what is occurring beyond these walls, only what I happen to overhear. I would be grateful if you could answer a few questions, Lady Maud. For example, I know the Patriarch of Jerusalem came to England to seek the king's aid for the defense of the Holy Land. Is it true that the king was offered the crown and actually turned it down? And is it true that Lady Matilda's daughter will not be accompanying her parents when they return to Saxony?"

Those questions seemed innocuous to Maud, and easy enough to answer. "I daresay you know that the King of Jerusalem is cousin to King Henry, and you know, too, that he has been afflicted by leprosy. He is a young man of great courage and ability, but he is also dying and when he does, the crown will pass to his sister's son, who is a small child. Patriarch Heraclius hoped that King Henry would agree to take the crown himself, believing that no one else could keep Outremer from falling to the infidels. King Henry put the proposal to his great council in London, but they did not want him to accept it."

"Why ever not?"

"The king asked them if they thought he could still fulfill his coronation oath to safeguard the realm if he were to accept the crown of Jerusalem, and they concluded that he could not," Maud said blandly, stifling a smile, for given such a broad hint by Henry, they could hardly have answered otherwise. "So the king told the patriarch nay, offering to provide money and soldiers for the defense of the Holy Land. The patriarch was distraught, and asked the king, then, to send his son. John was eager to go, from what I've heard, pleading for the chance, but the king would not agree to it. The patriarch was not mollified by the king's offer of gold and men, chastised him bluntly for failing in his duty as a Christian king. King Henry would not be swayed, though, saying he could not leave his kingdom. And when they met the French king at Vaudreuil, the patriarch had another failure, for your brother Philippe said that he could not take the cross at this time, either."

Alys seemed distressed. "Can the Holy Land survive without a new Christian quest, though?"

"God Willing," Maud murmured, wondering what else she could discuss with Alys. Surely personal news would be safe enough? "I am happy to report that your brother's queen is on the mend after her miscarriage." She saw at once that this was a mistake, that Alys had known neither that Isabelle was pregnant nor that she'd lost the baby. Did anyone even write to this girl? "I believe you asked about the Duchess of Saxony's daughter. It is true that Richenza—Matilda, I mean—will remain behind when her parents depart, but that is because she has a crown in her future. The Scots king has asked King Henry for her hand in marriage. They are distant cousins, so must receive a dispensation from His Holiness first, but the king has already sent a delegation to Rome to procure one. So it was for the best that she changed her name, for Richenza would not do at all for the Queen of Scotland!"

So far, so good, she thought. As long as they steered clear of any mention of Richard, the conversation should be smooth sailing. "Did you hear about Lord John? He was very disappointed when the king turned down the crown of Jerusalem on his behalf, and mayhap to make up for that, the king knighted him and put him in command of that long-planned expedition to Ireland. So it seems a crown is in the offing for him, too."

Alys did not show much interest in John's prospects, and Maud wondered if she even knew that Henry and Philippe had agreed after Hal's death that she should be wed to "whichever of the king's sons that he shall choose." Most likely not. Why should they bother to inform her that she might become John's bride rather than Richard's? Maud had always prided herself upon her pragmatic streak, knowing that if she'd been more sentimental, more of a starry-eyed romantic, she might have been unable to endure marriage to the Earl of Chester, a man surely burning in Hell Everlasting these thirty years past. She reminded herself now that Alys was none of her concern, but it was no longer that easy, for her sense of justice was offended by the young French-woman's plight.

Alys was glancing around nervously, worried that they could be interrupted at any moment, robbing her of her one chance to learn the truth. Worried, too, that her resolve might weaken, she leaned closer to Maud and blurted out in one great gasp, "Lady Maud, is it true that Richard is to wed the daughter of the Holy Roman Emperor?"

Maud had somehow known it would get to this. "Where did you hear that?" she temporized, wondering how to make such a bitter brew taste tolerable, and then she thought, *No, by God. The girl deserves the truth if nothing else.*

"One of my ladies overheard people gossiping about it and she came to me straightaway, of course. Is it true?"

"I am sorry you had to learn of it that way; you ought to have been told. A plight-troth was agreed upon, but the marriage will not take place. As much as it pleased the king and the emperor, it did not please God. The girl sickened soon after, and died ere the year was out."

Alys closed her eyes, her lips moving. It was the faintest of whispers, meant for no ears but those of the Almighty. Maud caught it, though, *"Deo gratias,"* most likely the only Latin Alys knew, and she felt a sharp pang of pity, but no surprise. Richard was a hero out of a minstrel's tale, highborn and handsome and courageous and dashing, a king in the making. Of course Alys wanted to marry him. What girl would not?

Alys soon excused herself, looking as if she'd been given a great gift. Maud knew better. Marriage was never easy, but she suspected that marriage to Richard would be more difficult than most. Men like Richard did not make good husbands; a wife would never be more than incidental, relegated to the outer edges of a life given over to war, duty, honor, and the pursuit of power. Sitting back in the window-seat, Maud considered approaching Henry on Alys's behalf. There was no deliberate cruelty in his nature; surely he could be made to see how unfairly he was treating Alys. But she was deluding herself and she knew it. There was a time when she could have taken her royal cousin to task for his transgressions and he would have heard her out, mayhap even heeded her. But that time had passed. She gazed around the hall, her eyes coming to rest upon the still elegant figure of her friend, the English queen. They'd all lost so much, Harry most of all.

E LEANOR SHOULD HAVE BEEN better pleased by Henry's summons, in-structing her, Tilda, Heinrich, and their children to take ship at Southampton and join him in Normandy as soon as possible; she'd like nothing better than to turn her back on England, the land she usually referred to as "that wet, wretched, and godforsaken isle." But instincts honed both by years of marriage and captivity alerted her to danger of some sort.

Nor was she reassured by the welcome they received upon their arrival at Bayeux. Henry had been as angry as she'd ever seen him when he'd learned of Richard's raiding into Brittany. But if he was still wroth, he no longer showed it, seemed to be in good spirits, teasing his granddaughter about needing to learn to speak Gaelic, shrugging off Tilda and Heinrich's effusive expressions of gratitude for ending their exile, even joking about the stern lecture he'd gotten from Patriarch Heraclius. His apparent equanimity merely served as further fuel for Eleanor's suspicions.

Unable to endure the suspense any longer, she cornered him in the great hall after a lavish meal in honor of the new archbishop of Rouen; Henry had not been won over by the campaigning of Rotrou's ambitious nephew and saw to it that his own choice was elected to the prestigious post, Walter de Coutances. When Henry amiably allowed her to steer him toward the relative privacy of a window-seat, Eleanor was utterly sure that he was up to something.

"You are looking much too smug for my peace of mind," she said bluntly. "If you were a cat, there'd be cream dripping from your whiskers. What are you plotting now, Harry? Why am I here?"

"Would you believe me if I said for the pleasure of your company?" he asked, fighting back a smile when she scowled. "Why are you here? A fair question. Your presence is required for upcoming events. As you never tire of reminding me, you are the Duchess of Aquitaine, after all."

Despite the warm spring night, Eleanor felt a sudden chill. "What are you going to do?"

He leaned back in the window-seat, regarding her with a smile that never reached his eyes. "I am going to answer all your prayers, love. I am going to restore your inheritance to you."

RICO FITZ RAINALD did not realize how much he'd had to drink until it was too late. Upon learning that Richard had no need of them that evening, he and André de Chauvigny had ventured into one of the more disreputable quarters of Poitiers in search of wine and whores. They found the first at several shabby taverns outside the old Roman walls and the second at a bawdy-house popular with the duke's soldiers. Their thirst slaked and their lust sated, they headed back toward the palace after curfew had rung, relying upon their prestige as the duke's knights should they have the bad luck to run into the Watch. Jesting and bantering and singing a ribald ditty about a lustful monk, they saved time by cutting through the ruins of the ancient Roman amphitheater, eerily bathed in May moonlight. André had drunk enough wine to become fanciful, and he launched into a disjointed tribute to all the men who'd died in this unholy arena, drawing heavily upon what Richard had told him of Roman blood-sports.

"A pity we do not have any more wine," he declared, "for we could drink to the memories of those brave men who fought and died on this very ground!"

"They were pagans, you fool!" Rico hooted, reaching out to steady André as he clambered onto a broken pillar.

"Brave men, nonetheless," André insisted hazily, "at least the gladiators were. Richard says they executed common criminals in the arena, too—" He stopped so abruptly that Rico took a quick step forward, thinking he'd lost his balance again. But he was staring over Rico's shoulder into the shadows behind them. "We have company," he said in a low voice that sounded as if he were beginning to sober up fast.

Rico spun around to see the men converging on them. They moved without haste, fanning out to cover any escape routes. "*Cagar*," Rico muttered, for Richard had recently begun to teach him to swear in the *lengua romana* of his duchy.

"Whatever you just said, I echo it," André said grimly, jumping from the pillar to the ground and unsheathing his sword. Rico's weapon had already cleared its leather scabbard. He did not like the odds, four against two, nor did he like the looks of these intruders, for they moved without haste, theirs a cockiness that bespoke an easy familiarity with violence and sudden death. Two of them had swords drawn; the other two wielding clubs studded with iron. They were close enough now for Rico to recognize one of them, a strapping, broad-chested brute with a close-cropped head. Rico had seen the man at two of the riverside taverns, and he cursed himself now for having drunk so much, for walking into this trap like a lamb to the slaughter. It never occurred to either knight to yield, though, for there would be great shame in letting themselves be robbed by these lowborn knaves.

"Give us your money and your rings and fine leather boots and we may spare your lives, young lordlings!"

"Come and get them," André challenged, as he and Rico braced themselves for the onslaught.

It didn't happen. The men were turning, looking off to the right. Risking a quick glance in case this was a trick, Rico saw what had attracted their attention—a glowing light that was moving steadily toward them. Holding a lantern aloft, a man was approaching, as casually as if encountering outlaws in a deserted, dark locale was a commonplace occurrence. "Is this a private game?" he asked. "Or can anyone play?"

The bandits regarded him with a mixture of surprise and scorn. "Oh, you can play, friend." The man who was apparently their leader took a menacing step in the newcomer's direction. "You can start by tossing your money pouch on the ground and then kneeling. If you beg for your life sweetly enough, we might spare it . . . or not. You'll have to wait and see."

His companions laughed, but the stranger continued to advance. He'd made no move to unsheathe his sword, though, and the bandit swaggered toward him, his naked blade leveled at the man's chest. "That is far enough, fool, unless you're truly eager to die."

Rico and André exchanged glances, agreeing that this might be as good a chance as they'd get. Before they could move, though, the lead outlaw lost patience and lunged at the newcomer. Rico had never seen anyone move as fast as the other man did. In one unbroken motion, he thrust the lantern into the bandit's face and stepped in as the outlaw recoiled from the flames. For the length of a breath, the two seemed frozen in an odd embrace, and then the brigand staggered back, sinking to his knees with a guttural cry. It was only then that they saw the bloodied dagger in the stranger's hand.

The stricken man's companions gaped at him as if they could not believe the evidence of their own eyes. They were no strangers to killings, but had never seen one done so swiftly, smoothly, and economically as this, and they hesitated, That brief instant of uncertainty was to prove decisive, for their new foe did not share it. He flung his dagger at the nearest of the men and then drew his sword while it was still in the air. The thrown knife missed its target, but not by much, and the man spun around, fled into the darkness. That was enough for the other outlaws; they, too, took to their heels.

Rico and André had yet to move, transfixed by the ease of the stranger's victory. They were not easily impressed by prowess, for they'd seen Richard on the battlefield, fought at his side as they'd grown to manhood. But as they looked at each other now, the same thought was in both their minds. This man was a master of the art of death. Then he moved within recognition range and they understood.

Mercadier and his band of routiers had been hired by Richard the past autumn, and he'd quickly earned the young duke's favor, for he was as fearless as Richard himself. Not all men were comfortable with him, though, for there was something unsettling about his very presence. He had the dark hair of a son of the south, but his eyes were so light they were almost colorless and utterly opaque, impossible to read. A jagged scar angled from the corner of one eye to his chin, leaving a bare patch of skin where his beard could not grow, and men accustomed to battle disfigurements nonetheless found themselves unwilling to look too long at Mercadier's sinister scar or those odd, pale eyes.

André and Rico felt awkward now that they knew the identity of their benefactor. Nevertheless, they could not deny they were now deeply in his debt, and lucky indeed that he'd happened to be passing by. When Rico said as much, he thought he caught the trace of a smile, but it was hard to tell for sure; the corner of Mercadier's mouth had been twisted awry as that fearsome facial wound had healed.

"I was not just 'passing by,'" he said. "I'd been looking for you both since Compline. You are wanted back at the palace, for the duke has need of you."

"Why? What happened?" André said warily, for neither he nor Rico could envision Mercadier as the bearer of good tidings. "What is wrong?"

"The duke got a message from his father. He has been ordered to surrender Aquitaine at once to its rightful ruler, the Duchess Eleanor, and if he balks, the old king threatens to send her into Poitou with an army, ravaging the land with fire and sword until he yields up the duchy to her."

They stared at him, dumbstruck. André was the first one to recover, lashing out bitterly against Richard's father, declaring that Henry Fitz Empress was truly the spawn of Satan. Rico was loath to say so aloud, for the same blood flowed in their veins, but he found himself in hearty agreement with André's emotional outburst. The old king was too clever by half, for how could Richard take up arms against his mother?

"How . . . how did the duke react?" he asked, and Mercadier's shoulders twitched in a half shrug.

"His face flamed, then he went white as chalk, and withdrew to his own chamber. It was his seneschal who sent me to find you, saying 'Go fetch his cousins,' hoping you two might be able to help. How, I do not know," Mercadier said candidly.

Rico and André did not know either. But they had to try, and when Mercadier turned to go, they were about to follow when a groan drew their attention back to the wounded bandit. Blood was soaking his tunic, and Rico flinched when he realized that it was coming from the man's groin. Sweet Jesus, no wonder the poor sod shrieked like a gutted weasel. "What about him?"

Mercadier glanced back over his shoulder. "Leave him. If he's lucky, his friends might come back for him. If not, there are plenty of stray dogs roaming the town, on the lookout for a meal."

That was not an image the young knights cared to dwell upon for long, and they hastened to catch up with Mercadier, leaving the outlaw sprawled in the ancient arena where so many others had fought and died.

THERE WERE ONLY A FEW TIMES when Eleanor's anger with Henry had burned so hotly that it had been indistinguishable from hatred. There was the afternoon she'd stood in the great hall at Limoges Castle and watched as the Count of Toulouse did homage to Hal. There were days of despairing rage in the early months of her captivity and the Michaelmas eve when he'd demanded that Richard yield Aquitaine to John. But this latest clash of wills was different. Nothing he'd ever done was as demeaning and unfair as this—using her as a weapon against her own son. Never had she felt as helpless as she had on that night at Bayeux, listening in stunned silence as he told her what he meant to do, utterly oblivious to the damage that might be done to her relationship with Richard. No, she could forgive him for making her his prisoner, but never his pawn.

Once she'd calmed down, though, she could see that there actually might be some benefits to his scheme. This was proof that he'd abandoned any hope of replacing Richard with John, for he knew she'd never agree to disinherit Richard. Richard would still be the heir to the duchy. Moreover, the transfer of authority would not be as hollow as Henry undoubtedly hoped. She had no illusions, knew he'd never trust her with real power. But the acknowledgment of her suzerainty was significant in and of itself. By recognizing her legal rights, he was bringing her from the shadows back into the light, restoring her identity in the eyes of the world. He'd not find it so easy to make her disappear again. And after eleven years of invisibility, she was eager for any taste of freedom, however circumscribed it might be.

The Duchess of Aquitaine had resources that a disgraced wife did not. She would be better able to protect herself, for she was a vassal of the French king. Most important of all, she'd be able to protect Richard's inheritance. As long as she drew breath, his succession was assured. And since she was sure her husband had considered that, too, she could only conclude it did not matter to him, further proof that he now knew he'd never coax or bully Richard into submission. It was enough for him to have the semblance of victory, to appear to have prevailed over his rebellious son. And if this man seemed utterly unlike the one she'd married, there was no surprise in that realization and only a little regret.

Her greatest fear was that Richard would not understand, that he'd be too outraged to see this Devil's deal was not such a one-sided bargain after all. What if he defied his father? If it came to war? If he blamed her, too, if he saw her as Harry's accomplice? In the days that followed, she told herself repeatedly that she was being foolish, that Richard knew she'd never put her own interests above his. But the truth was that she could not be sure. She'd been separated from her sons for so long, just as they came to manhood. She loved Richard dearly. But how well did she really know him?

ALTHOUGH IT WOULD HAVE GIVEN ELEANOR little consolation, Henry shared her unease as they awaited Richard's response. He thought he'd come up with a face-saving solution to an increasingly dangerous problem. He could not allow Richard to defy him so openly; no king could. By offering Richard a way to back down while still salvaging his pride, Henry hoped to resolve the impasse and restore peace to his family and realm. But he'd been bluffing, for he never had any intention of sending an army into Aquitaine. As a father, he found that prospect abhorrent, and as a king, sheer lunacy. So as time passed without word from Richard, he found himself confronting an unpleasant truth. Bluffing was an invaluable part of a ruler's arsenal, an integral aspect of statecraft, with one great flaw. If the bluff failed, what then?

RICHARD GAVE NO ADVANCE WARNING, arrived in Rouen with a large retinue of knights and clerics. He shared his brother Hal's sense of drama, and as he rode through the streets of the Norman city, people turned out in large numbers to watch, enjoying the visual spectacle that royalty was expected to provide; it was a source of disappointment to many that their duke had so little taste for pageantry and pomp. As they cheered his son—so handsome and splendidly attired, mounted on a magnificent white stallion—they agreed that Duke Richard was a worthy successor to his brother of blessed memory, the young king laid to rest in their great cathedral.

In addition to Richard's own imposing entourage, the king's court was filled to capacity with highborn visitors and vassals, so hundreds of avid eyes were upon him as he strode into the castle's great hall and approached his parents upon the dais. "My lord king," he said with flawless formality, kneeling gracefully before Henry, his respectful demeanor that of subject to sovereign. Having greeted his father, he turned then to acknowledge his mother, bending over her hand with a courtly flourish. "Madame, it is my privilege to return the governance of Aquitaine to your capable hands."

The curious spectators realized with disappointment that courtesy could be used as effectively as any shield of wood and leather, for none could tell what thoughts lay behind those inscrutable blue-grey eyes, not even the two people who'd given him life.

THE TABLE THAT EVENING was laden with venison from Henry's latest hunt, but Eleanor had no appetite and merely toyed with her food. Afterward she found no opportunity to speak privately with her son and retired to her own chamber in a foul mood. She was too tense to sleep and was still up and dressed several hours later when a knock sounded at the door. She nodded for Amaria to open it, assuming it would be Henry coming to discuss their son's submission. But it was Richard.

"Did your father's spies see you come here?"

He shrugged. "It hardly matters now, does it?" he said and reached out, enfolding her in a heartfelt hug. Eleanor's eyes misted and she blinked rapidly, not wanting him to see. Amaria had retreated to a far corner of the chamber and picked up some sewing, doing what she could to make herself as unobtrusive as possible. But she needn't have worried, for they'd already forgotten her presence.

"I was concerned," Eleanor admitted, "that you might be angry with me, too, thinking that I'd benefited at your expense."

Richard's surprise was obvious. "Why, Maman? You were given no more choice in this than I was."

"No, I was not. But I knew how difficult this would be for you and—"

"And you were probably scared to death that I was going to act like a damned fool and doom us all," he said with a fleeting smile. "I cannot say I was not tempted, but . . . well, here I am."

"And thank God for it," she said fervently. "Come sit down, Richard. We have much to talk about." Once they were seated, she reached over and laid her hand on his. "I know this is not what you want to do, but at least now you need not fear losing Aquitaine. By coming up with this scheme, your father is conceding defeat, admitting that he could not compel you to abdicate."

Richard tilted his head, looking at her in bemusement. Did she truly think he needed to have this pointed out? He almost reminded her that he was not the fool his brother had been. He did not, though, for even if he did not understand her grieving for Hal, he did respect it. "To give the Devil his due," he said, "Papa did come up with the only way to pry me loose from Aquitaine. He knew I would never deny your claim to the duchy."

He paused. "But this time he has been too clever for his own good, Maman. The old fox has finally outfoxed himself. He will have to grant you more liberty now, can no longer keep you sequestered in some remote stronghold out of sight and mind. I'll not deny that it is not easy for me, either to turn over the governance of the duchy or to let the world think he has won. But it will be a comfort to know that you are restored to your rightful place. And he is in for a rude surprise if he thinks he is going to get another tamed dog for his kennel. I will never follow in Hal's footsteps, never."

"I know," she said. "An argument can be made that Hal choked to death because he was kept on such a tight chain. But not only are you a very different man than your brother, your circumstances are different, too." She leaned forward, eager to explain why he need not fear Hal's fate, but he gave her no chance.

"I am looking forward to seeing his face when I tell him what I intend to do. He thinks I shall be dancing attendance upon him as Hal did. But if I am not to govern Aquitaine, then I am free to follow my heart. I am going to take the cross and do what Papa would not, answer Patriarch Heraclius's plea and lead my men to fight for the defense of the Holy Land."

Richard grinned, very pleased with himself for having found a way to honor his mother, thwart his father, and serve God, while having a grand adventure at the same time. Eleanor did not return his smile, though. She was regarding him gravely. "I fear that would be a great mistake, Richard."

"Why? What could be more important than securing the Kingdom of Jerusalem?"

"Securing the Kingdom of England. I know you want Aquitaine. But you want the crown, too, do you not?"

"Of course I do. It is my birthright now that Hal is dead. Why would taking the cross put it at risk?"

"Because your father will not want you to take the cross, no more than he wanted John to do so. He will forbid you to do it and will be outraged and distraught if you defy him in this. You will be giving him an entirely new grievance. He might even be dismayed enough to reconsider the succession, especially if you are not here to defend yourself."

Richard was frowning. "I know he has been favoring Geoffrey shamelessly of late, his way of reminding me that I am not an only child and nothing is writ in stone. I just took it as one of his usual threats, nothing more than that. You truly think . . . ?"

"I did not at first. Now . . . now I am not so sure. Geoffrey's governance of Normandy was cut short by your raids into Brittany, but Harry was pleased with the way he dealt with the Norman barons and clerics and he is equally pleased with the news coming out of Brittany."

"Why? What is Geoffrey up to now?"

"He and Constance just presided over an assize in Rennes, summoning the Breton lords to discuss the laws of inheritance in the duchy. They have made a compact in which all agree to pass their lands on to their eldest sons. Harry was quite impressed by reports of this assize, saying Geoffrey has shown considerable political skill in winning over perpetual rebels like Raoul de Fougères. They no longer view him as Constance's alien husband, the Angevin intruder forced upon them by their enemy, the English king. He's succeeded in earning their respect and their trust, no small feat considering the contentious nature of the Bretons. And I regret to say that your father has compared Geoffrey's assize to your own attempts to introduce the law of primogeniture, which resulted in a rebellion by the lords of Angoulême—"

"That is not fair! Primogeniture was already the custom in Brittany, so Geoffrey had an easier road to travel than I did."

"Be that as it may, your father likes what he has seen of your brother's rule in Brittany and he is troubled by the constant turmoil and antagonism between you and your vassals."

"I still say he gave Geoffrey power in Normandy to punish me, knowing how little I'd like it. You know how he is, Maman. Nothing is ever straightforward with him; the man has more coils than any serpent."

"And is he giving Geoffrey the county of Nantes just to vex you, too?"

Richard's eyes narrowed. "Geoffrey is getting Nantes?" When she nodded, he lapsed into silence for some moments. Eleanor was content to wait, wanting him to draw his own conclusions. "Would he truly do that?" he asked at last. "Would he dare to disregard the laws of primogeniture and pass over me in favor of my younger brother?"

"Would he dare? Oh, yes. Would he actually do it? That I do not know," she conceded, "but you ignore the possibility at your peril." Her hand closed on his again. "The crown is yours by right now that Hal is dead. But only you can decide if the price is too high, Richard. You will still have Aquitaine, come what may. If you can be content with that, then take the cross and leave for the Holy Land. But if you want to be king, then it would be wiser to remain here and fight for it."

He rose abruptly and began to pace. "I do want the crown. But I do not know if I could endure the humiliating apprenticeship Papa put Hal through. If he expects me to be at his beck and call like a pet spaniel . . ." He shook his head, turning back to face her. "I cannot do that, Maman."

"I do not think you will have to, dearest. Hal, may God assoil him, had no lands of his own, but you will still have Aquitaine. All will know this 'restoration' changes nothing in truth. You are still the heir to the duchy, and men will continue to come to you with petitions and appeals. In fact," she said, with a wry smile, "the poor souls wanting to have rights recognized will likely need to get charters from all three of us—you, me, and Harry—to make sure there are no ambiguities or uncertainties. And when rebellion breaks out again in Aquitaine, Harry will have to rely upon you to restore order in the duchy. He no longer has the boundless energy that he once had, for his youth is long gone and his health is not as robust as it used to be. You'll be the one he turns to for support—unless you are away in the Holy Land."

"And then it would be Geoffrey." He said no more after that, soon excused himself without telling her what he meant to do. There was no need, for she already knew.

It WAS A GOOD SUMMER FOR HENRY, for his domains were at peace and there was finally harmony at home, too. Richard treated him with deference, giving him no further reason for complaint. Now that he'd reconciled with his son, his anger with Eleanor soon cooled and he found himself enjoying her pleasure in her new status. She'd had her own household for a few years now, but she wasted no time in bringing her trusted clerk Jordan back into her service, and she bestowed lavish gifts upon favorite abbeys like Fontevrault, upon Tilda and Richenza, the loyal Amaria, her daughters in Castile and Sicily, and her new grandchild; Constance had given birth to another girl on the nativity of St John the Baptist, christened Matilda in honor of Geoffrey's sister and his formidable grandmother, the empress.

Henry shared Eleanor's joy in the birth of their granddaughter; the news helped him through a difficult time—the second anniversary of Hal's death. So, too, did the safe return of William Marshal from his pilgrimage to the Holy Land. Henry found he took surprising comfort in Will's presence. He knew Will was a man of honor, a valuable addition to the royal household, but what mattered more to him was Will's link to his son. For the first time in a long while, he could look upon his family with contentment. John was finally established in his own lands, and the new Pope had given permission to have him crowned as King of Ireland. Tilda and Heinrich were making ready to return to Saxony, grateful that he'd been able to end their exile. Richenza would soon be Scotland's queen. All in all, Henry thought the future looked brighter than it had in years.

But with the coming of autumn, these prospects dimmed. The Pope refused to grant the dispensation for Richenza's marriage to the Scots king, much to the girl's disappointment. Tilda and Heinrich had already departed, and Henry was glad that Eleanor was there to comfort Richenza, for he'd never been good at drying female tears. Then Henry fell seriously ill, and for more than a month, he found himself confined to Belvoir Castle, too weak to attend the truce conference he'd just brokered between the French king and the Count of Flanders.

Worst of all, the reports from Ireland were uniformly dismal. John's first taste of independence and authority had proven to be an unmitigated disaster. His companions, many of them younger sons, too, offended the Irish chieftains by mocking their dress, their customs, even their long beards. Instead of curbing such bad behavior, John had encouraged it. Having his own funds at long last, he'd spent money recklessly, squandering it on wine, entertainment, gambling, and frivolous whims. When he could no longer pay his routiers, they resorted to plunder and eventually deserted to the Irish. In just nine months John had managed to greatly diminish the long-standing hostility between the native Irish and the Anglo-Norman settlers, uniting them in their outrage with his inept rule. Very disappointed in his favorite son's first foray into manhood, Henry had finally been forced to recall him.

Henry passed a relatively quiet Christmas at Domfront, with only Richard, Eleanor, and Richenza, for John had just gotten back to England and Geoffrey and Constance remained in Brittany.

THAT SPRING Henry met the French king at Gisors, where they confirmed the settlement of 1183, again agreeing that Alys was to have the Vexin as her dowry and this time specifying that the son she was to wed would be Richard, which Philippe took to be an acknowledgment of Richard's status as Henry's heir. Richard took it that way, too, and was even more encouraged when Henry agreed to stake him in a campaign against the Count of Toulouse, who'd taken advantage of the Angevin family troubles to seize Cahors and Quercy. Now that he was no longer feuding with his father, Richard was determined to get them back and he was delighted to find that Henry was willing to finance the expedition.

Henry and Eleanor celebrated Easter at Rouen, and Henry invited Geoffrey and Constance to join them, for he was planning to return to England and wanted to see his granddaughters before he left. He and Eleanor were to be disappointed, though. Geoffrey came to Rouen, but he came alone, explaining that Constance felt their daughters were too young to make such a long journey. And Henry soon realized that Geoffrey was not there by choice. He behaved as a dutiful son, but a very distant one, and Henry was baffled by his aloof demeanor. He'd last seen Geoffrey that past summer, when he'd come to tell his parents of the birth of his daughter, and he'd seemed very pleased when Henry then turned Nantes over to him. So this change was as puzzling to Henry as it was unexpected.

He was disquieted enough to discuss it with Eleanor, who vexed him with her pithy response: "If you want to know what is troubling Geoffrey, you ought to be asking him." But somewhat to his own surprise, he eventually did. Putting aside his natural inclination for the oblique approach, he summoned Geoffrey to a private meeting in his bedchamber and asked his son bluntly what was wrong.

✦

HENRY HAD ALWAYS LAMENTED Hal's transparency, feeling that a king should not reveal his emotions as obviously as Hal invariably did. He was no better pleased, though, with Richard and Geoffrey's ability to guard their thoughts. Now he could only watch Geoffrey in frustration as his son said nothing was wrong, his face utterly unreadable.

"I do not believe you," he said at last, and Geoffrey shrugged.

"I do not know what you want me to say, Papa."

"I want you to give me a truthful answer." Crossing the chamber, he stopped in front of the younger man. "I would not be asking if I did not want to know, Geoffrey." And when his son continued to regard him blankly, he found it easier to express his concern in anger. "Why is it that none of you can be honest with me? Is that so much to ask?"

That seemed to strike a spark, to judge by the way Geoffrey's eyes began to glitter. "If you truly want an answer to that question, I would suggest you consult Scriptures."

"And what is that supposed to mean?"

"*Whatsoever a man soweth, that shall he also reap.* I am sorry I cannot cite the exact verse, but I daresay you've heard it before."

"You are hardly in a position to cast stones, Geoffrey. Do you think I've forgotten how frequently and convincingly you and Hal lied to me during the siege at Limoges? But when have I ever lied to you?"

"Lies are not always expressed in words, Papa. And in this past year, you have done nothing but lie to me!"

"I do not know what you are talking about!"

"I am talking about all you've done to convince me—to convince Richard and much of Christendom—that you might pass over him and make me your heir. I see now that it was just a ruse, a means of bringing Richard back into the fold. And of course you never gave a thought about how I'd feel. Why should I mind being used as bait to lure Richard home, after all?"

Henry was shaking his head vehemently. "That is not so. I never sought to mislead you, Geoffrey. Nor did I ever promise to choose you over your brother. I am indeed sorry if you took it that way—"

"But not sorry that Richard did, I daresay. You knew the only way to rein him in was to make him think the crown was in jeopardy. And as your schemes usually do, it worked. My congratulations."

Henry felt as if he were seeing a stranger, for Geoffrey had always been the controlled one, the son who never erupted into reckless fits of fury like his brothers. It was this realization that tempered his own anger. He ran his hand through his hair, impatiently pushed it back from his forehead as he tried to decide how best to handle this. Why was fatherhood so damnably hard? He was sure he'd never given his father the grief that his sons were constantly giving him.

"Geoffrey . . . listen, lad. I will not deny that I did think about it, that I considered whether you'd make a better king than Richard. Nor will I deny that I've occasionally wished you were the older brother. I've always understood you better than I did Richard. As I once told you, you are the son who most reminds me of my own father. If circumstances were different . . . but they are not. It would set a dangerous precedent to ignore the laws of inheritance, and Richard would never accept it. Many men would think he had the right of it, too, and you'd have no peace, not as long as he lived."

"I see. So you were actually looking out for my own good. How kind of you, Papa."

"I am sorry, Geoffrey, I truly am. And I do understand your disappointment. But this I swear to you, that I did not mean to deceive you or to raise false hopes. Had I only known . . ."

Geoffrey half-turned away, and Henry gave him the time he needed to master his emotions. When he swung around again, he did seem more composed, but his breathing was still swift and shallow, as if he'd been running a long and exhausting race. "You said I'd 'have no peace' if you'd passed over Richard. But what peace will I have once he is king? You think he'll not seek revenge as soon as you are safely gone to God?"

"That is why I intend to do all I can whilst I still live to bring about a genuine and lasting reconciliation between you and your brother."

The corner of Geoffrey's mouth twitched. "And since Richard is celebrated for his forgiving nature, how can you fail?" He made an indecisive movement and Henry feared he was about to go. But instead he reached out and grasped his father's arm. "We both know that not even God's own angels could make Richard and me anything but enemies. He is to be king. So be it, then. You said you were sorry that I'd 'misread' your intentions. You can prove it by giving me the means to defend my duchy."

"What do you need? Money?"

"I want Anjou." Geoffrey's grip tightened. "It makes sense, Papa, politically and geographically. I am more Angevin than Richard could ever hope to be, for he is Maman's son, not yours. He cares only for Aquitaine and for the crown. Anjou would never mean as much to him as it would to me. And if I held it, he'd be far less likely to declare war upon Brittany. You know that is so. Give me that much, Papa, give me Anjou so that I can honor your heritage and protect my family and my lands."

Henry was moved by Geoffrey's eloquence, and by his urgency. He wanted to say yes, to give his son what he wanted so desperately. He'd gladly have given Geoffrey Aquitaine if it were his to give. Anjou was dearest to his heart of all his domains, the land of his birth. He did not doubt that it would be in good hands if Geoffrey held it; he'd proven in Brittany that he could rule and rule well. But how could he rend his empire like that? Anjou and Normandy and England were his legacy, meant to be passed intact to his eldest son. Could he give up the dream that had sustained him through even the worst of times, the dream of establishing a dynasty that would endure long after he and all who'd known him were dust?

"I can see how much this means to you, Geoffrey. I cannot promise you that Anjou will be yours. But I can promise you this—that I will give it very serious consideration."

Geoffrey was silent for several long moments. "Yes," he said and smiled tightly. "I am sure you will."

CONSTANCE ADMITTED A SERVANT and instructed him to place the tray on a coffer. Following him to the door, she slid the bolt into place and then hurried over to her husband. Geoffrey was leaning back in his chair, his eyes half closed, his body as limp as if his bones were made of liquid. He looked utterly exhausted and she was not surprised, not after he'd told her he'd left Rouen just four days ago. That meant he and his men had covered more than forty miles a day, which sounded to her more like an escape than a departure.

"Denez has brought food and wine," she said. "Whilst you're eating, they'll heat water for a bath."

"Is that your subtle way of telling me that I reek?" he asked, opening his eyes long enough to give her a quick smile. But when she offered a wine cup, he shook his head. "I have not eaten all day, would be roaring drunk after three swallows." She reached for the plate of meat and bread, and he shook his head again. "Later . . . I'm not hungry."

She didn't insist, for she was scornful of women who hovered over their husbands as if they could not be trusted to take care of themselves. Geoffrey was a man grown, knew if he was hungry or not. Fetching a chair, she dragged it over and sat down beside him. "Do you want to talk about it? Or wait till the morrow?"

"You'd let me do that?"

"Of course," she said, and would have risen had he not caught her wrist. She sat down again and watched him as he seemed to doze. But then his lashes flickered and he turned his head to look directly at her.

"It is done, Constance." She waited and after another long silence, he said, "He wanted to know what was wrong. Can you believe that? When I told him, he seemed truly taken aback and swore that he'd never meant to mislead me, to make me think that I might be king."

"Did you believe him?"

"Does it matter?" He laughed, a sound that was not pleasant to hear. "He lies to everyone, even to himself. Especially to himself." He smothered a yawn, saying, "I'll have that wine, after all. I asked him for Anjou."

"What did he say?"

"What does he ever say? He fell back upon his usual stratagem—delay and evasion, promising to give it 'serious consideration.' He does not seem to realize that by now we understand the code and I know damned well that he turned me down."

After it had become obvious to them that their hopes of a crown were illusory, they'd had several sobering conversations about their future once Richard was king. Constance wanted to discuss their options now, but she held back, for she was not taken in by his bitter bravado, and she realized that his hurt went far deeper than he'd ever admit.

"I cannot believe that I let him play me for such a fool, Constance. I should have known better, should have known . . ." He drank slowly, and then startled her by flinging his cup against the wall.

Watching the wine stain the whitewash, looking eerily like blood to her, Constance said, "It may not be as hopeless as you think. How long ere your father and Richard start quarreling again? Who is to say that he will not turn to you, this time for true? In his way, he does love you, after all—"

"Indeed," he said, cracking the word like a lash. "Of course Hal comes first and then Johnny, but after that, yes, he finds space in his heart for me."

"Hal is dead and Johnny has just made a bloody botch of his Irish command," she pointed out. He surprised her then by coming to his younger brother's defense, saying that his father was as much to blame as Johnny, that he'd thrown the lad into deep water without first teaching him to swim.

"Mayhap it is better not to be loved by my father," he said after a time, "for it can be argued that Richard and I fared better than poor Hal and Johnny. He set us loose at eighteen and seventeen, sent us into Aquitaine and Brittany to learn how to fight, how to govern. He kept Hal and Johnny close, not giving them the chance to stand on their own. As God is my witness, Constance, I will never do that to my sons, never."

"I know you will not," she said, moving behind him and beginning to massage his shoulders; as she expected, his muscles were rigid, taut with tension. "Come to bed, Geoffrey, get some sleep. Our troubles will still be there on the morrow."

He did not seem to hear her. "I am glad he forced that talk, for now I see much more clearly. I'll play no more of his accursed games, leave that to Richard and Johnny, and good luck to them both. What I am going to do is to safeguard our future and our duchy. I'll need a few days to rest up . . . and then I think it is time you and I pay a visit to the French court."

This had always seemed like the obvious move to Constance. The French king had a keen interest in Brittany, an even keener interest in clipping Angevin wings, and Philippe was already showing signs of a ruthless will to rival Henry's. Philippe would make a useful ally, if not an entirely trustworthy one, but she felt confident that her husband was more than his match. She'd never urged Geoffrey to reach out to Philippe, even though she'd long thought it made political sense, for she understood that there'd be no going back. For Geoffrey, it would be a repudiation of his own blood and she'd not thought she had the right to ask that of him. She moved around the chair now so that she could see his face.

"Are you sure, Geoffrey? They are still your family and—"

"No," he said, "not anymore. You are my family, you and our children." His eyes sought hers. "So . . . what do you say?"

She leaned over, brushing her lips against his forehead and then cradling his head against her breasts. "Well, I have always wanted to see Paris."

CHAPTER FORTY-EIGHT

✦

February 1186
Paris, France

ONSTANCE WAS NOT IMPRESSED by the entertainment provided by the French king, although in fairness, she supposed she was spoiled. Geoffrey was an enthusiastic and generous patron of the troubadours of his mother's duchy, and as a result, he'd never had trouble attracting renowned performers to the Breton court. When she said as much to her husband, Geoffrey murmured, "Well, you get what you pay for," reminding her that Philippe had so far shown little interest in music or literature, forcing men of talent to look to others for support, to Henry and his sons, the Count of Flanders, or Marie, the Countess of Champagne, who'd been acting as regent since her husband's death five years ago.

Constance was willing to concede that Philippe's dinner in their honor was a culinary triumph; clearly the French monarch was more generous with his cooks than with his musicians. So far she'd not seen enough of Philippe to form any impressions of him, but that seemed about to change when they were summoned to join the French king and his queen upon the dais after the trestle tables had been cleared away and dancing begun. Isabelle was a pretty, slender blonde, who looked younger and acted older than her sixteen years. She was obviously attuned to her husband's wishes, for when Philippe asked Constance jovially if he could "borrow" her husband for a short while, Isabelle immediately chimed in with compliments about Constance's gown, saying that she would like to discuss the countess's seamstress with her.

Constance was not taken in by the flattery. How dare Philippe dismiss her as if she were an errant child? Had he forgotten that Brittany was hers? But as her eyes met Geoffrey's, he winked and she reconciled herself to playing the role Philippe cast for her, the dutiful, unobtrusive spouse. "Of course you may, my liege," she said, and then smiled sweetly. "As much as it grieves me to be deprived of your company, I know my husband will relate to me all that I miss. You see, we share everything."

As Isabelle did her part and drew Constance aside, Philippe said to Geoffrey with a bemused smile, "Your wife is rather spirited."

"Yes, she is," Geoffrey agreed with a grin. "I'm a lucky man." Philippe thought that was open to debate, but it would hardly be politic to insult the wife of a man whose good will he wanted. When he proposed now that they schedule a private meeting on the morrow, Geoffrey suggested instead that they take a stroll in the gardens. Such spontaneity was not Philippe's modus operandi, but he could see no reason not to go along with it and sent a servant for their mantles, then signaled to his bodyguards as the two men left the hall.

Geoffrey was quick to notice the men trailing at a discreet distance, for their presence seemed to confirm the tales he'd heard about Philippe's nervous disposition. He could not imagine that being said of any member of his family—male or female—and hoped the young French king's circumspection did not bode ill for his hopes of an alliance. In Geoffrey's view, statecraft and kingship were not for the faint of heart.

They walked in companionable silence through the gardens, dormant now in winter's grip. Daylight was a limited commodity in February and dusk was not far off. The Seine had not yet been closed to traffic for the night, and they could see boats bobbing past, their lanterns swaying in the wind, brief glimmers of light against the dimming sky and icy, dark river. When they reached the end of the island, Philippe sat down upon a wooden bench, but Geoffrey chose to perch on the garden wall, a position that seemed precarious enough to make Philippe uncomfortable.

"Do you mind sitting down here?" he said. "I'd have a difficult time explaining to the English king that his son drowned when he tumbled into the Seine." Although Geoffrey hid it well, Philippe suspected that the other man was humoring him when he obligingly switched seats. Philippe did not care, though; he never worried what others thought of him. "This is my first opportunity," he said, "to express my sorrow over the death of your brother, the young king. Hal's unexpected death was a great loss to us all."

"Yes," Geoffrey said, "indeed it was. It must have been a particularly sharp blow to .you, my liege."

Philippe thought that was an odd thing to say, for Hal had been merely a brother-in-law and they'd never been close. He made no comment, though, and when Geoffrey saw he was not going to respond, he said, "After all, Hal would have been the perfect king—for France." He saw Philippe's eyes flicker, and he bit back a smile as he continued blandly, "My brother had many admirable virtues. He never lacked for courage and he was remarkably good-natured and so generous that he'd literally give a man the shirt off his back. He was also one of the most malleable men I've ever known, easily led and easily bored. Given his lack of interest in the drudgery of governing, I am sure he'd have been grateful for any guidance offered by the French Crown. When you heard of his death at Martel and realized you'd now have to deal with Richard, you must have felt as if your affectionate, docile dog had been transformed by evil alchemy into a feral, ravening wolf."

"That is hardly a brotherly description of Richard." Philippe was rarely surprised by other men, and he regarded Geoffrey with suddenly sharpened interest. "So we are speaking candidly, are we?"

"Under the right circumstances, it can save a great deal of time."

Philippe glanced across the garden to reassure himself that his bodyguards were not within earshot. "Fair enough. Let me begin by saying that I've been expecting you. I've watched the brazen way your father used you to put the fear of God into Richard, and I knew it was only a matter of time until you turned your eyes in my direction."

"Yes," Geoffrey said dryly, "my brothers and I seem to look to Paris the way infidels look to Mecca. I am not Hal. I am not a king and I am neither malleable nor overly trusting. But that does not mean we could not forge an alliance that would be to our mutual benefit."

"Just what are you seeking?"

"Security." Geoffrey leaned closer, lowering his voice to evoke an intimacy more conducive to sharing secrets. "My father's health is beginning to fail."

Philippe nodded; he'd paid a sickbed visit to Henry that past November at Belvoir Castle. "Well, he is old," he said, from the comfortable vantage point of his twenty years, "so it is only to be expected."

"If you know a storm is coming, you do not wait until the wind is raging against your house ere you take protective measures. I want to be ready when that storm breaks over Brittany."

Philippe nodded again. "And what would make Brittany safe from the storm? Anjou? Mayhap even Normandy?"

Geoffrey was pleased that Philippe was so quick. "Anjou," he confirmed, "and an alliance that I can rely upon once Richard becomes king."

"It would certainly be in France's interests to have more reasonable leadership in .

Anjou or Normandy. I've long thought that the Bretons are natural allies of the French, not the English. Your father's meddling in Brittany was a shameless encroachment upon the suzerainty of the French Crown. I will not deny I find it offensive that you've done homage for your duchy to the Duke of Normandy and the King of England, but never to your rightful liege lord."

"Fortunately," Geoffrey said, "that can be remedied easily enough."

Now that they'd come to it, Philippe drew a deep breath to dampen down his rising excitement. "So you would be willing to do homage to me."

"I would."

"Well, then, I do not see why we cannot come to an understanding advantageous to us both. For example, I think it would be only fitting to name you, my lord duke, as the Seneschal of France."

As that office traditionally belonged to the Count of Anjou, Philippe could not have made Geoffrey a more welcome offer. He studied the French king intently and then startled Philippe by laughing. "I feel," he admitted, "as if I'd ventured into a foreign land, expecting to have difficulty making myself understood. Imagine my surprise to discover that we speak the same language."

Philippe thought that Geoffrey's reputation for eloquence was well deserved, for he'd just articulated perfectly what the French king was also feeling—that he'd finally found the ally of his dreams, one who shared his insight, shrewdness, and sangfroid. Philippe had long known that he was more intelligent than most of those around him, and while the knowledge was undeniably satisfying, it was occasionally lonely, too. For the first time in his young life, he was discovering the pleasure of finding a kindred spirit, and he joined in Geoffrey's laughter, laughter that sounded surprisingly carefree and gleeful to his bored bodyguards, not like Philippe's usual, guarded chuckle at all.

MORGAN FITZ RANULF could hardly believe he was at Lagny, site of some of the most famous tournaments of recent decades. When Geoffrey returned to the French court that August, Morgan had not expected such a marvelous surprise as Lagny. Tournaments were not frequently held in August, for even the most enthusiastic devotees of the tourney preferred not to have hundreds of men trampling through their fields and vineyards during the harvest season. But upon their arrival in Paris, Geoffrey and his men discovered that Philippe was absent from his capital, not likely to return from Senlis for another week. They also learned that a tournament was to be held that coming Monday at Lagny, just twenty miles from Paris, and suddenly Geoffrey no longer minded the wait, for while he'd never been as enamored of the sport as Hal, he enjoyed testing himself against men of equal skill. For Morgan, the Lagny tournament had even greater significance; he'd been knighted by Geoffrey in the past year and this would be his first chance to compete in one.

Morgan had just helped his squire to roll a wooden barrel up a slight incline, and was watching as Josse then rolled it back down, taking care not to let it get away from him. "You need to be quicker, lad, for it almost ran over your foot!" he joked, and then noticed that he had company. A small boy about six or seven was at his side, watching, too.

"What is he doing?"

"He is cleaning my hauberk. The best way to remove rust and dirt from mail is to shake it in a barrel of sand."

The boy's eyes fastened upon Morgan with flattering attention. "Are you going to fight in the tournament, Sir Knight?"

"I am." Because he believed the best knights were not braggarts, Morgan added frankly, "It will be my first. But that works to my advantage since I can take part in the jousting, which is reserved for newly made knights, and then fight in the mêlée, too."

Encouraged by Morgan's affability, the boy edged closer. "This will be my first tournament, too," he confided. "My mama thought I was too young in the past. But my brother is taking part in this one, and he spoke up for me. We'll be over there," he said, pointing across the field toward the wooden stands. "Will we be able to see everything?"

"Well, you'll be able to see the Vespers jousting tonight for those too eager to wait, and on the morrow you'll get to watch me joust, lucky lad," Morgan said, with a grin that the boy returned. "And you'll have a good view of the charge that will begin the mêlée. Both teams will try to stay together as long as possible, for that is the best strategy. But they'll eventually split up into smaller groups, and the fighting can range over several miles. This field will stretch between Lagny and the town of Torcy, and ere the day is done, you'll have knights laying ambushes in the woods and taking refuge in barns and chasing one another right into villages."

Seeing the look of disappointment on the child's face, Morgan said reassuringly, "You'll still get to see all the jousting and the lance charge and the start of the mêlée, and afterward, when the prize is awarded to the knight who was the most valiant, you'll be able to watch that, too. I've been told it is a fine Greenland falcon."

"My brother will win it. But I hope you do well, too."

"Thank you," Morgan said gravely, and when the boy continued to interrogate him, he answered readily enough, for he genuinely liked children and looked forward to the day when he'd have sons of his own. "The main rule is that there are no rules. Well, mayhap a few. You see that staked enclosure off to your right? That is the recet for our team; the one for our opponents is located near Torcy, since that is their base. If a knight is hard-pressed, he can take refuge in his recet, and there'll be men-at-arms to guard it and make sure the other side stays out. When a knight breaks his lance during the charge, he can ride over and get another one from his squires. But once the mêlée begins, lances are of no use in such close quarters and men rely upon swords and maces."

"How can you tell friend from foe?" the boy blurted out and then flushed. "That is a foolish question . . ."

"No, it is a very good one. Each lord will have his own banner and his knights will have his coat of arms emblazoned on their shields. And we all have our own battle cries, too. The French shout 'Montjoie' and the English cry 'Dex aie,' which means 'God our help.' The young king always used that one. My lord's men will be yelling 'Saint Malo,' a favorite Breton saint."

"You saw the young king fight?" the boy asked in awe. "My brother says he was a sight to behold."

Morgan thought that Geoffrey was as adept at arms as Hal, but it seemed mean-spirited to deny a dead man his due, and so he said, "Indeed he was, lad. One of his most celebrated fights was right here at Lagny. He'd become separated from his men, which is highly dangerous for a great lord. His foes swarmed him, eager for a king's ransom, and he was so hard pressed that his helmet was torn from his head. Fortunately his best knight, Will Marshal, was close by and he and another of the king's men rode to his rescue."

The child's eyes were as round as coins. "Do men die in tournaments?"

"Of course. Their weapons are not blunted and—" Morgan caught himself, remembering that the boy had a brother fighting on the morrow. "But any deaths would be by pure chance," he said hastily, "for that is not the goal. The idea is to capture your foe and his horse, hold him for a goodly ransom."

"Lord Thibault!" A plump, pink-cheeked woman was hastening toward them. "I have been looking everywhere for you!" Arms akimbo, she frowned down at the child, who scowled back, unrepentant.

Morgan gallantly came to Thibault's defense. "It is my fault, too, Dame," he said, with his most charming smile. "We were talking about the tournament and lost track of time." He kissed her hand then with a flourish. "I am Sir Morgan Fitz Ranulf, one of the mesnie of the Duke of Brittany."

Thibault's nurse was thawing quickly, soothed by the mention of Geoffrey's name. It had an immediate affect upon Thibault, too. "He is my uncle!" he exclaimed, looking up at Morgan with a pleased grin.

Morgan had known Thibault was from the upper classes; his clothing and speech and even his self-confidence all proclaimed him one of fortune's favorites. He'd not expected the boy to be quite so highly placed, though. If he was Geoffrey's nephew, he must be one of the sons of Geoffrey's half sister, Marie. That made perfect sense, for Lagny was on the border of Champagne. "Then your brother is Henri, Count of Champagne!"

Thibault nodded proudly but then bridled when his nurse sought to lead him away. Morgan again played the good knight and offered to escort them to Thibault's mother. That not only satisfied them both, but it would give Morgan a welcome chance to meet one of Christendom's great beauties, for all of Eleanor of Aquitaine's daughters were as physically blessed as she had been.

THIBAULT'S MOTHER was at that moment standing in the top tier of the spectator stands, checking out the view and bedeviling Geoffrey. "I recently discovered one of your dark secrets," she teased, "thanks to Gaucelm Faidit. He was performing at my court last month and he let it slip that you and he had composed an erotic tenso, with you singing in French and Gaucelm responding in the *lengua romana*. Naturally I had to hear it!"

"Oh, Lord . . . I was drunk at the time, Marie, I swear!"

"Actually it was rather good," she said, giving him a sidelong smile. "Richard is an occasional poet, too. Have you heard any of his songs?"

"Richard and I are more likely to share insults and threats than poetry."

"That is a pity," she said and meant it. She'd first met her mother's sons thirteen years ago, at the time of their first rebellion, and she'd become quite fond of all three of them; John, she'd yet to meet. She'd grieved for Hal and she was sorry that Richard and Geoffrey acted more like blood foes than blood brothers. Nor did she approve of Geoffrey's new rapport with her other half brother. Although she'd been compelled by the political realities of her world to make peace with Philippe, she neither liked nor trusted him, and she was sure that no good could come of his sudden friendship with Geoffrey.

Since no others were within hearing range, she took advantage of her status as Geoffrey's elder sister to speak her mind. "I find it curious that you and your men are fighting with the French instead of the Normans and Angevins."

"Merely a courtesy to my host," he said, and she gave him a skeptical glance that made her look uncannily like the mother she'd not seen since childhood.

"I am going to tell you a story, Geoffrey, about my father. Papa would often wander off by himself, and one time my brother-in-law Thibault found him dozing under a tree. When Thibault chided him for it, he said calmly, 'I may sleep alone quite safely for no one bears me any ill will.'"

"I know that story," Geoffrey said, grinning as he remembered how it had vexed his father, who found Louis's sanctimony hard to swallow. "I also heard about the time he said that the English king had men and horses and gold but in France they had only 'bread and wine and gaiety.' My parents called him 'Louis, Lamb of God' for some time after that one!"

"And did you hear what Philippe answered when he'd seemed lost in thought during a council? This is soon after he'd been crowned, so he was all of fourteen. He said that he'd been wondering if he'd be able to make France great again, as it had been in the days of Charlemagne."

"No, I had not heard that, but it does sound like Philippe. What is your point, Marie?"

"I am trying to warn you that Philippe might well be a changeling, for he could not be more unlike our father. I do not know what the two of you are up to, but I hope you take heed, Geoffrey. Despite his youth, Philippe is a clever, dangerous man."

"I agree with you. But you seem to have forgotten that I am a clever, dangerous man, too."

Marie rolled her eyes, but when Geoffrey laughed, she could not help laughing with him. "Very well. I've done my best, will say no more on it," she promised, and proved it by changing the subject. "Why did Constance not come with you? I would have liked to meet her."

"Come to our Christmas Court this year," Geoffrey said expansively, "and we'll show you that Breton hospitality is second to none. Constance had been suffering morning queasiness and she thought it best to remain in Rennes in case she might be pregnant. I keep telling her that all happens in God's Time, but she is impatient to give me a son."

"It's passing strange that you are the only one of the English king's sons to produce heirs so far."

He shrugged. "Well, Richard might get around to wedding poor Alys one of these days now that she will bring him the Vexin, and Johnny is keen to marry the Gloucester heiress. I wish him luck, for the last thing my father wants is to allow him to have incomes and lands of his own."

He sounded so bitter that she gave him a quick, searching look. "Far be it from me to offer a defense of Henry Fitz Empress, but you might keep this in mind. At least he has permitted contact with your mother, and that is more than my father did. Once their marriage was over, he did his best to exorcise her from my life and memories—"

She stopped then, having caught sight of the small boy running across the field, trailed by his nurse and a young knight. Leaning over the railing, she waved to Thibault and smiled. She loved all four of her children dearly, but she had a special fondness for Thibault, her youngest, and as she watched him race toward her, she felt a maternal pang, thinking that they grew up so fast, thankful that Thibault was only seven, years away from the time when he'd risk his life and honor in tournaments and war like her elder son, Henri, and her brothers Geoffrey and Richard.

GEOFFREY WAS WATCHING with amusement as his men teased, tormented, and chaffed his cousin Morgan, an initiation of sorts into the ranks of knighthood. Morgan bore it in good humor, fending off the jests and gibes with a becoming modesty that was belied by his wide grin and dancing dark eyes. Geoffrey knew his cousin would remember for the rest of his life that moment when his lance had unhorsed his foe; a knight never forgot his first joust.

Heralds were parading up and down, crying out "Helmets on!" Geoffrey adjusted his own helmet and then mounted his favorite destrier, a Spanish stallion he'd called Tempestad in recognition of the horse's silvery-grey coat and stormy temperament. Reaching for the lance that his squire was holding out, he playfully tapped the boy on the shoulder with it, a lighthearted reminder that Mikael might one day be dubbed a knight, too. The *estor*—the grand charge—was eagerly awaited by spectators and participants alike, and Geoffrey's breath quickened. This was the moment he most loved about tourneying, that first glorious sortie with banners streaming, trumpets blaring, and the earth atremble with pounding hooves as hundreds of knights came together in a spectacular clash of sound and fury.

They were close enough now to couch their lances under their arms, to home in upon targets. Geoffrey selected a knight on a rangy bay stallion. Unhorsing an opponent was as much an act of skill as it was luck, required steady nerves and perfect timing. As they closed with each other, Geoffrey veered at the last minute, just enough for his foe's lance to glance off his shield. He would then lean back in, hoping the Almighty would keep his own aim true. It was a maneuver he'd performed times beyond counting, both in tournaments and war, and indeed, the other knight's lance did not hit his shield full-on. But against all logic, the blow still slammed him back against the saddle cantle, with such force that he lost his balance and, unable to catch himself, crashed heavily to the ground.

The fall drove the breath from his lungs, but he reacted instinctively, rolling away from his horse's thrashing legs. His sense of danger was strong enough to override his body's pain, and by the time his foe turned his mount and circled back, Geoffrey had managed to get to his feet.

"Surrender!" the other knight cried out, flinging away his shattered lance and raising his sword menacingly over his head.

Geoffrey's shield had been ripped from his shoulder and his lance sent spinning

out of reach. Hastily unsheathing his own sword, he spat out one of his father's favorite Angevin oaths and made his refusal even more emphatic by slashing at the
other man's leg. His defiance was unthinking, dictated by pride. A knight unhorsed
was in grave peril, and he was a particularly tempting target; his opponents would
soon be trampling one another in their eagerness to capture the Duke of Brittany. He
knew, though, that he need not hold out for long. A knight's first duty was to protect
his liege lord and his Bretons would race to his rescue as soon as they noticed his
plight. It was just a question who would arrive first, friends or foes.

Sparks flew as he parried the other man's sword thrust and then jumped back,
forcing the knight to rein in his mount. "Do not be a fool," the man panted. "Yield and
if you give me your parole, I'll free you to rejoin the mêlée!" He swore bitterly then, not
at Geoffrey, but at the riders coming up fast. "Stay back! He's mine, to me!"

"You always were a greedy sod, Ancel," one of the new arrivals laughed. "A duke's
ransom is too much for one man!"

Geoffrey had seized his opportunity and snatched up his shield. Spurning Ancel's
repeated demands to surrender, he swung his sword in a sweeping arc to keep the
horses at bay, taking a blow on his shield that staggered him. Facing down three
knights, he despaired when he saw others galloping toward them. But then he heard
the sweetest sound this side of Heaven's golden harps. "Saint Malo! Saint Malo!" The
battle cry of the Bretons.

His attackers were turning to meet this new threat. Geoffrey recognized Gérard
de Fournival in the lead, with Matthew de Goulaine and his cousin Morgan only a few
strides behind him. More and more of his men were turning away from the mêlée,
too, starting to ride in his direction, and Geoffrey saw salvation was at hand. He had
no time to savor his reprieve, though. Gérard's destrier, screaming like a banshee,
smashed into the closest of its foes, and the other animal reared to meet the attack, unseating its rider. All was chaos, shouting men and slashing swords and maddened
horses. Acutely aware of his danger, Geoffrey darted for the closest open space. But before he could break free, the riderless stallion bolted and he was brushed by its
haunches as it turned, knocking him off his feet. Blinded by the clouds of dust being
churned up, he never saw the flailing hooves above his head.

"I THINK HE'S COMING AROUND!"

The voice seemed to echo from a great distance, and when Geoffrey opened his
eyes, he saw nothing but sky. The sun was so bright that he squeezed his eyes shut
again as he sought to orient himself, to understand why he was lying on the ground,
feeling as if every bone in his body was broken.

"Geoffrey . . . my lord!" This voice was familiar and so urgent that he tried to filter the glare through his lashes, enabling him to focus upon the circle of worried faces clustered around him. He was not surprised to see Gérard and Morgan, but he was puzzled by the presence of his sister. Although he did not remember what had happened, he sensed that she ought not to be here.

Seeing his confusion, Gérard knelt and leaned over so Geoffrey could hear. "You are in the recet. You were unhorsed and trampled . . . do you not remember? We drove them off and carried you to safety. The men-at-arms are guarding us, making sure none of those knaves make another try at capturing you."

It alarmed Geoffrey that he remembered none of this. He did not even remember the estor, the start of the tournament. "How . . . ?"

"Ancel de Vernon cheated!" Morgan came back into Geoffrey's line of vision. "That whoreson did not couch his lance, kept it in the fautré. He denied it, but he's done it in the past."

Geoffrey understood what Morgan was saying; it just did not seem very important at the moment. Marie obviously did not understand, though. " 'In the fautré'? What does that mean, Morgan?"

"The fautré is a spear rest, my lady, attached to the front of a man's saddle, enabling him to balance the lance upright whilst riding. He ought to have braced the lance under his arm when he charged. By leaving it in the fautré, he gave his thrust much more power. That is why he was able to knock the duke from his horse even though the lance did not strike my cousin's shield a direct blow."

One of the knights produced a wineskin, and Marie took it from him, tilting it to her brother's lips. Geoffrey swallowed gratefully. "You ought . . . not to be here . . ." he mumbled, surprised that his words sounded so slurred.

"I should have remained in the stands and watched the estor? When I did not know if you lived or not?"

Marie frowned down at him, and Geoffrey thought hazily that she looked like his mother, sounded like her, too. He was touched that they'd all been so concerned for him and he wanted to reassure them that his greatest injury was to his pride. "Are . . . are we winning?" he asked, and they burst out laughing, taking his question as proof that the legendary luck of the English king held true for his son, too.

MARIE HAD LOST ALL INTEREST in the tournament after Geoffrey's narrow escape. She'd accompanied him back to his tent, not departing until she was sure that he had indeed suffered no more than bruises, scrapes, and contusions. She'd have preferred to go to her lodgings at the abbey of St Pierre, but she'd left her young son in the stands with her ladies and his nurse, and she did not trust them to keep Thibault out of mischief. Upon her return, she found that the mêlée had long since broken up into smaller presses, continuing the fighting out of sight and sound of the spectators. But Thibault was still so excited that she had to promise she'd bring him back later to watch the awarding of the prize.

True to her word, Marie and Thibault were back in their seats several hours later. She knew they'd have a wait, but she did not have the heart to deny her son, whose enthusiasm for the tourney had not been diminished by his uncle's mishap. To Thibault, the day had exceeded his expectations, and he was soon proving to be a handful for his harried nurse, bouncing up on his seat to watch knights returning to the field, squirming and wriggling and demonstrating that no adults could hope to match the boundless energy of puppies, colts, and small boys. Marie kept a sharp eye upon him, for she was not a novice to motherhood, and her vigilance soon paid off, for she was able to stop Thibault from dashing down onto the field when he sighted her eldest son.

The young Count of Champagne rode over, delighting his little brother by swinging him up into the saddle and taking him for a slow gallop around the lists. After turning Thibault over to one of his knights, Henri reined in beside the stands and Marie hastened down the steps to meet him. His flaxen hair was tousled, his face smeared with sweat and dirt and there was a reddish stain on his hauberk that was worrying until she could be sure the blood was not his.

"Maman, I heard what happened to my uncle Geoffrey and so I stopped by his tent. He insisted that he was unhurt and said he means to attend the dinner tonight."

"What? Why must you men be so loath to use the brains God gave you?"

Henri grinned, for this was a conversation they'd had before; his mother was convinced that males were born without any common sense whatsoever. "I'd want to go, too, if I were in his place," he admitted. "It is a matter of pride. But . . ." Lowering his voice, he said, "The thing is that I do not think he is as well as he claims. He is very pale and hollow-eyed, like a man trying to pretend he's not suffering from a morning-after malaise. I think it would be best if he keeps away from the revelries tonight; they can last till dawn, after all. I thought mayhap if you talked to him . . ." Finding a smile, he joked that she was a force to be reckoned with and Geoffrey would not dare to defy her. But Marie was not misled by his attempt at humor; Geoffrey must look like Walking Death if her daredevil son Henri had taken notice.

TENTS OF THE NOBILITY were often so large that they had to be erected with winches, and Geoffrey's was a spacious one, but it was so crowded that Marie did not at once see her brother. Geoffrey knew most of the tournament participants and friends had quickly gathered once word spread of his fall. A number of French knights and lords were there, too, their presence confirming Marie's suspicions that Geoffrey and Philippe were plotting together. She finally found Geoffrey seated on the edge of his bed, talking with the renowned French knight Guillaume de Barres. One glance was enough to convince her that he was in pain; her husband had suffered from chronic headaches and she knew the signs: the tightness around Geoffrey's mouth, the vein throbbing in his temple, the ashen cast to his skin.

Marie was, at forty-one, still a beautiful woman and an accomplished flirt. She drew upon that charm now to disperse the men clustered around her brother. Sitting beside Geoffrey, she asked if he had seen a doctor. He swore he had, saying the physician had been impressed that his injuries were so trifling. Marie hoped he was right, but did not let that distract her from her purpose, and launched into her argument why he should not attend the night's dinner.

Much to her surprise, Geoffrey did not dispute her. "I am not feeling so good," he admitted. "My headache has gotten worse and I'm having some pain here." He gestured vaguely toward his abdomen. The mere thought of food roiled his stomach, but he saw no need to share that, saying with a flickering smile, "So you need not fret, Sister. I shall keep to my bed tonight, I promise."

"I am glad to hear that." But the more Marie scrutinized Geoffrey, the more uneasy she became. "I want you to come back with me to the abbey," she said. "Their infirmarian is experienced in the healing arts, and I can vouch for his skills, which I cannot do for your tourney leech. Do it for me, Geoffrey, I implore you."

"You're forgetting the Church's hostility to the tournament, Marie. I doubt that the abbot would be pleased if one of his monks tended to a sinful tourneyer."

"And you are forgetting that my husband's father was a great patron of St Pierre's. Not only is he interred in their church, his son Hugh was the abbot there for seven years. Trust me when I say the monks will bid you welcome."

Marie was both relieved and disquieted when Geoffrey raised no further objections, for if he was willing to see the infirmarian without being coaxed into it, he must be in considerable pain. "Henri promised to stay with Thibault through the ceremonies, so we can go straightaway," she said, determined not to give him a chance to change his mind. But then he turned to face her, and she felt a throb of fear, for the pupil of his left eye was so dilated that it looked black. "I'll be back," she said and jumped to her feet, going in search of Gérard de Fournival, for she knew the French knight better than the others in Geoffrey's mesnie.

Gérard did not protest when she told him Geoffrey was going to see the abbey infirmarian. He did balk, though, when she told him to find a horse litter or cart. "I cannot do that, Madame! The duke would be shamed to ride in a conveyance meant for women and the elderly. I'll order horses saddled—"

"We have more urgent concerns than the duke's pride," she snapped. "I fear he has suffered a serious head injury."

Gérard stared at her and then beckoned to the closest of Geoffrey's knights, Matthew de Goulaine and Morgan. After a brief murmured exchange, they both hastened toward Geoffrey. At their approach, Geoffrey started to rise, but he felt so dizzy that he had to grab Matthew's arm for support.

"I am all right," he insisted, "just a little light-headed." Releasing the knight's arm, he stepped back to show he'd regained his balance. But then his knees buckled. They caught him before he fell, maneuvered him toward the bed. Marie and Gérard were beside him now, and when his sister grasped his hand, Geoffrey tried to squeeze it reassuringly. "My head hurts . . ." he said indistinctly, and by the time they got him onto the bed, his eyes had rolled back in his head and he'd gone limp in their arms.

GÉRARD DE FOURNIVAL sat up with a start, surprised that he'd actually dozed off even though he'd slept little since Geoffrey's collapse. Getting stiffly to his feet, he glanced quickly toward the bed where his liege lord and friend lay motionless, as he'd done for the past two nights and a day. The infirmarian and another monk moved quietly about the chamber, but Gérard found their composure to be oddly comforting; these aged men of faith had seen too much to fear death. Some of the knights were napping, sprawled in the window-seat, slumped in chairs, or on the floor. A few of them—like Morgan and Matthew and Geoffrey's friend Ivo de la Baille—were still staving off sleep, for keeping vigil was all they could do for their duke now. Marie was not present, and Gérard assumed she'd gone to check upon her son, for only the duties of motherhood had taken her away from her brother's side.

Gérard stretched and winced as his knotted muscles protested, then crossed to the open window. Dawn was streaking the sky in delicate shades of pink and pearl, the last of the night stars flickering out like quenched candles. It took Gérard a moment to remember the day of the week . . . Wednesday, the feast day of St Bernard of Clairvaux. Gérard would normally have implored the saint's intercession on his day, but Bernard was a newly made saint, and the mortal Bernard had been a fierce foe of Geoffrey's parents. "From the Devil they came and to the Devil they'll go" had been Bernard's terse judgment upon the Angevins. Would he bestir himself on Geoffrey's behalf?

Geoffrey had been taken to a private chamber rather than to the large infirmary hall and, from the window, Gérard had a view of the abbey garth, watching without interest as riders were admitted. But then he leaned forward in amazement. "Jesu!"

That attracted the attention of the other men, and Morgan and Ivo came to stand beside him, though they saw nothing unusual about these new arrivals. "That man on the chestnut palfrey," Gérard cried. "It is my brother Roger!" They looked at him blankly, unable to understand how he could be so excited about a family reunion when their lord might be breathing his last. Seeing their lack of comprehension, Gérard said impatiently, "Roger is the French king's best physician!"

THE MEN WERE DISMOUNTING by the time Gérard came striding toward them, with Morgan and Ivo on his heels. Hastening forward, he enveloped his brother in a grateful embrace. "Never have I been so glad to lay eyes upon you, Roger! Your arrival here is so providential that the Almighty Himself must have directed you to Lagny!"

"Not the Almighty, the king." Roger handed his reins to one of his companions. "The countess's messenger reached Senlis late yesterday afternoon. King Philippe was sorely distressed to hear of the Breton duke's injury and dispatched me at once with orders to spare neither expense nor effort to save him. We rode all night," he said, sounding vaguely surprised that he'd proved up to such a great exertion, for a royal physician's life was not usually so arduous. "Now . . . tell me what you know."

"The infirmarian thinks Duke Geoffrey has a grave head injury. He cannot be sure if his skull has been fractured, for there was no open wound. He lost consciousness briefly when it happened, but once he came around, he was quite lucid, although he did complain of a headache that got worse as time went on. But we've not been able to rouse him since he collapsed in his tent. Can you help him, Roger?"

"God Willing," Roger said, reverting to the professional tone he used with patients. He did not like what he'd just been told, but he saw no need to share his misgivings with Gérard. If the duke's prognosis was as poor as he feared, there'd be time enough for that. "God Willing," he repeated resolutely. "Take me to him."

THEY WAITED IN THE ABBEY GUEST HALL while Roger conducted his examination, were soon joined by Marie and Henri. The hosteller sent servants over with food and wine, but none of them had any appetite. They sat without talking, for there was only one voice they wanted to hear now—that of the French king's physician. When Roger was escorted by one of the monks into the hall, they went to meet him in such haste that several benches were overturned.

A royal physician was expected to have the social skills of a courtier, and Roger greeted Marie and her son with the deference due their rank and the sympathy due their kinship to Geoffrey. Once the formalities had been observed, he looked from the countess to his brother and then said quietly, "Was the duke shriven?"

"Yes, he was. He heard a votive Mass of the Holy Spirit on Monday morning, and then my chaplain heard his confession ere the tournament began . . ." Marie's words faltered for she could still hear Geoffrey's laughing voice, joking that he never passed up an opportunity to seek absolution of his sins any more than he passed up an opportunity to sin anew. "Are you saying that there is no hope?"

"I am saying that he is in God's Hands, Madame," Roger said carefully, "for his wounds are beyond my abilities to heal."

Marie closed her eyes for a moment and then turned away without speaking. After a brief hesitation, Henri hurried after her. The other men were struggling with disbelief, for even though they'd known of the severity of Geoffrey's injuries, they'd been holding on to hope. Gérard and Morgan were the most incredulous, for Gérard had enormous confidence in his brother's medical skills and Morgan was by nature an optimist, always expecting the best outcome, never the worst.

"But . . . but there must be something you can do," he stammered, "I know head wounds are dangerous, but even so . . . One of the Breton lords, André de Vitré came back from pilgrimage last year and he told Duke Geoffrey about some miraculous surgeries performed in the Holy Land, about a Christian knight saved when the doctors bored into his skull. Can you not do something like that?"

"No, I cannot. I am not a surgeon—"

"But we could find one, Roger!" In his urgency, Gérard grabbed his brother's arm in an iron grip. "I know surgeons are not held in high regard by physicians, but surely that would not matter now? If there is nothing you can do and a surgeon could—"

"This has nothing to do with my well-founded misgivings about most surgeons. I know about the procedure in question. It is called trepanation, and is done to drain blood and pus and noxious humors from the skull. But it is rarely if ever successful when the patient is unconscious or feverish and the duke is both. I could not in good conscience recommend—"

"Surely it is worth trying!"

"If you would have me speak bluntly, Gérard, it is too late. Dilation of one or both pupils is a sign of bleeding in the brain, and the duke's other symptoms are not encouraging. His skin is cold and clammy to the touch, his pulse is weak, and his breathing has become shallow and uneven. Moreover, I fear that he has suffered damage to his liver or spleen—"

"That is not so," Morgan interrupted, "for I helped the infirmarian to undress my cousin. His body was badly bruised and scraped, but there were no contusions on his belly—"

"Internal injuries do not always show external signs. What I found far more significant than the presence or absence of bruises was the swelling of the duke's abdomen. This usually means that the liver has been lacerated and is bleeding into the abdominal cavity. Either injury would be grievous enough to kill a man."

They stared at him, momentarily stricken into silence. "What are you saying, Roger? That we just sit back and let him die!"

"I said nothing of the sort," Roger said testily. "We've been trying to get him to swallow yarrow and white willow, though that is obviously not easy. And there most certainly is something you can do for the duke. You can pray for him. Now, I need to see the hosteller about getting a meal."

They watched him go, and then, by common consent, headed for the abbey church, where they lit candles and prayed for Geoffrey's recovery. When they returned to the infirmary, they found Marie and the abbot standing by the bed. Marie clutched a jeweled reliquary, and they felt a flicker of hope, remembering that St Pierre had one of Christendom's most sacred treasures—a nail from the Holy Cross. Leaning over, Marie kissed her brother's forehead, then opened the reliquary and placed the nail in his hand, gently closing his fingers around the blessed relic. Then she and the abbot knelt by the bed and began to pray. Geoffrey's knights knelt, too, and added their voices to hers.

M ARIE WAS SITTING ON A BENCH not far from the infirmary hall. Several of her attendants hovered nearby, close enough to be summoned, far enough away to give her the semblance of privacy. The day had been a scorching one and dusk had not yet dispersed much of the heat. There was not even a breath of wind, and Marie's tears dried on her cheeks almost as soon as they trickled from the corners of her eyes. She'd lost track of time, would never know how long she sat there, so weary that her thoughts drifted without direction or purpose. She was heedless of passersby, the curious eyes of monastery guests, the silent solicitude of her own knights and ladies. It took a sudden stir of excitement and noise to dispel her sorrowful reverie, to bring her back to the August eve and the illusory peace of the abbey. Looking up, she gazed dully at the man coming toward her. It was only when he was several feet away that she rose to her feet and made a dutiful curtsy to her brother the French king.

She was puzzled by Philippe's presence at Lagny, but not enough to dwell upon it. He always looked rather untidy, but he seemed more disheveled than usual, his unruly brown hair flopping across his forehead, his clothes layered in dust, his eyes glazed with fatigue. He surprised her by reaching out, taking her hands in his. "Sister . . . is it true? The porter at the gate said that Geoffrey . . . ?"

"Yes, it is true. Geoffrey died as Vespers was ringing. Just like Hal . . ." She was not sure why that was relevant, but her tired mind was blurring her losses and she could not separate Geoffrey's death from Hal's, the brothers she'd loved, taken too soon.

Philippe released her hands and stepped back. She thought he would go, but instead he sat down heavily on the bench, gestured for her to do the same. Marie obeyed and they sat in silence for a time, while Philippe's men milled about in some confusion, unsure whether to wait or take their horses on to the abbey stables, sure only that Philippe would not welcome their intrusion. Marie glanced at him, thinking it was very unlike Philippe to ride all the way from Senlis in such haste; he'd shown no such compunction when their father lay dying. But his unexpected presence here might be a blessing, might forestall any unpleasantness with the Church.

"We must give him a fitting funeral," she said firmly, as if daring him to object. When he did not, she continued, less defiantly. "There might be trouble with the Church, though."

Philippe seemed lost in his own musings, but at that, he turned to look at her and she was stunned to see his eyes were wet with tears. "Why?"

"The Church forbids men who die in tournaments to be buried in consecrated ground," she reminded him. "The last Lateran Council reiterated the ban just five years ago."

"I'd forgotten that," he said, surprising her again, for Philippe had a memory to rival the English king's. "It is of no matter. None will protest, and if they do, they'll regret it."

"Thank you, my lord brother." Marie rose with another perfunctory curtsy. "Shall I take you to the abbot now?"

Philippe did not appear to have heard her. He was staring into space, scuffing the dirt with the toe of his boot, his head lowered so she could no longer see his face. "What a waste," he said thickly. "What a bloody waste . . ."

GEOFFREY DIED ON AUGUST 21, just a month from his twenty-eighth birthday. He was buried with great honors before the high altar in the cathedral of Notre Dame in Paris, with all the French court in attendance. Philippe grieved openly, and he and Marie each founded two chantries to pray for Geoffrey's soul.

CHAPTER FORTY-NINE

✦

August 1186
Rennes, Brittany

"M Y LADY?"

Always a light sleeper, Constance opened her eyes to see one of her attendants leaning over the bed. "What is it, Juvette?"

"The chamberlain is here, Madame. He says he must speak with you."

Sitting up, Constance reached for the bed robe that Blanche was holding out. She slid her feet into her slippers and was standing by the time Juvette admitted the chamberlain. He'd obviously been roused from sleep, too, for his clothing appeared to have been donned in haste. "I beg your pardon for disturbing you, Madame, but Sir Gérard de Fournival has just ridden in and he insists that he must speak with you straightaway, that it is urgent and cannot wait till morning. Will you see him?"

"I will." While the chamberlain went to fetch Gérard, Constance tightened the sash on her robe and smoothed back her hair. She wore it loose when she was sharing a bed with Geoffrey, for he liked to play with it during their lovemaking. Tonight Juvette had braided it neatly in a long plait so it would not tangle while Constance slept. Only a woman's husband and family usually saw her uncovered hair, but Constance was not about to bother with a wimple or veil for Gérard. She was striving to appear composed, but her pulse had begun to race. Geoffrey would not have used a man of Gérard's rank to deliver a routine letter. What had gone wrong in Paris? Did Philippe have a change of heart, deciding that Richard might make a more useful ally? Had Geoffrey's father learned of their plans? Or was the threat coming from Richard? Whatever Geoffrey's message, she did not doubt it would be a warning of some kind, and she was braced for bad news as Gérard was ushered into the bedchamber.

Gérard looked like a man who'd spent days in the saddle. His boots and mantle were travel-stained and muddy, his hair windblown. Constance saw only his eyes, though, bloodshot and red-rimmed, filled with pain. "My lady . . . I . . ."

"Tell me, Gérard," she said hoarsely, and he knelt at her feet, giving her a look of such naked misery that her breath stopped.

"Your lord husband . . ." He no longer met her eyes, saying in a rush, "He is dead, my lady. God help us all, he is dead . . ."

Constance heard Juvette's muffled scream, the chamberlain's gasp, the whining of her favorite spaniel. She saw Gérard's bowed head, the chalk-white faces of her ladies, even the toes of her felt slippers, peeping out from the hem of her robe. She was acutely aware of her surroundings, but none of it seemed familiar. She felt as if she were floating, no longer tethered to reality as she knew it. She found that she was sitting on a coffer and Gérard was kneeling beside her, clutching her hand in his. Now that he'd begun talking, he could not seem to stop, and she was being pelted with words. Gérard was gripping her fingers so tightly that her rings were being driven into her flesh, but she welcomed the pain, for it gave her something to focus upon, something to think about beside harrowing images of dust, blood, and plunging hooves.

They were all hovering around her now, fanning her as if she'd been made faint by the summer heat, trying to get her to take a few sips of wine, asking if they should send for a doctor, and Juvette, who knew her secret, made hesitant mention of a midwife. At that, Constance's head came up sharply. "No!"

Her face looked drained of all color, and she'd bitten her lower lip deeply enough to show flecks of blood. But her voice was infused with steel. "No . . . I want no one." She stared at them defiantly. "Leave me," she said, and they reluctantly obeyed.

After she was alone, she sat motionless while her spaniel whimpered and licked her hand. Moving like a sleepwalker, she finally rose and started toward the bed. But she could not bring herself to lie down upon it, to sleep alone in her marriage bed. Placing her hand protectively over her abdomen, she realized that Geoffrey had died not knowing for certes that she was pregnant. Her child would be born without a father, would never know Geoffrey. And her daughters were so young. How long would they remember him? How long would her own memories last? Would the day come when she could no longer see his face, hear his laughter, remember the feel of his arms around her? What a sad, dreary, dangerous place her world would be without Geoffrey.

She sank to her knees by the bed, but she could not pray. "It makes no sense," she whispered. "Why?" Even she was not sure if her cry was meant for the Almighty or for her husband. She knew only that there'd be no answer, and burying her face in her hands, she did something she'd once have thought impossible. She wept bitterly for a son of Henry Fitz Empress.

AFTER THE POPE HAD REFUSED to grant a dispensation for the marriage of Henry's granddaughter to the Scots king, Henry took it upon himself to find William another wife, the daughter of the Viscount of Beaumont, whose mother was a natural daughter of the first King Henry and therefore the English king's cousin. Not content with providing a highborn bride, Henry offered to host the wedding feast, and on this late August day, he was holding court at Woodstock, which would be the site of the Scots king's marriage in early September. Illustrious guests had already begun to arrive, and the great hall was crowded with bishops and barons and their ladies.

Henry was standing on the dais, dictating to a scribe at the same time that he was discussing Richard's campaign in Quercy with his son Geoff, the Earl of Essex, and his justiciar, Ralf de Glanville. Fortunately his clerk was a veteran of royal service and was able to distinguish between Henry's asides to his advisors and the thoughts to be set down in the letter.

"The last I heard, Richard and the King of Aragon were on the verge of capturing Cahors," Henry revealed with obvious satisfaction, and if the men found it odd that Richard was once again exercising authority in Aquitaine, they were too worldly to let such sentiments show on their faces. Interrupting himself to speak with a servant, Henry turned back to the others with a smile. "Morgan Fitz Ranulf has just ridden in," he told them, explaining for Ralf de Glanville's benefit that Morgan was his uncle's son. "He has been in my son Geoffrey's service for several years, is likely on his way to visit his parents in Wales."

"I am gladdened to see you, Morgan," he said, brushing aside the younger man's formal obeisance and waving him up onto the dais. "I assume you're heading for Wales, will give you a letter for your father. Ranulf is not ailing, is he? Or your mother?" He smiled again when Morgan shook his head and invited his cousin to dine with him that evening, thinking that would provide an opportunity to interrogate Morgan about Geoffrey, for he'd not heard from his son in months.

"My liege . . ." Morgan had never shouldered such a daunting responsibility, did not know how to go about it. Was it better just to blurt it out? Or ought he to lead up to it? "May I speak with you in a more private setting? I do not bring good news."

Morgan had no way of knowing it, but those were the same words that the prior of Grandmont had used to inform Henry of Hal's death. His memories of that dreadful day were never far from his mind, and as he looked now at his young cousin, his breath hissed through his teeth, for he read the truth of Morgan's mission in his forlorn, unhappy face.

M ORGAN SHIFTED FROM FOOT TO FOOT, uncomfortable with the silence. But when he glanced toward Geoff, the other man shook his head and he deferred to his cousin, keeping his eyes on Henry, though. He'd listened without speaking as Morgan had stumbled through an account of Geoffrey's last days and then moved across the solar to the window. Morgan yearned to slip away, for there were still awkward questions to be asked about Geoffrey's death and he did not want to be the one to answer them. He looked over again at Geoff and Willem. Neither one spoke; they seemed content to take their cues from Henry, and Morgan could not tell if they shared his fervent desire to disappear.

This was by far the most difficult task of his life, and yet he'd volunteered for it, for he'd soon realized that neither the French king nor the Countess of Champagne nor Geoffrey's knights cared about breaking the news gently to Henry. He was convinced that Henry had treated Geoffrey shabbily. But his own father had often insisted that Henry's love for his children was heartfelt, and Morgan thought the king deserved to hear of his son's death from a sympathetic source. Trapped now in Woodstock's solar and feeling more and more like Daniel in the lion's den, he found himself thinking that the bearers of such tragic tidings ought to have bells or clappers so they could warn others of their approach, much as lepers did.

When Henry finally spoke, Morgan flinched, for this was the question he'd been dreading. "Why was Geoffrey in Paris?"

"I . . . I do not . . ." he stammered, for he could neither lie to the king nor tell him the truth.

"He was there to take part in the tournament," Geoff said quickly, and both Morgan and Willem winced at the transparency of the falsehood, for that did not explain why Geoffrey had been given a lavish state funeral by the French king. Geoff soon saw the weaknesses inherent in his "explanation" and, realizing the futility of trying to protect his father from the truth, he said no more.

Henry had spoken with his back still to them. When he turned at last, Morgan was shocked by how ravaged he looked, and he knew that Henry was not taken in by talk of tournaments, that he understood what Geoffrey's presence in Paris meant. Once again a son had died in rebellion against him, and this time he'd been denied even a chance to make things right between them. For Geoffrey there'd been no sapphire rings, no promises of forgiveness, no avowals of affection. And as he realized what a burden this would be for Henry to bear, Morgan felt his own anger with the king ebbing away, replaced by an overwhelming sense of sorrow for his cousin and the father left to mourn him.

SEPTEMBER BEGAN WITH A PROMISE of perfection, and the women had been lured out into the gardens. They set up a trestle table under a shady chestnut tree and enjoyed wine, bread, cheese, and honeyed wafers. Afterward, Eleanor's granddaughter Richenza played the French game *jeu de paume* with her attendants and several of Maud's and Eleanor's ladies; even Amaria gamely joined in as they dashed about the gardens batting the ball back and forth. Eleanor and Maud prudently assumed the role of spectators, watching with amusement as the younger women laughed and shrieked and attracted several knights who were quite happy to join in the fun.

"This was an excellent idea, Maud. I have not seen Richenza so merry in a fortnight."

"I am glad to be of assistance." Eleanor had explained that Richenza was downcast as the nuptials of the Scots king drew near. Only fourteen, she'd set her heart upon becoming Queen of Scotland and she was not yet reconciled to the Pope's verdict. Pleased that she'd been able to cheer the girl up, Maud resolved to arrange for her granddaughters to spend some time at Winchester with Richenza. "Is Harry looking at another match for her?"

"Actually, he had an offer, one which would have made her a queen. Béla, the King of Hungary, expressed interest in wedding the English king's granddaughter. But Harry seemed to feel that Hungary was the back of beyond and he never gave Béla a definite response. Béla eventually grew tired of waiting and approached the French king for Marguerite. Philippe was happy to accept the offer, and she will be departing for Hungary at summer's end."

Eleanor sounded sad, and Maud easily understood why. The remarriage of Hal's widow was bound to stir up hurtful memories. "I've talked with my daughter-in-law about marrying again," she confided, "for it has been five years since Hugh died. She says she has no interest in taking another husband and reminded me that I've been a widow for more than thirty years!"

Eleanor had never been surprised that Maud had not remarried, for widowhood was the only time in a woman's life when she was not under a male's authority. Maud had obviously relished her independence, raising her children, traveling, and proving to be a generous patron of the Church; she'd even founded a priory at Repton in Derbyshire. Eleanor suspected that she'd also discreetly taken lovers. No, it was very easy to understand why Maud had found life more enjoyable as a widow than as a wife.

"I always appreciated the irony, Maud, that canon law includes widows in the class of *miserabiles personae,* the miserable wretches deserving of special protection. I suppose the Church fathers thought any woman without a husband had to be an object of pity. Speaking for myself, I expect to have the chance to discover the joys of widowhood, for I plan to outlive Harry if only from spite."

Eleanor grinned and Maud grinned back, but she was not completely sure that the queen was joking and she felt a pang of regret that their precarious rapprochement had been a casualty of Henry's double-dealing. She'd seen them take tentative steps toward a marital peace as the years passed, and then watched sadly as it all ended when Henry used Eleanor to win his clash of wills with their son. "Are we caught up now on family gossip?" she asked lightly. "So far I've learned that Richard is wreaking havoc on the Count of Toulouse's lands and your daughter in Castile has given birth to another girl and you have not heard lately from Geoffrey but you recently received a loving letter from Joanna in Sicily. Any other interesting rumors to relate?"

"I do have some news about my youngest son. Believe it or not, Harry has sent him back to Ireland." Eleanor grinned again at the expression on Maud's face. "For a man who rarely makes the same mistake twice, Harry acts like a dog chasing its tail where our sons are concerned. You may have heard that Hugh de Lacy, his justiciar for Ireland, was slain this summer. John had blamed de Lacy for much of his Irish follies, claiming the justiciar had acted to hinder his rule, and Harry of course accepted John's story as gospel. So when he learned of de Lacy's death, he decided it would be a good idea for John to return to Ireland and lay claim to de Lacy's estates in Meath." Her smile fading, she said, with real regret, "In all of Christendom, only Harry and John think that his second try will be any more successful than his first . . . and I am not even sure about John."

"Grandmother!" Richenza was back, followed by Denise, Eleanor's newest lady-in-waiting. "Grandfather is here! He just rode into the bailey!" Her duty done, the girl spun around and ran to greet Henry, with Denise right behind her. So only Maud there to hear Eleanor mouth a colorful profanity.

"That does not sound like the most loving of spousal greetings," she said dryly, and Eleanor summoned up a taut smile.

"The last time Harry was at Winchester, we had a particularly heated quarrel—about Richard, of course. We did not patch things up when he left, so I'd rather our first meeting not be a public one." .

"In other words, you've not yet forgiven him. Well, this is why friends have their uses. I'll go out and welcome him whilst you slip out the side gate and return to your own chambers. I happen to be very good at creating a distraction," Maud said with a wink and walked briskly along the path to the garden's main gateway.

There she saw Richenza, the ladies, knights, and other men clustered around a small group of riders dismounting in the bailey. Making her way through the growing crowd, she greeted her cousin with a graceful curtsy and a playful smile. "My liege, you came all this way to visit with me? I am very flattered."

She started to offer an explanation for Eleanor's absence, but Henry gave her no chance. Stepping forward, he drew her into a wordless embrace, holding her so tightly that she knew something was wrong even before he murmured against her ear, "Thank God you are here, Maud. Eleanor will have need of you."

Ignoring the other spectators, he moved toward the gardens. Maud trailed after him, but he gave her no chance to question him, opened the gate, and entered. When he closed the gate behind him, Maud took that to mean he did not want her to accompany him and she halted uncertainly, watching as he strode along the path. She was not surprised to see Eleanor emerge from the arbor, for the queen had finely honed instincts; on reflection, she'd probably concluded that his unexpected visits always boded ill.

"Cousin Maud?" Turning, she was delighted to recognize Morgan, and she kissed him fondly on both cheeks before asking him what she'd not had time to ask Henry. "We bring the worst news a mother could get," he said somberly. "Geoffrey was injured in a French tournament and died a few days later."

"Oh, no!" She clapped her hand to her mouth, staring at him in horror, and then swung back toward the gardens. Henry had reached Eleanor by now. Thankful they were out of earshot, Maud watched, tears stinging her eyes. She knew when Henry had revealed his heartbreaking message, for Eleanor spun away from him, then sank down on the nearest bench. When Henry followed, she flung up her hand, as if to hold him off, and Maud's tears flowed faster, for what could be sadder than parents unable to console each other over the death of a child?

Morgan did not know how to comfort her, but he did his best, putting his arm around her shoulders and sharing her sorrow. It was not long before Henry was heading back toward them, head down, steps heavy and plodding. As he came through the gate, Maud embraced him, pressing her wet cheek into his shoulder as she whispered the only words she could, a choked litany of "I am so sorry."

She'd lost both her sons, and Henry almost asked her how she'd survived such a loss, but Eleanor's need was greater and he said only, "Go to her, Maud."

As she slipped through the gate and hastened into the gardens, Henry glanced over at his young cousin. "Now is not the time, lad. But she'll want to hear about Geoffrey's last hours. Be sure to tell her that her daughter Marie was with him till the end. That might help . . . a little."

Morgan nodded, and they walked in silence back to the now subdued crowd of onlookers. Henry held out his arms and Richenza ran to him, wept against his chest as she told him how much she'd liked her uncle Geoffrey and how distraught her mother would be by his death. Henry had not been sure if he should be the one to tell Eleanor, at last concluding that he owed her that much. Despite her rebuff, he was glad now that he'd made the trip to Winchester; at least he could console their granddaughter. Holding the girl, he looked over her head, his eyes seeking Morgan's.

"You said you were returning to Wales. But what then, lad? What will you do?" When Morgan admitted that he did not know, Henry paused before saying quietly, "I would like you to come into my service, Morgan. I know you are not yet ready to consider your future. But when you do, remember that there will be a place for you here."

Caught off balance, Morgan murmured his thanks, then stood watching as the crowd parted to let Henry and his granddaughter pass. After a few moments, he sensed someone had come up beside him, and he turned, looked into the sympathetic eyes of Will Marshal.

"Did he ask you to be one of his household knights?" the older man said, and smiled when Morgan stared at him in surprise. "I thought he would, just as he did with me."

"His offer to you makes more sense, though, Will, for you are a renowned soldier. Whereas I am just . . ."

"One of his last links to his son," Will finished for him and Morgan finally began to understand.

THE SURRENDER OF CAHORS was a sweet victory for Richard and Alfonso of Aragon. For their armies, it was not as rewarding; they'd been forbidden to sack the city since it had not been taken by storm. Some of Alfonso's soldiers were tempted to see how much they could get away with, but Richard's men soon disabused them of that fancy, warning that even Mercadier's fierce routiers knew better than to defy their duke's orders. So the streets were reasonably calm as the Aragonese king rode into the city to meet Richard at the cathedral of St Étienne.

Alfonso was very pleased with their campaign so far. They had the Count of

Toulouse on the run, reduced to sending urgent pleas to his liege lord for help. But so far, Philippe had not responded and they'd retaken most of the lands seized by Count Raimon during Hal's rebellion. For Alfonso, it had been a satisfying summer. He enjoyed fighting alongside his friend and was relishing their mutual foe's humiliation. If they could be sure Philippe would stay out of it, they might even take the war to the russet rock walls of Toulouse.

Once he and his men reached the cathedral garth, Alfonso headed for the chapter house, where he expected to find Richard and the Bishop of Cahors. He suspected Bishop Gerald must be cursing his ill luck, as this was the second time his city had been taken by an Angevin army; Henry had captured Cahors when he'd sought to assert Eleanor's claim to Toulouse. Alfonso fervently hoped that Count Raimon was losing sleep now that Richard was in a position to finish what his father had begun.

They'd almost reached the cloisters when they encountered some of Richard's household knights. They seemed in high spirits and veered in Alfonso's direction as soon as they saw him. André de Chauvigny and Rico Fitz Rainald were arguing good-naturedly about which one got to "tell the king the good news," and Alfonso regarded them with a mixture of amusement and impatience. "Well, someone tell me!"

André's cousin Nicholas stepped into the breach. "The most remarkable occurrence, sire. Our lord's brother has died after being trampled during a tournament outside Paris."

Alfonso whistled in surprise. "The Duke of Brittany?" he said, just to be sure there were no misunderstandings, although he could not see why John's death would matter to anyone but Henry. And when they gleefully confirmed Geoffrey's identity, he continued on to the cloisters, marveling at Richard's great good luck.

The chapter house was crowded with men, but the bishop's woes had been forgotten in the excitement over the news from Paris. The prelate was standing off to the side with some of his canons, looking disgruntled. His sense of disapproval only intensified when Alfonso strolled in and greeted Richard with a breezy, "Well, the Lord God has been uncommonly busy on your behalf, separating the wheat from the chaff." And he was further scandalized when Richard laughed.

"Come on," Richard said, leading Alfonso back out into the cloisters, where his men dropped back to afford them a modicum of privacy. Richard gave Alfonso a concise summary of the report he'd gotten of Geoffrey's death, and then said, half seriously and half in jest, "I do think God is on my side, Alfonso, for Geoffrey was not in Paris by happenchance. It seems that he and Philippe discovered they shared many of the same vices: a taste for conspiracy and a hunger for lands not theirs."

"Lucky for you then that Geoffrey's aim was off."

"Not so lucky for my father, though," Richard said and smiled grimly, "for I am all the old man has left now." He paused and then added carelessly, "Except for the whelp, of course."

B ROTHER EUDDOGWY HAD DUTIFULLY SOUGHT to obey his Benedictine vows of obedience, poverty, and chastity. The last one had given him the most trouble and some sleepless nights, but those temptations were safely behind him, for lust was a sin more likely to afflict the young and Brother Euddogwy had gone grey in the service of his God and his Church. He'd never expected to be tripped up by obedience, but he'd been in a state of rebellious resentment ever since his prior had sent him to minister to the spiritual needs of the English king's son.

At first Brother Euddogwy had welcomed the novelty of it. His prior had explained that Count John's chaplain had fallen from his horse and broken his leg. Since he was confined to bed as his injuries healed, there was a need for a priest at the castle to say Mass and hear confessions. Since Brother Euddogwy was the only one of the brethren of Monkton Priory to have been ordained, he was the only possible choice. But the prior assured him that as their priory was within sight of Pembroke Castle, he need not sleep there, could return at nights to the monks' dorter. Moreover, his services would not be required for long. Count John and his men were sailing for Ireland as soon as they got favorable winds.

And so Brother Euddogwy had no misgivings, no forebodings as he'd begun his new duty. It took him only a few days, though, to become convinced that he'd been given an unwelcome glimpse of Hell. He knew he was not a worldly man, had passed all his years in this quiet corner of South Wales. The priory of St Nicholas had been his home since boyhood, for after his father died, his mother had pledged him to the Benedictine brothers as an oblate. Once he was old enough, he'd become a novice and in due time, he'd taken his holy vows, so impressing his superiors that he was encouraged to take the next step—priesthood. He'd always been content with his lot in life, kindly both by nature and experience, and when he heard the confessions of the townspeople and his brethren, he imposed light penances, never resorted to harangues and threats of eternal damnation as some of the other Pembroke priests did. He truly believed that most people wanted to do the right thing, just needed guidance to steer them away from sin.

His benign view of mankind was severely challenged, though, by the retainers and mesnie and soldiers of Count John. Like John, most of them were younger sons eager for a taste of independence, and many seemed to have confused freedom with disrespect, insolence, and provocation. They swaggered into town in search of trouble and usually found it. They certainly found women willing to barter their bodies for coins, wine, or a chance to socialize with these cocky young knights. It was Brother Eud-dogwy's shocked opinion that the behavior he'd seen in the castle's great hall was the sort of debauchery he imagined took place in bordels, those infamous houses for women of ill repute.

He was as distressed by their blatant bad manners as he was by their lechery. They bullied the castle servants and the burghers of Pembroke, shouted rudely at reputable wives and mothers, drank and gambled and squabbled among themselves. And they seemed to go out of their way to be offensive. His name attested to his dual heritage, Euddogwy from his Welsh mother and Huybeerecht from his father, who'd been a re-spected member of Pembroke's Flemish community. Count John's knights thought that was hilarious and insisted upon calling him Euddogwy Fitz Huybeerecht instead of Brother Euddogwy, competing with one another to mangle the names beyond recognition. They made no secret of their contempt for the Welsh, and Brother Eud-dogwy pitied the Irish, who would soon have these overweening hordes descending upon them.

The only light in this darkness was provided by an unexpected source—Father Bartholomew, the count's impaired chaplain. He was amiable, courteous, and had an inexhaustible store of spellbinding stories, for he'd spent a few years in the young king's household before being chosen to serve Count John. When the scandalous goings-on in the great hall would get to be too much for him, Brother Euddogwy would retreat to the chaplain's bedchamber, where Father Bartholomew mesmerized him with accounts of the royal court, convincing the monk that the Angevins truly were the Devil's brood.

There seemed no end to his trials, either, for the bad weather had yet to break. On this rainy September evening, it had been more than a fortnight since the prior had dispatched him to this dung heap of sin, and he was guilt-stricken to find himself struggling with rebellious impulses that no dutiful Benedictine ought ever to enter-tain. After getting John's permission to retire for the night, he took one last disap-proving look at the antics in the great hall and escaped out into the rain. He was trudging along the town's sludgy Main Street toward the Westgate when he was hailed by a mud-splattered rider on a lathered horse.

"A moment, Brother, if you will. Can you tell me if the Count of Mortain has sailed yet for Ireland?"

"No, he has been delayed by the foul weather." Brother Euddogwy suspected this was a royal messenger; he was young and fit and did not look as if he'd be daunted by bad roads, storms, or outlaws. "Are you one of the king's serjeants?" He was, indeed, the rider confirmed, and when he learned of Brother Euddogwy's connection to the castle, he leaned from the saddle and shared his news. He did not need directions, for the wooden paling of the stronghold's palisade loomed out of the damp mist. But when he continued on toward the gateway, Brother Euddogwy walked alongside him, for Count John might have need of spiritual comfort in light of the message he was about to receive.

The scene in the great hall was a raucous one, a cheerful mélange of knights, minstrels, servants, disreputable-looking women, and dogs, who were dicing, performing bawdy songs, responding to cries for wine, laughing shrilly, and barking. Brother Euddogwy flushed, as if this unseemly uproar somehow reflected badly on him, but the serjeant took it in stride. Weaving nimbly among the clots of merrymakers, he soon made his way to the dais, with the monk following in his wake.

John was lounging in a high-backed chair with a blonde in his lap; she was younger and prettier than most of the women in the hall, for a king's son naturally had the pick of the litter. He looked bored, seemed to be half listening to the girl's prattle and the fawning courtiers hovering at his side, but Brother Euddogwy had learned that his careless pose was deceptive; he missed little of what occurred around him. His gaze soon settled upon the bedraggled messenger, and he beckoned the man up onto the dais.

"I am Master Lucas, my lord. I come from your father the king, and alas, I am the bearer of sad tidings." He knelt and waited patiently until John shouted for silence, then drew out a sealed letter. "King Henry bids you return to England straightaway, as he no longer wants you to make the journey to Ireland."

That was not well received by John's mesnie, and they made their disappointment known with profanity-laced protests. John did not look pleased, either. "I wish my lord father would make up his mind," he said peevishly, reaching out to take the letter.

Since he seemed in no hurry to open it, the serjeant took it upon himself to speak up. "That is not the message, my lord, merely its consequences. I regret to tell you that the Duke of Brittany was fatally injured in a French tournament."

There was a shocked silence and then, to Brother Euddogwy's horror, the hall burst into tipsy cheering. He watched in disgust as John was mobbed by his knights and hangers-on, each one wanting to be the first to congratulate him that he was now second in line to the English throne. That had not even occurred to the monk, but John's men were euphoric, for this was every younger son's dream, to be elevated by the Almighty.

Whatever John might have said was drowned out in the riotous din. Brother Euddogwy could not read his face, but he did not seem in need of religious comfort, so the monk took the serjeant to find the steward, who'd arrange for a meal and a bed. He then went to see the bedridden chaplain, feeling that Father Bartholomew ought to be told of the duke's death.

He was heading again for the castle gateway when he heard footsteps behind him, and one of John's squires came running across the bailey. "Brother, wait! My lord wants to see you!"

That surprised the monk, and he was even more surprised when he was led, not back to the hall, but to John's private chamber. John was alone, pacing back and forth, his face shuttered and remote. "Come in, Brother. I want to ask you something."

"How may I serve you, my lord?"

"I would like to have a Requiem Mass for my brother. Can you make the arrangements?"

"Of course, my lord!" Brother Euddogwy beamed, delighted by a natural reaction to tragedy after what he'd seen in the hall. "The castle chapel is not large enough, but we can use the priory church. Or if you'd prefer, I am sure the priest at St Mary's will gladly make his church available."

"Whatever you think is best."

This was the first time that Brother Euddogwy found himself warming to the king's son, and since he'd not been dismissed, he ventured to express his regrets and offer solace if he could. "I am very sorry for your loss, my lord. You and the duke were close, then?"

"No," John said, "actually we were not. Whilst I was growing up, I thought my brothers were the spawn of Satan. But in the last few years, we'd gotten to know each other better. And when I needed him, he was there for me, providing generous support for my Poitevin campaign."

Brother Euddogwy did not know how to respond to that, for only the Angevins would see a rebellion as an opportunity for brotherly bonding. "I will ask my prior if we may say daily prayers for your brother's soul, my lord."

"Thank you." John moved to the only source of heat in the chamber, a brazier heaped with coals. He held his hands over the flames, glancing over his shoulder at the monk. "Does it ever stop raining in Wales?" he said, and then, "I wish it had been Richard."

P HILIPPE WASTED NO TIME in demanding the wardship of Geoffrey's daughters. Since Geoffrey had done homage to him for Brittany, he was the duke's rightful liege lord and ought to have custody of the little girls. Henry naturally did not agree, contending that the right of wardship was his. Neither king bothered to consult Constance.

CHAPTER FIFTY

✦

March 1187
Nantes, Brittany

*T*HE DUCAL CASTLE at Nantes was crowded with highborn Breton lords, their ladies, and retainers. Constance's mother Margaret had come from England for her daughter's confinement. Two of Constance's female friends, Clemencia de Fougères and Mathilde de Mayenne, were present, too, and both young women had been escorted by their male kin, Clemencia by her grandfather, Raoul, and Mathilde by her husband, André de Vitré. Clemencia's betrothed, Alain de Dinan-Vitré was also there, as was Maurice de Lire, the Seneschal of Nantes, and several churchmen.

Normally the men would not have accompanied the women at such a time. Not only were males barred from the birthing chamber, the process of childbirth was shrouded in female tradition and myth. But Raoul de Fougères and the de Vitré brothers, André and Alain, were men of power and influence, men with a keen interest in the future of their duchy, and they'd seized this opportunity to be among the first to learn the results of their duchess's confinement.

They were seated in chairs by the smoking central hearth in the great hall, passing the hours drinking and making idle conversation. The one subject they assiduously avoided was what was occurring in Constance's birthing chamber. They were superstitious enough not to want to discuss it beforehand, but they all knew what was at stake, possibly the very survival of their duchy. If Constance gave birth to a third daughter, it was just a matter of time until she'd be compelled to make another marriage, and she and her lords would have little say in the matter. The husband would be chosen by the English or French king, depending upon which one prevailed in their competing claims to lordship over Brittany.

They'd been very lucky in Constance's first husband, for Geoffrey had proven himself to be dedicated to the duchy's welfare and shrewd enough to ingratiate himself with the Breton barons. They doubted that they'd be so fortunate again, for it was Geoffrey's status as the king's son that had enabled him to assert so much independence. Constance's next husband was likely to be a mere puppet of the English or French king; they'd see to that.

If, however, Constance gave birth to a boy, that altered the dynamics, as the focus would shift to her son. Her role would change, and she'd be acting as regent for the infant duke. Henry and Philippe would still want her safely wed to a husband of their choosing. The new husband's influence would be circumscribed, though, for he would not be the father of the heir. Geoffrey's unexpected death had plunged his wife into grieving and the duchy into great peril, its future dependent upon the sex of the child being born on this Easter Sunday in late March.

The men thought it was a good omen that their duchess's pangs had begun on so holy a day, but their edginess increased as the hours dragged by. As evening drew nigh, they sought to distract themselves with an intent discussion of the dangers facing the Holy Land. André de Vitré had passed two years in Outremer, and he'd returned to Brittany with compelling stories of the tragic Baldwin IV, the Leper King. André had great admiration for Baldwin's courage and stoic acceptance of his affliction; he'd died at the age of twenty-three soon after André's departure, naming his nine-year-old nephew as king. But the boy was sickly and he'd died not long afterward, leaving the fate of the Kingdom of Jerusalem in the hands of his mother, Sybilla, and her much mistrusted husband, Guy, one of the notorious de Lusignan clan.

André had stories to tell, too, of the man many considered to be Outremer's most dangerous foe, Sultan Salah al-Din Yusuf ibn Ayyub, known to much of Christendom as Saladin. He'd been defeated by King Baldwin at Montgisard eight years ago, but had suffered few reverses since then, now ruled Syria as well as Egypt. He was one of those men about whom legends formed, and André was easily persuaded to recount the most famous of these tales, although he warned he could not vouch for its veracity.

"Saladin launched an attack upon Kerak, the stronghold of his blood enemy, Raynald de Châtillon. As it happened, a wedding had just taken place—Raynald's stepson and the young half sister of King Baldwin. The story goes that the groom's mother sent out some of the wedding dishes for Saladin, and he asked where the wedding-night chamber was located. He then ordered his men not to turn their siege engines upon that part of the castle, not wanting to disturb the newlywed couple."

The men laughed and André continued, relating that the king's army had arrived in time to lift the siege, with Baldwin too weak by then to ride, but insisting upon accompanying his men in a horse litter. "It is often thought that leprosy is the judgment of God," he said somberly, "but none who knew Baldwin could believe that his suffering was the result of sin. He was a man of honor and had he only been spared the scourge of leprosy, the Holy Land would not be in such peril—"

He stopped so abruptly that the others looked up in surprise. When he leaped to his feet, they followed his example, for they now saw what had drawn his attention: the woman just entering the hall. In recent hours, Clemencia and Matilde had made brief appearances to report on the progress of the birthing, assuring the men that all was going as it ought. But at the sight of Constance's mother, a stir swept the hall, for surely her presence must mean the child had been born.

Margaret's visage gave away nothing of her thoughts; she looked tired yet composed. But then she favored them with a smile resplendent enough to light the hall. "My daughter," she said, "has given birth to a fine, healthy son." And after that, there was such chaos that the rest of her words were drowned out.

MARGARET COULD STILL HEAR the clamor as she left the hall. By the sound of it, they'd be celebrating until dawn, she thought, and why not? God had been good to Brittany this Easter night, good to her daughter.

But as soon as she reentered Constance's chamber, she discovered there'd been a dramatic development. She'd left her daughter, exhausted and pale, smiling at her son. Now Constance was crumpled upon her bed, sobbing so despairingly that her entire body was trembling, while the other women clustered around her in dismay.

"Madame!" Juvette greeted her with obvious relief. "She just began weeping of a sudden and we've been unable to console her."

Marveling that the girl sounded so surprised, Margaret took charge, soon had the chamber cleared of all but the midwife, who was bathing the baby. Skirting the overturned birthing stool, she sat on the bed and gathered her daughter into her arms. "You go ahead, dearest, and cry," she said soothingly. "You've earned the right."

After a time, Constance's shudders eased, her breathing no longer as ragged and choked. Raising her wet face from her mother's lap, she regarded Margaret with swollen, dark eyes. "I was so happy, Maman, but then . . ." She swallowed with difficulty, hiccupped, and struggled to sit up. Margaret slid a supportive arm around her shoulders, helping her onto the pillows, before she rose and brought a wine cup back to the bed, watching as Constance obediently took a few sips.

"I would have been astonished if you'd not given way to tears, Constance. As great as your joy is, how could it not be bittersweet? You have what you most wanted in this world—a son, a son that Geoffrey will never get to see or hold or protect. You cannot exalt in what you've gained without mourning what you've lost."

That made sense to Constance. "Yes . . ." she said huskily, wiping away the last of her tears with the corner of the sheet, and Margaret looked over at the midwife, standing a few feet away with the newly swaddled infant. When she nodded, the midwife approached the bed and gently handed him to Constance. Geoffrey had often called Aenor his "perfect little pearl," and Constance thought now that their son was perfect, too, a warm, breathing blessing in her arms, a miraculous reprieve for her duchy.

The midwife stepped back, beaming. "Have you chosen a name, Madame?"

Constance smiled drowsily. "I was favoring Margaret for a daughter, Geoffrey for a son. But then my father-in-law the English king sent us word that if the baby was a boy, he would like him to be named Henry in his honor."

She glanced up briefly, finding it difficult to take her eyes away from her baby's face. "After that, my lords and I knew there could be but one name for my son. We shall name him after a great Breton king. We shall call him Arthur."

THE FRENCH KING demanded the wardship of Arthur, as he had done with the infant duke's sisters, and he insisted, too, that Henry stop Richard from making war upon his vassal, the Count of Toulouse. Philippe then ordered the arrest of any of Henry's subjects found in his domains, and Henry responded by arresting the French king's subjects. Skirmishing erupted in the Vexin, and an April meeting between the two kings resolved nothing. Both sides prepared for war. Henry divided up his army, giving separate commands to Richard, John, Geoff, and William de Mandeville. Philippe mustered his army at Bourges, and in June he invaded Berry, an ongoing source of contention between the French kings and the dukes of Aquitaine.

JOHN HAD LONG KNOWN he was uncomfortable in small or enclosed spaces, but he discovered in June that the worst sort of confinement was to be trapped in a castle under siege. Sent south by Henry to counter the threat in Berry, he and Richard had set up command in the castle at Châteauroux, and soon found themselves fending off an assault by the French army.

This was John's first taste of a siege, and so far he didn't care much for the experience. It bothered him more than he'd expected, to know he was a hostage of sorts; like a trout in a fish weir, he thought morosely. He was not truly worried that the castle might fall to Philippe, for they'd sent word to Henry of their plight. Richard would have been his last choice of company in a castle under siege, though. Moreover, he was soon utterly bored, for he did not share the pleasure Richard seemed to take in manning the castle's defenses. He'd heard of sieges lasting for months. How had such beleaguered men not gone stark mad out of the sheer tedium of their days?

He knew he should try to sleep, for with daybreak the bombardment would begin again. He was too restless to stay in his bedchamber, though, and eventually wandered over to the great hall, hoping that he might find some men still awake. A dice game seemed as good a way as any to pass the hours.

The hall was crowded with knights and soldiers, sleeping on pallets and blankets, using their boots as pillows. Rush-lights still burned in wall sconces, casting a smoky pall over air already stale and sweltering because of the shuttered windows. But a handful of men were still up, shooting dice in a corner, albeit without much enthusiasm. John headed toward them, only to stop when he spotted his brother. Richard was by himself in a window-seat, softly plucking the strings of a small harp. "So you cannot sleep either," he commented, so amiably that John found himself pausing, for most of the time his older brother treated him with offhand indifference or outright condescension.

"Why are you not abed?" he asked, for Richard had passed a very demanding day; when not up on the battlements, he was overseeing their mangonels, checking upon the wounded, handing out casual compliments to soldiers who acted—to John's annoyance—as if his words were gold, prowling the castle like a sheepdog keeping a watchful eye out for predators, determined to keep the flock safe.

"My body's tired enough," Richard acknowledged, "but my brain will not slow down. I keep thinking of possible weaknesses in our defenses or wondering how long our supplies will last or worrying that some of the sentries are too sleepy to stay alert."

"You think they might try a night assault?"

"I would in Philippe's place. But I doubt that he has the ballocks for it."

John sat down across from Richard in the window-seat, although he wasn't sure why. "You think our father will get here soon?"

Richard continued to strum the harp, but he gave John a curious look. "You are joking, right?"

"No . . . why?"

"Because you are trapped with me, of course. Now, if it were just me, he might be sorely tempted to take his time. But for you, he'll be killing horses in his haste to get here."

He laughed, but John remembered that Geoffrey had occasionally told bald truths in the guise of humor and he wondered if that were true for Richard, too. He started to remind his brother that their father had often ridden to his rescue in the past, but the words that emerged from his mouth seemed to come of their own volition. "Do you hate me for that?"

Richard blinked. "For what?'

John had been as surprised as Richard by what he'd said. He was committed now, though, and had no choice but to continue. "For Papa favoring me over you."

Richard didn't seem to have given the matter much thought before. He was quiet for a moment, considering. "No," he finally said. "I cannot say I was overly fond of Hal or Geoffrey, but I hold no grudge against you, lad."

"Why not?" John demanded, feeling somehow insulted by his brother's lack of rancor. "I did invade your duchy, after all!"

Richard was starting to look amused. "Far be it from me to deny you the credit for that bit of treachery."

"You just assumed that it was all Geoffrey's doing," John said accusingly, "the way Papa did! As if I could not possibly have formed the intent upon my own, even after you mocked me like that!"

"When did I mock you?"

"That day at Le Mans. When Papa said Aquitaine was mine if I could take it, you looked me up and down and then laughed."

"Did I? I'll take your word for it, Johnny. If it makes you feel better, though, I never imagined Geoffrey had dragged you along at knifepoint. The reason I am willing to let bygones be bygones is because you were all of . . . what? Sixteen? It was only to be expected that you'd act like a damned fool. God knows, I did at sixteen."

John did not share his amusement. "I was seventeen," he said sullenly, in that moment realizing that he resented Richard's indulgence more than his hostility. He also realized that he did not like to be called Johnny, not by Richard.

Richard had gone back to his song, frowning as he tried several chords. When he was finally satisfied, he glanced up, saying, "How does that sound to you?" But John was gone.

HENRY PROVED RICHARD RIGHT by reaching Châteauroux in record time. Philippe raised the siege, but to the surprise of all, he did not retreat, and with two armies separated only by the waters of the River Indre, it began to look as if a battle was inevitable. This was uncommon, for battles were usually a commander's action of last resort. Sensible men were not eager to submit themselves to the Judgment of the Almighty, and a decisive battle seemed to prove that the victor had God on his side. Most people preferred not to put the Lord's Favor to such a stringent, conclusive test. Nor were the barons of either army keen to fight with one another, for many had kin and friends in the opposing camps. These men did their best to persuade Henry and Philippe to resolve their differences by more reasonable means.

So, too, did the numerous clerics and prelates accompanying both armies, for the Church did not want to see two such powerful Christian kings at war when the real enemy was to be found in the Holy Land. In this way, a fortnight dragged by, with highborn messengers shuttling back and forth between encampments with proposals and counterproposals. No real progress had been made, however, and the fate of many continued to depend upon the whims of two strong-willed, unpredictable kings.

RICHARD HAD JUST RETURNED TO HIS TENT and his squire was helping him to remove his hauberk when he was informed that the Count of Flanders had ridden in under a flag of truce, asking to confer with him. Richard swore and then sighed, for by now he was thoroughly disgusted with the mummery masquerading as peace negotiations. He was tempted to tell Philip to go away, but he knew, of course, that he could not do that, and he directed that the count be brought to his tent.

He was somewhat surprised when Philip had his men wait outside, and as soon as they were seated, he could not resist a sardonic gibe at the Flemish ruler's expense. "Since you want to speak in private, should I assume, Cousin, that you are thinking of switching sides? There is little love lost between you and Philippe, after all."

Philip gave him a sharp look and then smiled, somewhat sourly. "True enough. My relationship with the French king is almost as stormy as yours with the English king." Taking a taste of his wine, he nodded approvingly. "It would be a shame to see your Poitevin vineyards go up in flames when you can produce wines like this. Look, Richard, let's speak plainly. Your interests are not being well served if this standoff results in a bloody battle. Despite your father's games-playing, we both know England will eventually be yours. But so will Normandy and Anjou. Is it truly wise to make an enemy of the man who will be your liege lord?"

"What would you suggest, instead? That I betray my father to court favor with Philippe? You're losing your touch, Cousin, if this is your idea of subtlety. Shall I also renounce my Christian faith whilst I am at it?"

Philip's smile did not waver, even as he marveled to himself that the genial Hal and this man could have come from the same womb. "Sheathe your sarcasm, Cousin. I am asking only that you talk directly with the French king, see if you can persuade him he will gain little and risk much by taking to the battlefield. I in turn will do what

I can to get your father to see reason." Adding wryly, "And may God have mercy upon us both."

RICHARD HAD BEEN ACQUAINTED with Philippe Capet since the latter was four, but as he studied the French king, he realized that he did not really know the younger man. They had little in common. Philippe was stiff-necked and judgmental, disapproved of swearing, had shown little interest in those pleasures that other men enjoyed. He denounced tournaments, disapproved of gambling and minstrels and troubadours, and did not even hunt much because he disliked horses. To Richard, a superb rider and swordsman who loved music and swore like a sailor, Philippe seemed as alien as a Carthusian monk. But he knew Philip of Flanders was right; he would eventually have to deal with this man and so it made sense to find out more about him.

So far they'd been dodging and weaving, using polite language and courtesy to guard their real thoughts, and Richard was growing tired of evasions and ambiguity. As he looked into the French king's pale blue eyes, he saw what his brother Geoffrey had also seen—a cool, calculating intelligence. Making up his mind then, he said, "Let's talk about my real reason for being here. You and my lord father are far from fools, so I assume you will eventually agree to a truce. How much longer must we wait?"

"What makes you think I am bluffing?"

Although Philippe's tone was composed, Richard noticed that his hands had briefly clenched upon the arms of his chair. So the French king was sensitive to slights upon his manhood. He marked that down as a useful fact to know and set his wine cup aside, leaning forward in his seat.

"You are bluffing for the same reason that my father is bluffing, because neither one of you wants to risk all upon one throw of the dice. I am paying you a compliment, for no capable commander commits his men to a pitched battle unless he is confident he will win or he has no other choice. Hellfire, Philippe, even I do not want to fight at Châteauroux and you know what they say of me—that I get drunk on bloodlust the way other men do on wine!"

Philippe looked taken aback, but when Richard grinned at him, he grinned back. "Let's talk then," he agreed, "about how your father and I save face and come away with enough to satisfy us both. And when this is done, I would like you to visit Paris . . . as my honored guest. I got to know both Hal and Geoffrey, would like to know you better, too."

I daresay you do, Richard thought, for what better weapons can you have against my father than his own sons? "I will give it serious consideration," he promised, and as soon as he said it, he realized that he meant it.

✛

"SO IF I AGREE to let Philippe hold on to the castles he took at Issoudun and Freteval, he will agree to a two-year truce?" When Richard confirmed it, Henry regarded him skeptically. "And what do I get out of it?"

"You get what you want," Richard said impatiently, "a chance to defer your reckoning with Philippe. That is your favorite tactic, after all, Papa . . . delay and delay and delay again. It has served you well in the past; think how long you've managed to keep Philippe in suspense over Alys and the Vexin."

"Are you telling me that you now want to wed the girl? Or that you're willing to hand over the Vexin?"

"I was not being critical of your stratagem," Richard insisted. "Of course I am not willing to yield the Vexin to Philippe. And since I have no great interest in wedding Alys, what else can we do but put Philippe off? What I am saying is what we both know, that you do not want to meet the French army on the field. So how much time are you willing to waste here whilst you and Philippe swap threats? Of course we can always go with one suggestion being bandied about—that you resolve your differences by choosing your best knights to joust on your behalf. The last I heard, men were proposing Philip of Flanders, Henri of Champagne, and the Count of Hainault as the French champions, and Will Marshal, your friend de Mandeville, and me as yours."

By now Henry and Richard were both laughing, for in that, they were in full agreement: that war was not a game and ought not to be treated like one. "Very well," Henry said, "let him keep those damned castles . . . at least for now. I've matters to deal with in Brittany, cannot spend the rest of the summer camping out here in Berry."

Henry paused then, looking pensively at his son. "We can accomplish a great deal when we are united, Richard. If there is trust between us, what could we not do together?"

If that was meant as an olive branch, Richard made no move to grasp it. "Yes," he said, "trust is essential," but he knew better, for he knew the old man would never trust him. Once that awareness had hurt, but no more. He no longer cared if he had his father's trust or respect. He wanted only what was his birthright, to be openly acknowledged as the heir to the English throne, and he meant to do whatever he must to secure his legacy . . . starting with a trip to Paris.

LÉON WAS ONE OF THE MOST REMOTE, inaccessible areas of Brittany, and its viscount had liked to boast that he "feared neither God nor man." He'd long posed a threat to ducal control of Brittany, and more than once Henry had led campaigns to quell his rebellions. He'd eventually broken faith one time too many and Geoffrey had seized the barony, compelling the viscount to make a penitential pilgrimage to atone for a lifetime of spectacular sins and disinheriting his sons. Upon Geoffrey's death in Paris, the sons promptly rebelled again, capturing two ducal strongholds. After concluding the truce with Philippe, Henry led an army into Brittany and retook the castles. He then visited Nantes in order to see his grandson.

Henry was cradling arthur in his arms, looking for the moment more like a doting grandfather than the man who cast such a formidable shadow over Brittany. Constance was neither charmed nor placated by this glimpse of her father-in-law's softer side and had to dig her nails into her palm to resist the urge to snatch her son out of his grasp. The Breton barons were just as unhappy and, like their duchess, more angry than grateful for his punitive expedition into Léon, as his campaign only underscored their subordination to the English Crown. Not that they needed a reminder, for after Geoffrey's death, Henry had dismissed Raoul de Fougères as Seneschal of Brittany and replaced him with the Angevin lord, Maurice de Craon.

Arthur, a curious, lively baby, seemed content in this stranger's embrace, but Constance was reaching her breaking point and signaled to the nurse, hoping Henry would take the hint. He did and reluctantly handed his grandson over to the woman, saying to Constance, "I think he looks like Geoffrey, don't you?"

"Yes."

Constance's elder daughter was tugging at Henry's tunic. He'd brought lavish gifts for the children: an expensive ivory rattle, carved wooden tops, whistles, felt puppets, balls, and poupées for the girls, one of linen and the other of wood, with yellow yarn hair and their own wardrobe. What had won Aenor over, though, was his willingness to kneel on the ground and show her how to spin the tops. Now she brandished her favorite new toy, a leather ball stuffed with wool and dyed a bright shade of red, entreating her grandfather to "play catch" with her.

Before Constance could intervene, Henry assured Aenor he'd like nothing better, and clasping her little hand in his, he suggested that he and Constance take a stroll in the gardens. This did not meet with the approval of her barons, who had been sticking closer to their duchess than her own shadow, but Henry had already started for the door, matching his pace to Aenor's toddler's steps, and Constance had no choice but to follow.

The day was overcast without even a hint of a breeze, for so far September had been as humid and sultry as August. With Constance's spaniel leading the way, they crossed the castle bailey and entered the gardens, fragrant with the last flowering of summer blossoms. Constance settled upon a turf bench, watching with a stiff smile as her daughter and the English king tossed the ball back and forth. He showed surprising patience with the little girl, continuing to play until she lost interest and began to throw the ball for the spaniel. Only then did he return to Constance and drew her to her feet, saying that they could talk as they walked.

They circled the grassy mead in silence, for Constance was not able to feign pleasure in his company; she thought he should count himself lucky that she managed to be civil. Henry paused in the shade of a pear tree, for it afforded them a good view of Aenor, but was distant enough to allow them to speak privately.

"I have been dealing with the duchess," he said, "but now I would talk with my daughter-in-law. You have never liked me, Constance, and in all honesty, you have not given me much reason to be fond of you either. But we share a common interest that matters more than our personal ill will."

"Yes . . . the Duchy of Brittany."

He ignored her sarcasm. "That, too. But I am speaking about your children, my grandchildren. Their future is inextricably entwined with that of the duchy, and I want to make sure that they do not suffer because of adult missteps or mistakes."

"What mistakes do you have in mind?"

"For one, the decision Geoffrey and you made to ally yourselves with the French king." Henry's voice was even, his face impassive, as if he were speaking of mundane matters, not the rebellion of his son. "As a stratagem, it had much to recommend it, with one great flaw. It had hopes of success only if Geoffrey lived to carry it out. Without him, you were likely to find yourself at Philippe's mercy, and that is indeed what happened."

Constance said nothing, and after a moment he resumed. "Philippe has made his intentions very clear. He means to deprive you of both legal and physical custody of your children. He will send the girls off to live in the households of their future husbands, men he will handpick for them. I would expect him to keep Arthur in Paris, ruling on his behalf until he comes of age. For your duchy, that will be more than twenty years with Philippe's hand firmly on the helm, twenty years in which to mold your son into a ruler who'd put the interests of France above those of Brittany. As for you, he'll marry you off as quickly as possible to a man of his sole choosing, possibly even one of inferior rank since his primary concern will be the loyalty of your new husband, and you can expect to live out your days on a remote manor far from the Breton borders—"

Constance could stand no more, for he was giving voice to all the fears that had haunted her nights since Geoffrey's death. "I know," she said sharply. "I know full well what I would have to look forward to—the loss of my children and my duchy and a miserable marriage to one of Philippe's lackeys. This is what always happens, is it not? What highborn widow gets the wardship of her own children? Even my mother, the Dowager Duchess of Brittany, sister to the Scots king. When her English husband died, the custody of their young son was not given to her. Why should I care whether my life is ruined by English or by French doing? What difference does it make to me?"

"Because it need not be that way. I do not want to take your children away from you—"

"And I am to believe that? Saint Henry, champion of widows and orphans! Say what you intend for me, for Brittany, but do not insult my intelligence, too. Why should I expect any more justice from you than I can from Philippe?"

"Because these are my grandchildren, of my blood. Can you truly doubt what family means to me? Surely I've proven it each time that I forgave my sons for betraying me yet again, as I would have forgiven Geoffrey for his conniving with the French king!"

He was no longer dispassionate, his voice rising, and Aenor stopped playing to look toward them in concern. "All is well, sweeting," Constance said hastily, and they both mustered up reassuring smiles for her benefit. Turning back to Henry, she said quietly, "You say you do not want to take my children away. What does that mean exactly?"

"It means that they remain with you. I want what is best for them and . . . and I know it is what my son would have wanted. This is what I am proposing, Constance. You retain the custody of Arthur, Aenor, and Matilda." The corner of his mouth curved in a hinted smile. "Arthur. Eleanor. How did you ever let Matilda slip in there? I'm surprised you did not call her Melisande since you seem to enjoy picking names sure to vex me."

"Geoffrey wanted to name Matilda after his sister," she said simply for she was not up to trading barbs with him, not now. "You say I can keep my children with me. And where would we all be? England?"

"Ruling Brittany from England would not make a great deal of sense." He heard her swift intake of breath, and said, "I expect you to continue to govern Brittany on Arthur's behalf. I also expect, of course, that you'll be willing to be guided by my counsel when necessary."

"And you would expect me to wed a man of your choosing."

"Naturally. I do not think you will be disappointed with my choice, though, for he is very highborn, my cousin, in fact. He holds a rich earldom in England, but he also has vast estates in Brittany, so the match makes sense. Moreover, he is a fine lad, clever and courtly and ought to make a satisfactory husband, a kind stepfather."

"You are talking about the Earl of Chester." When he nodded, she blurted out, "But . . . he is just a boy, fifteen or sixteen!"

"He is seventeen. I intend to knight him at year's end, so he will be eighteen or nigh on to it by the time of your marriage. I was thinking of a date sometime in February, ere the start of Lent, and I assume you would prefer that the ceremony be held in Brittany." When she did not respond, he reached out and tilted her chin up so that their eyes met. "I understand that you might not be ready to wed again, lass. Unfortunately, it is too dangerous to let you remain unmarried for long. If you were to fall into Philippe's hands, all our plans would be set at naught if he were able to marry you off to one of his 'lackeys,' as you so aptly put it."

He released her then and stepped back. "I daresay you want to give it some thought. You'll want to consult with your barons, too, of course."

Not trusting her voice, she merely nodded, but he did not press her for more. She sank down upon the edge of the freestone fountain as he crossed to her daughter, bent over to whisper in the little girl's ear. He then continued on along the pathway as Aenor came running toward her, with the dog yipping at her heels.

"Grandpapa said you wanted to give me a hug."

Constance gathered the child into her arms, holding her so tightly that Aenor soon started to squirm, protesting, "I cannot breathe, Maman!"

"I am sorry, poppet." Aenor stayed on her mother's lap, turning so she could splash her fingers in the fountain, and Constance watched her play, smoothing back the child's chestnut curls. When she whispered a name, though, Aenor looked up, her expression quizzical.

"Are you talking to Papa? I talk to him a lot, Maman."

"I am glad you do, Aenor." Constance smiled at her daughter, a smile that was edged in self-mockery. What was she going to do, ask for advice from a dead man? What did she expect Geoffrey to tell her? She already knew what she must do—what was best for her children and her duchy. The spaniel had begun to bark and she glanced up, saw Raoul de Fougères and André de Vitré coming toward her. She took several deliberate breaths, then rose to her feet and went to meet them.

Henry had been shocked and alarmed when Richard departed Châteauroux in the company of the French king. But worse was to come. Reports soon came from Paris about the newfound friendship of the two men, reports of a growing intimacy that could only bode ill for the English Crown. Henry did his best to coax Richard away from the French court, and when his messengers went unanswered, he delayed his planned return to England. By now his spies were warning him that Philippe had persuaded Richard his inheritance was in peril, that his father planned to disinherit him in favor of John, claiming that a plan was afoot to marry Alys to John. Richard's response was swift and characteristic. Leaving Paris, he rode for Chinon, where he seized the treasury and then withdrew into Poitou to fortify his castles. Henry eventually prevailed upon him to discuss their problems in person, and they held a tense meeting in Angers not long after Henry's return from Brittany. He was able to convince his son that Philippe's charges were untrue and Richard then did homage to him again. No one believed that a true and lasting reconciliation had been achieved, though, not even Henry.

But events were occurring in the Holy Land that were to have a profound effect upon the Angevin empire. In July, Guy de Lusignan had been lured into a disastrous battle against Saladin. The result was a catastrophic defeat for the Christian army. Guy was taken prisoner, over a thousand of his twelve hundred knights were either slain or captured, the knights of the military orders of the Templars and the Hospitallers were executed, and Saladin captured the most sacred of relics, the Holy Cross.

Word of the battle at the Horns of Hattin reached Europe by October. Pope Urban III died of a seizure upon hearing the news, and his successor at once urged another crusade to rescue the Holy Land and the city of Jerusalem. Richard learned of the defeat in early November. The next morning, he sought out the Archbishop of Tours and took the cross. Henry's multitude of enemies commented that he seemed more distraught by his son's action than he did by the news of Saladin's victory.

W ILLIAM DE MANDEVILLE wrapped himself in a blanket and slid out of bed. Caen Castle was filled to overflowing with guests attending Henry's Christmas Court, but Willem's rank and friendship with the king guaranteed him one of the better accommodations, and the chamber was spacious, heated by a wall fireplace that was now burning low. Willem's squires were stretched out on pallets close by the hearth, theirs the sound sleep of young men who'd downed more than their share of wine during the course of the evening. He hadn't the heart to awaken them and foraged for himself until he found a flagon of wine and a loaf of manchet bread, hastening back to the bed with his windfall.

"Bless you," his wife proclaimed, eagerly breaking off a chunk of the bread. "I ought not to be so hungry, for I ate a goodly amount of food at supper tonight, but I feel as if I've not had a decent meal in days."

"I'm glad to be of service," Willem said with a smile, for it amused him that Hawisa, who was as slender as a willow wand, had an appetite that would have put a burly quarryman to shame. "I am glad, too, that you are here for the Christmas Court." That was not something he could take for granted, as Hawisa had a mind of her own and was not one to be summoned like other, more docile wives. He supposed it was to be expected that a great heiress was strong-willed, and because he was easy-going by nature, her assertiveness had rarely caused troubles in their marriage. All in all, he was very satisfied with the wife that Henry had given him, marveling that their eighth anniversary was not far off. "I am very glad that you're here," he repeated and handed her the wine cup.

She took a swallow and then gave him a wine-flavored kiss. "So . . . tell me all the gossip. Is the king still swiving that wench with the red hair? Is it true that young Chester is going to wed the Duchess of Brittany? What sort of devilment has John been up to in Caen? Have you heard how the French king's baby is faring? They say he is as sickly and pitiful as a stray kitten, and I doubt that Philippe will get many more off that little queen of his; I heard that she almost bled to death expelling the after-birth."

She paused for another swallow of wine and another quick kiss. "And is it true that the king was in a tearing rage when he was told that Richard had taken the cross? I heard that he would not come out of his chamber for days, just like when Archbishop Thomas was slain!"

Willem chose to address her last query first, reaching over to steady her grip on the wine cup. "That is not so. The king was not happy about it—I'll not deny that. And he did some brooding for a few days, but he was not so much angered as he was troubled. He was also vexed, of course, that Richard had done this without consulting him first."

"If he thinks Richard will ever be as biddable as John, he is blinder than old Peter, my almoner. Some hawks are too wild to be tamed, can never be broken to the creance and jesses." Hawisa devoted herself then to eating the bread but was soon ready to resume her interrogation of her husband. "I know you have a great fondness for the king, love, and I'll not deny he has been right good to you. But I do not understand why he has so little interest in the Holy Land. Most men would be proud that their son had taken the cross as Richard did. As I recall, he was not happy when Hal took the cross, either, and he would not let John go back with the Patriarch of Jerusalem. Nor has he fulfilled his own vow to go on pilgrimage to atone for the archbishop's death."

This was their one serious bone of contention, that Hawisa did not see the king as Willem did. He did not want another argument on the subject, but he could not keep a defensive note from entering his voice. "Yes, Harry did vow to take the cross, but soon after, his sons and queen rebelled, and he could hardly leave, then, could he? And since then his kingdom has been in ferment thanks to those same sons. He has been extremely generous, though, with his financial support, has given the vast sum of thirty thousand silver marks for the defense of the Holy Land."

"Yes, but you told me once that the money is being held by the Templars and Hospitallers, cannot be dispensed without the king's consent. Is that not like giving a gift with the proviso that you can always change your mind and take it back?"

"Indeed it is not. The bulk of the money was to be spent when the king was able to travel himself to the Holy Land. In any event, Guy de Lusignan and his barons drew heavily upon the funds this year to increase their army in the face of Saladin's growing threat."

"And that was a great success," Hawisa said caustically. "I daresay the king considers that money well spent."

"I assume the rest of it is being used to defend Jerusalem, and Harry would never begrudge a penny of that," Willem insisted. Seeing that his wife did not look convinced, he said, "You cannot blame the king for fearing for the safety of his sons in so dangerous a place as Outremer. And as it happens, I did ask him why he was not more concerned about the threat to the Holy Land."

Hawisa's eyes brightened with interest. "Did you now? And what did he say?"

"He gave me one of those looks of his, where he cannot believe anyone could ask so foolish a question. And then he said, 'Of course I care about the fate of the Kingdom of Jerusalem. But I care more about the fate of the Kingdom of England.'"

CHAPTER FIFTY-ONE

✦

January 1188
Gisors, Normandy

ENRY WAS AT BARFLEUR waiting for favorable winds when he learned of the French king's new threats. It seemed that Philippe was no more pleased than Henry by Richard's decision to take the cross, for he was warning that Richard must wed Alys before he departed for the Holy Land or Gisors must be returned at once to the French Crown. If not, he would lay waste to Normandy. Henry reluctantly delayed his return to England and agreed to confer with Philippe at their traditional meeting place, the ancient elm tree near Gisors Castle.

Henry was not sanguine about their chances of reaching an accord. He could not really blame Philippe, for in the latter's place, he'd have been making the same demands. But he was not about to yield up Gisors, for he was convinced the Vexin was rightfully part of Normandy. Neither he nor Richard wanted the marriage, though. Richard had never shown any interest in Alys, and Henry had learned to his cost how dangerous a marital alliance with the French was, for he was convinced that Hal would not have been so easily led into rebellion had he not been the French king's son-in-law. The last thing he wanted was to give Philippe an opportunity to suborn another one of his sons. He felt some pity for Alys, but if the price of her freedom was the loss of the Vexin or outright war, it was too high to pay. A king must do what was best for his realm.

The conference started badly with Philippe insisting at the onset that there'd be no compromises on this issue, and Henry saw they were in for a long, difficult day. Only half listening to arguments he'd heard many times before, he found his attention wandering: to the crowd of onlookers eager to watch the spectacle of two kings in conflict, to the lowering winter sky that was threatening snow, and then to approaching riders. Even at a distance he could see they were well mounted and richly garbed, his gaze drawn to a man wearing a stiff linen miter that marked him as a prince of the Church.

No longer even making a pretense of listening to Philippe, Henry watched as they dismounted, the spectators parting to let them pass. The prelate was resplendent in a blue chasuble and purple dalmatic, both of finely spun silk, brandishing a crozier with a delicate ivory crook. But his face was unfamiliar. By now Philippe had paused to watch, too, and shook his head when Henry asked, "Is he one of yours?"

Identification came from the Count of Flanders. "I know him!" he exclaimed in surprise. "We met in the Holy Land . . . Joscius, the Bishop of Acre."

"No," Henry corrected, for he'd spotted the lamb's wool pallium around the man's shoulders. "He's no longer a bishop, Cousin. We're being honored by a visit from the Archbishop of Tyre."

Greetings were prolonged for the archbishop was accompanied by a number of high-ranking churchmen and the two kings by many of their lords and barons. But once the amenities had been observed, the archbishop drew Philippe, Henry, and Philip aside and shared with them the heavy burden he'd been carrying since leaving Outremer that autumn. As dire as the news of the battle at the Horns of Hattin had been, this was far worse. After a brief siege, the Holy City of Jerusalem had been captured by the Saracens.

As word began to spread, the grieving swept through the crowd like a rogue wave, engulfing men and women alike. People wept openly, cursed aloud, fell to their knees on the frozen ground to pray. It had been less than a hundred years since the first crusaders had retaken Jerusalem for Christendom, but no one had expected the city to fall to the infidels. Surely the Almighty would never let such an atrocity happen?

The kings and their highborn vassals were no less stunned than the spectators. The Count of Flanders was striding up and down, slamming his fist into his palm again and again. Philippe was making the archbishop repeat the story, as if he expected the ending to change upon hearing it again. And Henry's shock was giving way to horror, for he was a student of history and he knew what had happened when Jerusalem had been captured by the Christian army in God's Year 1099. It had been a massacre. Men, women, and children alike were shown no mercy, and it was reported that the bodies of the slain Muslims and Jews had been stacked up in the streets like kindling and knights rode in blood up to their horses' ankles. The archbishop was still occupied with Philippe, and Henry beckoned to one of his companions, clad in the distinctive red cross and white mantle of the Knights Templar, the warrior monks who prided themselves upon being the soldiers of God.

"Tell me the worst," he demanded. "How many died when Jerusalem fell to Saladin?"

To his amazement, the knight shook his head. "There was no slaughter of the citizens."

"Are you saying that Saladin allowed the city to surrender peacefully?"

This time the Templar nodded. "Balian de Ibelin, the Lord of Nablus, was commanding the defense of Jerusalem. When he saw they were doomed, he went to Saladin under a truce and asked to be permitted to surrender. Saladin refused, reminding him of the thousands of Muslims who'd died when the Christians had taken the city. Lord Balian warned him that if they had nothing left to lose, they would kill all of the Muslim prisoners they held, then they would destroy the Dome of the Rock and all the Holy Places in the city, those sacred to Christians and Muslims both, and burn Jerusalem to the ground. Saladin then agreed to ransom the citizens. You saved thousands from slavery or death, my lord king."

"Me? Ah . . . Balian paid for the ransoms with the money I'd provided for the Holy Land."

"Yes, my liege. We paid ten dinars for a man, five for a woman, and two for a child." The knight paused, for it was not easy to speak well of his infidel enemies, not after the blood of his brother Templars had flowed so freely at the Horns of Hattin. But he was an honorable man and felt compelled to admit that "they did show some mercy. Saladin protected patients at the Hospital of St John, and he freed hundreds at Lord Balian's behest and spared the elderly. His brother asked him for a thousand Christians and then set them free. About seven thousand men and eight thousand women and children were still sold as slaves. With your money, though, we were able to buy the freedom for seven thousand of the city's poor."

"Thank God for that," Henry said softly. He was pragmatic by nature and could take comfort from the fact that it could have been so much worse. As he looked around, though, he saw that few would see the loss of Jerusalem in that light. For them, all that mattered was that the Holy City was now in the hands of the infidels.

And it was only then that he realized what this dreadful defeat would mean for him. He glanced quickly toward Philippe, saw that the French king had not yet recognized how adroitly they'd been ambushed, and he smiled grimly. Philippe would not long remain in ignorance.

And indeed, Archbishop Joscius was already stepping forward. "It is only fitting that I speak to the people, tell them what has occurred," he said, and gestured to some of his companions, who began to shout for silence. When the throng finally quieted, he took up a jeweled cross and raised it high.

"Behold the cross of our salvation," he cried in a rich, resonant voice that confirmed Henry's suspicions; the archbishop was a polished orator. "But alas, this is not the most precious of Christendom's holy relics. This is not the fragment of the True Cross. That was stolen by the infidels at the Horns of Hattin, and we've heard it was paraded through the streets of Damascus to jeers and mockery."

He paused for his audience to react and then held his hand up to quiet them. "When I was chosen to tell the Holy Father in Rome of the dreadful calamity that has befallen us, our galley had black sails so that all would know we were the bearers of evil tidings. Everywhere on our journey, we have left wailing and lamentations in our wake. Men and women of faith cried out to Mary, Mother of Mercy, we poor banished children of Eve, mourning and weeping in this vale of tears."

Again he flourished the cross aloft. "You know those words of the Salve Regina, have sung it in our churches for the feasts of the Purification, Annunciation, and Nativity of Our Lady. But how many of you know its origin? How many know it was composed by the Bishop of Puy-en-Velay or that he was the first to take the cross from Pope Urban of blessed memory?

"For that is the message I bring to you this day, good people. The time for tears is past. More is demanded of you, of us all. Because of our sins, the enemy of the cross has devastated with the sword the Promised Land, has dared to invade the Holy City itself. But we must not lose faith, for when God Almighty has been soothed by our repentance, He will bring us gladness after our grief.

"I say to you," he thundered, turning suddenly to face the assembled kings and nobles, "'you soldiers of Hell, become soldiers of the Living God. It is Christ Himself who issues from His tomb and presents to you His Cross. Wear it upon your shoulders. It will remind you that Christ died for you and that it is your duty to die for Him.' So said Pope Urban when he first called upon men to take the cross. His plea is echoed by our Holy Father today. He has charged me to remind you of your duty as sons of the Faith. And to those who undertake this quest with a humble heart and who die in repentance for their sins, he promises a plenary indulgence for all their sins and eternal life."

The crowd was cheering wildly now, but he never took his eyes from his true audience, the men of rank and power, the two kings and their vassals. "Who will answer the call? Who will come to the defense of Zion? Who will free the Holy City from men who do not know God?"

Henry looked around appraisingly. Philippe appeared impassive, showing the public stoicism expected of royalty, but a muscle was twitching in his cheek. The Duke of Burgundy and the Counts of Flanders, Blois, Champagne, Sancerre, and Ponthieu were listening to the archbishop with as much outrage as the prelate could have wished. Henry was sure they'd be trampling one another in their eagerness to answer the archbishop's call. But now all eyes were turning to him and to his adversary, the French king. Suppressing a sigh, Henry stepped forward and in silence utterly remarkable for such a large crowd, he knelt before the archbishop.

"I, Henry, by God's Grace King of the English, Duke of Normandy and Aquitaine, Count of Anjou, do hereby pledge myself to the recovery of the Holy City. My lord archbishop, I ask to be allowed to enter the way of God and to take the cross from your hand."

There was a roar from those watching, as loud a sound as Henry had ever heard, and within momonto tho fiold woo ochoing with tho chant that had launchod tho firot crusade. Even those who knew no Latin but the response to the Mass knew this, the battle cry of their Church: "*Deus vult!*" God wills it!

"Nothing would give me greater pleasure, my lord king," the archbishop said smoothly as one of his archdeacons appeared at his side. Crusader crosses were usually small and crudely cut from whatever cloth was available. The one that the archbishop offered Henry now was of fine linen embroidered with gold thread. The eyes of the two men caught and held, Henry conveying an ironic appreciation of the archbishop's tactical talents and the latter offering an equally ironic acknowledgment of the unspoken compliment. And then Henry rose and raised his cross high for all to see, setting off another spate of cheering.

Philippe stepped forward hastily then, giving Henry a look sharp enough to stab before he knelt and he, too, asked for the cross. Philip of Flanders could barely contain himself, rushing toward the archbishop as soon as Philippe was done, followed by Marie's son, the young Count of Champagne, his uncle the Count of Blois, the Duke of Burgundy, and other men of rank, jostling as they awaited their turns. So many men sought to answer the archbishop's call that he dispatched the other prelates to accept these vows, and for a time there was considerable chaos. An emotional day became even more so when some people cried out that they saw a cross shimmering in the sky above them and this celestial sign of Divine Providence encouraged even more men to volunteer for God's army. The response was so great that the more practical-minded among them suggested that crosses be assigned according to realm, and it was soon agreed that the men of Flanders would bear green crosses, the French would bear red ones, and Henry's vassals would wear white.

It was some time before the archbishop had a moment to himself, and he accepted gratefully when one of his archdeacons proffered a wineskin, for by then his throat was sore and his voice hoarse. He could not remember ever being so exhausted, both physically and emotionally. Nor could he ever remember feeling such a sense of peace. The Bishop of Tripoli had joined him, saying, "I confess I did not see the cross in the sky myself. By the time I looked, it was gone. But none would argue that this has been a day for miracles."

The archbishop glanced at his friend and then across the field, where the kings of England and France were being mobbed by their supporters. "The greatest miracle," he said with a smile, "was getting those two to take the cross."

CONSTANCE KNEW she was sprinkling salt into an open wound, but she could not seem to help herself. Lying awake in the dark of a cold February night, sharing her bed with a stranger, she could not keep her memories at bay, could not stop comparing her two wedding days. She remembered well how unhappy she'd been as she struggled to play the role of Geoffrey's blushing bride. Looking back upon it, she realized that her barons had not shared her discontent. By then they'd had six years to take Geoffrey's measure, had a better idea of the man she was marrying than she did.

This time around, the Bretons and she were of one mind—embittered that the English king had forced his own man upon them. They'd not bothered to make much of a pretense of amiability either, proof that they expected the young Earl of Chester's influence to be limited in scope. The duchy was bilingual, with Breton and French both in widespread use. The Breton tongue was more likely to be heard in the western areas such as Léon; lords such as the de Vitrés and the barons of Fougères were native French-speakers, as Constance herself was. But the wedding feast had resonated with the sounds of Breton, an effective means of isolating their new duke, for Randolph of Chester spoke only French. He had spent enough time in Brittany, though, to understand the insult he was being offered by his wife's vassals.

Randolph stirred and Constance stiffened, listening intently until his soft, even breathing assured her that he still slept. Even though their initial coupling had not been a success, giving her no pleasure and him very little, she knew that with youths of eighteen, the flesh was always willing and a naked woman in his bed would be a temptation he was not likely to resist. His eagerness had been part of their problem; she could tell he was embarrassed by how quickly he'd spilled his seed. Geoffrey had taught her well and she could easily have shown him those tricks a man could use to prolong his pleasure. But why should she? She'd wanted only to get it over with as quickly as possible, for it had been harder than she'd expected—having to submit to the wrong man's intimate caresses. Her mind may have accepted the unwelcome reality of her marriage, but her body still felt violated.

It had not helped that she'd felt Geoffrey's presence so strongly, that her memories had been so merciless. It was too easy to envision Geoffrey watching from the shadows, offering a sardonic commentary on Randolph's lovemaking. She knew she had to exorcise him from her head and heart if there was any hope of reaching an accord with her new husband. She knew, too, that she might even feel a flicker of pity for Randolph if she let herself, for he was laboring under some severe handicaps—thrust into a land that was not his own, having to cope with vassals who did not want him there and a worldly older wife who did not want him, either.

But if his plight was awkward, what of her own? Widowed at twenty-five, left with three young children to raise and protect on her own, caught between the French and English kings like those ancient sailors forced to brave the perils of Scylla and Charybdis. Where was the fairness in that? Was it fair that Geoffrey had died so needlessly? That he'd left his wife and family in such peril? Was it fair that she must now share her body and her bed with this callow lordling? That she would never again know the pleasures to be found in a man's arms?

Unlike her first wedding, when she'd abstained from wine to be sure she'd be able to govern her tongue, she'd lost track of the cups she'd drained this night, hoping that if she were tipsy enough, she'd find it easier to submit to Randolph. It hadn't helped much. She was definitely not sober, but all that wine had done little to dilute her misery. If she ever did get to sleep, she'd likely awaken in the morning with a wretched headache, too, what Geoffrey had called "the drunkard's penance."

Was he going to haunt her like this for the rest of her days? Go away, Geoffrey, she entreated silently. Please go away. *Do you truly want me to go away, darling?* She knew it was not really his voice that was echoing in her ears, but it sounded so real, so like him. "No," she whispered, "no . . ." and shut her eyes tightly as she tried to squeeze back her tears.

LATER IN THE MONTH, Henry convened a council at Le Mans, where it was decided that a tax would be levied upon a tenth of all the movable property and revenues of his subjects, what would be known as the Saladin Tithe and would become extremely unpopular even among churchmen. Those who took the cross were exempt from the tithe; any debts they owed were postponed until their return, and their property was taken under the protection of the Church. Men found themselves under increasing pressure to take the cross, and those who did not were mocked and presented with distaff and wool as an obvious slur upon their manhood. Crusading fervor swept through Christendom, and rulers vowed to set their differences aside and unite for the defense of the Holy Land.

It was expected to take well over a year to make the necessary preparations, but Richard was not willing to wait that long, and he sought Henry's permission to raise money on the security of Poitou and to receive public acknowledgment of his status as heir apparent before he departed. But Henry insisted that Richard wait, arguing that they should travel to the Holy Land together. Richard's demand for official recognition was once more brushed aside. Richard was not dissuaded and began to make his own arrangements for an early departure. It was then, though, that another rebellion broke out in Poitou, begun when a friend of Richard's was slain by Joffroi de Lusignan and quickly joined by the Count of Angoulême and Geoffrey de Rançon. Richard swooped down upon them, once again captured the impregnable castle of Taillebourg, sparing the captured rebels only when they agreed to take the cross.

Richard had little time to enjoy the resumption of peace in his duchy, for his old enemy, the Count of Toulouse, seized this opportunity to make trouble, maltreating Poitevin merchants passing through his lands. Richard retaliated by capturing one of Count Raimon's closest advisors and refusing all of the count's offers to ransom the man. Count Raimon then arrested two English knights making their way home from a pilgrimage to Santiago de Compostela. Outraged by this sacrilegious attack upon pilgrims, Richard launched a major assault upon Toulouse, capturing seventeen castles with impressive speed and driving his army into the heart of Raimon's domains.

An alarmed French king then came to the defense of his liegeman and raided into Berry. To the dismay of the Church and those men who'd pledged to recover the Holy City, the accord reached at Gisors seemed about to go up in the smoke of burning towns in Toulouse and Berry.

JULY HAD BEEN AN INCLEMENT MONTH so far, and the castle at Sarum was being buffeted by high winds and thunderstorms. Eleanor had been surprised by Henry's unexpected arrival that week, for Sarum was out of his way; he was planning to sail for Normandy in response to the latest crisis and his fleet was awaiting him at Portsea. Her transfer to Sarum had shown Eleanor that she was back in her husband's bad graces, because of his deteriorating relationship with Richard; each time his son dared to defy him, his suspicions invariably spilled over onto her, too. But during his brief stay at Sarum, she'd come to the startling conclusion that he'd made a deliberate detour in order to bid her farewell. She'd attempted to find out if he was ailing again, to no avail. No one was better than Henry at giving evasive responses to questions he did not want to answer, and she finally decided that as he aged, he was coming to share the natural anxiety of all sensible people when making a Channel crossing.

That theory lasted no longer than his announcement that he planned to sail if the winds were in his favor, the rain and choppy seas notwithstanding. Gazing at her husband in exasperation, she could only shake her head in feigned disbelief. "If it is your destiny to drown, why do you need to give fate a helping hand?"

Her scolding sounded so familiar that Henry could not help smiling. "Since when have I let bad weather interfere with my plans? Have you forgotten that we sailed in a God-awful storm to claim the English crown?"

Eleanor remembered that turbulent voyage all too well, although it seemed so long ago that it might have happened to two other people. Knowing it was futile to argue once he'd made up his mind, she focused instead upon the crusader's emblem stitched to the shoulder of his mantle. "Well, they say the Almighty looks after those who've taken the cross, however halfheartedly they took their vows."

He was not offended by her gibe, for Eleanor was the only one with whom he could be truly honest about the crusade. Even with close friends like Willem, he could not confess his misgivings, for Willem had already undertaken one pilgrimage of his own and was eager to undertake another. Nor could he confide in his sons, for Richard's crusading fever burned fiercely and he did not feel comfortable talking to John man-to-man, his instincts still to shelter his last-born.

"If you think I was halfhearted," he said, "you ought to have seen Philippe Capet trying to hide his lack of enthusiasm. I think he was convinced that I'd taken the cross just to spite him. But one of the few advantages of aging is that you learn to recognize when defeat is staring you in the face, wearing an archbishop's miter. Not even Merlin himself could have escaped that trap." Moving to the window, he pulled the shutter back to gaze out at the dismal, rain-drenched bailey. "I do care about the recovery of Jerusalem, Eleanor. But I cannot help putting the interests of my own kingdom first. Philippe and I are struggling against the tide, though, and all we can do is try to stay afloat."

Eleanor could sympathize, for Poitiers mattered more to her than the Holy City. Moreover, Louis's disastrous crusade had raised doubts in her mind about the efficacy of such a quest. "It is not always easy to be a good Christian and a good king." Unable to resist adding, "Or a good father and a good king."

"Or to be a good mother and a good wife," he shot back, and she acknowledged his riposte with a wry smile.

"That is not as difficult as you seem to think, Harry. Let me prove it. Let me tell you a simple way to resolve your differences with Richard and restore peace, both to our family and your empire."

He raised a brow. "Can you also turn water into wine?"

"No, nor can I turn a rebellious, resentful son into a respectful, contented one. But you can, Harry, and it would be so easy. You need only make a public declaration that Richard is your heir, to be king after you. That is all it would take."

"You just proved my argument for me. If I were foolish enough to take your advice, Richard would benefit greatly, all at my expense. If there were no longer any doubts about the succession, I'd have no leverage at all, no way to exert any influence over Richard."

"But you'd not need leverage if you formally named Richard as your heir, for he would have no grievances then. All he wants is his birthright. As your eldest surviving son, he is entitled to inherit the kingdom in his turn. You need only say so, without evasions or equivocations, and you remove the main cause of contention between you."

"I'd like to give you the benefit of the doubt, assume that you honestly believe what you're saying. How can I, though, when you know the sorry story of Richard's past history fully as well as I do. Does your memory really need refreshing, Eleanor? Must I remind you that last year's near-war with Philippe ended with Richard riding off with him to Paris? Or that all reports had them acting closer than brothers? Have you forgotten what Richard did next? He rode to Chinon, seized the treasury I kept there, and hastened into Poitou to fortify all his castles against me."

Henry had been endeavoring to sound matter-of-fact, but he betrayed his inner agitation by the color rising in his face. "And that is not the half of it. Richard never fails to believe the worst of me. Indeed, I think it gives him pleasure. He nurses his suspicions the way a miser hoards his coins, and nothing seems too far-fetched for him to believe. I have even heard that he suspects me of providing money to the Poitevin rebels and the Count of Toulouse. Supposedly I am the mastermind behind all the strife in his duchy, hoping to create enough unrest to keep him from going to the Holy Land."

"Oh, my," Eleanor said, biting her lip to keep from smiling. "You know, that sounds just devious enough to have come from your brain, Harry."

"I did nothing of the sort!" he snapped, so indignantly that she could not doubt his sincerity on this much, at least.

"I believe you. But you cannot blame Richard for giving it some credence. You've always been too clever by half, Harry, and now you are reaping what you've sown.

You've spun such fine webs over the years that I suppose it was inevitable you'd eventually ensnare yourself in one."

"I am glad that you find this so amusing."

"Believe me, my lord husband, I find nothing even remotely amusing about any of this. I will not deny that Richard trusts you no more than you trust him. But why is that? Because of your determination to keep him in suspense about his heritage. Because you gave him reason to think you were considering Geoffrey in his stead and you continue to raise suspicions with the favor you show John. Because you even sought to take Aquitaine away from him!"

"I meant to deprive him of nothing! I was only trying to provide properly for Johnny, as any father would. You keep blaming me for not acknowledging Richard as my heir. Well, I offered to do just that after Hal died. But Richard scorned the offer, surely the only man in Christendom who'd choose a duchy over a kingdom!"

"Dear God in Heaven!" Eleanor was staring at him in dismay. "You have not given up on that, have you? You still hope to coax or coerce Richard into yielding up Aquitaine to John!"

He was too angry to deny it. "What if I do? As you delight in reminding me, Aquitaine is your legacy. It makes more political sense to have it ruled by its own duke, as Brittany is. If Richard becomes king, he'll have little time for personal rule over that hornet's nest of rebels and malcontents!"

" 'If Richard becomes king?' That truly goes to the heart of the matter, to your reluctance to anoint your successor. The only thing worse than not learning from your mistakes is learning the wrong lessons. Richard is not Hal, and your refusal to see that may end up costing you dearly!"

He glared at her, then swung around to stalk out. He halted at the door, though, standing motionless for a moment and then slamming his fist into the heavy oaken wood. When he turned back to face her, his mask was gone. "Do you think I wanted it this way? I loved my father dearly, never imagined that my sons would not love me."

"Ah, Harry . . ."

"I lost Hal and then Geoffrey, and Richard . . . he was always yours, never mine. If it were not for Johnny . . . Can you not see why I want to do right by him? He is all I have left."

She was shocked by what he'd just done, dropping his defenses to give her a glimpse of an open, bleeding wound. Crossing the chamber, she came into his arms. He held her so tightly that it hurt and they stood like that for a timeless moment, one in which they recognized all that still bound them together and mourned all that had been lost.

When Henry released her and stepped back, he was once more in control of himself. "I would ask you to come with me to the Holy Land," he said lightly, "but it has been agreed that women are to be banned from the expedition, save only laundresses of good character."

"My legacy, I daresay," she said with a smile. "Apparently the stories of my pilgrimage with Louis have passed into legend." He smiled, too, encouraging her to make one last attempt. "Harry, I am imploring you to give some thought to what I've said. There is still time to make things right with Richard."

She'd half expected him to react in anger again. Instead, he took her hand in his, pressed his lips to her palm, wondering if their marriage might have been different if she'd given to him the utter, unconditional loyalty that she gave to Richard. "I hope Richard realizes how fortunate he is to have you as his advocate."

She almost told him the truth, that her fears were not for Richard. Time was Richard's ally, not his. But she knew he'd never forgive her if she admitted that she saw him now as the vulnerable one. So she said only, "I will pray for your safe voyage to Barfleur."

Henry sailed in a violent storm, but he found conditions no less turbulent upon his return to Normandy and the rest of the summer was taken up with skirmishing, raids, threats, and futile peace conferences. At one held near Gisors that August, it went so badly that Philippe angrily ordered the ancient elm tree be chopped down. A second meeting in October at Châtillon-sur-Indre was no more successful. It began promisingly, with the agreement that Philippe would return the gains he'd made in Berry and Richard would relinquish his conquests in Toulouse. But then Philippe demanded that Henry surrender his castle at Pacy as a "good faith pledge," and the council broke up in acrimony.

Richard's frustration grew by the day, for he could not depart for the Holy Land as long as this sporadic war raged between England and France. He received some unexpected support that autumn when the Count of Flanders, the Counts of Blois and Champagne, and other French lords balked at continuing to wage war against their fellow crusaders, and faced with the defection of a large part of his army, Philippe reluctantly agreed when Richard proposed another peace council at Bonsmoulins in November. Henry was willing, too, and Richard set the plans in motion. But he was determined to end this impasse one way or another, and he had a secret parley with the French king before they were to gather at Bonsmoulins.

CHAPTER FIFTY-TWO

✝

November 1188
Bonsmoulins, Normandy

ICHARD'S NEW CHANCELLOR, Guillaume de Longchamp, was meeting his duke at the Cistercian abbey of La Trappe, not far from the conference site at Bonsmoulins. He was unpopular with Richard's knights, partly because of their natural distrust of clerks and partly because of Longchamp's physical flaws. The young men agreed that Longchamp was one of the ugliest individuals they'd ever seen: short and swarthy, with close-set black eyes, a flat nose, and a receding chin. Moreover, he was crippled, lame in both legs, and theirs was a world in which deformity was often seen as the outer manifestation of inner evil.

As the chancellor limped toward the abbey guest hall, he was aware of the hostile scrutiny of a handful of Richard's knights. He knew what was said of him, that they referred to him behind his back as a "dwarf" and "elf" and "gargoyle." He knew, too, that they resented him all the more because he was not meek and obsequious, because he refused to act like one of society's misfits. He believed that his superior intellect mattered more than his physical defects and saw no reason why he must defer to these fortunate young men with handsome faces and healthy bodies and empty heads. He could hear their muttering as he was admitted into Richard's presence without delay; it vexed them no end that he stood so high in the duke's favor.

Richard smiled at the sight of him. "Come with me, Guillaume," he directed. "We need to talk in private."

As he followed Richard across the hall, Longchamp took satisfaction in the disgruntled expressions on the faces around him. Let them call him arrogant and presumptuous. Their enmity did not change the fact that he was the duke's confidant, viewed as utterly trustworthy by a man who did not find it easy to trust.

Once they were alone in Richard's chamber, he waved his chancellor toward a seat even though he remained on his feet. The only way that he ever indicated his awareness of Longchamp's physical frailty was by this casual concern for the older man's comfort, acknowledging Longchamp's special needs without making a fuss about it. It was as close as Longchamp had come to acceptance in a life of rejection and he valued it almost as much as he did the chancellorship. His ambition had drawn him to Richard, after an earlier stint as a chancery clerk. But his fierce absolute loyalty was rooted in these small acts of unexpected kindness.

"How did your meeting with the French king go, my lord?" And when Richard said it had gone well, Longchamp felt secure enough to venture a small jest. "Has he forgiven you, then, for calling him a 'vile recreant' at Châtillon-sur-Indre?"

Richard grinned. "He'd have forgiven much worse, Guillaume. I made an interesting discovery at Mantes. Philippe is not only eager to ally himself with me. He is downright desperate to bring it about. He is a very clever lad, the French king. But he shares the same weakness that my father does—a tendency to undervalue his adversaries."

"Will he support you at the Bonsmoulins conclave?"

"Yes, he will. We are going to demand that my father formally recognize me as his heir. I can no longer abide his infernal games-playing, need to have this settled ere I can depart for the Holy Land. If my foes think I may not become king, they'll take advantage of my absence to stir up rebellions in Aquitaine and start courting my little brother's favor in hopes of playing king-maker."

"Do you truly think your lord father would dare to disinherit you in favor of John?"

Richard took his time in answering. "I am not sure, Guillaume. I do not doubt that he'd rather see John succeed him than me. Would he actually do it? If he thought he could get away with it, probably. He must know that I'd never accept it, though, and John's reign would be the shortest in English history. Of course Philippe swears by all the saints that there is no doubt whatsoever, that he means to put John in my place even if it means war."

Richard had been pacing as he talked. Stopping abruptly, he glanced toward his chancellor with an expression Longchamp could not easily read. "Philippe never misses an opportunity to sing that song. To hear him tell it, my father spends every waking moment scheming to rob me of my rightful heritage. But according to what I was told at Mantes, that is not exactly true. Apparently he found time to pay some nocturnal visits to my betrothed."

Longchamp could not believe he'd heard correctly. "I . . . I am not sure I understand, my lord."

"I think you do. Philip of Flanders was the one to break the news to me, but he was doing Philippe's bidding. They claim that my father seduced Alys a few years back and this is the real reason why he is loath to allow our marriage. I suppose he thought I might balk at sharing her favors once we were wed."

The chancellor was dumbfounded and suddenly fearful, feeling as if he were teetering upon the edge of a cliff where the slightest movement might send him plunging into a fatal fall. He'd not have thought the discord between the king and the duke could get any worse . . . until now. Adding a woman to the mix would do it, though. But how was he supposed to react to such news? What did Richard want him to say?

"My lord, I . . ." Should he express outrage? Horror at the king's depravity? But what if Richard did not believe the story? What if he did want to marry the girl? He could find no clues in Richard's face. If he erred, there would be no recovery. Oh, the duke might not dismiss him, but the wrong answer was bound to affect his prospects, to impair his credibility. He took several deep breaths to steady his nerves, and then made the only choice he could. Since he did not know the "right answer" to this deadly riddle, all he could do was speak the truth. "I have my doubts about that, my lord."

Richard showed no reaction. "Why is that?"

Longchamp knotted his fingers together in his lap. "If I may speak candidly, my lord duke? From what I've heard said of the English king, he is a man given to sins of the flesh. He has violated his marriage vows time and time again. I would not find it easy to defend his sense of honor. But I have never heard him called a fool. And to have taken your betrothed, the sister of the French king, as his concubine would be an act beyond foolhardy. It would be quite mad."

He could feel sweat trickling down his ribs, could taste it on his upper lip. He even imagined his thudding heartbeat must be audible to Richard in the endless silence that greeted his words. When he could endure it no longer, he said hoarsely, "If I have offended you, my lord . . ."

"You have not," Richard said composedly. As their eyes met, Longchamp saw that he had guessed right, and he went limp with relief, understanding just how much had been at stake. Richard agreed with him, did not credit this malicious rumor. But more important, this had been a test, both of his judgment and of his willingness to speak honestly, to tell the duke what he really thought. And he had passed it, had proven himself worthy of the duke's trust.

Richard sat down in a high-backed chair, stretching his long legs toward the warmth of the hearth. "Your logic is impeccable, Guillaume," he said approvingly. "My father is, as you say, 'given to sins of the flesh.' But he has never been one for thinking with his cock. And Alys Capet is no Helen of Troy. Philippe ought to have known better."

Longchamp had no interest whatsoever in the French princess; he neither liked nor trusted women. But he said now what he thought was expected of a man of God and shook his head disapprovingly. "It is indeed shameful that the French king would besmirch his own sister's honor for political gain."

"Shameful, indeed," Richard echoed, so dryly that Longchamp realized the duke was not taken in by his sham indignation, knew it was feigned and did not care in the least. "It is not as if Philippe has ever been the soul of sentiment. And I do not think he has even seen Alys since she was handed over to my parents at the time of our betrothal, when he was all of four, five at the most. It would not surprise me, though, if my cousin Philip was the one to suggest the idea to Philippe. That is how Philip got control of his wife's inheritance, after all, by accusing her of adultery."

"We are dealing with some very unscrupulous men, my lord."

"Yes, the gathering at Bonsmoulins ought to be a most interesting encounter. It is all such hypocrisy, Guillaume. Any peace between my father and Philippe would last as long as ice on a summer's day, for there is not enough trust between them to fill a walnut shell. The both of them are born liars, but I will do whatever I must to patch up a peace, for without it, I dare not leave for the Holy Land. So I will let the French king think that he is using me. I will even overlook the fact that he clearly believes me to be as easily duped as my brother Hal. I'll admit I was somewhat insulted at first by that. But then I realized what a convenient excuse he has given me for refusing to wed his sister. He wants that wedding, you see, for the same reason that my father does not want it: Hal's sorry example. But I have no intention of taking Alys as my wife. I do not need her to hold on to the Vexin, and I can do better for England. The marriage would not turn Philippe into an ally. It could be revealed that he is really one of my father's bastards and he'd still hate the Angevins."

Richard debated telling his chancellor that he was thinking of a marital alliance with Navarre, which made a great deal of strategic sense, but he decided he'd shared enough of his secrets with the cleric this day. "So," he concluded, "should Philippe ever attempt to compel me to honor the plight-troth with Alys, I would be quite indignant. How could he expect me, after all, to wed my father's bedmate?"

"I think the English and French kings are going to find you are more than a match for either one of them," Longchamp said admiringly. What a formidable team they were going to make. And since Richard's future held the promise of a crown, mayhap he could dare to dream of a bishop's miter.

Longchamp had learned that Richard's moods were mercurial, and like his father, he was as changeable as the winds. He was not surprised now when Richard's acerbic amusement gave way without warning to a far grimmer humor. "I am not going to let him win, Guillaume," he said. "Not this time. I could not keep him from making my mother pay the price for our failed rebellion. Fifteen years she has been his prisoner, fifteen years! And she *is* his prisoner, for all that she no longer wants for a queen's comforts. I have had to submit to his demands and subject myself to his whims and endure the indignity of having him brandish the crown before me as he would tease a dog with a bone. But no more. I will not let him rob me of my birthright, and I will not let him keep me from honoring my vow to defend the Holy Land. I do think he is behind that very opportune rebellion in my duchy, and I would not put it past him to be conniving with the Count of Toulouse, either. And if by chance, he did not, it is only because he did not think of it. No, a reckoning is long overdue, and we will have it at Bonsmoulins."

THE PEACE CONFERENCE at Bonsmoulins would prove to be one of the worst experiences of Henry's life. His suspicions were immediately ignited when Richard and the French king arrived together, not believing for a moment Richard's nonchalant claim that they'd just happened to meet on the way. Still brooding over the offer Richard had made at Châtillon-sur-Indre, declaring that he was willing to submit his dispute with the Count of Toulouse to the judgment of the French court if that would end the hostilities, Henry needed little to convince himself that they were secretly in league against him, for Eleanor's charge had been right. He did not trust his eldest son.

The first day had gone well enough, with all parties maintaining civility. By the second day, tempers had begun to fray, and by the third day, negotiations had become so heated that Henry and Philippe's knights were keeping their hands on their sword hilts. As was customary, they were meeting in an open field not far from Bonsmoulins Castle, and the blustery November weather only added to the general sense of discontent and distrust. But even Henry's bleak expectations had not prepared him for what was to come.

The cold and the damp seemed to have penetrated to the very marrow of his bones and his bad leg was aching, but Henry would not show weakness by requesting a chair. His physical discomfort was just one more aggravation on a day of many. So far little progress had been made, despite the best efforts of the Norman and French bishops, who feared that their holy crusade might be doomed before it even began. And by mid-afternoon, Henry's patience had run out.

"This is a waste of all our time," he said curtly. "For three days we have been wrangling like barn cats, and what have we accomplished? We've agreed on a truce to last till St Hilary's Day! Unless you have a new proposal to make, my lord king of the French, I suggest we put an end to this trumpery, resume once you are truly interested in reaching terms."

"We can settle our differences here and now," Philippe said coolly. "We have but two demands to make and are willing to overlook all our other grievances if you are prepared to concede on these two points."

Henry's eyes turned accusingly toward Richard. "Does he speak for you now?"

"In this, he does." Before Philippe could continue, though, Richard stepped forward. "But first I would have a private word with you, my lord father."

This was the first time that Richard had even acknowledged their blood bond, and Henry nodded his agreement. They walked away from the others, coming to a stop under a gnarled oak, stripped bare by the winter winds. "I want to caution you," Richard said bluntly, "to think carefully ere you answer us. There is no room for compromise here, and more rides upon your response than you could ever know."

Henry scowled. "Is this why you took me aside—to threaten me?"

Richard started to speak, stopped himself. "So be it," he said, and turned on his heel, leaving his father to return on his own to the waiting circle.

"I am willing to make a true and lasting peace with England," Philippe demanded, "and to return all of the lands I've claimed in this past year. But in return, my lord king, you must at once hand over the Lady Alys to our keeping so that we may make arrangements for her marriage to the Duke of Aquitaine. And you must also order your barons and vassals to swear an oath of fealty to the duke, as your heir and king-to-be. Do this and we will be content."

"I daresay you would be content," Henry jeered, "and why not? You would be dictating terms to another king, meddling in English internal matters, and using the threat of war to gain your own way. I would be a poor king indeed if I yielded to French extortion or allowed you to crown my heir apparent. I'd sooner abdicate than betray my coronation oath and the promises I made to preserve and protect the English kingdom."

Before Philippe could respond, Richard strode over to confront his father. "Are you denying that I am your rightful heir?"

"I am saying that I will not be coerced or compelled. Any declarations I might make today would be suspect and bring shame to me and to my subjects, for it would seem as if I were not acting of my own free will."

For a long moment, they stared at each other, and then Richard slowly shook his head. "Now at last I must believe what I had always thought was impossible." Turning his back upon his father, he unfastened his mantle, let it slip to the ground, removed his hat, and unbuckled his scabbard, handing his sword to the closest of his men. He then crossed to the French king and knelt before him.

"My lord king and liege lord. As Duke of Aquitaine and rightful heir to the English throne, I do willingly enter into your homage and faith and become your sworn man for the Duchy of Aquitaine, the Duchy of Normandy, for Anjou, Maine, Berry, Toulouse, and all my other fiefs on this side of the sea, saving only the fealty that I owe to my lord father, the English king."

Philippe had listened with the glimmer of a smile. "We do promise you, my vassal and liegeman, that we and our heirs will guarantee to you and your heirs those lands that you now hold of us, against all others. And we do hereby promise to return to your keeping those lands we'd taken in Berry and to assure your possession of those lands you now hold in Toulouse."

Rising, Richard accepted the kiss of peace from his new liege lord and then reclaimed his sword. "We are done here, then," he said, and walked away without once looking back at his father.

MORGAN'S FAMILY WAS NOT PLEASED by his belated decision to accept Henry's offer. His mother had been very happy to have him home again, his brother could not imagine why he'd want to leave Wales, and his father was wary of him becoming entangled in the political turmoil roiling the Angevin Empire. When it became apparent that he was determined, though, Ranulf insisted upon giving him a letter for the English king, pointing out that Henry may have forgotten all about his young Welsh cousin by now in light of the ongoing crisis. "But I've always been his favorite uncle," he said, "and if I ask it of him, he'll be sure to find a place for you." Morgan accepted the letter with thanks, but he doubted that he'd have to use it. He was convinced that he needed no other credentials than his link to Henry's son.

And when he finally caught up with the king, holding his Christmas Court at Saumur in Anjou, his confidence was justified by the warmth of his welcome. Henry seemed genuinely pleased to see him, so much so that some of the other knights looked askance at this newcomer thrust into their midst. Morgan had always heard

that royal courts were breeding grounds for intrigue, envy, and rivalry, and those stories seemed confirmed by the coolness of the king's household mesnie. His first few
days were lonely ones, and he began to wonder if he'd made a mistake. But he'd grown
bored in Wales, missing the energy and excitement of the Breton court. In truth, he'd
been tempted from the first by Henry's offer. He could not in good conscience join the
king's service, though, until he was sure Henry would not be making war on Geoffrey's
lady. When word had finally trickled into Wales that Constance had thrown her lot in
with Henry rather than Philippe, he felt free then to offer his services to Geoffrey's father.

He'd not expected to be treated like an interloper. Outgoing and sociable, he was
accustomed to making friends easily. The rules seemed different at the royal court,
though. It was shaping up, he thought, to be a bleak Christmas indeed, for the king's
anxieties naturally filtered down to his followers. But things changed for the better
with the arrival of William Marshal, returning from a diplomatic mission to the Flemish court. To Morgan's surprised pleasure, the celebrated older knight greeted him as
if they were comrades of long standing and his approval was enough to win acceptance for the king's newest knight.

Morgan was very flattered by Will's friendliness because the older man had risen
in the world since their last meeting. He'd always been acclaimed for his battle and
tourney skills, but now he was a man of substance, too. Henry had given him the
wardship of an heiress and the manor of Cartmel in northern England upon his return from fulfilling Hal's pilgrimage pledge in the Holy Land. But that past July, Henry
had bestowed upon him a far greater prize, Denise de Deols, the heiress who would
bring Will the Honour of Châteauroux. The castle itself had fallen to Philippe that
summer, but Denise was safe in England, lodged with Richard's unhappy betrothed
Alys and John's bride-to-be, Avisa of Gloucester. She was too young for marriage yet,
Will explained to Morgan, but his future was now assured, and all agreed he'd done remarkably well for a younger son with no lands of his own.

As Christmas drew nigh, the weather took a nasty turn, and on this Friday
evening, snow was falling thickly upon the ancient castle perched high above the River
Loire. The night's fish meal had been a modest one by royal standards, for Henry was
ailing again and his cooks were taking advantage of his failing appetite to slack off. At
least that was the view of the knights gathered around the hall's center hearth. Hours
later, they were still complaining about the inferior quality of the fish that had been
served, grumbling that the sauce had been too salty and the bread hard enough to
pound nails. Will and Morgan and several of the Marshal's friends were listening to
these laments with amusement, for soldiers had griped about such matters since the
dawn of time.

"In one breath they'll be claiming the wine tastes like goat's piss and in the next breath asking for more," Will said with a wry smile. "Though it is true that this was a meager meal to serve at a king's table. I've talked to the steward about it, but he insists the cooks and kitchen servants are doing the best they can, pointing out that they'd not expected the king to celebrate Christmas at Saumur when Chinon is so close at hand."

"I once knew a traveling player, and he told me one of the tricks of their trade. When they arrived in a town, they liked to give their performances in as crowded a site as possible to make it look as if they'd drawn twice the audience they actually did."

Morgan looked curiously at the speaker, for this was not the first time that he'd heard comments about the poor turnout for a royal Christmas Court. The king's son John was present as was his other son, the chancellor, the steadfast Earl of Essex and his wife, Maurice de Craon, and some Norman barons and bishops. But many more were conspicuous by their absence, either keeping to their own hearths or paying court to Henry's rebel son Richard.

Morgan had been stunned to learn that Richard had done homage to the French king, for he'd not realized how serious their rupture was until his arrival at Saumur. The king had gone "white as death," Will told him sadly, and since then not a one of them had heard him so much as mention Richard's name. Unlike many of the king's knights, Morgan was not personally hostile toward Richard. If Geoffrey's rebellion was understandable, then in fairness he could not hold Richard to a higher standard of accountability, for he had genuine grievances, too. Still, he regretted Richard's public repudiation of his father, for that seemed like such a drastic step to take.

The other knights were still discussing the lords and barons who'd chosen to stay away from Saumur. The more he listened, the more unsettled Morgan became. "You make it sound," he protested, "as if the king will not be able to rely upon his own vassals. Surely that is not so?"

There was a telling silence, and then Will said stoutly, "Men of honor will stand by the king."

"And the others will wait to see who is likely to win, the king or his son. Anyone want to wager that the second band far outnumbers the first?"

This was the same man who'd implied that Henry had chosen Saumur over Chinon to make the disappointing attendance at his Christmas Court less noticeable. Renaud was one of the sons of the Count of Dammartin, a young man with a sardonic tongue, a swagger, and a disconcerting habit of saying what was on his mind.

Some of the others viewed him with mistrust for he'd been raised with Philippe in Paris, but Will Marshal's look of disapproval now was aimed at Renaud's cynical appraisal of Henry's chances of victory. "I have more faith in the king's vassals than you do," he insisted, but he saw Renaud's pessimism mirrored on many of the other faces.

Renaud himself did not look impressed by the rebuke. "If you are right, Sir William, Saumur ought to be swarming with men eager to display their loyalty to the king. But the hall does not look all that crowded, does it? Whether we like it or not, rats rarely swim toward a sinking ship."

There was another awkward silence, for most of the men were not comfortable with such blunt speaking. If Henry's ship was floundering, they were at peril, too. Once again it was Will Marshal who took charge. "I cannot speak for any others," he said brusquely. "But I will not be amongst those who abandon their liege lord, and if you are right, Renaud, it is a shameful commentary upon our times. As I said, no man of honor would betray the king."

Renaud de Dammartin opened his mouth to argue further. But before he could speak, Baldwin de Bethune leaned over and clamped his hand warningly upon the younger man's wrist. Baldwin was a close friend of the Marshal's. Renaud considered him a friend, too, though, and he looked at the Flemish knight in surprise.

Baldwin shook his head, almost imperceptibly, and Renaud saw several of the men were gazing over his shoulder toward the stairwell. He turned in time to catch a movement in the shadows, and felt a sudden unease that he could not explain. No one spoke for several moments, not until Baldwin said softly, "He's gone."

"Who is gone?" Renaud demanded, though he was not sure he wanted the answer to that question.

"The king's son. I saw him standing in the stairwell, listening to us."

Renaud cursed softly. "You do not think he thought I was advocating a wait-and-see approach, do you? I am here with the king now, am I not?" He was more disquieted than he wanted to admit, though, so much so that it did not occur to him to ask the natural question. Will did, and Renaud felt some relief when Baldwin said it was the Count of Mortain, not the chancellor, for Geoff's fiery loyalty to the king was legendary. Lord John was more of an unknown quantity, and Renaud assured himself that there was no reason to think he'd go to the old king with what he'd heard.

After that, they found safer topics of conversation. Morgan was among those listening to a minstrel's plaintive song of lost love when he received an unexpected summons to the king's bedchamber. Baffled and a little bit nervous, Morgan followed a servant from the hall. The snow was coming down so heavily now that when he glanced over his shoulder, he could no longer see the footprints they'd tracked across the bailey. Why would the king want to see him?

Flames were crackling in the hearth, and Morgan was grateful when Henry instructed him to warm himself by the fire. The king was seated in a cushioned chair, his leg propped up on a stool. He looked very tired and caught up in thoughts that were far from pleasant. "I had sorrowful news today, Morgan," he said, his voice so low that Morgan could barely hear his words. "A message from Brittany, from the Lady Constance."

Morgan felt a flicker of unease. "The duchess . . . she is well, my lord?"

"No . . . she is heartsick. Her daughter is dead."

Morgan gasped, then said haltingly, "Which . . . which one?"

"Matilda, her younger. A sudden fever." Henry closed his eyes for a moment. "Constance says she was not sick long . . ."

"Sire, I am so sorry. I hope it is of some comfort to the duchess and to you that she is with her father now."

Henry looked up, his eyes glistening. "At least Geoffrey was spared this. It is an awful thing to lose a child, Morgan. I hope you never learn what it is like."

Morgan nodded mutely, not knowing what to say. "I will pray for her soul," he promised at last, but Henry did not reply. It soon became apparent to him that the king had forgotten he was there. He waited a while longer and then quietly withdrew. Henry did not seem to notice, continuing to gaze into the flickering, wavering flames.

CHAPTER FIFTY-THREE

✦

June 1189
La Ferté-Bernard, Maine

IN THE MONTHS since Richard's dramatic public repudiation at Bons-moulins, Henry tried in vain to reestablish communications between them, en-treating his son to return to the English court. But even when he dispatched the Archbishop of Canterbury as his messenger, Richard refused to meet with the prelate. The truce between the English and French kings had expired when Henry was too ill to attend the conference, and that spring Philippe and Richard began to stage raids into Henry's domains, much to the dismay of those who'd taken the cross and were eager to depart for the Holy Land. The arrival of a papal legate, the Cardinal John of Anagni, rekindled hope, though, for the Church was determined to make peace between the warring crusader-kings. The cardinal succeeded in gaining their agreement to arbitration, and a meet-ing was set up at Whitsuntide at which time their grievances would be submitted to the cardinal himself and the Archbishops of Rheims, Bourges, Rouen, and Canterbury.

THE CARDINAL WAS A TALL, elegant figure in a silk cappa magna and linen miter banded in gold, his impressive bearing enhanced by his regal aplomb. This was obviously not a man to be intimidated by those who wielded secular power and many of the witnesses took heart, daring to hope that the Peace of God would prevail.

It was soon evident, though, that neither Philippe nor Richard was in a conciliatory frame of mind. Philippe wasted no time in articulating their position, that war was inevitable unless Henry acceded to their demands. They reiterated the conditions they'd set forth at Bonsmoulins, that Alys be wed at once to Richard and that Richard be formally recognized as the rightful heir to the English crown. And they added a new proviso, insisting that John take the cross and accompany them to Outremer.

John looked startled to find himself suddenly the center of attention. Henry ignored Philippe, although he had been the speaker, and looked coolly at his elder son. "Are you saying that the success of our holy war depends upon the presence of the Count of Mortain? That is indeed a great compliment, one I am sure he appreciates. But I do not believe that the Blessed Mother Church approves of compelling a man to take the cross."

Richard was quick to take up the challenge. "I'll let you worry about the state of his soul. But his body will be in the Holy Land with me. I will not even consider departing myself unless he goes, too, for reasons I am sure you well know, my lord king."

John flushed, the cardinal frowned, and Henry gave Richard a look that was far from fatherly. Before he could respond, though, Philippe stepped in, not wanting Richard to openly accuse Henry of seeking to disinherit him. That was at the heart of Richard's quarrel, of course, but Philippe thought that it was important to couch their complaints in more elevated terms. He'd taken the cardinal's measure and did not think the prideful papal legate would want to be dragged into a family squabble. It must seem that greater issues were at stake, just as he and Richard must seem reasonable and sincere.

Thinking that there were definite drawbacks to having an ally as impetuous as Richard, Philippe said quickly, "My lord cardinal, I would hope that we'll not be distracted from the true purpose of this meeting. I do indeed support the Duke of Aquitaine's insistence that his brother accompany us to the Holy Land. And justice demands that the duke be acknowledged as the English king's heir. The law of primogeniture very clearly states that an inheritance is passed on to the eldest son, and since the death of the young king, that son is Duke Richard. But our greatest grievance lies in the shameful treatment of my sister, the Lady Alys."

He paused deliberately to give Henry a look that was both indignant and sorrowful before turning back to the papal legate and the bishops. "My sister was betrothed to the English king's son in God's Year 1169 . . . nigh on twenty years ago, Your Grace. She is now twenty-eight years old, well past the accepted age for matrimony. My lord father of blessed memory was greatly troubled by the English king's refusal to honor the plight-troth and tried repeatedly to remedy her predicament, and I in my turn have done what I could for my unfortunate sister. Again and again I have implored the English king either to marry her to the duke as he promised or return her and her dowry to France."

Philippe shook his head sadly. "In truth, my lords, I do not know why the English king continues to be so arbitrary and unfair. Those are questions best addressed to him. I can say only that I will no longer abide her continuing exile. She deserves better than this, and as her closest male kin, it is my duty to act on her behalf. She must marry the English king's son, or she must come home and Gisors and the Vexin must be returned to the French Crown."

As he glanced around at their intently listening audience, Philippe was gratified by what he saw: heads nodding in agreement and challenging looks being directed in Henry's direction by members of the cardinal's retinue. Let the old fox talk his way out of this snare!

Seeing that all were waiting for his response, Henry let his gaze linger upon the French king's face, not even glancing toward Richard. "So the Lady Alys's marriage is what matters most to you, my lord king?" When Philippe nodded gravely, Henry smiled, with such satisfaction that the French king felt a prickle of foreboding.

"I am pleased to hear that," Henry said, "for this means we can resolve our differences here and now and turn our attention to what matters most—going to the rescue of the Holy City. You would have your sister wed, my lord king? Fine. I am quite willing to see it done and with no further delay. But let her wed the Count of Mortain."

There was a stunned silence and then pandemonium. Richard's shock gave way almost at once to utter outrage, and he cried out angrily that this insulting proposal justified all of his past suspicions. Philippe was no longer feigning indignation, glaring at Henry as he scornfully rejected the English king's "games-playing." Richard's men and the French were voicing support for their lords, the assembled prelates were murmuring among themselves, and John was gazing at his father in disbelief. Was it too much to have expected Papa to mention this beforehand?

"I do not understand why you refuse even to consider it, my liege," Henry said, looking at the French king with a puzzled air. "If the marriage of the Lady Alys to my son will put an end to this needless strife between us, what are your objections?"

"You've just proved that all my suspicions were correct," Richard snarled. "Your intent has always been to put John in my rightful place!"

Henry gave Richard a dismissive glance, keeping his eyes on Philippe. "It is for you to answer, my liege," he said, "not one of your vassals."

Philippe was as angry now as Richard. "Your duplicity knows no bounds, my lord! You expect us to forget your years of bad faith and double-dealing as you play us for fools? I daresay you'll be bargaining with the Devil on your deathbed . . . but not with me. I've had enough, will waste no more time here today."

But as Philippe turned to stalk off, he found his way barred by the papal legate. The cardinal was also furious, but his anger was not directed at Henry. "The English king told me that you were using your sister's marriage as a pretext, an excuse for aggression against his Norman lands. I was doubtful, but I see now that he was right. If your sole concern is your sister's welfare, why would you refuse his offer? If you suspect that he intends to name the Count of Mortain as his successor, I would think that ought to make the marriage even more valuable in your eyes. Of course if your real interest is in continuing this war, then your refusal makes deplorable sense."

"I am surprised, my lord cardinal, that you are so trusting, so easily swayed. You do not truly think he'll let Alys marry John, do you? This is a bluff!"

"Prove it, then, by accepting his offer," the cardinal challenged, and waited for a response that was not coming. "Your silence speaks for itself, my liege. Let me now speak for the Holy Church. If you persist in this war and thus doom the Holy City, I will lay your lands under Interdict until you come to your senses."

"You dare to threaten me with an Interdict?" Philippe said incredulously. "As a good son of the Church, I will match my history against the English king's any day of the week! But I will not allow you to meddle in this matter. I have every right to punish a rebellious vassal, and lest you forget, he is indeed my vassal."

"You have been warned, my lord king."

"And you have been bought, my lord cardinal. Take your threats and your saddle bags filled with English gold and go back to Rome."

Philippe's accusation set off another uproar, and arguments began to break out all over the field. Richard shouldered his way forward to voice his own anger with the cardinal, the exchange becoming so heated that the bishops hastened to intercede between the two men. Fuming, Richard finally allowed the Archbishop of Rouen to draw him away, but he was only half listening as the prelate assured him that the cardinal bore him no malice, that his sole concern was the coming quest to the Holy Land. His eyes searched the crowd and when he found his father, he was not surprised to see Henry standing apart, watching the commotion like a playwright observing a drama of his making. And despite his fury, Richard felt a flicker of grudging admiration.

Philippe was storming off, trailed by his lords and clerics, and the cardinal was preparing to depart, too. One of Richard's squires had brought his stallion up and he reached for the reins, swinging easily into the saddle. Before he could signal to his men, though, he noticed his brother, standing by himself a few feet away. On impulse, he nudged his mount in John's direction.

"To give the Devil his due," he said, "he does know how to stir a pot."

John shrugged and Richard leaned from the saddle so that his words reached his brother's ears alone. "A bit of advice, Johnny. An infidel who converts at knifepoint will not be valued as much as one who converts of his own free will."

John looked up at him, his face unreadable. "I do not know what you mean, Richard."

"A pity," Richard said laconically, and turned his horse away. John stood motionless, watching him go.

H ENRY WITHDREW SOUTH to Le Mans after the conference fell apart, hoping that Philippe would heed the cardinal's warning once his anger cooled. He'd gambled all upon one throw of the dice, having concluded that his only chance was to drive a wedge between Richard and Philippe. Without the French king backing him up, Richard's threat would be blunted, and he'd either have to accept Henry's olive branch or depart on his own for the Holy Land. But he'd underestimated the intensity of Philippe's hostility; either that or Philippe considered Richard so useful an ally that he was willing to defy the Church in order to safeguard that alliance. At least he'd been able to win the cardinal's support. But it would not count for much if Philippe was willing to wage war even under the threat of an Interdict. Henry found it hard to believe that the young French king would be so reckless.

He soon learned that his hopes of a peaceful settlement were no more substantial than shadows and smoke. The very next day, Philippe and Richard launched a surprise and successful assault upon his castle at La Ferté-Bernard. In quick succession, they moved on to capture the castles of Montfort, Maletable, Beaumont, and Ballon. The loss of Ballon was particularly disturbing, for it was just fifteen miles from Le Mans.

W HEN JOHN WAS ADMITTED to his father's chamber, he found Henry playing chess with Geoff. Henry greeted him with a smile and pushed his chair back from the table, but John was not impressed that his father would interrupt the game for him. When other men told him how lucky he was to stand so high in the king's favor, he was hard put not to point out that a diet of promises was a thin gruel. For all his father's fondness and fine talk, he had yet to grant the incomes of Mortain, and the Gloucester heiress seemed likely to join Alys in a chaste old age.

"I heard that some of the Breton lords have thrown their lot in with Richard and Philippe, joining them at Ballon," he said. "Is it true?"

"Yes," Henry admitted. "You know Raoul de Fougères. He's never one to miss a rebellion."

John was not cheered by Henry's humor, not with their scouts reporting that the French king and Richard were heading south, toward Le Mans. "I do not understand why you insist upon staying in Le Mans, Papa. Surely it would make more sense to withdraw into Normandy where your army is gathering. Here you have only your household knights and your Welsh routiers. Why put yourself needlessly at risk?"

Henry had already had this discussion with Willem and Geoff and several others, all of whom had advocated a retreat into the greater safety of Normandy. "Le Mans has always been the city closest to my heart, Johnny. I was born here and my father is buried in the cathedral. I have promised the citizens that I will not abandon them."

His father's logic eluded John altogether. He looked at Henry in frustration, but he had no chance to continue the argument, for it was then that Will Marshal was announced. John stepped aside so Will could confer with Henry, just in time to catch Geoff surreptitiously shifting several of the chess pieces on the board. John did not like his half brother any more than Richard did, and when he realized what Geoff was up to, he shook his head, thinking that only Geoff would cheat to lose.

Henry beckoned Will into the chamber. "Will, my scouts report that Philippe and Richard have turned in the direction of Tours. But I want to be sure it is not a trick. On the morrow, take several of our men and find out if they are indeed heading away from Le Mans."

Will promised to leave at first light and then asked about the defensive ditches they'd dug outside the city walls. John saw that Henry was going to be occupied for some time and quietly slipped from the chamber.

THERE WERE TWO ROYAL RESIDENCES in Le Mans, the ancient castle near the cathedral of St Julien and the palace in the Place St Pierre, where Henry was lodging. Willem was standing on the town walls, looking down at the sprawling suburb that had grown up around the city. Sheltered on two sides by the rivers Sarthe and Huisne, Le Mans had an ancient past and its walls dated back to the time when it had been a Roman outpost. It had long been the heart of Anjou, but Willem was scrutinizing it now with a soldier's eye, his only concern the defenses it offered against assault. He would have been more content had the city not held such a great prize—the king himself.

It was that ephemeral hour between day and night, clouds still tinted with the red hues of sunset, the sky taking on the deepening haze of a summer twilight. Willem was too tense, too preoccupied to appreciate the quiet beauty of a country eventide, and he started visibly at the sound of his name. Turning, he saw Henry's youngest son approaching along the battlement walkway, not a welcome sight, for he was sure John was seeking reassurance he could not in all honesty provide.

John's greeting was perfunctory, and he wasted no time in social amenities. "I have just come from my father, and he is still balking at withdrawing into Normandy. I do not understand him at all anymore, Willem. How can he be so lethargic in the face of such danger? He has always been acclaimed for the speed of his campaigns, and yet now he does nothing!"

"What would you have him do, John? He does not want to make war upon his son."

"The choice is no longer his," John pointed out impatiently. "Surely he means to defend himself? He showed no such reticence during the first rebellion, nor when Hal and Geoffrey sought to overthrow Richard. I know he is older now, but even so . . ."

"He is fifty and six, which is hardly doddering." Part of Willem's annoyance was due to the fact that he and Henry were born in the same year. But he was also thoroughly disillusioned with the ingratitude of the king's sons. After years of witnessing Henry's strife with Hal and Geoffrey and Richard, he'd decided that a fertile queen might well pose a greater danger than a barren one. And so far he'd seen nothing in John to soften that harsh judgment, for Henry's youngest seemed like a typical spoiled and callow young princeling to him, not likely to be the staff of his father's old age.

"Has it never occurred to you, John, that heart-wounds can be more dangerous than those inflicted with lance or sword? Especially now . . ."

"What do you mean by 'especially now'?"

Willem stared at him. How could he not know? "I am talking of your lord father's failing health, of course."

John frowned. "I know he is troubled by that recurring leg injury. And he suffered greatly this spring from an abscess in his groin. But as painful as they are, they are not mortal ailments. He always gets better, does he not?"

Willem's hesitation was brief. John was not a child, after all. He was a man grown of twenty and two. It was time for him to look at the world with a man's eyes, time to realize how greatly his father needed him. "He is loath to speak openly of his ills, but he has been troubled for months by an ulcer and he has a wound in his heel that is not healing as it ought. Constant pain saps a man's strength, all the more so when he must endure one family crisis after another."

John was silent for a time. "Then this is why so many of his barons are deserting him? They fear he might die?"

"They fear he cannot win this war, and for a king, death and defeat are one and the same. I do not mean to alarm you, unduly, John. But I felt you had the right to know how serious your father's maladies are."

"Thank you," John said softly, "for telling me the truth." Willem patted him on the shoulder and then moved on, heading for the ladder. John remained where he was, gazing over the walls at the deceptively tranquil scene below. Candles had begun to glow through the open windows of the houses, and bobbing beacons appeared on the streets as lanterns were struck. But these cheerful flickers of light were soon swallowed up by the encroaching dark.

D URING THE NIGHT, thick fog drifted into the valley, and when Will and his companions set out, they could barely see more than a few yards ahead of them. They almost ran into an advance party of French scouts, but since they were not armed for combat, they let the French riders pass by in peace. Will led the way toward the River Huisne, and there he found that Henry's caution had been well warranted. Using the fog as camouflage, the French and Poitevins had stealthily advanced as far as the river and were now encamped on the other bank, with the obvious intent of laying siege to Le Mans.

E NTERING THE GREAT HALL, John made his way toward the dais, where Henry was talking quietly and intently with Will Marshal and several of his knights. "You sent for me, my lord?"

Henry nodded, said "Come with me," and led the way behind the oaken partition that screened off one end of the hall. "The French army is gathering for an attack upon Le Mans. I have given orders to break down the Pontlieu bridge over the River Huisne, to place stakes in the places where the river can be forded, and to scatter caltrops and sharpened stones in the riverbed. We are deepening the ditches and pulling down those houses closest to the city gates."

John nodded; he'd already heard about the French army's advance, for rumors were sweeping the city. "What do you want me to do?"

Henry hesitated, then reached out and placed his hands on his son's shoulders. "I want you to go, Johnny. I expect to be able to withstand the siege long enough for my army to reach us. But it would be foolish for both of us to be trapped in Le Mans, so I want you safely away from here."

John caught his breath. "Papa . . . are you sure?"

Henry felt a vast relief, for he'd feared that John would balk. Nothing ever came easily if one of his sons was involved. Thank God Almighty that Johnny could be reasoned with, unlike Richard. "Very sure, lad. It makes the most sense to have you in Normandy to take charge of the army and lead them back to lift the siege."

"I'd rather not leave you," John said slowly, "but if that is your wish, I will obey."

Henry pretended to reel back in shock. "That is a word I never thought to hear from the lips of a son of mine," he joked. "Bless you, lad, for not arguing with me." Keeping his arm around John's shoulders, he steered the young man toward the door. "Take your household knights, Johnny, and go at once."

The sooner his son was on the road to safety, the sooner he could draw an easy breath. He was not about to admit that, though, knowing that too much fatherly concern would sting John's pride, make him more likely to insist upon staying. So he continued to banter with John, bidding him farewell as nonchalantly as if this were a routine separation, and only once did they acknowledge more was at stake. John had turned to go, then came back and gave Henry a quick hug.

Henry's eyes misted, but he then gave his son a playful push. "Be off with you, Johnny. And try not to get lost!"

THE NEXT MORNING Henry decided to venture out to reconnoiter the French camp. Confident that there'd be no immediate assault since he'd had the bridge destroyed, neither he nor any of the men with him wore their hauberks. Only Will Marshal was insistent upon fully arming himself, and Henry was both amused and irked by the knight's stubbornness. Exiting the city through a postern gate between the palace and the church of St Pierre de la Coeur, they rode through the suburb known as Bourg Dom Guy. The streets were eerily empty now as the residents had taken refuge within the city walls. Even the Maison Dieu de Coeffort, the hospital Henry had founded nine years ago, had been evacuated, a sight so mournful that he had to avert his eyes as they passed.

They had agreed that if the French did attack, the suburb would have to be set on fire, and the knowledge that these poor people might lose all they had only dragged Henry's spirits down further. When he'd first learned that Richard and Philippe meant to attack the city of his birth, Henry had been sustained by the intensity of his rage. But it had not continued to burn at white heat, and this morning he felt numb and exhausted after another sleepless night and uncomfortably aware of his body's aches and pains with every step his stallion took.

"My lords!" One of the scouts they'd sent ahead was racing toward them, spurring his mount without mercy. "They have found a ford, are making ready to cross!"

When Henry galloped past him, several of his companions cried out in protest. But he had to see for himself. French knights had ridden out into the River Huisne, using their lances to test its depth, and discovered a ford by the remains of Pontlieu

Bridge. They were already lining up to cross, and Henry thought he caught a glimpse of Richard, mounted on a favorite roan stallion, not yet armed, but shouting commands, making order of chaos.

"Papa!" Geoff had reined in beside him, swinging his mount around as if to block Henry from view. "We have to get back into the city! None of us are armed, so we cannot engage them, and if they see you, they'll be on us like a hawk on a thrush!"

Indeed, no sooner were the words out of his mouth than they heard shouts and men were pointing in their direction. As the first French knights splashed into the river, Henry and his men wheeled their horses about and raced for safety.

WILL MARSHAL HAD BEEN LEFT BEHIND to guard the postern gate, and as it opened to admit the king and his knights, Will charged toward the pursuing riders, for he knew that Taillebourg had fallen when Richard had gotten into the city with the fleeing garrison. At first he was alone, but men on the parapet began shouting, "Over here, for God and the Marshal!" and some of Will's knights came galloping through the gate to fight at his side. Soon a number of Henry's men, now armed, joined the fray and before long a sharp battle was taking place in the streets under the city walls.

One of Will's knights, Hugh de Malanny, was struck with such force that his horse lost its footing and rider and animal both toppled into the marshy moat. Will promptly shattered his own lance on the French knight's shield and the man also splashed into the moat. Casting aside his lance, Will soon spotted another worthy foe and spurred his stallion toward André de Chauvigny.

Will was famed in tournaments for his ability to capture knights by seizing their bridles, using his own considerable strength and his horse's momentum to drag his helpless opponents off the field. The maneuver worked perfectly now with Richard's knight. To his horror, André suddenly found himself being towed toward the gate, faced with several choices, all of them unpalatable. He could try to cut his mount's bridle, which would give him no way to control the animal. He could fling himself from a galloping horse. Or he could become the Marshal's prisoner.

Drawing his dagger, André leaned forward in an attempt to slash the reins before they reached the gate. Men up on the parapet were heaving large rocks down upon the French, and one of them hit André's arm while another stone struck his mount in the head. The horse reared, screaming, and suddenly Will found himself holding the bridle, while André found himself clinging desperately to his saddle as his stallion bolted back toward the river. By now he was in such pain that he knew his arm was broken and he felt a surge of fear, for he'd not be able to halt the panicked animal. But hoof-beats were thudding behind him and from the corner of his eye, he saw Rico ranging up alongside.

André took no time to consider, kicked his feet free of his stirrups, and leaped. This was a maneuver he'd often practiced in the tiltyard, but he'd never tried it with an injured arm, and sprawled awkwardly across the destrier's rump. For several terrifying seconds, he hung there, holding on for dear life until Rico, displaying fine horseman-ship, managed to halt his stallion. André slid to the ground and sank down in the grass. He was chalk-white, in such agony that he was on the verge of blacking out. But he was alive, and so had no complaints.

At the gate, Will looked for new quarry and, in quick succession, he used his bri-dle trick upon two other knights, but both men preferred runaway horses to captivity and cut themselves free. Will's third foe was not so lucky and was hauled through the city gate where he was quickly disarmed and turned over to Will's excited squire. Will then switched horses with his prisoner, for his own stallion had been lamed after step-ping on a broken lance. Returning to the combat, he led a charge that soon had the French in flight toward the river.

By now Will was drenched in sweat and finding it hard to catch his breath, for the Seneschal of Anjou had set fire to the suburbs and smoke and flames were adding to the dangers of the battlefield. "I think we've beaten them back for now," Will panted, looking at his comrades with pride, for Baldwin de Bethune and Renaud de Dam-martin and Morgan Fitz Ranulf and Peter Fitz Guy were men he was honored to fight with, even to die with if need be.

The French had retreated across the river, but Henry's knights knew they'd soon be trying again, and they turned their mounts back toward the city. It was an exceed-ingly hot and humid day, and they were all exhausted, winded, and badly bruised from deflected blows. But they were triumphant, too, for the first onslaught had been a vic-tory for the English. They'd almost reached the gate when Morgan gave a sudden shout of alarm.

"Jesu, look! The wind is shifting!" And as they watched, appalled, sparks and cin-ders and burning embers were caught by the wind, sent spiraling up into the sky. Many of them came down within the city, and screams warned the men of Le Mans's peril even before they saw the smoke.

Nᴏᴛ ꜰɪɴᴅɪɴɢ ʜᴇɴʀʏ ᴀᴛ ᴛʜᴇ ᴘᴀʟᴀᴄᴇ, Will was heading for the cas-tle when he heard a woman crying for help. One of the flying embers had set her roof afire, and she was frantically trying to drag her belongings from the house before it went up in flames. Will at once dismounted, and he and his squires came to her aid. She wept with gratitude as they were able to recover a table and bed-frame and a coffer chest of her family's clothing. Carrying out a smoldering feather quilt, Will found himself choking on the acrid fumes coming from the bedding and after dropping it into a horse trough, he knelt, pulled off his helmet, and splashed water on his face. He could tell from the noise that the citizens were doing their best to put out the fires, but he could see smoke staining the sky in several quarters of the city and he feared that Le Mans was doomed.

Riders were coming up the street, and he recognized the Earl of Essex in the lead. When Willem reined in his horse, Will felt as if he were looking at a stranger, for the normally imperturbable earl was as alarmed as Will had ever seen him. "The French crossed the Sarthe downstream and circled around to the west. They have taken the Perrin bridge and will soon be in the city. We must get the king away whilst we still can!"

"No!" Henry looked defiantly from Willem to Geoff, but there was more despair in his voice than anger. "I have never run from a fight in my life, am not about to start now."

Geoff grasped Henry's arm, desperate enough to try to take his father from the city by force if need be. "Papa, you cannot stay!"

"You must make a choice, Harry." Willem took advantage of years of friendship to speak bluntly now, no longer as subject to sovereign, but as one battle commander to another. "We cannot hold the city, cannot fight the fire and the French, too. So you must retreat . . . or you must surrender to the French king and your son. And you've precious little time to make up your mind."

Henry turned away. He, who had always prided himself upon his swift response to a crisis, now found himself crippled by indecision, by a paralyzing sense of unreality. How could it have come to this? How could he lose Le Mans, the city dearest to his heart?

"We will retreat," he agreed at last, and they sprang into action, not wanting to give him a chance to reconsider.

With the French forcing their way into the city through the west gate and the body of their army just an arrow's flight to the south, the only escape still open to Henry was through the north gate, out onto the road to Alençon. Having shed their hauberks and helmets so they could make better speed, they galloped out of the city, heading north. But Henry was already having second thoughts. How could he abandon the townsmen, always so steadfast and loyal? How could he let himself be chased away by that paltry French stripling and his wretched ingrate of a son?

To the dismay of his men, he insisted on drawing rein upon the crest of a hill, and as he looked back at the burning city, his anguish gave way to a wild, unholy rage. "O God, since You have taken away from me the city that I loved most on earth, the city where I was born and bred, the city where my father is buried, I will repay You as best I can. I will deny You what You love best in me, my soul!"

His listeners shivered in horror, hastily making the sign of the cross to distance themselves from Henry's bitter, blasphemous rant. Geoff pleaded with him to ride on, but it was only when they saw the horsemen galloping after them that he let himself be pulled away from the sight of the smoke-shrouded city.

RICHARD HAD NOT TAKEN a personal role in the assault upon Le Mans, feeling it would be unseemly to lead an attack upon his own father. He was not clad in armor, therefore, when he entered the city and learned that Henry and his knights had fled. Without stopping to think it through, Richard at once led his men in pursuit. His was an instinctive response, wanting to put an end to this once and for all, wanting the satisfaction of being the one to take his father prisoner, and perhaps sensing, too, that it would be better if he caught up with Henry rather than the men of the French king.

Not burdened with hauberk, helmet, or shield, wearing only an iron cap—a cervellier—he rapidly gained ground on them, was soon in sight of the retreating rearguard. One of Henry's knights had once been a friend, and when he saw him jousting with a Poitevin knight, Richard could not resist jeering as he swept by. "You are foolish to waste your time with tournament tactics, des Roches, would do better to put on a bit of speed!"

At the sound of Richard's voice, another knight turned back and charged straight at him. Richard was suddenly acutely aware of his vulnerability, for the man riding at him with lance leveled at his chest was one of the best of their age, his mentor who now seemed likely to be his nemesis. His mouth went dry, as for the first time he experienced the purely physical fear of death.

In desperation, he tried to ward off the lance with his arm, shouting out, "God's Legs, Marshal, do not kill me! I am unarmed!" They were close enough now for him to see the grim expression on the other man's face, to anticipate the lance driving into his chest with all the force of the Marshal's body behind it. But at the last possible moment, Will shifted his aim and plunged the weapon into Richard's stallion. Death was instantaneous and as the animal fell, Richard was thrown to the ground. Gasping from the impact, struggling for breath, he looked up at the knight, who'd reined in only a few feet away.

"Let the Devil be the one to kill you," Will said, and he then spurred his horse, rode to catch up with his king.

By now several of Richard's knights had reached him and were dismounting in haste to make sure he was unharmed. Waving their helping hands aside, Richard insisted upon struggling to his feet by himself. More shaken than he'd ever admit, he stood watching as Marshal disappeared into the distance, suddenly able to appreciate the kind of courage that was not fearless, that owed nothing to bravado or daredevil abandon, but was the pure product of the will.

"No," he said, when they asked if they should resume the pursuit. "It is done."

THEIR FLIGHT FROM LE MANS was a hellish journey for Henry and his knights. They were never out of danger, for they had to pass several of the castles that had been seized by the French. Men and horses collapsed in the scorching heat, as they dared not slacken their pace. By the time they reached Fresnay-sur-Sarthe that evening, Henry was in such pain that he could barely stay in the saddle. Geoff and Willem would have preferred to press on to Alençon, for Fresnay was a small castle, unable to accommodate hundreds of knights. But they knew Henry could go no farther.

Fresnay was one of the castles of the Viscount Beaumont; in happier days Henry had played host to the wedding of his daughter to the Scots king. He was with Henry's army at Alençon, but his castellan did all he could to make them welcome, turning over the best bedchamber to Henry, offering to feed as many as he could, and suggesting that some of their men could lodge in the town's three priories. Henry needed Geoff's help to climb the stairs, for that hard ride had inflamed his old leg injury. Sinking down on the bed, he stirred only when Geoff would have departed, saying he meant to pass the night in the town, keeping vigil in case the French found them.

"No," Henry whispered, "stay here, stay with me . . ." Not closing his eyes until Geoff promised he would remain.

Henry's young squire, Hugh de Sandford, had shown the presence of mind to bring along a sumpter horse and Geoff gladly accepted a change of clothing, for he'd left everything behind in Le Mans. Henry did not have the energy to remove his dusty tunic and sweat-soaked shirt, so Geoff covered him with his own mantle, then settled down in a nearby chair to keep watch while he slept.

Awakening the next morning, Geoff was so stiff and sore that he could not move without wincing. To his relief, Henry still slept, and after instructing Hugh to let him sleep, he stumbled downstairs. The great hall had been used as a bedchamber by some of Henry's knights. They were up by now, though, consuming bread, cheese, and wine, talking and even laughing among themselves, for their spirits had risen with the sun. Geoff shared their sense of rejuvenation, for they were less than ten miles from the Norman border and safety. He wished that he could convince his father to return to England to recover, but he knew that was a lost cause, and so contented himself that at least Henry would find security and time to convalesce in Rouen.

Morgan was also feeling much more cheerful, for he was still young enough to be restored by a good night's sleep and a meal. He and several of his friends were prodding Will Marshal to tell them again about his clash with Richard, and Will, who had no false modesty when it came to his knightly skills, was happy to oblige. He soon had a large and enthusiastic audience, but their laughter had a nervous edge, for Richard was not known for his forgiving nature and few doubted that he would be king one day.

When Henry entered the hall, a sudden silence fell, for the past day's ordeal was writ plainly in his face for all to see; his complexion was livid, his eyes sunken, his mouth tightly clamped. Morgan was so shocked by the king's haggard appearance that he soon fled the hall, feeling as if he were reliving a nightmare, thrust back in time to those wretched days at Lagny, forced to stand by and watch helplessly as Geoffrey's life ebbed away.

In his misery, he turned to the Almighty and headed for the chapel on the far side of the bailey. There he offered up a fervent prayer for his cousin the king and then lingered to talk with the chaplain. The chapel priory was a cell of the abbey of St Aubin in Angers, and the young priest was passionately loyal to the Count of Anjou; with him, as with so many Angevins, the fact that their count was also England's king was an interesting irrelevancy. Morgan found it comforting to speak to another one of Henry's partisans, and it was some time before he emerged from the church.

He was immediately hailed by two of his friends and fellow knights, Peter Fitz Guy and Robert de Tresgoz. "Morgan! We've been looking all over for you!" As soon as he joined them, they both blurted out their news at once. "You'll not believe what happened!" Peter exclaimed while Rob declared that he feared the king's wits had been affected. They paused for breath, and this time Rob deferred to Peter. "The king is not going on to Alençon, Morgan. He is sending his son and the Earl of Essex into Normandy with our men, but he says he is going back into Anjou!"

Morgan was staggered. "But that makes no sense!"

"We know! You should have heard the others when he told them that. I thought Geoff would go as mad as the king. They all decried it, speaking more frankly than he is accustomed to hear, first arguing and then pleading, to no avail. He told them this was not open for debate and in the end, he got his own way, as he usually does. He made the Earl of Essex promise not to turn any of his castles in Normandy over to anyone but Count John and insisted that Geoff continue on to Alençon. Geoff was so distraught, though, that the king did agree he could join him in Anjou after leading our men to Alençon."

Morgan did not understand Henry's rash decision any more than his friends did, and he remained silent as they told him that Will Marshal had begged to come, but the king was adamant. "You see why I wonder if he is in his right senses?" Rob said unhappily. "He escapes Le Mans by a hairbreadth and God's Grace, and now he wants to go right back into Hell!"

Morgan didn't reply, for he'd just spotted Geoff and Willem leaving the hall. Geoff at once swerved in their direction, with Willem following. Giving Morgan no chance to speak, Geoff reached out and grasped the younger man's arm, hard enough to hurt. "You heard?" When Morgan nodded solemnly, Geoff's grip tightened. "You must promise me, Cousin Morgan, promise that you'll not leave him. He will not let me come with him, so it is up to you. To all of you," he added, his gaze now including Peter and Rob. "You were steadfast in your loyalty to Geoffrey, and you two were just as faithful to Hal. I want you to swear to me, on the surety of your souls, that you will give the king the same devotion you gave his sons."

Wide-eyed, they all pledged their fidelity to the king, vowed not to abandon him. Morgan then took advantage of his kinship to the chancellor and confessed, "Cousin, we do not understand. Why is the king doing this?"

Geoff looked at him mutely and then turned away, but not before they saw his despair. They watched him stride toward the chapel, and then glanced imploringly at the Earl of Essex. Willem did not reply at once. "He is going home to Anjou," he said at last, his voice muffled, "going home to die."

CHAPTER FIFTY-FOUR

✦

June 1189
Chinon, Anjou

OR THE REST OF HIS LIFE, Morgan would remember that harrowing journey through lands now occupied by the French army. They had to swing well to the west of Le Mans, passed two nights at the small hilltop castle of Sainte-Suzanne, and then, avoiding the main roads and enemy patrols, ventured on into Anjou. Much of the time they had to traverse narrow forest paths where Henry had hunted since his youth, and there were a few nights when they'd had to camp out in the woods, which Henry had done before, but never when he was feverish and in constant pain. It was easy for Morgan to imagine them as a small band of outlaws on the run from the law, an astonishing image for one of the most powerful rulers in Christendom.

The handful of young knights who were accompanying their king were impressed by his knowledge of the back roads and byways of Anjou, for he was often the one acting as their guide, and impressed, too, by his stoic endurance of his suffering. They were greatly relieved when they got safely to Angers, but after a brief stay to husband his waning strength, Henry insisted upon continuing on toward Saumur. Geoff caught up with them at Savigny, for he'd remained at Alençon only long enough to select one hundred handpicked knights and then set out after Henry. They finally reached Chinon in late June. As the crow flies, their journey was over a hundred miles, but they'd had to detour and sidetrack and veer off so often that they agreed they'd probably ridden twice that distance. A man famed for the speed of his travels, a man who'd once covered two hundred miles in four days, Henry had taken fully a fortnight to get home to the Loire Valley.

AT THE END OF JUNE, William Marshal and his household knights arrived at Chinon, in response to Henry's summons. The Angevin baron Maurice de Craon also joined them. But the royal army remained at Alençon, for many of the Norman barons were loath to fight for a king who might be dying against the man most likely to succeed him.

HENRY HAD BEEN RUNNING a high fever for days. He was propped up with pillows, not having the strength to get out of bed, but he was lucid and determined to do this, to express his gratitude to the men gathered in his bedchamber. "Have you heard, Will, what has happened? My city of Tours has fallen to the French."

"Yes, sire, I know."

"And my barons and vassals are cravenly keeping away, fearful of offending a rebel duke and the false, shameless whelp who sits on the French throne. But you *did* come, Will." Henry had to pause, overcome with gratitude and affection for these loyal, courageous, honorable men. "I am grateful beyond words to you," he said huskily, "above all to you, my dearest son. I pray that the Almighty grants me enough time to reward you as you deserve, with the archbishopric of York." His cracked lips twitched in what was almost a smile. "Even though I know you have never burned to take holy orders."

"I want only your return to health and prosperity, my lord father," Geoff managed to get out before his throat closed up.

"At least I can reward the rest of you," Henry murmured, "and nothing has given me greater pleasure than what I do now." A scribe had been standing off to the side, ready to capture the king's words with pen and ink. One by one, Henry called upon the young knights who'd shared such adversity with him, and made grants and conferred wardships and heiresses upon them. He bestowed the castle and forest of Lillebonne upon Renaud de Dammartin, rendering that cocksure young man speechless for once. He gave a Marcher castle to his Welsh cousin Morgan. He rewarded Peter Fitz Guy and the other knights who'd stayed with Hal at Martel. And then he shocked them all by giving to Baldwin de Bethune the rich heiress Denise de Deols, whom he'd once promised to Will.

"No, Will, I am not growing forgetful in my old age," he said, smiling at the dumbfounded expression on the Marshal's face. "I have another highborn lady in mind for you."

Will had quickly recovered his aplomb, for he was courtier as well as soldier, and he assured Henry that he asked no more than to enjoy the king's favor, a courteous and blatant falsehood that amused them all, including Henry. But he was growing very tired, and so he did not tease Will by dragging out the suspense. "It is my great joy to bestow upon the Marshal the hand of Isabella de Clare, heiress of Richard Strongbow, Earl of Pembroke and Lord of Striguil and Leinster."

Will gasped and his friends forgot for a moment that they were at a king's sickbed. They cheered and thumped him boisterously on the back, excited by his great good fortune, for Isabella de Clare was the richest heiress in England, would bring Will vast estates in England, Normandy, Wales, and Ireland. They soon subsided, though, realizing the insensitivity of celebrating Will's bright prospects when the king's were so bleak. Will had begun to stammer his thanks, but Henry stopped him.

"You served my son well," he said softly, "just as you've served me. Hal would have wanted me to do this for you." And Will had to swallow a sudden lump in his throat, for Henry's words had conjured up a beguiling ghost, his manifest flaws expunged by death, handsome and dashing and forever young.

On the first of July, the Archbishop of Tours arrived to give Henry an eyewitness account of the capture of his city. He was also able to tell them what had happened in Le Mans after they'd fled. It had not been sacked, most likely due to the duke's orders, he reported diffidently, nervous at having to say anything complimentary about Richard under the circumstances. All of Henry's Welsh routiers had been massacred, save only those who'd retreated into the castle and withstood a three-day siege. The fire damage was not as great as first feared, he said, hoping that might give Henry some comfort, but seeing that it did not.

Geoff and Will begged Henry to let the archbishop shrive him of his sins, for they greatly feared that he might die before he could atone for his blasphemy on the hill overlooking Le Mans. But Henry refused, for he was not yet ready, either to forgive the Almighty or to ask His forgiveness. As his fever continued to spike, he found himself drifting back in time, although his memories were fragmented and random, flashes of his boyhood and his garden courtship of the beautiful French queen, whispers of past triumphs and echoes of unhealed sorrows. His father and Eleanor and Hal wandered through his dreams, as did Thomas Becket, miraculously young again, the king's chancellor and loyal friend, laughing and telling him that the lucky man was one who died without regrets. Upon awakening, Henry found that his face was wet with tears, for he had regrets beyond counting. One of his greatest was that he'd not have the chance to explain to John why he'd never taken any measures to secure the crown for him. You could not have held it, lad, not against Richard, and your kingship would be as brief as it was bloody. He'd wanted to spare his son's pride, but now he wished he'd been more forthright, sought to make John understand. He was beginning to worry about him, for John's whereabouts were still unknown nigh on three weeks after the retreat from Le Mans. Geoff and Will had not seen him at Alençon, and while Henry thought he was likely safe in Normandy, the silence was one more burden to take to his grave.

THE NEXT DAY HENRY HAD MORE VISITORS, the Count of Flanders, the Archbishop of Rheims, and the Count of Blois riding in under a flag of truce. "Do you wish to see them, Papa?" Geoff asked. "Shall I bring them up to your chamber?"

"No," Henry said and only when he tried to rise did his son realize he was not refusing to see the men, but unwilling to see them at his sickbed. Geoff argued against it in vain, insisting Henry did not have to do this. By now Henry had managed to swing his legs over the side of the bed. "Yes, Geoff, I do," he said, and beckoned for Hugh to help him dress.

Henry felt no surprise when they seemed so taken aback as he limped into the hall; by now he was used to having people react to his appearance with poorly concealed shock. "I know," he said, sinking down into the chair that Will was holding out for him. "I look like a corpse that is overdue for burial. So spare me the solicitous queries about my health and tell me why you are here."

Thibault of Blois and the archbishop seemed disconcerted by such candor, but Philip of Flanders gave Henry a grimly approving smile. "Fair enough," he said and leaned across the table. "We never wanted this war, Cousin. We ought to have been halfway to Jerusalem by now, but Philippe has the bit between his teeth. I fear he's in danger of getting drunk on battlefield glory, blissfully unaware that he is drinking from Richard's cup. We have been urging him to make peace, without success. And yes, I know I seem like an unlikely peacemaker. But my vow to take the cross apparently means more to me than his does to Philippe. And it is not in any of our interests to have the balance of power turned on its head like this. An overly mighty French king is no improvement over an overly mighty English one."

Henry could believe them, for all three men had been involved in rebellions against Philippe during the early years of his reign, years in which he'd come to the boy's rescue time and time again. No one ought ever to doubt that the Almighty had a sense of humor. "Then if you bring no peace offers, what exactly do you have for me, Cousin?"

Once Philip would have relished this moment, but he discovered now that he could take no pleasure in Henry's defeat and humiliation. "Philippe and Richard wish you to come to Colombières the day after tomorrow," he said, doing his best to transform a command into a request.

Henry was not misled, knew full well that this was no invitation. "Tell the French king and the Duke of Aquitaine that I will be there."

THEY'D BROUGHT OUT A STOOL to assist Henry in mounting, for he'd adamantly refused to use a horse litter. His squires stood by, as it was obvious to them that he'd still need help in getting securely into the saddle. Geoff waved them aside, though.

"Let me lend a hand, Papa," he said, and then, "I am such a coward, for I cannot bear to accompany you to Colombières, cannot watch as you must humble yourself before men not worthy of your spit. I am sorry to fail you like this, so sorry . . ."

"You owe me no apologies, Geoff, for your reluctance is proof of the love you bear me. In truth," Henry said, trying to smile, "I would as soon miss this spectacle myself. As much as I fancied hunting, I never cared for a bear-baiting."

His attempt at humor only made it harder for Geoff, who hugged him tightly, then boosted him up into the saddle. Geoff then retreated back into the great hall to grieve and to curse his brothers, the French king, and himself for not being there when his father had such need of him.

HENRY SOMEHOW MADE IT ALL THE WAY to Colombières, actually was the first to arrive. By now he was in such pain that his men insisted he await their coming in the commandery of the Knights Templar at Ballan just a few miles to the east. They should have been relieved when he agreed, but his acquiescence only alarmed them all the more, for it proved how ill he truly was. Upon reaching the commandery, Henry almost fell when dismounting and had to lean against a wall for support. When he opened his eyes, Will Marshal was at his side, looking so concerned that he could hide the truth no longer.

"The pain has gotten so bad, Will. It began in my heel, then it spread to my legs. Now my whole body is afire."

"Come inside, sire, and rest for a while," Will said firmly, and giving Henry no chance to object, he put his arm around the older man, helped him into the commandery and into bed. They'd brought along the doctor they'd engaged in Angers, but there was little he could do. The Templars fetched a basin of cool water and they took turns putting compresses upon Henry's forehead, while sending one of his knights to inform Richard and Philippe that Henry was too ill to attend the conference.

Morgan was leaning over the bed, trying to coax Henry into taking a few swallows of wine when the knight returned. One look at his face and they knew the news he brought was not good.

"Gilbert, let's go outside," Will said quickly, but he was not in time. Gilbert Pipard hastened toward the bed, where he knelt and looked at Henry with tears in his eyes. "I am so sorry, my liege. I failed you. I told them you were ill, but they did not believe me. Duke Richard . . ." His mouth twisted, as if he'd tasted something rancid. "He told the French king that you were feigning this sickness, that it was just another one of your tricks, and they demand that you come to Colombières straightaway."

Henry's knights were outraged and began to swear, calling Richard and Philippe every vile name they could think of, and most of them had a considerable vocabulary of obscenities. Henry said nothing, though. Struggling to sit up, he managed to lurch to his feet, retaining his balance only with Morgan's help. The Templars had been watching in dismay, and they sought now to persuade Henry to remain abed, warning him that it might be the death of him to get back on his horse.

Henry had bitten his lower lip so deeply that he tasted blood on his tongue. "It does not sound," he said hoarsely, "that I am being given a choice."

"Jesus wept!" The involuntary cry came from Philippe, genuinely shocked by his first sight of the English king. This man was not feigning illness. He was dying. After glancing at Richard, who showed no emotion, Philippe hastily ordered one of his men to spread a cloak upon the ground. "My lord, there is no question whatsoever of your standing. Do seat yourself on this mantle."

"I have no need to sit," Henry said stonily. "I am here to learn what you want from me."

Philippe shrugged. "As you wish. But ere we speak of peace, you must first submit yourself utterly to my mercy, agree to be guided in all matters by my counsel and advice and not gainsay whatsoever I have decreed."

Henry looked at him, saying nothing, for he did not trust his voice, feeling as if he would choke on his rage and humiliation. Philippe was waiting for his response, though. He opened his mouth, not sure what he would say, when thunder sounded directly overhead. Both Henry and Philippe flinched, as did many of their men, none sure what this meant. Was thunder in an empty sky a sign of Divine displeasure? And if so, who was the object of the Lord's Wrath? A second thunderclap rumbled, and Henry was almost thrown when his stallion shied and bucked nervously. With Morgan on one side and Renaud de Dammartin on the other, holding on to his legs to keep him erect in the saddle, he agreed to place himself at the mercy of the French king.

"Very well," Philippe said, with a brief satisfied smile. "These are the terms you must meet. You will agree to do homage to me for all of your lands on this side of the channel. You will surrender custody of my sister, the Lady Alys, to a guardian chosen by the Duke of Aquitaine, and agree that he shall marry her upon his return from Jerusalem."

For the first time, Henry looked over at his son. Richard was standing a short distance away, listening impassively, his face revealing nothing of his thoughts. Had the circumstances been different, Henry might have appreciated the irony of it. So Richard had talked Philippe into delaying the wedding yet again. Philippe was going to find that it would be no easy task to get Richard and Alys to the altar.

Philippe waited until he had Henry's attention again before continuing. "You shall pay the French Crown an indemnity of twenty thousand silver marks to compensate me for the expenses I incurred in this war. You will have your barons on both sides of the channel swear fealty to Duke Richard, acknowledging he is your rightful heir. You may not avenge yourself upon those of your lords or knights who have withdrawn their allegiance to you and pledged themselves to the duke. To make sure of this, none of them need return to your service until the month ere we set out for Jerusalem. The departure date for this journey will be mid-Lent of the coming year."

Philippe paused, as if realizing how pointless this last provision was, for few of the men at Colombières imagined that Henry would ever be able to fulfill his crusading vow. "All of your barons shall swear that their allegiance to you is contingent upon your compliance with the terms of this treaty. And as a pledge of your good faith, you are to surrender to me and to the duke your city of Le Mans and your castles of Château-du-Loire and Trou until these terms have been honored. If you would prefer to yield the castles of Gisors, Pacy, and Nonancourt, that is also acceptable to us."

"I agree to your terms," Henry said tersely. "Is there anything else you demand of me?"

"You may defer your act of homage until your health is on the mend," Philippe said, with such an air of magnanimity that Henry's men seethed in silence. "But you must openly acknowledge your reconciliation with Duke Richard by giving him the kiss of peace."

Until now Richard had been regarding Henry's surrender as dispassionately as if he were merely a spectator, not actively involved in the proceedings. A shadow crossed his face and then he stepped forward, obviously intending to approach Henry so he need not dismount. But Henry was already struggling from the saddle, held upright with some discreet assistance from Morgan and Renaud.

Richard reached out to offer support, but Henry ignored the gesture. As commanded, he gave his son a brief kiss of peace, but as he pulled back, he hissed in Richard's ear, "God grant that I live long enough to avenge myself upon you!"

Henry's lacerated pride then suffered another wound, for it was evident even to him that he could not ride back to Chinon, and a horse litter had to be found. Philippe and some of the French lords joined Richard, and they all stood watching in silence as Henry was borne away from Colombières.

Upon his arrival at Chinon, Henry found a delegation of Canterbury monks awaiting his return. They were feuding with their archbishop and, undeterred by war and rebellion, they'd managed to track him down to seek his support in their quarrel. Henry once would have been amused by the ludicrous incongruity of it, but now he was past finding humor in anything, and after promising curtly to dictate a letter to the Canterbury chapter, he took to his bed.

One of his men had remained behind to be given the list of those who'd disavowed allegiance to him and could not be punished, not returning to Chinon until after nightfall. Henry had refused to eat, speaking little and staring into some dark vista that only he could see. But he showed a flicker of interest when Roger Malchael was ushered into his bedchamber.

"You have the names of those who betrayed me, Roger? Read them to me."

Geoff and Will frowned, not wanting Henry to deal with still more misery in his weakened state. But there was nothing enfeebled about Henry's will, and they knew better than to object. Roger was already obeying, approaching the bed and breaking the seal on the parchment roll. Once he looked down at the list, though, he sucked in his breath before glancing up at Henry in dismay.

"May Jesus Christ help me, sire! The first name written here is Count John, your son!"

Henry jerked upright in the bed, then fell back, gasping. "I do not believe it!"

"I am sure Roger has misread the name," Geoff said swiftly, but Will said nothing, standing apart and watching sadly as the last act of the tragedy was played out.

"Let me see it," Henry demanded and Roger obeyed, looking as stricken as if he were handing over a draught of lethal poison. For a long time, Henry stared down at John's name without speaking, and then he crumpled the list in his fist, let it flutter into the floor rushes. When Geoff tried to offer comfort, he muttered, "Say no more," and turned his face away from them, toward the wall.

T HAT NIGHT HENRY'S FEVER FLARED even higher, and he lapsed into delirium. Geoff stayed by his side, putting wet cloths on his burning skin, fanning him and flicking away the flies; it was too hot to close the windows. Will and Morgan and Maurice de Craon also kept vigil at his bedside. Most of the time they could make no sense of his feverish mumblings, but occasionally he said something intelligible, and when he did, they winced and fought back tears, for he was cursing his sons, cursing himself and the day he was born, in his anguish mumbling over and over, "Shame on a conquered king."

Wednesday evening, he surprised them by regaining his senses. He whispered words of love to Geoff, calling him his "true son," and asking that a ring be bequeathed to his son-in-law and another one to Geoff. But when Geoff urged him to confess so he could be absolved of his sins, Henry closed his eyes again, saying nothing. Geoff began to sob, and the other men were just as distraught, appalled that Henry was putting his immortal soul at risk.

Deliverance came from an unlikely source. Renaud de Dammartin had been watching from the shadows, so quiet that the others had assumed he'd fallen asleep. But now he rose and approached the bed, leaning over to whisper something in Henry's ear. Henry's lashes flickered, and he looked at the young knight, then murmured his son's name. Geoff bent over, listened intently, and straightened up with a radiant smile.

"Yes, Papa, I will!" Turning toward the others, he said joyfully, "He wants to be shriven!"

A T HENRY'S OWN REQUEST, a bed was made up for him before the altar in the chapel of Ste Melanie, and he was carried down the stairs and across the bailey by his son and knights. There he made his confession, his voice so faint that the arch-bishop had to put his ear close to Henry's mouth, and was absolved of his sins, while outside the chapel, Geoff leaned against the wall and wept.

It was Will who eventually pulled Renaud aside, demanding to know what he'd said to change the king's mind. Renaud gave Will an enigmatic look and then grinned. "You really want to know? I asked him if he wanted to be trapped in Hell for all eternity with Richard."

Will didn't know whether to laugh or cry. He shook his head, managed a bemused smile, and then started back toward the chapel, for he wanted to keep vigil with Geoff. But his steps began to flag, and instead he swung about and disappeared into the shadows of the vast yew tree in the middle bailey, where he grieved privately and alone for his dying king and for his young lord, who'd also joked in those final moments of his mortal life in that stifling chamber at Martel.

HENRY'S DELIRIUM SOON RETURNED, and he did not speak coherently again, dying the next day after a hemorrhage that stained his bedding with dark blood. He was fifty-six, had ruled almost thirty-five years as King of England and even longer as Duke of Normandy and Count of Anjou.

CHAPTER FIFTY-FIVE

✦

July 1189
Fontevrault Abbey, Anjou

*T*HE NUNS HAD NEVER seen their self-possessed abbess so fretful. Gillette's position was one without parallel in Christendom, for she ruled over no less than four monasteries, including the male priory of St Jean de l'Habit, the priory of St Lazare, which had been founded to treat those unfortunates afflicted with leprosy, and the priory of Ste Marie-Madeleine, which offered sanctuary and salvation to women who'd sinned and repented. Only at Fontevrault were men subject to the authority of a woman, and there had been occasional discipline problems caused by resentful or rebellious monks in the early years.

But these minor scandals had ceased during the kingship of Henry Fitz Empress, for he had taken a keen, personal interest in the welfare of the Angevin abbey. And Abbess Gillette had soon shown herself to be a fair but firm mother superior, rising through the ranks from cellarer to mistress of novices to grand prioress and eventually to the ultimate office. There was no doubt, though, that she was now faced with the most daunting challenge of her nine-year reign.

There could be no greater honor than to have their abbey chosen for the burial of a king, particularly one who'd been such a generous patron of Fontevrault. Henry had exempted them from royal taxes, conferred an annual stipend, founded one of their sister houses in England as penitence for the murder of St Thomas, entrusted the nuns with the education of two of his children, and provided in his will for a bequest of two thousand silver marks. He deserved a royal funeral that was one for the ages, but they had neither the time nor the resources for such a majestic pageantry. They'd gotten word only that morning that the king was dead.

IT WAS A MEAGER AND MELANCHOLY FUNERAL cortege that made its way from the castle at Chinon. It was with great difficulty that Henry's men had found for him the trappings of sovereignty, for much had been left behind at Le Mans. They were deeply distressed that they were unable to dispense alms to the poor, and to Will Marshal, there was a dreary familiarity about the straitened circumstances, evoking painful memories of Hal's unhappy death. They moved slowly in the summer heat, bearing the funeral bier upon their shoulders, somber crowds gathering by the roadside to watch them pass. They were not yet within sight of Fontevrault when they heard the tolling of the abbey bells, and then the wind brought to them the melodic sound of prayer. The nuns were coming out to meet them in solemn procession, with flaring torches and pealing bells and the sacred music of the Benedictus, reverently chanted by the sisters and monks as they advanced to welcome the king to his last resting place. And Will and Geoff, who'd been anguishing over the selection of Fontevrault, knowing that Henry had wanted to be buried at Grandmont, felt a sweet sense of relief, sure now that they'd chosen well for him.

GEOFF HAD INSISTED UPON ACCOMPANYING his father's body into the church, but his knights had gathered in the guest hall to quench their thirst, ease their hunger, and fortify themselves for the night's vigil. They found, though, that most of them had little appetite. Renaud de Dammartin was one of the few able to eat with relish, and one of the few, too, to dare to broach the subject of their uncertain prospects as men who'd been on the wrong side of a bitter internecine war.

"Do you think Richard will attend the funeral?" he asked, stabbing a chunk of bream with his knife.

"I do not know," Will said honestly. "I sent him word, and now it is up to him."

Renaud drained his wine cup before sighing melodramatically. "A pity," he said, "that my lordship of Lillebonne Castle should be so brief. I was looking forward to having my own hunting preserve."

The other men could not help feeling a sense of personal loss, too, midst their mourning for Henry. Their hopes of the promised heiresses and wardships and grants had died with the king, and that disappointment might be the least of their troubles. Their eyes sought Will, for he had the most to fear. Not only had he lost a great heiress and a king's favor, he'd bested Richard in combat, inflicting a public humiliation upon a man no less prideful and hot-tempered than his sire. At least Will already had the manor of Cartmel, given to him by Henry upon his return from the Holy Land. Assuming that Richard let him keep it.

Maurice de Craon had less to fear, for he was a powerful baron in his own right, and therefore not as vulnerable as Henry's household knights. He'd eaten little, absently crumbling a piece of bread as he regarded the Marshal. "We might as well speak candidly," he said. "You are the most likely to suffer from the new king's displeasure, Will. I want you to know that I would be pleased to offer you horses or money, whatever you need to get through the bad days ahead."

"I cannot offer you as much as Lord Maurice," Baldwin said quickly, "but all I have is yours, Will."

Several others chimed in, touching Will with their loyalty and generosity. But he could not help feeling shamed, too, that he should, at this time in his life, be dependent upon the charity of friends. He knew he'd not have to beg his bread by the roadside, could always find a place in the Count of Flanders's mesnie. But it would not be easy to become a landless knight again, not at his age.

"I thank you, my lord, thank you all. But I cannot accept, not knowing if I could repay you. I shall put my trust in the Almighty, as I've always done." He cocked his head then, listening. "They are pealing the bells for Vespers," he said, getting to his feet. The others did, too, following him back toward the abbey church for evensong.

THE OFFICE OF THE DEAD SERVICE known as the Placebo had ended, but the abbey church was still full. The nuns were kneeling by the funeral bier, set up before the high altar, and many of Henry's knights had also lingered to pray. Morgan said a prayer for Geoff, too, asking the Almighty to give him strength, for his grieving was painful to see. He was admiring the elegant marble columns and domed roof, thinking this was one of the most beautiful churches he'd ever seen, when Henry's squire Hugh came dashing into the nave. He paused by Morgan long enough to gasp out, "He is here!" before hurrying to warn Will and the others. Morgan spun around to see Richard framed in the nave entranceway.

The men hastily made their obeisances, but he acknowledged only the Abbess Gillette and the Archbishop of Tours before continuing on into the choir and halting by the candlelit bier. For a time, Richard gazed down at his father, and then he knelt. Barely long enough to say one pater noster, some thought indignantly. Richard's face was inscrutable, a mask of royal reserve. Rising to his feet, he did not speak to his brother Geoff, who was kneeling on the other side of the bier. He did signal to Will Marshal and Maurice de Craon, though, gesturing for them to follow him as he strode through the door leading out into the cloisters.

Although Compline had been rung, summer daylight was not easy to rout and was still holding the night at bay, so the men had no need for torches or lanterns yet. Richard was regarding Will in silence, grey eyes giving away nothing. "The other day you intended to kill me, Marshal, and would have had I not deflected your lance with my arm."

Maurice started to speak, thought better of it. Will's nervousness was washed away by the rising tide of his indignation. "My lord duke, it was never my intent to kill you. I am still strong enough to direct my lance where I want it to go. Had I wished, I could have struck you instead of your horse. And I cannot repent of that, for it ended the pursuit of the king." He raised his head, then, meeting Richard's eyes steadily, bracing for the worst. But the duke's mouth was curving, ever so slightly, at the corners.

"You are forgiven, Marshal. I bear you no malice."

"I am gladdened to hear that, my lord," Will said, knowing Richard must be able to see his relief, but too thankful to care.

Richard was looking over Will's shoulder. Turning, Will saw that some of the knights had followed them out into the cloisters and were hovering at a discreet distance. They came forward quickly when Richard beckoned to them.

"That is true for the rest of you, too," he said. "You have nothing to fear. Loyalty to the king is an admirable trait, not one I'd want to discourage." And now that inkling of a smile was unmistakable. "Indeed," he continued, "I value men such as you more highly than those who abandoned my father to be on the winning side." Glancing back toward Will then, he said, "After the funeral on the morrow, I want you to leave at once for Sarum. I will have letters for you to deliver to my lady mother and others, naming her as regent until my return to England. I want it known that her wishes are to be obeyed in all matters."

Will was promising that he would when there was a stir and some of the men parted to let Geoff pass. "My lord duke," he said coldly, managing to make his very formality sound insulting. "I am gratified to hear that you are following the noble example set by our father in showing magnanimity to defeated foes."

"Brother," Richard said, and he somehow turned that fraternal greeting into an insult, too.

Geoff's eyes softened as he glanced toward Will and the other knights. "I think you should know that our lord father gave the lady of Pembroke and Striguil to the Marshal in recognition of his steadfast and admirable loyalty."

Richard looked over at Will, and then shook his head. "No, he did not give her to the Marshal. Rather, he promised her to him. I am the one who will give her to him, sure that she will be safe in his hands."

Will dropped to his knees. "Thank you, my lord!"

"Sire," Renaud prompted, "the king your father made gifts to the rest of us, too."

Richard's gaze moved from face to face. "I will honor his promises. You need not fear. Now I would take my leave of the lady abbess and my lord archbishop. I shall pass the night at Saumur, will return on the morrow for the funeral." Richard started to turn away, then paused. "Bury richly the king my father, Will."

E LEANOR'S RELATIVE FREEDOM had been curtailed once Richard declared war on Henry. She no longer had such easy and unquestioned access to visitors, her household was reduced, and surveillance was once more intrusive. Her confinement was not as stringent as in the early years of her captivity, but she very much resented these new restrictions, saying bitterly to Amaria that she felt like a hawk with clipped wings, cruelly kept from flight within sight of the sky.

The windows of her chamber were unshuttered, open to the humid Sarum air. Eleanor was playing chess with Amaria when Sir Ralph Fitz Stephen and the justiciar, Ralf de Glanville, sought admittance. Rising, Eleanor stood watching as they came toward her, their faces grave, their eyes apprehensive.

"The king is dead," she said before either man could speak.

Their mouths dropped open, and they regarded her for a moment with awe and unease before the justiciar rallied. "Yes, Madame, that is so. The lord king died at Chinon on the sixth of July, not long after being compelled to make peace with the Duke of Aquitaine and the French king. I regret we can tell you no more than that, for we've had word only of his mortal illness and his funeral at Fontevrault Abbey."

"Fontevrault," Eleanor said softly. The abbey where he'd meant to exile her, now his burial site. "I would have a Requiem Mass said on the morrow for the repose of his soul."

"Of course, Madame."

"Afterward, I shall return to Winchester, for Sarum has never been to my liking." Eleanor looked at them challengingly, but they raised no objections whatsoever, to the contrary, seemed eager to oblige her.

"It shall be as the queen commands."

Once they'd gone, Eleanor moved to the window, stood gazing out at the starless summer night. Amaria was watching her uncertainly, not sure what—if any—comfort to offer. "My lady, it must be a great relief to recover your liberty and my heart rejoices for you. And of course you are gladdened that Lord Richard will now be king, as am I. But . . . do you not . . . not . . ."

"Mourn?" Eleanor did not turn around. "I've been mourning for months, Amaria, ever since I learned about Bonsmoulins. After that, I knew it could only end like this."

WILL MARSHAL WAITED as the queen read her son's letter. She'd moved to the open window for better light, and Will marveled that a woman of her age could take the harsh glare of the sun and still look so handsome. He found it hard to believe she was just five years away from her biblical three score and ten. But then he found it hard to remember that he was past forty. He'd loved Hal, had developed a great respect for Henry, and was very grateful to Richard for bearing no grudges. But he'd always had a special bond with the queen, who'd ransomed a young knight of no consequence, not only saving his life but putting him on the path that now led to Isabella de Clare and possibly even an earldom. He deeply regretted the king's unhappy death. He was glad, though, that Eleanor would flourish now that her son ruled, very glad, indeed.

"It seems congratulations are in order, Will." Eleanor glanced up from Richard's letter, a smile playing about her mouth. "So you are to be married?"

"Indeed, my lady. From here I go to seek out the damsel in London." His smile was joyful, but wry, too. "She is very young, seventeen or so. I hope she'll not be disappointed to find herself wed to a man so much older than she."

Eleanor was touched, surprised that a boy's shyness could still survive under the polished, worldly mien of this accomplished courtier and knight. "Dearest Will," she said, "you think your renown has not reached English shores? Isabella will be so bedazzled to wed the famed Will Marshal that she'll never notice a grey hair or two at your temples." She grinned then, and he had to grin back. "I am loath to cut short your time with your bride, but do not tarry with her too long, Will. There is much to be done, and I shall have need of your services."

"Of course, Madame. I assume you will be making the arrangements for the duke's coronation?"

She inclined her head. "But that is only one of the tasks I must undertake. My son is not that well known in England, for he has passed little time here. I want to do what I can to make sure his welcome will be a warm one."

Will did not doubt she would succeed; he'd known few men with the shrewdness and political acumen of the queen. He'd begun to hope that he might actually evade the question he'd been dreading, but it was then that Eleanor said, "You were with my husband until the end. Tell me about those last days."

Will was quiet for a moment. "How much do you want to know, Madame?"

Her eyes narrowed. "As bad as that?"

"Yes, my lady, as bad as that."

Eleanor found herself hesitating, uncharacteristically irresolute. She did not truly want to know how Henry had suffered; she already had enough bad memories to last a lifetime. Yet she felt oddly obligated to hear it all. One final act of atonement? Irony was not likely to be an effective shield, though. "Tell me," she repeated, and Will did. He'd have spared her if he could, but he respected her too much to lie to her after she'd asked for the truth.

She listened in silence, but when he told her of John's betrayal, her eyes burned with tears. "I'd been told that John and Richard had made their peace, but I assumed it had happened after Harry died . . ."

Will shook his head grimly. "I would to God it had been like that, Madame, for this was the true mortal blow. I know the king made mistakes, many of them, but he did not deserve a death like this."

"No," she said, very low, "he did not."

Neither spoke for a time, and then Will roused himself to tell her the rest, the most shameful part of this sad story. "By ill chance, neither Geoff nor I were with him when he died, and whilst we were being summoned, some of his servants and men stole what they could. They'd dared to search his body, and when we entered the chapel, we found him lying there on the bed without even a blanket to cover him. One of his knights at once removed his own mantle and wrapped the king in that. We did the best we could, found a fine robe to bury him in, and a scepter, and lacking a crown, we made do with gold embroidery. We were distraught that we had no ring for his finger, but fortunately he'd given one to his squire for safekeeping, and Hugh produced a jeweled ring of great beauty. We had no money for alms, though, and several thousand of Christ's poor had gathered as word spread. Stephen de Marcay, the king's seneschal, insisted that there was no money left in Chinon's treasury, and I reminded him how much he'd benefited from the king's favor, saying that he may have none of the king's money but he had plenty of his own which he'd amassed in the royal service. But the ungrateful wretch claimed he could do nothing, and so we had to turn the people away, which would have grieved King Henry greatly . . ."

He waited, and when she said nothing, he crossed to her side, kissed her hand,

and bade her farewell. She did not speak until he reached the door. "Will . . . tell the Lady Amaria that I would be alone."

"I will, my lady," he said and closed the door quietly behind him.

Eleanor moved to the table and poured wine with an unsteady hand. But she did not drink, for her chest felt congested, her throat too tight to swallow. Her hand tightened around the cup and then she dashed it to the floor, sent the flagon flying with another sweep of her arm.

"Damn you, Harry, I am not going to let you do this! After all the grief you gave me over the years, I am not going to let you torment me from the grave, too!"

Sitting down upon the edge of her bed, she closed her eyes and counted her scars as if they were pater noster beads. The expression on his face during their dreadful confrontation at Falaise. *Look upon the sun, you'll not be seeing it again. I will never forgive you, never. I offered to make you the abbess of Fontevrault, but it can just as easily be an impoverished Irish convent, so remote and secluded that not even God could find you.*

No, she did not lack for reasons to curse his memory. She had sixteen of them. She need only think of all those lonely Christmases, all those wasted years. She need only remember how he'd used her to compel Richard to surrender Aquitaine, careless of the damage he might be doing between mother and son, or the awful sound of the key turning in the lock on her first night of captivity at Loches Castle.

But memories were as elusive as quicksilver, as hard to control. Other images jostled for attention. Harry holding her as they grieved for Joanna's baby. Despairing together over Hal's follies. A lifetime of tears and laughter. Lusting after crowns and each other. Their wedding night, his first words after their lovemaking. *Good God, woman . . . Forget what I told you in Paris; I would have married you without Aquitaine.* Laughing when she called him a gallant liar, and laughing, too, when she related scandalous stories of her grandfather, exclaiming gleefully, *Between the two of us, we've got a family tree rooted in Hell!*

Yes, there were good memories, too, thirty-seven years of good and bad. Quarrels and reconciliations. Eight cradles and too many gravestones and Rosamund Clifford and power that rivaled Caesar's, an empire that stretched from the Scots border to the Mediterranean Sea. She lay back on the bed, hot tears seeping through her lashes and trickling across her cheeks until she tasted salt on her lips. One more memory was taking shape, with painful clarity. Another bitter argument, angry words traded back and forth, accusations and reproaches and her scornful warning that echoed now across the years as the Final Judgment upon their marriage.

We've schemed and fought and loved until we are so entangled in hearts and minds that there is no way to set us free. God help us both, Harry, for we will never be rid of each other. Not even death will do that.

F ROM THE TWELFTH-CENTURY *Annals of Roger de Hoveden:*

Queen Eleanor, the mother of the before-named duke, moved her royal court from city to city, and from castle to castle, just as she thought proper; and sending messengers throughout all the counties of England, ordered that all captives should be liberated from prison and confinement, for the good of the soul of Henry, her lord inasmuch as, in her own person, she had learnt by experience that confinement is distasteful to mankind, and that it is a most delightful refreshment to the spirits to be liberated therefrom.

RICHARD SOON MET THE ARCHBISHOPS of Rouen and Canterbury and sought pardon for taking up arms against his father after taking the cross. He was then girded with the ducal sword of Normandy on July 20 in Rouen. Two days later he met with the French king near Chaumont and reached terms that would prevent a further delay of their crusade.

In the meantime, Eleanor was very active in England on his behalf. After securing the treasury in Winchester, she rode to London and then began a royal progress through the southern shires. She issued edicts establishing uniform weights and measures for corn, liquid, and cloth, as well as a currency valid anywhere in England. She freed the English abbeys from their obligation to stable and provide for the king's reserve horses and magnanimously gave these mounts to the monks. She continued to release those imprisoned for offenses against Henry's harsh and unpopular forest laws, and she allowed those who'd been outlawed under these laws to return, "for the good of King Henry's soul." And wherever she went, she demanded oaths of fealty from all free men in the name of Lord Richard and the Lady Eleanor.

Her efforts were so effective that Richard was given a tumultuous welcome upon arriving at Portsmouth on August 13. Two days later he got an equally enthusiastic reception in Winchester and was reunited with his mother, the queen.

RICHARD WAS LAUGHING. "You know, Maman, your enemies are going to accuse you of practicing the Black Arts. How else explain how you emerged from sixteen years of confinement still looking so elegant and comely, not to mention having more energy than a kennel full of greyhounds. I hear that between your travels and councils and proclamations, you managed to find time to found a hospital for the poor in Surrey. I assume that upon the seventh day, you rested?"

"Not for long," she said, laughing, too. "If you want your coronation to be as splendid as I suspect you do, that is going to take a great deal more work." Sitting beside him in the window-seat, she exercised a mother's prerogative and reached over to brush his hair back from his forehead. "You were telling me about the meeting with Philippe."

Richard made a mock-sour face. "I had to bribe him with another four thousand marks, and that in addition to the twenty thousand he extorted from my father at Colombières, then agree to relinquish my rights in Auvergne and give up two fiefs in Berry. I had no choice, though, not if I hope to depart for the Holy Land ere I am too old to fight. But Philippe is going to be troublesome. It is hard to believe that one came from Louis's loins. You think he could be a foundling?"

He laughed again; laughter came very easily to them both on this August afternoon. "I have made a good match for Richenza; I do not know why we bothered to change the lass's name when none of us call her Matilda. I am wedding her to the son of the Count of Perche."

Eleanor nodded approvingly; she'd be marrying into a highborn family and the marital alliance would strengthen their northeast borders. "And what of John's marriage to Avisa of Gloucester?" She kept her voice noncommittal; John had arrived with Richard, but she'd yet to have a private moment with him.

"I'll be in Marlborough ere the end of the month to give the bride away. In addition to the Gloucester estates, I am settling upon him lands worth four thousand a year in the counties of Cornwall, Devon, Dorset, and Somerset. Our father had promised it to him again and again, but not surprisingly, he never got around to actually doing it."

Eleanor regarded him thoughtfully. "I know you've been implacable with the men who abandoned Harry toward the last, dismissing them from your service in favor of those who'd stayed loyal, even seizing the lands of Raoul de Fougères and Juhel de Mayenne. It is always wise policy to reward loyalty to the Crown, of course. But you seem to have made one exception, are showing John great generosity."

Richard shrugged. "I can hardly do less for him, Maman. Until I have a son of my own, he is my heir—unless you'd rather I pick Arthur in Brittany. So he must be provided for, but you notice all his new lands are located in England, not Normandy or Anjou. I'd as soon keep the Channel between him and my good friend, the French king."

"So in effect you are buying John's loyalty."

He shrugged again. "Well, my father kept him hanging, too, with little to call his own. So he deserves a chance to show he can be trusted if I play fair with him. And if he proves himself to be unreliable, I'll deal with it. I cannot say I see him as any great threat. Now Geoffrey . . . he would have borne watching. But I'm not likely to lose sleep fretting about Johnny."

He paused to take a sip from his wine cup. "I did not tell you, did I? I am honoring my father's last wishes, and one of them was to see Geoff as Archbishop of York."

"And you are going to follow through? Is that wise, Richard? Geoff will not be grateful to you, will never forgive you, and I think you know that."

"Of course I do. Hellfire, I could buy him the papacy, and he'd still act like I am Saladin. But there are advantages to having him wear a miter. Once he is ordained as a priest, he cannot harbor any illusions about laying claim to my throne. You look dubious, Maman. Geoff is an able man, and an ambitious one. You cannot tell me it has not crossed his mind that William the Bastard was born out of wedlock, too. So I'd as soon he kept his eye upon Heaven's Crown and not my own. Besides," he added with a sudden grin, "he is not at all happy about it, so how could I resist?"

He continued to confide his plans, pleasing her with most of them. So far he'd yet to take a misstep. She would have felt better, though, if he were not intending to journey to the other side of the world, leaving his kingdom for God knows how long. "So I mean to name the Earl of Essex as one of my justiciars whilst I am away. Willem is a good man, and if he serves me half as well as he served my father, I will be content. I hear there will soon be a vacant bishopric at Ely, as the current occupant of the see is ailing. Once he goes to God, I will name Guillaume Longchamp in his stead. I intend to give Longchamp Geoff's chancellorship, too, for I want to make sure that I have men I can trust to watch over my kingdom whilst I am gone. Of course you will be the one I'll truly depend upon to keep order and quench any rebellious sparks ere they can take fire."

Eleanor assured him that she would do whatever he asked of her, and he smiled, but then startled her by saying, "You know, Maman, you'll have to see Johnny sooner or later. He's as nervous as a treed cat, so why not put him out of his misery and let me get him?"

She hadn't realized that he'd sensed her ambivalence about John. "You are too sharp-eyed for my own good. Very well, go and fetch him."

"If you do not mind, I'll send someone for him. I am a king now," he joked, "and it is not seemly to be running my own errands." He got to his feet, but took only a few steps toward the door before he halted. "Do you blame me for my father's death?"

Eleanor was taken aback. "No, Richard, I do not." She studied his face intently, and then said quietly, "Do you?"

"No! No, I do not." But despite the vehemence of his denial, she was not convinced and waited for him to reveal more. "Others do, though," he said, with enough heat to tell her that this had been preying on his mind. "No one dares say it to my face, of course, but I know what is being whispered behind my back. There is even talk that when I stood beside Papa's body, he began to bleed from the nose and mouth. That is not so!"

Eleanor was not surprised by the story, for it was a widely accepted belief that a murder victim would often bleed in the presence of his killer. "That is foolish folklore, Richard. No one of any sense would believe it."

"I would hope not," he said brusquely, obviously vexed with himself for paying any heed to superstition. He was not yet ready to let it go, though, shooting her a searching glance. "I did not believe Papa was ill," he said abruptly. "I was positive he was feigning, that this was yet another of his cunning tricks, and I assured Philippe of that. It was only when he dragged himself from his bed to ride to Colombières that we saw he'd not been lying."

"Well, your father gave you reason to suspect his good faith. He was always too clever by half, and it was inevitable that it would eventually catch up with him."

Richard nodded as if agreeing, but he was gnawing his lower lip. "But I still did not believe he was dying, Maman. It was obvious at Colombières that he was ailing. I still expected him to recover, though. How did I not see what everyone else did?"

Eleanor smiled sadly. "Sons always find it difficult to see their fathers as they truly are, and how much more true that would be for a living legend like Harry. Now wives rarely have that defect of vision, but I suspect most sons are like you, finding it hard to realize their fathers are mere mortal beings, no longer the all-powerful patriarchs they remember from childhood."

"So you are saying I was not willfully blind, merely immature," he said wryly. "Philippe insisted that he give me the kiss of peace. For the first time, I saw how frail he'd become, almost feeble. But then he growled that he asked only to live long enough to revenge himself upon me, and I found myself looking into a hawk's eyes, fierce and proud and still defiant."

"Yes," she said, "according to Will, his spirit burned brightly to the end. It was his body that failed him."

Richard was silent for a moment. "I truly did not think I had a choice but to do what I did."

"I know."

He tossed his head then, as if shaking off the past. "Well, let me get Johnny for you." He stepped forward, gave her a brief hug, and then strode from the chamber.

Eleanor paced as she waited, still not sure what she would say to John. With her other sons, she could argue convincingly that they'd had legitimate grievances, especially in Richard's case. It was not that easy to absolve her lastborn, for he'd been the best-loved by Henry and his betrayal seemed the cruelest of all.

When John entered the chamber, she saw what Richard meant. His unease was evident. What struck her most forcefully, though, was how young he seemed. At his age, Henry had already made himself England's king, and Geoffrey and Richard were putting down rebellions in Brittany and Poitou; even Hal had carved out a niche for himself upon the tournament circuit. Why had John not crossed the border from boyhood to manhood by now? She reminded herself this was Harry's doing, not hers. But she had her own sins to answer for, and she owed a debt, if not to this faithless young prince, to the wounded child he'd once been.

When he greeted her formally and warily, she smiled and held out her hand to him. "We are alone," she said. "Greet me as your mother, not the queen." John's relief was as obvious as his discomfort had been. He came quickly toward her, took her hand in his.

"Mother . . . I want to explain, to make you understand why—"

"Hush, John," she said, stopping his words by putting her fingers to his lips. "We need not talk of it."

THE SUMMER HEAT that had seared France and England did not reach North Wales. August was cool and rainy, but on the day the message arrived from Morgan, the sky was clear of clouds and the manor at Trefriw was dappled with mellow sun. Ranulf regarded his son's missive with some trepidation. He knew of Henry's dismal death at Chinon, thanks to his niece Emma. He sensed, though, that this news was not likely to be good. Escorting his wife out into their hillside garden, he seated her on a wooden bench and only then did he break the seal, scan the contents.

Rhiannon waited patiently until he was ready to read it to her. "Morgan is not coming home, is he?" she said at last, and Ranulf nodded before remembering that his wife needed verbal, not visual cues. Passing strange that after so many years of marriage, he occasionally forgot that.

"No, love, I think not. He does not say so, but I expect he will take the cross and accompany Richard to the Holy Land."

Sitting beside her on the bench, he slipped his arm around her shoulders and read her their son's letter. They were regretful, but resigned, for they'd realized long ago that Wales was too small to hold their youngest. Rhiannon's fears were more immediate, her concern for her aging husband, not her adventuresome son. "I suppose . . ." she began, trying to sound matter-of-fact, not wanting him to hear any echoes of reproach in her voice. "I suppose you will want to go back to England, to attend Richard's coronation."

Ranulf did not answer at once, regarding her fondly, this brave woman who'd done so much to heal his wounds, who'd assured him on their wedding night that she understood his loyalties would always be divided, understood that England would always exert a powerful pull upon his soul.

"No, Rhiannon," he said, "I will not be going back to England. I can grieve for Harry here in Gwynedd. I wish Richard well, but that is Morgan's world now, not mine. I am home."

Her smile was luminous. He read Morgan's letter again for her, and they lingered in the garden afterward, sharing the quiet contentment that had no need of words.

As SHE RODE ALONG WINCHESTER'S HIGH STREET, Eleanor soon drew a cheering crowd. She smiled and waved before turning into the narrow street that led into the cathedral close. Later that day, she and her sons would be departing the city for Sarum and then Marlborough. This visit to the cathedral of St Swithun's had been an impulsive one; she was still enjoying being able to indulge her whims as she chose. It amused her that she was being escorted by her erstwhile gaolers, Ralf de Glanville and Sir Ralph Fitz Stephen. Richard had given her the right to punish them if she wished, but she could not blame them for merely obeying Henry's orders, and in his unobtrusive way, Sir Ralph had done what he could to mitigate the severity of those early years of confinement.

The bishopric of Winchester was presently vacant and so it was the prior of St Swithun's and his monks who'd gathered in the garth to bid her welcome. When she explained that she'd come to offer prayers for the success of her son's reign, the prior personally led her toward the west door and then showed unexpected sensitivity by asking if she'd prefer to pray alone.

She would, and leaving her companions outside, Eleanor moved up the nave, pausing briefly at the font of black Tournai marble before turning into the north transept. The small chapel of St Saviour had always been a favorite of hers, for she greatly admired the vibrant biblical scenes painted on the wall above the altar. She noticed now that several of them were looking dull and faded, though. She resolved to give the prior money for their restoration, and then smiled, thinking that she'd not take her privileged life for granted again.

Kneeling before the altar, she said a prayer for Richard's safety in the Holy Land, and murmured prayers for the repose of Hal and Geoffrey's souls. Rising, she lit a votive candle, then, for her husband.

"I've been doing good for the sake of your soul, Harry," she said, laughing soundlessly as she imagined his pithy response to that. What a twisted road they'd traveled together. "What is so very sad," she said softly, "is that it did not have to end like this. We had chances to turn aside, to find our way again. Ah, Harry, we were so well-matched, you and I. If only we could have learned to forgive each other. 'If only' and 'what if,' fitting epitaphs for both our tombs. Well, you'll have all eternity to learn to forgive us and yourself. Knowing you, it is likely to take that long, too."

The candle flickered and seemed about to go out, but then it steadied and she smiled again. "At least it was never dull, my darling. And you will be remembered long after we've all turned to dust. But so will I."

The sound of footsteps drew her attention then, and she glanced out into the nave, saw a monk approaching. "Forgive me for disturbing your prayers, Madame, but your son the lord duke has sent a messenger to inquire when you'll be returning to the castle."

Eleanor sighed, thinking her husband and son were much more alike than they'd been willing to admit. Like Henry, Richard had no patience for delays, was eager to be on the road. "Thank you, Brother," she said. "I am coming." And she walked with a sure step from the shadows of the cathedral out into the sunlit priory garth.

ACKNOWLEDGMENTS

For a time I feared that *Devil's Brood* would become a literary Flying Dutchman, doomed never to reach port or print. I am so grateful to so many for their support and encouragement when I most needed it. No writer ever had a better midwife for her books than Valerie Ptak LaMont. Lowell LaMont has exorcised more of my computer demons than either of us can count. My readers have patiently endured the long delay with understanding and humor; my all-time favorite query is the one that said simply, "Did Eleanor get lost in Aquitaine?" I have been blessed with wonderful agents, Molly Friedrich and Paul Cirone of the Friedrich Agency, and Mic Cheetham of the Mic Cheetham Agency. I owe so much to my editors, Clare Ledingham at Penguin and Kate Davis and the incomparable Marian Wood at G. P. Putnam's Sons. I thank M. Markowski for translating the letter that Peter of Blois wrote on behalf of the Archbishop of Rouen to Queen Eleanor and then for generously posting it on the Internet Medieval Sourcebook website so that others might make use of it; I am grateful, too, to Dr. Paul Halsall, the ORB Sources editor for the Internet Medieval Sourcebook website, www.fordham.edu/halsall/sbook.html, for giving me permission to use this translation. I am very grateful to Dr. Diego Fiorentino, who was kind enough to act as my "medical consultant" for Geoffrey's accident. I do not think I could have done without Dr. David Crouch's masterly work on *L'Histoire de Guillaume le Maréchal,* for William Marshal was an eyewitness to many of the events in *Devil's Brood.* Lastly, I would like to thank Antony and Genie, two young French knights-errant in blue jeans who came to our rescue when our car broke down on a rainy autumn night in Saumur.

DEVIL'S BROOD

Sharon Kay Penman

A READER'S GUIDE

AUTHOR'S NOTE

First of all, I want to address the queries of fans of *The Lion in Winter*, that classic film about the Devil's Brood, with Henry and Eleanor memorably portrayed by Peter O'Toole and Katharine Hepburn. As I was writing this novel, I could hear their puzzled voices echoing in my ears. *Then Henry did not take Alys as his concubine? And Richard was not gay? He did not have an affair with the French king?*

I defer to none in my admiration for James Goldman; *The Lion in Winter* remains one of my all-time favorite films. But it came out in 1969, and what was accepted as gospel forty years ago is not necessarily true today. I have to confess that I was quite disappointed to conclude that Henry's purported affair with Alys was a political calumny, for writers are irresistibly drawn to high drama, and what could be more dramatic than a man seducing his son's betrothed? Oh my, the scenes I could have written . . . But once I'd researched the accusation, I realized that it would not withstand close scrutiny.

Sexual slander was as common a weapon in the Middle Ages as it is today. Henry was accused of lechery and adultery, Eleanor of incest and adultery, Richard of rape, and John of virtually every crime known to man. Many of the more unsavory stories involving Henry and Eleanor come from a very untrustworthy source, the man known as Giraldus Cambrensus or Gerald the Welshman, a Norman-Welsh cleric who has made brief appearances in both *Time and Chance* and *Devil's Brood* as Gerald de Barri. Giraldus was a gifted and prolific writer, and his books about Wales are a treasure trove of information about medieval life. But Giraldus had a sharp axe to grind when it came to the Angevins; he bitterly blamed them for thwarting his ambition to become Bishop of St David's. Most of Giraldus's scandalous stories about Henry and Eleanor are better read as fiction; his literary career is aptly summed up by the eminent historian Hans Eberhard Mayer, who described Giraldus's writings as "always delightful to read, but often hard to believe."

Rumors of a liaison between Henry and Alys were mentioned by several English chroniclers, but there is no evidence to support them. I am not alone in reaching this conclusion. Dr. W. L. Warren, author of the definitive biography of Henry, did not find the story credible. Most of Henry's biographers are skeptical of the charge, although Eleanor's biographers are inclined to accept it. This is interesting but not surprising, for her biographers tend to become her partisans and Henry suffers accordingly. I plan to discuss this in greater detail on my website, but will confine myself here to pointing out the implausibility of these rumors. Henry would have had limited opportunities even to be with Alys, given his peripatetic lifestyle. Alys was at Winchester for a while and then apparently resided at the Tower of London with two other highborn heiresses, Isabella de Clare and Denise de Deols. Not even Giraldus suggests that Alys accompanied Henry on his unending excursions through his domains. But apart from the difficult logistics of it, such an action on Henry's part would have been sheer insanity. And while Henry did not lack for flaws, he was always a pragmatist and never a fool.

Richard was able to benefit from these rumors, though. When the French king objected to his plan to wed Berengaria, the daughter of the King of Navarre, he expressed shock that Philippe could expect him to wed his father's mistress. If Philippe had indeed made use of the gossip to try to worsen Richard's precarious relationship with Henry, he was hoist with his own petard. All we can say for absolute certainty is that Alys was the true victim in these political machinations, a pawn caught up in a cold-blooded game of kings, treated very shabbily by Henry, Richard, and Philippe. When she was finally returned to France, Philippe married her off to the Count of Ponthieu, and we can only hope that she found some contentment in that union.

Now . . . on to Richard. He and Philippe were never lovers. This notion stems from a patent misreading of medieval culture and custom. Richard's sexuality was first questioned in the second half of the twentieth century, and this speculation can be traced in large measure to a passage in *The Annals of Roger de Hoveden,* who described Richard's visit to the French court in 1187 as follows: "After peace was made, Richard, earl of Poitou, remained with the King of France, though much against the will of his father, and the King of France held him in such high esteem that every day they ate at the same table and from the same dish, and at night had not separate chambers. In consequence of this strong attachment which seemed to have arisen between them, the King of England was struck with great astonishment and wondered what it could mean, and taking precautions for the future, frequently sent messengers into France for the purpose of recalling his son Richard."

To us, this clearly indicates a sexual relationship. But in the Middle Ages, sharing a bed did not have the same meaning that we would place on it today. Medieval people were accustomed to sharing beds, often with strangers. More to the point, this was an accepted means of bestowing honor and demonstrating royal favor. Throughout the Middle Ages, and beyond, kings used such ostentatious intimacy to flaunt political alliances and mend political fences; for example, Edward IV, surely the greatest womanizer ever to sit on the English throne, with the possible exception of Charles II, shared his chamber with the rebel Earl of Somerset to dramatize their reconciliation. And while our tabloids would go into meltdown mode in comparable circumstances, neither Philippe's nor Edward's subjects would have read something sexual in such familiarity.

So Richard was not the French king's lover. But was he homosexual? In her insightful book *Sexuality in Medieval Europe,* Dr. Ruth Mazo Karras explores this challenging subject, setting forth the reasons why sexual mores in the Middle Ages cannot be easily compared to the beliefs of our more secular society. They saw sodomy as an act not an orientation, and they were unaware that sexual identity is biologically determined. We must bear this in mind when trying to answer questions about Richard's sexuality.

What little we know of Richard's sex life is as follows: He had an unhappy marriage, and an illegitimate son, and was accused of lechery in his lifetime; a chronicler writing in the thirteenth century reported that he'd scandalized his doctors on his deathbed by demanding that he be provided with women. We also know that he made a flamboyant and public confession of his sins in Messina, en route to the Holy Land, and that in 1195 he was accosted by a hermit who chastised him for his sinful ways, warning, "Be thou mindful of the destruction of Sodom, and abstain from what is unlawful, for if thou dost not, a vengeance worthy of God shall overtake thee." According to Roger de Hoveden, Richard remained "intent upon the things of this world and not those which are of God," not taking the warning seriously until he became gravely ill, after which "he was not ashamed to confess the guiltiness of his life, and after receiving absolution, took back his wife, whom for a long time he had not known, and putting away all illicit intercourse, he remained constant to his wife."

This is all we know for certain. Anything else is conjecture. Was the hermit admonishing him for the sin of adultery or the sin of sodomy? John Gillingham, Richard's preeminent biographer, contends that the Sodom warning does not refer to homosexuality, arguing that in the Middle Ages it referred to the terrible nature of the punishment, not the nature of the offense. Not every historian agrees with his interpretation, and so there is no academic consensus about Richard's sex life. How could there be? He may have been heterosexual. He may have been bisexual. The only person who could answer the question with certainty has been dead for eight hundred years, and in any event, those were terms that would have been foreign to him.

Geoffrey has always been the son who interested me most, perhaps because he was the most enigmatic and the one most neglected by historians. Unfortunately for him, there were no Breton chroniclers writing during the years that he governed the duchy, and he was mentioned by English chroniclers only in passing, and always in connection with his rebellions against his father. Modern historians have tended to rely on Roger de Hoveden's colorful quotation—that Geoffrey was a "son of perdition"—and on Giraldus Cambrensus's condemnation of him as an eloquent dissembler, making no attempt to delve into the reasons for his rebellions. I have even seen his motives dismissed as mere "mindless malice," and I always knew there was more to his story than that! He had to wait more than eight hundred years, but in 2000 a historian finally examined Geoffrey's career in the context of his role as Duke of Brittany, giving us a much more nuanced and logical explanation for his actions.

The book is *Brittany and the Angevins: Province and Empire, 1158–1203,* by Judith A. Everard, and I recommend it highly for anyone interested in medieval Brittany. Dr. Everard demonstrates very convincingly that Geoffrey's goal was to secure the full possession of his wife's inheritance, the county of Nantes and the Honour of Richmond. Seen in that light, his actions make sense. And it can be argued that his conspiracy with the French king in the last months of his life may not be admirable, but it is understandable under the circumstances, for he saw the possession of Anjou as essential to protect his duchy against his hostile brother Richard.

Just as controversy swirled around Geoffrey during his lifetime, it followed him faithfully to the grave. Roger de Hoveden reported that he died of injuries received in a French tournament, while Philippe's French clerk, Rigord, recorded that he died in Paris after enduring "a bed of suffering." Until recently, it was accepted that Geoffrey died after being unhorsed in a tournament. But Dr. Everard argues that he really died of a fever, as reported by Rigord, and she postulates that the tournament was a "cover story" to explain his presence in Paris and to allay Henry's suspicions. While I admire Dr. Everard's work enormously, I did not find this argument persuasive. There was nothing secretive about Geoffrey's presence in Paris; he issued his last charter there. And immediately after his death, Philippe claimed wardship of his daughters as his liege lord, thus revealing to Henry that his son had done homage to the French king. I could see the French king offering a false account of Geoffrey's death, however, to avoid any difficulties with the Church over Geoffrey's state funeral in Notre Dame cathedral, for men who died in tournaments were to be denied Christian burial. (Nor does it seem to me that there is an inherent conflict between Roger de Hoveden's account and the one offered by Rigord. The English chronicler says Geoffrey was unhorsed and trampled after refusing to yield to his foes, and it is quite possible that he survived for hours or days. Rigord then focused on his actual death, rather than the circumstances of it, to spare his king any awkward conflict with the Bishop of Paris.)

Very little is known of the circumstances of Eleanor's capture, other than the fact that she was disguised as a man. We do not know when it occurred or where. Some historians place her flight in the spring of 1173, but I do not agree. She had too much pride to run, until there was no other choice. I am convinced that she did not leave Poitou until Henry's army was driving into the heart of her duchy in November. The French historian Alfred Richard was the first to contend that she had been betrayed, having discovered the generous grants that Henry bestowed on four of her Poitevin barons. Since Henry went so far as to name Porteclie de Mauzé as Seneschal of Poitou in 1174, he seemed the most likely suspect to me. I set the ambush at Loches because of its proximity to Chinon, where she was apparently taken after her capture.

Roland de Dinan's attack on Geoffrey's castle at Rennes is often dated to 1182, which makes no sense, for Roland would not have acted on his own and Henry had no reason to launch such an assault at a time when he and Geoffrey were on good terms. But it is quite logical for the attack to have been made during the rebellion of 1183, as a means of drawing Geoffrey back to Brittany.

Only one significant fictional character has ever infiltrated my books—Ranulf Fitz Roy, Henry's uncle in the trilogy. Henry I is known to have sired at least twenty illegitimate children, so what is one more? Otherwise, I prefer to use actual historical figures even in minor roles, such as the provost of Loches and the novice monk Jocelin of Brakelond. Often I have only a name to work with and must create a history on my own, as with Amaria. She is briefly mentioned in the Pipe Rolls, as when Henry paid for a gilt saddle with scarlet for Eleanor and a plainer one for Amaria, "her maid." Obviously I often had to invent attendants, squires, and servants, although I was fortunate enough to find the actual household knights serving Henry, Hal, Richard, and Geoffrey. I arbitrarily picked the name Nicholas de Chauvigny for Eleanor's loyal household knight, and was later delighted to discover that the de Chauvignys were stalwart supporters of the duchess and her son; I then made my fictional Nicholas kinsman to Richard's real cousin André de Chauvigny.

Readers of my previous books know that I try not to tamper with established historical facts. I took a few liberties, but only those that kept my conscience clear: Hal's presence at Henry's Christmas Court in 1178; Eleanor's presence at Woodstock in the summer of 1179. I indulged a whim and placed John of Salisbury on the scene when his friend the Bishop of Poitiers saved Hal's hapless vice-chancellor, Adam de Churchedune, and since we don't know who alerted the bishop to Adam's peril, I gave that honor to Marguerite. I occasionally allowed my characters to receive news faster than their real-life counterparts. And I committed a minor sin of plagiarism, giving to Henry's cousin Roger a sardonic assessment of the Archbishop of Canterbury when the acerbic judgment really came from the English chronicler William of Newburgh. It was simply too good not to use: "The man is laudably inoffensive, with the virtue of realizing his limitations."

There is still so much that I want to share: the obvious cause of death for Hal and likely cause of death for Henry, personal details gleaned from the chronicles, discussion of the ways an individual's death can alter the course of history, Eleanor's age and Geoffrey's actual date of death, my guidelines for creating medieval dialogue and the problems of writing of a bilingual society. But even I think a ten-page Author's Note would be pushing the limits. So once *Devil's Brood* is published, I will post some of these additional musings on my website, www.sharonkaypenman.com. Readers who do not have access to the Internet but who share my curiosity about the Angevins may write to me at PO Box 1134, Mays Landing, New Jersey 08330, and I will send you copies of the website material.

On the last page of the book, I could not resist having Eleanor comment that she and Henry would be remembered long after their deaths. Henry is judged to be one of England's greatest kings, and Eleanor continues to bewitch and confound us just as surely as she bewitched and confounded her contemporaries. Even people with no interest in medieval history have heard of Richard Lionheart and Robin Hood's nemesis, evil King John, for they have long since moved into the land of myth and legend. Even after spending more than a decade immersed in the compelling, improbable lives of this fascinating and dysfunctional family, I am not ready to let them go. So my next book will continue the story of Eleanor, Richard, John, Joanna, Constance, Will Marshal, Philippe Capet, and Saladin.

SKP

May 2008

QUESTIONS AND TOPICS
FOR DISCUSSION

1. Whom do you blame more for the destruction of their family, Henry or Eleanor?

2. Eleanor learned from her mistakes during her long confinement. Why do you think Henry was unable to learn from his?

3. Henry's three elder sons all had legitimate grievances against their father. Do you think these grievances justified their rebellion?

4. John would prove to be the most emotionally damaged of Henry and Eleanor's children. Why do you think this was so?

5. Discuss the medieval custom of betrothing or marrying royal daughters at an early age and sending them away to be raised at the courts of their husbands. Do you think this made it easier for the girls to adapt to their new lives in foreign countries?

6. Had Geoffrey not died, it is likely that he rather than John would have succeeded Richard in 1199. What sort of a king do you think he would have made?

7. Was Hal's kingship doomed by his very nature? Was he simply unsuited to rule, or was he molded by his parents' mistakes?

8. Richard would prove to be the most ruthless of Henry's sons. What factors do you think helped shape his character?

9. What were Henry and Eleanor's greatest failings as parents? Who do you think was ultimately more successful as a parent?

10. Though Henry is disappointed by his sons' betrayal, he is heartbroken by Eleanor's. How do you think love factored into her decision? What would you have done in her place?

11. Though Sharon Kay Penman writes about the Middle Ages, many of the themes in *Devil's Brood* are still applicable today. How do you think Henry would have fared as a ruler today? Would he have had the same downfall?

PHOTO: WILLIAM J. PENMAN, JR.

Sharon Kay Penman is the author of six previous historical novels (including *When Christ and His Saints Slept* and *Time and Chance*, the first two books in the Henry and Eleanor trilogy) and four medieval mysteries set during the reign of Eleanor of Aquitaine. She lives in Mays Landing, New Jersey.